PENGUIN POPULAR CLASSICS

# WAVERLEY

## BY SIR WALTER SCOTT

SIR WALTER SCOTT (1771–1832). Scottish novelist, ballad-collector, poet, critic and man of letters – but probably of all these Scott is best remembered as a writer of picaresque novels of chivalry and romance. In Thomas Love Peacock's words, 'He has the rare talent of pleasing all ranks and classes of men, from the peer to the peasant.'

The son of a solicitor, Scott was born in College Wynd in Edinburgh in 1771. He spent his formative years between the city and Roxburghshire before attending the famed Edinburgh High School in 1779. After this he took some classes at Edinburgh University in order to follow his father's profession, which he duly did, being called to the Bar in 1792. Despite his subsequent literary triumphs Scott never entirely gave up the legal profession. He became Sheriff-Depute of Selkirkshire in 1799, and he remained Clerk of the Court of Session in Edinburgh from 1806 to within a year or two of his death. His interest in the old Border tales and ballads was stimulated from an early age by his mother, who, less austere than her husband, had a love of poetry. Although left lame by a childhood illness, Scott devoted much of his leisure time to the exploration of the Border country and it is a combination of these two interests that led to his initial success. In 1797, the same year as Scott married Catherine Carpenter, his first literary efforts, anonymous translations of some German plays and poems, were published. It wasn't until five years later that a collection of popular ballads entitled *The Minstrelsy of the Scottish Border* appeared under his own name. From this time on Scott's literary achievements were vast and his most memorable poems include *The Lady of the Lake*, *The Bridal of Triermain* and *Harold the Dauntless*, his last long poem, written in 1818. Although Scott began the Waverley novels in 1805, he abandoned them for more marketable work until 1814, when *Waverley* appeared. The first nine novels he published (all appeared anonymously) drew on Scottish settings and on recent Scottish history,

but with the publication of *Ivanhoe* in 1819 Scott turned increasingly to England and Europe and to the Middle Ages and the Renaissance for his subject matter. Among his most famous novels are *Waverley* (1814), *Old Mortality* (1816), *Rob Roy* (1817), *The Heart of Midlothian* (1818), *The Bride of Lammermoor* (1819), *Ivanhoe* (1819), *Perveril of the Peak* (1823) and *Castle Dangerous* (1831). Scott was, for most of his life, accepted as an outstanding member of the literary establishment, not only for his poetry and novels but also for the important historical, literary and antiquarian works written by him or issued under his editorship. Although he refused the title of Poet Laureate in 1813 he did accept a baronetcy in 1820. Living like a landed magnate at Abbotsford from 1811 onwards, Scott spent extensively on rebuilding his estate, a decision which was to prove both expensive and unwise. In 1826 the company of Ballantyne & Co (in which Scott had been a secret partner for many years) collapsed, and Scott found himself liable for debts of about £114,000. It is well known that he shouldered the whole burden himself and worked at a tremendous rate for the rest of his life in an attempt to pay off the creditors. They were finally paid in full from the proceeds of the sale of his copyrights after his death in September 1832.

*Waverley* (1814), Scott's first novel, is often regarded as the first historical novel ever written and is one of the most significant books of the nineteenth century. In addition to the influence it had on the history of the novel, its impact on the reading public was like nothing before and possibly nothing since – it is said that everyone who read, read Scott.

Readers may also find the following books of interest: James Anderson, *Sir Walter Scott and History* (1981); Iain Gordon Brown, *Scott's Interleaved Waverley Novels* (1987); James Kerr, *Fiction Against History: Scott as Storyteller* (1989); John O. Hayden, *Scott: The Critical Heritage* (1970); Jane Millgate, *Walter Scott: The Making of the Novelist* (1984); Jill Rubenstein, *Sir Walter Scott: A Reference Guide* (1978); A. N. Wilson, *The Laird of Abbotsford: A View of Sir Walter Scott* (1980); and Judith Wilt, *Secret Leaves: The Novels of Walter Scott* (1985).

PENGUIN POPULAR CLASSICS

# WAVERLEY

## SIR WALTER SCOTT

PENGUIN BOOKS
A PENGUIN/GODFREY CAVE EDITION

PENGUIN BOOKS

Published by the Penguin Group
Penguin Books Ltd, 27 Wrights Lane, London w8 5tz, England
Penguin Books USA Inc., 375 Hudson Street, New York, New York 10014, USA
Penguin Books Australia Ltd, Ringwood, Victoria, Australia
Penguin Books Canada Ltd, 10 Alcorn Avenue, Toronto, Ontario, Canada m4v 3b2
Penguin Books (NZ) Ltd, 182–190 Wairau Road, Auckland 10, New Zealand

Penguin Books Ltd, Registered Offices: Harmondsworth, Middlesex, England

First published 1814
Published in Penguin Popular Classics 1994
1 3 5 7 9 10 8 6 4 2

Printed in England by Clays Ltd, St Ives plc

# ADVERTISEMENT

*To the Author's Edition of the Waverley Novels, published in 1829-33.*

————————

IT has been the occasional occupation of the Author of *Waverley* for several years past, to revise and correct the voluminous series of Novels which pass under that name; in order that, if they should ever appear as his avowed productions, he might render them in some degree deserving of a continuance of the public favour with which they have been honoured ever since their first appearance. For a long period, however, it seemed likely that the improved and illustrated edition which he meditated would be a posthumous publication. But the course of the events which occasioned the disclosure of the Author's name, having, in a great measure, restored to him a sort of parental control over these Works, he is naturally induced to give them to the press in a corrected, and, he hopes, an improved form, while life and health permit the task of revising and illustrating them. Such being his purpose, it is necessary to say a few words on the plan of the proposed Edition.

In stating it to be revised and corrected, it is not to be inferred that any attempt is made to alter the tenor of the stories, the character of the actors, or the spirit of the dialogue. There is no doubt ample room for emendation in all these points,—but where the tree falls it must lie. Any attempt to obviate criticism, however just, by altering a work already in the hands of the public is generally unsuccessful. In the most improbable fiction, the reader still desires some air of *vraisemblance*, and does not relish that the incidents of a tale familiar to him should be altered to suit the taste of critics, or the caprice of the author himself. This process of feeling is so natural, that it may be observed even in children, who cannot endure that a nursery story should be repeated to them differently from the manner in which it was first told.

But without altering, in the slightest degree, either the story or the mode of telling it, the Author has taken this opportunity to correct errors of the press and slips of the pen. That such should exist cannot be wondered at, when it is considered that the Publishers found it their interest to hurry through the press a succession of the early editions of the various Novels, and that the Author had not the usual opportunity of revision. It is hoped that the present edition will be found free from errors of that accidental kind.

The Author has also ventured to make some emendations of a different character, which, without being such apparent deviations from the original stories as to disturb the reader's old associations, will, he thinks, add something to the spirit of the dialogue, narrative, or description. These consist in occasional pruning where the language is redundant, compression where the style is loose, infusion of vigour where it is languid, the exchange of less forcible for more appropriate epithets—slight alterations in short, like the last touches of an Artist, which contribute to heighten and finish the picture, though an inexperienced eye can hardly detect in what they consist.

The General Preface to the new Edition, and the Introductory Notices to each separate work, will contain an account of such circumstances attending the first publication of the Novels and Tales, as may appear interesting in themselves, or proper to be communicated to the public. The Author also proposes to publish, on this occasion, the various legends, family traditions, or obscure historical facts, which have formed the ground-work of these Novels, and to give some account of the places where the scenes are laid, when these are altogether, or in part, real; as well as a statement of particular incidents founded on fact; together with a more copious Glossary, and Notes explanatory of the ancient customs, and popular superstitions, referred to in the Romances.

Upon the whole, it is hoped that the Waverley Novels, in their new dress, will not be found to have lost any part of their attractions in consequence of receiving illustrations by the Author, and undergoing his careful revision.

ABBOTSFORD, *January* 1829.

# GENERAL PREFACE.

---

———And must I ravel out
My weaved-up follies?
*Richard II.*, Act *IV.*

HAVING undertaken to give an Introductory Account of the compositions which are here offered to the public, with Notes and Illustrations, the Author, under whose name they are now for the first time collected, feels that he has the delicate task of speaking more of himself and his personal concerns, than may perhaps be either graceful or prudent. In this particular, he runs the risk of presenting himself to the public in the relation that the dumb wife in the jest-book held to her husband, when, having spent half of his fortune to obtain the cure of her imperfection, he was willing to have bestowed the other half to restore her to her former condition. But this is a risk inseparable from the task which the Author has undertaken, and he can only promise to be as little of an egotist as the situation will permit. It is perhaps an indifferent sign of a disposition to keep his word, that having introduced himself in the third person singular, he proceeds in the second paragraph to make use of the first. But it appears to him that the seeming modesty connected with the former mode of writing, is overbalanced by the inconvenience of stiffness and affectation which attends it during a narrative of some length, and which may be observed less or more in every work in which the third person is used, from the *Commentaries of Cæsar*, to the *Autobiography of Alexander the Corrector*.

I must refer to a very early period of my life, were I to point out my first achievements as a tale-teller—but I believe some of my old schoolfellows can still bear witness that I had a distinguished character for that talent, at a time when the applause of my companions was my recompense for the disgraces and punishments which the future romance-writer incurred for being idle himself, and keeping others idle, during hours that should have

been employed on our tasks. The chief enjoyment of my
holidays was to escape with a chosen friend, who had the
same taste with myself, and alternately to recite to each
other such wild adventures as we were able to devise.
We told, each in turn, interminable tales of knight-
errantry and battles and enchantments, which were continued from one day to another as opportunity offered,
without our ever thinking of bringing them to a conclusion. As we observed a strict secrecy on the subject
of this intercourse, it acquired all the character of a
concealed pleasure, and we used to select, for the scenes
of our indulgence, long walks through the solitary and
romantic environs of Arthur's Seat, Salisbury Crags,
Braid Hills, and similar places in the vicinity of Edinburgh ; and the recollection of those holidays still forms
an *oasis* in the pilgrimage which I have to look back
upon. I have only to add, that my friend still lives, a
prosperous gentleman, but too much occupied with
graver business, to thank me for indicating him more
plainly as a confident of my childish mystery.

When boyhood advancing into youth required more
serious studies and graver cares, a long illness threw me
back on the kingdom of fiction, as if it were by a species
of fatality. My indisposition arose, in part at least, from
my having broken a blood-vessel ; and motion and speech
were for a long time pronounced positively dangerous.
For several weeks I was confined strictly to my bed,
during which time I was not allowed to speak above a
whisper, to eat more than a spoonful or two of boiled
rice, or to have more covering than one thin counterpane.
When the reader is informed that I was at this time a
growing youth, with the spirits, appetite, and impatience
of fifteen, and suffered, of course, greatly under this
severe regimen, which the repeated return of my disorder
rendered indispensable, he will not be surprised that I
was abandoned to my own discretion, so far as reading
(my almost sole amusement) was concerned, and still less
so, that I abused the indulgence which left my time so
much at my own disposal.

There was at this time a circulating library in Edinburgh, founded, I believe, by the celebrated Allan
Ramsay, which, besides containing a most respectable
collection of books of every description, was, as might
have been expected, peculiarly rich in works of fiction.
It exhibited specimens of every kind, from the romances
of chivalry, and the ponderous folios of Cyrus and

Cassandra, down to the most approved works of later times. I was plunged into this great ocean of reading without compass or pilot; and unless when some one had the charity to play at chess with me, I was allowed to do nothing save read, from morning to night. I was, in kindness and pity, which was perhaps erroneous, however natural, permitted to select my subjects of study at my own pleasure, upon the same principle that the humours of children are indulged to keep them out of mischief. As my taste and appetite were gratified in nothing else, I indemnified myself by becoming a glutton of books. Accordingly, I believe I read almost all the romances, old plays, and epic poetry, in that formidable collection, and no doubt was unconsciously amassing materials for the task in which it has been my lot to be so much employed.

At the same time I did not in all respects abuse the license permitted me. Familiar acquaintance with the specious miracles of fiction brought with it some degree of satiety, and I began, by degrees, to seek in histories, memoirs, voyages and travels, and the like, events nearly as wonderful as those which were the work of imagination, with the additional advantage that they were at least in a great measure true. The lapse of nearly two years, during which I was left to the exercise of my own free will, was followed by a temporary residence in the country, where I was again very lonely but for the amusement which I derived from a good though old-fashioned library. The vague and wild use which I made of this advantage I cannot describe better than by referring my reader to the desultory studies of Waverley in a similar situation; the passages concerning whose course of reading were imitated from recollections of my own.—It must be understood that the resemblance extends no farther.

Time, as it glided on, brought the blessings of confirmed health and personal strength, to a degree which had never been expected or hoped for. The severe studies necessary to render me fit for my profession occupied the greater part of my time; and the society of my friends and companions who were about to enter life along with me, filled up the interval, with the usual amusements of young men. I was in a situation which rendered serious labour indispensable; for, neither possessing, on the one hand, any of those peculiar advantages which are supposed to favour a hasty advance in the profession of the law, nor being, on the other hand, exposed to unusual obstacles to interrupt my progress, I might reasonably expect to succeed according to the greater or less degree of trouble which I should take to qualify myself as a pleader.

It makes no part of the present story to detail how the success of a few ballads had the effect of changing all the purpose and tenor of my life, and of converting a pains-taking lawyer of some years' standing into a follower of literature. It is enough to say, that I had assumed the latter character for several years before I seriously thought of attempting a work of imagination in prose, although one or two of my poetical attempts did not differ from romances otherwise than by being written in verse. But yet, I may observe, that about this time (now, alas! thirty years since) I had nourished the ambitious desire of composing a tale of chivalry, which was to be in the style of the *Castle of Otranto*, with plenty of Border characters, and supernatural incident. Having found unexpectedly a chapter of this intended work among some old papers, I have subjoined it to this introductory essay, thinking some readers may account as curious, the first attempts at romantic composition by an author, who has since written so much in that department.[1] And those who complain, not unreasonably, of the profusion of the Tales which have followed *Waverley*, may bless their stars at the narrow escape they have made, by the commencement of the inundation which had so nearly taken place in the first year of the century, being post-poned for fifteen years later.

This particular subject was never resumed, but I did not abandon the idea of fictitious composition in prose, though I determined to give another turn to the style of the work.

My early recollections of the Highland scenery and customs made so favourable an impression in the poem called the *Lady of the Lake*, that I was induced to think of attempting something of the same kind in prose. I had been a good deal in the Highlands at a time when they were much less accessible, and much less visited, than they have been of late years, and was acquainted with many of the old warriors of 1745, who were, like most veterans, easily induced to fight their battles over again, for the benefit of a willing listener like myself. It naturally occurred to me that the ancient traditions and

[1] See the Fragment alluded to, in the Appendix, No. I.

high spirit of a people, who, living in a civilized age and country, retained so strong a tincture of manners belonging to an early period of society, must afford a subject favourable for romance, if it should not prove a curious tale marred in the telling.

It was with some idea of this kind, that, about the year 1805, I threw together about one-third part of the first volume of *Waverley*. It was advertised to be published by the late Mr John Ballantyne, bookseller in Edinburgh, under the name of "Waverley, or 'tis Fifty Years since," —a title afterwards altered to "'Tis Sixty Years since," that the actual date of publication might be made to correspond with the period in which the scene was laid. Having proceeded as far, I think, as the Seventh Chapter, I showed my work to a critical friend, whose opinion was unfavourable ; and having then some poetical reputation, I was unwilling to risk the loss of it by attempting a new style of composition. I therefore threw aside the work I had commenced, without either reluctance or remonstrance. I ought to add, that though my ingenious friend's sentence was afterwards reversed, on an appeal to the public, it cannot be considered as any imputation on his good taste ; for the specimen subjected to his criticism did not extend beyond the departure of the hero for Scotland, and, consequently, had not entered upon the part of the story which was finally found most interesting.

Be that as it may, this portion of the manuscript was laid aside in the drawers of an old writing desk, which, on my first coming to reside at Abbotsford, in 1811, was placed in a lumber garret, and entirely forgotten. Thus, though I sometimes, among other literary avocations, turned my thoughts to the continuation of the romance which I had commenced, yet as I could not find what I had already written, after searching such repositories as were within my reach, and was too indolent to attempt to write it anew from memory, I as often laid aside all thoughts of that nature.

Two circumstances, in particular, recalled my recollection of the mislaid manuscript. The first was the extended and well-merited fame of Miss Edgeworth, whose Irish characters have gone so far to make the English familiar with the character of their gay and kind-hearted neighbours of Ireland, that she may be truly said to have done more towards completing the Union, than perhaps all the legislative enactments by which it has been followed up.

Without being so presumptuous as to hope to emulate the rich humour, pathetic tenderness, and admirable tact, which pervade the works of my accomplished friend, I felt that something might be attempted for my own country, of the same kind with that which Miss Edgeworth so fortunately achieved for Ireland—something which might introduce her natives to those of the sister kingdom, in a more favourable light than they had been placed hitherto, and tend to procure sympathy for their virtues and indulgence for their foibles. I thought also, that much of what I wanted in talent, might be made up by the intimate acquaintance with the subject which I could lay claim to possess, as having travelled through most parts of Scotland, both Highland and Lowland; having been familiar with the elder, as well as more modern race; and having had from my infancy free and unrestrained communication with all ranks of my countrymen, from the Scottish peer to the Scottish ploughman. Such ideas often occurred to me, and constituted an ambitious branch of my theory, however far short I may have fallen of it in practice.

But it was not only the triumphs of Miss Edgeworth which worked in me emulation, and disturbed my indolence. I chanced actually to engage in a work which formed a sort of essay piece, and gave me hope that I might in time become free of the craft of Romance-writing, and be esteemed a tolerable workman.

In the year 1807-8, I undertook, at the request of John Murray, Esq. of Albemarle Street, to arrange for publication some posthumous productions of the late Mr Joseph Strutt, distinguished as an artist and an antiquary, amongst which was an unfinished romance, entitled *Queen-Hoo-Hall*. The scene of the tale was laid in the reign of Henry VI., and the work was written to illustrate the manners, customs, and language of the people of England during that period. The extensive acquaintance which Mr Strutt had acquired with such subjects in compiling his laborious "Horda Angel Cynnan," his "Royal and Ecclesiastical Antiquities," and his "Essay on the Sports and Pastimes of the People of England," had rendered him familiar with all the antiquarian lore necessary for the purpose of composing the projected romance; and although the manuscript bore the marks of hurry and incoherence natural to the first rough draft of the author, it evinced (in my opinion) considerable powers of imagination.

As the Work was unfinished, I deemed it my duty, as
Editor, to supply such a hasty and inartificial conclusion
as could be shaped out from the story, of which Mr Strutt
had laid the foundation. This concluding chapter[1] is
also added to the present Introduction, for the reason
already mentioned regarding the preceding fragment.
It was a step in my advance towards romantic composition ; and to preserve the traces of these is in a great
measure the object of this Essay.

*Queen-Hoo-Hall* was not, however, very successful. I
thought I was aware of the reason, and supposed that, by
rendering his language too ancient, and displaying his
antiquarian knowledge too liberally, the ingenious author
had raised up an obstacle to his own success. Every
work designed for mere amusement must be expressed in
language easily comprehended ; and when, as is sometimes the case in *Queen-Hoo-Hall*, the author addresses
himself exclusively to the Antiquary, he must be content
to be dismissed by the general reader with the criticism
of Mungo, in the *Padlock*, on the Mauritanian music,
" What signifies me hear, if me no understand ?"

I conceived it possible to avoid this error ; and by
rendering a similar work more light and obvious to
general comprehension, to escape the rock on which my
predecessor was shipwrecked. But I was, on the other
hand, so far discouraged by the indifferent reception of
Mr Strutt's romance, as to become satisfied that the
manners of the Middle Ages did not possess the interest
which I had conceived ; and was led to form the opinion
that a romance, founded on a Highland story, and more
modern events, would have a better chance of popularity
than a tale of chivalry. My thoughts, therefore, returned
more than once to the tale which I had actually commenced, and accident at length threw the lost sheets in
my way.

I happened to want some fishing-tackle for the use
of a guest, when it occurred to me to search the old
writing-desk already mentioned, in which I used to keep
articles of that nature. I got access to it with some
difficulty ; and, in looking for lines and flies, the long-lost
manuscript presented itself. I immediately set to work
to complete it, according to my original purpose. And
here I must frankly confess, that the mode in which I
conducted the story scarcely deserved the success which
the Romance afterwards attained. The tale of *Waverley*

[1] See Appendix, No. II.

was put together with so little care, that I cannot boast of having sketched any distinct plan of the work. The whole adventures of Waverley, in his movements up and down the country with the Highland cateran Bean Lean, are managed without much skill. It suited best, however, the road I wanted to travel, and permitted me to introduce some descriptions of scenery and manners, to which the reality gave an interest which the powers of the Author might have otherwise failed to attain for them. And though I have been in other instances a sinner in this sort, I do not recollect any of these Novels, in which I have transgressed so widely as in the first of the Series.

Among other unfounded reports, it has been said that the copyright of *Waverley* was, during the book's progress through the press, offered for sale to various booksellers in London at a very inconsiderable price. This was not the case. Messrs Constable & Caddell, who published the work, were the only persons acquainted with the contents of the publication, and they offered a large sum for it while in the course of printing, which, however, was declined, the Author not choosing to part with the copyright.

The origin of the story of *Waverley* and the particular facts on which it is founded, are given in the separate introduction prefixed to that romance in this edition, and require no notice in this place.

*Waverley* was published in 1814, and as the title-page was without the name of the Author, the work was left to win its way in the world without any of the usual recommendations. Its progress was for some time slow; but after the first two or three months, its popularity had increased in a degree which must have satisfied the expectations of the Author, had these been far more sanguine than he ever entertained.

Great anxiety was expressed to learn the name of the Author, but on this no authentic information could be attained. My original motive for publishing the work anonymously, was the consciousness that it was an experiment on the public taste which might very probably fail, and therefore there was no occasion to take on myself the personal risk of discomfiture. For this purpose considerable precautions were used to preserve secrecy. My old friend and schoolfellow, Mr James Ballantyne, who printed these Novels, had the exclusive task of corresponding with the Author, who thus had not only the advantage of his professional talents, but also of his critical abilities. The original manuscript, or, as it is technically called, copy, was transcribed under Mr Ballantyne's eye by confidential persons; nor was there an instance of treachery during the many years in which these precautions were resorted to, although various individuals were employed at different times. Double proof-sheets were regularly printed off. One was forwarded to the Author by Mr Ballantyne, and the alterations which it received were, by his own hand, copied upon the other proof-sheet for the use of the printers, so that even the corrected proofs of the Author were never seen in the printing-office; and thus the curiosity of such eager enquirers as made the most minute investigation, was entirely at fault.

But although the cause of concealing the Author's name in the first instance, when the reception of *Waverley* was doubtful, was natural enough, it is more difficult, it may be thought, to account for the same desire for secrecy during the subsequent editions, to the amount of betwixt eleven and twelve thousand copies, which followed each other close, and proved the success of the work. I am sorry I can give little satisfaction to queries on this subject. I have already stated elsewhere, that I can render little better reason for choosing to remain anonymous, than by saying with Shylock, that such was my humour. It will be observed, that I had not the usual stimulus for desiring personal reputation, the desire, namely, to float amidst the conversation of men. Of literary fame, whether merited or undeserved, I had already as much as might have contented a mind more ambitious than mine; and in entering into this new contest for reputation, I might be said rather to endanger what I had, than to have any considerable chance of acquiring more. I was affected, too, by none of those motives which, at an earlier period of life, would doubtless have operated upon me. My friendships were formed,—my place in society fixed,—my life had attained its middle course. My condition in society was higher perhaps than I deserved, certainly as high as I wished, and there was scarce any degree of literary success which could have greatly altered or improved my personal condition.

I was not, therefore, touched by the spur of ambition, usually stimulating on such occasions; and yet I ought to stand exculpated from the charge of ungracious or unbecoming indifference to public applause. I did not the less feel gratitude for the public favour, although I did not proclaim it,—as the lover who wears his mistress's favour in his bosom, is as proud, though not so vain of possessing it, as another who displays the token of her grace upon his bonnet. Far from such an ungracious state of mind, I have seldom felt more satisfaction than when, returning from a pleasure voyage, I found *Waverley* in the zenith of popularity, and public curiosity in full cry after the name of the Author. The knowledge that I had the public approbation, was like having the property of a hidden treasure, not less gratifying to the owner than if all the world knew that it was his own. Another advantage was connected with the secrecy which I observed. I could appear, or retreat from the stage at pleasure, without attracting any personal notice or attention, other than what might be founded on suspicion only. In my own person also, as a successful Author in another department of literature, I might have been charged with too frequent intrusions on the public patience; but the Author of *Waverley* was in this respect as impassible to the critic as the Ghost of Hamlet to the partisan of Marcellus. Perhaps the curiosity of the public, irritated by the existence of a secret, and kept afloat by the discussions which took place on the subject from time to time, went a good way to maintain an unabated interest in these frequent publications. There was a mystery concerning the Author, which each new novel was expected to assist in unravelling, although it might in other respects rank lower than its predecessors.

I may perhaps be thought guilty of affectation, should I allege as one reason of my silence, a secret dislike to enter on personal discussions concerning my own literary labours. It is in every case a dangerous intercourse for an author to be dwelling continually among those who make his writings a frequent and familiar subject of conversation, but who must necessarily be partial judges of works composed in their own society. The habits of self-importance, which are thus acquired by authors, are highly injurious to a well-regulated mind; for the cup of flattery, if it does not, like that of Circe, reduce men to the level of beasts, is sure, if eagerly drained, to bring the best and the ablest down to that of fools. This risk was in some degree prevented by the mask which I wore; and my own stores of self-conceit were left to their natural course, without being enhanced by the partiality of friends, or adulation of flatterers.

If I am asked further reasons for the conduct I have long observed, I can only resort to the explanation supplied by a critic as friendly as he is intelligent; namely, that the mental organization of the Novelist must be characterised, to speak craniologically, by an extraordinary development of the passion for delitescency! I the rather suspect some natural disposition of this kind; for, from the instant I perceived the extreme curiosity manifested on the subject, I felt a secret satisfaction in baffling it, for which, when its unimportance is considered, I do not well know how to account.

My desire to remain concealed, in the character of the Author of these Novels, subjected me occasionally to awkward embarrassments, as it sometimes happened that those who were sufficiently intimate with me, would put the question in direct terms. In this case, only one of three courses could be followed. Either I must have surrendered my secret,—or have returned an equivocating answer,—or, finally, must have stoutly and boldly denied the fact. The first was a sacrifice which I conceive no one had a right to force from me, since I alone was concerned in the matter. The alternative of rendering a doubtful answer must have left me open to the degrading suspicion that I was not unwilling to assume the merit (if there was any) which I dared not absolutely lay claim to; or those who might think more justly of me, must have received such an equivocal answer as an indirect avowal. I therefore considered myself entitled, like an accused person put upon trial, to refuse giving my own evidence to my own conviction, and flatly to deny all that could not be proved against me. At the same time I usually qualified my denial by stating, that, had I been the Author of these works, I would have felt myself quite entitled to protect my secret by refusing my own evidence, when it was asked for to accomplish a discovery of what I desired to conceal.

The real truth is, that I never expected or hoped to disguise my connection with these Novels from any one who lived on terms of intimacy with me. The number of coincidences which necessarily existed between narratives recounted, modes of expression, and opinions broached in these Tales, and such as were used by their Author in the intercourse of private life, must have been far too great to permit any of my familiar acquaintances to doubt the identity betwixt their friend and the Author of *Waverley;* and I believe, they were all morally convinced of it. But

while I was myself silent, their belief could not weigh
much more with the world than that of others; their
opinions and reasoning were liable to be taxed with
partiality, or confronted with opposing arguments and
opinions; and the question was not so much, whether I
should be generally acknowledged to be the author, in
spite of my own denial, as whether even my own avowal
of the works, if such should be made, would be sufficient
to put me in undisputed possession of that character.

I have been often asked concerning supposed cases, in
which I was said to have been placed on the verge of
discovery; but, as I maintained my point with the composure of a lawyer of thirty years' standing, I never
recollect being in pain or confusion on the subject. In
Captain Medwyn's *Conversations* of Lord Byron, the
reporter states himself to have asked my noble and
highly-gifted friend, "If he was certain about these
Novels being Sir Walter Scott's?" To which Lord Byron
replied, "Scott as much as owned himself the Author of
*Waverley* to me in Murray's shop. I was talking to him
about that novel, and lamented that its author had not
carried back the story nearer to the time of the Revolution—Scott, entirely off his guard, replied, 'Ay, I might
have done so; but—' there he stopped. It was in vain to
attempt to correct himself; he looked confused, and
relieved his embarrassment by a precipitate retreat." I
have no recollection whatever of this scene taking place,
and I should have thought that I was more likely to have
laughed than to appear confused, for I certainly never
hoped to impose upon Lord Byron in a case of the kind;
and from the manner in which he uniformly expressed
himself, I knew his opinion was entirely formed, and that
any disclamations of mine would only have savoured of
affectation. I do not mean to insinuate that the incident did not happen, but only that it could hardly have
occurred exactly under the circumstances narrated,
without my recollecting something positive on the
subject. In another part of the same volume, Lord
Byron is reported to have expressed a supposition that
the cause of my not avowing myself the Author of
*Waverley* may have been some surmise that the reigning
family would have been displeased with the work. I can
only say, it is the last apprehension I should have entertained, as indeed the inscription to these volumes
sufficiently proves. The sufferers of that melancholy
period have, during the last and present reign, been

honoured both with the sympathy and protection of the reigning family, whose magnanimity can well pardon a sigh from others, and bestow one themselves, to the memory of brave opponents, who did nothing in hate, but all in honour.

While those who were in habitual intercourse with the real author had little hesitation in assigning the literary property to him, others, and those critics of no mean rank, employed themselves in investigating with persevering patience any characteristic features which might seem to betray the origin of these Novels. Amongst these, one gentleman, equally remarkable for the kind and liberal tone of his criticism, the acuteness of his reasoning, and the very gentlemanlike manner in which he conducted his enquiries, displayed not only powers of accurate investigation, but a temper of mind deserving to be employed on a subject of much greater importance ; and I have no doubt made converts to his opinion of almost all who thought the point worthy of consideration.[1] Of those *Letters*, and other attempts of the same kind, the Author could not complain, though his incognito was endangered. He had challenged the public to a game at bo-peep, and if he was discovered in his "hiding-hole," he must submit to the shame of detection.

Various reports were of course circulated in various ways ; some founded on an inaccurate rehearsal of what may have been partly real, some on circumstances having no concern whatever with the subject, and others on the invention of some importunate persons, who might perhaps imagine, that the readiest mode of forcing the Author to disclose himself, was to assign some dishonourable and discreditable cause for his silence.

It may be easily supposed that this sort of inquisition was treated with contempt by the person whom it principally regarded ; as, among all the rumours that were current, there was only one, and that as unfounded as the others, which had nevertheless some alliance to probability, and indeed might have proved in some degree true.

I allude to a report which ascribed a great part, or the whole, of these Novels to the late Thomas Scott, Esq., of the 70th Regiment, then stationed in Canada. Those who remembered that gentleman will readily grant, that, with talents at least equal to those of his elder brother, he added a power of social humour, and a deep insight into

[1] *Letters on the Author of Waverley;* Rodwell & Martin, London, 1822.

human character, which rendered him an universally
delightful member of society, and that the habit of composition alone was wanting to render him equally successful as a writer. The Author of *Waverley* was so
persuaded of the truth of this, that he warmly pressed
his brother to make such an experiment, and willingly
undertook all the trouble of correcting and superintend-
ing the press. Mr Thomas Scott seemed at first very well
disposed to embrace the proposal, and had even fixed on
a subject and a hero. The latter was a person well known
to both of us in our boyish years, from having displayed
some strong traits of character. Mr T. Scott had determined to represent his youthful acquaintance as emi-
grating to America, and encountering the dangers and
hardships of the New World, with the same dauntless
spirit which he had displayed when a boy in his native
country. Mr Scott would probably have been highly successful, being familiarly acquainted with the manners of
the native Indians, of the old French settlers in Canada,
and of the Brules or Woodsmen, and having the power
of observing with accuracy what, I have no doubt, he
could have sketched with force and expression. In short,
the Author believes his brother would have made himself
distinguished in that striking field, in which, since that
period, Mr Cooper has achieved so many triumphs. But
Mr T. Scott was already affected by bad health, which
wholly unfitted him for literary labour, even if he could
have reconciled his patience to the task. He never, I
believe, wrote a single line of the projected work; and I
only have the melancholy pleasure of preserving in the
Appendix,[1] the simple anecdote on which he proposed to
found it.

To this I may add, I can easily conceive that there may
have been circumstances which gave a colour to the general report of my brother being interested in these works;
and in particular that it might derive strength from my
having occasion to remit to him, in consequence of certain
family transactions, some considerable sums of money
about that period. To which it is to be added that if any
person chanced to evince particular curiosity on such a
subject, my brother was likely enough to divert himself
with practising on their credulity.

It may be mentioned, that while the paternity of these
Novels was from time to time warmly disputed in Britain,
the foreign booksellers expressed no hesitation on the

[1] See Appendix, No. III.

matter, but affixed my name to the whole of the novels, and to some besides to which I had no claim. The volumes, therefore, to which the present pages form a Preface, are entirely the composition of the Author by whom they are now acknowledged, with the exception, always, of avowed quotations, and such unpremeditated and involuntary plagiarisms as can scarce be guarded against by any one who has read and written a great deal. The original manuscripts are all in existence, and entirely written (*horresco referens*) in the Author's own hand, excepting during the years 1818 and 1819, when, being affected with severe illness, he was obliged to employ the assistance of a friendly amanuensis.

The number of persons to whom the secret was necessarily intrusted, or communicated by chance, amounted I should think to twenty at least, to whom I am greatly obliged for the fidelity with which they observed their trust, until the derangement of the affairs of my publishers, Messrs Constable & Co., and the exposure of their accompt books, which was the necessary consequence, rendered secrecy no longer possible. The particulars attending the avowal have been laid before the public in the Introduction to the *Chronicles of the Canongate*.

The Preliminary Advertisement has given a sketch of the purpose of this Edition. I have some reason to fear that the Notes which accompany the Tales, as now published, may be thought too miscellaneous and too egotistical. It may be some apology for this, that the publication was intended to be posthumous, and still more, that old men may be permitted to speak long, because they cannot in the course of nature have long time to speak. In preparing the present edition, I have done all that I can do to explain the nature of my materials, and the use I have made of them; nor is it probable that I shall again revise or even read these Tales. I was therefore desirous rather to exceed in the portion of new and explanatory matter which is added to this edition, than that the reader should have reason to complain that the information communicated was of a general and merely nominal character. It remains to be tried whether the public (like a child to whom a watch is shown) will, after having been satiated with looking at the outside, acquire some new interest in the object when it is opened, and the internal machinery displayed to them.

If, like a spoiled child, the Author has sometimes abused or trifled with the indulgence of the public, he feels himself entitled to full belief, when he exculpates himself from the charge of having been at any time insensible of their kindness.

ABBOTSFORD, 1st January 1829.

---

# APPENDIX.

## No. I.[1]

FRAGMENT OF A ROMANCE WHICH WAS TO HAVE BEEN ENTITLED,

# THOMAS THE RHYMER.

### CHAPTER I.

THE sun was nearly set behind the distant mountains of Liddesdale, when a few of the scattered and terrified inhabitants of the village of Hersildoun, which had four days before been burned by a predatory band of English Borderers, were now busied in repairing their ruined dwellings. One high tower in the centre of the village alone exhibited no appearance of devastation. It was surrounded with court walls, and the outer gate was barred and bolted. The bushes and brambles which grew around, and had even insinuated their branches beneath the gate, plainly showed that it must have been many years since it had been opened. While the cottages around lay in smoking ruins, this pile, deserted and desolate as it seemed to be, had suffered nothing from the violence of the invaders; and the wretched beings who were endeavouring to repair their miserable huts against nightfall, seemed to neglect the preferable shelter which it might have afforded them, without the necessity of labour.

Before the day had quite gone down, a knight, richly armed, and mounted upon an ambling hackney, rode slowly into the village. His attendants were a lady, apparently young and beautiful, who rode by his side upon a dappled palfrey; his squire, who carried his helmet and lance, and led his battle-horse, a noble steed, richly caparisoned. A page and four yeomen, bearing bows and quivers, short swords, and targets of a span breadth, completed his equipage, which, though small, denoted him to be a man of high rank.

---

[1] It is not to be supposed that these fragments are given as possessing any intrinsic value of themselves; but there may be some curiosity attached to them, as to the first etchings of a plate, which are accounted interesting by those who have, in any degree, been interested in the more finished works of the artist.

He stopped and addressed several of the inhabitants whom curiosity had withdrawn from their labour to gaze at him ; but at the sound of his voice, and still more on perceiving the St George's Cross in the caps of his followers, they fled, with a loud cry, "that the Southrons were returned." The knight endeavoured to expostulate with the fugitives, who were chiefly aged men, women, and children ; but their dread of the English name accelerated their flight, and in a few minutes, excepting the knight and his attendants, the place was deserted by all. He paced through the village to seek a shelter for the night, and despairing to find one either in the inaccessible tower, or the plundered huts of the peasantry, he directed his course to the left hand, where he spied a small decent habitation, apparently the abode of a man considerably above the common rank. After much knocking, the proprietor at length showed himself at the window, and speaking in the English dialect, with great signs of apprehension, demanded their business. The warrior replied, that his quality was an English knight and baron, and that he was travelling to the court of the King of Scotland on affairs of consequence to both kingdoms.

"Pardon my hesitation, noble Sir Knight," said the old man, as he unbolted and unbarred his doors—"Pardon my hesitation, but we are here exposed to too many intrusions, to admit of our exercising unlimited and unsuspicious hospitality. What I have is yours ; and God send your mission may bring back peace and the good days of our old Queen Margaret !"

"Amen, worthy Franklin," quoth the Knight—"Did you know her ?"

"I came to this country in her train," said the Franklin ; "and the care of some of her jointure lands which she devolved on me, occasioned my settling here."

"And how do you, being an Englishman," said the Knight, "protect your life and property here, when one of your nation cannot obtain a single night's lodging, or a draught of water, were he thirsty ?"

"Marry, noble sir," answered the Franklin, "use, as they say, will make a man live in a lion's den ; and as I settled here in a quiet time, and have never given cause of offence, I am respected by my neighbours, and even, as you see, by our *forayers* from England."

"I rejoice to hear it, and accept your hospitality.—Isabella, my love, our worthy host will provide you a bed. My daughter, good Franklin, is ill at ease. We will occupy your house till the Scottish King shall return from his northern expedition—meanwhile call me Lord Lacy of Chester."

The attendants of the Baron, assisted by the Franklin, were now busied in disposing of the horses, and arranging the table for some refreshment for Lord Lacy and his fair companion. While they sat down to it, they were attended by their host and his daughter, whom custom did not permit to eat in their presence, and who afterwards withdrew to an outer chamber, where the squire and page (both young men of noble birth) partook of supper, and were accommodated with beds. The yeomen, after doing honour to the rustic cheer of Queen Margaret's bailiff, withdrew to the stable, and each, beside his favourite horse, snored away the fatigues of their journey.

Early on the following morning, the travellers were roused by a thundering knocking at the door of the house, accompanied with many demands for instant admission, in the roughest tone. The squire and page of Lord Lacy, after buckling on their arms, were about to sally out to chastise these intruders, when the old host, after looking out at a private casement, contrived for reconnoitring his visitors, entreated them, with great signs of terror, to be quiet, if they did not mean that all in the house should be murdered.

He then hastened to the apartment of Lord Lacy, whom he met dressed in a long furred gown and the knightly cap called a *mortier*, irritated at the noise, and demanding to know the cause which had disturbed the repose of the household.

"Noble sir," said the Franklin, "one of the most formidable and bloody of the Scottish Border riders is at hand—he is never seen," added he, faltering with terror, "so far from the hills, but with some bad purpose, and the power of accomplishing it, so hold yourself to your guard, for"——

A loud crash here announced that the door was broken down, and the knight just descended the stair in time to prevent bloodshed betwixt his attendants and the intruders. They were three in number—their chief was tall, bony, and athletic, his spare and muscular frame, as well as the hardness of his features, marked the course of his life to have been fatiguing and perilous. The effect of his appearance was aggravated by his dress, which consisted of a jack or jacket, composed of thick buff leather, on which small plates of iron of a lozenge form were stitched, in such a manner as to overlap each other, and form a coat of mail, which swayed with every motion of the wearer's body. This defensive armour covered a doublet of coarse grey cloth, and the Borderer had a few half-rusted plates of steel on his shoulders, a two-edged sword, with a dagger hanging beside it, in a buff belt —a helmet, with a few iron bars, to cover the face instead of a visor, and a lance of tremendous and uncommon length, completed his appointments. The looks of the man were as wild and rude as his attire—his keen black eyes never rested one moment fixed upon a single object, but constantly traversed all around, as if they ever sought some danger to oppose, some plunder to seize, or some insult to revenge. The latter seemed to be his present object, for, regardless of the dignified presence of Lord Lacy, he uttered the most incoherent threats against the owner of the house and his guests.

"We shall see—ay, marry shall we—if an English hound is to harbour and reset the Southrons here. Thank the Abbot of

Melrose, and the good Knight of Coldingnow, that have so long
kept me from your skirts. But those days are gone, by St Mary,
and you shall find it!"

It is probable the enraged Borderer would not have long
continued to vent his rage in empty menaces, had not the
entrance of the four yeomen, with their bows bent, convinced
him that the force was not at this moment on his own side.

Lord Lacy now advanced towards him. "You intrude upon
my privacy, soldier; withdraw yourself and your followers—
there is peace betwixt our nations, or my servants should chastise
thy presumption."

"Such peace as ye give such shall you have," answered the
moss-trooper, first pointing with his lance towards the burned
village, and then almost instantly levelling it against Lord Lacy.
The squire drew his sword, and severed at one blow the steel
head from the truncheon of the spear.

"Arthur Fitzherbert," said the baron, "that stroke has
deferred thy knighthood for one year—never must that squire
wear the spurs whose unbridled impetuosity can draw unbidden
his sword in the presence of his master. Go hence, and think on
what I have said."

The squire left the chamber abashed.

"It were vain," continued Lord Lacy, "to expect that courtesy
from a mountain churl which even my own followers can forget.
Yet, before thou drawest thy brand (for the intruder laid his
hand upon the hilt of his sword), thou wilt do well to reflect
that I came with a safe-conduct from thy king, and have no time
to waste in brawls with such as thou."

"From *my* king—from my king!" re-echoed the mountaineer.
"I care not that rotten truncheon (striking the shattered spear
furiously on the ground) for the King of Fife and Lothian. But
Habby of Cessford will be here belive; and we shall soon know
if he will permit an English churl to occupy his hostelrie."

Having uttered these words, accompanied with a lowering
glance from under his shaggy black eye-brows, he turned on his
heel, and left the house with his two followers;—they mounted
their horses, which they had tied to an outer fence, and vanished
in an instant.

"Who is this discourteous ruffian?" said Lord Lacy to the
Franklin, who had stood in the most violent agitation during this
whole scene.

"His name, noble lord, is Adam Kerr of the Moat, but he is
commonly called by his companions, the Black Rider of Cheviot.
I fear, I fear, he comes hither for no good—but if the Lord of
Cessford be near, he will not dare offer any unprovoked out-
rage."

"I have heard of that chief," said the Baron—"let me know
when he approaches, and do thou, Rodulph, (to the eldest
yeoman,) keep a strict watch. Adelbert, (to the page,) attend
to arm me." The page bowed, and the Baron withdrew to the

chamber of the Lady Isabella, to explain the cause of the disturbance.

\*     \*     \*     \*     \*     \*

No more of the proposed tale was ever written; but the author's purpose was, that it should turn upon a fine legend of superstition, which is current in the part of the Borders where he had his residence; where in the reign of Alexander III. of Scotland, that renowned person Thomas of Hersildoune, called the Rhymer, actually flourished. This personage, the Merlin of Scotland, and to whom some of the adventures which the British bards assigned to Merlin Caledonius, or the Wild, have been transferred by tradition, was, as is well known, a magician, as well as a poet and prophet. He is alleged still to live in the land of Faery, and is expected to return at some great convulsion of society, in which he is to act a distinguished part, a tradition common to all nations, as the belief of the Mahomedans respecting their twelfth Imaum demonstrates.

Now, it chanced many years since, that there lived on the Borders a jolly, rattling horse-cowper, who was remarkable for a reckless and fearless temper, which made him much admired, and a little dreaded, amongst his neighbours. One moonlight night, as he rode over Bowden Moor, on the west side of the Eildon Hills, the scene of Thomas the Rhymer's prophecies, and often mentioned in his story, having a brace of horses along with him which he had not been able to dispose of, he met a man of venerable appearance, and singularly antique dress, who, to his great surprise, asked the price of his horses, and began to chaffer with him on the subject. To Canobie Dick, for so shall we call our Border dealer, a chap was a chap, and he would have sold a horse to the devil himself, without minding his cloven hoof, and would have probably cheated Old Nick into the bargain The stranger paid the price they agreed on, and all that puzzled Dick in the transaction was, that the gold which he received was in unicorns, bonnet-pieces, and other ancient coins, which would have been invaluable to collectors, but were rather troublesome in modern currency. It was gold, however, and therefore Dick contrived to get better value for the coin, than he perhaps gave to his customer. By the command of so good a merchant, he brought horses to the same spot more than once; the purchaser only stipulating that he should always come by night, and alone. I do not know whether it was from mere curiosity, or whether some hope of gain mixed with it, but after Dick had sold several horses in this way, he began to complain that dry bargains were unlucky, and to hint, that since his chap must live in the neighbourhood, he ought, in the courtesy of dealing, to treat him to half a mutchkin.

"You may see my dwelling if you will," said the stranger; "but if you lose courage at what you see there, you will rue it all your life."

Dicken, however, laughed the warning to scorn, and having alighted to secure his horse, he followed the stranger up a narrow foot-path, which led them up the hills to the singular eminence stuck betwixt the most southern and the centre peaks, and called from its resemblance to such an animal in its form, the Lucken Hare. At the foot of this eminence, which is almost as famous for witch meetings as the neighbouring wind-mill of Kippilaw, Dick was somewhat startled to observe that his conductor entered the hill side by a passage or cavern, of which he himself, though well acquainted with the spot, had never seen or heard.

"You may still return," said his guide, looking ominously back upon him; but Dick scorned to show the white feather, and on they went. They entered a very long range of stables; in every stall stood a coal-black horse; by every horse lay a knight in coal-black armour, with a drawn sword in his hand, but all were as silent, hoof and limb, as if they had been cut out of marble. A great number of torches lent a gloomy lustre to the hall, which, like those of the Caliph Vathek, was of large dimensions. At the upper end, however, they at length arrived, where a sword and horn lay on an antique table.

"He that shall sound that horn and draw that sword," said the stranger, who now intimated that he was the famous Thomas of Hersildoune, "shall, if his heart fail him not, be king over all broad Britain. So speaks the tongue that cannot lie. But all depends on courage, and much on your taking the sword or the horn first."

Dick was much disposed to take the sword, but his bold spirit was quailed by the supernatural terrors of the hall, and he thought to unsheath the sword first, might be construed into defiance, and give offence to the powers of the Mountain. He took the bugle with a trembling hand, and a feeble note, but loud enough to produce a terrible answer. Thunder rolled in stunning peals through the immense hall; horses and men started to life; the steeds snorted, stamped, grinded their bits, and tossed on high their heads—the warriors sprung to their feet, clashed their armour, and brandished their swords. Dick's terror was extreme at seeing the whole army, which had been so lately silent as the grave, in uproar, and about to rush on him. He dropped the horn, and made a feeble attempt to seize the enchanted sword; but at the same moment a voice pronounced aloud the mysterious words:

> "Woe to the coward, that ever he was born,
> Who did not draw the sword before he blew the horn!"

At the same time a whirlwind of irresistible fury howled through the long hall, bore the unfortunate horse-jockey clear out of the mouth of the cavern, and precipitated him over a steep bank of loose stones, where the shepherds found him the next morning, with just breath sufficient to tell his fearful tale, after concluding which he expired.

This legend, with several variations, is found in many parts of Scotland and England—the scene is sometimes laid in some favourite glen of the Highlands, sometimes in the deep coal-mines of Northumberland and Cumberland, which run so far beneath the ocean. It is also to be found in Reginald Scott's book on Witchcraft, which was written in the 16th century. It would be in vain to ask what was the original of the tradition. The choice between the horn and sword may, perhaps, include as a moral, that it is fool-hardy to awaken danger before we have arms in our hands to resist it.

Although admitting of much poetical ornament, it is clear that this legend would have formed but an unhappy foundation for a prose story, and must have degenerated into a mere fairy tale. Dr John Leyden has beautifully introduced the tradition in his Scenes of Infancy :

> " Mysterious Rhymer, doom'd by fate's decree,
>   Still to revisit Eildon's fated tree;
>   Where oft the swain, at dawn of Hallow-day.
>   Hears thy fleet barb with wild impatience neigh;
>   Say who is he, with summons long and high,
>   Shall bid the charmed sleep of ages fly,
>   Roll the long sound through Eildon's caverns vast,
>   While each dark warrior kindles at the blast:
>   The horn, the falchion grasp with mighty hand,
>   And peal proud Arthur's march from Fairy-land ?"
>                               *Scenes of Infancy*, Part 1.

In the same cabinet with the preceding fragment, the following occurred among other *disjecta membra*. It seems to be an attempt at a tale of a different description from the last, but was almost instantly abandoned. The introduction points out the time of the composition to have been about the end of the 18th century.

## THE LORD OF ENNERDALE.

IN A FRAGMENT OF A LETTER FROM JOHN B——, ESQ., OF THAT ILK,
TO WILLIAM G——, F.R.S.E.

"Fill a bumper," said the Knight; "the ladies may spare us a little longer—Fill a bumper to the Archduke Charles."

The company did due honour to the toast of their landlord.

"The success of the Archduke," said the muddy Vicar, "will tend to further our negotiation at Paris ; and if——"

"Pardon the interruption, Doctor," quoth a thin emaciated figure, with somewhat of a foreign accent; "but why should you connect those events unless to hope that the bravery and victories of our allies may supersede the necessity of a degrading treaty ?"

"We begin to feel, Monsieur L'Abbé," answered the Vicar, with some asperity, "that a Continental war entered into for the defence of an ally who was unwilling to defend himself, and for the restoration of a royal family, nobility, and priesthood, who tamely abandoned their own rights, is a burden too much even for the resources of this country."

"And was the war then on the part of Great Britain," rejoined the Abbé, "a gratuitous exertion of generosity? Was there no fear of the wide-wasting spirit of innovation which had gone abroad? Did not the laity tremble for their property, the clergy for their religion, and every loyal heart for the Constitution? Was it not thought necessary to destroy the building which was on fire, ere the conflagration spread around the vicinity?"

"Yet, if upon trial," said the Doctor, "the walls were found to resist our utmost efforts, I see no great prudence in persevering in our labour amid the smouldering ruins."

"What, Doctor," said the Baronet, "must I call to your recollection your own sermon on the late general fast?—did you not encourage us to hope that the Lord of Hosts would go forth with our armies, and that our enemies, who blasphemed him, should be put to shame?"

"It may please a kind father to chasten even his beloved children," answered the Vicar.

"I think," said a gentleman near the foot of the table, "that the Covenanters made some apology of the same kind for the failure of their prophecies at the battle of Dunbar, when their mutinous preachers compelled the prudent Lesley to go down against the Philistines in Gilgal."

The Vicar fixed a scrutinizing and not a very complacent eye upon this intruder. He was a young man of mean stature, and rather a reserved appearance. Early and severe study had quenched in his features the gaiety peculiar to his age, and impressed upon them a premature cast of thoughtfulness. His eye had, however, retained its fire, and his gesture its animation. Had he remained silent, he would have been long unnoticed; but when he spoke, there was something in his manner which arrested attention.

"Who is this young man?" said the Vicar in a low voice, to his neighbour.

"A Scotchman called Maxwell, on a visit to Sir Henry," was the answer.

"I thought so, from his accent and his manners," said the Vicar.

It may be here observed, that the northern English retain rather more of the ancient hereditary aversion to their neighbours than their countrymen of the South. The interference of other disputants, each of whom urged his opinion with all the vehemence of wine and politics, rendered the summons to the drawing-room agreeable to the more sober part of the company.

The company dispersed by degrees, and at length the Vicar and the young Scotchman alone remained, besides the Baronet, his lady, daughters, and myself. The clergyman had not, it would seem, forgot the observation which ranked him with the false prophets of Dunbar, for he addressed Mr Maxwell upon the first opportunity.

"Hem! I think, sir, you mentioned something about the civil wars of last century? You must be deeply skilled in them indeed, if you can draw any parallel betwixt those and the present evil days—days which I am ready to maintain are the most gloomy that ever darkened the prospects of Britain."

"God forbid, Doctor, that I should draw a comparison between the present times and those you mention. I am too sensible of the advantages we enjoy over our ancestors. Faction and ambition have introduced division among us; but we are still free from the guilt of civil bloodshed, and from all the evils which flow from it. Our foes, sir, are not those of our own household; and while we continue united and firm, from the attacks of a foreign enemy, however artful, or however inveterate, we have, I hope, little to dread."

"Have you found any thing curious, Mr Maxwell, among the dusty papers?" said Sir Henry, who seemed to dread a revival of political discussion.

"My investigation amongst them led to reflections which I have just now hinted," said Maxwell; "and I think they are pretty strongly exemplified by a story which I have been endeavouring to arrange from some of your family manuscripts."

"You are welcome to make what use of them you please," said Sir Henry; "they have been undisturbed for many a day, and I have often wished for some person as well skilled as you in these old pot-hooks, to tell me their meaning."

"Those I just mentioned," answered Maxwell, "relate to a piece of private history, savouring not a little of the marvellous, and intimately connected with your family; if it is agreeable, I can read to you the anecdotes in the modern shape into which I have been endeavouring to throw them, and you can then judge of the value of the originals."

There was something in this proposal, agreeable to all parties. Sir Henry had family pride, which prepared him to take an interest in whatever related to his ancestors. The ladies had dipped deeply into the fashionable reading of the present day. Lady Ratcliff and her fair daughters had climbed every pass, viewed every pine-shrouded ruin, heard every groan, and lifted every trap-door, in company with the noted heroine of Udolpho. They had been heard, however, to observe, that the famous incident of the Black Veil, singularly resembled the ancient apologue of the Mountain in labour, so that they were unquestionably critics, as well as admirers. Besides all this, they had valorously mounted *en croupe* behind the ghostly horseman of Prague, through all his seven translators, and followed the footsteps of Moor through the forest of Bohemia. Moreover, it was even hinted (but this was a greater mystery than all the rest), that a certain performance called the *Monk*, in three neat volumes, had been seen, by a prying eye, in the right-hand drawer of the Indian cabinet of Lady Ratcliff's dressing room. Thus predisposed for wonders and signs, Lady Ratcliff and her nymphs drew their chairs round a large blazing wood-fire, and arranged themselves to listen to the tale. To that fire I also approached, moved thereunto partly by the inclemency of the season, and partly that my deafness, which you know, cousin, I acquired during my campaign under Prince Charles Edward, might be no obstacle to the gratification of my curiosity, which was awakened by what had any reference to the fate of such faithful followers of royalty, as you well know the house of Ratcliff have ever been. To this wood-fire the Vicar likewise drew near, and reclined himself conveniently in his chair, seemingly disposed to testify his disrespect for the narration and narrator by falling asleep as soon as he conveniently could. By the side of Maxwell (by the way, I cannot learn that he is in the least related to the Nithsdale family) was placed a small table and couple of lights, by the assistance of which he read as follows :—

*"Journal of Jan Von Eulen.*

"On the 6th November, 1645, I, Jan Von Eulen, merchant in Rotterdam, embarked with my only daughter on board of the good vessel Vryheid of Amsterdam, in order to pass into the unhappy and disturbed kingdom of England. 7th November—a brisk gale—daughter sea-sick—myself unable to complete the calculation which I have begun, of the inheritance left by Jane Lansache of Carlisle, my late dear wife's sister, the collection of which is the object of my voyage.—8th November, wind still stormy and adverse—a horrid disaster nearly happened—my dear child washed overboard as the vessel lurched to leeward.—Memorandum, to reward the young sailor who saved her, out of the first moneys which I can recover from the inheritance of her aunt Lansache.—9th November, calm—P.M. light breezes from N.N.W. I talked with the captain about the inheritance of my sister-in-law, Jane Lansache.—He says he knows the principal subject, which will not exceed L.1000 in value. N.B. He is a cousin to a family of Petersons, which was the name of the husband of my sister-in-law ; so there is room to hope it may be worth more than he reports.—10th November, 10 A.M. May God pardon all our sins—An English frigate, bearing the Parliament flag, has appeared in the offing, and gives chase.—11 A.M. She nears us every moment, and the captain of our vessel prepares to clear for action.—May God again have mercy upon us !"

\* \* \* \* \* \* \* \*

"Here," said Maxwell, "the journal with which I have opened the narration ends somewhat abruptly."

"I am glad of it," said Lady Ratcliff.

"But, Mr Maxwell," said young Frank, Sir Henry's grandchild, "shall we not hear how the battle ended ?"

I do not know, cousin, whether I have not formerly made you acquainted with the abilities of Frank Ratcliff. There is not a battle fought between the troops of the Prince and of the Government, during the years 1745-6, of which he is not able to give an account. It is true, I have taken particular pains to fix the events of this important period upon his memory by frequent repetition.

"No, my dear," said Maxwell, in answer to young Frank Ratcliff.—"No, my dear, I cannot tell you the exact particulars of the engagement, but its consequences appear from the following letter, dispatched by Garbonete Von Eulen, daughter of our journalist, to a relation in England, from whom she implored assistance. After some general account of the purpose of the voyage, and of the engagement, her narrative proceeds thus :—

"The noise of the cannon had hardly ceased, before the sounds of a language to me but half known, and the confusion on board our vessel, informed me that the captors had boarded us, and taken possession of our vessel. I went on deck, where the first spectacle that met my eyes was a young man, mate of our vessel, who, though disfigured and covered with blood, was loaded with irons, and whom they were forcing over the side of the vessel into a boat. The two principal persons among our enemies appeared to be a man of a tall thin figure, with a high-crowned hat and long neck-band, and short-cropped head of hair, accompanied by a bluff open-looking elderly man in a naval uniform. 'Yarely! yarely! pull away, my hearts,' said the latter, and the boat bearing the unlucky young man soon carried him on board the frigate. Perhaps you will blame me for mentioning this circumstance ; but consider, my dear cousin, this man saved my life, and his fate, even when my own and my father's were in the balance, could not but affect me nearly.

"'In the name of him who is jealous, even to slaying,' said the first"———

\*　　\*　　\*　　\*　　\*　　\*　　\*　　\*

*Cetera desunt.*

# No. II.

### CONCLUSION OF MR STRUTT'S ROMANCE OF

## QUEENHOO-HALL.

### BY THE AUTHOR OF "WAVERLEY."

### CHAPTER IV.

#### A HUNTING PARTY—AN ADVENTURE—A DELIVERANCE.

THE next morning the bugles were sounded by day-break in the court of Lord Boteler's mansion, to call the inhabitants from

their slumbers, to assist in a splendid chase, with which the
Baron had resolved to entertain his neighbour Fitzallen, and his
noble visitor St Clere. Peter Lanaret, the falconer, was in
attendance, with falcons for the knights, and teircelets for the
ladies, if they should choose to vary their sport from hunting to
hawking. Five stout yeomen keepers, with their attendants,
called Ragged Robins, all meetly arrayed in Kendal green, with
bugles and short hangers by their sides, and quarter-staffs in
their hands, led the slow-hounds or brachets, by which the deer
were to be put up. Ten brace of gallant greyhounds, each of
which was fit to pluck down, singly, the tallest red deer, were
led in leashes by as many of Lord Boteler's foresters. The pages,
squires, and other attendants of feudal splendour, well attired in
their best hunting-gear, upon horseback or foot, according to
their rank, with their boar-spears, long bows, and cross-bows,
were in seemly waiting.

A numerous train of yeomen, called in the language of the
times, retainers, who yearly received a livery coat, and a small
pension for their attendance on such solemn occasions, appeared
in cassocks of blue, bearing upon their arms the cognizance of
the house of Boteler, as a badge of their adherence. They were
the tallest men of their hands that the neighbouring villages
could supply, with every man his good buckler on his shoulder,
and a bright burnished broadsword dangling from his leathern
belt. On this occasion, they acted as rangers for beating up the
thickets, and rousing the game. These attendants filled up the
court of the castle, spacious as it was.

On the green without, you might have seen the motley
assemblage of peasantry convened by report of the splendid
hunting, including most of our old acquaintances from Tewin,
as well as the jolly partakers of good cheer at Hob Filcher's.
Gregory the jester, it may well be guessed, had no great mind to
exhibit himself in public, after his recent disaster; but Oswald
the steward, a great formalist in whatever concerned the public
exhibition of his master's household state, had positively enjoined
his attendance. "What," quoth he, "shall the house of the
brave Lord Boteler, on such a brave day as this, be without a
fool? Certes, the good Lord St Clere, and his fair lady sister,
might think our housekeeping as niggardly as that of their
churlish kinsman at Gay Bowers, who sent his father's jester to
the hospital, sold the poor sot's bells for hawk-jesses, and made
a nightcap of his long-eared bonnet. And, sirrah, let me see
thee fool handsomely—speak squibs and crackers, instead of that
dry, barren, musty gibing, which thou hast used of late; or, by
the bones! the porter shall have thee to his lodge, and cob thee
with thine own wooden sword, till thy skin is as motley as thy
doublet." To this stern injunction, Gregory made no reply, any
more than to the courteous offer of old Albert Drawslot, the
chief park-keeper, who proposed to blow vinegar in his nose, to
sharpen his wit, as he had done that blessed morning to Bragger,

the old hound, whose scent was failing.   There was indeed little
time for reply, for the bugles, after a lively flourish, were now
silent, and Peretto, with his two attendant minstrels, stepping
beneath the windows of the stranger's apartments, joined in the
following roundelay, the deep voices of the rangers and falconers
making up a chorus that caused the very battlements to ring
again.

> Waken, lords and ladies gay,
> On the mountain dawns the day;
> All the jolly chase is here,
> With hawk and horse, and hunting spear:
> Hounds are in their couples yelling,
> Hawks are whistling, horns are knelling,
> Merrily, merrily, mingle they,
> " Waken, lords and ladies gay."
>
> Waken, lords and ladies gay,
> The mist has left the mountain grey;
> Springlets in the dawn are streaming,
> Diamonds on the brake are gleaming,
> And foresters have busy been,
> To track the buck in thicket green;
> Now we come to chant our lay,
> " Waken, lords and ladies gay."
>
> Waken, lords and ladies gay,
> To the green-wood haste away;
> We can show you where he lies,
> Fleet of foot, and tall of size;
> We can show the marks he made,
> When 'gainst the oak his antlers frayed;
> You shall see him brought to bay,
> "Waken  lords and ladies gay."
>
> Louder, louder chant the lay,
> Waken, lords and ladies gay;
> Tell them, youth, and mirth, and glee,
> Run a course as well as we,
> Time, stern huntsman! who can baulk,
> Stanch as hound, and fleet as hawk?
> Think of this, and rise with day,
> Gentle lords and ladies gay.

By the time this lay was finished, Lord Boteler, with his
daughter and kinsman, Fitzallen of Marden, and other noble
guests, had mounted their palfreys, and the hunt set forward in
due order.   The huntsmen, having carefully observed the traces
of a large stag on the preceding evening, were able, without loss
of time, to conduct the company, by the marks which they had
made upon the trees, to the side of the thicket, in which, by the
report of Drawslot, he had harboured all night.   The horsemen
spreading themselves along the side of the cover, waited
until the keeper entered, leading his bandog, a large blood-hound
tied in a leam or band, from which he takes his name.

But it befell thus.   A hart of the second year, which was in
the same cover with the proper object of their pursuit, chanced
to be unharboured first, and broke cover very near where the
Lady Emma and her brother were stationed.   An inexperienced

varlet, who was nearer to them, instantly unloosed two tall grey-hounds, who sprung after the fugitive with all the fleetness of the north wind. Gregory, restored a little to spirits by the enlivening scene around him, followed, encouraging the hounds with a loud tayout,[1] for which he had the hearty curses of the huntsman; as well as of the Baron, who entered into the spirit of the chase with all the juvenile ardour of twenty. "May the foul fiend, booted and spur'd, ride down his bawling throat, with a scythe at his girdle," quoth Albert Drawslot; "here have I been telling him, that all the marks were those of a buck of the first head, and he has halloo'd the hounds upon a velvet-headed knobbler! By Saint Hubert, if I break not his pate with my cross-bow, may I never cast off hound more! But to it, my lords and masters! the noble beast is here yet, and, thank the saints, we have enough of hounds."

The cover being now thoroughly beat by the attendants, the stag was compelled to abandon it, and trust to his speed for his safety. Three greyhounds were slipped upon him, whom he threw out, after running a couple of miles, by entering an extensive furzy brake, which extended along the side of a hill. The horsemen soon came up, and casting off a sufficient number of slow-hounds, sent them with the prickers into the cover, in order to drive the game from his strength. This object being accomplished, afforded another severe chase of several miles, in a direction almost circular, during which, the poor animal tried every wile to get rid of his persecutors. He crossed and traversed all such dusty paths as were likely to retain the least scent of his footsteps; he laid himself close to the ground, drawing his feet under his belly, and clapping his nose close to the earth, lest he should be betrayed to the hounds by his breath and hoofs. When all was in vain, and he found the hounds coming fast in upon him, his own strength failing, his mouth embossed with foam, and the tears dropping from his eyes, he turned in despair upon his pursuers, who then stood at gaze, making an hideous clamour, and awaiting their two-footed auxiliaries. Of these, it chanced that the Lady Eleanor, taking more pleasure in the sport than Matilda, and being a less burden to her palfrey than the Lord Boteler, was the first who arrived at the spot, and taking a cross-bow from an attendant, discharged a bolt at the stag. When the infuriated animal felt himself wounded, he pushed frantically towards her from whom he had received the shaft, and Lady Eleanor might have had occasion to repent of her enterprise, had not young Fitzallen, who had kept near her during the whole day, at that instant galloped briskly in, and ere the stag could change his object of assault, dispatched him with his short hunting-sword.

Albert Drawslot, who had just come up in terror for the young lady's safety, broke out into loud encomiums upon Fitzallen's

---

[1] *Tailliers-hors*, in modern phrase, Tally-ho!

strength and gallantry. "By'r Lady," said he, taking off his
cap, and wiping his sun-burnt face with his sleeve, "well
struck, and in good time!—But now, boys, doff your bonnets,
and sound the mort."

The sportsmen then sounded a treble mort, and set up a
general whoop, which, mingled with the yelping of the dogs, made
the welkin ring again. The huntsman then offered his knife to Lord
Boteler, that he might take the say of the deer, but the Baron
courteously insisted upon Fitzallen going through that ceremony.
The Lady Matilda was now come up, with most of the
attendants; and the interest of the chase being ended, it excited
some surprise, that neither St Clere nor his sister made their
appearance. The Lord Boteler commanded the horns again to
sound the recheat, in hopes to call in the stragglers, and said to
Fitzallen, "Methinks St Clere, so distinguished for service in
war, should have been more forward in the chase."

"I trow," said Peter Lanaret, "I know the reason of the
noble lord's absence; for when that mooncalf, Gregory, hallooed
the dogs upon the knobbler, and galloped like a green hilding, as
he is, after them, I saw the Lady Emma's palfrey follow apace
after that varlet, who should be trashed for overrunning, and
I think her noble brother has followed her, lest she should come
to harm.—But here, by the rood, is Gregory to answer for
himself."

At this moment Gregory entered the circle which had been
formed round the deer, out of breath, and his face covered with
blood. He kept for some time uttering inarticulate cries of
"Harrow!" and "Wellaway!" and other exclamations of
distress and terror, pointing all the while to a thicket at some
distance from the spot where the deer had been killed.

"By my honour," said the Baron, "I would gladly know who
has dared to array the poor knave thus; and I trust he should
dearly abye his outrecuidance, were he the best, save one, in
England."

Gregory, who had now found more breath, cried, "Help, an
ye be men! Save Lady Emma and her brother, whom they are
murdering in Brockenhurst thicket."

This put all in motion. Lord Boteler hastily commanded a
small party of his men to abide for the defence of the ladies,
while he himself, Fitzallen, and the rest, made what speed they
could towards the thicket, guided by Gregory, who for that
purpose was mounted behind Fabian. Pushing through a
narrow path, the first object they encountered was a man of
small stature lying on the ground, mastered and almost strangled
by two dogs, which were instantly recognized to be those that
had accompanied Gregory. A little farther was an open space,
where lay three bodies of dead or wounded men; beside these
was Lady Emma, apparently lifeless, her brother and a young
forester bending over and endeavouring to recover her. By
employing the usual remedies, this was soon accomplished;

while Lord Boteler, astonished at such a scene, anxiously enquired at St Clere the meaning of what he saw, and whether more danger was to be expected?

"For the present, I trust not," said the young warrior, who they now observed was slightly wounded; "but I pray you, of your nobleness, let the woods here be searched; for we were assaulted by four of these base assassins, and I see three only on the sward."

The attendants now brought forward the person whom they had rescued from the dogs, and Henry, with disgust, shame, and astonishment, recognised his kinsman, Gaston St Clere. This discovery he communicated in a whisper to Lord Boteler, who commanded the prisoner to be conveyed to Queenhoo-Hall, and closely guarded; meanwhile he anxiously enquired of young St Clere about his wound.

"A scratch, a trifle!" cried Henry; "I am in less haste to bind it than to introduce to you one, without whose aid that of the leech would have come too late.—Where is he? where is my brave deliverer?"

"Here, most noble lord," said Gregory, sliding from his palfrey, and stepping forward, "ready to receive the guerdon which your bounty would heap on him."

"Truly, Friend Gregory," answered the young warrior, "thou shalt not be forgotten; for thou didst run speedily, and roar manfully for aid, without which, I think verily, we had not received it.—But the brave forester, who came to my rescue when these three ruffians had nigh overpowered me, where is he?"

Every one looked around, but though all had seen him on entering the thicket, he was not now to be found. They could only conjecture that he had retired during the confusion occasioned by the detention of Gaston.

"Seek not for him," said the Lady Emma, who had now in some degree recovered her composure; "he will not be found of mortal, unless at his own season."

The Baron, convinced from this answer that her terror had, for the time, somewhat disturbed her reason, forbore to question her; and Matilda and Eleanor, to whom a message had been despatched with the result of this strange adventure, arriving, they took the Lady Emma between them, and all in a body returned to the castle.

The distance was, however, considerable, and, before reaching it, they had another alarm. The prickers, who rode foremost in the troop, halted, and announced to the Lord Boteler, that they perceived advancing towards them a body of armed men. The followers of the Baron were numerous, but they were arrayed for the chase, not for battle; and it was with great pleasure that he discerned, on the pennon of the advancing body of men-at-arms, instead of the cognizance of Gaston as he had some reason to expect, the friendly bearings of Fitzosborne of Diggswell, the

same young lord who was present at the May-games with Fitzallen of Marden. The knight himself advanced, sheathed in
armour, and, without raising his visor, informed Lord Boteler,
that having heard of a base attempt made upon a part of his
train by ruffianly assassins, he had mounted and armed a small
party of his retainers, to escort them to Queenhoo-Hall. Having
received and accepted an invitation to attend them thither, they
prosecuted their journey in confidence and security, and arrived
safe at home without any further accident.


## CHAPTER V.

### INVESTIGATION OF THE ADVENTURE OF THE HUNTING—A DISCOVERY —GREGORY'S MANHOOD—FATE OF GASTON ST CLERE—CON-CLUSION.

So soon as they arrived at the princely mansion of Boteler, the
Lady Emma craved permission to retire to her chamber, that she
might compose her spirits after the terror she had undergone.
Henry St Clere, in a few words, proceeded to explain the adventure to the curious audience. "I had no sooner seen my sister's
palfrey, in spite of her endeavours to the contrary, entering with
spirit into the chase set on foot by the worshipful Gregory than
I rode after to give her assistance. So long was the chase, that
when the greyhounds pulled down the knobbler, we were out of
hearing of your bugles; and having rewarded and coupled the
dogs, I gave them to be led by the jester, and we wandered in
quest of our company, whom it would seem the sport had led in
a different direction. At length, passing through the thicket
where you found us, I was surprised by a cross-bow bolt whizz-
ing past mine head. I drew my sword, and rushed into the
thicket, but was instantly assailed by two ruffians, while other
two made towards my sister and Gregory. The poor knave fled,
crying for help, pursued by my false kinsman, now your prisoner;
and the designs of the other on my poor Emma (murderous no
doubt) were prevented by the sudden apparition of a brave
woodsman, who, after a short encounter, stretched the miscreant
at his feet, and came to my assistance. I was already slightly
wounded, and nearly over-laid with odds. The combat lasted
some time, for the caitiffs were both well armed, strong, and
desperate; at length, however, we had each mastered our antag-
onist, when your retinue, my Lord Boteler, arrived to my relief.
So ends my story; but, by my knighthood, I would give an earl's
ransom for an opportunity of thanking the gallant forester by
whose aid I live to tell it."

"Fear not," said Lord Boteler, "he shall be found, if this or
the four adjacent counties hold him.—And now Lord Fitzosborne
will be pleased to doff the armour he has so kindly assumed for
our sakes, and we will all bowne ourselves for the banquet."

When the hour of dinner approached, the Lady Matilda and

her cousin visited the chamber of the fair Darcy. They found her in a composed but melancholy posture. She turned the discourse upon the misfortunes of her life, and hinted, that having recovered her brother, and seeing him look forward to the society of one who would amply repay to him the loss of hers, she had thoughts of dedicating her remaining life to Heaven, by whose providential interference it had been so often preserved.

Matilda coloured deeply at something in this speech, and her cousin inveighed loudly against Emma's resolution. "Ah, my dear Lady Eleanor," replied she, "I have to-day witnessed what I cannot but judge a supernatural visitation, and to what end can it call me but to give myself to the altar? That peasant who guided me to Baddow through the Park of Danbury, the same who appeared before me at different times, and in different forms, during that eventful journey,—that youth, whose features are imprinted on my memory, is the very individual forester who this day rescued us in the forest. I cannot be mistaken; and, connecting these marvellous appearances with the spectre which I saw while at Gay Bowers, I cannot resist the conviction that Heaven has permitted my guardian angel to assume mortal shape for my relief and protection."

The fair cousins, after exchanging looks which implied a fear that her mind was wandering, answered her in soothing terms, and finally prevailed upon her to accompany them to the banqueting-hall. Here the first person they encountered was the Baron Fitzosborne of Diggswell, now divested of his armour; at the sight of whom the Lady Emma changed colour, and exclaiming, "It is the same!" sunk senseless into the arms of Matilda.

"She is bewildered by the terrors of the day," said Eleanor; "and we have done ill in obliging her to descend."

"And I," said Fitzosborne, "have done madly in presenting before her one, whose presence must recall moments the most alarming in her life."

While the ladies supported Emma from the hall, Lord Boteler and St Clere requested an explanation from Fitzosborne of the words he had used.

"Trust me, gentle lords," said the Baron of Diggswell, "ye shall have what ye demand, when I learn that Lady Emma Darcy has not suffered from my imprudence."

At this moment Lady Matilda returning, said, that her fair friend, on her recovery, had calmly and deliberately insisted that she had seen Fitzosborne before, in the most dangerous crisis of her life.

"I dread," said she, "her disordered mind connects all that her eye beholds with the terrible passages that she has witnessed."

"Nay," said Fitzosborne, "if noble St Clere can pardon the unauthorized interest which, with the purest and most honourable intentions, I have taken in his sister's fate, it is easy for me to explain this mysterious impression."

He proceeded to say, that, happening to be in the hostelry called the Griffin, near Baddow, while upon a journey in that country, he had met with the old nurse of the Lady Emma Darcy, who, being just expelled from Gay Bowers, was in the height of her grief and indignation, and made loud and public proclamation of Lady Emma's wrongs. From the description she gave of the beauty of her foster-child, as well as from the spirit of chivalry, Fitzosborne became interested in her fate. This interest was deeply enhanced when, by a bribe to old Gaunt the Reve, he procured a view of the Lady Emma, as she walked near the castle of Gay Bowers. The aged churl refused to give him access to the castle; yet dropped some hints, as if he thought the lady in danger, and wished she were well out of it. His master, he said, had heard she had a brother in life, and since that deprived him of all chance of gaining her domains by purchase, he—in short, Gaunt wished they were safely separated. "If any injury," quoth he, "should happen to the damsel here, it were ill for us all. I tried, by an innocent stratagem, to frighten her from the castle, by introducing a figure through a trap-door, and warning her, as if by a voice from the dead, to retreat from thence; but the giglet is wilful, and is running upon her fate."

Finding Gaunt, although covetous and communicative, too faithful a servant to his wicked master to take any active steps against his commands, Fitzosborne applied himself to old Ursely, whom he found more tractable. Through her he learned the dreadful plot Gaston had laid to rid himself of his kinswoman, and resolved to effect her deliverance. But aware of the delicacy of Emma's situation, he charged Ursely to conceal from her the interest he took in her distress, resolving to watch over her in disguise, until he saw her in a place of safety. Hence the appearance he made before her in various dresses during her journey, in the course of which he was never far distant; and he had always four stout yeomen within hearing of his bugle, had assistance been necessary. When she was placed in safety at the lodge, it was Fitzosborne's intention to have prevailed upon his sisters to visit, and take her under their protection; but he found them absent from Diggswell, having gone to attend an aged relation, who lay dangerously ill in a distant county. They did not return until the day before the May-games; and the other events followed too rapidly to permit Fitzosborne to lay any plan for introducing them to Lady Emma Darcy. On the day of the chase, he resolved to preserve his romantic disguise, and attend the Lady Emma as a forester, partly to have the pleasure of being near her, and partly to judge whether, according to an idle report in the country, she favoured his friend and comrade Fitzallen of Marden. This last motive, it may easily be believed, he did not declare to the company. After the skirmish with the ruffians, he waited till the Baron and the hunters arrived, and then, still doubting the farther designs of Gaston, hastened to his castle, to arm the band which had escorted them to Queenhoo-Hall.

Fitzosborne's story being finished, he received the thanks of all the company, particularly of St Clere, who felt deeply the respectful delicacy with which he had conducted himself towards his sister. The lady was carefully informed of her obligations to him; and it is left to the well-judging reader, whether even the raillery of Lady Eleanor made her regret, that Heaven had only employed natural means for her security, and that the guardian angel was converted into a handsome, gallant, and enamoured knight.

The joy of the company in the hall extended itself to the buttery, where Gregory the jester narrated such feats of arms done by himself in the fray of the morning, as might have shamed Bevis and Guy of Warwick. He was, according to his narrative, singled out for destruction by the gigantic Baron himself, while he abandoned to meaner hands the destruction of St Clere and Fitzosborne.

"But certes," said he, "the foul paynim met his match; for, ever as he foined at me with his brand, I parried his blows with my bauble, and closing with him upon the third veny, threw him to the ground, and made him cry recreant to an unarmed man."

"Tush, man," said Drawslot, "thou forgettest thy best auxiliaries, the good greyhounds, Help and Holdfast! I warrant thee, that when the humpbacked Baron caught thee by the cowl, which he hath almost torn off, thou hadst been in a fair plight had they not remembered an old friend, and come in to the rescue. Why, man, I found them fastened on him myself; and there was odd staving and stickling to make them 'ware haunch!' Their mouths were full of the flex, for I pulled a piece of the garment from their jaws. I warrant thee, that when they brought him to ground, thou fledst like a frighted pricket."

"And as for Gregory's gigantic paynim," said Fabian, "why, he lies yonder in the guard-room, the very size, shape, and colour of a spider in a yew-hedge."

"It is false!" said Gregory; "Colbrand the Dane was a dwarf to him."

"It is as true," returned Fabian, "as that the Tasker is to be married, on Tuesday, to pretty Margery. Gregory, thy sheet hath brought them between a pair of blankets."

"I care no more for such a gillflirt," said the Jester, "than I do for thy leasings. Marry, thou hop-o'-my-thumb, happy wouldst thou be could thy head reach the captive Baron's girdle."

"By the mass," said Peter Lanaret, "I will have one peep at this burly gallant;" and, leaving the buttery, he went to the guard-room where Gaston St Clere was confined. A man-at-arms, who kept sentinel on the strong studded door of the apartment, said, he believed he slept; for that, after raging, stamping, and uttering the most horrid imprecations, he had been of late perfectly still. The Falconer gently drew back a sliding board, of a foot square, towards the top of the door, which covered a hole of the same size, strongly latticed, through which the warder, without opening the door, could look in upon his prisoner. From this aperture he beheld the wretched Gaston suspended by the neck, by his own girdle, to an iron ring in the side of his prison. He had clambered to it by means of the table on which his food had been placed; and, in the agonies of shame, and disappointed malice, had adopted this mode of ridding himself of a wretched life. He was found yet warm, but totally lifeless. A proper account of the manner of his death was drawn up and certified. He was buried that evening, in the chapel of the castle, out of respect to his high birth; and the chaplain of Fitzallen of Marden, who said the service upon the occasion, preached, the next Sunday, an excellent sermon upon the text, Radix malorum est cupiditas, which we have here transcribed.——

\*        \*        \*        \*        \*        \*        \*

[Here the manuscript, from which we have painfully transcribed, and frequently, as it were, translated this tale, for the reader's edification, is so indistinct and defaced, that, excepting certain howbeits, nathlesses, lo ye's! &c., we can pick out little that is intelligible, saving that avarice is defined "a likourishness of heart after earthly things." A little farther, there seems to have been a gay account of Margery's wedding with Ralph the Tasker; the running at the quintain, and other rural games practised on the occasion. There are also fragments of a mock sermon preached by Gregory upon that occasion, as for example:

"My dear cursed caitiffs, there was once a king, and he wedded a young old queen, and she had a child; and this child was sent to Solomon the Sage, praying he would give it the same blessing which he got from the witch of Endor when she bit him by the heel. Hereof speaks the worthy Dr Radigundus Potator; why should not mass be said for all the roasted shoe souls served up in the king's dish on Saturday; for true it is, that St Peter asked father Adam, as they journeyed to Camelot, an high, great, and doubtful question, 'Adam, Adam, why eated'st thou the apple without paring'?" \*

---

\* This tirade of gibberish is literally taken or selected from a mock discourse pronounced by a professed jester, which occurs in an ancient manuscript in the Advocates' Library, the same from which the late ingenious Mr Weber published the curious comic romance of the Hunting of the Hare. It was introduced in compliance with Mr Strutt's plan of rendering his tale an illustration of ancient manners. A similar burlesque sermon is pronounced by the Fool in Sir David Lindesay's satire of the Three Estates. The nonsense and vulgar burlesque of that composition illustrate the ground of Sir Andrew Aguecheek's eulogy on the exploits of the jester in Twelfth Night, who, reserving his sharper jests for Sir Toby, had doubtless enough of the jargon of his calling to captivate the imbecility

With much goodly gibberish to the same effect; which display of Gregory's ready wit not only threw the whole company into convulsions of laughter, but made such an impression on Rose, the Potter's daughter, that it was thought it would be the Jester's own fault if Jack was long without his Jill. Much pithy matter, concerning the bringing the bride to bed—the loosing the bridegroom's points—the scramble which ensued for them—and the casting of the stocking, is also omitted from its obscurity.

The following song, which has been since borrowed by the worshipful author of the famous "History of Fryar Bacon," has been with difficulty deciphered. It seems to have been sung on occasion of carrying home the bride.

### BRIDAL SONG.

*To the tune of—" I have been a Fiddler," &c.*

And did you not hear of a mirth befell
    The morrow after a wedding day,
And carrying a bride at home to dwell?
    And away to Tewin, away, away!

The quintain was set, and the garlands were made,
    'Tis pity old customs should ever decay;
And wo be to him that was horsed on a jade,
    For he carried no credit away, away.

We met a concert of fiddle-de-dees;
    We set them a cockhorse, and made them play
The winning of Bullen, and Upsey-frees,
    And away to Tewin, away, away!

There was ne'er a lad in all the parish
    That would go to the plough that day;
But on his fore-horse his wench he carries,
    And away to Tewin, away, away!

The butler was quick, and the ale he did tap,
    The maidens did make the chamber full gay;
The servants did give me a fuddling cup,
    And I did carry't away, away.

The smith of the town his liquor so took,
    That he was persuaded that the ground look'd blew;
And I dare boldly be sworn on a book,
    Such smiths as he there's but a few.

A posset was made, and the women did sip,
    And simpering said, they could eat no more;
Full many a maiden was laid on the lip,—
    I'll say no more, but give o'er, (give o'er.)

But what our fair readers will chiefly regret, is the loss of three declarations of love; the first by St Clere to Matilda;

of his brother knight, who is made to exclaim—"In sooth, thou wast in very gracious fooling last night, when thou spokest of Pigrogremitus, and of the vapours passing the equinoctials of Quenbus; 'twas very good, i' faith!" It is entertaining to find commentators seeking to discover some meaning in the professional jargon of such a passage as this.

which, with the lady's answer, occupies fifteen closely written
pages of manuscript. That of Fitzosborne to Emma is not much
shorter; but the amours of Fitzallen and Eleanor, being of a less
romantic cast, are closed in three pages only. The three noble
couples were married in Queenhoo-Hall upon the same day, being
the twentieth Sunday after Easter. There is a prolix account of
the marriage-feast, of which we can pick out the names of a few
dishes, such as peterel, crane, sturgeon, swan, &c., &c., with a
profusion of wild-fowl and venison. We also see, that a suitable
song was produced by Peretto on the occasion; and that the
bishop, who blessed the bridal beds which received the happy
couples, was no niggard of his holy water, bestowing half a
gallon upon each of the couches. We regret we cannot give
these curiosities to the reader in detail, but we hope to expose
the manuscript to abler antiquaries, so soon as it shall be framed
and glazed by the ingenious artist who rendered that service to
Mr Ireland's Shakespeare MSS. And so, (being unable to lay
aside the style to which our pen is habituated,) gentle reader,
we bid thee heartily farewell.]

## No. III.

## ANECDOTE OF SCHOOL DAYS,

UPON WHICH MR THOMAS SCOTT PROPOSED TO FOUND A TALE
OF FICTION.

It is well known in the South that there is little or no boxing at
the Scottish schools. About forty or fifty years ago, however, a
far more dangerous mode of fighting, in parties or factions, was
permitted in the streets of Edinburgh, to the great disgrace of
the police, and danger of the parties concerned. These parties
were generally formed from the quarters of the town in which
the combatants resided, those of a particular square or district
fighting against those of an adjoining one. Hence it happened
that the children of the higher classes were often pitted against
those of the lower, each taking their side according to the
residence of their friends. So far as I recollect, however, it was
unmingled either with feelings of democracy, or aristocracy, or
indeed with malice or ill-will of any kind towards the opposite
party. In fact, it was only a rough mode of play. Such
contests were, however, maintained with great vigour with
stones, and sticks, and fisticuffs, when one party dared to charge,
and the other stood their ground. Of course mischief sometimes
happened, boys are said to have been killed at these *Bickers*, as
they were called, and serious accidents certainly took place, as
many contemporaries can bear witness.

The author's father, residing in George Square, in the southern
side of Edinburgh, the boys belonging to that family, with
others in the square, were arranged into a sort of company, to

which a lady of distinction presented a handsome set of colours. Now this company or regiment, as a matter of course, was engaged in weekly warfare with the boys inhabiting the Cross-causeway, Bristo-street, the Potterrow,—in short, the neighbouring suburbs. These last were chiefly of the lower rank, but hardy loons, who threw stones to a hair's-breadth, and were very rugged antagonists at close quarters. The skirmish sometimes lasted for a whole evening, until one party or the other was victorious, when, if ours were successful, we drove the enemy to their quarters, and were usually chased back by the reinforcement of bigger lads who came to their assistance. If, on the contrary, we were pursued, as was often the case, into the precincts of our square, we were in our turn supported by our elder brothers, domestic servants, and similar auxiliaries.

It followed, from our frequent opposition to each other, that though not knowing the names of our enemies, we were yet well acquainted with their appearance, and had nicknames for the most remarkable of them. One very active and spirited boy might be considered as the principal leader in the cohort of the suburbs. He was, I suppose, thirteen or fourteen years old, finely made, tall, blue-eyed, with long fair hair, the very picture of a youthful Goth. This lad was always first in the charge, and last in the retreat—the Achilles, at once, and Ajax, of the Crosscauseway. He was too formidable to us not to have a cognomen, and, like that of a knight of old, it was taken from the most remarkable part of his dress, being a pair of old green livery breeches, which was the principal part of his clothing; for, like Pentapolin, according to Don Quixote's account, Green-Breeks, as we called him, always entered the battle with bare arms, legs, and feet.

It fell, that once upon a time, when the combat was at the thickest, this plebeian champion headed a sudden charge, so rapid and furious, that all fled before him. He was several paces before his comrades, and had actually laid his hands on the patrician standard, when one of our party, whom some misjudging friend had intrusted with a *couteau de chasse*, or hanger, inspired with a zeal for the honour of the corps, worthy of Major Sturgeon himself, struck poor Green-Breeks over the head, with strength sufficient to cut him down. When this was seen, the casualty was so far beyond what had ever taken place before, that both parties fled different ways, leaving poor Green-Breeks with his bright hair plentifully dabbled in blood, to the care of the watchman, who (honest man) took care not to know who had done the mischief. The bloody hanger was flung into one of the Meadow ditches, and solemn secrecy was sworn on all hands; but the remorse and terror of the actor were beyond all bounds, and his apprehensions of the most dreadful character. The wounded hero was for a few days in the Infirmary, the case being only a trifling one. But though enquiry was strongly pressed on him, no argument could make him indicate the person from whom he had received the wound, though he must have been perfectly well known to him. When he recovered, and was dismissed, the author and his brothers opened a communication with him, through the medium of a popular gingerbread baker, of whom both parties were customers, in order to tender a subsidy in name of smart-money. The sum would excite ridicule were I to name it ; but sure I am, that the pockets of the noted Green-Breeks never held as much money of his own. He declined the remittance, saying that he would not sell his blood ; but at the same time reprobated the idea of being an informer, which he said was *clam, i.e.* base or mean. With much urgency he accepted a pound of snuff for the use of some old woman,—aunt, grandmother, or the like,—with whom he lived. We did not become friends, for the *bickers* were more agreeable to both parties than any more pacific amusement ; but we conducted them ever after under mutual assurances of the highest consideration for each other.

Such was the hero whom Mr Thomas Scott proposed to carry to Canada, and involve in adventures with the natives and colonists of that country. Perhaps the youthful generosity of the lad will not seem so great in the eyes of others, as to those whom it was the means of screening from severe rebuke and punishment. But it seemed to those concerned, to argue a nobleness of sentiment far beyond the pitch of most minds ; and however obscurely the lad, who showed such a frame of noble spirit, may have lived or died, I cannot help being of opinion, that if fortune had placed him in circumstances calling for gallantry or generosity, the man would have fulfilled the promises of the boy. Long afterwards, when the story was told to my father, he censured us severely for not telling the truth at the time, that he might have attempted to be of use to the young man in entering on life. But our alarms for the consequences of the drawn sword, and the wound inflicted with such a weapon, were far too predominant at the time for such a pitch of generosity.

Perhaps I ought not to have inserted this school-boy tale ; but, besides the strong impression made by the incident at the time, the whole accompaniments of the story are matters to me of solemn and sad recollection. Of all the little band who were concerned in those juvenile sports or brawls, I can scarce recollect a single survivor. Some left the ranks of mimic war to die in the active service of their country. Many sought distant lands to return no more. Others, dispersed in different paths of life, "my dim eyes now seek for in vain." Of five brothers, all healthy and promising, in a degree far beyond one whose infancy was visited by personal infirmity, and whose health after this period seemed long very precarious, I am, nevertheless, the only survivor. The best loved, and the best deserving to be loved, who had destined this incident to be the foundation of literary composition, died "before his day," in a distant and foreign land ; and trifles assume an importance not their own, when connected with those who have been loved and lost.

# INTRODUCTION TO WAVERLEY.

THE plan of this edition leads me to insert in this place some account of the incidents on which the Novel of WAVERLEY is founded. They have been already given to the public, by my late lamented friend, William Erskine, Esq. (afterwards Lord Kinneder), when reviewing the *Tales of My Landlord* for the *Quarterly Review*, in 1817. The particulars were derived by the critic from the author's information. Afterwards they were published in the preface to the *Chronicles of the Canongate*. They are now inserted in their proper place.

The mutual protection afforded by Waverley and Talbot to each other, upon which the whole plot depends, is founded upon one of those anecdotes which soften the features even of civil war; and as it is equally honourable to the memory of both parties, we have no hesitation to give their names at length. When the Highlanders, on the morning of the battle of Preston, 1745, made their memorable attack on Sir John Cope's army, a battery of four field-pieces was stormed and carried by the Camerons and the Stewarts of Appine. The late Alexander Stewart of Invernahyle was one of the foremost in the charge, and observing an officer of the King's forces, who, scorning to join the flight of all around, remained with his sword in his hand, as if determined to the very last to defend the post assigned to him, the Highland gentleman commanded him to surrender, and received for reply a thrust, which he caught in his target. The officer was now defenceless, and the battle-axe of a gigantic Highlander (the miller of Invernahyle's mill) was uplifted to dash his brains out, when Mr Stewart with difficulty prevailed on him to yield. He took charge of his enemy's property, protected his person, and finally obtained him liberty on his parole. The officer proved to be Colonel Whitefoord, an Ayrshire gentleman of high character and influence, and warmly attached to the House of Hanover; yet such was the confidence existing between these two honourable men, though of different political principles, that while the civil war was raging, and straggling officers from the Highland army were executed without mercy, Invernahyle hesitated not to pay his late captive a visit, as he returned to the Highlands to raise fresh recruits, on which occasion he spent a day or two in Ayrshire among Colonel Whitefoord's Whig friends, as pleasantly and as good-humouredly as if all had been at peace around him

After the battle of Culloden had ruined the hopes of Charles Edward, and dispersed his proscribed adherents, it was Colonel Whitefoord's turn to strain every nerve to obtain Mr Stewart's pardon.  He went to the Lord Justice Clerk, to the Lord Advocate, and to all the officers of state, and each application was answered by the production of a list, in which Invernahyle (as the good old gentleman was wont to express it) appeared "marked with the sign of the beast!" as a subject unfit for favour or pardon.

At length Colonel Whitefoord applied to the Duke of Cumberland in person.  From him, also, he received a positive refusal. He then limited his request, for the present, to a protection for Stewart's house, wife, children, and property.  This was also refused by the Duke; on which Colonel Whitefoord, taking his commission from his bosom, laid it on the table before his Royal Highness with much emotion, and asked permission to retire from the service of a sovereign who did not know how to spare a vanquished enemy.  The Duke was struck, and even affected. He bade the Colonel take up his commission, and granted the protection he required.  It was issued just in time to save the house, corn, and cattle at Invernahyle from the troops, who were engaged in laying waste what it was the fashion to call "the country of the enemy."  A small encampment of soldiers was formed on Invernahyle's property, which they spared while plundering the country around, and searching in every direction for the leaders of the insurrection, and for Stewart in particular. He was much nearer them than they suspected; for, hidden in a cave (like the Baron of Bradwardine) he lay for many days so near the English sentinels, that he could hear their muster-roll called.  His food was brought to him by one of his daughters, a child of eight years old, whom Mrs Stewart was under the necessity of intrusting with this commission; for her own motions, and those of all her elder inmates, were closely watched. With ingenuity beyond her years, the child used to stray about among the soldiers, who were rather kind to her, and thus seize the moment when she was unobserved, and steal into the thicket, when she deposited whatever small store of provisions she had in charge, at some marked spot, where her father might find it. Invernahyle supported life for several weeks by means of these precarious supplies; and as he had been wounded in the battle of Culloden, the hardships which he endured were aggravated by great bodily pain.  After the soldiers had removed their quarters, he had another remarkable escape.

As he now ventured to his own house at night, and left it in the morning, he was espied during the dawn by a party of the enemy, who fired at and pursued him.  The fugitive being fortunate enough to escape their search, they returned to the house, and charged the family with harbouring one of the proscribed traitors.  An old woman had presence of mind enough to maintain that the man they had seen was the shepherd.

"Why did he not stop when we called to him?" said the soldier. —"He is as deaf, poor man, as a peat stack," answered the ready-witted domestic.—"Let him be sent for directly." The real shepherd accordingly was brought from the hill, and as there was time to tutor him by the way, he was as deaf when he made his appearance, as was necessary to sustain his character. Invernahyle was afterwards pardoned under the Act of Indemnity.

The author knew him well, and has often heard these circumstances from his own mouth. He was a noble specimen of the old Highlander, far descended, gallant, courteous, and brave, even to chivalry. He had been *out*, I believe, in 1715 and 1745, was an active partaker in all the stirring scenes which passed in the Highlands, betwixt these memorable eras; and I have heard, was remarkable, among other exploits, for having fought a duel with the broadsword with the celebrated Rob Roy MacGregor, at the Clachan of Balquhidder.

Invernahyle chanced to be in Edinburgh when Paul Jones came into the Frith of Forth, and though then an old man, I saw him in arms, and heard him exult (to use his own words), in the prospect of "drawing his claymore once more before he died." In fact, on that memorable occasion, when the capital of Scotland was menaced by three trifling sloops or brigs, scarce fit to have sacked a fishing village, he was the only man who seemed to propose a plan of resistance. He offered to the magistrates, if broadswords and dirks could be obtained, to find as many Highlanders among the lower classes, as would cut off any boat's crew who might be sent into a town, full of narrow and winding passages, in which they were like to disperse in quest of plunder. I know not if his plan was attended to; I rather think it seemed too hazardous to the constituted authorities, who might not, even at that time, desire to see arms in Highland hands. A steady and powerful west wind settled the matter, by sweeping Paul Jones and his vessels out of the Frith.

If there is something degrading in this recollection, it is not unpleasant to compare it with those of the last war, when Edinburgh, besides regular forces and militia, furnished a volunteer brigade of cavalry, infantry, and artillery, to the amount of six thousand men and upwards, which was in readiness to meet and repel a force of a far more formidable description, than was commanded by the adventurous American. Time and circumstances change the character of nations, and the fate of cities; and it is some pride to a Scotchman to reflect, that the independent and manly character of a country, willing to intrust its own protection to the arms of its children, after having been obscured for half a century, has, during the course of his own lifetime, recovered its lustre.

Other illustrations of Waverley will be found in the Notes at the foot of the pages to which they belong. Those which appeared too long to be so placed, are given at the end of this Volume.

# Waverley

OR

## 'TIS SIXTY YEARS SINCE

BY

SIR WALTER SCOTT, Bart.

"Under which king, Bezonian? Speak, or die."
*Henry IV. Part II*

EDINBURGH

WILLIAM PATERSON

# PREFACE

## TO THE THIRD EDITION OF WAVERLEY.

To this slight attempt at a sketch of ancient Scottish manners, the public have been more favourable than the Author durst have hoped or expected. He has heard, with a mixture of satisfaction and humility, his work ascribed to more than one respectable name. Considerations, which seem weighty in his particular situation, prevent his releasing those gentlemen from suspicion by placing his own name in the title page; so that, for the present at least, it must remain uncertain, whether WAVERLEY be the work of a poet or a critic, a lawyer or a clergyman, or whether the writer, to use Mrs Malaprop's phrase, be, "like Cerberus—three gentlemen at once." The Author, as he is unconscious of any thing in the work itself (except perhaps its frivolity) which prevents its finding an acknowledged father, leaves it to the candour of the public to choose among the many circumstances peculiar to different situations in life, such as may induce him to suppress his name on the present occasion. He may be a writer new to publication, and unwilling to avow a character to which he is unaccustomed; or he may be a hackneyed author, who is ashamed of too frequent appearance, and employs this mystery, as the heroine of the old comedy used her mask, to attract the attention of those to whom her face had become too familiar. He may be a man of a grave profession, to whom the reputation of being a novel-writer might be prejudicial; or he may be a man of fashion, to whom writing of any kind might appear pedantic. He may be too young to assume the character of an author, or so old as to make it advisable to lay it aside.

The Author of Waverley has heard it objected to this novel, that, in the character of Callum Beg, and in the account given by the Baron of Bradwardine of the petty trespasses of the Highlanders upon trifling articles of property, he has borne hard, and unjustly so, upon their national character. Nothing could be farther from his wish or intention. The character of Callum Beg is that of a spirit naturally turned to daring evil, and determined, by the circumstances of his situation, to a particular species of mischief. Those who have perused the curious Letters from the Highlands, published about 1726, will find instances of such atrocious characters which fell under the writer's own observation, though it would be most unjust to consider such villains as representatives of the Highlanders of that period, any more than the murderers of Marr and Williamson can be supposed to represent the English of the present day. As for the plunder supposed to have been picked up by some of the insurgents in 1745, it must be remembered, that although the way of that unfortunate little army was neither marked by devastation nor bloodshed, but, on the contrary, was orderly and quiet in a most wonderful degree, yet *no* army marches through a country in a hostile manner without committing some depredations; and several, to the extent, and of the nature, jocularly imputed to them by the Baron, were really laid to the charge of the Highland insurgents; for which many traditions, and particularly one respecting the Knight of the Mirror, may be quoted as good evidence. *

* A homely metrical narrative of the events of the period, which contains some striking particulars, and is still a great favourite with the lower classes, gives a very correct statement of the behaviour of the mountaineers respecting this same military license; and as the verses are little known, and contain some good sense, we venture to insert them.

THE AUTHOR'S ADDRESS TO ALL IN GENERAL.

Now, gentle readers, I have let you ken
My very thoughts, from heart and pen,
'Tis needless for to conten'
        Or yet controule,
For there's not a word o't I can men'—
        So ye must thole.

For on both sides, some were not good;
I saw them murd'ring in cold blood,
Not the gentlemen, but wild and rude,
        The baser sort,
Who to the wounded had no mood
        But murd'ring sport!

Ev'n both at Preston and Falkirk,
That fatal night ere it grew mirk,
Piercing the wounded with their durk,
        Caused many cry!
Such pity's shown from Savage and Turk
        As peace to die.

A woe be to such hot zeal,
To smite the wounded on the fiell!
It's just they got such groats in kail,
        Who do the same.
It only teaches cruelty's real
        To them again.

I've seen the men call'd Highland Rogues,
With Lowland men make *shangs* a brojs,
Sup kail and brose, and fling the cogs
        Out at the door,
Take cocks, hens, sheep, and hogs,
        And pay nought for.

I saw a Highlander, 'twas right-drole,
With a string of puddings hung on a pole,
Whip'd o'er his shoulder, skipped like a fole,
  Caus'd Maggy bann,
Lap o'er the midden and midden-hole,
  And aff he ran.

When check'd for this, they'd often tell ye—
Indeed *her nainsell's* a tume belly;
You'll no gie't wanting bought, nor sell me;
  *Hersell* will hae't;
Go tell King Shorge, and Shordy's Willie,
  I'll hae a meat.

I saw the soldiers at Linton-brig,
Because the man was not a Whig,
Of meat and drink leave not a skig,
  Within his door;
They burnt his very hat and wig,
  And thump'd him sore.

And through the Highlands they were so rude,
As leave them neither clothes nor food,
Then burnt their houses to conclude;
  'T was tit for tat.
How can *her nainsell* e'er be good,
  To think on that?

And after all, O, shame and grief!
To use some worse than murd'ring thief,
Their very gentleman and chief,
  Unhumanly!
Like Popish tortures, I believe,
  Such cruelty.

Ev'n what was act on open stage
At Carlisle, in the hottest rage,
When mercy was clapt in a cage,
  And pity dead.
Such cruelty approv'd by every age,
  I shook my head.

So many to curse, so few to pray,
And some aloud huzza did cry:
They cursed the Rebel Scots that day,
  As they'd been nowt
Brought up for slaughter, as that way
  Too many rowt.

Therefore, alas! dear countrymen,
O never do the like again,
To thirst for vengeance, never ben'
  Your gun nor pa',
But with the English e'en borrow and len',
  Let anger fa'.

Their boasts and bullying, not worth a louse,
As our King's the best about the house.
'T is ay good to be sober and douce,
  To live in peace;
For many, I see, for being o'er crouse.
  Gets broken face.

# WAVERLEY;

## OR,

## 'T IS SIXTY YEARS SINCE.

—o—

## CHAPTER I.

### *Introductory.*

THE title of this work has not been chosen without the
grave and solid deliberation, which matters of importance
demand from the prudent. Even its first, or general
denomination, was the result of no common research or
selection, although, according to the example of my
predecessors, I had only to seize upon the most sounding
and euphonic surname that English history or topo-
graphy affords, and elect it at once as the title of my
work, and the name of my hero. But alas! what could
my readers have expected from the chivalrous epithets of
Howard, Mordaunt, Mortimer, or Stanley, or from the
softer and more sentimental sounds of Belmour, Belville,
Belfield, and Belgrave, but pages of inanity, similar to
those which have been so christened for half a century
past? I must modestly admit I am too diffident of my
own merit to place it in unnecessary opposition to preconceived associations; I have, therefore, like a maiden
knight with his white shield, assumed for my hero,
WAVERLEY, an uncontaminated name, bearing with its
sound little of good or evil, excepting what the reader
shall hereafter be pleased to affix to it. But my second
or supplemental title was a matter of much more difficult
election, since that, short as it is, may be held as pledging
the author to some special mode of laying his scene,
drawing his characters, and managing his adventures.
Had I, for example, announced in my frontispiece,
"Waverley, a Tale of other Days," must not every novel-

reader have anticipated a castle scarce less than that of
Udolpho, of which the eastern wing had long been unin-
habited, and the keys either lost, or consigned to the care
of some aged butler or housekeeper, whose trembling
steps, about the middle of the second volume, were
doomed to guide the hero, or heroine, to the ruinous
precincts? Would not the owl have shrieked and the
cricket cried in my very title-page? and could it have
been possible for me, with a moderate attention to decorum, to introduce any scene more lively than might be
produced by the jocularity of a clownish but faithful
valet, or the garrulous narrative of the heroine's fille-de-
chambre, when rehearsing the stories of blood and horror
which she had heard in the servants' hall? Again, had
my title borne, "Waverley, a Romance from the German,"
what head so obtuse as not to image forth a profligate
abbot, an oppressive duke, a secret and mysterious
association of Rosycrucians and Illuminati, with all their
properties of black cowls, caverns, daggers, electrical
machines, trap-doors, and dark-lanterns? Or if I had
rather chosen to call my work a "Sentimental Tale,"
would it not have been a sufficient presage of a heroine
with a profusion of auburn hair, and a harp, the soft
solace of her solitary hours, which she fortunately finds
always the means of transporting from castle to cottage,
although she herself be sometimes obliged to jump out of
a two-pair-of-stairs window, and is more than once bewildered on her journey, alone and on foot, without any
guide but a blowzy peasant girl, whose jargon she hardly
can understand? Or again, if my *Waverley* had been
entitled "A Tale of the Times," wouldst thou not, gentle
reader, have demanded from me a dashing sketch of the
fashionable world, a few anecdotes of private scandal
thinly veiled, and if lusciously painted, so much the
better? a heroine from Grosvenor Square, and a hero
from the Barouche Club or the Four-in-Hand, with a set
of subordinate characters from the elegantes of Queen
Anne Street East, or the dashing heroes of the Bow-
Street Office? I could proceed in proving the importance
of a title-page, and displaying at the same time my own
intimate knowledge of the particular ingredients necessary
to the composition of romances and novels of various descriptions: But it is enough, and I scorn to tyrannize longer
over the impatience of my reader, who is doubtless already
anxious to know the choice made by an author, so profoundly versed in the different branches of his art.

By fixing, then, the date of my story Sixty Years before this present 1st November 1805, I would have my readers understand, that they will meet in the following pages neither a romance of chivalry, nor a tale of modern manners; that my hero will neither have iron on his shoulders, as of yore, nor on the heels of his boots, as is the present fashion of Bond Street; and that my damsels will neither be clothed "in purple and in pall," like the Lady Alice of an old ballad, nor reduced to the primitive nakedness of a modern fashionable at a rout. From this my choice of an era the understanding critic may farther presage, that the object of my tale is more a description of men than manners. A tale of manners, to be interesting, must either refer to antiquity so great as to have become venerable, or it must bear a vivid reflection of those scenes which are passing daily before our eyes, and are interesting from their novelty. Thus the coat-of-mail of our ancestors, and the triple-furred pelisse of our modern beaux, may, though for very different reasons, be equally fit for the array of a fictitious character; but who, meaning the costume of his hero to be impressive, would willingly attire him in the court dress of George the Second's reign, with its no collar, large sleeves, and low pocket-holes? The same may be urged, with equal truth, of the Gothic hall, which, with its darkened and tinted windows, its elevated and gloomy roof, and massive oaken table garnished with boars-head and rosemary, pheasants and peacocks, cranes and cygnets, has an excellent effect in fictitious description. Much may also be gained by a lively display of a modern fete, such as we have daily recorded in that part of a newspaper entitled the *Mirror of Fashion*, if we contrast these, or either of them, with the splendid formality of an entertainment given Sixty Years since; and thus it will be readily seen how much the painter of antique or of fashionable manners gains over him who delineates those of the last generation.

Considering the disadvantages inseparable from this part of my subject, I must be understood to have resolved to avoid them as much as possible, by throwing the force of my narrative upon the characters and passions of the actors;—those passions common to men in all stages of society, and which have alike agitated the human heart, whether it throbbed under the steel corslet of the fifteenth century, the brocaded coat of the eighteenth, or the blue

frock and white dimity waistcoat of the present day.[1]
Upon these passions it is no doubt true that the state of
manners and laws casts a necessary colouring; but the
bearings, to use the language of heraldry, remain the
same, though the tincture may be not only different, but
opposed in strong contradistinction. The wrath of our
ancestors, for example, was coloured *gules;* it broke forth
in acts of open and sanguinary violence against the
objects of its fury. Our malignant feelings, which must
seek gratification through more indirect channels, and
undermine the obstacles which they cannot openly bear
down, may be rather said to be tinctured *sable*. But the
deep-ruling impulse is the same in both cases; and the
proud peer, who can now only ruin his neighbour according to law, by protracted suits, is the genuine descendant
of the baron, who wrapped the castle of his competitor in
flames, and knocked him on the head as he endeavoured
to escape from the conflagration. It is from the great
book of Nature, the same through a thousand editions,
whether of black-letter, or wire-wove and hot-pressed,
that I have venturously essayed to read a chapter to the
public. Some favourable opportunities of contrast have
been afforded me, by the state of society in the northern
part of the island at the period of my history, and may
serve at once to vary and to illustrate the moral lessons,
which I would willingly consider as the most important
part of my plan; although I am sensible how short these
will fall of their aim, if I shall be found unable to mix
them with amusement,—a task not quite so easy in this
critical generation as it was "Sixty Years since."

## CHAPTER II.

### *Waverley-Honour.—A Retrospect.*

IT is, then, sixty years since Edward Waverley, the hero
of the following pages, took leave of his family, to join
the regiment of dragoons in which he had lately obtained
a commission. It was a melancholy day at Waverley-
Honour when the young officer parted with Sir Everard,

[1] Alas! that attire, respectable and gentlemanlike in 1805, or thereabouts, is
now as antiquated as the Author of *Waverley* has himself become since that
period! The reader of fashion will please to fill up the costume with an embroidered waistcoat of purple velvet or silk, and a coat of whatever colour he
pleases. (S.)

the affectionate old uncle to whose title and estate he was presumptive heir.

A difference in political opinions had early separated the Baronet from his younger brother Richard Waverley, the father of our hero. Sir Everard had inherited from his sires the whole train of Tory or High-church predilections and prejudices, which had distinguished the house of Waverley since the Great Civil War. Richard, on the contrary, who was ten years younger, beheld himself born to the fortune of a second brother, and anticipated neither dignity nor entertainment in sustaining the character of Will Wimble. He saw early, that, to succeed in the race of life, it was necessary he should carry as little weight as possible. Painters talk of the difficulty of expressing the existence of compound passions in the same features at the same moment: It would be no less difficult for the moralist to analyze the mixed motives which unite to form the impulse of our actions. Richard Waverley read and satisfied himself from history and sound argument that, in the words of the old song,

> Passive obedience was a jest,
> And pshaw! was non-resistance ;

yet reason would have probably been unable to combat and remove hereditary prejudice could Richard have anticipated that his elder brother, Sir Everard, taking to heart an early disappointment, would have remained a bachelor at seventy-two. The prospect of succession, however remote, might in that case have led him to endure dragging through the greater part of his life as "Master Richard at the Hall, the baronet's brother," in the hope that ere its conclusion he should be distinguished as Sir Richard Waverley of Waverley-Honour, successor to a princely estate, and to extended political connections as head of the county interest in the shire where it lay. But this was a consummation of things not to be expected at Richard's outset, when Sir Everard was in the prime of life, and certain to be an acceptable suitor in almost any family, whether wealth or beauty should be the object of his pursuit, and when, indeed, his speedy marriage was a report which regularly amused the neighbourhood once a-year. His younger brother saw no practicable road to independence save that of relying upon his own exertions, and adopting a political creed more consonant both to reason and his own interest than the hereditary faith of Sir Everard in High-church and in the house of

Stewart. He therefore read his recantation at the beginning of his career, and entered life as an avowed
Whig, and friend of the Hanover succession.

The ministry of George the First's time were prudently
anxious to diminish the phalanx of opposition. The Tory
nobility, depending for their reflected lustre upon the
sunshine of a court, had for some time been gradually
reconciling themselves to the new dynasty. But the
wealthy country gentlemen of England, a rank which
retained, with much of ancient manners and primitive
integrity, a great proportion of obstinate and unyielding
prejudice, stood aloof in haughty and sullen opposition,
and cast many a look of mingled regret and hope to Bois
le Duc, Avignon, and Italy.[1] The accession of the near
relation of one of those steady and inflexible opponents
was considered as a means of bringing over more converts,
and therefore Richard Waverley met with a share of
ministerial favour, more than proportioned to his talents
or his political importance. It was, however, discovered
that he had respectable talents for public business, and
the first admittance to the minister's levee being negotiated, his success became rapid. Sir Everard learned
from the public *News-Letter*, first, that Richard Waverley,
Esquire, was returned for the ministerial borough of
Barterfaith ; next, that Richard Waverley, Esquire, had
taken a distinguished part in the debate upon the Excise
bill in the support of government ; and, lastly, that
Richard Waverley, Esquire, had been honoured with a
seat at one of those boards, where the pleasure of serving
the country is combined with other important gratifica-
tions, which, to render them the more acceptable, occur
regularly once a-quarter.

Although these events followed each other so closely
that the sagacity of the editor of a modern newspaper
would have presaged the two last even while he announced
the first, yet they came upon Sir Everard gradually, and
drop by drop, as it were, distilled through the cool and
procrastinating alembic of *Dyer's Weekly Letter*.[2] For
it may be observed in passing, that instead of those mail-
coaches, by means of which every mechanic at his six-

[1] Where the Chevalier Saint George, or, as he was termed, the Old Pretender, held
his exiled court, as his situation compelled him to shift his place of residence.  (S.)
[2] Long the oracle of the country gentlemen of the high Tory party. The ancient
*News-Letter* was written in manuscript and copied by clerks, who addressed the
copies to the subscribers.  The politician by whom they were compiled picked up
his intelligence at Coffee-houses, and often pleaded for an additional gratuity, in
consideration of the extra expense attached to frequenting such places of fashionable resort.  (S.)

penny club may nightly learn from twenty contradictory
channels the yesterday's news of the capital, a weekly
post brought, in those days, to Waverley-Honour, a
*Weekly Intelligencer*, which, after it had gratified Sir
Everard's curiosity, his sister's, and that of his aged
butler, was regularly transferred from the Hall to the
Rectory, from the Rectory to Squire Stubbs's at the
Grange, from the Squire to the Baronet's steward at his
neat white house on the heath, from the steward to the
bailiff, and from him through a huge circle of honest
dames and gaffers, by whose hard and horny hands it
was generally worn to pieces in about a month after its
arrival.

This slow succession of intelligence was of some
advantage to Richard Waverley in the case before us;
for, had the sum total of his enormities reached the ears
of Sir Everard at once, there can be no doubt that the
new commissioner would have had little reason to pique
himself on the success of his politics. The Baronet,
although the mildest of human beings, was not without
sensitive points in his character; his brother's conduct
had wounded these deeply; the Waverley estate was
fettered by no entail, (for it had never entered into the
head of any of its former possessors that one of their
progeny could be guilty of the atrocities laid by *Dyer's
Letter* to the door of Richard,) and if it had, the marriage
of the proprietor might have been fatal to a collateral
heir. These various ideas floated through the brain of
Sir Everard, without, however, producing any determined
conclusion.

He examined the tree of his genealogy, which, emblazoned with many an emblematic mark of honour
and heroic achievement, hung upon the well-varnished
wainscot of his hall. The nearest descendants of Sir
Hildebrand Waverley, failing those of his eldest son
Wilfred, of whom Sir Everard and his brother were the
only representatives, were, as this honoured register
informed him, (and, indeed, as he himself well knew,) the
Waverleys of Highley Park, com. Hants; with whom the
main branch, or rather stock, of the house had renounced
all connection, since the great law-suit in 1670.

This degenerate scion had committed a farther offence
against the head and source of their gentility, by the
intermarriage of their representative with Judith, heiress
of Oliver Bradshawe, of Highley Park, whose arms, the
same with those of Bradshawe the regicide, they had

quartered with the ancient coat of Waverley. These
offences, however, had vanished from Sir Everard's
recollection in the heat of his resentment; and had
Lawyer Clippurse, for whom his groom was despatched
express, arrived but an hour earlier, he might have had
the benefit of drawing a new settlement of the lordship
and manor of Waverley-Honour, with all its dependencies.
But an hour of cool reflection is a great matter, when
employed in weighing the comparative evil of two
measures, to neither of which we are internally partial.
Lawyer Clippurse found his patron involved in a deep
study, which he was too respectful to disturb, otherwise
than by producing his paper and leathern ink-case, as
prepared to minute his honour's commands. Even this
slight manœuvre was embarrassing to Sir Everard, who
felt it as a reproach to his indecision. He looked at the
attorney with some desire to issue his fiat, when the sun,
emerging from behind a cloud, poured at once its
chequered light through the stained window of the
gloomy cabinet in which they were seated. The Baronet's
eye, as he raised it to the splendour, fell right upon the
central scutcheon, impressed with the same device which
his ancestor was said to have borne in the field of Hastings;
three ermines passant, argent, in a field azure, with its
appropriate motto, *sans tache*. "May our name rather
perish," exclaimed Sir Everard, "than that ancient and
loyal symbol should be blended with the dishonoured
insignia of a traitorous Roundhead!"

All this was the effect of the glimpse of a sunbeam,
just sufficient to light Lawyer Clippurse to mend his pen.
The pen was mended in vain. The attorney was dismissed, with directions to hold himself in readiness on
the first summons.

The apparition of Lawyer Clippurse at the Hall
occasioned much speculation in that portion of the world
to which Waverley-Honour formed the centre: But the
more judicious politicians of this microcosm augured yet
worse consequences to Richard Waverley from a movement which shortly followed his apostacy. This was no
less than an excursion of the Baronet in his coach-and-six,
with four attendants in rich liveries, to make a visit of
some duration to a noble peer on the confines of the
shire, of untainted descent, steady Tory principles, and
the happy father of six unmarried and accomplished
daughters.

Sir Everard's reception in this family was, as it may

be easily conceived, sufficiently favourable; but of the six young ladies, his taste unfortunately determined him in favour of Lady Emily, the youngest, who received his attentions with an embarrassment, which showed, at once, that she durst not decline them, and that they afforded her anything but pleasure.

Sir Everard could not but perceive something uncommon in the restrained emotions which the young lady testified at the advances he hazarded; but, assured by the prudent Countess that they were the natural effects of a retired education, the sacrifice might have been completed, as doubtless has happened in many similar instances, had it not been for the courage of an elder sister, who revealed to the wealthy suitor that Lady Emily's affections were fixed upon a young soldier of fortune, a near relation of her own. Sir Everard manifested great emotion on receiving this intelligence, which was confirmed to him, in a private interview, by the young lady herself, although under the most dreadful apprehensions of her father's indignation.

Honour and generosity were hereditary attributes of the house of Waverley. With a grace and delicacy worthy the hero of a romance, Sir Everard withdrew his claim to the hand of Lady Emily. He had even, before leaving Blandeville Castle, the address to extort from her father a consent to her union with the object of her choice. What arguments he used on this point cannot exactly be known, for Sir Everard was never supposed strong in the powers of persuasion; but the young officer, immediately after this transaction, rose in the army with a rapidity far surpassing the usual pace of unpatronised professional merit, although, to outward appearance, that was all he had to depend upon.

The shock which Sir Everard encountered upon this occasion, although diminished by the consciousness of having acted virtuously and generously, had its effect upon his future life. His resolution of marriage had been adopted in a fit of indignation; the labour of courtship did not quite suit the dignified indolence of his habits; he had but just escaped the risk of marrying a woman who could never love him, and his pride could not be greatly flattered by the termination of his amour, even if his heart had not suffered. The result of the whole matter was his return to Waverley-Honour without any transfer of his affections, notwithstanding the sighs and languishments of the fair tell-tale, who had revealed, in mere

sisterly affection, the secret of Lady Emily's attachment,
and in despite of the nods, winks, and innuendoes of the
officious lady mother, and the grave eulogiums which the
Earl pronounced successively on the prudence, and good
sense, and admirable dispositions, of his first, second,
third, fourth, and fifth daughters. The memory of his
unsuccessful amour was with Sir Everard, as with many
more of his temper, at once shy, proud, sensitive, and
indolent, a beacon against exposing himself to similar
mortification, pain, and fruitless exertion for the time to
come. He continued to live at Waverley-Honour in the
style of an old English gentleman, of an ancient descent
and opulent fortune. His sister, Miss Rachel Waverley,
presided at his table ; and they became, by degrees, an
old bachelor and an ancient maiden lady, the gentlest
and kindest of the votaries of celibacy.

The vehemence of Sir Everard's resentment against his
brother was but short-lived ; yet his dislike to the Whig
and the placeman, though unable to stimulate him to
resume any active measures prejudicial to Richard's
interest, in the succession to the family estate, continued
to maintain the coldness between them. Richard knew
enough of the world, and of his brother's temper, to
believe that by any ill-considered or precipitate advances
on his part, he might turn passive dislike into a more
active principle. It was accident, therefore, which at
length occasioned a renewal of their intercourse. Richard
had married a young woman of rank, by whose family
interest and private fortune he hoped to advance his
career. In her right, he became possessor of a manor of
some value, at the distance of a few miles from Waverley-
Honour.

Little Edward, the hero of our tale, then in his fifth
year, was their only child. It chanced that the infant
with his maid had strayed one morning to a mile's
distance from the avenue of Brere-wood Lodge, his
father's seat. Their attention was attracted by a carriage
drawn by six stately longtailed black horses, and with as
much carving and gilding as would have done honour to
my lord mayor's. It was waiting for the owner, who was
at a little distance inspecting the progress of a half-built
farm-house. I know not whether the boy's nurse had
been a Welsh or a Scotch woman, or in what manner he
associated a shield emblazoned with three ermines with
the idea of personal property, but he no sooner beheld
this family emblem, than he stoutly determined on

vindicating his right to the splendid vehicle on which it was displayed. The Baronet arrived while the boy's maid was in vain endeavouring to make him desist from his determination to appropriate the gilded coach and six. The rencontre was at a happy moment for Edward, as his uncle had been just eyeing wistfully, with something of a feeling like envy, the chubby boys of the stout yeoman whose mansion was building by his direction. In the round-faced rosy cherub before him, bearing his eye and his name, and vindicating [a hereditary title to his family, affection, and patronage, by means of a tie which Sir Everard held as sacred as either Garter or Blue-mantle, Providence seemed to have granted to him the very object best calculated to fill up the void in his hopes and affections. Sir Everard returned to Waverley-Hall upon a led horse, which was kept in readiness for him, while the child and his attendant were sent home in the carriage to Brere-wood Lodge, with such a message as opened to Richard Waverley a door of reconciliation with his elder brother.

Their intercourse, however, though thus renewed, continued to be rather formal and civil, than partaking of brotherly cordiality; yet it was sufficient to the wishes of both parties. Sir Everard obtained, in the frequent society of his little nephew, something on which his hereditary pride might found the anticipated pleasure of a continuation of his lineage, and where his kind and gentle affections could at the same time fully exercise themselves. For Richard Waverley, he beheld in the growing attachment between the uncle and nephew the means of securing his son's if not his own, succession to the hereditary estate which he felt would be rather endangered than promoted by any attempt on his own part towards a closer intimacy with a man of Sir Everard's habits and opinions.

Thus, by a sort of tacit compromise, little Edward was permitted to pass the greater part of the year at the Hall, and appeared to stand in the same intimate relation to both families, although their mutual intercourse was otherwise limited to formal messages, and more formal visits. The education of the youth was regulated alternately by the taste and opinions of his uncle and of his father. But more of this in a subsequent chapter.

## CHAPTER III.

### *Education.*

THE education of our hero, Edward Waverley, was of a nature somewhat desultory. In infancy, his health suffered, or was supposed to suffer, (which is quite the same thing,) by the air of London. As soon, therefore, as official duties, attendance on Parliament, or the prosecution of any of his plans of interest or ambition, called his father to town, which was his usual residence for eight months in the year, Edward was transferred to Waverley-Honour, and experienced a total change of instructors and of lessons, as well as of residence. This might have been remedied, had his father placed him under the superintendence of a permanent tutor. But he considered that one of his choosing would probably have been unacceptable at Waverley-Honour, and that such a selection as Sir Everard might have made, were the matter left to him, would have burdened him with a disagreeable inmate, if not a political spy, in his family. He, therefore, prevailed upon his private secretary, a young man of taste and accomplishments, to bestow an hour or two on Edward's education while at Brere-wood Lodge, and left his uncle answerable for his improvement in literature while an inmate at the Hall.

This was in some degree respectably provided for. Sir Everard's chaplain, an Oxonian, who had lost his fellowship for declining to take the oaths at the accession of George I., was not only an excellent classical scholar, but reasonably skilled in science, and master of most modern languages. He was, however, old and indulgent, and the recurring interregnum, during which Edward was entirely freed from his discipline, occasioned such a relaxation of authority, that the youth was permitted, in a great measure, to learn as he pleased, what he pleased, and when he pleased. This slackness of rule might have been ruinous to a boy of slow understanding, who, feeling labour in the acquisition of knowledge, would have altogether neglected it, save for the command of a taskmaster; and it might have proved equally dangerous to a youth whose animal spirits were more powerful than his imagination or his feelings, and whom the irresistible influence of Alma would have engaged in field-sports from morning till night. But the character of Edward

Waverley was remote from either of these. His powers
of apprehension were so uncommonly quick, as almost to
resemble intuition, and the chief care of his preceptor was
to prevent him, as a sportsman would phrase it, from
over-running his game, that is, from acquiring his knowledge in a slight, flimsy, and inadequate manner. And
here the instructor had to combat another propensity too
often united with brilliancy of fancy and vivacity of
talent,—that indolence, namely, of disposition, which can
only be stirred by some strong motive of gratification,
and which renounces study as soon as curiosity is
gratified, the pleasure of conquering the first difficulties
exhausted, and the novelty of pursuit at an end. Edward
would throw himself with spirit upon any classical author
of which his preceptor proposed the perusal, make himself master of the style so far as to understand the story,
and, if that pleased or interested him, he finished the
volume. But it was in vain to attempt fixing his attention on critical distinctions of philology, upon the
difference of idiom, the beauty of felicitous expression, or
the artificial combinations of syntax. "I can read and
understand a Latin author," said young Edward, with the
self-confidence and rash reasoning of fifteen, "and Scaliger
or Bentley could not do much more." Alas! while he
was thus permitted to read only for the gratification of
his amusement, he foresaw not that he was losing for ever
the opportunity of acquiring habits of firm and assiduous
application, of gaining the art of controlling, directing,
and concentrating the powers of his mind for earnest
investigation,—an art far more essential than even that
intimate acquaintance with classical learning which is the
primary object of study.

I am aware I may be here reminded of the necessity of
rendering instruction agreeable to youth, and of Tasso's
infusion of honey into the medicine prepared for a child;
but an age in which children are taught the driest doctrines by the insinuating method of instructive games,
has little reason to dread the consequences of study being
rendered too serious or severe. The history of England
is now reduced to a game at cards,—the problems of
mathematics to puzzles and riddles,—and the doctrines of
arithmetic may, we are assured, be sufficiently acquired,
by spending a few hours a-week at a new and complicated edition of the Royal Game of the Goose. There
wants but one step further, and the Creed and Ten
Commandments may be taught in the same manner,

without the necessity of the grave face, deliberate tone of
recital, and devout attention, hitherto exacted from the
well-governed childhood of this realm. It may, in the
meantime, be subject of serious consideration, whether
those who are accustomed only to acquire instruction
through the medium of amusement, may not be brought
to reject that which approaches under the aspect of
study; whether those who learn history by the cards,
may not be led to prefer the means to the end; and
whether, were we to teach religion in the way of sport,
our pupils may not thereby be gradually induced to
make sport of their religion. To our young hero, who
was permitted to seek his instruction only according to
the bent of his own mind, and who, of consequence, only
sought it so long as it afforded him amusement, the
indulgence of his tutors was attended with evil consequences, which long continued to influence his character,
happiness, and utility.

Edward's power of imagination and love of literature,
although the former was vivid, and the latter ardent,
were so far from affording a remedy to this peculiar evil,
that they rather inflamed and increased its violence.
The library at Waverley-Honour, a large Gothic room,
with double arches and a gallery, contained such a
miscellaneous and extensive collection of volumes as had
been assembled together, during the course of two hundred years, by a family which had been always wealthy,
and inclined, of course, as a mark of splendour, to furnish
their shelves with the current literature of the day,
without much scrutiny, or nicety of discrimination.
Throughout this ample realm Edward was permitted to
roam at large. His tutor had his own studies; and
church politics and controversial divinity, together with
a love of learned ease, though they did not withdraw his
attention at stated times from the progress of his patron's
presumptive heir, induced him readily to grasp at any
apology for not extending a strict and regulated survey
towards his general studies. Sir Everard had never been
himself a student, and, like his sister Miss Rachel Waverley, held the common doctrine, that idleness is incom-
patible with reading of any kind, and that the mere
tracing the alphabetical characters with the eye, is in
itself a useful and meritorious task, without scrupulously
considering what ideas or doctrines they may happen to
convey. With a desire of amusement, therefore, which
better discipline might soon have converted into a thirst

for knowledge, young Waverley drove through the sea of books, like a vessel without a pilot or a rudder. Nothing perhaps increases by indulgence more than a desultory habit of reading, especially under such opportunities of gratifying it. I believe one reason why such numerous instances of erudition occur among the lower ranks is, that, with the same powers of mind, the poor student is limited to a narrow circle for indulging his passion for books, and must necessarily make himself master of the few he possesses ere he can acquire more. Edward, on the contrary, like the epicure who only deigned to take a single morsel from the sunny side of a peach, read no volume a moment after it ceased to excite his curiosity or interest; and it necessarily happened, that the habit of seeking only this sort of gratification rendered it daily more difficult of attainment, till the passion for reading, like other strong appetites, produced by indulgence a sort of satiety.

Ere he attained this indifference, however, he had read, and stored in a memory of uncommon tenacity, much curious, though ill-arranged and miscellaneous information. In English literature he was master of Shakspeare and Milton, of our earlier dramatic authors, of many picturesque and interesting passages from our old historical chronicles, and was particularly well acquainted with Spenser, Drayton, and other poets who have exercised themselves on romantic fiction, of all themes the most fascinating to a youthful imagination, before the passions have roused themselves, and demand poetry of a more sentimental description. In this respect his acquaintance with Italian opened him yet a wider range. He had perused the numerous romantic poems, which, from the days of Pulci, have been a favourite exercise of the wits of Italy, and had sought gratification in the numerous collections of *novelle*, which were brought forth by the genius of that elegant though luxurious nation, in emulation of the Decameron. In classical literature, Waverley had made the usual progress, and read the usual authors; and the French had afforded him an almost exhaustless collection of memoirs, scarcely more faithful than romances, and of romances so well written as hardly to be distinguished from memoirs. The splendid pages of Froissart, with his heart-stirring and eye-dazzling descriptions of war and of tournaments, were among his chief favourites; and from those of Brantome and De la Noue he learned to compare the wild and loose

yet superstitious character of the nobles of the League,
with the stern, rigid, and sometimes turbulent disposition
of the Huguenot party. The Spanish had contributed to
his stock of chivalrous and romantic lore. The earlier
literature of the northern nations did not escape the
study of one who read rather to awaken the imagination
than to benefit the understanding. And yet, knowing
much that is known but to few, Edward Waverley might
justly be considered as ignorant, since he knew little of
what adds dignity to man, and qualifies him to support
and adorn an elevated situation in society.

The occasional attention of his parents might indeed
have been of service, to prevent the dissipation of mind
incidental to such a desultory course of reading. But his
mother died in the seventh year after the reconciliation
between the brothers, and Richard Waverley himself,
who, after this event, resided more constantly in London,
was too much interested in his own plans of wealth and
ambition, to notice more respecting Edward, than that he
was of a very bookish turn, and probably destined to be
a bishop. If he could have discovered and analyzed his
son's waking dreams, he would have formed a very
different conclusion.

## CHAPTER IV.

### Castle-Building.

I HAVE already hinted, that the dainty, squeamish, and
fastidious taste acquired by a surfeit of idle reading, had
not only rendered our hero unfit for serious and sober
study, but had even disgusted him in some degree with
that in which he had hitherto indulged.

He was in his sixteenth year, when his habits of
abstraction and love of solitude became so much marked,
as to excite Sir Everard's affectionate apprehension. He
tried to counterbalance these propensities, by engaging
his nephew in field-sports, which had been the chief
pleasure of his own youthful days. But although Edward
eagerly carried the gun for one season, yet when practice
had given him some dexterity, the pastime ceased to
afford him amusement.

In the succeeding spring, the perusal of old Isaac
Walton's fascinating volume determined Edward to

become "a brother of the angle." But of all diversions which ingenuity ever devised for the relief of idleness, fishing is the worst qualified to amuse a man who is at once indolent and impatient; and our hero's rod was speedily flung aside. Society and example, which, more than any other motives, master and sway the natural bent of our passions, might have had their usual effect upon the youthful visionary. But the neighbourhood was thinly inhabited, and the home-bred young squires whom it afforded, were not of a class fit to form Edward's usual companions, far less to excite him to emulation in the practice of those pastimes which composed the serious business of their lives.

There were a few other youths of better education, and a more liberal character, but from their society also our hero was in some degree excluded. Sir Everard had, upon the death of Queen Anne, resigned his seat in Parliament, and, as his age increased and the number of his contemporaries diminished, had gradually withdrawn himself from society; so that when, upon any particular occasion, Edward mingled with accomplished and well-educated young men of his own rank and expectations, he felt an inferiority in their company, not so much from deficiency of information, as from the want of the skill to command and to arrange that which he possessed. A deep and increasing sensibility added to this dislike of society. The idea of having committed the slightest solecism in politeness, whether real or imaginary, was agony to him; for perhaps even guilt itself does not impose upon some minds so keen a sense of shame and remorse, as a modest, sensitive, and inexperienced youth feels from the consciousness of having neglected etiquette, or excited ridicule. Where we are not at ease, we cannot be happy; and therefore it is not surprising, that Edward Waverley supposed that he disliked and was unfitted for society, merely because he had not yet acquired the habit of living in it with ease and comfort, and of reciprocally giving and receiving pleasure.

The hours he spent with his uncle and aunt were exhausted in listening to the oft-repeated tale of narrative old age. Yet even there his imagination, the predominant faculty of his mind, was frequently excited. Family tradition and genealogical history, upon which much of Sir Everard's discourse turned, is the very reverse of amber, which, itself a valuable substance, usually includes flies, straws, and other trifles; whereas

these studies, being themselves very insignificant and
trifling, do nevertheless serve to perpetuate a great deal
of what is rare and valuable in ancient manners, and to
record many curious and minute facts which could have
been preserved and conveyed through no other medium.
If, therefore, Edward Waverley yawned at times over the
dry deduction of his line of ancestors, with their various
intermarriages, and inwardly deprecated the remorseless
and protracted accuracy with which the worthy Sir
Everard rehearsed the various degrees of propinquity
between the house of Waverley-Honour and the doughty
barons, knights, and squires, to whom they stood allied ;
if (notwithstanding his obligations to the three ermines
passant) he sometimes cursed in his heart the jargon of
heraldry, its griffins, its moldwarps, its wyverns, and its
dragons, with all the bitterness of Hotspur himself, there
were moments when these communications interested his
fancy and rewarded his attention.

The deeds of Wilibert of Waverley in the Holy Land,
his long absence and perilous adventures, his supposed
death, and his return on the evening when the betrothed
of his heart had wedded the hero who had protected her
from insult and oppression during his absence ; the
generosity with which the Crusader relinquished his
claims, and sought in a neighbouring cloister that peace
which passeth not away ; [1]—to these and similar tales he
would hearken till his heart glowed and his eye glistened.
Nor was he less affected, when his aunt, Mrs Rachel,
narrated the sufferings and fortitude of Lady Alice
Waverley during the Great Civil War. The benevolent
features of the venerable spinster kindled into more
majestic expression, as she told how Charles had, after
the field of Worcester, found a day's refuge at Waverley-
Honour, and how, when a troop of cavalry were approaching to search the mansion, Lady Alice dismissed her
youngest son with a handful of domestics, charging them
to make good with their lives an hour's diversion, that
the king might have that space for escape. "And, God
help her," would Mrs Rachel continue, fixing her eyes
upon the heroine's portrait as she spoke, "full dearly did

[1] There is a family legend to this purpose, belonging to the knightly family of
Bradshaigh, the proprietors of Haigh-hall, in Lancashire, where, I have been
told, the event is recorded on a painted glass window. The German ballad of the
Noble Moringer turns upon a similar topic. But undoubtedly many such incidents
may have taken place, where, the distance being great and the intercourse
infrequent, false reports concerning the fate of the absent Crusaders must have
been commonly circulated, and sometimes perhaps rather hastily credited at
home. (S.)

she purchase the safety of her prince with the life of her darling child. They brought him here a prisoner, mortally wounded; and you may trace the drops of his blood from the great hall door along the little gallery, and up to the saloon, where they laid him down to die at his mother's feet. But there was comfort exchanged between them; for he knew, from the glance of his mother's eye, that the purpose of his desperate defence was attained. Ah! I remember," she continued, "I remember well to have seen one that knew and loved him. Miss Lucy St Aubin lived and died a maid for his sake, though one of the most beautiful and wealthy matches in this country; all the world ran after her, but she wore widow's mourning all her life for poor William, for they were betrothed though not married, and died in ——, I cannot think of the date; but I remember, in the November of that very year, when she found herself sinking, she desired to be brought to Waverley-Honour once more, and visited all the places where she had been with my grand-uncle, and caused the carpets to be raised that she might trace the impression of his blood, and if tears could have washed it out, it had not been there now; for there was not a dry eye in the house. You would have thought, Edward, that the very trees mourned for her, for their leaves dropt around her without a gust of wind; and, indeed, she looked like one that would never see them green again."

From such legends our hero would steal away to indulge the fancies they excited. In the corner of the large and sombre library, with no other light than was afforded by the decaying brands on its ponderous and ample hearth, he would exercise for hours that internal sorcery, by which past or imaginary events are presented in action, as it were, to the eye of the muser. Then arose in long and fair array the splendour of the bridal feast at Waverley-Castle; the tall and emaciated form of its real lord, as he stood in his pilgrim's weeds, an unnoticed spectator of the festivities of his supposed heir and intended bride; the electrical shock occasioned by the discovery; the springing of the vassals to arms; the astonishment of the bridegroom; the terror and confusion of the bride; the agony with which Wilibert observed, that her heart as well as consent was in these nuptials; the air of dignity, yet of deep feeling with which he flung down the half-drawn sword, and turned away for ever from the house of his ancestors. Then

would he change the scene, and fancy would at his wish
represent Aunt Rachel's tragedy.  He saw the Lady
Waverley seated in her bower, her ear strained to every
sound, her heart throbbing with double agony, now
listening to the decaying echo of the hoofs of the king's
horse, and when that had died away, hearing in every
breeze that shook the trees of the park, the noise of the
remote skirmish.  A distant sound is heard like the
rushing of a swoln stream ; it comes nearer, and Edward
can plainly distinguish the galloping of horses, the cries
and shouts of men, with straggling pistol-shots between,
rolling forwards to the hall.  The lady starts up—a
terrified menial rushes in—but why pursue such a description ?

As living in this ideal world became daily more delect-
able to our hero, interruption was disagreeable in proportion.  The extensive domain that surrounded the
Hall, which, far exceeding the dimensions of a park, was
usually termed Waverley-Chase, had originally been forest
ground, and still, though broken by extensive glades, in
which the young deer were sporting, retained its pristine
and savage character.  It was traversed by broad
avenues, in many places half grown up with brushwood,
where the beauties of former days used to take their
stand to see the stag coursed with greyhounds, or to gain
an aim at him with the cross-bow.  In one spot, distinguished by a moss-grown Gothic monument, which retained the name of Queen's Standing, Elizabeth herself
was said to have pierced seven bucks with her own
arrows.  This was a very favourite haunt of Waverley.
At other times, with his gun and his spaniel, which
served as an apology to others, and with a book in his
pocket, which perhaps served as an apology to himself,
he used to pursue one of these long avenues, which, after
an ascending sweep of four miles, gradually narrowed
into a rude and contracted path through the cliffy and
woody pass called Mirkwood Dingle, and opened suddenly
upon a deep, dark, and small lake, named, from the same
cause, Mirkwood-Mere.  There stood, in former times, a
solitary tower upon a rock almost surrounded by the
water, which had acquired the name of the Strength of
Waverley, because, in perilous times, it had often been the
refuge of the family.  There, in the wars of York and
Lancaster, the last adherents of the Red Rose who dared
to maintain her cause, carried on a harassing and predatory warfare, till the strong-hold was reduced by the

celebrated Richard of Gloucester. Here, too, a party of cavaliers long maintained themselves under Nigel Waverley, elder brother of that William whose fate Aunt Rachel commemorated. Through these scenes it was that Edward loved to "chew the cud of sweet and bitter fancy," and, like a child among his toys, culled and arranged, from the splendid yet useless imagery and emblems with which his imagination was stored, visions as brilliant and as fading as those of an evening sky. The effect of this indulgence upon his temper and character will appear in the next chapter.

## CHAPTER V.

### *Choice of a Profession.*

FROM the minuteness with which I have traced Waverley's pursuits, and the bias which these unavoidably communicated to his imagination, the reader may perhaps anticipate, in the following tale, an imitation of the romance of Cervantes. But he will do my prudence injustice in the supposition. My intention is not to follow the steps of that inimitable author, in describing such total perversion of intellect as misconstrues the objects actually presented to the senses, but that more common aberration from sound judgment, which apprehends occurrences indeed in their reality, but communicates to them a tincture of its own romantic tone and colouring. So far was Edward Waverley from expecting general sympathy with his own feelings, or concluding that the present state of things was calculated to exhibit the reality of those visions in which he loved to indulge, that he dreaded nothing more than the detection of such sentiments as were dictated by his musings. He neither had nor wished to have a confident, with whom to communicate his reveries ; and so sensible was he of the ridicule attached to them, that, had he been to choose between any punishment short of ignominy, and the necessity of giving a cold and composed account of the ideal world in which he lived the better part of his days, I think he would not have hesitated to prefer the former infliction. This secrecy became doubly precious, as he felt in advancing life the influence of the awakening passions. Female forms of exquisite grace and beauty began to mingle in his mental adventures ;

nor was he long without looking abroad to compare the
creatures of his own imagination with the females of
actual life.

The list of the beauties who displayed their hebdomadal
finery at the parish church of Waverley was neither
numerous nor select. By far the most passable was Miss
Sissly, or, as she rather chose to be called, Miss Cecilia
Stubbs, daughter of Squire Stubbs at the Grange. I
know not whether it was by the "merest accident in the
world," a phrase which, from female lips, does not always
exclude *malice prepense*, or whether it was from a con-
formity of taste, that Miss Cecilia more than once crossed
Edward in his favourite walks through Waverley-Chase.
He had not as yet assumed courage to accost her on these
occasions; but the meeting was not without its effect.
A romantic lover is a strange idolater, who sometimes
cares not out of what log he frames the object of his
adoration; at least, if nature has given that object any
passable proportion of personal charms, he can easily play
the Jeweller and Dervise in the Oriental tale,[1] and supply
her richly, out of the stores of his own imagination, with
supernatural beauty, and all the properties of intellectual
wealth.

But ere the charms of Miss Cecilia Stubbs had erected
her into a positive goddess, or elevated her at least to a
level with the saint her namesake, Mrs Rachel Waverley
gained some intimation which determined her to prevent
the approaching apotheosis. Even the most simple and
unsuspicious of the female sex have (God bless them!) an
instinctive sharpness of perception in such matters, which
sometimes goes the length of observing partialities that
never existed, but rarely misses to detect such as pass
actually under their observation. Mrs Rachel applied
herself with great prudence, not to combat, but to elude,
the approaching danger, and suggested to her brother the
necessity that the heir of his house should see something
more of the world than was consistent with constant residence at Waverley-Honour.

Sir Everard would not at first listen to a proposal which
went to separate his nephew from him. Edward was a
little bookish, he admitted; but youth, he had always
heard, was the season for learning, and, no doubt, when
his rage for letters was abated, and his head fully stocked
with knowledge, his nephew would take to field-sports
and country business. He had often, he said, himself re-

[1] See Hoppner's tale of the Seven Lovers.

gretted that he had not spent some time in study during his youth ; he would neither have shot nor hunted with less skill, and he might have made the roof of St Stephen's echo to longer orations than were comprised in those zealous Noes, with which, when a member of the House during Godolphin's administration, he encountered every measure of government.

Aunt Rachel's anxiety, however, lent her address to carry her point. Every representative of their house had visited foreign parts, or served his country in the army, before he settled for life at Waverley-Honour, and she appealed for the truth of her assertion to the genealogical pedigree ; an authority which Sir Everard was never known to contradict. In short, a proposal was made to Mr Richard Waverley, that his son should travel, under the direction of his present tutor, Mr Pembroke, with a suitable allowance from the Baronet's liberality. The father himself saw no objection to this overture ; but upon mentioning it casually at the table of the minister, the great man looked grave. The reason was explained in private. The unhappy turn of Sir Everard's politics, the minister observed, was such as would render it highly improper that a young gentleman of such hopeful prospects should travel on the Continent with a tutor doubtless of his uncle's choosing, and directing his course by his instructions. What might Mr Edward Waverley's society be at Paris, what at Rome, where all manner of snares were spread by the Pretender and his sons—these were points for Mr Waverley to consider. This he could himself say, that he knew his Majesty had such a just sense of Mr Richard Waverley's merits, that if his son adopted the army for a few years, a troop, he believed, might be reckoned upon in one of the dragoon regiments lately returned from Flanders.

A hint thus conveyed and enforced was not to be neglected with impunity ; and Richard Waverley, though with great dread of shocking his brother's prejudices, deemed he could not avoid accepting the commission thus offered him for his son. The truth is, he calculated much, and justly, upon Sir Everard's fondness for Edward, which made him unlikely to resent any step that he might take in due submission to parental authority. Two letters announced this determination to the Baronet and his nephew. The latter barely communicated the fact, and pointed out the necessary preparations for joining his regiment. To his brother, Richard was more diffuse and circuitous. He coincided with him, in the most flattering manner, in the propriety of his son's seeing a little more of the world, and was even humble in expressions of gratitude for his proposed assistance ; was however, deeply concerned that it was now, unfortunately, not in Edward's power exactly to comply with the plan which had been chalked out by his best friend and benefactor. He himself had thought with pain on the boy's inactivity, at an age when all his ancestors had borne arms ; even Royalty itself had deigned to inquire whether young Waverley was not now in Flanders, at an age when his grandfather was already bleeding for his king in the Great Civil War. This was accompanied by an offer of a troop of horse. What could he do ? There was no time to consult his brother's inclinations, even if he could have conceived there might be objections on his part to his nephew's following the glorious career of his predecessors. And, in short, that Edward was now (the intermediate steps of cornet and lieutenant being over-leapt with great agility) Captain Waverley, of Gardiner's regiment of dragoons, which he must join in their quarters at Dundee in Scotland, in the course of a month.

Sir Everard Waverley received this intimation with a mixture of feelings. At the period of the Hanoverian succession he had withdrawn from parliament, and his conduct, in the memorable year 1715, had not been altogether unsuspected. There were reports of private musters of tenants and horses in Waverley-Chase by moonlight, and of cases of carbines and pistols purchased in Holland, and addressed to the Baronet, but intercepted by the vigilance of a riding officer of the excise, who was afterwards tossed in a blanket on a moonless night, by an association of stout yeomen, for his officiousness. Nay, it was even said, that at the arrest of Sir William Wynd-ham, the leader of the Tory party, a letter from Sir Everard was found in the pocket of his night-gown. But there was no overt act which an attainder could be founded on, and government, contented with suppressing the insurrection of 1715, felt it neither prudent nor safe to push their vengeance farther than against those unfortunate gentlemen who actually took up arms.

Nor did Sir Everard's apprehensions of personal consequences seem to correspond with the reports spread among his Whig neighbours. It was well known that he had supplied with money several of the distressed

Northumbrians and Scotchmen, who, after being made
prisoners at Preston in Lancashire, were imprisoned in
Newgate and the Marshalsea, and it was his solicitor and
ordinary counsel who conducted the defence of some of
these unfortunate gentlemen at their trial. It was
generally supposed, however, that, had ministers possessed
any real proof of Sir Everard's accession to the rebellion,
he either would not have ventured thus to brave the
existing government, or at least would not have done so
with impunity. The feelings which then dictated his
proceedings, were those of a young man, and at an agitating period. Since that time Sir Everard's jacobitism had
been gradually decaying, like a fire which burns out for
want of fuel. His Tory and High-church principles were
kept up by some occasional exercise at elections and
quarter-sessions ; but those respecting hereditary right
were fallen into a sort of abeyance. Yet it jarred severely
upon his feelings, that his nephew should go into the
army under the Brunswick dynasty ; and the more so, as,
independent of his high and conscientious ideas of
paternal authority, it was impossible, or at least highly
imprudent, to interfere authoritatively to prevent it.
This suppressed vexation gave rise to many poohs and
pshaws, which were placed to the account of an incipient
fit of gout, until, having sent for the Army List, the
worthy Baronet consoled himself with reckoning the
descendants of the house of genuine loyalty, Mordaunts,
Granvilles, and Stanleys, whose names were to be found
in that military record ; and, calling up all his feelings of
family grandeur and warlike glory, he concluded, with
logic something like Falstaff's, that when war was at
hand, although it were shame to be on any side but one, it
were worse shame to be idle than to be on the worst side,
though blacker than usurpation could make it. As for
aunt Rachel, her scheme had not exactly terminated
according to her wishes, but she was under the necessity
of submitting to circumstances ; and her mortification
was diverted by the employment she found in fitting out
her nephew for the campaign, and greatly consoled by the
prospect of beholding him blaze in complete uniform.

Edward Waverley himself received with animated and
undefined surprise this most unexpected intelligence. It
was, as a fine old poem expresses it, "like a fire to
heather set," that covers a solitary hill with smoke, and
illumines it at the same time with dusky fire. His tutor,
or I should say, Mr Pembroke, for he scare assumed the

name of tutor, picked up about Edward's room some
fragments of irregular verse, which he appeared to have
composed under the influence of the agitating feelings
occasioned by this sudden page being turned up to him
in the book of life. The doctor, who was a believer in all
poetry which was composed by his friends, and written
out in fair straight lines, with a capital at the beginning
of each, communicated this treasure to Aunt Rachel, who,
with her spectacles dimmed with tears, transferred them
to her common-place book, among choice receipts for
cookery and medicine, favourite texts, and portions from
High-church divines, and a few songs, amatory and
jacobitical, which she had carroll'd in her younger days,
from whence her nephew's poetical *tentamina* were
extracted when the volume itself, with other authentic
records of the Waverley family, were exposed to the
inspection of the unworthy editor of this memorable
history. If they afford the reader no higher amusement,
they will serve, at least, better than narrative of any
kind, to acquaint him with the wild and irregular spirit
of our hero :—

Late, when the Autumn evening fell
On Mirkwood-Mere's romantic dell,
The lake return'd, in chasten'd gleam,
The purple cloud, the golden beam :
Reflected in the crystal pool,
Headland and bank lay fair and cool;
The weather-tinted rock and tower,
Each drooping tree, each fairy flower,
So true, so soft, the mirror gave,
As if there lay beneath the wave,
Secure from trouble, toil, and care,
A world than earthly world more fair.

But distant winds began to wake,
And roused the Genius of the Lake!
He heard the groaning of the oak,
And donn'd at once his sable cloak,
As warrior, at the battle-cry.
Invests him with his panoply :
Then as the whirlwind nearer press'd,
He 'gan to shake his foamy crest
O'er furrow'd brow and blacken'd cheek,
And bade his surge in thunder speak.
In wild and broken eddies whirl'd
Flitted that fond ideal world,
And to the shore in tumult tost,
The realms of fairy bliss were lost.

Yet, with a stern delight and strange,
I saw the spirit-stirring change.
As warr'd the wind with wave and wood,
Upon the ruin'd tower I stood,
And felt my heart more strongly bound,
Responsive to the lofty sound,
While, joying in the mighty roar,
I mourn'd that tranquil scene no more.

So, on the idle dreams of youth,
Breaks the loud trumpet-call of truth,
Bids each fair vision pass away,
Like landscape on the lake that lay,
As fair, as flitting, and as frail,
As that which fled the Autumn gale—
For ever dead to fancy's eye
Be each gay form that glided by,
While dreams of love and lady's charms
Give place to honour and to arms!

In sober prose, as perhaps these verses intimate less decidedly, the transient idea of Miss Cecilia Stubbs passed from Captain Waverley's heart amid the turmoil which his new destinies excited. She appeared, indeed, in full splendour in her father's pew upon the Sunday when he attended service for the last time at the old parish church, upon which occasion, at the request of his uncle and Aunt Rachel, he was induced (nothing loth, if the truth must be told) to present himself in full uniform.

There is no better antidote against entertaining too high an opinion of others, than having an excellent one of ourselves at the very same time. Miss Stubbs had indeed summoned up every assistance which art could afford to beauty; but alas! hoop, patches, frizzled locks, and a new mantua of genuine French silk, were lost upon a young officer of dragoons, who wore, for the first time, his gold-laced hat, jack-boots, and broadsword. I know not whether, like the champion of an old ballad,

His heart was all on honour bent,
He could not stoop to love;
No lady in the land had power
His frozen heart to move;

or whether the deep and flaming bars of embroidered gold, which now fenced his breast, defied the artillery of Cecilia's eyes; but every arrow was launched at him in vain.

Yet did I mark where Cupid's shaft did light;
It lighted not on little western flower,
But on bold yeoman, flower of all the west,
Hight Jonas Culbertfield, the steward's son.

Craving pardon for my heroics, (which I am unable in certain cases to resist giving way to,) it is a melancholy fact, that my history must here take leave of the fair Cecilia, who, like many a daughter of Eve, after the departure of Edward, and the dissipation of certain idle visions which she had adopted, quietly contented herself with a *pis-aller*, and gave her hand, at the distance of six

months, to the aforesaid Jonas, son of the Baronet's
steward, and heir (no unfertile prospect) to a steward's
fortune; besides the snug probability of succeeding to
his father's office. All these advantages moved Squire
Stubbs, as much as the ruddy brow and manly form of
the suitor influenced his daughter, to abate somewhat in
the article of their gentry; and so the match was concluded. None seemed more gratified than Aunt Rachel,
who had hitherto looked rather askance upon the presumptuous damsel, (as much so, peradventure, as her
nature would permit,) but who, on the first appearance of
the new-married pair at church, honoured the bride with
a smile and a profound curtsey, in presence of the
rector, the curate, the clerk, and the whole congregation
of the united parishes of Waverley *cum* Beverley.

I beg pardon, once and for all, of those readers who
take up novels merely for amusement, for plaguing them
so long with old-fashioned politics, and Whig and Tory,
and Hanoverians and Jacobites. The truth is, I cannot
promise them that this story shall be intelligible, not to
say probable, without it. My plan requires that I should
explain the motives on which its action proceeded; and
these motives necessarily arose from the feelings, prejudices, and parties, of the times. I do not invite my fair
readers, whose sex and impatience give them the greatest
right to complain of these circumstances, into a flying
chariot drawn by hippogriffs, or moved by enchantment.
Mine is a humble English post-chaise, drawn upon four
wheels, and keeping his majesty's highway. Such as
dislike the vehicle may leave it at the next halt, and wait
for the conveyance of Prince Hussein's tapestry, or Malek
the Weaver's flying sentry-box. Those who are contented
to remain with me will be occasionally exposed to the
dulness inseparable from heavy roads, steep hills, sloughs,
and other terrestrial retardations; but, with tolerable
horses and a civil driver, (as the advertisements have it,)
I engage to get as soon as possible into a more picturesque and romantic country, if my passengers incline to
have some patience with me during my first stages.[1]

[1] These Introductory Chapters have been a good deal censured as tedious and
unnecessary. Yet there are circumstances recorded in them which the author
has not been able to persuade himself to retract or cancel. (S.)

## CHAPTER VI.

### *The Adieus of Waverley.*

IT was upon the evening of this memorable Sunday that Sir Everard entered the library, where he narrowly missed surprising our young hero as he went through the guards of the broadsword with the ancient weapon of old Sir Hildebrand, which, being preserved as an heir-loom, usually hung over the chimney in the library, beneath a picture of the knight and his horse, where the features were almost entirely hidden by the knight's profusion of curled hair, and the Bucephalus which he bestrode concealed by the voluminous robes of the Bath with which he was decorated. Sir Everard entered, and after a glance at the picture and another at his nephew, began a little speech, which, however, soon dropt into the natural simplicity of his common manner, agitated upon the present occasion by no common feeling. "Nephew," he said; and then, as mending his phrase, "My dear Edward, it is God's will, and also the will of your father, whom, under God, it is your duty to obey, that you should leave us to take up the profession of arms, in which so many of your ancestors have been distinguished I have made such arrangements as will enable you to take the field as their descendant, and as the probable heir of the house of Waverley; and, sir, in the field of battle you will remember what name you bear. And, Edward, my dear boy, remember also that you are the last of that race, and the only hope of its revival depends upon you; therefore, as far as duty and honour will permit, avoid danger—I mean unnecessary danger—and keep no company with rakes, gamblers, and Whigs, of whom, it is to be feared, there are but too many in the service into which you are going. Your colonel, as I am informed, is an excellent man—for a Presbyterian; but you will remember your duty to God, the Church of England, and the"——(this breach ought to have been supplied, according to the rubrick, with the word *king :* but as, unfortunately, that word conveyed a double and embarrassing sense, one meaning *de facto*, and the other *de jure*, the knight filled up the blank otherwise)—"the Church of England, and all constituted authorities." Then, not trusting himself with any further oratory, he carried his nephew to his stables to see the horses destined for his campaign. Two were black, (the regimental colour,) superb chargers both ; the other three were stout active hacks, designed for the road, or for his domestics, of whom two were to attend him from the Hall ; an additional groom, if necessary, might be picked up in Scotland.

"You will depart with but a small retinue," quoth the Baronet, "compared to Sir Hildebrand, when he mustered before the gate of the Hall a larger body of horse than your whole regiment consists of. I could have wished that these twenty young fellows from my estate, who have enlisted in your troop, had been to march with you on your journey to Scotland. It would have been something, at least ; but I am told their attendance would be thought unusual in these days, when every new and foolish fashion is introduced to break the natural dependence of the people upon their landlords."

Sir Everard had done his best to correct this unnatural disposition of the times ; for he had brightened the chain of attachment between the recruits and their young captain, not only by a copious repast of beef and ale, by way of parting feast, but by such a pecuniary donation to each individual, as tended rather to improve the conviviality than the discipline of their march. After inspecting the cavalry, Sir Everard again conducted his nephew to the library, where he produced a letter, carefully folded, surrounded by a little stripe of flox-silk, according to ancient form, and sealed with an accurate impression of the Waverley coat-of-arms. It was addressed, with great formality, "To Cosmo Comyne Bradwardine, Esq. of Bradwardine, at his principal mansion of Tully-Veolan, Perthshire, North Britain. These—By the hands of Captain Edward Waverley, nephew of Sir Everard Waverley, of Waverley-Honour, Bart."

The gentleman to whom this enormous greeting was addressed, of whom we shall have more to say in a sequel, had been in arms for the exiled family of Stewart in the year 1715, and was made prisoner at Preston in Lancashire. He was of a very ancient family, and somewhat embarrassed fortune ; a scholar, according to the scholarship of Scotchmen, that is, his learning was more diffuse than accurate, and he was rather a reader than a grammarian. Of his zeal for the classic authors he is said to have given an uncommon instance. On the road between Preston and London he made his escape from his guards ;

but being afterwards found loitering near the place where
they had lodged the former night, he was recognised, and
again arrested. His companions, and even his escort,
were surprised at his infatuation, and could not help inquiring, why, being once at liberty, he had not made the
best of his way to a place of safety ; to which he replied,
that he had intended to do so, but, in good faith, he had
returned to seek his Titus Livius, which he had forgot in
the hurry of his escape.[1] The simplicity of this anecdote
struck the gentleman, who, as we before observed, had
managed the defence of some of those unfortunate persons, at the expense of Sir Everard, and perhaps some
others of the party. He was, besides, himself a special
admirer of the old Patavinian, and though probably his
own zeal might not have carried him such extravagant
lengths, even to recover the edition of Sweynheim and
Pannartz, (supposed to be the princeps,) he did not the
less estimate the devotion of the North Briton, and in
consequence exerted himself to so much purpose to
remove and soften evidence, detect legal flaws, *et cetera*,
that he accomplished the final discharge and deliverance
of Cosmo Comyne Bradwardine from certain very awkward consequences of a plea before our sovereign lord the
king in Westminster.

The Baron of Bradwardine, for he was generally so
called in Scotland, (although his intimates, from his place
of residence, used to denominate him Tully-Veolan, or,
more familiarly, Tully,) no sooner stood *rectus in curia*,
than he posted down to pay his respects and make his
acknowledgments at Waverley-Honour. A congenial
passion for field-sports, and a general coincidence in
political opinions, cemented his friendship with Sir
Everard, notwithstanding the difference of their habits
and studies in other particulars ; and, having spent
several weeks at Waverley-Honour, the Baron departed
with many expressions of regard, warmly pressing the
Baronet to return his visit, and partake of the diversion
of grouse-shooting upon his moors in Perthshire next
season. Shortly after, Mr Bradwardine remitted from
Scotland a sum in reimbursement of expenses incurred in
in the King's High Court of Westminster, which, although
not quite so formidable when reduced to the English denomination, had, in its original form of Scotch pounds,
shillings and pence, such a formidable effect upon the
frame of Duncan Macwheeble, the laird's confidential

[1] Note 1. Titus Livius.

factor, baron-bailie, and man of resource, that he had a
fit of the cholic which lasted for five days, occasioned, he
said, solely and utterly by becoming the unhappy instrument of conveying such a serious sum of money out of
his native country into the hands of the false English.
But patriotism, as it is the fairest, so it is often the most
suspicious mask of other feelings ; but many who knew
Bailie Macwheeble, concluded that his professions of regret were not altogether disinterested, and that he would
have grudged the moneys paid to the *loons* at Westminster
much less had they not come from Bradwardine estate,
a fund which he considered as more particularly his own.
But the Bailie protested he was absolutely disinterested—

"Woe, woe, for Scotland, not a whit for me!"

The laird was only rejoiced that his worthy friend Sir
Everard Waverley of Waverley-Honour, was reimbursed
of the expenditure which he had outlaid on account of
the house of Bradwardine.  It concerned, he said, the
credit of his own family, and of the kingdom of Scotland,
at large, that these disbursements should be repaid forthwith, and, if delayed, it would be a matter of national
reproach.  Sir Everard, accustomed to treat much larger
sums with indifference, received the remittance of £294,
13s. 6d., without being aware that the payment was an
international concern, and, indeed, would probably have
forgot the circumstance altogether, if Bailie Macwheeble
had thought of comforting his cholic by intercepting the
subsidy.  A yearly intercourse took place, of a short
letter, and a hamper or a cask or two, between Waverley-
Honour and Tully-Veolan, the English exports consisting
of mighty cheeses and mightier ale, pheasants, and venison, and the Scottish returns being vested in grouse,
white hares, pickled salmon, and usquebaugh.  All which
were meant, sent, and received, as pledges of constant
friendship and amity between two important houses.  It
followed as a matter of course, that the heir-apparent of
Waverley-Honour could not with propriety visit Scotland
without being furnished with credentials to the Baron of
Bradwardine.

When this matter was explained and settled, Mr Pembroke expressed his wish to take a private and particular
leave of his dear pupil.  The good man's exhortations to
Edward to preserve an unblemished life and morals, to
hold fast the principles of the Christian religion, and to
eschew the profane company of scoffers and latitudin-

arians, too much abounding in the army, were not unmingled with his political prejudices. It had pleased
Heaven, he said, to place Scotland (doubtless for the sins
of their ancestors in 1642) in a more deplorable state of
darkness than even this unhappy kingdom of England.
Here, at least, although the candlestick of the Church of
England had been in some degree removed from its place,
it yet afforded a glimmering light; there was a heirarchy,
though schismatical, and fallen from the principles maintained by those great fathers of the church, Sancroft and
his brethren; there was a liturgy, though wofully perverted in some of the principal petitions. But in Scotland it was utter darkness; and, excepting a sorrowful,
scattered, and persecuted remnant, the pulpits were
abandoned to Presbyterians, and, he feared, to sectaries
of every description. It should be his duty to fortify his
dear pupil to resist such unhallowed and pernicious
doctrines in church and state, as must necessarily be
forced at times upon his unwilling ears.

Here he produced two immense folded packets, which
appeared each to contain a whole ream of closely written
manuscript. They had been the labour of the worthy
man's whole life; and never were labour and zeal more
absurdly wasted. He had at one time gone to London,
with the intention of giving them to the world, by the
medium of a bookseller in Little Britain, well known to
deal in such commodities, and to whom he was instructed
to address himself in a particular phrase, and with a
certain sign, which, it seems, passed at that time current
among the initiated Jacobites. The moment Mr Pembroke
had uttered the Shibboleth, with the appropriate gesture,
the bibliopolist greeted him, notwithstanding every dis-
clamation, by the title of Doctor, and conveying him into
his back shop, after inspecting every possible and impossible place of concealment, he commenced: "Eh,
doctor!—Well—all under the rose—snug—I keep no holes
here even for a Hanoverian rat to hide in. And, what—
eh! any good news from our friends over the water?—
and how does the worthy King of France?—Or perhaps
you are more lately from Rome? it must be Rome will do
it at last—the church must light its candle at the old
lamp.—Eh—what, cautious? I like you the better; but
no fear."

Here Mr Pembroke with some difficulty stopt a torrent
of interrogations, eked out with signs, nods, and winks;
and, having at length convinced the bookseller that he

did him too much honour in supposing him an emissary
of exiled royalty, he explained his actual business.

The man of books with a much more composed air
proceeded to examine the manuscripts. The title of the
first was "A Dissent from Dissenters, or the Comprehension confuted; showing the Impossibility of any Composition between the Church and Puritans, Presbyterians,
or Sectaries of any Description; illustrated from the
Scriptures, the Fathers of the Church, and the soundest
Controversial Divines." To this work the bookseller
positively demurred. "Well meant," he said, "and learned,
doubtless; but the time had gone by. Printed on small-
pica it would run to eight hundred pages, and could never
pay. Begged therefore to be excused — Loved and
honoured the true church from his soul, and, had it been
a sermon on the martyrdom, or any twelve-penny touch
—why I would venture something for the honour of the
cloth—But come, let's see the other. 'Right Hereditary
righted!'—Ah! there's some sense in this. Hum—hum
—hum—pages so many, paper so much, letter-press——
Ah—I'll tell you, though, doctor, you must knock out
some of the Latin and Greek; heavy, doctor, damn'd
heavy—(beg your pardon) and if you throw in a few
grains more pepper—I am he that never peached my
author—I have published for Drake and Charlwood Law-
ton, and poor Amhurst[1]—Ah, Caleb! Caleb! Well, it
was a shame to let poor Caleb starve, and so many fat
rectors and squires among us. I gave him a dinner once
a-week; but, Lord love you, what's once a-week, when a
man does not know where to go the other six days?—
Well, but I must show the manuscript to little Tom Alibi
the solicitor, who manages all my law affairs—must keep
on the windy side—the mob were very uncivil the last
time I mounted in Old Palace Yard—all Whigs and
Roundheads every man of them, Williamites and Hanover
rats."

The next day Mr Pembroke again called on the publisher, but found Tom Alibi's advice had determined him
against undertaking the work. "Not but what I would
go to—(what was I going to say?) to the Plantations for
the Church with pleasure—but, dear doctor, I have a wife
and family; but, to show my zeal, I'll recommend the job
to my neighbour Trimmel—he is a bachelor, and leaving
off business, so a voyage in a western barge would not
inconvenience him." But Mr Trimmel was also obdurate,

---

[1] Note 2. Nicholas Amhurst.

and Mr Pembroke, fortunately perchance for himself, was compelled to return to Waverley-Honour with his treatise in vindication of the real fundamental principles of church and state safely packed in his saddle-bags.

As the public were thus likely to be deprived of the benefit arising from his lucubrations by the selfish cowardice of the trade, Mr Pembroke resolved to make two copies of these tremendous manuscripts for the use of his pupil. He felt that he had been indolent as a tutor, and, besides, his conscience checked him for complying with the request of Mr Richard Waverley, that he would impress no sentiments upon Edward's mind inconsistent with the present settlement in church and state.—But now, thought he, I may, without breach of my word, since he is no longer under my tuition, afford the youth the means of judging for himself, and have only to dread his reproaches for so long concealing the light which the perusal will flash upon his mind.—While he thus indulged the reveries of an author and a politician, his darling proselyte, seeing nothing very inviting in the title of the tracts, and appalled by the bulk and compact lines of the manuscript, quietly consigned them to a corner of his travelling trunk.

Aunt Rachel's farewell was brief and affectionate. She only cautioned her dear Edward, whom she probably deemed somewhat susceptible, against the fascination of Scottish beauty. She allowed that the northern part of the island contained some ancient families, but they were all Whigs and Presbyterians except the Highlanders ; and respecting them she must needs say, there could be no great delicacy among the ladies, where the gentlemen's usual attire was, as she had been assured, to say the least, very singular, and not at all decorous. She concluded her farewell with a kind and moving benediction, and gave the young officer, as a pledge of her regard, a valuable diamond ring, (often worn by the male sex at that time,) and a purse of broad gold pieces, which also were more common Sixty Years since than they have been of late.

## CHAPTER VII.

### *A Horse-Quarter in Scotland.*

THE next morning, amid varied feelings, the chief of
which was a predominant, anxious, and even solemn
impression, that he was now in a great measure abandoned
to his own guidance and direction, Edward Waverley
departed from the Hall amid the blessings and tears of all
the old domestics and the inhabitants of the village,
mingled with some sly petitions for sergeantcies and
corporal-ships, and so forth, on the part of those who
professed that "they never thoft to ha' seen Jacob, and
Giles, and Jonathan, go off for soldiers, save to attend his
honour, as in duty bound." Edward, as in duty bound,
extricated himself from the supplicants with the pledge
of fewer promises than might have been expected from a
young man so little accustomed to the world. After a
short visit to London, he proceeded on horseback, then
the general mode of travelling, to Edinburgh, and from
thence to Dundee, a seaport on the eastern coast of
Angus-shire, where his regiment was then quartered.

He now entered upon a new world, where, for a time,
all was beautiful because all was new. Colonel Gardiner,
the commanding officer of the regiment, was himself a
study for a romantic, and at the same time an inquisitive,
youth. In person he was tall, handsome, and active,
though somewhat advanced in life. In his early years,
he had been what is called, by manner of palliative, a
very gay young man, and strange stories were circulated
about his sudden conversion from doubt, if not infidelity,
to a serious and even enthusiastic turn of mind. It was
whispered that a supernatural communication, of a nature
obvious even to the exterior senses, had produced this
wonderful change; and though some mentioned the
proselyte as an enthusiast, none hinted at his being a
hypocrite. This singular and mystical circumstance gave
Colonel Gardiner a peculiar and solemn interest in the
eyes of the young soldier.[1] It may be easily imagined
that the officers of a regiment, commanded by so respectable a person, composed a society more sedate and orderly
than a military mess always exhibits; and that Waverley
escaped some temptations to which he might otherwise
have been exposed.

[1] Note 3.   Colonel Gardiner.

Meanwhile his military education proceeded. Already a good horseman, he was now initiated into the arts of the manege, which, when carried to perfection, almost realize the fable of the Centaur, the guidance of the horse appearing to proceed from the rider's mere volition, rather than from the use of any external and apparent signal of motion. He received also instructions in his field duty; but I must own, that when his first ardour was past, his progress fell short in the latter particular of what he wished and expected. The duty of an officer, the most imposing of all others to the inexperienced mind, because accompanied with so much outward pomp and circumstance, is in its essence a very dry and abstract task, depending chiefly upon arithmetical combinations, requiring much attention, and a cool and reasoning head to bring them into action. Our hero was liable to fits of absence, in which his blunders excited some mirth, and called down some reproof. This circumstance impressed him with a painful sense of inferiority in those qualities which appeared most to deserve and obtain regard in his new profession. He asked himself in vain, why his eye could not judge of distance or space so well as those of his companions; why his head was not always successful in disentangling the various partial movements necessary to execute a particular evolution; and why his memory, so alert upon most occasions, did not correctly retain technical phrases, and minute points of etiquette or field discipline. Waverley was naturally modest, and therefore did not fall into the egregious mistake of supposing such minuter rules of military duty beneath his notice, or conceiting himself to be born a general, because he made an indifferent subaltern. The truth was, that the vague and unsatisfactory course of reading which he had pursued, working upon a temper naturally retired and abstracted, had given him that wavering and unsettled habit of mind, which is most averse to study and riveted attention. Time, in the meanwhile, hung heavily on his hands. The gentry of the neighbourhood were disaffected, and showed little hospitality to the military guests; and the people of the town, chiefly engaged in mercantile pursuits, were not such as Waverley chose to associate with. The arrival of summer, and a curiosity to know something more of Scotland than he could see in a ride from his quarters, determined him to request leave of absence for a few weeks. He resolved first to visit his uncle's ancient friend and correspondent, with the purpose of extending or shortening the time of his residence according to circumstances. He travelled of course on horseback, and with a single attendant, and passed his first night at a miserable inn, where the land-lady had neither shoes nor stockings, and the landlord, who called himself a gentleman, was disposed to be rude to his guest, because he had not bespoke the pleasure of his society to supper.[1] The next day, traversing an open and unenclosed country, Edward gradually approached the Highlands of Perthshire, which at first had appeared a blue outline in the horizon, but now swelled into huge gigantic masses, which frowned defiance over the more level country that lay beneath them. Near the bottom of this stupendous barrier, but still in the Lowland country, dwelt Cosmo Comyne Bradwardine of Brad-wardine; and, if grey-haired eld can be in aught believed, there had dwelt his ancestors, with all their heritage, since the days of the gracious King Duncan.

## CHAPTER VIII.

### A Scottish Manor-House Sixty Years since.

IT was about noon when Captain Waverley entered the straggling village, or rather hamlet, of Tully-Veolan, close to which was situated the mansion of the proprietor. The houses seemed miserable in the extreme, especially to an eye accustomed to the smiling neatness of English cottages. They stood, without any respect for regularity, on each side of a straggling kind of unpaved street, where children, almost in a primitive state of nakedness, lay sprawling, as if to be crushed by the hoofs of the first passing horse. Occasionally, indeed, when such a consummation seemed inevitable, a watchful old gran-dam, with her close cap, distaff, and spindle, rushed like a sibyl in frenzy out of one of these miserable cells, dashed into the middle of the path, and snatching up her own charge from among the sun-burnt loiterers, saluted him with a sound cuff, and transported him back to his dungeon, the little white-headed varlet screaming all the while from the very top of his lungs, a shrilly treble to the growling remonstrances of the enraged matron. Another part in this concert was sustained by the

[1] Note 4. Scottish Inns.

incessant yelping of a score of idle useless curs, which
followed, snarling, barking, howling, and snapping at the
horses' heels ; a nuisance at that time so common in
Scotland, that a French tourist, who, like other travellers,
longed to find a good and rational reason for every thing
he saw, has recorded, as one of the memorabilia of
Caledonia, that the state maintained in each village a
relay of curs, called *collies*, whose duty it was to chase
the *chevaux de poste* (too starved and exhausted to move
without such a stimulus) from one hamlet to another, till
their annoying convoy drove them to the end of their
stage. The evil and remedy (such as it is) still exist :
But this is remote from our present purpose, and is only
thrown out for consideration of the collectors under Mr
Dent's dog-bill.

As Waverley moved on, here and there an old man,
bent as much by toil as years, his eyes bleared with age
and smoke, tottered to the door of his hut, to gaze on the
dress of the stranger and the form and motions of the
horses, and then assembled, with his neighbours, in a
little group at the smithy, to discuss the probabilities of
whence the stranger came, and where he might be going.
Three or four village girls, returning from the well or
brook with pitchers and pails upon their heads, formed
more pleasing objects, and, with their thin short-gowns
and single petticoats, bare arms, legs, and feet, uncovered
heads and braided hair, somewhat resembled Italian
forms of landscape. Nor could a lover of the picturesque
have challenged either the elegance of their costume, or
the symmetry of their shape ; although, to say the truth,
a mere Englishman, in search of the *comfortable*, a word
peculiar to his native tongue, might have wished the
clothes less scanty, the feet and legs somewhat protected
from the weather, the head and complexion shrouded
from the sun, or perhaps might even have thought the
whole person and dress considerably improved, by a
plentiful application of spring water, with a *quantum
sufficit* of soap. The whole scene was depressing ; for it
argued, at the first glance, at least a stagnation of
industry, and perhaps of intellect. Even curiosity, the
busiest passion of the idle, seemed of a listless cast in the
village of Tully-Veolan : the curs aforesaid alone showed
any part of its activity ; with the villagers it was passive.
They stood and gazed at the handsome young officer and
his attendant, but without any of those quick motions
and eager looks, that indicate the earnestness with which

those who live in monotonous ease at home, look out for amusement abroad. Yet the physiognomy of the people, when more closely examined, was far from exhibiting the indifference of stupidity; their features were rough, but remarkably intelligent; grave, but the very reverse of stupid; and from among the young women, an artist might have chosen more than one model, whose features and form resembled those of Minerva. The children also, whose skins were burnt black, and whose hair was bleached white, by the influence of the sun, had a look and manner of life and interest. It seemed, upon the whole, as if poverty, and indolence, its too frequent companion, were combining to depress the natural genius and acquired information of a hardy, intelligent, and reflecting peasantry.

Some such thoughts crossed Waverley's mind as he paced his horse slowly through the rugged and flinty street of Tully-Veolan, interrupted only in his meditations by the occasional caprioles which his charger exhibited at the reiterated assaults of those canine Cossacks, the *collies* before mentioned. The village was more than half a mile long, the cottages being irregularly divided from each other by gardens, or yards, as the inhabitants called them, of different sizes, where (for it is Sixty Years since) the now universal potato was unknown, but which were stored with gigantic plants of *kale* or colewort, encircled with groves of nettles, and exhibited here and there a huge hemlock, or the national thistle, overshadowing a quarter of the petty inclosure. The broken ground on which the village was built had never been levelled; so that these inclosures presented declivities of every degree, here rising like terraces, there sinking like tan-pits. The dry-stone walls which fenced, or seemed to fence, (for they were sorely breached,) these hanging gardens of Tully-Veolan, were intersected by a narrow lane leading to the common field, where the joint labour of the villagers cultivated alternate ridges and patches of rye, oats, barley, and pease, each of such minute extent, that at a little distance the unprofitable variety of the surface resembled a tailor's book of patterns. In a few favoured instances, there appeared behind the cottages a miserable wigwam, compiled of earth, loose stones, and turf, where the wealthy might perhaps shelter a starved cow or sorely galled horse. But almost every hut was fenced in front by a huge black stack of turf on one side of the door, while on the other the family dunghill ascended in noble emulation.

About a bowshot from the end of the village appeared the inclosures, proudly denominated the Parks of Tully-Veolan, being certain square fields, surrounded and divided by stone walls five feet in height. In the centre of the exterior barrier was the upper gate of the avenue, opening under an archway, battlemented on the top, and adorned with two large weather-beaten mutilated masses of upright stone, which, if the tradition of the hamlet could be trusted, had once represented, at least had been once designed to represent, two rampant Bears, the supporters of the family of Bradwardine. This avenue was straight, and of moderate length, running between a double row of very ancient horse-chestnuts, planted alternately with sycamores, which rose to such huge height, and flourished so luxuriantly, that their bows completely over-arched the broad road beneath. Beyond these venerable ranks, and running parallel to them, were two high walls, of apparently the like antiquity, overgrown with ivy, honey-suckle, and other climbing plants. The avenue seemed very little trodden, and chiefly by foot-passengers; so that being very broad, and enjoying a constant shade, it was clothed with grass of a deep and rich verdure, excepting where a footpath, worn by occasional passengers, tracked with a natural sweep the way from the upper to the lower gate. This nether portal, like the former, opened in front of a wall ornamented with some rude sculpture, with battlements on the top, over which were seen, half-hidden by the trees of the avenue, the high steep roofs and narrow gables of the mansion, with lines indented into steps, and corners decorated with small turrets. One of the folding leaves of the lower gate was open, and as the sun shone full into the court behind, a long line of brilliancy was flung upon the aperture up the dark and gloomy avenue. It was one of those effects which a painter loves to represent, and mingled well with the struggling light which found its way between the boughs of the shady arch that vaulted the broad green alley.

The solitude and repose of the whole scene seemed almost monastic; and Waverley, who had given his horse to his servant on entering the first gate, walked slowly down the avenue, enjoying the grateful and cooling shade, and so much pleased with the placid ideas of rest and seclusion excited by this confined and quiet scene,

that he forgot the misery and dirt of the hamlet he had
left behind him.  The opening into the paved court-yard
corresponded with the rest of the scene.  The house,
which seemed to consist of two or three high, narrow, and
steep-roofed buildings, projecting from each other at
right angles, formed one side of the inclosure.  It had
been built at a period when castles were no longer
necessary, and when the Scottish architects had not yet
acquired the art of designing a domestic residence.  The
windows were numberless, but very small ; the roof had
some nondescript kind of projections, called bartizans,
and displayed at each frequent angle a small turret,
rather resembling a pepper-box than a Gothic watch-
tower.  Neither did the front indicate absolute security
from danger.  There were loop-holes for musketry, and
iron stancheons on the lower windows, probably to repel
any roving band of gipsies, or resist a predatory visit
from the Caterans of the neighbouring Highlands.  Stables
and other offices occupied another side of the square.
The former were low vaults, with narrow slits instead of
windows, resembling, as Edward's groom observed, "rather
a prison for murderers, and larceners, and such like as
are tried at 'sizes, than a place for any Christian cattle."
Above these dungeon-looking stables were granaries,
called girnels, and other offices, to which there was access
by outside stairs of heavy masonry.  Two battlemented
walls, one of which faced the avenue, and the other
divided the court from the garden, completed the inclosure.

Nor was the court without its ornaments.  In one
corner was a tun-bellied pigeon-house, of great size and
rotundity, resembling in figure and proportion the curious
edifice called Arthur's Oven, which would have turned the
brains of all the antiquaries in England, had not the
worthy proprietor pulled it down for the sake of mending
a neighbouring dam-dyke.  This dovecot, or *columbarium*,
as the owner called it, was no small resource to a Scottish
laird of that period, whose scanty rents were eked out by
the contributions levied upon the farms by these light
foragers, and the conscriptions exacted from the latter
for the benefit of the table.

Another corner of the court displayed a fountain,
where a huge bear, carved in stone, predominated over a
large stone-basin, into which he disgorged the water.
This work of art was the wonder of the country ten miles
round.  It must not be forgotten, that all sorts of bears,

small and large, demi or in full proportion, were carved
over the windows, upon the ends of the gables, terminated
the spouts, and supported the turrets, with the ancient
family motto, "Bewar the Bar," cut under each hyper-
borean form.  The court was spacious, well paved, and
perfectly clean, there being probably another entrance
behind the stables for removing the litter.  Everything
around appeared solitary, and would have been silent,
but for the continued plashing of the fountain; and the
whole scene still maintained the monastic illusion which
the fancy of Waverley had conjured up.—And here we
beg permission to close a chapter of still life.[1]

## CHAPTER IX.

### More of the Manor-House and its Environs.

AFTER having satisfied his curiosity by gazing around
him for a few minutes, Waverley applied himself to the
massive knocker of the hall-door, the architrave of which
bore the date 1594.   But no answer was returned, though
the peal resounded through a number of apartments, and
was echoed from the court-yard walls without the house,
startling the pigeons from the venerable rotunda which
they occupied, and alarming anew even the distant
village curs, which had retired to sleep upon their
respective dunghills.   Tired of the din which he created,
and the unprofitable responses which it excited, Waverley
began to think that he had reached the castle of Orgoglio,
as entered by the victorious Prince Arthur,

When 'gan he loudly through the house to call,
    But no man cared to answer to his cry;
  There reign'd a solemn silence over all,
Nor voice was heard, nor wight was seen in bower or hall.

Filled almost with expectation of beholding some "old,
old man, with beard as white as snow," whom he might
question concerning this deserted mansion, our hero

[1] There is no particular mansion described under the name of Tully-Veolan;
but the peculiarities of the description occur in various old Scottish Seats.  The
House of Warrender upon Burntsfield links, and that of Old Ravelston, belonging, the former to Sir George Warrender, the latter to Sir Alexander Keith, have
both contributed several hints to the description in the text.   The House of Dean,
near Edinburgh, has also some points of resemblance with Tully-Veolan.  The
author has, however, been informed, that the House of Grandtully resembles
that of the Baron of Bradwardine still more than any of the above.  (S.)

turned to a little oaken wicket-door, well clenched with
iron-nails, which opened in the court-yard wall at its
angle with the house. It was only latched, notwithstanding its fortified appearance, and, when opened, admitted
him into the garden, which presented a pleasant scene.[1]
The southern side of the house, clothed with fruit-trees,
and having many evergreens trained upon its walls,
extended its irregular yet venerable front, along a
terrace, partly paved, partly gravelled, partly bordered
with flowers and choice shrubs. This elevation descended
by three several flights of steps, placed in its centre and
at the extremities, into what might be called the garden
proper, and was fenced along the top by a stone parapet
with a heavy balustrade, ornamented from space to space
with huge grotesque figures of animals seated upon their
haunches, among which the favourite bear was repeatedly
introduced. Placed in the middle of the terrace, between
a sashed-door opening from the house and the central
flight of steps, a huge animal of the same species supported on his head and forepaws a sun-dial of large
circumference, inscribed with more diagrams than
Edward's mathematics enabled him to decipher.

The garden, which seemed to be kept with great
accuracy, abounded in fruit-trees, and exhibited a profusion of flowers and evergreens, cut into grotesque forms.
It was laid out in terraces, which descended rank by rank
from the western wall to a large brook, which had a
tranquil and smooth appearance, where it served as a
boundary to the garden; but, near the extremity, leapt
in tumult over a strong dam, or wear-head, the cause of
its temporary tranquillity, and there forming a cascade,
was overlooked by an octangular summer-house, with a
gilded bear on the top by way of vane. After this feat,
the brook, assuming its natural rapid and fierce character,
escaped from the eye down a deep and wooded dell, from
the copse of which arose a massive, but ruinous tower,
the former habitation of the Barons of Bradwardine.
The margin of the brook, opposite to the garden, displayed a narrow meadow, or haugh, as it was called,
which formed a small washing-green; the bank, which
retired behind it, was covered by ancient trees.

The scene, though pleasing, was not quite equal to the

---

[1] At Ravelston may be seen such a garden, which the taste of the proprietor,
the author's friend and kinsman, Sir Alexander Keith, Knight Mareschal, has
judiciously preserved. That, as well as the house, is, however, of smaller
dimensions than the Baron of Bradwardine's mansion and garden are presumed to
have been. (S.)

gardens of Alcina; yet wanted not the "*due donzelette garrule*" of that enchanted paradise, for upon the green aforesaid two bare-legged damsels, each standing in a spacious tub, performed with their feet the office of a patent washing-machine. These did not, however, like the maidens of Armida, remain to greet with their harmony the approaching guest, but, alarmed at the appearance of a handsome stranger on the opposite side, dropped their garments (I should say garment, to be quite correct) over their limbs, which their occupation exposed somewhat too freely, and, with a shrill exclamation of "Eh, sirs!" uttered with an accent between modesty and coquetry, sprung off like deer in different directions.

Waverley began to despair of gaining entrance into this solitary and seemingly enchanted mansion, when a man advanced up one of the garden alleys, where he still retained his station. Trusting this might be a gardener, or some domestic belonging to the house, Edward descended the steps in order to meet him; but as the figure approached, and long before he could descry its features, he was struck with the oddity of its appearance and gestures. Sometimes this mister wight held his hands clasped over his head, like an Indian Jogue in the attitude of penance; sometimes he swung them perpendicularly, like a pendulum, on each side; and anon he slapped them swiftly and repeatedly across his breast, like the substitute used by a hackney-coachman for his usual flogging exercise, when his cattle are idle upon the stand, in a clear frosty day. His gait was as singular as his gestures, for at times he hopp'd with great perseverance on the right foot, then exchanged that supporter to advance in the same manner on the left, and then putting his feet close together, he hopp'd upon both at once. His attire also was antiquated and extravagant. It consisted in a sort of grey jerkin, with scarlet cuffs and slash'd sleeves showing a scarlet lining; the other parts of the dress corresponded in colour, not forgetting a pair of scarlet stockings, and a scarlet bonnet, proudly surmounted with a turkey's feather. Edward, whom he did not seem to observe, now perceived confirmation in his features of what the mien and gestures had already announced. It was apparently neither idiocy nor insanity which gave that wild, unsettled, irregular expression to a face which naturally was rather handsome, but something that resembled a compound of both, where the simplicity of the fool was mixed with the extravagance of a crazed

imagination.   He sung with great earnestness, and not
without some taste, a fragment of an old Scottish ditty:

> False love, and hast thou play'd me this
>    In summer among the flowers?
> I will repay thee back again
>    In winter among the showers.
> Unless again, again, my love,
>    Unless you turn again;
> As you with other maidens rove,
>    I'll smile on other men.[1]

Here lifting up his eyes, which had hitherto been fixed
in observing how his feet kept time to the tune, he beheld
Waverley, and instantly doff'd his cap, with many
grotesque signals of surprise, respect, and salutation.
Edward, though with little hope of receiving an answer
to any constant question, requested to know whether Mr
Bradwardine were at home, or where he could find any of
the domestics.  The questioned party replied,—and, like
the witch of Thalaba, "still his speech was song,"—

> The Knight's to the mountain
>    His bugle to wind;
> The Lady's to greenwood
>    ·Her garland to bind.
> The bower of Burd Ellen
>    Has moss on the floor,
> That the step of Lord William
>    Be silent and sure.

This conveyed no information, and Edward, repeating
his queries, received a rapid answer, in which, from the
haste and peculiarity of the dialect, the word "butler"
was alone intelligible.  Waverley then requested to see
the butler; upon which the fellow, with a knowing look
and nod of intelligence, made a signal to Edward to
follow, and began to dance and caper down the alley up
which he had made his approaches.—A strange guide this,
thought Edward, and not much unlike one of Shakspeare's
roynish clowns.  I am not over prudent to trust to his
pilotage; but wiser men have been led by fools.—By this
time he reached the bottom of the alley, where, turning
short on a little parterre of flowers, shrouded from the
east and north by a close yew hedge, he found an old man
at work without his coat, whose appearance hovered
between that of an upper servant and gardener; his red
nose and ruffled shirt belonging to the former profession;
his hale and sunburnt visage, with his green apron,
appearing to indicate

> Old Adam's likeness, set to dress this garden.

The major domo, for such he was, and indisputably the

----
[1] This is a genuine ancient fragment, with some alteration in the two last lines. (S.)

second officer of state in the barony, (nay, as chief minister of the interior, superior even to Bailie Mac-wheeble, in his own department of the kitchen and cellar,) —the major domo laid down his spade, slipped on his coat in haste, and with a wrathful look at Edward's guide, probably excited by his having introduced a stranger while he was engaged in this laborious, and, as he might suppose it, degrading office, requested to know the gentle-man's commands. Being informed that he wished to pay his respects to his master, that his name was Waverley, and so forth, the old man's countenance assumed a great deal of respectful importance. "He could take it upon his conscience to say, his honour would have exceeding pleasure in seeing him. Would not Mr Waverley choose some refreshment after his journey? His honour was with the folk who were getting doon the dark hag[1]; the twa gardener lads (an emphasis on the word *twa*) had been ordered to attend him; and he had been just amusing himself in the mean time with dressing Miss Rose's flower-bed, that he might be near to receive his honour's orders, if need were : he was very fond of a garden, but had little time for such divertisements."

"He canna get it wrought in abune twa days in the week at no rate whatever," said Edward's fantastic con-ductor.

A grim look from the butler chastised his interference, and he commanded him, by the name of Davie Gellatley, in a tone which admitted no discussion, to look for his honour at the dark hag, and tell him there was a gentle-man from the south had arrived at the Ha'.

"Can this poor fellow deliver a letter?" asked Edward.

"With all fidelity, sir, to any one whom he respects. I would hardly trust him with a long message by word of mouth—though he is more knave than fool."

Waverley delivered his credentials to Mr Gellatley, who seemed to confirm the butler's last observation, by twisting his features at him, when he was looking another way, into the resemblance of the grotesque face on the bole of a German tobacco-pipe; after which, with an odd congé to Waverley, he danced off to discharge his errand.

"He is an innocent, sir," said the butler; "there is one such in almost every town in the country, but ours is brought far ben.[2] He used to work a day's turn weel eneugh ; but he help'd Miss Rose when she was flemit[3]

---

[1] Fellin the oak copse.  [2] Made much of.  [3] Chased.

with the Laird of Killancureit's new English bull, and
since that time we ca' him Davie Do-little; indeed we
might ca' him Davie Do-naething, for since he got that
gay clothing, to please his honour and my young mistress,
(great folks will have their fancies,) he has done naething
but dance up and down about the *toun*,[1] without doing a
single turn, unless trimming the laird's fishing-wand or
busking his flies, or may be catching a dish of trouts at
an orra-time.[2]  But here comes Miss Rose, who, I take
burden upon me for her, will be especial glad to see
one of the house of Waverley at her father's mansion of
Tully-Veolan."

But Rose Bradwardine deserves better of her unworthy historian, than to be introduced at the end of
a chapter.

In the meanwhile it may be noticed, that Waverley
learned two things from this colloquy; that in Scotland
a single house was called a *town*, and a natural fool an
*innocent*.[3]

## CHAPTER X.

### Rose Bradwardine and her Father.

MISS BRADWARDINE was but seventeen; yet, at the last
races of the county town of ——, upon her health being
proposed among a round of beauties, the Laird of
Bumperquaigh, permanent toastmaster and croupier of
the Bautherwhillery Club, not only said *More* to the
pledge in a pint bumper of Bourdeaux, but, ere pouring
forth the libation, denominated the divinity to whom it
was dedicated, "the Rose of Tully-Veolan;" upon which
festive occasion, three cheers were given by all the sitting
members of that respectable society, whose throats the

[1] A dwelling-house with surrounding buildings.          [2] Spare time.
[3] I am ignorant how long the ancient and established custom of keeping fools
has been disused in England.  Swift writes an epitaph on the Earl of Suffolk's
fool,—

"Whose name was Dickie Pearce."

In Scotland the custom subsisted till late in the last century; at Glammis Castle, is
preserved the dress of one of the jesters, very handsome, and ornamented with
many bells.  It is not above thirty years since such a character stood by the sideboard of a nobleman of the first rank in Scotland, and occasionally mixed in the
conversation, till he carried the joke rather too far, in making proposals to one of
the young ladies of the family, and publishing the bans betwixt her and himself in
the public church.  (S.)

wine had left capable of such exertion. Nay, I am well assured, that the sleeping partners of the company snorted applause, and that although strong bumpers and weak brains had consigned two or three to the floor, yet even these, fallen as they were from their high estate, and weltering—I will carry the parody no farther—uttered divers inarticulate sounds, intimating their assent to the motion.

Such unanimous applause could not be extorted but by acknowledged merit; and Rose Bradwardine not only deserved it, but also the approbation of much more rational persons than the Bautherwhillery Club could have mustered, even before discussion of the first *magnum.* She was indeed a very pretty girl of the Scotch cast of beauty, that is, with a profusion of hair of paley gold, and a skin like the snow of her own mountains in whiteness. Yet she had not a pallid or pensive cast of countenance; her features, as well as her temper, had a lively expression; her complexion, though not florid, was so pure as to seem transparent, and the slightest emotion sent her whole blood at once to her face and neck. Her form, though under the common size, was remarkably elegant, and her motions light, easy, and unembarrassed. She came from another part of the garden to receive Captain Waverley, with a manner that hovered between bashfulness and courtesy.

The first greetings past, Edward learned from her that the *dark hag,* which had somewhat puzzled him in the butler's account of his master's avocations, had nothing to do either with a black cat or a broomstick, but was simply a portion of oak copse which was to be felled that day. She offered, with diffident civility, to show the stranger the way to the spot, which, it seems, was not far distant; but they were prevented by the appearance of the Baron of Bradwardine in person, who, summoned by David Gellatley, now appeared, "on hospitable thoughts intent," clearing the ground at a prodigious rate with swift and long strides, which reminded Waverley of the seven-league boots of the nursery fable. He was a tall, thin, athletic figure, old indeed and grey-haired, but with every muscle rendered as tough as whip-cord by constant exercise. He was dressed carelessly, and more like a Frenchman than an Englishman of the period, while, from his hard features and perpendicular rigidity of stature, he bore some resemblance to a Swiss officer of the guards, who had resided some time at Paris, and caught the

*costume*, but not the ease or manner, of its inhabitants.
The truth was, that his language and habits were as
heterogeneous as his external appearance.

Owing to his natural disposition to study, or perhaps
to a very general Scottish fashion of giving young men of
rank a legal education, he had been bred with a view to
the bar. But the politics of his family precluding the
hope of his rising in that profession, Mr Bradwardine
travelled with high reputation for several years, and
made some campaigns in foreign service. After his
démêlée with the law of high treason in 1715, he had
lived in retirement, conversing almost entirely with those
of his own principles in the vicinage. The pedantry of
the lawyer, superinduced upon the military pride of the
soldier, might remind a modern of the days of the zealous
volunteer service, when the bar-gown of our pleaders was
often flung over a blazing uniform. To this must be
added the prejudices of ancient birth and Jacobite
politics, greatly strengthened by habits of solitary and
secluded authority, which, though exercised only within
the bounds of his half-cultivated estate, was there indis-
putable and undisputed. For, as he used to observe,
"the lands of Bradwardine, Tully-Veolan, and others, had
been erected into a free barony by a charter from David
the First, *cum liberali potest. habendi curias et justicias,
cum fossa et furca* (LIE pit and gallows) *et saka et soka, et
thol et theam, et infang-thief et outfang-thief, sive hand-
habend. sive bak-barand.*" The peculiar meaning of all
these cabalistical words few or none could explain ; but
they implied, upon the whole, that the Baron of Bradwardine might, in case of delinquency, imprison, try, and
execute his vassals at his pleasure. Like James the First,
however, the present possessor of this authority was more
pleased in talking about prerogative than in exercising
it ; and excepting that he imprisoned two poachers in the
dungeon of the old tower of Tully-Veolan, where they
were sorely frightened by ghosts, and almost eaten by
rats, and that he set an old woman in the *jougs* (or
Scottish pillory) for saying "there were mair fules in the
laird's ha' house than Davie Gellatley," I do not learn
that he was accused of abusing his high powers. Still,
however, the conscious pride of possessing them gave
additional importance to his language and deportment.

At his first address to Waverley, it would seem that the
hearty pleasure he felt to behold the nephew of his friend
had somewhat discomposed the stiff and upright dignity

of the Baron of Bradwardine's demeanour, for the tears stood in the old gentleman's eyes, when, having first shaken Edward heartily by the hand in the English fashion, he embraced him *à-la-mode Française*, and kissed him on both sides of his face ; while the hardness of his gripe, and the quantity of Scotch snuff which his *accolade* communicated, called corresponding drops of moisture to the eyes of his guest.

"Upon the honour of a gentleman," he said, "but it makes me young again to see you here, Mr Waverley ! A worthy scion of the old stock of Waverley-Honour— *spes altera*, as Maro hath it—and you have the look of the old line, Captain Waverley ; not so portly yet as my old friend Sir Everard—*mais cela viendra avec le temps*, as my Dutch acquaintance, Baron Kikkitbroeck, said of the *sagesse* of *Madame son epouse*.—And so ye have mounted the cockade ? Right, right ; though I could have wished the colour different, and so I would ha' deemed might Sir Everard. But no more of that ; I am old, and times are changed.—And how does the worthy knight baronet, and the fair Mrs Rachel ?—Ah, ye laugh, young man ! In troth she was the fair Mrs Rachel in the year of grace seventeen hundred and sixteen ; but time passes—*et singula prædantur anni*—that is most certain. But once again ye are most heartily welcome to my poor house of Tully-Veolan !—Hie to the house, Rose, and see that Alexander Saunderson looks out the old Chateau Margoux, which I sent from Bourdeaux to Dundee in the year 1713."

Rose tripped off demurely enough till she turned the first corner, and then ran with the speed of a fairy, that she might gain leisure, after discharging her father's commission, to put her own dress in order, and produce all her little finery, an occupation for which the approaching dinner-hour left but limited time.

"We cannot rival the luxuries of your English table, Captain Waverley, or give you the *epulæ lautiores* of Waverley-Honour—I say *epulæ* rather than *prandium*, because the latter phrase is popular ; *Epulæ ad senatum, prandium vero ad populum attinet*, says Suetonius Tranquillus. But I trust ye will applaud my Bourdeaux ; *c'est des deux oreilles*, as Captain Vinsauf used to say— *Vinum primæ notæ*, the Principal of St Andrews denominated it. And, once more, Captain Waverley, right glad am I that ye are here to drink the best my cellar can make forthcoming."

This speech, with the necessary interjectional answers, continued from the lower alley where they met, up to the door of the house, where four or five servants in old-fashioned liveries, headed by Alexander Saunderson, the butler, who now bore no token of the sable stains of the garden, received them in grand *costume*,

In an old hall hung round with pikes and with bows,
With old bucklers and corslets that had borne many shrewd blows.

With much ceremony, and still more real kindness, the Baron, without stopping in any intermediate apartment, conducted his guest through several into the great dining parlour, wainscotted with black oak, and hung round with the pictures of his ancestry, where a table was set forth in form for six persons, and an old-fashioned buffet displayed all the ancient and massive plate of the Bradwardine family. A bell was now heard at the head of the avenue; for an old man, who acted as porter upon gala days, had caught the alarm given by Waverley's arrival, and, repairing to his post, announced the arrival of other guests.

These, as the Baron assured his young friend, were very estimable persons. "There was the young Laird of Balmawhapple, a Falconer by surname, of the house of Glenfarquhar, given right much to field-sports—*gaudet equis et canibus*—but a very discreet young gentleman. Then there was the Laird of Killancureit, who had devoted his leisure *untill* tillage and agriculture, and boasted himself to be possessed of a bull of matchless merit, brought from the county of Devon (the Damnonia of the Romans, if we can trust Robert of Cirencester.) He is, as ye may well suppose from such a tendency, but of yeoman extraction—*servabit odorem testa diu*—and I believe, between ourselves, his grandsire was from the wrong side of the Border—one Bullsegg, who came hither as a steward, or bailiff, or ground-officer, or something in that department, to the last Girnigo of Killancureit, who died of an atrophy. After his master's death, sir,—ye would hardly believe such a scandal,—but this Bullsegg, being portly and comely of aspect, intermarried with the lady dowager, who was young and amorous, and possessed himself of the estate, which devolved on this unhappy woman by a settlement of her umwhile[1] husband, in direct contravention of an unrecorded taillie,[2] and to the prejudice of the disponer's own flesh and blood, in the person

[1] Late.  [2] Agreement.

of his natural heir and seventh cousin, Girnigo of Tipperhewit, whose family was so reduced by the ensuing law-suit, that his representative is now serving as a private gentleman-sentinel in the Highland Black Watch. But this gentleman, Mr Bullsegg of Killancureit that now is, has good blood in his veins by the mother and grand-mother, who were both of the family of Pickletillim, and he is well liked and looked upon, and knows his own place. And God forbid, Captain Waverley, that we of irreproach-able lineage should exult over him, when it may be, that in the eighth, ninth, or tenth generation, his progeny may rank, in a manner, with the old gentry of the country. Rank and ancestry, sir, should be the last words in the mouths of us of unblemished race—*vix ea nostra voco*, as Naso saith.—There is, besides, a clergyman of the true (though suffering) Episcopal church of Scotland. He was a confessor in her cause after the year 1715, when a Whiggish mob destroyed his meeting-house, tore his surplice, and plundered his dwelling-house of four silver spoons, intromitting also with his mart and his meal-ark, and with two barrels, one of single, and one of double ale, besides three bottles of brandy.[1] My Baron-Bailie and doer, Mr Duncan Macwheeble, is the fourth on our list. There is a question, owing to the incertitude of ancient orthography, whether he belongs to the clan of Wheedle or of Quibble, but both have produced persons eminent in the law."—

> As such he described them by person and name,
> They enter'd, and dinner was served as they came.

# CHAPTER XI.

## *The Banquet.*

THE entertainment was ample, and handsome, according to the Scotch ideas of the period, and the guests did great honour to it. The Baron eat like a famished soldier, the Laird of Balmawhapple like a sportsman, Bullsegg of Kil-

---

* After the Revolution of 1688, and on some occasions when the spirit of the Presbyterians had been unusually animated against their opponents, the Episcopal clergymen, who were chiefly non-jurors, were exposed to be mobbed, as we should now say, or *rabbled*, as the phrase then went, to expiate their political heresies. But notwithstanding that the Presbyterians had the persecution in Charles II., and his brother's time, to exasperate them, there was little mischief done beyond the kind of petty violence mentioned in the text. (S.)

lancureit like a farmer, Waverley himself like a traveller,
and Bailie Macwheeble like all four together; though,
either out of more respect, or in order to preserve that
proper declination of person which showed a sense that
he was in the presence of his patron, he sat upon the
edge of his chair, placed at three feet distance from the
table, and achieved a communication with his plate by
projecting his person towards it in a line which obliqued
from the bottom of his spine, so that the person who sat
opposite to him could only see the foretop of his riding
periwig.

This stooping position might have been inconvenient to
another person; but long habit made it, whether seated
or walking, perfectly easy to the worthy Bailie. In the
latter posture, it occasioned, no doubt, an unseemly pro-
jection of the person towards those who happened to walk
behind; but those being at all times his inferiors, (for Mr
Macwheeble was very scrupulous in giving place to all
others,) he cared very little what inference of contempt or
slight regard they might derive from the circumstance.
Hence, when he waddled across the court to and from his
old grey pony, he somewhat resembled a turnspit walking
upon its hind legs.

The nonjuring clergyman was a pensive and interesting
old man, with much the air of a sufferer for conscience
sake. He was one of those,

*Who, undeprived, their benefice forsook.*

For this whim, when the Baron was out of hearing, the
Bailie used sometimes gently to rally Mr Rubrick, upbraiding him with the nicety of his scruples. Indeed, it
must be owned, that he himself, though at heart a keen
partisan of the exiled family, had kept pretty fair with
all the different turns of state in his time; so that Davie
Gellatley once described him as a particularly good man,
who had a very quiet and peaceful conscience, *that never
did him any harm.*

When the dinner was removed, the Baron announced
the health of the King, politely leaving to the consciences
of his guests to drink to the sovereign *de facto* or *de jure*,
as their politics inclined. The conversation now became
general; and, shortly afterwards, Miss Bradwardine, who
had done the honours with natural grace and simplicity,
retired, and was soon followed by the clergyman. Among
the rest of the party, the wine, which fully justified the
encomiums of the landlord, flowed freely round, although

Waverley, with some difficulty, obtained the privilege of sometimes neglecting the glass. At length, as the evening grew more late, the Baron made a private signal to Mr Saunders Saunderson, or, as he facetiously denominated him, *Alexander ab Alexandro*, who left the room with a nod, and soon after returned, his grave countenance mantling with a solemn and mysterious smile, and placed before his master a small oaken casket, mounted with brass ornaments of curious form. The Baron, drawing out a private key, unlocked the casket, raised the lid, and produced a golden goblet of a singular and antique appearance, moulded into the shape of a rampant bear, which the owner regarded with a look of mingled reverence, pride, and delight, that irresistibly reminded Waverley of Ben Jonson's Tom Otter, with his Bull, Horse, and Dog, as that wag wittily denominated his chief carousing cups. But Mr Bradwardine, turning towards him with complacency, requested him to observe this curious relic of the olden time.

"It represents," he said, "the chosen crest of our family, a bear, as ye observe, and *rampant ;* because a good herald will depict every animal in its noblest posture ; as a horse *salient*, a greyhound *currant*, and, as may be inferred, a ravenous animal *in actu ferociori*, or in a voracious, lacerating, and devouring posture. Now, sir, we hold this most honourable achievement by the wappenbrief, or concession of arms, of Frederick Red-beard, Emperor of Germany, to my predecessor, Godmund Bradwardine, it being the crest of a gigantic Dane, whom he slew in the lists in the Holy Land, on a quarrel touching the chastity of the emperor's spouse or daughter, tradition saith not precisely which, and thus, as Virgilius hath it—

> Mutemus clypeos, Danaumque insignia nobis
> Aptemus.

Then for the cup, Captain Waverley, it was wrought by the command of St Duthac, Abbot of Aberbrothoc, for behoof of another baron of the house of Bradwardine, who had valiantly defended the patrimony of that monastery against certain encroaching nobles. It is properly termed the Blessed Bear of Bradwardine, (though old Dr Doubleit used jocosely to call it Ursa Major,) and was supposed, in old and Catholic times, to be invested with certain properties of a mystical and supernatural quality. And though I give not in to such *anilia*, it is certain it has always been esteemed a solemn standard cup and heirloom

of our house; nor is it ever used but upon seasons of high
festival, and such I hold to be the arrival of the heir of
Sir Everard under my roof ; and I devote this draught to
the health and prosperity of the ancient and highly-to-be-
honoured house of Waverley."

During this long harangue, he carefully decanted a
cobwebbed bottle of claret into the goblet, which held
nearly an English pint; and, at the conclusion, delivering
the bottle to the butler, to be held carefully in the same
angle with the horizon, he devoutly quaffed off the contents of the Blessed Bear of Bradwardine.

Edward, with horror and alarm, beheld the animal
making his rounds, and thought with great anxiety upon
the appropriate motto, "Beware the Bear;" but, at the
same time, plainly foresaw, that, as none of the guests
scrupled to do him this extraordinary honour, a refusal
on his part to pledge their courtesy would be extremely
ill received. Resolving, therefore, to submit to this last
piece of tyranny, and then to quit the table, if possible,
and confiding in the strength of his constitution, he did
justice to the company in the contents of the Blessed
Bear, and felt less inconvenience from the draught than
he could possibly have expected. The others, whose time
had been more actively employed, began to show symptoms of innovation,—"the good wine did its good office."[1]
The frost of etiquette, and pride of birth, began to give
way before the genial blessings of this benign constellation, and the formal appellatives with which the three
dignitaries had hitherto addressed each other, were now
familiarly abbreviated into Tully, Bally, and Killie.
When a few rounds had passed, the two latter, after
whispering together, craved permission (a joyful hearing
for Edward) to ask the grace cup. This, after some delay,
was at length produced, and Waverley concluded the
orgies of Bacchus were terminated for the evening. He
was never more mistaken in his life.

As the guests had left their horses at the small inn, or
*change-house*, as it was called, of the village, the Baron
could not, in politeness, avoid walking with them up the
avenue, and Waverley, from the same motive, and to
enjoy, after this feverish revel, the cool summer evening,
attended the party. But when they arrived at Luckie
Macleary's the Lairds of Balmawhapple and Killancureit
declared their determination to acknowledge their sense
of the hospitality of Tully-Veolan, by partaking, with

───────────
[1] Southey's *Madoc*. (S )

their entertainer and his guest Captain Waverley, what they technically called *deoch an doruis*, a stirrup-cup, to the honour of the Baron's roof-tree.[1]

It must be noticed, that the Bailie, knowing by experience that the day's joviality, which had been hitherto sustained at the expense of his patron, might terminate partly at his own, had mounted his spavined grey pony, and, between gaiety of heart, and alarm for being hooked into a reckoning, spurred him into a hobbling canter, (a trot was out of the question,) and had already cleared the village. The others entered the change-house, leading Edward in unresisting submission; for his landlord whispered him, that to demur to such an overture would be construed into a high misdemeanour against the *leges conviviales*, or regulations of genial compotation. Widow Macleary seemed to have expected this visit, as well she might, for it was the usual consummation of merry bouts, not only at Tully-Veolan, but at most other gentlemen's houses in Scotland, Sixty Years since. The guests thereby at once acquitted themselves of their burden of gratitude for their entertainer's kindness, encouraged the trade of his change-house, did honour to the place which afforded harbour to their horses, and indemnified themselves for the previous restraints imposed by private hospitality, by spending, what Falstaff calls the sweet of the night, in the genial licence of a tavern.

Accordingly, in full expectation of these distinguished guests, Luckie Macleary had swept her house for the first time this fortnight, tempered her turf-fire to such a heat as the season required in her damp hovel even at Midsummer, set forth her deal table newly washed, propped its lame foot with a fragment of turf, arranged four or five stools of huge and clumsy form upon the sites which best suited the inequalities of her clay floor; and having, moreover, put on her clean toy, rokelay, and scarlet plaid, gravely awaited the arrival of the company, in full hope of custom and profit. When they were seated under the sooty rafters of Luckie Macleary's only apartment, thickly tapestried with cobwebs, their hostess, who had already taken her cue from the Laird of Balmawhapple, appeared with a huge pewter measuring-pot, containing at least three English quarts, familiarly denominated *a Tappit Hen*, and which, in the language of the hostess, reamed, (*i. e.* mantled) with excellent claret just drawn from the cask.

It was soon plain that what crumbs of reason the Bear
had not devoured, were to be picked up by the Hen; but
the confusion which appeared to prevail favoured Edward's
resolution to evade the gaily circling glass. The others
began to talk thick and at once, each performing his own
part in the conversation, without the least respect to his
neighbour. The Baron of Bradwardine sung French
*chansons-à-boire,* and spouted pieces of Latin; Killancureit talked, in a steady unalterable dull key, of top-
dressing and bottom-dressing,[1] and year-olds, and gim-
mers, and dinmonts, and stots, and runts, and kyloes, and
a proposed turnpike-act; while Balmawhapple, in notes
exalted above both, extolled his horse, his hawks, and a
greyhound called Whistler. In the middle of this din, the
Baron repeatedly implored silence; and when at length
the instinct of polite discipline so far prevailed, that for
a moment he obtained it, he hastened to beseech their
attention "unto a military ariette, which was a particular
favourite of the Marechal Duc de Berwick;" then,
imitating, as well as he could, the manner and tone of a
French musquetaire, he immediately commenced,—

> Mon coeur volage, dit elle,
>   N'est pas pour vous, garçon;
> Est pour un homme de guerre,
>   Qui a barbe au menton.
>     Lon, Lon, Laridon.
>
> Qui port chapeau à plume,
>   Soulier à rouge talon,
> Qui joue de la flute,
>   Aussi de violon.
>     Lon, Lon, Laridon.

Balmawhapple could hold no longer, but broke in with
what he called a d—d good song, composed by Gibby
Gaethroughwi't, the piper of Cupar; and, without wasting
more time, struck up,—

> It's up Glenbarchan's braes I gaed,[2]
> And o'er the bent of Killiebraid,
> And mony a weary cast I made,
> To cuittle[3] the moor-fowl's tail.[4]

The Baron, whose voice was drowned in the louder and
more obstreperous strains of Balmawhapple, now dropped
the competition, but continued to hum, Lon, Lon, Laridon,
and to regard the successful candidate for the attention

---

[1] This has been censured as an anachronism; and it must be confessed that
agriculture of this kind was unknown to the Scotch Sixty Years since. (S.)
[2] Went.       [3] Tickle.
[4] *Suum cuique.* This snatch of a ballad was composed by Andrew MacDonald,
the ingenious and unfortunate author of *Vimonda* (S.)

of the company with an eye of disdain, while Balmawhapple proceeded,—

> If up a bonny black-cock should spring,
> To whistle him down wi' a slug in his wing,
> And strap him on to my lunzie[1] string
> Right seldom would I fail.

After an ineffectual attempt to recover the second verse,
he sung the first over again; and, in prosecution of his
triumph, declared there was "more sense in that than in
all the *derry-dongs* of France, and Fifeshire to the boot of
it." The Baron only answered with a long pinch of snuff,
and a glance of infinite contempt. But those noble allies,
the Bear and the Hen, had emancipated the young laird
from the habitual reverence in which he held Bradwardine
at other times. He pronounced the claret *shilpit*,[2] and
demanded brandy with great vociferation. It was
brought; and now the Demon of Politics envied even the
harmony arising from this Dutch concert, merely because
there was not a wrathful note in the strange compound
of sounds which it produced. Inspired by her, the Laird
of Balmawhapple, now superior to the nods and winks
with which the Baron of Bradwardine, in delicacy to
Edward, had hitherto checked his entering upon political
discussion, demanded a bumper, with the lungs of a
Stentor, "to the little gentleman in black velvet who did
such service in 1702, and may the white horse break his
neck over a mound of his making!"

Edward was not at that moment clear-headed enough
to remember that King William's fall, which occasioned
his death, was said to be owing to his horse stumbling at
a mole-hill; yet felt inclined to take umbrage at a toast,
which seemed, from the glance of Balmawhapple's eye, to
have a peculiar and uncivil reference to the Government
which he served. But, ere he could interfere, the Baron
of Bradwardine had taken up the quarrel. "Sir," he said,
"whatever my sentiments, *tanquam privatus*, may be in
such matters, I shall not tamely endure your saying anything that may impinge upon the honourable feelings of
a gentleman under my roof. Sir, if you have no respect
for the laws of urbanity, do ye not respect the military
oath, the *sacramentum militare*, by which every officer is
bound to the standards under which he is enrolled? Look
at Titus Livius what he says of those Roman soldiers who
were so unhappy as *exuere sacramentum*,—to rénounce

---

[1] Wallet.    [2] Insipid.

their legionary oath; but you are ignorant, sir, alike of ancient history and modern courtesy."

"Not so ignorant as ye would pronounce me," roared Balmawhapple. "I ken weel that you mean the Solemn League and Covenant; but if a' the Whigs in hell had taken the "———

Here the Baron and Waverley both spoke at once, the former calling out, "Be silent, sir! ye not only show your ignorance, but disgrace your native country before a stranger and an Englishman;" and Waverley, at the same moment, entreating Mr Bradwardine to permit him to reply to an affront which seemed levelled at him personally. But the Baron was exalted by wine, wrath, and scorn, above all sublunary considerations.

"I crave you to be hushed, Captain Waverley; you are elsewhere, peradventure, *sui juris*,—forisfamiliated, that is, and entitled, it may be, to think and resent for yourself; but in my domain, in this poor Barony of Bradwardine, and under this roof, which is *quasi* mine, being held by tacit relocation by a tenant at will, I am *in loco parentis*, to you and bound to see you scatheless.— And for you, Mr Falconer of Balmawhapple, I warn ye, let me see no more aberrations from the paths of good manners."

"And I tell you, Mr Cosmo Comyne Bradwardine, of Bradwardine and Tully-Veolan," retorted the sportsman, in huge disdain, "that I'll make a moor-cock of the man that refuses my toast, whether it be a crop-eared English Whig wi' a black ribband at his lug[1] or ane wha deserts his ain friends to claw[2] favour wi' the rats of Hanover."

In an instant both rapiers were brandished, and some desperate passes exchanged. Balmawhapple was young, stout, and active; but the Baron, infinitely more master of his weapon, would, like Sir Toby Belch, have tickled his opponent other gates than he did, had he not been under the influence of Ursa Major.

Edward rushed forward to interfere between the combatants, but the prostrate bulk of the Laird of Killancureit, over which he stumbled, intercepted his passage. How Killancureit happened to be in this recumbent posture at so interesting a moment, was never accurately known. Some thought he was about to ensconce himself under the table; he himself alleged that he stumbled in the act of lifting a joint-stool, to prevent mischief, by

[1] Ear.    [2] Curry

knocking down Balmawhapple. Be that as it may, if readier aid than either his or Waverley's had not interposed, there would certainly have been bloodshed. But the well-known clash of swords, which was no stranger to her dwelling, aroused Luckie Macleary as she sat quietly beyond the hallan, or earthen partition of the cottage, with eyes employed in Boston's *Crook of the Lot*, while her ideas were engaged in summing up the reckoning. She boldly rushed in, with the shrill expostulation, "Wad their honours slay ane another there, and bring discredit on a honest widow-woman's house, when there was a' the lee-land [1] in the country to fight upon?" a remonstrance which she seconded by flinging her plaid with great dexterity over the weapons of the combatants. The servants by this time rushed in, and being, by great chance, tolerably sober, separated the incensed opponents, with the assistance of Edward and Killancureit. The latter led off Balmawhapple, cursing, swearing, and vowing revenge against every Whig, Presbyterian, and fanatic in England and Scotland, from John-o'-Groat's to the Land's End, and with difficulty got him to horse. Our hero, with the assistance of Saunders Saunderson, escorted the Baron of Bradwardine to his own dwelling, but could not prevail upon him to retire to bed until he had made a long and learned apology for the events of the evening, of which, however, there was not a word intelligible, except something about the Centaurs and the Lapithæ.

## CHAPTER XII.

### Repentance and a Reconciliation.

WAVERLEY was unaccustomed to the use of wine, excepting with great temperance. He slept therefore soundly till late in the succeeding morning, and then awakened to a painful recollection of the scene of the preceding evening. He had received a personal affront,—he, a gentleman, a soldier, and a Waverley. True, the person who offered it was not, at the time it was given, possessed of the moderate share of sense which nature had allotted him; true also, in resenting this insult, he would break the laws of Heaven, as well as of his country; true, in doing so, he might take the life of a young man

[1] Open land

who perhaps respectably discharged the social duties,
and render his family miserable ; or he might lose his
own ;—no pleasant alternative even to the bravest,
when it is debated coolly and in private.

All this pressed on his mind ; yet the original statement
recurred with the same irresistible force.  He had received
a personal insult ; he was of the house of Waverley ; and
he bore a commission.  There was no alternative ; and he
descended to the breakfast parlour with the intention of
taking leave of the family, and writing to one of his
brother officers to meet him at the inn mid-way between
Tully-Veolan and the town where they were quartered, in
order that he might convey such a message to the Laird
of Balmawhapple as the circumstances seemed to demand.
He found Miss Bradwardine presiding over the tea and
coffee, the table loaded with warm bread, both of flour,
oatmeal, and barleymeal, in the shape of loaves, cakes,
biscuits, and other varieties, together with eggs, rein-deer
ham, mutton and beef ditto, smoked salmon, marmalade,
and all the other delicacies which induced even Johnson
himself to extol the luxury of a Scotch breakfast above
that of all other countries.  A mess of oatmeal porridge,
flanked by a silver jug, which held an equal mixture of
cream and butter-milk, was placed for the Baron's share
of this repast ; but Rose observed he had walked out early
in the morning, after giving orders that his guest should
not be disturbed.

Waverley sat down almost in silence, and with an air
of absence and abstraction, which could not give Miss
Bradwardine a favourable opinion of his talents for conversation.  He answered at random one or two observations which she ventured to make upon ordinary topics ;
so that feeling herself almost repulsed in her efforts at
entertaining him, and secretly wondering that a scarlet
coat should cover no better breeding, she left him to his
mental amusement of cursing Dr Doubleit's favourite
constellation of Ursa Major, as the cause of all the mischief
which had already happened, and was likely to ensue.  At
once he started, and, his colour heightened, as, looking
toward the window he beheld the Baron and young
Balmawhapple pass arm in arm, apparently in deep conversation ; and he hastily asked, "Did Mr Falconer sleep
here last night ?"  Rose, not much pleased with the abrupt-
ness of the first question which the young stranger had
addressed to her, answered drily in the negative, and the
conversation again sunk into silence.

At this moment Mr Saunderson appeared, with a message from his master, requesting to speak with Captain Waverley in another apartment. With a heart which beat a little quicker, not indeed from fear, but from uncertainty and anxiety, Edward obeyed the summons. He found the two gentlemen standing together, an air of complacent dignity on the brow of the Baron, while something like sullenness or shame, or both, blanked the bold visage of Balmawhapple. The former slipped his arm through that of the latter, and thus seeming to walk with him, while in reality he led him, advanced to meet Waverley, and, stopping in the midst of the apartment, made in great state the following oration : "Captain Waverley,— my young and esteemed friend, Mr Falconer of Balmawhapple, has craved of my age and experience, as of one not wholly unskilled in the dependencies and punctilios of the duello or monomachia, to be his interlocutor in expressing to you the regret with which he calls to remembrance certain passages of our symposion last night, which could not but be highly displeasing to you, as serving for the time under this present existing government. He craves you, sir, to drown in oblivion the memory of such solecisms against the laws of politeness, as being what his better reason disavows, and to receive the hand which he offers you in amity; and I must needs assure you that nothing less than a sense of being *dans son tort*, as a gallant French chevalier, Mons. Le Bretailleur, once said to me on such an occasion, and an opinion also of your peculiar merit, could have extorted such concessions; for he and all his family are, and have been, time out of mind, *Mavortia pectora*, as Buchanan saith, a bold and warlike sept, or people."

Edward immediately, and with natural politeness, accepted the hand which Balmawhapple, or rather the Baron in his character of mediator, extended towards him. "It was impossible," he said, "for him to remember what a gentleman expressed his wish he had not uttered; and he willingly imputed what had passed to the exuberant festivity of the day."

"That is very handsomely said," answered the Baron; "for undoubtedly, if a man be *ebrius*, or intoxicated, an incident which on solemn and festive occasions may and will take place in the life of a man of honour; and if the same gentleman, being fresh and sober, recants the contumelies which he hath spoken in his liquor, it must be held *vinum locutum est;* the words cease to be his own.

Yet would I not find this exculpation relevant in the case
of one who was *ebriosus*, or an habitual drunkard; because,
if such a person choose to pass the greater part of his
time in the predicament of intoxication, he hath no title
to be exeemed from the obligations of the code of politeness, but should learn to deport himself peaceably and
courteously when under influence of the vinous stimulus.—
And now let us proceed to breakfast, and think no more
of this daft business."

I must confess, whatever inference may be drawn from
the circumstance, that Edward, after so satisfactory an
explanation, did much greater honour to the delicacies of
Miss Bradwardine's breakfast-table than his commencement had promised. Balmawhapple, on the contrary,
seemed embarrassed and dejected; and Waverley now,
for the first time, observed that his arm was in a sling,
which seemed to account for the awkward and embarrassed manner with which he had presented his hand.
To a question from Miss Bradwardine, he muttered, in
answer, something about his horse having fallen; and,
seeming desirous to escape both from the subject and the
company, he arose as soon as breakfast was over, made
his bow to the party, and, declining the Baron's invitation to tarry till after dinner, mounted his horse and
returned to his own home.

Waverley now announced his purpose of leaving Tully-
Veolan early enough after dinner to gain the stage at
which he meant to sleep; but the unaffected and deep
mortification with which the good-natured and affectionate
old gentleman heard the proposal, quite deprived him of
courage to persist in it. No sooner had he gained Waverley's consent to lengthen his visit for a few days, than he
laboured to remove the grounds upon which he conceived
he had meditated a more early retreat. "I would not
have you opine, Captain Waverley, that I am by practice
or precept an advocate of ebriety, though it may be that,
in our festivity of last night, some of our friends, if not
perchance altogether *ebrii*, or drunken, were, to say the
least, *ebrioli*, by which the ancients designed those who
were fuddled, or, as your English vernacular and meta-
phorical phrase goes, half-seas-over. Not that I would so
insinuate respecting you, Captain Waverley, who, like a
prudent youth, did rather abstain from potation; nor can
it be truly said of myself, who, having assisted at the
tables of many great generals and mareschals at their
solemn carousals, have the art to carry my wine discreetly,

and did not, during the whole evening, as ye must have
doubtless observed, exceed the bounds of a modest
hilarity."

There was no refusing assent to a proposition so
decidedly laid down by him, who undoubtedly was the
best judge ; although, had Edward formed his opinion
from his own recollections, he would have pronounced
that the Baron was not only *ebriolus*, but verging to
become *ebrius;* or, in plain English, was incomparably
the most drunk of the party, except perhaps his anta-
gonist the Laird of Balmawhapple. However, having
received the expected, or rather the required, compliment
on his sobriety, the Baron proceeded—"No, sir, though I
am myself of a strong temperament, I abhor ebriety, and
detest those who swallow wine *gulæ causa*, for the oblec-
tation of the gullet ; albeit I might deprecate the law
of Pittacus of Mitylene, who punished doubly a crime
committed under the influence of *Liber Pater;* nor would
I utterly accede to the objurgation of the younger Plinius,
in the fourteenth book of his 'Historia Naturalis.' No,
sir, I distinguish, I discriminate, and approve of wine so
far only as it maketh glad the face, or, in the language of
Flaccus, *recepto amico.*"

Thus terminated the apology which the Baron of
Bradwardine thought it necessary to make for the super-
abundance of his hospitality ; and it may be easily
believed that he was neither interrupted by dissent, nor
any expression of incredulity.

He then invited his guest to a morning ride, and
ordered that Davie Gellatley should meet them at the
*dern*[1] *path* with Ban and Buscar. "For, until the shooting
season commence, I would willingly show you some sport,
and we may, God willing, meet with a roe. The roe,
Captain Waverley, may be hunted at all times alike ; for
never being in what is called *pride of grease*, he is also
never out of season, though it be a truth that his venison
is not equal to that of either the red or fallow deer.[2] But
he will serve to show how my dogs run ; and therefore
they shall attend us with David Gellatley."

Waverley expressed his surprise that his friend Davie
was capable of such trust ; but the Baron gave him to
understand that this poor simpleton was neither fatuous,
*nec naturaliter idiota*, as is expressed in the brieves of

---

[1] Secluded.

[2] The learned in cookery dissent from the Baron of Bradwardine, and hold the
roe venison dry and indifferent food, unless when dressed in soup and Scotch
collops. (S.)

furiosity, but simply a crack-brained knave, who could execute very well any commission which jumped with his own humour, and made his folly a plea for avoiding every other. "He has made an interest with us," continued the Baron, "by saving Rose from a great danger with his own proper peril; and the roguish loon must therefore eat of our bread and drink of our cup, and do what he can, or what he will; which, if the suspicions of Saunderson and the Bailie are well founded, may perchance in his case be commensurate terms."

Miss Bradwardine then gave Waverley to understand, that this poor simpleton was dotingly fond of music, deeply affected by that which was melancholy, and transported into extravagant gaiety by light and lively airs. He had in this respect a prodigious memory, stored with miscellaneous snatches and fragments of all tunes and songs, which he sometimes applied, with considerable address, as the vehicles of remonstrance, explanation, or satire. Davie was much attached to the few who showed him kindness; and both aware of any slight or ill usage which he happened to receive, and sufficiently apt, where he saw opportunity, to revenge it. The common people, who often judge hardly of each other, as well as of their betters, although they had expressed great compassion for the poor *innocent* while suffered to wander in rags about the village, no sooner beheld him decently clothed, provided for, and even a sort of favourite, than they called up all the instances of sharpness and ingenuity, in action and repartee, which his annals afforded, and charitably bottomed thereupon a hypothesis, that David Gellatley was no farther fool than was necessary to avoid hard labour. This opinion was not better founded than that of the Negroes, who, from the acute and mischievous pranks of the monkeys, suppose that they have the gift of speech, and only suppress their powers of elocution to escape being set to work. But the hypothesis was entirely imaginary; David Gellatley was in good earnest the half-crazed simpleton which he appeared, and was incapable of any constant and steady exertion. He had just so much solidity as kept on the windy side of insanity; so much wild wit as saved him from the imputation of idiocy; some dexterity in field-sports, (in which we have known as great fools excel,) great kindness and humanity in the treatment of animals intrusted to him, warm affections, a prodigious memory, and an ear for music.

The stamping of horses was now heard in the court, and Davie's voice singing to the two large deer greyhounds,

> Hie away, hie away,
> Over bank and over brae,
> Where the copsewood is the greenest,
> Where the fountains glisten sheenest,
> Where the lady-fern grows strongest,
> Where the morning dew lies longest.
> Where the black-cock sweetest sips it,
> Where the fairy latest trips it:
> Hie to haunts right seldom seen,
> Lovely, lonesome, cool and green,
> Over bank and over brae,
> Hie away, hie away.

"Do the verses he sings," asked Waverley, "belong to old Scottish poetry, Miss Bradwardine?"

"I believe not," she replied. "This poor creature had a brother, and Heaven, as if to compensate to the family Davie's deficiencies, had given him what the hamlet thought uncommon talents. An uncle contrived to educate him for the Scottish kirk, but he could not get preferment because he came from our *ground*. He returned from college hopeless and broken-hearted, and fell into a decline. My father supported him till his death, which happened before he was nineteen. He played beautifully on the flute, and was supposed to have a great turn for poetry. He was affectionate and compassionate to his brother, who followed him like his shadow, and we think that from him Davie gathered many fragments of songs and music unlike those of this country. But if we ask him where he got such a fragment as he is now singing, he either answers with wild and long fits of laughter, or else breaks into tears of lamentation; but was never heard to give any explanation, or to mention his brother's name since his death."

"Surely," said Edward, who was readily interested by a tale bordering on the romantic, "surely more might be learned by more particular inquiry."

"Perhaps so," answered Rose; "but my father will not permit any one to practise on his feelings on this subject."

By this time the Baron, with the help of Mr Saunderson, had indued a pair of jack-boots of large dimensions, and now invited our hero to follow him as he stalked clattering down the ample stair-case, tapping each huge balustrade as he passed with the but of his massive horsewhip, and humming, with the air of a chasseur of Louis Quatorze,

> Pour la chasse ordonnée il faut preparer tout,
> Ho la ho! Vite! vite debout.

## CHAPTER XIII.

### *A more rational Day than the last.*

THE Baron of Bradwardine, mounted on an active and
well-managed horse, and seated on a demi-pique saddle,
with deep housings to agree with his livery, was no bad
representative of the old school. His light-coloured
embroidered coat, and superbly barred waistcoat, his
brigadier wig, surmounted by a small gold-laced cocked
hat, completed his personal costume; but he was attended
by two well-mounted servants on horseback, armed with
holster-pistols.

In this guise he ambled forth over hill and valley, the
admiration of every farm-yard which they passed in their
progress, till, "low down in a grassy vale," they found
David Gellatley leading two very tall deer greyhounds,
and presiding over half a dozen curs, and about as many
bare-legged and bare-headed boys, who, to procure the
chosen distinction of attending on the chase, had not
failed to tickle his ears with the dulcet appellation of
*Maister Gellatley*, though probably all and each had
hooted him on former occasions in the character of *daft
Davie*. But this is no uncommon strain of flattery to
persons in office, nor altogether confined to the bare-
legged villagers of Tully-Veolan; it was in fashion Sixty
Years since, is now, and will be six hundred years hence,
if this admirable compound of folly and knavery, called
the world, shall be then in existence.

These *gillie-wet-foots*,[1] as they were called, were destined
to beat the bushes, which they performed with so much
success, that, after half an hour's search, a roe was
started, coursed, and killed; the Baron following on his
white horse, like Earl Percy of yore, and magnanimously
flaying and embowelling the slain animal (which, he
observed, was called by the French chasseurs, *faire la
curée*) with his own baronial couteau de chasse. After
this ceremony, he conducted his guest homeward by a
pleasant and circuitous route, commanding an extensive
prospect of different villages and houses, to each of which
Mr Bradwardine attached some anecdote of history or
genealogy, told in language whimsical from prejudice
and pedantry, but often respectable for the good sense

---

[1] A bare-footed Highland lad is called a gillie-wet-foot. Gillie, in general,
means servant or attendant. (S.)

and honourable feelings which his narrative displayed, and almost always curious, if not valuable, for the information they contained.

The truth is, the ride seemed agreeable to both gentlemen, because they found amusement in each other's conversation, although their characters and habits of thinking were in many respects totally opposite. Edward, we have informed the reader, was warm in his feelings, wild and romantic in his ideas and in his taste of reading, with a strong disposition towards poetry. Mr Bradwardine was the reverse of all this, and piqued himself upon stalking through life with the same upright, starched, stoical gravity which distinguished his evening promenade upon the terrace of Tully-Veolan, where for hours together—the very model of old Hardyknute—

> Stately stepp'd he east the wa',
> And stately stepp'd he west.

As for literature, he read the classic poets to be sure, and the Epithalamium of Georgius Buchanan, and Arthur Johnstone's Psalms, of a Sunday; and the Deliciæ Poetarum Scotorum, and Sir David Lindsay's Works, and Barbour's Bruce, and Blind Harry's Wallace, and the Gentle Shepherd, and the Cherry and the Slae. But though he thus far sacrificed his time to the Muses, he would, if the truth must be spoken, have been much better pleased had the pious or sapient apothegms, as well as the historical narratives, which these various works contained, been presented to him in the form of simple prose. And he sometimes could not refrain from expressing contempt of the "vain and unprofitable art of poem-making," in which, he said, "the only one who had excelled in his time was Allan Ramsay, the periwigmaker."[1]

But although Edward and he differed *toto cœlo*, as the Baron would have said, upon this subject, yet they met upon history as on a neutral ground, in which each claimed an interest. The Baron, indeed, only cumbered his memory with matters of fact; the cold, dry, hard outlines which history delineates. Edward, on the contrary, loved to fill up and round the sketch with the colouring of a warm and vivid imagination, which gives light and

---

[1] The Baron ought to have remembered that the joyous Allan literally drew his blood from the house of the noble Earl, whom he terms—

> Dalhousie of an old descent,
> My stoup, my pride, my ornament.                    (S.)

life to the actors and speakers in the drama of past ages.
Yet with tastes so opposite, they contributed greatly to
each other's amusement. Mr Bradwardine's minute
narratives and powerful memory supplied to Waverley
fresh subjects of the kind upon which his fancy loved to
labour, and opened to him a new mine of incident and of
character. And he repaid the pleasure thus communicated, by an earnest attention, valuable to all story-
tellers, more especially to the Baron, who felt his habits
of self-respect flattered by it; and sometimes also by
reciprocal communications, which interested Mr Bradwardine, as confirming or illustrating his own favourite
anecdotes. Besides, Mr Bradwardine loved to talk of the
scenes of his youth, which had been spent in camps and
foreign lands, and had many interesting particulars to
tell of the generals under whom he had served, and the
actions he had witnessed.

Both parties returned to Tully-Veolan in great good-
humour with each other; Waverley desirous of studying
more attentively what he considered as a singular and
interesting character, gifted with a memory containing a
curious register of ancient and modern anecdotes; and
Bradwardine disposed to regard Edward as *puer* (or
rather *juvenis*) *bonæ spei et magnæ indolis,* a youth devoid
of that petulant volatility, which is impatient of, or
vilipends, the conversation and advice of his seniors, from
which he predicted great things of his future success and
deportment in life. There was no other guest except Mr
Rubrick, whose information and discourse, as a clergyman and a scholar, harmonized very well with that of the
Baron and his guest.

Shortly after dinner, the Baron, as if to show that his
temperance was not entirely theoretical, proposed a visit
to Rose's apartment, or, as he termed it, her *Troisième
Etage.* Waverley was accordingly conducted through one
or two of those long awkward passages with which
ancient architects studied to puzzle the inhabitants of the
houses which they planned, at the end of which Mr Bradwardine began to ascend, by two steps at once, a very
steep, narrow, and winding stair, leaving Mr Rubrick and
Waverley to follow at more leisure, while he should
announce their approach to his daughter.

After having climbed this perpendicular corkscrew
until their brains were almost giddy, they arrived in a
little matted lobby, which served as an anteroom to
Rose's *sanctum sanctorum,* and through which they entered

her parlour. It was a small, but pleasant apartment, opening to the south, and hung with tapestry; adorned besides with two pictures, one of her mother, in the dress of a shepherdess, with a bell-hoop; the other of the Baron, in his tenth year, in a blue coat, embroidered waistcoat, laced hat, and bag-wig, with a bow in his hand. Edward could not help smiling at the costume, and at the odd resemblance between the round, smooth, red-cheeked, staring visage in the portrait, and the gaunt, bearded, hollow-eyed, swarthy features, which travelling, fatigues of war, and advanced age, had bestowed on the original. The Baron joined in the laugh. "Truly," he said, "that picture was a woman's fantasy of my good mother's; (a daughter of the Laird of Tulliellum, Captain Waverley; I indicated the house to you when we were on the top of the Shinnyheuch; it was burnt by the Dutch auxiliaries brought in by the Government in 1715;) I never sate for my pourtraiture but once since that was painted, and it was at the special and reiterated request of the Mareschal Duke of Berwick."

The good old gentleman did not mention what Mr Rubrick afterwards told Edward, that the Duke had done him this honour on account of his being the first to mount the breach of a fort in Savoy during the memorable campaign of 1709, and his having there defended himself with his half-pike for nearly ten minutes before any support reached him. To do the Baron justice, although sufficiently prone to dwell upon, and even to exaggerate his family dignity and consequence, he was too much a man of real courage ever to allude to such personal acts of merit as he had himself manifested.

Miss Rose now appeared from the interior room of her apartment, to welcome her father and his friends. The little labours in which she had been employed obviously showed a natural taste, which required only cultivation. Her father had taught her French and Italian, and a few of the ordinary authors in those languages ornamented her shelves. He had endeavoured also to be her preceptor in music; but as he began with the more abstruse doctrines of the science, and was not perhaps master of them himself, she had made no proficiency farther than to be able to accompany her voice with the harpsichord; but even this was not very common in Scotland at that period. To make amends, she sung with great taste and feeling, and with a respect to the sense of what she uttered, that might be proposed in example to ladies of much superior musical talent. Her natural good sense taught her, that if, as we are assured by high authority, music be "married to immortal verse," they are very often divorced by the performer in a most shameful manner. It was perhaps owing to this sensibility to poetry, and power of combining its expression with those of the musical notes, that her singing gave more pleasure to all the unlearned in music, and even to many of the learned, than could have been communicated by a much finer voice and more brilliant execution, unguided by the same delicacy of feeling.

A bartizan, or projecting gallery, before the windows of her parlour, served to illustrate another of Rose's pursuits; for it was crowded with flowers of different kinds, which she had taken under her special protection. A projecting turret gave access to this Gothic balcony, which commanded a most beautiful prospect. The formal garden, with its high bounding walls, lay below, contracted, as it seemed, to a mere parterre; while the view extended beyond them down a wooded glen, where the small river was sometimes visible, sometimes hidden in copse. The eye might be delayed by a desire to rest on the rocks, which here and there rose from the dell with massive or spiry fronts, or it might dwell on the noble, though ruined tower, which was here beheld in all its dignity, frowning from a promontory over the river. To the left were seen two or three cottages, a part of the village; the brow of the hill concealed the others. The glen, or dell, was terminated by a sheet of water, called Loch Veolan, into which the brook discharged itself, and which now glistened in the western sun. The distant country seemed open and varied in surface, though not wooded; and there was nothing to interrupt the view until the scene was bounded by a ridge of distant and blue hills, which formed the southern boundary of the strath or valley. To this pleasant station Miss Bradwardine had ordered coffee.

The view of the old tower, or fortalice, introduced some family anecdotes and tales of Scottish chivalry, which the Baron told with great enthusiasm. The projecting peak of an impending crag which rose near, it had acquired the name of St Swithin's Chair. It was the scene of a peculiar superstition, of which Mr Rubrick mentioned some curious particulars, which reminded Waverley of a rhyme quoted by Edgar in King Lear; and Rose was

called upon to sing a little legend, in which they had been
interwoven by some village poet,

> Who, noteless as the race from which he sprung,
> Saved others' names, but left his own unsung.

The sweetness of her voice, and the simple beauty of
her music, gave all the advantage which the minstrel
could have desired, and which his poetry so much wanted.
I almost doubt if it can be read with patience, destitute
of these advantages; although I conjecture the following
copy to have been somewhat corrected by Waverley, to
suit the taste of those who might not relish pure antiquity.

### St Swithin's Chair.

> On Hallow-Mass Eve, ere ye boune[1] ye to rest,
> Ever beware that your couch be bless'd;
> Sign it with cross, and sain[2] it with bead,
> Sing the Ave, and say the Creed.
>
> For on Hallow-Mass Eve the Night-Hag will ride,
> And all her nine-fold sweeping on by her side,
> Whether the wind sing lowly or loud,
> Sailing through moonshine or swath'd in the cloud.
>
> The Lady she sat in St Swithin's Chair,
> The dew of the night has damp'd her hair:
> Her cheek was pale—but resolved and high
> Was the word of her lip and the glance of her eye.
>
> She mutter'd the spell of Swithin bold,
> When his naked foot traced the midnight wold,
> When he stopp'd the Hag as she rode the night,
> And bade her descend, and her promise plight.
>
> He that dare sit on St Swithin's Chair,
> When the Night-Hag wings the troubled air,
> Questions three, when he speaks the spell,
> He may ask, and she must tell.
>
> The Baron has been with King Robert his liege,
> These three long years in battle and siege;
> News are there none of his weal or his woe,
> And fain the Lady his fate would know.
>
> She shudders and stops as the charm she speaks;—
> Is it the moody owl that shrieks?
> Or is it that sound, betwixt laughter and scream,
> The voice of the Demon who haunts the stream?
>
> The moan of the wind sunk silent and low,
> And the roaring torrent has ceased to flow;
> The calm was more dreadful than raging storm,
> When the cold grey mist brought the ghastly Form!

x      *      *      *      *

"I am sorry to disappoint the company, especially
Captain Waverley, who listens with such laudable
gravity; it is but a fragment, although I think there

---

[1] Make ready.      [2] Bless.

are other verses, describing the return of the Baron from
the wars, and how the lady was found 'clay-cold upon the
grounsill ledge.'"

"It is one of those figments," observed Mr Bradwardine,
"with which the early history of distinguished families
was deformed in the times of superstition; as that of
Rome, and other ancient nations, had their prodigies, sir,
the which you may read in ancient histories, or in the
little work compiled by Julius Obsequens, and inscribed
by the learned Scheffer, the editor, to his patron, Bene-
dictus Skytte, Baron of Dudershoff."

"My father has a strange defiance of the marvellous,
Captain Waverley," observed Rose, "and once stood firm
when a whole synod of Presbyterian divines were put to
the rout by a sudden apparition of the foul fiend."

Waverley looked as if desirous to hear more.

"Must I tell my story as well as sing my song?—Well
—Once upon a time there lived an old woman, called
Janet Gellatley, who was suspected to be a witch, on the
infallible grounds that she was very old, very ugly, very
poor, and had two sons, one of whom was a poet, and the
other a fool, which visitation, all the neighbourhood
agreed, had come upon her for the sin of witchcraft.
And she was imprisoned for a week in the steeple of the
parish church, and sparely supplied with food, and not
permitted to sleep until she herself became as much
persuaded of her being a witch as her accusers; and in
this lucid and happy state of mind was brought forth to
make a clean breast, that is, to make open confession of
her sorceries, before all the Whig gentry and ministers in
the vicinity, who were no conjurors themselves.  My
father went to see fair play between the witch and the
clergy; for the witch had been born on his estate.  And
while the witch was confessing that the Enemy appeared,
and made his addresses to her as a handsome black man,
—which, if you could have seen poor old blear-eyed Janet,
reflected little honour on Apollyon's taste,—and while
the auditors listened with astonished ears, and the clerk
recorded with a trembling hand, she, all of a sudden,
changed the low mumbling tone with which she spoke
into a shrill yell, and exclaimed, 'Look to yourselves!
look to yourselves! I see the Evil One sitting in the
midst of ye.'  The surprise was general, and terror and
flight its immediate consequences.  Happy were those
who were next the door; and many were the disasters
that befel hats, bands, cuffs, and wigs, before they could

get out of the church, where they left the obstinate prelatist to settle matters with the witch and her admirer, at his own peril or pleasure."

"*Risu solvuntur tabulæ*," said the Baron; "when they recovered their panic trepidation, they were too much ashamed to bring any wakening of the process against Janet Gellatley." [1]

This anecdote led into a long discussion of

> All those idle thoughts and fantasies,
>   Devices, dreams, opinions unsound,
>   Shows, visions, soothsays, and prophecies,
>   And all that feigned is, as leasings, tales, and lies.

With such conversation, and the romantic legends which it introduced, closed our hero's second evening in the house of Tully-Veolan.


# CHAPTER XIV.

### *A Discovery—Waverley becomes domesticated at Tully-Veolan.*

THE next day Edward arose betimes, and in a morning walk around the house and its vicinity, came suddenly upon a small court in front of the dog-kennel, where his friend Davie was employed about his four-footed charge. One quick glance of his eye recognised Waverley, when, instantly turning his back, as if he had not observed him, he began to sing part of an old ballad:

> Young men will love thee more fair and more fast;
>   *Heard ye so merry the little bird sing?*
> Old men's love the longest will last,
>   *And the throstle-cock's head is under his wing.*
>
> The young man's wrath is like light straw on fire;
>   *Heard ye so merry the little bird sing?*
> But like red-hot steel is the old man's ire,
>   *And the throstle-cock's head is under his wing.*
>
> The young man will brawl at the evening board;
>   *Heard ye so merry the little bird sing?*
> But the old man will draw at the dawning the sword,
>   *And the throstle-cock's head is under his wing.*

Waverley could not avoid observing that Davie laid something like a satirical emphasis on these lines. He

---

[1] The story last told was said to have happened in the south of Scotland; but — *cedant arma togæ*—and let the gown have its dues. It was an old clergyman, who had wisdom and firmness enough to resist the panic which seized his brethren, who was the means of rescuing a poor insane creature from the cruel fate which would otherwise have overtaken her. The accounts of the trials for witchcraft form one of the most deplorable chapters in Scottish story. (S.)

therefore approached, and endeavoured, by sundry queries, to elicit from him what the innuendo might mean ; but Davie had no mind to explain, and had wit enough to make his folly cloak his knavery. Edward could collect nothing from him, excepting that the Laird of Balma-whapple had gone home yesterday morning, "wi' his boots fu' o' bluid." In the garden, however, he met the old butler, who no longer attempted to conceal, that, having been bred in the nursery line with Sumack & Co. of Newcastle, he sometimes wrought a turn in the flower-borders to oblige the Laird and Miss Rose. By a series of queries, Edward at length discovered, with a painful feeling of surprise and shame, that Balmawhapple's sub-mission and apology had been the consequence of a ren-contre with the Baron before his guest had quitted his pillow, in which the younger combatant had been dis-armed and wounded in the sword arm.

Greatly mortified at this information, Edward sought out his friendly host, and anxiously expostulated with him upon the injustice he had done him in anticipating his meeting with Mr Falconer, a circumstance, which, considering his youth and the profession of arms which he had just adopted, was capable of being represented much to his prejudice. The Baron justified himself at greater length than I choose to repeat. He urged, that the quarrel was common to them, and that Balmawhapple could not, by the code of honour, *evite* giving satisfaction to both, which he had done in his case by an honourable meeting, and in that of Edward by such a *palinode* as rendered the use of the sword unnecessary, and which, being made and accepted, must necessarily *sopite* the whole affair.

With this excuse, or explanation, Waverley was silenced, if not satisfied ; but he could not help testifying some displeasure against the Blessed Bear, which had given rise to the quarrel, nor refrain from hinting, that the sanctified epithet was hardly appropriate. The Baron ob-served, he could not deny that "The Bear, though allowed by heralds as a most honourable ordinary, had, never-theless, somewhat fierce, churlish, and morose in his dis-position, (as might be read in Archibald Simson, pastor of Dalkeith's *Hieroglyphica Animalium*,) and had thus been the type of many quarrels and dissensions which had occurred in the house of Bradwardine ; of which," he continued, "I might commemorate mine own unfortunate dissension with my third cousin by the mother's side Sir

Hew Halbert, who was so unthinking as to deride my
family name, as if it had been *quasi Bear-Warden;* a
most uncivil jest, since it not only insinuated that the
founder of our house occupied such a mean situation as
to be a custodier of wild beasts, a charge which, ye must
have observed, is only intrusted to the very basest
plebeians; but, moreover, seemed to infer that our coat-
armour had not been achieved by honourable actions in
war, but bestowed by way of *paranomasia,* or pun, upon
our family appellation,—a sort of bearing which the
French call *armoires parlantes;* the Latins *arma cantantia;*
and your English authorities, canting heraldry; being
indeed a species of emblazoning more befitting canters,
gaberlunzies, and such like mendicants, whose gibberish is
formed upon playing upon the word, than the noble,
honourable, and useful science of heraldry, which assigns
armorial bearings as the reward of noble and generous
actions, and not to tickle the ear with vain quodlibets,
such as are found in jest-books."[1] Of his quarrel with Sir
Hew he said nothing more, than that it was settled in a
fitting manner.

Having been so minute with respect to the diversions
of Tully-Veolan, on the first days of Edward's arrival, for
the purpose of introducing its inmates to the reader's
acquaintance, it becomes less necessary to trace the
progress of his intercourse with the same accuracy. It is
probable that a young man, accustomed to more cheerful
society, would have tired of the conversation of so violent
an assertor of the "boast of heraldry" as the Baron; but
Edward found an agreeable variety in that of Miss Bradwardine, who listened with eagerness to his remarks upon
literature, and showed great justness of taste in her
answers. The sweetness of her disposition had made her
submit with complacency, and even pleasure, to the
course of reading prescribed by her father, although it
not only comprehended several heavy folios of history,
but certain gigantic tomes in high-church polemics. In
heraldry he was fortunately contented to give her only

---

[1] Although canting heraldry is generally reprobated, it seems nevertheless to
have been adopted in the arms and mottos of many honourable families. Thus
the motto of the Vernons, *Ver non semper viret,* is a perfect pun, and so is that
of the Onslows, *Festina lente.* The *Periissem ni per-iissem* of the Anstruthers
is liable to a similar objection. One of that ancient race, finding that an antago-
nist, with whom he had fixed a friendly meeting, was determined to take the first
opportunity of assassinating him, prevented the hazard by dashing out his brains
with a battle-axe. Two sturdy arms, brandishing such a weapon, form the usual
crest of the family, with the above motto—*Periissem ni per-iissem*—(I had died,
unless I had gone through with it.) (S.)

such a slight tincture as might be acquired by perusal of
the two folio volumes of Nisbet. Rose was indeed the
very apple of her father's eye. Her constant liveliness,
her attention to all those little observances most gratifying to those who would never think of exacting them,
her beauty, in which he recalled the features of his beloved
wife, her unfeigned piety, and the noble generosity of her
disposition, would have justified the affection of the most
doting father.

His anxiety on her behalf did not, however, seem to
extend itself in that quarter, where, according to the
general opinion, it is most efficiently displayed; in
labouring, namely, to establish her in life, either by a
large dowry or a wealthy marriage. By an old settlement, almost all the landed estates of the Baron went,
after his death, to a distant relation; and it was supposed
that Miss Bradwardine would remain but slenderly
provided for, as the good gentleman's cash matters had
been too long under the exclusive charge of Bailie Macwheeble, to admit of any great expectations from his
personal succession. It is true, the said Bailie loved his
patron and his patron's daughter next (though at an
incomparable distance) to himself. He thought it was
possible to set aside the settlement on the male line, and
had actually procured an opinion to that effect (and, as
he boasted, without a fee) from an eminent Scottish
counsel, under whose notice he contrived to bring the
point while consulting him regularly on some other
business. But the Baron would not listen to such a
proposal for an instant. On the contrary, he used to
have a perverse pleasure in boasting that the barony of
Bradwardine was a male fief, the first charter having been
given at that early period when women were not deemed
capable to hold a feudal grant; because, according to
*Les coutumes de Normandie, c'est l'homme qui se bast et qui
conseille;* or, as is yet more ungallantly expressed by
other authorities, all of whose barbarous names he
delighted to quote at full length, because a woman could
not serve the superior, or feudal lord, in war, on account
of the decorum of her sex, nor assist him with advice,
because of her limited intellect, nor keep his counsel,
owing to the infirmity of her disposition. He would
triumphantly ask, how it would become a female, and
that female a Bradwardine, to be seen employed *in
servitio exuendi, seu detrahendi, caligas regis post batta-
liam?* that is, in pulling off the king's boots after an

engagement, which was the feudal service by which he held the barony of Bradwardine. "No," he said, "beyond hesitation, *procul dubio*, many females, as worthy as Rose, had been excluded, in order to make way for my own succession, and Heaven forbid that I should do aught that might contravene the destination of my forefathers, or impinge upon the right of my kinsman, Malcolm Bradwardine of Inchgrabbit, an honourable, though decayed branch of my own family."

The Bailie, as prime minister, having received this decisive communication from his sovereign, durst not press his own opinion any farther, but contented himself with deploring, on all suitable occasions, to Saunderson, the minister of the interior, the Laird's self-willedness, and with laying plans for uniting Rose with the young Laird of Balmawhapple, who had a fine estate, only moderately burdened, and was a faultless young gentleman, being as sober as a saint—if you keep brandy from him, and him from brandy—and who, in brief, had no imperfection but that of keeping light company at a time; such as Jinker, the horse-couper, and Gibby Gaethroughwi't, the piper o' Cupar; "o' whilk follies, Mr Saunderson, he'll mend, he'll mend."—pronounced the Bailie.

"Like sour ale in simmer," added Davie Gellatley, who happened to be nearer the conclave than they were aware of.

Miss Bradwardine, such as we have described her, with all the simplicity and curiosity of a recluse, attached herself to the opportunities of increasing her store of literature which Edward's visit afforded her. He sent for some of his books from his quarters, and they opened to her sources of delight of which she had hitherto had no idea. The best English poets, of every description, and other works on belles lettres, made a part of this precious cargo. Her music, even her flowers, were neglected, and Saunders not only mourned over, but began to mutiny against the labour for which he now scarce received thanks. These new pleasures became gradually enhanced by sharing them with one of a kindred taste. Edward's readiness to comment, to recite, to explain difficult passages, rendered his assistance invaluable; and the wild romance of his spirit delighted a character too young and inexperienced to observe its deficiencies. Upon subjects which interested him, and when quite at ease, he possessed that flow of natural, and somewhat florid eloquence, which has been supposed as powerful even as figure, fashion, fame, or fortune, in winning the female heart. There was, therefore, an increasing danger, in this constant intercourse, to poor Rose's peace of mind, which was the more imminent, as her father was greatly too much abstracted in his studies, and wrapped up in his own dignity, to dream of his daughter's incurring it. The daughters of the house of Bradwardine were, in his opinion, like those of the house of Bourbon or Austria, placed high above the clouds of passion which might obfuscate the intellects of meaner females; they moved in another sphere, were governed by other feelings, and amenable to other rules, than those of idle and fantastic affection. In short, he shut his eyes so resolutely to the natural consequences of Edward's intimacy with Miss Bradwardine, that the whole neighbourhood concluded that he had opened them to the advantages of a match between his daughter and the wealthy young Englishman, and pronounced him much less a fool than he had generally shown himself in cases where his own interest was concerned.

If the Baron, however, had really meditated such an alliance, the indifference of Waverley would have been an insuperable bar to his project. Our hero, since mixing more freely with the world, had learned to think with great shame and confusion upon his mental legend of Saint Cecilia, and the vexations of these reflections was likely, for some time at least, to counterbalance the natural susceptibility of his disposition. Besides, Rose Bradwardine, beautiful and amiable as we have described her, had not precisely the sort of beauty or merit, which captivates a romantic imagination in early youth. She was too frank, too confiding, too kind; amiable qualities, undoubtedly, but destructive of the marvellous, with which a youth of imagination delights to dress the empress of his affections. Was it possible to bow, to tremble, and to adore, before the timid, yet playful little girl, who now asked Edward to mend her pen, now to construe a stanza in Tasso, and now how to spell a very —very long word in her version of it? All these incidents have their fascination on the mind at a certain period of life, but not when a youth is entering it, and rather looking out for some object whose affection may dignify him in his own eyes, than stooping to one who looks up to him for such distinction. Hence, though there can be no rule in so capricious a passion, early love is frequently

ambitious in choosing its object; or, which comes to
the same, selects her (as in the case of Saint Cecilia
aforesaid) from a situation that gives fair scope for *le
beau idéal*, which the reality of intimate and familiar
life rather tends to limit and impair. I knew a very
accomplished and sensible young man cured of a violent
passion for a pretty woman, whose talents were not
equal to her face and figure, by being permitted to bear
her company for a whole afternoon. Thus, it is certain,
that had Edward enjoyed such an opportunity of conversing with Miss Stubbs, Aunt Rachel's precaution would
have been unnecessary, for he would as soon have fallen
in love with the dairy-maid. And although Miss Bradwardine was a very different character, it seems probable
that the very intimacy of their intercourse prevented his
feeling for her other sentiments than those of a brother
for an amiable and accomplished sister; while the
sentiments of poor Rose were gradually, and without
her being conscious, assuming a shade of warmer
affection.

I ought to have said that Edward, when he sent to
Dundee for the books before mentioned, had applied for,
and received permission, extending his leave of absence.
But the letter of his commanding-officer contained a
friendly recommendation to him, not to spend his time
exclusively with persons, who, estimable as they might
be in a general sense, could not be supposed well affected
to a government, which they declined to acknowledge by
taking the oath of allegiance. The letter further insinuated, though with great delicacy, that although some
family connections might be supposed to render it
necessary for Captain Waverley to communicate with
gentlemen who were in this unpleasant state of suspicion,
yet his father's situation and wishes ought to prevent his
prolonging those attentions into exclusive intimacy. And
it was intimated, that while his political principles were
endangered by communicating with laymen of this
description, be might also receive erroneous impressions
in religion from the prelatic clergy, who so perversely
labour to set up the royal prerogative in things sacred.

This last insinuation probably induced Waverley to
set both down to the prejudices of his commanding officer.
He was sensible that Mr Bradwardine had acted with the
most scrupulous delicacy, in never entering upon any
discussion that had the most remote tendency to bias his
mind in political opinions, although he was himself not

only a decided partizan of the exiled family, but had
been trusted at different times with important commissions for their service. Sensible, therefore, that there
was no risk of his being perverted from his allegiance,
Edward felt as if he should do his uncle's old friend
injustice in removing from a house where he gave and
received pleasure and amusement, merely to gratify a
prejudiced and ill-judged suspicion. He therefore wrote
a very general answer, assuring his commanding officer
that his loyalty was not in the most distant danger of
contamination, and continued an honoured guest and
inmate of the house of Tully-Veolan.


## CHAPTER XV.

### A Creagh,[1] and its consequences.

WHEN Edward had been a guest at Tully-Veolan nearly
six weeks, he descried, one morning, as he took his usual
walk before the breakfast-hour, signs of uncommon per-
turbation in the family. Four bare-legged dairy-maids,
with each an empty milk-pail in her hand, ran about with
frantic gestures, and uttering loud exclamations of surprise, grief, and resentment. From their appearance, a
pagan might have conceived them a detachment of the
celebrated Belides, just come from their baleing penance.
As nothing was to be got from this distracted chorus,
excepting "Lord guide us!" and "Eh sirs!" ejaculations
which threw no light upon the cause of their dismay,
Waverley repaired to the fore-court, as it was called,
where he beheld Bailie Macwheeble cantering his white
pony down the avenue with all the speed it could muster.
He had arrived, it would seem, upon a hasty summons,
and was followed by half a score of peasants from the
village, who had no great difficulty in keeping pace with
him.

The Bailie, greatly too busy, and too important, to
enter into explanations with Edward, summoned forth
Mr Saunderson, who appeared with a countenance in
which dismay was mingled with solemnity, and they
immediately entered into close conference. Davie
Gellatley was also seen in the group, idle as Diogenes at.

---

[1] A *creagh* was an incursion for plunder. termed on the Borders a *raid*.  (S.)

Sinope, while his countrymen were preparing for a siege. His spirits always rose with anything, good or bad, which occasioned tumult, and he continued frisking, hopping, dancing, and singing the burden of an old ballad,—

"Our gear's a' gane,"

until, happening to pass too near the Bailie, he received an admonitory hint from his horse-whip, which converted his songs into lamentation.

Passing from thence towards the garden, Waverley beheld the Baron in person, measuring and re-measuring, with swift and tremendous strides, the length of the terrace; his countenance clouded with offended pride and indignation, and the whole of his demeanour such as seemed to indicate, that any inquiry concerning the cause of his discomposure would give pain at least, if not offence. Waverley therefore glided into the house, without addressing him, and took his way to the breakfast-parlour, where he found his young friend Rose, who, though she neither exhibited the resentment of her father, the turbid importance of Bailie Macwheeble, nor the despair of the handmaidens, seemed vexed and thoughtful. A single word explained the mystery. "Your breakfast will be a disturbed one, Captain Waverley. A party of Caterans have come down upon us last night, and have driven off all our milch cows."

"A party of Caterans?"

"Yes; robbers from the neighbouring Highlands. We used to be quite free from them while we paid black-mail to Fergus Mac-Ivor Vich Ian Vohr; but my father thought it unworthy of his rank and birth to pay it any longer, and so this disaster has happened. It is not the value of the cattle, Captain Waverley, that vexes me; but my father is so much hurt at the affront, and is so bold and hot, that I fear he will try to recover them by the strong hand; and if he is not hurt himself, he will hurt some of these wild people, and then there will be no peace between them and us perhaps for our life-time; and we cannot defend ourselves as in old times, for the government have taken all our arms; and my dear father is so rash—O what will become of us!"——Here poor Rose lost heart altogether, and burst into a flood of tears.

The Baron entered at this moment, and rebuked her with more asperity than Waverley had ever heard him use to any one. "Was it not a shame," he said, "that she

should exhibit herself before any gentleman in such a
light, as if she shed tears for a drove of horned nolt and
milch kine, like the daughter of a Cheshire yeoman!—
Captain Waverley, I must request your favourable
construction of her grief, which may, or ought to proceed,
solely from seeing her father's estate exposed to *spulzie*[1]
and depredation from common thieves and sornars,[2] while
we are not allowed to keep half a score of muskets,
whether for defence or rescue."

Bailie Macwheeble entered immediately afterwards, and
by his report of arms and ammunition confirmed this
statement, informing the Baron, in a melancholy voice,
that though the people would certainly obey his honour's
orders, yet there was no chance of their following the
gear to ony guid purpose, in respect there were only his
honour's body servants who had swords and pistols, and
the depredators were twelve Highlanders, completely
armed after the manner of their country.—Having
delivered this doleful annunciation, he assumed a posture
of silent dejection, shaking his head slowly with the
motion of a pendulum when it is ceasing to vibrate, and
then remained stationary, his body stooping at a more
acute angle than usual, and the latter part of his person
projecting in proportion.

The Baron, meanwhile, paced the room in silent
indignation, and at length fixing his eye upon an old
portrait, whose person was clad in armour, and whose
features glared grimly out of a huge bush of hair, part of
which descended from his head to his shoulders, and part
from his chin and upper-lip to his breast-plate,—"That
gentleman, Captain Waverley, my grandsire," he said,
"with two hundred horse, whom he levied within his own
bounds, discomfited and put to rout more than five
hundred of these Highland reivers,[3] who have been ever
*lapis offensionis, et petra scandali*, a stumbling-block and
a rock of offence to the Lowland vicinage—he discomfited
them, I say, when they had the temerity to descend to
harry this country, in the time of the civil dissensions, in
the year of grace, sixteen hundred forty and two. And
now, sir, I, his grandson, am thus used at such unworthy
hands!"

Here there was an awful pause; after which all the

---

[1] Spoil.
[2] *Sornars* may be translated sturdy beggars, more especially indicating those
unwelcome visitors who exact lodgings and victuals by force, or something
approaching to it.  (S.)                          [3] Robbers.

company, as is usual in cases of difficulty, began to give
separate and inconsistent counsel. Alexander ab Alexandro proposed they should send some one to compound
with the Caterans, who would readily, he said, give up
their prey for a dollar a-head. The Bailie opined that
this transaction would amount to theft-boot, or composition of felony; and he recommended that some *canny
hand* should be sent up to the glens to make the best
bargain he could, as it were for himself, so that the Laird
might not be seen in such a transaction. Edward proposed to send off to the nearest garrison for a party of
soldiers and a magistrate's warrant; and Rose, as far as
she dared, endeavoured to insinuate the course of paying
the arrears of tribute money to Fergus Mac-Ivor Vich Ian
Vohr, who, they all knew, could easily procure restoration
of the cattle, if he were properly propitiated.

None of these proposals met the Baron's approbation.
The idea of composition, direct or implied, was absolutely
ignominious; that of Waverley only showed that he did
not understand the state of the country, and of the
political parties which divided it; and, standing matters
as they did with Fergus Mac-Ivor Vich Ian Vohr, the
Baron would make no concession to him, were it, he said,
"to procure restitution *in integrum* of every stirk and
stot that the chief, his forefathers, and his clan, had
stolen since the days of Malcolm Canmore."

In fact, his voice was still for war, and he proposed to
send expresses to Balmawhapple, Killancureit, Tulliellum,
and other lairds, who were exposed to similar depredations, inviting them to join in the pursuit; "and then,
sir, shall these *nebulones nequissimi*, as Leslæus calls them,
be brought to the fate of their predecessor Cacus,

'Elisos oculos, et siccum sanguine guttur.'"

The Bailie, who by no means relished these warlike
counsels, here pulled forth an immense watch, of the
colour, and nearly of the size, of a pewter warming-pan,
and observed it was now past noon, and that the Caterans
had been seen in the pass of Ballybrough soon after sun-
rise; so that before the allied forces could assemble, they
and their prey would be far beyond the reach of the
most active pursuit, and sheltered in those pathless
deserts, where it was neither advisable to follow, nor
indeed possible to trace them.

This proposition was undeniable. The council therefore broke up without coming to any conclusion, as has

occurred to councils of more importance; only it was
determined that the Bailie should send his own three
milk cows down to the Mains for the use of the Baron's
family, and brew small ale, as a substitute for milk, in
his own. To this arrangement, which was suggested by
Saunderson, the Bailie readily assented, both from
habitual deference to the family, and an internal consciousness that his courtesy would, in some mode or other,
be repaid tenfold.

The Baron having also retired to give some necessary
directions, Waverley seized the opportunity to ask,
whether this Fergus, with the unpronounceable name, was
the chief thief-taker of the district?

"Thief-taker!" answered Rose, laughing; "he is a
gentleman of great honour and consequence; the
chieftain of an independent branch of a powerful Highland clan, and is much respected, both for his own power,
and that of his kith, kin, and allies."

"And what has he to do with the thieves, then? Is he
a magistrate, or in the commission of the peace?" asked
Waverley.

"The commission of war rather, if there be such a
thing," said Rose; "for he is a very unquiet neighbour to
his un-friends, and keeps a greater *following* on foot than
many that have thrice his estate. As to his connection
with the thieves, that I cannot well explain; but the
boldest of them will never steal a hoof from any one that
pays black-mail to Vich Ian Vohr"

"And what is black-mail?"

"A sort of protection-money that Low-country gentlemen and heritors, lying near the Highlands, pay to some
Highland chief, that he may neither do them harm
himself, nor suffer it to be done to them by others; and
then if your cattle are stolen, you have only to send him
word, and he will recover them; or it may be, he will
drive away cows from some distant place, where he has a
quarrel, and give them to you to make up your loss."

"And is this sort of Highland Jonathan Wild admitted
into society, and called a gentleman?"

"So much so," said Rose, "that the quarrel between
my father and Fergus Mac-Ivor began at a county
meeting, where he wanted to take precedence of all the
Lowland gentlemen then present, only my father would
not suffer it. And then he upbraided my father that he
was under his banner, and paid him tribute; and my
father was in a towering passion, for Bailie Macwheeble,

who manages such things his own way, had contrived to keep this black-mail a secret from him, and passed it in his account for cess-money. And they would have fought; but Fergus Mac-Ivor said, very gallantly, he would never raise his hand against a grey head that was so much respected as my father's.—O I wish, I wish they had continued friends!"

"And did you ever see this Mr Mac-Ivor, if that be his name, Miss Bradwardine?"

"No, that is not his name; and he would consider *master* as a sort of affront, only that you are an Englishman, and know no better. But the Lowlanders call him, like other gentlemen, by the name of his estate, Glennaquoich; and the Highlanders call him Vich Ian Vohr, that is, the son of John the Great; and we upon the braes here call him by both names indifferently."

"I am afraid I shall never bring my English tongue to call him by either one or other."

"But he is a very polite, handsome man," continued Rose; "and his sister Flora is one of the most beautiful and accomplished young ladies in this country: she was bred in a convent in France, and was a great friend of mine before this unhappy dispute. Dear Captain Waverley, try your influence with my father to make matters up. I am sure this is but the beginning of our troubles; for Tully-Veolan has never been a safe or quiet residence when we have been at feud with the Highlanders. When I was a girl about ten, there was a skirmish fought between a party of twenty of them, and my father and his servants, behind the Mains; and the bullets broke several panes in the north windows, they were so near. Three of the Highlanders were killed, and they brought them in wrapped in their plaids, and laid them on the stone floor of the hall; and next morning, their wives and daughters came, clapping their hands, and crying the coronach, and shrieking, and carried away the dead bodies, with the pipes playing before them. I could not sleep for six weeks without starting, and thinking I heard these terrible cries, and saw the bodies lying on the steps, all stiff and swathed up in their bloody tartans. But since that time there came a party from the garrison at Stirling, with a warrant from the Lord Justice-Clerk, or some such great man, and took away all our arms; and now, how are we to protect ourselves if they come down in any strength?"

Waverley could not help starting at a story which bore

so much resemblance to one of his own day dreams.
Here was a girl scarce seventeen, the gentlest of her sex,
both in temper and appearance, who had witnessed with
her own eyes such a scene as he had used to conjure up
in his imagination, as only occurring in ancient times,
and spoke of it coolly, as one very likely to recur. He
felt at once the impulse of curiosity, and that slight
sense of danger which only serves to heighten its interest.
He might have said with Malvolio, "'I do not now
fool myself, to let imagination jade me!' I am actually
in the land of military and romantic adventures, and
it only remains to be seen what will be my own share in
them.'

The whole circumstances now detailed concerning the
state of the country, seemed equally novel and extraordinary. He had indeed often heard of Highland
thieves, but had no idea of the systematic mode in which
their depredations were conducted; and that the practice
was connived at, and even encouraged, by many of the
Highland chieftains, who not only found the creaghs, or
forays, useful for the purpose of training individuals of
their clan to the practice of arms, but also of maintaining
a wholesome terror among their Lowland neighbours,
and levying, as we have seen, a tribute from them, under
colour of protection-money.

Bailie Macwheeble, who soon afterwards entered, ex-
patiated still more at length upon the same topic. This
honest gentleman's conversation was so formed upon his
professional practice, that Davie Gellatley once said his
discourse was like a "charge of horning." He assured
our hero, that "from the maist ancient times of record,
the lawless thieves, limmers,[1] and broken men of the
Highlands, had been in fellowship together by reason of
their surnames, for the committing of divers thefts, reifs,
and herships[2] upon the honest men of the Low Country,
when they not only intromitted with their whole goods
and gear, corn, cattle, horse, nolt, sheep, outsight and insight plenishing, at their wicked pleasure, but moreover
made prisoners, ransomed them, or concussed them into
giving borrows (pledges) to enter into captivity again:
All which was directly prohibited in divers parts of the
Statute Book, both by the act one thousand five hundred
and sixty-seven, and various others; the whilk statutes,
with all that had followed and might follow thereupon,
were shamefully broken and vilipended by the said sor-

[1] Scoundrels.          [2] Robbing and devastation.

nars, limmers, and broken men, associated into fellow-
ships, for the aforesaid purposes of theft, stouthreef,[1] fire-
raising, murther, *raptus mulierum*, or forcible abduction
of women, and such like as aforesaid."

It seemed like a dream to Waverley that these deeds
of violence should be familiar to men's minds, and
currently talked of, as falling within the common order
of things, and happening daily in the immediate vicinity,
without his having crossed the seas, and while he was yet
in the otherwise well-ordered island of Great Britain.[2]


## CHAPTER XVI.

### *An unexpected Ally appears.*

THE Baron returned at the dinner-hour, and had in a
great measure recovered his composure and good-humour.
He not only confirmed the stories which Edward had
heard from Rose and Bailie Macwheeble, but added many
anecdotes from his own experience, concerning the state
of the Highlands and their inhabitants. The chiefs, he
pronounced to be, in general, gentlemen of great honour
and high pedigree, whose word was accounted as a law
by all those of their own sept, or clan. "It did not
indeed," he said, "become them, as had occurred in late
instances, to propone their *prosapia*, a lineage which
rested for the most part on the vain and fond rhymes
of their Seannachies or Bhairds, as æquiponderate with the
evidence of ancient charters and royal grants of antiquity,
conferred upon distinguished houses in the Low Country

---

[1] Theft with violence.
[2] Mac-Donald of Barrisdale, one of the very last Highland gentlemen who
carried on the plundering system to any great extent, was a scholar and a well-
bred gentleman. He engraved on his broadswords the well-known lines—

Hæ tibi erunt artes—pacisque imponere morem,
Parcere subjectis, et debellare superbos.

Indeed, the levying of black-mail was, before 1745, practised by several chiefs
of very high rank, who, in doing so, contended that they were lending the laws
the assistance of their arms and swords, and affording a protection which could
not be obtained from the magistracy in the disturbed state of the country. The
author has seen a Memoir of Mac-Pherson of Cluny, Chief of that ancient clan,
from which it appears that he levied protection-money to a very large amount,
which was willingly paid even by some of his most powerful neighbours. A
gentleman of this clan hearing a clergyman hold forth to his congregation on the
crime of theft, interrupted the preacher to assure him, he might leave the en-
forcement of such doctrines to Cluny Mac-Pherson, whose broadsword would put
a stop to theft sooner than all the sermons of all the ministers of the Synod.   (S.)

by divers Scottish monarchs; nevertheless, such was
their *outrecuidance* and presumption, as to undervalue
those who possessed such evidents, as if they held their
lands in a sheep's skin."

This, by the way, pretty well explained the cause of
quarrel between the Baron and his Highland ally. But
he went on to state so many curious particulars concerning the manners, customs, and habits of this patriarchal
race, that Edward's curiosity became highly interested,
and he inquired whether it was possible to make with
safety an excursion into the neighbouring Highlands,
whose dusky barrier of mountains had already excited
his wish to penetrate beyond them. The Baron assured
his guest that nothing would be more easy, providing
this quarrel were first made up, since he could himself
give him letters to many of the distinguished Chiefs,
who would receive him with the utmost courtesy and
hospitality.

While they were on this topic, the door suddenly opened,
and, ushered by Saunders Saunderson, a Highlander, fully
armed and equipped, entered the apartment. Had it not
been that Saunders acted the part of master of the
ceremonies to this martial apparition, without appearing
to deviate from his usual composure, and that neither Mr
Bradwardine nor Rose exhibited any emotion, Edward
would certainly have thought the intrusion hostile. As
it was, he started at the sight of what he had not yet
happened to see, a mountaineer in his full national
costume. The individual Gael was a stout, dark, young
man, of low stature, the ample folds of whose plaid added
to the appearance of strength which his person exhibited.
The short kilt, or petticoat, showed his sinewy and clean-
made limbs; the goat-skin purse, flanked by the usual
defences, a dirk and steel-wrought pistol, hung before
him; his bonnet had a short feather, which indicated his
claim to be treated as a Duinhé-wassel, or sort of gentleman; a broadsword dangled by his side, a target hung
upon his shoulder, and a long Spanish fowling-piece
occupied one of his hands. With the other hand he
pulled off his bonnet, and the Baron, who well knew
their customs, and the proper mode of addressing them,
immediately said, with an air of dignity, but without
rising, and much, as Edward thought, in the manner
of a prince receiving an embassy, "Welcome, Evan Dhu
Maccombich; what news from Fergus Mac-Ivor Vich Ian
Vohr?"

"Fergus Mac-Ivor Vich Ian Vohr," said the ambassador, in good English, "greets you well, Baron of Bradwardine and Tully-Veolan, and is sorry there has been a thick cloud interposed between you and him, which has kept you from seeing and considering the friendship and alliances that have been between your houses and fore-bears of old; and he prays you that the cloud may pass away, and that things may be as they have been hereto-fore between the clan Ivor and the house of Bradwardine, when there was an egg between them for a flint, and a knife for a sword. And he expects you will also say, you are sorry for the cloud, and no man shall hereafter ask whether it descended from the hill to the valley, or rose from the valley to the hill; for they never struck with the scabbard who did not receive with the sword, and woe to him who would lose his friend for the stormy cloud of a spring morning."

To this the Baron of Bradwardine answered with suitable dignity, that he knew the chief of clan Ivor to be a well-wisher to the *King*, and he was sorry there should have been a cloud between him and any gentleman of such sound principles, "for when folks are banding together, feeble is he who hath no brother."

This appearing perfectly satisfactory, that the peace between these august persons might be duly solemnized, the Baron ordered a stoup of usquebaugh, and, filling a glass, drank to the health and prosperity of Mac-Ivor of Glennaquoich; upon which the Celtic ambassador, to requite his politeness, turned down a mighty bumper of the same generous liquor, seasoned with his good wishes to the house of Bradwardine.

Having thus ratified the preliminaries of the general treaty of pacification, the envoy retired to adjust with Mr Macwheeble some subordinate articles with which it was not thought necessary to trouble the Baron. These pro-bably referred to the discontinuance of the subsidy, and apparently the Bailie found means to satisfy their ally, without suffering his master to suppose that his dignity was compromised. At least, it is certain, that after the plenipotentiaries had drunk a bottle of brandy in single drams, which seemed to have no more effect upon such seasoned vessels, than if it had been poured upon the two bears at the top of the avenue, Evan Dhu Maccombich having possessed himself of all the information which he could procure respecting the robbery of the preceding night, declared his intention to set off immediately in pursuit of the cattle, which he pronounced to be "no that far off;—they have broken the bone," he observed, "but they have had no time to suck the marrow."

Our hero, who had attended Evan Dhu during his perquisitions, was much struck with the ingenuity which he displayed in collecting information, and the precise and pointed conclusions which he drew from it. Evan Dhu, on his part, was obviously flattered with the attention of Waverley, the interest he seemed to take in his inquiries, and his curiosity about the customs and scenery of the Highlands. Without much ceremony he invited Edward to accompany him on a short walk of ten or fifteen miles into the mountains, and see the place where the cattle were conveyed to; adding, "If it be as I suppose, you never saw such a place in your life, nor ever will, unless you go with me or the like of me."

Our hero, feeling his curiosity considerably excited by the idea of visiting the den of a Highland Cacus, took, however, the precaution to inquire if his guide might be trusted. He was assured, that the invitation would on no account have been given had there been the least danger, and that all he had to apprehend was a little fatigue; and as Evan proposed he should pass a day at his Chieftain's house in returning, where he would be sure of good accommodation and an excellent welcome, there seemed nothing very formidable in the task he undertook. Rose, indeed, turned pale when she heard of it; but her father, who loved the spirited curiosity of his young friend, did not attempt to damp it by an alarm of danger which really did not exist, and a knapsack, with a few necessaries, being bound on the shoulders of a sort of deputy gamekeeper, our hero set forth with a fowling-piece in his hand, accompanied by his new friend Evan Dhu, and followed by the gamekeeper aforesaid, and by two wild Highlanders, the attendants of Evan, one of whom had upon his shoulder a hatchet at the end of a pole, called a Lochaber-axe,[1] and the other a long ducking-gun. Evan, upon Edward's inquiry, gave him to understand that this martial escort was by no means necessary as a guard, but merely, as he said, drawing up

---

[1] The Town-guard of Edinburgh were, till a late period, armed with this weapon when on their police-duty. There was a hook at the back of the axe, which the ancient Highlanders used to assist them to climb over walls, fixing the hook upon it, and raising themselves by the handle. The axe, which was also much used by the natives of Ireland, is supposed to have been introduced into both countries from Scandinavia. (S.)

and adjusting his plaid with an air of dignity, that he might appear decently at Tully-Veolan, and as Vich Ian Vohr's foster-brother ought to do. "Ah!" said he, "if you Saxon Duinhé-wassel (English gentlemen) saw but the Chief with his tail on!"

"With his tail on?" echoed Edward, in some surprise.

"Yes—that is, with all his usual followers, when he visits those of the same rank. There is," he continued, stopping and drawing himself proudly up, while he counted upon his fingers the several officers of his chief's retinue—"there is his *hanchman*, or right-hand man; then his *bàrd*, or poet; then his *bladier*, or orator, to make harangues to the great folks whom he visits; then his *gilly-more*, or armour-bearer, to carry his sword and target, and his gun; then his *gilly-casfliuch*, who carries him on his back through the sikes and brooks; then his *gilly-comstrian*, to lead his horse by the bridle in steep and difficult paths; then his *gilly-trushharnish*, to carry his knapsack; and the piper and the piper's man, and it may be a dozen young lads beside, that have no business, but are just boys of the belt, to follow the laird, and do his honour's bidding."

"And does your Chief regularly maintain all these men?" demanded Waverley.

"All these?" replied Evan; "ay, and many a fair head beside, that would not ken where to lay itself, but for the mickle barn at Glennaquoich."

With similar tales of the grandeur of the Chief in peace and war, Evan Dhu beguiled the way till they approached more closely those huge mountains which Edward had hitherto only seen at a distance. It was towards evening as they entered one of the tremendous passes which afford communication between the high and low country; the path, which was extremely steep and rugged, winded up a chasm between two tremendous rocks, following the passage which a foaming stream, that brawled far below, appeared to have worn for itself in the course of ages. A few slanting beams of the sun, which was now setting, reached the water in its darksome bed, and showed it partially, chafed by a hundred rocks, and broken by a hundred falls. The descent from the path to the stream was a mere precipice, with here and there a projecting fragment of granite, or a scathed tree, which had warped its twisted roots into the fissures of the rock. On the right hand, the mountain rose above the path with almost equal inaccessibility; but the hill on the opposite side

displayed a shroud of copsewood, with which some pines
were intermingled.

"This," said Evan, "is the pass of Bally-Brough, which
was kept in former times by ten of the clan Donnochie
against a hundred of the Low Country carles. The
graves of the slain are still to be seen in that little corri,
or bottom, on the opposite side of the burn—if your eyes
are good, you may see the green specks among the
heather—See, there is an earn, which you Southrons call
an eagle—you have no such birds as that in England—he
is going to fetch his supper from the Laird of Bradwardine's braes, but I'll send a slug after him."

He fired his piece accordingly, but missed the superb
monarch of the feathered tribes, who, without noticing
the attempt to annoy him, continued his majestic flight
to the southward. A thousand birds of prey, hawks,
kites, carrion-crows, and ravens, disturbed from the
lodgings which they had just taken up for the evening,
rose at the report of the gun, and mingled their hoarse
and discordant notes with the echoes which replied to it,
and with the roar of the mountain cataracts. Evan, a
little disconcerted at having missed his mark, when he
meant to have displayed peculiar dexterity, covered his
confusion by whistling part of a pibroch as he reloaded
his piece, and proceeded in silence up the pass.

It issued in a narrow glen, between two mountains,
both very lofty, and covered with heath. The brook
continued to be their companion, and they advanced up
its mazes, crossing them now and then, on which occasions
Evan Dhu uniformly offered the assistance of his attendants to carry over Edward; but our hero, who had
been always a tolerable pedestrian, declined the accommodation, and obviously rose in his guide's opinion, by
showing that he did not fear wetting his feet. Indeed he
was anxious, so far as he could without affectation, to
remove the opinion which Evan seemed to entertain of
the effeminacy of the Lowlanders, and particularly of the
English.

Through the gorge of this glen they found access to a
black bog, of tremendous extent, full of large pit-holes,
which they traversed with great difficulty and some
danger, by tracks which no one but a Highlander could
have followed. The path itself, or rather the portion of
more solid ground on which the travellers half walked,
half waded, was rough, broken, and in many places
quaggy and unsound. Sometimes the ground was so

completely unsafe, that it was necessary to spring from
one hillock to another, the space between being incapable
of bearing the human weight. This was an easy matter
to the Highlanders, who wore thin-soled brogues fit for
the purpose, and moved with a peculiar springing step;
but Edward began to find the exercise, to which he was
unaccustomed, more fatiguing than he expected. The
lingering twilight served to show them through this
Serbonian bog, but deserted them almost totally at the
bottom of a steep and very stony hill, which it was the
travellers' next toilsome task to ascend. The night,
however, was pleasant, and not dark; and Waverley,
calling up mental energy to support personal fatigue,
held on his march gallantly, though envying in his heart
his Highland attendants, who continued, without a
symptom of abated vigour, the rapid and swinging pace,
or rather trot, which, according to his computation, had
already brought them fifteen miles upon their journey.

After crossing this mountain, and descending on the
other side towards a thick wood, Evan Dhu held some
conference with his Highland attendants, in consequence
of which Edward's baggage was shifted from the shoulders
of the gamekeeper to those of one of the gillies, and the
former was sent off with the other mountaineer in a
direction different from that of the three remaining
travellers. On asking the meaning of this separation,
Waverley was told that the Lowlander must go to a
hamlet about three miles off for the night; for unless it
was some very particular friend, Donald Bean Lean, the
worthy person whom they supposed to be possessed of
the cattle, did not much approve of strangers approaching his retreat. This seemed reasonable, and silenced a
qualm of suspicion which came across Edward's mind,
when he saw himself, at such a place and such an hour,
deprived of his only Lowland companion. And Evan
immediately afterwards added, "that indeed he himself
had better get forward, and announce their approach to
Donald Bean Lean, as the arrival of a *sidier roy* (red
soldier) might otherwise be a disagreeable surprise."
And without waiting for an answer, in jockey phrase, he
trotted out, and putting himself to a very round pace,
was out of sight in an instant.

Waverley was now left to his own meditations, for his
attendant with the battle-axe spoke very little English.
They were traversing a thick, and, as it seemed, an
endless wood of pines, and consequently the path was

altogether indiscernible in the murky darkness which
surrounded them. The Highlander, however, seemed to
trace it by instinct, without the hesitation of a moment,
and Edward followed his footsteps as close as he could.

After journeying a considerable time in silence, he
could not help asking, "Was it far to the end of their
journey?"

"Ta cove was tree, four mile; but as Duinhé-wassel
was a wee taiglit,[1] Donald could, tat is, might—would—
should send ta curragh."[2]

This conveyed no information. The *curragh* which was
promised might be a man, a horse, a cart, or chaise; and
no more could be got from the man with the battle-axe,
but a repetition of "Aich ay! ta curragh."

But in a short time Edward began to conceive his
meaning, when, issuing from the wood, he found himself
on the banks of a large river or lake, where his conductor
gave him to understand they must sit down for a little
while. The moon, which now began to rise, showed
obscurely the expanse of water which spread before them,
and the shapeless and indistinct forms of mountains with
which it seemed to be surrounded. The cool, and yet
mild air of the summer night, refreshed Waverley after
his rapid and toilsome walk; and the perfume which it
wafted from the birch trees,[3] bathed in the evening dew,
was exquisitely fragrant.

He had now time to give himself up to the full romance
of his situation. Here he sate on the banks of an unknown lake, under the guidance of a wild native, whose
language was unknown to him, on a visit to the den of
some renowned outlaw, a second Robin Hood, perhaps, or
Adam o' Gordon, and that at deep midnight, through
scenes of difficulty and toil, separated from his attendant,
left by his guide:—What a variety of incidents for the
exercise of a romantic imagination, and all enhanced by
the solemn feeling of uncertainty, at least, if not of
danger! The only circumstance which assorted ill with
the rest, was the cause of his journey—the Baron's milk
cows! this degrading incident he kept in the background.

While wrapt in these dreams of imagination, his companion gently touched him, and, pointing in a direction
nearly straight across the lake, said, "Yon's ta cove."
A small point of light was seen to twinkle in the direction

---

[1] Wearied.        [2] Skiff.
[3] It is not the weeping birch, the most common species in the Highlands, but
the woolly-leaved Lowland birch, that is distinguished by this fragrance. (S.)

in which he pointed, and, gradually increasing in size and lustre, seemed to flicker like a meteor upon the verge of the horizon. While Edward watched this phenomenon, the distant dash of oars was heard. The measured sound approached near and more near, and presently a loud whistle was heard in the same direction. His friend with the battle-axe immediately whistled clear and shrill, in reply to the signal, and a boat, manned with four or five Highlanders, pushed for a little inlet, near which Edward was sitting. He advanced to meet them with his attendant, was immediately assisted into the boat by the officious attention of two stout mountaineers, and had no sooner seated himself than they resumed their oars, and began to row across the lake with great rapidity.

## CHAPTER XVII.

### The Hold of a Highland Robber.

THE party preserved silence, interrupted only by the monotonous and murmured chant of a Gaelic song, sung in a kind of low recitative by the steersman, and by the dash of the oars, which the notes seemed to regulate, as they dipped to them in cadence. The light, which they now approached more nearly, assumed a broader, redder, and more irregular splendour. It appeared plainly to be a large fire, but whether kindled upon an island or the mainland, Edward could not determine. As he saw it, the red glaring orb seemed to rest on the very surface of the lake itself, and resembled the fiery vehicle in which the Evil Genius of an Oriental tale traverses land and sea. They approached nearer, and the light of the fire sufficed to show that it was kindled at the bottom of a huge dark crag or rock, rising abruptly from the very edge of the water; its front, changed by the reflection to dusky red, formed a strange, and even awful contrast to the banks around, which were from time to time faintly and partially illuminated by pallid moonlight.

The boat now neared the shore, and Edward could discover that this large fire, amply supplied with branches of pine-wood by two figures, who, in the red reflection of its light, appeared like demons, was kindled in the jaws of a lofty cavern, into which an inlet from the lake seemed to advance; and he conjectured, which was

indeed true, that the fire had been lighted as a beacon to
the boatmen on their return. They rowed right for the
mouth of the cave, and then, shipping their oars, permitted the boat to enter in obedience to the impulse
which it had received. The skiff passed the little point
or platform of rock, on which the fire was blazing, and
running about two boats' length farther, stopped where
the cavern (for it was already arched overhead) ascended
from the water by five or six broad ledges of rocks, so
easy and regular that they might be termed natural
steps. At this moment a quantity of water was suddenly
flung upon the fire, which sunk with a hissing noise, and
with it disappeared the light it had hitherto afforded.
Four or five active arms lifted Waverley out of the boat,
placed him on his feet, and almost carried him into the
recesses of the cave. He made a few paces in darkness,
guided in this manner; and advancing towards a hum of
voices, which seemed to sound from the centre of the
rock, at an acute turn Donald Bean Lean and his whole
establishment were before his eyes.

The interior of the cave, which here rose very high, was
illuminated by torches made of pine-tree, which emitted
a bright and bickering light, attended by a strong, though
not unpleasant odour. Their light was assisted by the red
glare of a large charcoal fire, round which were seated
five or six armed Highlanders, while others were indistinctly seen couched on their plaids, in the more remote
recesses of the cavern. In one large aperture, which the
robber facetiously called his *spence*, (or pantry,) there
hung by the heels the carcasses of a sheep, or ewe, and
two cows lately slaughtered. The principal inhabitant of
this singular mansion, attended by Evan Dhu as master
of the ceremonies, came forward to meet his guest, totally
different in appearance and manner from what his imagination had anticipated. The profession which he followed
—the wilderness in which he dwelt—the wild warrior
forms that surrounded him, were all calculated to inspire
terror. From such accompaniments, Waverley prepared
himself to meet a stern, gigantic, ferocious figure, such as
Salvator would have chosen to be the central object of a
group of banditti.[1]

Donald Bean Lean was the very reverse of all these.
He was thin in person and low in stature, with light
sandy-coloured hair, and small pale features, from which
he derived his agnomen of *Bean*, or white; and although

his form was light, well-proportioned, and active, he appeared, on the whole, rather a diminutive and insignificant figure. He had served in some inferior capacity in the French army, and in order to receive his English visitor in great form, and probably meaning, in his way, to pay him a compliment, he had laid aside the Highland dress for the time, to put on an old blue and red uniform, and a feathered hat, in which he was far from showing to advantage, and indeed looked so incongruous, compared with all around him, that Waverley would have been tempted to laugh, had laughter been either civil or safe. The robber received Captain Waverley with a profusion of French politeness and Scottish hospitality, seemed perfectly to know his name and connections, and to be particularly acquainted with his uncle's political principles. On these he bestowed great applause, to which Waverley judged it prudent to make a very general reply.

Being placed at a convenient distance from the charcoal fire, the heat of which the season rendered oppressive, a strapping Highland damsel placed before Waverley, Evan, and Donald Bean, three cogues, or wooden vessels composed of staves and hoops, containing *eanaruich*[1] a sort of strong soup, made out of a particular part of the inside of the beeves. After this refreshment, which, though coarse, fatigue and hunger rendered palatable, steaks, roasted on the coals, were supplied in liberal abundance, and disappeared before Evan Dhu and their host with a promptitude that seemed like magic, and astonished Waverley, who was much puzzled to reconcile their voracity with what he had heard of the abstemiousness of the Highlanders. He was ignorant that this abstinence was with the lower ranks wholly compulsory, and that, like some animals of prey, those who practise it were usually gifted with the power of indemnifying themselves to good purpose, when chance threw plenty in their way. The whisky came forth in abundance to crown the cheer. The Highlanders drank it copiously and undiluted; but Edward, having mixed a little with water, did not find it so palatable as to invite him to repeat the draught. Their host bewailed himself exceedingly that he could offer him no wine: "Had he but known four-and-twenty hours before, he would have had some, had it been within the circle of forty miles round him. But no gentleman could do more to show his sense

---

[1] This was the regale presented by Rob Roy to the Laird of Tullibody. (S.)

of the honour of a visit from another, than to offer him
the best cheer his house afforded. Where there are no
bushes there can be no nuts, and the way of those you
live with is that you must follow."

He went on regretting to Evan Dhu the death of an
aged man, Donnacha an Amrigh, or Duncan with the
Cap, "a gifted seer," who foretold, through the second
sight, visitors of every description who haunted their
dwelling, whether as friends or foes.

"Is not his son Malcolm *taishatr* (a second-sighted
person)?" asked Evan.

"Nothing equal to his father," replied Donald Bean.
"He told us the other day we were to see a great gentleman riding on a horse, and there came nobody that whole
day but Shemus Beg, the blind harper, with his dog.
Another time he advertised us of a wedding, and behold
it proved a funeral; and on the creagh, when he foretold
to us we should bring home a hundred head of horned
cattle, we gripped nothing but a fat bailie of Perth."

From this discourse he passed to the political and
military state of the country; and Waverley was astonished, and even alarmed, to find a person of this
description so accurately acquainted with the strength of
the various garrisons and regiments quartered north of
the Tay. He even mentioned the exact number of
recruits who had joined Waverley's troop from his uncle's
estate, and observed they were *pretty men*, meaning, not
handsome, but stout warlike fellows. He put Waverley
in mind of one or two minute circumstances which had
happened at a general review of the regiment, which
satisfied him that the robber had been an eye-witness of
it; and Evan Dhu having by this time retired from the
conversation, and wrapped himself up in his plaid to take
some repose, Donald asked Edward, in a very significant
manner, whether he had nothing particular to say to him.

Waverley, surprised and somewhat startled at this
question from such a character, answered he had no
motive in visiting him but curiosity to see his extraordinary place of residence. Donald Bean Lean looked him
steadily in the face for an instant, and then said, with a
significant nod, "You might as well have confided in me;
I am as much worthy of trust as either the Baron of
Bradwardine, or Vich Ian Vohr:—But you are equally
welcome to my house."

Waverley felt an involuntary shudder creep over him
at the mysterious language held by this outlawed and

lawless bandit, which, in despite of his attempts to master it, deprived him of the power to ask the meaning of his insinuations. A heath pàllet, with the flowers stuck uppermost, had been prepared for him in the recess of the cave, and here, covered with such spare plaids as could be mustered, he lay for some time watching the motions of the other inhabitants of the cavern. Small parties of two or three entered or left the place without any other ceremony than a few words in Gaelic to the principal outlaw, and, when he fell asleep, to a tall Highlander who acted as his lieutenant, and seemed to keep watch during his repose. Those who entered, seemed to have returned from some excursion, of which they reported the success, and went without farther ceremony to the larder, where cutting with their dirks their rations from the carcasses which were there suspended, they proceeded to broil and eat them at their own pleasure and leisure. The liquor was under strict regulation, being served out either by Donald himself, his lieutenant, or the strapping Highland girl aforesaid, who was the only female that appeared. The allowance of whisky, however, would have appeared prodigal to any but Highlanders, who, living entirely in the open air, and in a very moist climate, can consume great quantities of ardent spirits without the usual baneful effects either upon the brain or constitution.

At length the fluctuating groups began to swim before the eyes of our hero as they gradually closed ; nor did he re-open them till the morning sun was high on the lake without, though there was but a faint and glimmering twilight in the recesses of Uaimh an Ri, or the King's Cavern, as the abode of Donald Bean Lean was proudly denominated.

## CHAPTER XVIII.

### *Waverley proceeds on his Journey.*

WHEN Edward had collected his scattered recollection, he was surprised to observe the cavern totally deserted. Having arisen and put his dress in some order, he looked more accurately round him ; but all was still solitary. If it had not been for the decayed brands of the fire, now sunk into grey ashes, and the remnants of the festival,

consisting of bones half burnt and half gnawed, and an
empty keg or two, there remained no traces of Donald
and his band.  When Waverley sallied forth to the entrance of the cave, he perceived that the point of rock, on
which remained the marks of last night's beacon, was
accessible by a small path, either natural, or roughly
hewn in the rock, along the little inlet of water which
ran a few yards up into the cavern, where, as in a wet-
dock, the skiff which brought him there the night before,
was still lying moored.    When he reached the small
projecting platform on which the beacon had been established, he would have believed his farther progress by
land impossible, only that it was scarce probable but
what the inhabitants of the cavern had some mode of
issuing from it otherwise than by the lake.  Accordingly,
he soon observed three or four shelving steps, or ledges
of rock, at the very extremity of the little platform ; and,
making use of them as a staircase, he clambered by their
means around the projecting shoulder of the crag on
which the cavern opened, and, descending with some
difficulty on the other side, he gained the wild and
precipitous shores of a Highland loch, about four miles
in length, and a mile and a half across, surrounded by
heathy and savage mountains, on the crests of which the
morning mist was still sleeping.

Looking back to the place from which he came, he
could not help admiring the address which had adopted a
retreat of such seclusion and secrecy.  The rock, round
the shoulder of which he had turned by a few imperceptible notches, that barely afforded place for the foot,
seemed, in looking back upon it, a huge precipice, which
barred all farther passage by the shores of the lake in
that direction.  There could be no possibility, the breadth
of the lake considered, of descrying the entrance of the
narrow and low-browed cave from the other side ; so that,
unless the retreat had been sought for with boats, or dis-
closed by treachery, it might be a safe and secret residence
to its garrison as long as they were supplied with provisions.  Having satisfied his curiosity in these particulars,
Waverley looked around for Evan Dhu and his attendant,
who, he rightly judged, would be at no great distance,
whatever might have become of Donald Bean Lean and
his party, whose mode of life was, of course, liable to
sudden migrations of abode.  Accordingly, at the distance
of about half a mile, he beheld a Highlander (Evan apparently) angling in the lake, with another attending

him, whom, from the weapon which he shouldered, he recognised for his friend with the battle-axe.

Much nearer to the mouth of the cave he heard the notes of a lively Gaelic song, guided by which, in a sunny recess, shaded by a glittering birch-tree, and carpeted with a bank of firm white sand, he found the damsel of the cavern, whose lay had already reached him, busy, to the best of her power, in arranging to advantage a morning repast of milk, eggs, barley-bread, fresh butter, and honey-comb. The poor girl had already made a circuit of four miles that morning in search of the eggs, of the meal which baked her cakes, and of the other materials of the breakfast, being all delicacies which she had to beg or borrow from distant cottagers. The followers of Donald Bean Lean used little food except the flesh of the animals which they drove away from the Lowlands ; bread itself was a delicacy seldom thought of, because hard to be obtained, and all the domestic accommodations of milk, poultry, butter, &c., were out of the question in this Scythian camp. Yet it must not be omitted, that although Alice had occupied a part of the morning in providing those accommodations for her guest which the cavern did not afford, she had secured time also to arrange her own person in her best trim. Her finery was very simple. A short russet-coloured jacket, and a petticoat, of scanty longitude, was her whole dress ; but these were clean, and neatly arranged. A piece of scarlet embroidered cloth, called the *snood*, confined her hair, which fell over it in a profusion of rich dark curls. The scarlet plaid, which formed part of her dress, was laid aside, that it might not impede her activity in attending the stranger. I should forget Alice's proudest ornament, were I to omit mentioning a pair of gold ear-rings, and a golden rosary, which her father (for she was the daughter of Donald Bean Lean) had brought from France, the plunder, probably, of some battle or storm.

Her form, though rather large for her years, was very well proportioned, and her demeanour had a natural and rustic grace, with nothing of the sheepishness of an ordinary peasant. The smiles, displaying a row of teeth of exquisite whiteness, and the laughing eyes, with which, in dumb show, she gave Waverley that morning greeting which she wanted English words to express, might have been interpreted by a coxcomb, or perhaps by a young soldier, who, without being such, was conscious of a handsome person, as meant to convey more than the courtesy

of an hostess. Nor do I take it upon me to say, that the
little wild mountaineer would have welcomed any staid
old gentleman advanced in life, the Baron of Bradwardine,
for example, with the cheerful pains which she bestowed
upon Edward's accommodation. She seemed eager to
place him by the meal which she had so sedulously
arranged, and to which she now added a few bunches of
cran-berries, gathered in an adjacent morass. Having
had the satisfaction of seeing him seated at his breakfast,
she placed herself demurely upon a stone at a few yards'
distance, and appeared to watch with great complacency
for some opportunity of serving him.

Evan and his attendant now returned slowly along the
beach, the latter bearing a large salmon-trout, the produce
of the morning's sport, together with the angling-rod,
while Evan strolled forward, with an easy, self-satisfied,
and important gait, towards the spot where Waverley was
so agreeably employed at the breakfast-table. After
morning greetings had passed on both sides, and Evan,
looking at Waverley, had said something in Gaelic to
Alice, which made her laugh, yet colour up to her eyes,
through a complexion well embrowned by sun and wind,
Evan intimated his commands that the fish should be prepared for breakfast. A spark from the lock of his pistol
produced a light, and a few withered fir branches were
quickly in flame, and as speedily reduced to hot embers,
on which the trout was broiled in large slices. To crown
the repast, Evan produced from the pocket of his short
jerkin, a large scallop shell, and from under the folds of
his plaid, a ram's horn full of whisky. Of this he took a
copious dram, observing, he had already taken his *morning*
with Donald Bean Lean, before his departure ; he offered
the same cordial to Alice and to Edward, which they both
declined. With the bounteous air of a lord, Evan then
proffered the scallop to Dugald Mahony, his attendant,
who, without waiting to be asked a second time, drank it
off with great gusto. Evan then prepared to move
towards the boat, inviting Waverley to attend him.
Meanwhile Alice had made up in a small basket what she
thought worth removing, and flinging her plaid around
her, she advanced up to Edward, and with the utmost
simplicity, taking hold of his hand, offered her cheek to
his salute, dropping, at the same time, her little courtesy.
Evan, who was esteemed a wag among the mountain fair,
advanced, as if to secure a similar favour ; but Alice,
snatching up her basket, escaped up the rocky bank as

fleetly as a roe, and, turning round and laughing, called
something out to him in Gaelic, which he answered in the
same tone and language ; then, waving her hand to
Edward, she resumed her road, and was soon lost among
the thickets, though they continued for some time to hear
her lively carol, as she proceeded gaily on her solitary
journey.

They now again entered the gorge of the cavern, and
stepping into the boat, the Highlander pushed off, and,
taking advantage of the morning breeze, hoisted a clumsy
sort of sail, while Evan assumed the helm, directing their
course, as it appeared to Waverley, rather higher up the
lake than towards the place of his embarkation on the
preceding night. As they glided along the silver mirror,
Evan opened the conversation with a panegyric upon
Alice, who, he said, was both *canny* and *fendy ;* [1] and
was, to the boot of all that, the best dancer of a strathspey in the whole strath. Edward assented to her praises
so far as he understood them, yet could not help regretting
that she was condemned to such a perilous and dismal
life.

"Oich! for that," said Evan, "there is nothing in
Perthshire that she need want, if she ask her father to
fetch it, unless it be too hot or too heavy."

"But to be the daughter of a cattle-stealer—a common
thief!"

"Common thief!—No such thing : Donald Bean Lean
never *lifted* [2] less than a drove in his life."

"Do you call him an uncommon thief, then ?"

"No—he that steals a cow from a poor widow, or a
stirk from a cottar, is a thief ; he that lifts a drove from
a Sassenach laird, is a gentleman-drover. And, besides,
to take a tree from the forest, a salmon from the river, a
deer from the hill, or a cow from a Lowland strath, is
what no Highlander need ever think shame upon."

"But what can this end in, were he taken in such an
appropriation ?"

"To be sure he would *die for the law*, as many a pretty
man has done before him."

"Die for the law !"

"Ay ; that is, with the law, or by the law ; be strapped
up on the *kind* gallows of Crieff, [3] where his father died,
and his goodsire died, and where I hope he'll live to die
himsell, if he's not shot, or slashed, in a creagh." [4]

---

[1] Prudent and handy.     [2] Carried off cattle by theft.     [3] Note 7.   Kind
Gallows of Crieff.     [4] Expedition for plunder.

"You *hope* such a death for your friend, Evan?"

"And that do I e'en; would you have me wish him to die on a bundle of wet straw in yon den of his, like a mangy tyke?"[1]

"But what becomes of Alice, then?"

"Troth, if such an accident were to happen, as her father would not need her help ony langer, I ken nought to hinder me to marry her mysell."

"Gallantly resolved," said Edward;—"but, in the meanwhile, Evan, what has your father-in-law (that shall be, if he have the good fortune to be hanged) done with the Baron's cattle?"

"Oich," answered Evan, "they were all trudging before your lad and Allan Kennedy before the sun blinked ower Ben-Lawers this morning; and they'll be in the pass of Bally-Brough by this time, in their way back to the parks of Tully-Veolan, all but two, that were unhappily slaughtered before I got last night to Uaimh an Ri."

"And where are we going, Evan, if I may be so bold as to ask?" said Waverley.

"Where would you be ganging, but to the laird's ain house of Glennaquoich? Ye would not think to be in his country, without ganging to see him? It would be as much as a man's life's worth."

"And are we far from Glennaquoich?"

"But five bits of miles; and Vich Ian Vohr will meet us."

In about half an hour they reached the upper end of the lake, where, after landing Waverley, the two Highlanders drew the boat into a little creek among thick flags and reeds, where it lay perfectly concealed. The oars they put in another place of concealment, both for the use of Donald Bean Lean probably, when his occasions should next bring him to that place.

The travellers followed for some time a delightful opening into the hills, down which a little brook found its way to the lake. When they had pursued their walk a short distance, Waverley renewed his questions about their host of the cavern.

"Does he always reside in that cave?"

"Out, no! it's past the skill of man to tell where he's to be found at a' times; there's not a dern[2] nook, or cove, or corri, in the whole country, that he's not acquainted with."

"And do others beside your master shelter him?"

_____
[1] Dog.    [2] Hidden.

"My master?—*My* master is in Heaven," answered Evan, haughtily; and then immediately assuming his usual civility of manner, "but you mean my Chief;—no, he does not shelter Donald Bean Lean, nor any that are like him; he only allows him (with a smile) wood and water."

"No great boon, I should think, Evan, when both seem to be very plenty."

"Ah! but ye dinna see through it. When I say wood and water, I mean the loch and the land; and I fancy Donald would be put till't if the laird were to look for him wi' threescore men in the wood of Kailychat yonder; and if our boats, with a score of twa mair, were to come down the loch to Uaimh an Ri, headed by mysell, or ony other pretty man."

"But suppose a strong party came against him from the Low Country, would not your Chief defend him?"

"Na, he would not ware the spark of a flint for him—if they came with the law."

"And what must Donald do, then?"

"He behoved to rid this country of himsell, and fall back, it may be, over the mount upon Letter Scriven."

"And if he were pursued to that place?"

"I'se warrant he would go to his cousin's at Rannoch."

"Well, but if they followed him to Rannoch?"

"That," quoth Evan, "is beyond all belief; and, indeed, to tell you the truth, there durst not a Lowlander in all Scotland follow the fray a gun-shot beyond Bally-Brough, unless he had the help of the *Sidier Dhu*."

"Whom do you call so?"

"The *Sidier Dhu?* the black soldier; that is what they call the independent companies that were raised to keep peace and law in the Highlands. Vich Ian Vohr commanded one of them for five years, and I was sergeant myself, I shall warrant ye. They call them *Sidier Dhu*, because they wear the tartans, as they call your men—King George's men,—*Sidier Roy*, or red soldiers."

"Well, but when you were in King George's pay, Evan, you were surely King George's soldiers?"

"Troth, and you must ask Vich Ian Vohr about that; for we are for his king, and care not much which o' them it is. At ony rate, nobody can say we are King George's men now, when we have not seen his pay this twelve-month."

This last argument admitted of no reply, nor did Edward attempt any: he rather chose to bring back the discourse to Donald Bean Lean. "Does Donald confine himself to cattle, or does he *lift*, as you call it, anything else that comes in his way?"

"Troth, he's nae nice body, and he'll just tak ony thing, but most readily cattle, horse, or live Christians; for sheep are slow of travel, and inside plenishing is cumbrous to carry, and not easy to put away for siller in this country."

"But does he carry off men and women?"

"Out, ay. Did not ye hear him speak o' the Perth bailie? It cost that body five hundred merks ere he got to the south of Bally-Brough.—And ance Donald played a pretty sport.[1] There was to be a blythe bridal between the Lady Cramfeezer, in the howe o' the Mearns, (she was the auld laird's widow, and no sae young as she had been hersell,) and young Gilliewhackit, who had spent his heirship and moveables, like a gentleman, at cock-matches, bull-baitings, horse-races, and the like. Now, Donald Bean Lean, being aware that the bridegroom was in request, and wanting to cleik the cunzie (that is, to hook the siller,) he cannily carried off Gilliewhackit ae night when he was riding *dovering*[2] hame, (wi' the malt rather abune the meal,) and with the help of his gillies he gat him into the hills with the speed of light, and the first place he wakened in was the cove of Uaimh an Ri. So there was old to do about ransoming the bridegroom; for Donald would not lower a farthing of a thousand punds."——

"The Devil!"

"Punds Scottish, ye shall understand. And the lady had not the siller if she had pawned her gown; and they applied to the governor o' Stirling castle, and to the major o' the Black Watch; and the governor said, it was ower far to the northward, and out of his district; and the major said, his men were gane hame[3] to the shearing, and he would not call them out before the victual was got in for all the Cramfeezers in Christendom, let alane the Mearns, for that it would prejudice the country. And in the meanwhile ye'll no hinder Gilliewhackit to take the small-pox. There was not the doctor in Perth or Stirling would look near the poor lad; and I cannot blame them, for Donald had been misguggled[4] by ane of these doctors about Paris, and he swore he would fling the first into the loch that he catched beyond the Pass. However, some cailliachs, (that is, old women,) that were about Donald's hand, nursed Gilliewhackit sae weel, that between the free open air in the cove and the fresh whey, deil an he did not recover may be as weel as if he had been closed in a glazed chamber and a bed with curtains, and fed with red wine and white meat. And Donald was sae vexed about it, that when he was stout and weel, he even sent him free home, and said he would be pleased with ony thing they would like to gie him for the plague and trouble which he had about Gilliewhackit to an unkenn'd[1] degree. And I cannot tell you precisely how they sorted; but they agreed sae right that Donald was invited to dance at the wedding in his Highland trews, and they said that there was never sae meikle siller clinked in his purse either before or since. And to the boot of all that, Gilliewhackit said, that, be the evidence what it liked, if he had the luck to be on Donald's inquest, he would bring him in guilty of nothing whatever, unless it were wilful arson, or murder under trust."

With such bold and disjointed chat Evan went on illustrating the existing state of the Highlands, more perhaps to the amusement of Waverley than that of our readers. At length, after having marched over bank and brae, moss and heather, Edward, though not unacquainted with the Scottish liberality in computing distance, began to think that Evan's five miles were nearly doubled. His observation on the large measure which the Scottish allowed of their land, in comparison to the computation of their money, was readily answered by Evan, with the old jest, "The deil take them wha have the least pint stoup."[2]

And now the report of a gun was heard, and a sportsman was seen, with his dogs, and attendant, at the upper end of the glen. "Shough," said Dugald Mahony, "tat's ta Chief."

"It is not," said Evan, imperiously. "Do you think he would come to meet a Sassenach Duinhé-wassel in such a way as that?"

But as they approached a little nearer, he said, with an appearance of mortification, "And it is even he, sure enough; and he has not his tail on after all;—there is no living creature with him but Callum Beg."

In fact, Fergus Mac-Ivor, of whom a Frenchman might

[1] Unknown.
[2] The Scotch are liberal in computing their land and liquor the Scottish pint corresponds to two English quarts. As for their coin, every one knows the couplet—

How can the rogues pretend to sense ?—
Their pound is only twenty pence. (S.)

have said, as truly as of any man in the Highlands, *"Qu'il connait bien ses gens,"* had no idea of raising himself in the eyes of an English young man of fortune, by appearing with a retinue of idle Highlanders, disproportioned to the occasion. He was well aware that such an unnecessary attendance would seem to Edward rather ludicrous than respectable; and while few men were more attached to ideas of chieftainship and feudal power, he was, for that very reason, cautious of exhibiting external marks of dignity, unless at the time and in the manner when they were most likely to produce an imposing effect. Therefore, although, had he been to receive a brother chieftain, he would probably have been attended by all that retinue which Evan described with so much unction, he judged it more respectable to advance to meet Waverley with a single attendant, a very handsome Highland boy, who carried his master's shooting-pouch and his broadsword, without which he seldom went abroad.

When Fergus and Waverley met, the latter was struck with the peculiar grace and dignity of the Chieftain's figure. Above the middle size, and finely proportioned, the Highland dress, which he wore in its simplest mode, set off his person to great advantage. He wore the trews, or close trousers, made of tartan, chequed scarlet and white; in other particulars, his dress strictly resembled Evan's, excepting that he had no weapon save a dirk, very richly mounted with silver. His page, as we have said, carried his claymore; and the fowling-piece which he held in his hand, seemed only designed for sport. He had shot in the course of his walk some young wild-ducks, as, though *close-time* was then unknown, the broods of grouse were yet too young for the sportsman. His countenance was decidedly Scottish, with all the peculiarities of the northern physiognomy, but yet had so little of its harshness and exaggeration, that it would have been pronounced in any country extremely handsome. The martial air of the bonnet, with a single eagle's feather as a distinction, added much to the manly appearance of his head, which was besides ornamented with a far more natural and graceful cluster of close black curls than ever were exposed to sale in Bond-Street.

An air of openness and affability increased the favourable impression derived from this handsome and dignified exterior. Yet a skilful physiognomist would have been less satisfied with the countenance on the second than on the first view. The eye-brow and upper lip bespoke something of the habit of peremptory command and decisive superiority. Even his courtesy, though open, frank, and unconstrained, seemed to indicate a sense of personal importance; and, upon any check or accidental excitation, a sudden, though transient lour of the eye, showed a hasty, haughty, and vindictive temper, not less to be dreaded because it seemed much under its owner's command. In short, the countenance of the Chieftain resembled a smiling summer's day, in which, notwithstanding, we are made sensible by certain, though slight signs, that it may thunder and lighten before the close of evening.

It was not, however, upon their first meeting that Edward had an opportunity of making these less favourable remarks. The Chief received him as a friend of the Baron of Bradwardine, with the utmost expression of kindness and obligation for the visit; upbraided him gently with choosing so rude an abode as he had done the night before; and entered into a lively conversation with him about Donald Bean's housekeeping, but without the least hint as to his predatory habits, or the immediate occasion of Waverley's visit, a topic which, as the Chief did not introduce it, our hero also avoided. While they walked merrily on towards the house of Glennaquoich, Evan, who now fell respectfully into the rear, followed with Callum Beg and Dugald Mahony.

We shall take the opportunity to introduce the reader to some particulars of Fergus Mac-Ivor's character and history, which were not completely known to Waverley till after a connection, which, though arising from a circumstance so casual, had for a length of time the deepest influence upon his character, actions, and prospects. But this, being an important subject, must form the commencement of a new chapter.

## CHAPTER XIX.

### The Chief and his Mansion.

THE ingenious licentiate Francisco de Ubeda, when he commenced his history of La Picara Justina Diez,—which, by the way, is one of the most rare books of Spanish literature,—complained of his pen having caught up a hair, and forthwith begins, with more eloquence than

common sense, an affectionate expostulation with that
useful implement, upbraiding it with being the quill of a
goose,—a bird inconstant by nature, as frequenting the
three elements of water, earth, and air, indifferently, and
being, of course, "to one thing constant never." Now I
protest to thee, gentle reader, that I entirely dissent from
Francisco de Ubeda in this matter, and hold it the most
useful quality of my pen, that it can speedily change
from grave to gay, and from description and dialogue to
narrative and character. So that if my quill display no
other properties of its mother-goose than her mutability,
truly I shall be well pleased ; and I conceive that you, my
worthy friend, will have no occasion for discontent.
From the jargon, therefore, of the Highland gillies, I pass
to the character of their Chief. It is an important
examination, and therefore, like Dogberry, we must spare
no wisdom.

The ancestor of Fergus Mac-Ivor, about three centuries
before, had set up a claim to be recognised as chief of the
numerous and powerful clan to which he belonged, the
name of which it is unnecessary to mention. Being
defeated by an opponent who had more justice, or at
least more force, on his side, he moved southwards, with
those who adhered to him, in quest of new settlements,
like a second Æneas. The state of the Perthshire Highlands favoured his purpose. A great baron in that
country had lately become traitor to the crown ; Ian,
which was the name of our adventurer, united himself
with those who were commissioned by the king to
chastise him, and did such good service, that he obtained
a grant of the property, upon which he and his posterity
afterwards resided. He followed the king also in war
to the fertile regions of England, where he employed his
leisure hours so actively in raising subsidies among the
boors of Northumberland and Durham, that upon his
return he was enabled to erect a stone tower, or fortalice,
so much admired by his dependents and neighbours, that
he, who had hitherto been called Ian Mac-Ivor, or John
the son of Ivor, was thereafter distinguished, both in
song and genealogy, by the high title of *Ian nan Chaistel*,
or John of the Tower. The descendants of this worthy
were so proud of him, that the reigning chief always
bore the patronymic title of Vich Ian Vohr, *i.e.* the son of
John the Great ; while the clan at large, to distinguish
them from that from which they had seceded, were
denominated *Sliochd nan Ivor*, the race of Ivor.

The father of Fergus, the tenth in direct descent from John of the Tower, engaged heart and hand in the insurrection of 1715, and was forced to fly to France, after the attempt of that year in favour of the Stewarts had proved unsuccessful. More fortunate than other fugitives, he obtained employment in the French service, and married a lady of rank in that kingdom, by whom he had two children, Fergus and his sister Flora. The Scottish estate had been forfeited and exposed to sale, but was repurchased for a small price in the name of the young proprietor, who in consequence came to reside upon his native domains.[1]  It was soon perceived that he possessed a character of uncommon acuteness, fire, and ambition, which, as he became acquainted with the state of the country, gradually assumed a mixed and peculiar tone, that could only have been acquired Sixty Years since.

Had Fergus Mac-Ivor lived Sixty Years sooner than he did, he would, in all probability, have wanted the polished manner and knowledge of the world which he now possessed ; and had he lived Sixty Years later, his ambition and love of rule would have lacked the fuel which his situation now afforded.  He was indeed, within his little circle, as perfect a politician as Castruccio Castrucani himself.  He applied himself with great earnestness to appease all the feuds and dissensions which often arose among other clans in his neighbourhood, so that he became a frequent umpire in their quarrels.  His own patriarchal power he strengthened at every expense which his fortune would permit, and indeed stretched his means to the uttermost to maintain the rude and plentiful hospitality, which was the most valued attribute of a chieftain.  For the same reason, he crowded his estate with a tenantry, hardy indeed, and fit for the purposes of war, but greatly outnumbering what the soil was calculated to maintain.  These consisted chiefly of his own clan, not one of whom he suffered to quit his lands if he could possibly prevent it.  But he maintained, besides, many adventurers from the mother sept, who

[1] This happened on many occasions.  Indeed, it was not till after the total destruction of the clan influence, after 1745, that purchasers could be found, who offered a fair price for the estates forfeited in 1715, which were then brought to sale by the creditors of the York Buildings Company, who had purchased the whole or greater part from government at a very small price.  Even so late as the period first mentioned, the prejudices of the public in favour of the heirs of the forfeited families threw various impediments in the way of intending purchasers of such property.  (S.)

deserted a less warlike, though more wealthy chief, to do homage to Fergus Mac-Ivor. Other individuals, too, who had not even that apology, were nevertheless received into his allegiance, which indeed was refused to none who were, like Poins, proper men of their hands, and were willing to assume the name of Mac-Ivor.

He was enabled to discipline these forces, from having obtained command of one of the independent companies, raised by government to preserve the peace of the Highlands. While in this capacity he acted with vigour and spirit, and preserved great order in the country under his charge. He caused his vassals to enter by rotation into his company, and serve for a certain space of time, which gave them all in turn a general notion of military discipline. In his campaigns against the banditti, it was observed that he assumed and exercised to the utmost the discretionary power, which, while the law had no free course in the Highlands, was conceived to belong to the military parties who were called in to support it. He acted, for example, with great and suspicious lenity to those freebooters who made restitution on his summons, and offered personal submission to himself, while he rigorously pursued, apprehended, and sacrificed to justice, all such interlopers as dared to despise his admonitions or commands. On the other hand, if any officers of justice, military parties, or others, presumed to pursue thieves or marauders through his territories, and without applying for his consent and concurrence, nothing was more certain than that they would meet with some notable foil or defeat; upon which occasions Fergus Mac-Ivor was the first to condole with them, and, after gently blaming their rashness, never failed deeply to lament the lawless state of the country. These lamentations did not exclude suspicion, and matters were so represented to government, that our Chieftain was deprived of his military command.[1]

Whatever Fergus Mac-Ivor felt on this occasion, he had the art of entirely suppressing every appearance of discontent; but in a short time the neighbouring country began to feel bad effects from his disgrace. Donald Bean Lean, and others of his class, whose depredations had hitherto been confined to other districts, appeared from thenceforward to have made a settlement on this devoted

---

[1] Note 9. Highland Policy.

border; and their ravages were carried on with little opposition, as the Lowland gentry were chiefly Jacobites, and disarmed. This forced many of the inhabitants into contracts of black-mail with Fergus Mac-Ivor, which not only established him their protector, and gave him great weight in all their consultations, but, moreover, supplied funds for the waste of his feudal hospitality, which the discontinuance of his pay might have otherwise essentially diminished.

In following this course of conduct, Fergus had a further object than merely being the great man of his neighbourhood, and ruling despotically over a small clan. From his infancy upward, he had devoted himself to the cause of the exiled family, and had persuaded himself, not only that their restoration to the crown of Britain would be speedy, but that those who assisted them would be raised to honour and rank. It was with this view that he laboured to reconcile the Highlanders among themselves, and augmented his own force to the utmost, to be prepared for the first favourable opportunity of rising. With this purpose also he conciliated the favour of such Lowland gentlemen in the vicinity as were friends to the good cause; and for the same reason, having incautiously quarrelled with Mr Bradwardine, who, notwithstanding his peculiarities, was much respected in the country, he took advantage of the foray of Donald Bean Lean to solder up the dispute in the manner we have mentioned. Some, indeed, surmised that he caused the enterprise to be suggested to Donald, on purpose to pave the way to a reconciliation, which, supposing that to be the case, cost the Laird of Bradwardine two good milch cows. This zeal in their behalf the House of Stewart repaid with a considerable share of their confidence, an occasional supply of louis d'or, abundance of fair words, and a parchment, with a huge waxen seal appended, purporting to be an earl's patent, granted by no less a person than James the Third King of England, and Eighth King of Scotland, to his right feal, trusty, and well-beloved Fergus Mac-Ivor of Glennaquoich, in the county of Perth, and kingdom of Scotland.

With this future coronet glittering before his eyes, Fergus plunged deeply into the correspondence and plots of that unhappy period; and, like all such active agents, easily reconciled his conscience to going certain lengths in the service of his party, from which honour and pride would have deterred him, had his sole object been the

direct advancement of his own personal interest. With
this insight into a bold, ambitious, and ardent, yet artful and politic character, we resume the broken thread of
our narrative.

The Chief and his guest had by this time reached the
house of Glennaquoich, which consisted of Ian nan
Chaistel's mansion, a high rude-looking square tower,
with the addition of a *lofted* house, that is, a building of
two stories, constructed by Fergus's grandfather when he
returned from that memorable expedition, well remembered by the western shires, under the name of the
Highland Host. Upon occasion of this crusade against
the Ayrshire Whigs and Covenanters, the Vich Ian Vohr
of the time had probably been as successful as his predecessor was in harrying Northumberland, and therefore left to his posterity a rival edifice, as a monument of
his magnificence.

Around the house, which stood on an eminence in the
midst of a narrow Highland valley, there appeared none
of that attention to convenience, far less to ornament and
decoration, which usually surrounds a gentleman's habitation. An inclosure or two, divided by dry-stone walls,
were the only part of the domain that was fenced ; as to
the rest, the narrow slips of level ground which lay by
the side of the brook exhibited a scanty crop of barley,
liable to constant depredations from the herds of wild
ponies and black cattle that grazed upon the adjacent
hills. These ever and anon made an incursion upon the
arable ground, which was repelled by the loud, uncouth,
and dissonant shouts of half a dozen Highland swains, all
running as if they had been mad, and every one hallooing
a half-starved dog to the rescue of the forage. At a little
distance up the glen was a small and stunted wood of
birch ; the hills were high and heathy, but without any
variety of surface ; so that the whole view was wild and
desolate, rather than grand and solitary. Yet, such as it
was, no genuine descendant of Ian nan Chaistel would
have changed the domain for Stow or Blenheim.

There was a sight, however, before the gate, which perhaps would have afforded the first owner of Blenheim
more pleasure than the finest view in the domain assigned
to him by the gratitude of his country. This consisted of
about a hundred Highlanders, in complete dress and
arms ; at sight of whom the Chieftain apologised to Waverley in a sort of negligent manner. "He had forgot," he
said, "that he had ordered a few of his clan out, for the

purpose of seeing that they were in a fit condition to protect the country, and prevent such accidents as, he was sorry to learn, had befallen the Baron of Bradwardine. Before they were dismissed, perhaps Captain Waverley might choose to see them go through a part of their exercise."

Edward assented, and the men executed with agility and precision some of the ordinary military movements. They then practised individually at a mark, and showed extraordinary dexterity in the management of the pistol and firelock. They took aim, standing, sitting, leaning, or lying prostrate, as they were commanded, and always with effect upon the target. Next, they paired off for the broadsword exercise; and, having manifested their individual skill and dexterity, united in two bodies, and exhibited a sort of mock encounter, in which the charge, the rally, the flight, the pursuit, and all the current of a heady fight, were exhibited to the sound of the great war bagpipe.

On a signal made by the Chief, the skirmish was ended. Matches were then made for running, wrestling, leaping, pitching the bar, and other sports, in which this feudal militia displayed incredible swiftness, strength, and agility; and accomplished the purpose which their Chieftain had at heart, by impressing on Waverley no light sense of their merit as soldiers, and of the power of him who commanded them by his nod.[1]

"And what number of such gallant fellows have the happiness to call you leader?" asked Waverley.

"In a good cause, and under a chieftain whom they loved, the race of Ivor have seldom taken the field under five hundred claymores. But you are aware, Captain Waverley, that the disarming act, passed about twenty years ago, prevents their being in the complete state of preparation as in former times; and I keep no more of my clan under arms than may defend my own or my friend's property, when the country is troubled with such men as your last night's landlord; and government, which has removed other means of defence, must connive at our protecting ourselves."

"But, with your force, you might soon destroy, or put down, such gangs as that of Donald Bean Lean."

"Yes, doubtless; and my reward would be a summons to deliver up to General Blakeney, at Stirling, the few broadswords they have left us: there were little policy

in that methinks.—But come, captain, the sound of the
pipes informs me that dinner is prepared—Let me have
the honour to show you into my rude mansion."


## CHAPTER XX.

### A Highland Feast.

ERE Waverley entered the banqueting hall, he was
offered the patriarchal refreshment of a bath for the feet,
which the sultry weather, and the morasses he had
traversed, rendered highly acceptable.   He was not,
indeed, so luxuriously attended upon this occasion as the
heroic travellers in the Odyssey ; the task of ablution and
abstersion being performed, not by a beautiful damsel,
trained

To chafe the limb, and pour the fragrant oil,

but by a smoke-dried skinny old Highland woman, who
did not seem to think herself much honoured by the duty
imposed upon her, but muttered between her teeth, "Our
father's herds did not feed so near together, that I should
do you this service."   A small donation, however, amply
reconciled this ancient handmaiden to the supposed
degradation ; and, as Edward proceeded to the hall, she
gave him her blessing, in the Gaelic proverb, "May the
open hand be filled the fullest."
   The hall, in which the feast was prepared, occupied all
the first story of Ian nan Chaistel's original erection, and
a huge oaken table extended through its whole length.
The apparatus for dinner was simple, even to rudeness,
and the company numerous, even to crowding.   At the
head of the table was the Chief himself, with Edward, and
two or three Highland visitors of neighbouring clans ;
the elders of his own tribe, wadsetters and tacksmen, as
they were called, who occupied portions of his estate as
mortgagers or lessees, sat next in rank ;  beneath them,
their sons and nephews, and foster-brethren ;  then the
officers of the Chief's household, according to their order ;
and, lowest of all, the tenants who actually cultivated the
ground.   Even beyond this long perspective, Edward
might see upon the green, to which a huge pair of folding
doors opened, a multitude of Highlanders of a yet inferior
description, who, nevertheless, were considered as guests,

and had their share both of the countenance of the entertainer, and of the cheer of the day. In the distance, and fluctuating round this extreme verge of the banquet, was a changeful group of women, ragged boys and girls, beggars, young and old, large greyhounds, and terriers, and pointers, and curs of low degree; all of whom took some interest, more or less immediate, in the main action of the piece.

This hospitality, apparently unbounded, had yet its line of economy. Some pains had been bestowed in dressing the dishes of fish, game, &c., which were at the upper end of the table, and immediately under the eye of the English stranger. Lower down stood immense clumsy joints of mutton and beef, which, but for the absence of pork,[1] abhorred in the Highlands, resembled the rude festivity of the banquet of Penelope's suitors. But the central dish was a yearling lamb, called "a hog in har'st," roasted whole. It was set upon its legs, with a bunch of parsley in its mouth, and was probably exhibited in that form to gratify the pride of the cook, who piqued himself more on the plenty than the elegance of his master's table. The sides of this poor animal were fiercely attacked by the clansmen, some with dirks, others with the knives which were usually in the same sheath with the dagger, so that it was soon rendered a mangled and rueful spectacle. Lower down still, the victuals seemed of yet coarser quality, though sufficiently abundant. Broth, onions, cheese, and the fragments of the feast, regaled the sons of Ivor who feasted in the open air.

The liquor was supplied in the same proportion, and under similar regulations. Excellent claret and champagne were liberally distributed among the Chief's immediate neighbours; whisky, plain or diluted, and strong-beer, refreshed those who sat near the lower end. Nor did this inequality of distribution appear to give the least offence. Every one present understood that his taste was to be formed according to the rank which he held at table; and, consequently, the tacksmen and their dependents always professed the wine was too cold for their stomachs, and called, apparently out of choice, for the liquor which was assigned to them from economy.[2] The bagpipers, three in number, screamed, during the whole time of dinner, a tremendous war-tune; and the echoing of the vaulted roof, and clang of the Celtic

---

[1] Note 11. Dislike of the Scotch to Pork.
[2] Note 12. A Scottish Dinner Table.

tongue, produced such a Babel of noises, that Waverley
dreaded his ears would never recover it. Mac-Ivor,
indeed, apologized for the confusion occasioned by so
large a party, and pleaded the necessity of his situation,
on which unlimited hospitality was imposed as a para-
mount duty. "These stout idle kinsmen of mine," he
said, "account my estate as held in trust for their
support; and I must find them beef and ale, while the
rogues will do nothing for themselves but practise the
broadsword, or wander about the hills, shooting, fishing,
hunting, drinking, and making love to the lasses of the
strath. But what can I do, Captain Waverley? every
thing will keep after its kind, whether it be a hawk or a
Highlander." Edward made the expected answer, in a
compliment upon his possessing so many bold and
attached followers.

"Why, yes," replied the Chief, "were I disposed, like
my father, to put myself in the way of getting one blow
on the head, or two on the neck, I believe the loons would
stand by me. But who thinks of that in the present day,
when the maxim is,—'Better an old woman with a purse
in her hand, than three men with belted brands?'"
Then, turning to the company, he proposed the "Health
of Captain Waverley, a worthy friend of his kind neighbour and ally, the Baron of Bradwardine."

"He is welcome hither," said one of the elders, "if he
come from Cosmo Comyne Bradwardine."

"I say nay to that," said an old man, who apparently
did not mean to pledge the toast; "I say nay to that;—
while there is a green leaf in the forest, there will be
fraud in a Comyne."

"There is nothing but honour in the Baron of Bradwardine," answered another ancient; "and the guest
that comes hither from him should be welcome, though he
came with blood on his hand, unless it were blood of the
race of Ivor."

The old man, whose cup remained full, replied, "There
has been blood enough of the race of Ivor on the hand of
Bradwardine."

"Ah! Ballenkeiroch," replied the first, "you think
rather of the flash of the carbine at the Mains of Tully-
Veolan, than the glance of the sword that fought for the
cause at Preston."

"And well I may," answered Ballenkeiroch; "the flash
of the gun cost me a fair-haired son, and the glance of the
sword has done but little for King James."

The Chieftain, in two words of French, explained to Waverley, that the Baron had shot this old man's son in a fray near Tully-Veolan about seven years before; and then hastened to remove Ballenkeiroch's prejudice, by informing him that Waverley was an Englishman, unconnected by birth or alliance with the family of Bradwardine; upon which the old gentleman raised the hitherto-untasted cup, and courteously drank to his health. This ceremony being requited in kind, the Chieftain made a signal for the pipes to cease, and said, aloud, "Where is the song hidden, my friends, that Mac-Murrough cannot find it?"

Mac-Murrough, the family *bhairdh*, an aged man, immediately took the hint, and began to chant, with low and rapid utterance, a profusion of Celtic verses, which were received by the audience with all the applause of enthusiasm. As he advanced in his declamation, his ardour seemed to increase. He had at first spoken with his eyes fixed on the ground; he now cast them around as if beseeching, and anon as if commanding, attention, and his tones rose into wild and impassioned notes, accompanied with appropriate gestures. He seemed to Edward, who attended to him with much interest, to recite many proper names, to lament the dead, to apostrophize the absent, to exhort, and entreat, and animate those who were present. Waverley thought he even discerned his own name, and was convinced his conjecture was right, from the eyes of the company being at that moment turned towards him simultaneously. The ardour of the poet appeared to communicate itself to the audience. Their wild and sun-burnt countenances assumed a fiercer and more animated expression; all bent forward towards the reciter, many sprung up and waved their arms in ecstasy, and some laid their hands on their swords. When the song ceased, there was a deep pause, while the aroused feelings of the poet and of the hearers gradually subsided into their usual channel.

The Chieftain, who, during this scene, had appeared rather to watch the emotions which were excited, than to partake their high tone of enthusiasm, filled with claret a small silver cup which stood by him. "Give this," he said to an attendant, "to Mac-Murrough nan Fonn, (*i. e.* of the songs,) and when he has drank the juice, bid him keep, for the sake of Vich Ian Vohr, the shell of the gourd which contained it." The gift was received by Mac-Murrough with profound gratitude; he drank the

wine, and, kissing the cup, shrouded it with reverence in
the plaid which was folded on his bosom. He then burst
forth into what Edward justly supposed to be an extemporaneous effusion of thanks, and praises of his Chief.
It was received with applause, but did not produce the
effect of his first poem. It was obvious, however, that the
clan regarded the generosity of their Chieftain with high
approbation. Many approved Gaelic toasts were then
proposed, of some of which the Chieftain gave his guest
the following versions :—

"To him that will not turn his back on friend or foe."
"To him that never forsook a comrade." "To him that
never bought or sold justice." "Hospitality to the exile,
and broken bones to the tyrant." "The lads with the
kilts." "Highlanders, shoulder to shoulder,"—with many
other pithy sentiments of the like nature.

Edward was particularly solicitous to know the meaning of that song which appeared to produce such effect
upon the passions of the company, and hinted his curiosity
to his host. "As I observe," said the Chieftain, "that you
have passed the bottle during the last three rounds, I was
about to propose to you to retire to my sister's tea-table,
who can explain these things to you better than I can.
Although I cannot stint my clan in the usual current of
their festivity, yet I neither am addicted myself to exceed
in its amount, nor do I," added he, smiling, "keep a Bear
to devour the intellects of such as can make good use of
them."

Edward readily assented to this proposal, and the
Chieftain, saying a few words to those around him, left
the table, followed by Waverley. As the door closed
behind them, Edward heard Vich Ian Vohr's health invoked with a wild and animated cheer, that expressed the
satisfaction of the guests, and the depth of their devotion
to his service.

## CHAPTER XXI.

### The Chieftain's Sister.

THE drawing-room of Flora Mac-Ivor was furnished in
the plainest and most simple manner; for at Glennaquoich every other sort of expenditure was retrenched as
much as possible, for the purpose of maintaining, in its
full dignity, the hospitality of the Chieftain, and retain-

ing and multiplying the number of his dependents and adherents. But there was no appearance of this parsimony in the dress of the lady herself, which was in texture elegant, and even rich, and arranged in a manner which partook partly of the Parisian fashion, and partly of the more simple dress of the Highlands, blended together with great taste. Her hair was not disfigured by the art of the friseur, but fell in jetty ringlets on her neck, confined only by a circlet, richly set with diamonds. This peculiarity she adopted in compliance with the Highland prejudices, which could not endure that a woman's head should be covered before wedlock.

Flora Mac-Ivor bore a most striking resemblance to her brother Fergus; so much so, that they might have played Viola and Sebastian with the same exquisite effect produced by the appearance of Mrs Henry Siddons and her brother, Mr William Murray, in these characters. They had the same antique and regular correctness of profile; the [same dark eyes, eye-lashes, and eye-brows; the same clearness of complexion, excepting that Fergus's was embrowned by exercise, and Flora's possessed the utmost feminine delicacy. But the haughty, and somewhat stern regularity of Fergus's features, was beautifully softened in those of Flora. Their voices were also similar in tone, though differing in the key. That of Fergus, especially while issuing orders to his followers during their military exercise, reminded Edward of a favourite passage in the description of Emetrius:

———whose voice was heard around,
Loud as a trumpet with a silver sound.

That of Flora, on the contrary, was soft and sweet,—"an excellent thing in woman;" yet, in urging any favourite topic, which she often pursued with natural eloquence, it possessed as well the tones which impress awe and conviction, as those of persuasive insinuation. The eager glance of the keen black eye, which, in the Chieftain, seemed impatient even of the material obstacles it encountered, had, in his sister, acquired a gentle pensiveness. His looks seemed to seek glory, power, all that could exalt him above others in the race of humanity; while those of his sister, as if she were already conscious of mental superiority, seemed to pity, rather than envy, those who were struggling for any farther distinction. Her sentiments corresponded with the expression of her countenance. Early education had impressed upon her mind, as well as on that of the Chieftain, the most devoted attachment to the exiled family of Stewart. She believed it the duty of her brother, of his clan, of every man in Britain, at whatever personal hazard, to contribute to that restoration which the partizans of the Chevalier St George had not ceased to hope for. For this she was prepared to do all, to suffer all, to sacrifice all. But her loyalty, as it exceeded her brother's in fanaticism, excelled it also in purity. Accustomed to petty intrigue, and necessarily involved in a thousand paltry and selfish discussions, ambitious also by nature, his political faith was tinctured, at least, if not tainted, by the views of interest and advancement so easily combined with it; and at the moment he should unsheathe his claymore, it might be difficult to say whether it would be most with the view of making James Stewart, a king, or Fergus Mac-Ivor an earl. This, indeed, was a mixture of feeling which he did not avow even to himself, but it existed, nevertheless, in a powerful degree.

In Flora's bosom, on the contrary, the zeal of loyalty burnt pure and unmixed with any selfish feeling; she would have as soon made religion the mask of ambitious and interested views, as have shrouded them under the opinions which she had been taught to think patriotism. Such instances of devotion were not uncommon among the followers of the unhappy race of Stewart, of which many memorable proofs will recur to the mind of most of my readers. But peculiar attention on the part of the Chevalier de St George and his princess to the parents of Fergus and his sister, and to themselves, when orphans, had riveted their faith. Fergus, upon the death of his parents, had been for some time a page of honour in the train of the Chevalier's lady, and, from his beauty and sprightly temper, was uniformly treated by her with the utmost distinction. This was also extended to Flora, who was maintained for some time at a convent of the first order, at the princess's expense, and removed from thence into her own family, where she spent nearly two years. Both brother and sister retained the deepest and most grateful sense of her kindness.

Having thus touched upon the leading principle of Flora's character, I may dismiss the rest more slightly. She was highly accomplished, and had acquired those elegant manners to be expected from one who, in early youth, had been the companion of a princess; yet she had not learned to substitute the gloss of politeness for the reality of feeling. When settled in the lonely regions of Glennaquoich, she found that her resources in French, English, and Italian literature, were likely to be few and interrupted ; and, in order to fill up the vacant time, she bestowed a part of it upon the music and poetical traditions of the Highlanders, and began really to feel the pleasure in the pursuit, which her brother, whose perceptions of literary merit were more blunt, rather affected for the sake of popularity than actually experienced. Her resolution was strengthened in these researches, by the extreme delight which her inquiries seemed to afford those to whom she resorted for information.

Her love of her clan, an attachment which was almost hereditary in her bosom, was, like her loyalty, a more pure passion than that of her brother. He was too thorough a politician, regarded his patriarchal influence too much as the means of accomplishing his own aggrandizement, that we should term him the model of a Highland Chieftain. Flora felt the same anxiety for cherishing and extending their patriarchal sway, but it was with the generous desire of vindicating from poverty, or at least from want and foreign oppression, those whom her brother was by birth, according to the notions of the time and country, entitled to govern. The savings of her income, for she had a small pension from the Princess Sobieski, were dedicated, not to add to the comforts of the peasantry, for that was a word which they neither knew, nor apparently wished to know, but to relieve their absolute necessities, when in sickness or extreme old age. At every other period, they rather toiled to procure something which they might share with the Chief, as a proof of their attachment, than expected other assistance from him save what was afforded by the rude hospitality of his castle, and the general division and subdivision of his estate among them. Flora was so much beloved by them, that when Mac-Murrough composed a song, in which he enumerated all the principal beauties of the district, and intimated her superiority by concluding, that "the fairest apple hung on the highest bough," he received, in donatives from the individuals of the clan, more seed-barley than would have sowed his Highland Parnassus, the *Bard's croft*, as it was called, ten times over.

From situation, as well as choice, Miss Mac-Ivor's society was extremely limited. Her most intimate friend had been Rose Bradwardine, to whom she was much

attached; and when seen together, they would have
afforded an artist two admirable subjects for the gay and
the melancholy muse. Indeed Rose was so tenderly
watched by her father, and her circle of wishes was so
limited, that none arose but what he was willing to
gratify, and scarce any which did not come within the
compass of his power. With Flora it was otherwise.
While almost a girl, she had undergone the most complete
change of scene, from gaiety and splendour to absolute
solitude and comparative poverty; and the ideas and
wishes which she chiefly fostered, respected great national
events, and changes not to be brought round without
both hazard and bloodshed, and therefore not to be
thought of with levity. Her manner, consequently, was
grave, though she readily contributed her talents to
the amusement of society, and stood very high in the
opinion of the old Baron, who used to sing along with
her such French duets of Lindor and Cloris, &c., as
were in fashion about the end of the reign of old Louis le
Grand.

It was generally believed, though no one durst have
hinted it to the Baron of Bradwardine, that Flora's
intreaties had no small share in allaying the wrath of
Fergus upon occasion of their quarrel. She took her
brother on the assailable side, by dwelling first upon
the Baron's age, and then representing the injury which
the cause might sustain, and the damage which must
arise to his own character in point of prudence, so
necessary to a political agent, if he persisted in carrying
it to extremity. Otherwise it is probable it would have
terminated in a duel, both because the Baron had, on a
former occasion, shed blood of the clan, though the matter
had been timely accommodated, and on account of his
high reputation for address at his weapon, which Fergus
almost condescended to envy. For the same reason she
had urged their reconciliation, which the Chieftain the
more readily agreed to, as it favoured some ulterior
projects of his own.

To this young lady, now presiding at the female empire
of the tea-table, Fergus introduced Captain Waverley,
whom she received with the usual forms of politeness.

## CHAPTER XXII.

### *Highland Minstrelsy.*

WHEN the first salutations had passed, Fergus said to his sister, "My dear Flora, before I return to the barbarous ritual of our forefathers, I must tell you that Captain Waverley is a worshipper of the Celtic muse, not the less so perhaps that he does not understand a word of her language. I have told him you are eminent as a translator of Highland poetry, and that Mac-Murrough admires your version of his songs upon the same principle that Captain Waverley admires the original,—because he does not comprehend them. Will you have the goodness to read or recite to our guest in English, the extraordinary string of names which Mac-Murrough has tacked together in Gaelic?—My life to a moorfowl's feather, you are provided with a version; for I know you are in all the bard's councils, and acquainted with his songs long before he rehearses them in the hall."

"How can you say so, Fergus? You know how little these verses can possibly interest an English stranger, even if I could translate them as you pretend."

"Not less than they interest me, lady fair. To-day your joint composition, for I insist you had a share in it, has cost me the last silver cup in the castle, and I suppose will cost me something else next time I hold *cour plénière*, if the muse descends on Mac-Murrough; for you know our proverb,—When the hand of the chief ceases to bestow, the breath of the bard is frozen in the utterance. —Well, I would it were even so: there are three things that are useless to a modern Highlander,—a sword which he must not draw,—a bard to sing of deeds which he dare not imitate,—and a large goat-skin purse without a louis-d'or to put into it."

"Well, brother, since you betray my secrets, you cannot expect me to keep yours.—I assure you, Captain Waverley, that Fergus is too proud to exchange his broad sword for a mareschal's baton; that he esteems Mac-Murrough a far greater poet than Homer, and would not give up his goat-skin purse for all the louis-d'or which it could contain."

"Well pronounced, Flora; blow for blow, as Conan[1]

Note 13. Conan the Jester.

said to the devil. Now do you two talk of bards and
poetry, if not of purses and claymores, while I return to
do the final honours to the senators of the tribe of Ivor."
So saying, he left the room.

The conversation continued between Flora and Waverley ; for two well-dressed young women, whose character
seemed to hover between that of companions and dependents, took no share in it. They were both pretty girls,
but served only as foils to the grace and beauty of their
patroness. The discourse followed the turn which the
Chieftain had given it, and Waverley was equally amused
and surprised with the account which the lady gave him
of Celtic poetry.

"The recitation," she said, "of poems, recording the
feats of heroes, the complaints of lovers, and the wars of
contending tribes, forms the chief amusement of a winter
fire-side in the Highlands. Some of these are said to be
very ancient, and if they are ever translated into any of
the languages of civilized Europe, cannot fail to produce
a deep and general sensation. Others are more modern,
the composition of those family bards whom the chieftains
of more distinguished name and power retain as the poets
and historians of their tribes. These, of course, possess
various degrees of merit ; but much of it must evaporate
in translation, or be lost on those who do not sympathize
with the feelings of the poet."

"And your bard, whose effusions seemed to produce
such effect upon the company to-day, is he reckoned
among the favourite poets of the mountains?"

"That is a trying question. His reputation is high
among his countrymen, and you must not expect me to
depreciate it."[1]

"But the song, Miss Mac-Ivor, seemed to awaken all
those warriors, both young and old."

"The song is little more than a catalogue of names of
the Highland clans under their distinctive peculiarities,
and an exhortation to them to remember and to emulate
the actions of their forefathers."

"And am I wrong in conjecturing, however extraordinary the guess appears, that there was some allusion to me
in the verses which he recited?"

"You have a quick observation, Captain Waverley,
which in this instance has not deceived you. The Gaelic
anguage, being uncommonly vocalic, is well adapted for

[1] The Highland poet almost always was an improvisatore. Captain Burt met one
of them at Lovat's table. (S.)

sudden and extemporaneous poetry; and a bard seldom fails to augment the effects of a premeditated song, by throwing in any stanzas which may be suggested by the circumstances attending the recitation."

"I would give my best horse to know what the Highland bard could find to say of such an unworthy Southron as myself."

"It shall not even cost you a lock of his mane.—Una, *Mavourneen!* (She spoke a few words to one of the young girls in attendance, who instantly curtsied, and tripped out of the room.)—I have sent Una to learn from the bard the expressions he used, and you shall command my skill as dragoman."

Una returned in a few minutes, and repeated to her mistress a few lines in Gaelic. Flora seemed to think for a moment, and then, slightly colouring, she turned to Waverley—"It is impossible to gratify your curiosity, Captain Waverley, without exposing my own presumption. If you will give me a few moments for consideration, I will endeavour to engraft the meaning of these lines upon a rude English translation, which I have attempted, of a part of the original. The duties of the tea-table seem to be concluded, and, as the evening is delightful, Una will show you the way to one of my favourite haunts, and Cathleen and I will join you there."

Una, having received instructions in her native language, conducted Waverley out by a passage different from that through which he had entered the apartment. At a distance he heard the hall of the Chief still resounding with the clang of bagpipes and the high applause of his guests. Having gained the open air by a postern door, they walked a little way up the wild, bleak, and narrow valley in which the house was situated, following the course of the stream that winded through it. In a spot, about a quarter of a mile from the castle, two brooks, which formed the little river, had their junction. The larger of the two came down the long bare valley, which extended, apparently without any change or elevation of character, as far as the hills which formed its boundary permitted the eye to reach. But the other stream, which had its source among the mountains on the left hand of the strath, seemed to issue from a very narrow and dark opening betwixt two large rocks. These streams were different also in character. The larger was placid, and even sullen in its course, wheeling in deep eddies, or sleeping in dark blue pools; but the motions of the lesser brook were rapid and

furious, issuing from between precipices, like a maniac
from his confinement, all foam and uproar.

It was up the course of this last stream that Waverley,
like a knight of romance, was conducted by the fair Highland damsel, his silent guide. A small path, which had
been rendered easy in many places for Flora's accommodation, led him through scenery of a very different
description from that which he had just quitted. Around
the castle, all was cold, bare, and desolate, yet tame even
in desolation; but this narrow glen, at so short a distance, seemed to open into the land of romance. The
rocks assumed a thousand peculiar and varied forms. In
one place, a crag of huge size presented its gigantic bulk,
as if to forbid the passenger's farther progress; and it
was not until he approached its very base, that Waverley
discerned the sudden and acute turn by which the pathway wheeled its course around this formidable obstacle.
In another spot, the projecting rocks from the opposite
sides of the chasm had approached so near to each other,
that two pine-trees laid across, and covered with turf,
formed a rustic bridge at the height of at least one
hundred and fifty feet. It had no ledges, and was barely
three feet in breadth.

While gazing at this pass of peril, which crossed, like a
single black line, the small portion of blue sky not intercepted by the projecting rocks on either side, it was with
a sensation of horror that Waverley beheld Flora and her
attendant appear, like inhabitants of another region,
propped, as it were, in mid air, upon this trembling
structure. She stopped upon observing him below, and,
with an air of graceful ease, which made him shudder,
waved her handkerchief to him by way of signal. He
was unable, from the sense of dizziness which her situation conveyed, to return the salute; and was never more
relieved than when the fair apparition passed on from
the precarious eminence which she seemed to occupy with
so much indifference, and disappeared on the other side.

Advancing a few yards, and passing under the bridge
which he had viewed with so much terror, the path
ascended rapidly from the edge of the brook, and the
glen widened into a silvan amphitheatre, waving with
birch, young oaks, and hazels, with here and there a
scattered yew-tree. The rocks now receded, but still
showed their grey and shaggy crests rising among the
copse-wood. Still higher, rose eminences and peaks, some
bare, some clothed with wood, some round and purple

with heath, and others splintered into rocks and crags. At a short turning, the path, which had for some furlongs lost sight of the brook, suddenly placed Waverley in front of a romantic waterfall. It was not so remarkable either for great height or quantity of water, as for the beautiful accompaniments which made the spot interesting. After a broken cataract of about twenty feet, the stream was received in a large natural basin filled to the brim with water, which, where the bubbles of the fall subsided, was so exquisitely clear, that although it was of great depth, the eye could discern each pebble at the bottom. Eddying round this reservoir, the brook found its way over a broken part of the ledge, and formed a second fall, which seemed to seek the very abyss; then, wheeling out beneath from among the smooth dark rocks, which it had polished for ages, it wandered murmuring down the glen, forming the stream up which Waverley had just ascended.[1] The borders of this romantic reservoir corresponded in beauty; but it was beauty of a stern and commanding cast, as if in the act of expanding into grandeur. Mossy banks of turf were broken and interrupted by huge fragments of rock, and decorated with trees and shrubs, some of which had been planted under the direction of Flora, but so cautiously that they added to the grace, without diminishing the romantic wildness of the scene.

Here, like one of those lovely forms which decorate the landscapes of Poussin, Waverley found Flora gazing on the waterfall. Two paces farther back stood Cathleen, holding a small Scottish harp, the use of which had been taught to Flora by Rory Dall, one of the last harpers of the Western Highlands. The sun, now stooping in the west, gave a rich and varied tinge to all the objects which surrounded Waverley, and seemed to add more than human brilliancy to the full expressive darkness of Flora's eye, exalted the richness and purity of her complexion, and enhanced the dignity and grace of her beautiful form. Edward thought he had never, even in his wildest dreams, imagined a figure of such exquisite and interesting loveliness. The wild beauty of the retreat, bursting upon him as if by magic, augmented the mingled feeling of delight and awe with which he approached her, like a fair enchantress of Boiardo or Ariosto, by whose nod the scenery around seemed to have been created, an Eden in the wilderness.

[1] Note 14. Waterfall.

Flora, like every beautiful woman, was conscious of her
own power, and pleased with its effects, which she could
easily discern from the respectful, yet confused address
of the young soldier.   But, as she possessed excellent
sense, she gave the romance of the scene, and other
accidental circumstances, full weight in appreciating the
feelings with which Waverley seemed obviously to be
impressed; and, unacquainted with the fanciful and
susceptible peculiarities of his character, considered
his homage as the passing tribute which a woman of
even inferior charms might have expected in such a
situation.  She therefore quietly led the way to a spot
at such a distance from the cascade, that its sound
should rather accompany than interrupt that of her
voice and instrument, and, sitting down upon a mossy
fragment of rock, she took the harp from Cathleen.

"I have given you the trouble of walking to this
spot, Captain Waverley, both because I thought the
scenery would interest you, and because a Highland
song would suffer still more from my imperfect translation, were I to introduce it without its own wild and
appropriate accompaniments.  To speak in the poetical
language of my country, the seat of the Celtic Muse
is in the midst of the secret and solitary hill, and her
voice in the murmur of the mountain stream.  He who
woos her must love the barren rock more than the
fertile valley, and the solitude of the desert better than
the festivity of the hall.

Few could have heard this lovely woman make this
declaration, with a voice where harmony was exalted by
pathos, without exclaiming that the muse whom she
invoked could never find a more appropriate representative.  But Waverley, though the thought rushed on his
mind, found no courage to utter it.   Indeed, the wild feeling of romantic delight with which he heard the few first
notes she drew from her instrument, amounted almost to
a sense of pain.  He would not for worlds have quitted his
place by her side ; yet he almost longed for solitude, that
he might decipher and examine at leisure the complication
of emotions which now agitated his bosom.

Flora had exchanged the measured and monotonous
recitative of the bard for a lofty and uncommon Highland
air, which had been a battle-song in former ages.  A few
irregular strains introduced a prelude of a wild and
peculiar tone, which harmonized well with the distant
waterfall, and the soft sigh of the evening breeze in the

rustling leaves of an aspen which overhung the seat of the fair harpess. The following verses convey but little idea of the feelings with which, so sung and accompanied, they were heard by Waverley:

There is mist on the mountain, and night on the vale,
But more dark is the sleep of the sons of the Gael.
A stranger commanded—it sunk on the land,
It has frozen each heart, and benumb'd every hand!

The dirk and the target lie sordid with dust,
The bloodless claymore is but redden'd with rust;
On the hill or the glen if a gun should appear,
It is only to war with the heath-cock or deer.

The deeds of our sires if our bards should rehearse,
Let a blush or a blow be the meed of their verse!
Be mute every string, and be hush'd every tone,
That shall bid us remember the fame that is flown.

But the dark hours of night and of slumber are past,
The morn on our mountains is dawning at last;
Glenaladale's peaks are illumed with the rays,
And the streams of Glenfinnan [1] leap bright in the blaze.

O high-minded Moray! [2]—the exiled—the dear!—
In the blush of the dawning the STANDARD uprear!
Wide, wide on the winds of the north let it fly,
Like the sun's latest flash when the tempest is nigh!

Ye sons of the strong, when that dawning shall break,
Need the harp of the aged remind you to wake?
That dawn never beam'd on your forefather's eye,
But it roused each high chieftain to vanquish or die.

O, sprung from the Kings who in Islay kept state,
Proud chiefs of Clan Ranald, Glengarry, and Sleat!
Combine like three streams from one mountain of snow,
And resistless in union rush down on the foe!

True son of Sir Evan, undaunted Lochiel,
Place thy targe on thy shoulder and burnish thy steel!
Rough Keppoch, give breath to thy bugle's bold swell,
Till far Coryarrick resound to the knell!

Stern son of Lord Kenneth, high chief of Kintail,
Let the stag in thy standard bound wild in the gale!
May the race of Clan Gillean, the fearless and free,
Remember Glenlivat, Harlaw, and Dundee!

Let the clan of grey Fingon, whose offspring has given
Such heroes to earth, and such martyrs to heaven,
Unite with the race of renown'd Rorri More,
To launch the long galley, and stretch to the oar.

How Mac-Shimei will joy when their chief shall display
The yew-crested bonnet o'er tresses of grey!
How the race of wrong'd Alpine and murder'd Glencoe
Shall shout for revenge when they pour on the foe!

[1] The young and daring Adventurer, Charles Edward, landed at Glenaladale, in Moidart, and displayed his standard in the valley of Glenfinnan, mustering around it the Mac-Donalds, the Camerons, and other less numerous clans, whom he had prevailed on to join him. There is a monument erected on the spot, with a Latin inscription by the late Doctor Gregory. (S.)

[2] The Marquis of Tullibardine's elder brother, who, long exiled, returned to Scotland with Charles Edward in 1745. (S.)

> Ye sons of brown Dermid, who slew the wild boar,
> Resume the pure faith of the great Callum-More!
> Mac-Neil of the Islands, and Moy of the Lake,
> For honour, for freedom, for vengeance awake!

Here a large greyhound bounding up the glen, jumped upon Flora, and interrupted her music by his importunate caresses.  At a distant whistle, he turned, and shot down the path again with the rapidity of an arrow.  "That is Fergus's faithful attendant, Captain Waverley, and that was his signal.  He likes no poetry but what is humorous, and comes in good time to interrupt my long catalogue of the tribes, whom one of your saucy English poets calls

> Our bootless host of high-born beggars,
> Mac-Leans, Mac-Kenzies, and Mac-Gregors. "

Waverley expressed his regret at the interruption.

"O you cannot guess how much you have lost!  The bard, as in duty bound, has addressed three long stanzas to Vich Ian Vohr of the Banners, enumerating all his great properties, and not forgetting his being a cheerer of the harper and bard—'a giver of bounteous gifts.'  Besides, you should have heard a practical admonition to the fair-haired son of the stranger, who lives in the land where the grass is always green—the rider on the shining pampered steed, whose hue is like the raven, and whose neigh is like the scream 'of the eagle for battle.  This valiant horseman is affectionately conjured to remember that his ancestors were distinguished by their loyalty, as well as by their courage.—All this you have lost; but, since your curiosity is not satisfied, I judge, from the distant sound of my brother's whistle, I may have time to sing the concluding stanzas before he comes to laugh at my translation."

> Awake on your hills, on your islands awake,
> Brave sons of the mountain, the frith, and the lake!
> 'Tis the bugle—but not for the chase is the call;
> 'Tis the pibroch's shrill summons—but not to the hall.
>
> 'Tis the summons of heroes for conquest or death,
> When the banners are blazing on mountain and heath:
> They call to the dirk, the claymore, and the targe,
> To the march and the muster, the line and the charge.
>
> Be the brand of each Chieftain like Fin's in his ire!
> May the blood through his veins flow like currents of fire!
> Burst the base foreign yoke as your sires did of yore,
> Or die like your sires, and endure it no more!

## CHAPTER XXIII.

### *Waverley continues at Glennaquoich.*

As Flora concluded her song, Fergus stood before them. "I knew I should find you here, even without the assistance of my friend Bran. A simple and unsublimed taste now, like my own, would prefer a jet d'eau at Versailles to this cascade, with all its accompaniments of rock and roar; but this is Flora's Parnassus, Captain Waverley, and that fountain her Helicon. It would be greatly for the benefit of my cellar if she could teach her coadjutor, Mac-Murrough, the value of its influence: he has just drunk a pint of usquebaugh to correct, he said, the coldness of the claret—Let me try its virtues." He sipped a little water in the hollow of his hand, and immediately commenced, with a theatrical air,—

> "O Lady of the desert, hail!
> That lovest the harping of the Gael,
> Through fair and fertile regions borne,
> Where never yet grew grass or corn.

But English poetry will never succeed under the influence of a Highland Helicon—*Allons, courage*—

> O vous, qui buvez, à tasse pleine,
> A cette heureuse fontaine,
> Ou on ne voit, sur le rivage,
> Que quelques vilains troupeaux,
> Suivis de nymphes de village,
> Qui les escortent sans sabots "——

"A truce, dear Fergus! spare us those most tedious and insipid persons of all Arcadia. Do not, for Heaven's sake bring down Coridon and Lindor upon us."

"Nay, if you cannot relish *la houlette et le chalumeau*, have with you in heroic strains."

"Dear Fergus, you have certainly partaken of the inspiration of Mac-Murrough's cup, rather than of mine."

"I disclaim it, *ma belle demoiselle*, although I protest it would be the more congenial of the two. Which of your crack-brained Italian romancers is it that says,

> Io d'Elicona niente
> Mi curo, in fe de Dio, che'l bere d'acque
> (Bea chi ber ne vuol) sempre mi spiacque ! [1]

But if you prefer the Gaelic, Captain Waverley, here is

[1] Good sooth, I reck nought of your Helicon;
Drink water whoso will, in faith I will drink none.

little Cathleen shall sing you Drimmindhu.—Come, Cathleen, *astore*, (*i.e.* my dear,) begin; no apologies to the *Cean-kinné.*"

Cathleen sung with much liveliness a little Gaelic song, the burlesque elegy of a countryman on the loss of his cow, the comic tones of which, though he did not understand the language, made Waverley laugh more than once.[1]

"Admirable, Cathleen!" cried the Chieftain; "I must find you a handsome husband among the clansmen one of these days."

Cathleen laughed, blushed, and sheltered herself behind her companion.

In the progress of their return to the castle, the Chieftain warmly pressed Waverley to remain for a week or two in order to see a grand hunting party, in which he and some other Highland gentlemen proposed to join. The charms of melody and beauty were too strongly impressed in Edward's breast to permit his declining an invitation so pleasing. It was agreed, therefore, that he should write a note to the Baron of Bradwardine, expressing his intention to stay a fortnight at Glennaquoich, and requesting him to forward by the bearer (a *gilly* of the Chieftain's) any letters which might have arrived for him.

This turned the discourse upon the baron, whom Fergus highly extolled as a gentleman and soldier. His character was touched with yet more discrimination by Flora, who observed he was the very model of the old Scottish cavalier, with all his excellencies and peculiarities. "It is a character, Captain Waverley, which is fast disappearing; for its best point was a self-respect which was never lost sight of till now   But, in the present time, the gentlemen whose principles do not permit them to pay court to the existing government, are neglected and degraded, and many conduct themselves accordingly; and, like some of the persons you have seen at Tully-Voelan, adopt habits and companions inconsistent with their birth and breeding. The ruthless proscription of party seems to degrade the victims whom it brands, however unjustly. But let us hope a brighter day is approaching, when a Scottish country-gentleman may be a scholar without the pedantry of our friend the Baron, a sportsman without the low habits of Mr Falconer, and a judicious improver of his

---

[1] This ancient Gaelic ditty is still well known, both in the Highlands and in Ireland. It was translated into English, and published, if I mistake not, under the auspices of the facetious Tom D'Urfey, by the title of " Colley, my Cow." (S.)

property without becoming a boorish two-legged steer like Killancureit."

Thus did Flora prophesy a revolution, which time indeed has produced, but in a manner very different from what she had in her mind.

The amiable Rose was next mentioned, with the warmest encomium on her person, manners, and mind. "That man," said Flora, "will find an inestimable treasure in the affections of Rose Bradwardine, who shall be so fortunate as to become their object. Her very soul is in home, and in the discharge of all those quiet virtues of which home is the centre. Her husband will be to her what her father now is, the object of all her care, solicitude, and affection. She will see nothing, and connect herself with nothing, but by him and through him. If he is a man of sense and virtue, she will sympathise in his sorrows, divert his fatigue, and share his pleasures. If she becomes the property of a churlish or negligent husband she will suit his taste also, for she will not long survive his unkindness. And, alas! how great is the chance that some such unworthy lot may be that of my poor friend!—O that I were a queen this moment, and could command the most amiable and worthy youth of my kingdom to accept happiness with the hand of Rose Bradwardine!"

"I wish you would command her to accept mine *en attendant*," said Fergus, laughing.

I don't know by what caprice it was that this wish, however jocularly expressed, rather jarred on Edward's feelings, notwithstanding his growing inclination to Flora, and his indifference to Miss Bradwardine. This is one of the inexplicabilities of human nature, which we leave without comment.

"Yours, brother?" answered Flora, regarding him steadily. "No; you have another bride—Honour; and the dangers you must run in pursuit of her rival would break poor Rose's heart."

With this discourse they reached the castle, and Waverley soon prepared his despatches for Tully-Veolan. As he knew the Baron was punctilious in such matters, he was about to impress his billet with a seal on which his armorial bearings were engraved, but he did not find it at his watch, and thought he must have left it at Tully-Veolan. He mentioned his loss, borrowing at the same time the family seal of the Chieftain.

"Surely," said Miss Mac-Ivor, "Donald Bean Lean would not"———

"My life for him, in such circumstances," answered her brother;—"besides, he would never have left the watch behind."

"After all, Fergus," said Flora, "and with every allowance, I am surprised you can countenance that man."

"I countenance him?—This kind sister of mine would persuade you, Captain Waverley, that I take what the people of old used to call 'a steakraid,' that is, a 'collop of the foray,' or, in plainer words, a portion of the robber's booty, paid by him to the Laird, or Chief, through whose grounds he drove his prey. O, it is certain, that unless I can find some way to charm Flora's tongue, General Blakeney will send a sergeant's party from Stirling (this he said with haughty and emphatic irony) to seize Vich Ian Vohr, as they nickname me, in his own castle."

"Now, Fergus, must not our guest be sensible that all this is folly and affectation? You have men enough to serve you without enlisting banditti, and your own honour is above taint—Why don't you send this Donald Bean Lean, whom I hate for his smoothness and duplicity, even more than for his rapine, out of your country at once? No cause should induce me to tolerate such a character."

"*No* cause, Flora?" said the Chieftain, significantly.

"No cause, Fergus! not even that which is nearest to my heart. Spare it the omen of such evil supporters!"

"O but, sister," rejoined the Chief, gaily, "you don't consider my respect for *la belle passion*. Evan Dhu Maccombich is in love with Donald's daughter, Alice, and you cannot expect me to disturb him in his amours. Why, the whole clan would cry shame on me. You know it is one of their wise sayings, that a kinsman is part of a man's body, but a foster-brother is a piece of his heart."

"Well, Fergus, there is no disputing with you; but I would all this may end well."

"Devoutly prayed, my dear and prophetic sister, and the best way in the world to close a dubious argument.— But hear ye not the pipes, Captain Waverley? Perhaps you will like better to dance to them in the hall, than to be deafened with their harmony without taking part in the exercise they invite us to."

Waverley took Flora's hand. The dance, song, and merry-making proceeded, and closed the day's entertain--

ment at the castle of Vich Ian Vohr. Edward at length
retired, his mind agitated by a variety of new and conflicting feelings, which detained him from rest for some
time, in that not unpleasing state of mind in which fancy
takes the helm, and the soul rather drifts passively along
with the rapid and confused tide of reflections, than
exerts itself to encounter, systematize, or examine them.
At a late hour he fell asleep, and dreamed of Flora Mac
Ivor.

## CHAPTER XXIV.

### A Stag-hunt and its Consequences.

SHALL this be a long or a short chapter?—This is a
question in which you, gentle reader, have no vote,
however much you may be interested in the consequences;
just as you may (like myself) probably have nothing to
do with the imposing a new tax, excepting the trifling
circumstance of being obliged to pay it. More happy
surely in the present case, since, though it lies within my
arbitrary power to extend my materials as I think
proper, I cannot call you into Exchequer if you do not
think proper to read my narrative. Let me therefore
consider. It is true, that the annals and documents in
my hands say but little of this Highland chase; but then
I can find copious materials for description elsewhere.
There is old Lindsay of Pitscottie ready at my elbow,
with his Athole hunting, and his "lofted and joisted
palace of green timber; with all kind of drink to be had
in burgh and land, as ale, beer, wine, muscadel, malvaise,
hippocras, and aquavitæ; with wheat-bread, main-bread,
ginge-bread, beef, mutton, lamb, veal, venison, goose,
grice, capon, coney, crane, swan, partridge, plover, duck,
drake, brissel-cock, pawnies, black-cock, muir-fowl, and
capercailzies;" not forgetting the "costly bedding,
vaiselle, and napry," and least of all the "excelling
stewards, cunning baxters, excellent cooks, and pottin-
gars, with confections and drugs for the desserts."
Besides the particulars which may be thence gleaned for
this Highland feast, (the splendour of which induced the
Pope's legate to dissent from an opinion which he had
hitherto held, that Scotland, namely, was the—the—the
latter end of the world)—besides these, might I not

illuminate my pages with Taylor the Water Poet's
hunting in the braes of Mar, where,

> "Through heather, mosse, 'mong frogs, and bogs, and fogs,
>   'Mongst craggy cliffs and thunder-batter'd hills,
> Hares, hinds, bucks, roes, are chased by men and dogs,
>   Where two hours' hunting fourscore fat deer kills.
> Lowland, your sports are low as is your seat;
> The Highland games and minds are high and great."

But without further tyranny over my readers, or
display of the extent of my own reading, I shall content
myself with borrowing a single incident from the memorable hunting at Lude, commemorated in the ingenious Mr
Gunn's "Essay on the Caledonian Harp," and so proceed
in my story with all the brevity that my natural style of
composition, partaking of what scholars call the peri-
phrastic and ambagitory, and the vulgar the circumben-
dibus, will permit me.

The solemn hunting was delayed, from various causes,
for about three weeks. The interval was spent by
Waverley with great satisfaction at Glennaquoich; for
the impression which Flora had made on his mind at
their first meeting grew daily stronger. She was precisely the character to fascinate a youth of romantic
imagination. Her manners, her language, her talents for
poetry and music, gave additional and varied influence to
her eminent personal charms. Even in her hours of
gaiety, she was in his fancy exalted above the ordinary
daughters of Eve, and seemed only to stoop for an
instant to those topics of amusement and gallantry
which others appear to live for. In the neighbourhood
of this enchantress, while sport consumed the morning,
and music and the dance led on the hours of evening,
Waverley became daily more delighted with his hospitable landlord, and more enamoured of his bewitching
sister.

At length, the period fixed for the grand hunting
arrived, and Waverley and the Chieftain departed for
the place of rendezvous, which was a day's journey to
the northward of Glennaquoich. Fergus was attended
on this occasion by about three hundred of his clan, well
armed, and accoutred in their best fashion. Waverley
complied so far with the custom of the country as to
adopt the trews, (he could not be reconciled to the kilt,)
brogues, and bonnet, as the fittest dress for the exercise
in which he was to be engaged, and which least exposed
him to be stared at as a stranger when they should reach

the place of rendezvous. They found, on the spot appointed, several powerful Chiefs, to all of whom Waverley was formally presented, and by all cordially received. Their vassals and clansmen, a part of whose feudal duty it was to attend on these parties, appeared in such numbers as amounted to a small army. These active assistants spread through the country far and near, forming a circle, technically called the *tinchel*, which, gradually closing, drove the deer in herds together towards the glen where the Chiefs and principal sportsmen lay in wait for them. In the meanwhile, these distinguished personages bivouacked among the flowery heath, wrapped up in their plaids; a mode of passing a summer's night which Waverley found by no means unpleasant.

For many hours after sun-rise, the mountain ridges and passes retained their ordinary appearance of silence and solitude, and the Chiefs, with their followers, amused themselves with various pastimes, in which the joys of the shell, as Ossian has it, were not forgotten. "Others apart sate on a hill retired;" probably as deeply engaged in the discussion of politics and news, as Milton's spirits in metaphysical disquisition. At length signals of the approach of the game were descried and heard. Distant shouts resounded from valley to valley, as the various parties of Highlanders, climbing rocks, struggling through copses, wading brooks, and traversing thickets, approached more and more near to each other, and compelled the astonished deer, with the other wild animals that fled before them, into a narrower circuit. Every now and then the report of muskets was heard, repeated by a thousand echoes. The baying of the dogs was soon added to the chorus, which grew ever louder and more loud. At length the advanced parties of the deer began to show themselves; and as the stragglers came bounding down the pass by two or three at a time, the Chiefs showed their skill by distinguishing the fattest deer, and their dexterity in bringing them down with their guns. Fergus exhibited remarkable address, and Edward was also so fortunate as to attract the notice and applause of the sportsmen.

But now the main body of the deer appeared at the head of the glen, compelled into a very narrow compass, and presenting such a formidable phalanx, that their antlers appeared at a distance, over the ridge of the steep pass, like a leafless grove. Their number was very great, and from a desperate stand which they made, with the tallest of the red-deer stags arranged in front, in a sort of battle-array, gazing on the group which barred their passage down the glen, the more experienced sportsmen began to augur danger. The work of destruction, however, now commenced on all sides. Dogs and hunters were at work, and muskets and fusees resounded from every quarter. The deer, driven to desperation, made at length a fearful charge right upon the spot where the more distinguished sportsmen had taken their stand. The word was given in Gaelic to fling themselves upon their faces; but Waverley, on whose English ears the signal was lost, had almost fallen a sacrifice to his ignorance of the ancient language in which it was communicated. Fergus, observing his danger, sprung up and pulled him with violence to the ground, just as the whole herd broke down upon them. The tide being absolutely irresistible, and wounds from a stag's horn highly dangerous,[1] the activity of the Chieftain may be considered, on this occasion, as having saved his guest's life. He detained him with a firm grasp until the whole herd of deer had fairly run over them. Waverley then attempted to rise, but found that he had suffered several very severe contusions, and, upon a further examination, discovered that he had sprained his ankle violently.

This checked the mirth of the meeting, although the Highlanders, accustomed to such incidents, and prepared for them, had suffered no harm themselves. A wigwam was erected almost in an instant, where Edward was deposited on a couch of heather. The surgeon, or he who assumed the office, appeared to unite the characters of a leech and a conjuror. He was an old smoke-dried Highlander, wearing a venerable grey beard, and having for his sole garment a tartan frock, the skirts of which descended to the knee, and, being undivided in front, made the vestment serve at once for doublet and breeches.[2] He observed great ceremony in approaching Edward; and though our hero was writhing with pain, would not proceed to any operation which might assuage

---

[1] The thrust from the tynes, or branches, of the stag's horns, were accounted far more dangerous than those of the boar's tusk:—

> If thou be hurt with horn of stag, it brings thee to thy bier,
> But barber's hand shall boar's hurt heal; thereof have thou no fear. (S.)

[2] This garb, which resembled the dress often put on children in Scotland, called a polonie (i.e. polonaise), is a very ancient modification of the Highland garb. It was, in fact, the hauberk or shirt of mail, only composed of cloth instead of rings of armour. (S.)

it until he had perambulated his couch three times, moving from east to west, according to the course of the sun. This, which was called making the *deasil*,[1] both the leech and the assistants seemed to consider as a matter of the last importance to the accomplishment of a cure ; and Waverley, whom pain rendered incapable of expostulation, and who indeed saw no chance of its being attended to, submitted in silence.

After this ceremony was duly performed, the old Esculapius let his patient blood with a cupping-glass with great dexterity, and proceeded, muttering all the while to himself in Gaelic, to boil on the fire certain herbs, with which he compounded an embrocation. He then fomented the parts which had sustained injury, never failing to murmur prayers or spells, which of the two Waverley could not distinguish, as his ear only caught the words *Gasper-Melchior-Balthazer-max-prax-fax*, and similar gibberish. The fomentation had a speedy effect in alleviating the pain and swelling, which our hero imputed to the virtue of the herbs, or the effect of the chafing, but which was by the bystanders unanimously ascribed to the spells with which the operation had been accompanied. Edward was given to understand, that not one of the ingredients had been gathered except during the full moon, and that the herbalist had, while collecting them, uniformly recited a charm, which, in English, ran thus :

> Hail to thee, thou holy herb,
> That sprung on holy ground!
> All in the Mount Olivet
> First wert thou found:
> Thou art boot for many a bruise,
> And healest many a wound;
> In our Lady's blessed name,
> I take thee from the ground.[2]

Edward observed, with some surprise, that even Fergus, notwithstanding his knowledge and education, seemed to fall in with the superstitious ideas of his countrymen, either because he deemed it impolitic to affect scepticism on a matter of general belief, or more probably because, like most men who do not think deeply or accurately on such subjects, he had in his mind a reserve of superstition which balanced the freedom of his expressions

---

[1] Old Highlanders will still make the *deasil* around those whom they wish well to. To go round a person in the opposite direction, or *wither-shins* (German *wider-shins*), is unlucky, and a sort of incantation. (S.)

[2] This metrical spell, or something very like it, is preserved by Reginald Scott, in his work on Witchcraft. (S.)

and practice upon other occasions. Waverley made no
commentary, therefore, on the manner of the treatment,
but rewarded the professor of medicine with a liberality
beyond the utmost conception of his wildest hopes. He
uttered, on the occasion, so many incoherent blessings in
Gaelic and English, that Mac-Ivor, rather scandalized at
the excess of his acknowledgments, cut them short by
exclaiming, *Ceud mile mhalloich ort! i.e.* "A hundred
thousand curses on you!" and so pushed the helper of
men out of the cabin.

After Waverley was left alone, the exhaustion of pain
and fatigue,—for the whole day's exercise had been severe,
threw him into a profound, but yet a feverish sleep, which
he chiefly owed to an opiate draught administered by the
old Highlander from some decoction of herbs in his phar-
macopœia.

Early the next morning, the purpose of their meeting being over, and their sports damped by the un-
toward accident, in which Fergus and all his friends
expressed the greatest sympathy, it became a question
how to dispose of the disabled sportsman. This was
settled by Mac-Ivor, who had a litter prepared, of "birch
and hazel-grey," [1] which was borne by his people with
such caution and dexterity as renders it not improbable
that they may have been the ancestors of some of those
sturdy Gael, who have now the happiness to transport
the belles of Edinburgh, in their sedan-chairs, to ten
routs in one evening. When Edward was elevated upon
their shoulders, he could not help being gratified with the
romantic effect produced by the breaking up of this
silvan camp. [2]

The various tribes assembled, each at the pibroch of
their native clan, and each headed by their patriarchal
ruler. Some, who had already begun to retire, were seen
winding up the hills, or descending the passes which led
to the scene of action, the sound of their bagpipes dying
upon the ear. Others made still a moving picture upon
the narrow plain, forming various changeful groups, their

[1]                     On the morrow they made their biers
                        Of birch and hazel grey.

                                              *Chevy Chase.* (S.)

[2] The author has been sometimes accused of confounding fiction with reality.
He therefore thinks it necessary to state, that the circumstance of the hunting
described in the text as preparatory to the insurrection of 1745, is, so far as he
knows, entirely imaginary. But it is well known such a great hunting was held
in the Forest of Brae-Mar, under the auspices of the Earl of Mar, as preparatory
to the Rebellion of 1715; and most of the Highland chieftains who afterwards
engaged in that civil commotion were present on this occasion. (S.)

feathers and loose plaids waving in the morning breeze, and their arms glittering in the rising sun. Most of the Chiefs came to take farewell of Waverley, and to express their anxious hope they might again, and speedily, meet ; but the care of Fergus abridged the ceremony of taking leave. At length, his own men being completely assembled and mustered, Mac-Ivor commenced his march, but not towards the quarter from which they had come. He gave Edward to understand, that the greater part of his followers, now on the field, were bound on a distant expedition, and that when he had deposited him in the house of a gentleman, who he was sure would pay him every attention, he himself should be under the necessity of accompanying them the greater part of the way, but would lose no time in rejoining his friend.

Waverley was rather surprised that Fergus had not mentioned this ulterior destination when they set out upon the hunting-party ; but his situation did not admit of many interrogatories. The greater part of the clans-men went forward under the guidance of old Ballen-keiroch, and Evan Dhu Maccombich, apparently in high spirits. A few remained for the purpose of escorting the Chieftain, who walked by the side of Edward's litter, and attended him with the most affectionate assiduity. About noon, after a journey which the nature of the conveyance, the pain of his bruises, and the roughness of the way, rendered inexpressibly painful, Waverley was hospitably received into the house of a gentleman related to Fergus, who had prepared for him every accommodation which the simple habits of living then universal in the Highlands, put in his power. In this person, an old man about seventy, Edward admired a relic of primitive simplicity. He wore no dress but what his estate afforded ; the cloth was the fleece of his own sheep, woven by his own ser-vants, and stained into tartan by the dyes produced from the herbs and lichens of the hills around him. His linen was spun by his daughters and maid-servants, from his own flax, nor did his table, though plentiful, and varied with game and fish, offer an article but what was of native produce.

Claiming himself no rights of clanship or vassalage, he was fortunate in the alliance and protection of Vich Ian Vohr, and other bold and enterprising chieftains, who protected him in the quiet unambitious life he loved. It is true, the youth born on his grounds were often enticed to leave him for the service of his more active friends ;

but a few old servants and tenants used to shake their
grey locks when they heard their master censured for
want of spirit, and observed, "When the wind is still, the
shower falls soft." This good old man, whose charity and
hospitality were unbounded, would have received Waverley with kindness, had he been the meanest Saxon
peasant, since his situation required assistance. But his
attention to a friend and guest of Vich Ian Vohr was
anxious and unremitted. Other embrocations were
applied to the injured limb, and new spells were put in
practice. At length, after more solicitude than was perhaps for the advantage of his health, Fergus took farewell of Edward for a few days, when, he said, he would
return to Tomanrait, and hoped by that time Waverley
would be able to ride one of the Highland ponies of his
landlord, and in that manner return to Glennaquoich.

The next day, when his good old host appeared, Edward
learned that his friend had departed with the dawn,
leaving none of his followers except Callum Beg, the sort
of foot-page who used to attend his person, and who had
now in charge to wait upon Waverley. On asking his
host, if he knew where the Chieftain was gone? the old
man looked fixedly at him, with something mysterious
and sad in the smile which was his only reply. Waverley
repeated his question, to which his host answered in a
proverb,—

> "What sent the messengers to hell,
> Was asking what they knew full well." [1]

He was about to proceed, but Callum Beg said, rather
pertly, as Edward thought, that "Ta Tighearnach (*i.e.*
the Chief) did not like ta Sassenagh Duinhé-wassel to be
pingled wi' mickle speaking, as she was na tat weel."
From this Waverley concluded he should disoblige his
friend by enquiring of a stranger the object of a journey
which he himself had not communicated.

It is unnecessary to trace the progress of our hero's
recovery. The sixth morning had arrived, and he was
able to walk about with a staff, when Fergus returned
with about a score of his men. He seemed in the highest
spirits, congratulated Waverley on his progress towards
recovery, and finding he was able to sit on horseback,
proposed their immediate return to Glennaquoich. Waverley joyfully acceded, for the form of its fair mistress

[1] Corresponding to the Lowland saying, "Mony ane speirs the gate they ken
fu weel." (S.)

had lived in his dreams during all the time of his confinement.

> Now he has ridden o'er moor and moss,
> O'er hill and many a glen,

Fergus, all the while, with his myrmidons, striding stoutly by his side, or diverging to get a shot at a roe or a heath-cock. Waverley's bosom beat thick when they approached the old tower of Ian nan Chaistel, and could distinguish the fair form of its mistress advancing to meet them.

Fergus began immediately, with his usual high spirits, to exclaim, "Open your gates, incomparable princess, to the wounded Moor Abindarez, whom Rodrigo de Narvez, constable of Antiquera, conveys to your castle ; or open them, if you like it better, to the renowned Marquis of Mantua, the sad attendant of his half-slain friend, Baldovinos of the mountain.—Ah, long rest to thy soul, Cervantes ! without quoting thy remnants, how should I frame my language to befit romantic ears ! "

Flora now advanced, and welcoming Waverley with much kindness, expressed her regret for his accident, of which she had already heard particulars, and her surprise that her brother should not have taken better care to put a stranger on his guard against the perils of the sport in which he engaged him. Edward easily exculpated the Chieftain, who, indeed, at his own personal risk, had probably saved his life.

This greeting over, Fergus said three or four words to his sister in Gaelic. The tears instantly sprung to her eyes, but they seemed to be tears of devotion and joy, for she looked up to heaven, and folded her hands as in a solemn expression of prayer or gratitude. After the pause of a minute, she presented to Edward some letters which had been forwarded from Tully-Veolan during his absence, and, at the same time, delivered some to her brother. To the latter she likewise gave three or four numbers of the *Caledonian Mercury*, the only newspaper which was then published to the north of the Tweed.

Both gentlemen retired to examine their despatches, and Edward speedily found that those which he had received contained matters of very deep interest.

## CHAPTER XXV.

### *News from England.*

The letters which Waverley had hitherto received from his relations in England, were not such as required any particular notice in this narrative. His father usually wrote to him with the pompous affectation of one who was too much oppressed by public affairs to find leisure to attend to those of his own family. Now and then he mentioned persons of rank in Scotland to whom he wished his son should pay some attention; but Waverley, hitherto occupied by the amusements which he had found at Tully-Veolan and Glennaquoich, dispensed with paying any attention to hints so coldly thrown out, especially as distance, shortness of leave of absence, and so forth, furnished a ready apology. But latterly the burden of Mr Richard Waverley's paternal epistles consisted in certain mysterious hints of greatness and influence which he was speedily to attain, and which would ensure his son's obtaining the most rapid promotion, should he remain in the military service. Sir Everard's letters were of a different tenor. They were short; for the good Baronet was none of your illimitable correspondents, whose manuscript overflows the folds of their large post paper, and leaves no room for the seal; but they were kind and affectionate, and seldom concluded without some allusion to our hero's stud, some question about the state of his purse, and a special enquiry after such of his recruits as had preceded him from Waverley-Honour. Aunt Rachel charged him to remember his principles of religion, to take care of his health, to beware of Scotch mists, which, she had heard, would wet an Englishman through and through; never to go out at night without his great-coat; and, above all, to wear flannel next to his skin.

Mr Pembroke only wrote to our hero one letter, but it was of the bulk of six epistles of these degenerate days, containing, in the moderate compass of ten folio pages, closely written, a precis of a supplementary quarto manuscript of *addenda, delenda, et corrigenda*, in reference to the two tracts with which he had presented Waverley. This he considered as a mere sop in the pan to stay the appetite of Edward's curiosity, until he should find an opportunity of sending down the volume itself, which was much too heavy for the post, and which he proposed to accompany with certain interesting pamphlets, lately published by his friend in Little Britain, with whom he had kept up a sort of literary correspondence, in virtue of which the library shelves of Waverley-Honour were loaded with much trash, and a good round bill, seldom summed in fewer than three figures, was yearly transmitted, in which Sir Edward Waverley of Waverley-Honour, Bart., was marked Dr. to Jonathan Grubbet, bookseller and stationer, Little Britain. Such had hitherto been the style of the letters which Edward had received from England; but the packet delivered to him at Glenna-quoich was of a different and more interesting complexion. It would be impossible for the reader, even were I to insert the letters at full length, to comprehend the real cause of their being written, without a glance into the interior of the British Cabinet at the period in question.

The ministers of the day happened (no very singular event) to be divided into two parties; the weakest of which, making up by assiduity of intrigue their inferiority in real consequence, had of late acquired some new proselytes, and with them the hope of superseding their rivals in the favour of their sovereign, and overpowering them in the House of Commons. Amongst others, they had thought it worth while to practise upon Richard Waverley. This honest gentleman, by a grave mysterious demeanour, an attention to the etiquette of business, rather more than to its essence, a facility in making long dull speeches, consisting of truisms and common-places, hashed up with a technical jargon of office, which prevented the inanity of his orations from being discovered, had acquired a certain name and credit in public life, and even established, with many, the character of a profound politician; none of your shining orators, indeed, whose talents evaporate in tropes of rhetoric and flashes of wit, but one possessed of steady parts for business, which would wear well, as the ladies say in choosing their silks, and ought in all reason to be good for common and every-day use, since they were confessedly formed of no holiday texture.

This faith had become so general, that the insurgent party in the cabinet of which we have made mention, after sounding Mr Richard Waverley, were so satisfied with his sentiments and abilities, as to propose, that, in case of a certain revolution in the ministry, he should take an ostensible place in the new order of things, not indeed of the very first rank, but greatly higher, in point both of emolument and influence, than that which he now enjoyed. There was no resisting so tempting a proposal, notwithstanding that the Great Man, under whose patronage he had enlisted, and by whose banner he had hitherto stood firm, was the principal object of the proposed attack by the new allies. Unfortunately this fair scheme of ambition was blighted in the very bud, by a premature movement. All the official gentlemen concerned in it, who hesitated to take the part of a voluntary resignation, were informed that the king had no farther occasion for their services; and, in Richard Waverley's case, which the minister considered as aggravated by ingratitude, dismissal was accompanied by something like personal contempt and contumely. The public, and even the party of whom he shared the fall, sympathised little in the disappointment of this selfish and interested statesman; and he retired to the country under the comfortable reflection, that he had lost, at the same time, character, credit, and,—what he at least equally deplored,—emolument.

Richard Waverley's letter to his son upon this occasion was a masterpiece of its kind. Aristides himself could not have made out a harder case. An unjust monarch, and an ungrateful country, were the burden of each rounded paragraph. He spoke of long services, and unrequited sacrifices; though the former had been overpaid by his salary, and nobody could guess in what the latter consisted, unless it were in his deserting, not from conviction, but for the lucre of gain, the Tory principles of his family. In the conclusion, his resentment was wrought to such an excess by the force of his own oratory, that he could not repress some threats of vengeance, however vague and impotent, and finally acquainted his son with his pleasure that he should testify his sense of the ill-treatment he had sustained, by throwing up his commission as soon as the letter reached him. This, he said, was also his uncle's desire, as he would himself intimate in due course.

Accordingly, the next letter which Edward opened was from Sir Everard. His brother's disgrace seemed to have removed from his well-natured bosom all recollection of their differences, and, remote as he was from every means of learning that Richard's disgrace was in reality only the just, as well as natural consequence, of his own unsuccessful intrigues, the good, but credulous Baronet at once set it down as a new and enormous instance of the injustice of the existing government. It was true, he said, and he must not disguise it even from Edward, that his father could not have sustained such an insult as was now, for the first time, offered to one of his house, unless he had subjected himself to it by accepting of an employment under the present system. Sir Everard had no doubt that he now both saw and felt the magnitude of this error, and it should be his (Sir Everard's) business, to take care that the cause of his regret should not extend itself to pecuniary consequences. It was enough for a Waverley to have sustained the public disgrace; the patrimonial injury could easily be obviated by the head of their family. But it was both the opinion of Mr Richard Waverley and his own, that Edward, the representative of the family of Waverley-Honour, should not remain in a situation which subjected him also to such treatment as that with which his father had been stigmatized. He requested his nephew therefore to take the fittest, and, at the same time, the most speedy opportunity, of transmitting his resignation to the War-Office, and hinted, moreover, that little ceremony was necessary where so little had been used to his father. He sent multitudinous greetings to the Baron of Bradwardine.

A letter from aunt Rachel spoke out even more plainly. She considered the disgrace of brother Richard as the just reward of his forfeiting his allegiance to a lawful, though exiled sovereign, and taking the oaths to an alien; a concession which her grandfather, Sir Nigel Waverley, refused to make, either to the Round-head Parliament or to Cromwell, when his life and fortune stood in the utmost extremity. She hoped her dear Edward would follow the footsteps of his ancestors, and as speedily as possible get rid of the badge of servitude to the usurping family, and regard the wrongs sustained by his father as an admonition from Heaven, that every desertion of the line of loyalty becomes its own punishment. She also concluded with her respects to Mr Bradwardine, and begged Waverley would inform her whether his daughter, Miss Rose, was old enough to wear a pair of very handsome ear-rings, which she proposed to send as a token of her affection. The good lady also desired to be informed whether Mr Bradwardine took as much Scotch snuff, and danced as unweariedly, as he did when he was at Waverley-Honour about thirty years ago.

These letters, as might have been expected, highly
excited Waverley's indignation. From the desultory style
of his studies, he had not any fixed political opinion to
place in opposition to the movements of indignation
which he felt at his father's supposed wrongs. Of the
real cause of his disgrace, Edward was totally ignorant;
nor had his habits at all led him to investigate the politics
of the period in which he lived, or remark the intrigues
in which his father had been so actively engaged. Indeed,
any impressions which he had accidentally adopted concerning the parties of the times, were (owing to the
society in which he had lived at Waverley-Honour) of a
nature rather unfavourable to the existing government
and dynasty. He entered, therefore, without hesitation,
into the resentful feeling of the relations who had the
best title to dictate his conduct; and not perhaps the
less willingly, when he remembered the tædium of his
quarters, and the inferior figure which he had made
among the officers of his regiment. If he could have had
any doubt upon the subject, it would have been decided
by the following letter from his commanding officer,
which, as it is very short, shall be inserted verbatim :

"SIR,

"Having carried somewhat beyond the line of my duty,
an indulgence which even the lights of nature, and much
more those of Christianity, direct towards errors which
may arise from youth and inexperience, and that altogether without effect, I am reluctantly compelled, at the
present crisis, to use the only remaining remedy which is
in my power. You are, therefore, hereby commanded to
repair to ——, the head-quarters of the regiment, within
three days after the date of this letter  If you shall fail
to do so, I must report you to the War-Office as absent
without leave, and also take other steps, which will be
disagreeable to you, as well as to,

"Sir,

"Your obedient Servant,

"J. GARDINER, Lieut.-Col.
"Commanding the —— Regt. Dragoons."

Edward's blood boiled within him as he read this letter.
He had been accustomed from his very infancy to
possess, in a great measure, the disposal of his own time,

and thus acquired habits which rendered the rules of military discipline as unpleasing to him in this as they were in some other respects. An idea that in his own case they would not be enforced in a very rigid manner, had also obtained full possession of his mind, and had hitherto been sanctioned by the indulgent conduct of his lieutenant-colonel. Neither had anything occurred, to his knowledge, that should have induced his commanding officer, without any other warning than the hints we noticed at the end of the fourteenth chapter, so suddenly to assume a harsh, and, as Edward deemed it, so insolent a tone of dictatorial authority. Connecting it with the letters he had just received from his family, he could not but suppose, that it was designed to make him feel, in his present situation, the same pressure of authority which had been exercised in his father's case, and that the whole was a concerted scheme to depress and degrade every member of the Waverley family.

Without a pause, therefore, Edward wrote a few cold lines, thanking his lieutenant-colonel for past civilities, and expressing regret that he should have chosen to efface the remembrance of them, by assuming a different tone towards him. The strain of his letter, as well as what he (Edward) conceived to be his duty, in the present crisis, called upon him to lay down his commission; and he therefore inclosed the formal resignation of a situation which subjected him to so unpleasant a correspondence, and requested Colonel Gardiner would have the goodness to forward it to the proper authorities.

Having finished this magnanimous epistle, he felt somewhat uncertain concerning the terms in which his resignation ought to be expressed, upon which subject he resolved to consult Fergus Mac-Ivor. It may be observed in passing, that the bold and prompt habits of thinking, acting, and speaking, which distinguished this young Chieftain, had given him a considerable ascendency over the mind of Waverley. Endowed with at least equal powers of understanding, and with much finer genius, Edward yet stooped to the bold and decisive activity of an intellect which was sharpened by the habit of acting on a preconceived and regular system, as well as by extensive knowledge of the world.

When Edward found his friend, the latter had still in his hand the newspaper which he had perused, and advanced to meet him with the embarrassment of one who has unpleasing news to communicate. "Do your letters,

Captain Waverley, confirm the unpleasing information which I find in this paper?"

He put the paper into his hand, where his father's disgrace was registered in the most bitter terms, transferred probably from some London journal. At the end of the paragraph was this remarkable innuendo:

"We understand that 'this same *Richard* who hath done all this,' is not the only example of the *Wavering Honour* of W-v-r-ly H-n-r. See the *Gazette* of this day."

With hurried and feverish apprehension our hero turned to the place referred to, and found therein recorded, "Edward Waverley, captain in —— regiment dragoons, superseded for absence without leave;" and in the list of military promotions, referring to the same regiment, he discovered this farther article, "Lieut. Julius Butler, to be captain, *vice* Edward Waverley superseded."

Our hero's bosom glowed with the resentment which undeserved and apparently premeditated insult was calculated to excite in the bosom of one who had aspired after honour, and was thus wantonly held up to public scorn and disgrace. Upon comparing the date of his colonel's letter with that of the article in the *Gazette*, he perceived that his threat of making a report upon his absence had been literally fulfilled, and without inquiry, as it seemed, whether Edward had either received his summons, or was disposed to comply with it. The whole, therefore, appeared a formed plan to degrade him in the eyes of the public; and the idea of its having succeeded filled him with such ¦bitter emotions, that, after various attempts to conceal them, he at length threw himself into Mac-Ivor's arms, and gave vent to tears of shame and indignation.

It was none of this Chieftain's faults to be indifferent to the wrongs of his friends; and for Edward, independent of certain plans with which he was connected, he felt a deep and sincere interest. The proceeding appeared as extraordinary to him as it had done to Edward. He indeed knew of more motives than Waverley was privy to for the peremptory order that he should join his regiment. But that, without farther inquiry into the circumstances of a necessary delay, the commanding officer, in contradiction to his known and established character, should have proceeded in so harsh and unusual a manner, was a mystery which he could not penetrate. He soothed our hero, however, to the best of his power, and began to turn his thoughts on revenge for his insulted honour.

Edward eagerly grasped at the idea. "Will you carry a message for me to Colonel Gardiner, my dear Fergus, and oblige me for ever?"

Fergus paused; "It is an act of friendship which you should command, could it be useful, or lead to the righting your honour; but in the present case, I doubt if your commanding officer would give you the meeting on account of his having taken measures, which, however harsh and exasperating, were still within the strict bounds of his duty. Besides, Gardiner is a precise Huguenot, and has adopted certain ideas about the sinfulness of such rencontres, from which it would be impossible to make him depart, especially as his courage is beyond all suspicion. And besides, I—I, to say the truth—I dare not at this moment, for some very weighty reasons, go near any of the military quarters or garrisons belonging to this government."

"And am I," said Waverley, "to sit down quiet and contented under the injury I have received?"

"That will I never advise my friend," replied Mac-Ivor. "But I would have vengeance to fall on the head, not on the hand; on the tyrannical and oppressive government which designed and directed these premeditated and reiterated insults, not on the tools of office which they employed in the execution of the injuries they aimed at you."

"On the government!" said Waverley.

"Yes," replied the impetuous Highlander, "on the usurping House of Hanover, whom your grandfather would no more have served than he would have taken wages of red-hot gold from the great fiend of hell!"

"But since the time of my grandfather two generations of this dynasty have possessed the throne," said Edward, coolly.

"True," replied the Chieftain; "and because we have passively given them so long the means of showing their native character,—because both you and I myself have lived in quiet submission, have even truckled to the times so far as to accept commissions under them, and thus have given them an opportunity of disgracing us publicly by resuming them, are we not on that account to resent injuries which our fathers only apprehended, but which we have actually sustained? Or is the cause of the unfortunate Stewart family become less just,

because their title has devolved upon an heir who is
innocent of the charges of misgovernment brought
against his father?—Do you remember the lines of your
favourite poet?—

> Had Richard unconstrain'd resign'd the throne,
> A king can give no more than is his own;
> The title stood entail'd had Richard had a son.

You see, my dear Waverley, I can quote poetry as well as
Flora and you. But come, clear your moody brow, and
trust to me to show you an honourable road to a speedy
and glorious revenge. Let us seek Flora, who perhaps
has more news to tell us of what has occurred during our
absence. She will rejoice to hear that you are relieved of
your servitude. But first add a postscript to your letter,
marking the time when you received this calvinistical
Colonel's first summons, and express your regret that the
hastiness of his proceedings prevented your anticipating
them by sending your resignation. Then let him blush
for his injustice."

The letter was sealed accordingly, covering a formal resignation of the commission, and Mac-Ivor despatched it
with some letters of his own by a special messenger,
with charge to put them into the nearest post-office in
the Lowlands.

## CHAPTER XXVI.

### An Eclaircissement.

THE hint which the Chieftain had thrown out respecting
Flora was not unpremeditated. He had observed with
great satisfaction the growing attachment of Waverley to
his sister, nor did he see any bar to their union, excepting the situation which Waverley's father held in the
ministry, and Edward's own commission in the army of
George II. These obstacles were now removed, and in a
manner which apparently paved the way for the son's
becoming reconciled to another allegiance. In every
other respect the match would be most eligible. The
safety, happiness, and honourable provision of his sister,
whom he dearly loved, appeared to be ensured by the
proposed union; and his heart swelled when he considered how his own interest would be exalted in the
eyes of the ex-monarch to whom he had dedicated his
service, by an alliance with one of those ancient, power-

ful, and wealthy English families of the steady cavalier faith, to awaken whose decayed attachment to the Stewart family was now a matter of such vital import-ance to the Stewart cause. Nor could Fergus perceive any obstacle to such a scheme. Waverley's attachment was evident; and as his person was handsome, and his taste apparently coincided with her own, he anticipated no opposition on the part of Flora. Indeed, between his ideas of patriarchal power, and those which he had acquired in France respecting the disposal of females in marriage, any opposition from his sister, dear as she was to him, would have been the last obstacle on which he would have calculated, even had the union been less eligible.

Influenced by these feelings, the Chief now led Waver-ley in quest of Miss Mac-Ivor, not without the hope that the present agitation of his guest's spirits might give him courage to cut short what Fergus termed the romance of the courtship. They found Flora, with her faithful attendants, Una and Cathleen, busied in preparing what appeared to Waverley to be white bridal favours. Dis-guising as well as he could the agitation of his mind, Waverley asked for what joyful occasion Miss Mac-Ivor made such ample preparation.

"It is for Fergus's bridal," she said, smiling.

"Indeed!" said Edward; "he has kept his secret well. I hope he will allow me to be his bride's man."

"That is a man's office, but not yours, as Beatrice says," retorted Flora.

"And who is the fair lady, may I be permitted to ask, Miss Mac-Ivor?"

"Did not I tell you long since, that Fergus wooed no bride but Honour?" answered Flora.

"And am I then incapable of being his assistant and counsellor in the pursuit of honour?" said our hero, colouring deeply. "Do I rank so low in your opinion?"

"Far from it, Captain Waverley. I would to God you were of our determination! and made use of the expres-sion which displeased you, solely

> Because you are not of our quality,
> But stand against us as an enemy."

"That time is past, sister," said Fergus; "and you may wish Edward Waverley (no longer captain) joy of being freed from the slavery to an usurper, implied in that sable and ill-omened emblem."

"Yes," said Waverley, undoing the cockade from his

hat, "it has pleased the king who bestowed this badge upon me, to resume it in a manner which leaves me little reason to regret his service."

"Thank God for that!" cried the enthusiast; "and O that they may be blind enough to treat every man of honour who serves them with the same indignity, that I may have less to sigh for when the struggle approaches!"

"And now, sister," said the Chieftain, "replace his cockade with one of a more lively colour  I think it was the fashion of the ladies of yore to arm and send forth their knights to high achievement."

"Not," replied the lady, "till the knight adventurer had well weighed the justice and the danger of the cause, Fergus.  Mr Waverley is just now too much agitated by feelings of recent emotion, for me to press upon him a resolution of consequence."

Waverley felt half-alarmed at the thought of adopting the badge of what was by the majority of the kingdom esteemed rebellion, yet he could not disguise his chagrin at the coldness with which Flora parried her brother's hint.  "Miss Mac-Ivor, I perceive, thinks the knight unworthy of her encouragement and favour," said he, somewhat bitterly.

"Not so, Mr Waverley," she replied, with great sweetness.  "Why should I refuse my brother's valued friend a boon which I am distributing to his whole clan?  Most willingly would I enlist every man of honour in the cause to which my brother has devoted himself.  But Fergus has taken his measures with his eyes open.  His life has been devoted to this cause from his cradle; with him its call is sacred, were it even a summons to the tomb.  But how can I wish you, Mr Waverley, so new to the world, so far from every friend who might advise and ought to influence you,—in a moment too of sudden pique and indignation,—how can I wish you to plunge yourself at once into so desperate an enterprise?"

Fergus, who did not understand these delicacies, strode through the apartment biting his lip, and then, with a constrained smile, said, "Well, sister, I leave you to act your new character of mediator between the Elector of Hanover and the subjects of your lawful sovereign and benefactor," and left the room.

There was a painful pause, which was at length broken by Miss Mac-Ivor.  "My brother is unjust," she said, "because he can bear no interruption that seems to thwart his loyal zeal."

"And do you not share his ardour!" asked Waverley.

"Do I not?" answered Flora—"God knows mine exceeds his, if that be possible. But I am not, like him, rapt by the bustle of military preparation, and the infinite detail necessary to the present undertaking, beyond consideration of the grand principles of justice and truth, on which our enterprise is grounded; and these, I am certain, can only be furthered by measures in themselves true and just. To operate upon your present feelings, my dear Mr Waverley, to induce you to an irretrievable step, of which you have not considered either the justice or the danger, is, in my poor judgment, neither the one nor the other."

"Incomparable Flora!" said Edward, taking her hand, "how much do I need such a monitor!"

"A better one by far," said Flora, gently withdrawing her hand, "Mr Waverley will always find in his own bosom, when he will give its small still voice leisure to be heard."

"No, Miss Mac-Ivor, I dare not hope it; a thousand circumstances of fatal self-indulgence have made me the creature rather of imagination than reason. Durst I but hope—could I but think—that you would deign to be to me that affectionate, that condescending friend, who would strengthen me to redeem my errors, my future life"——

"Hush, my dear sir! now you carry your joy at escaping the hands of a Jacobite recruiting officer to an unparalleled excess of gratitude."

"Nay, dear Flora, trifle with me no longer; you cannot mistake the meaning of those feelings which I have almost involuntarily expressed; and since I have broken the barrier of silence, let me profit by my audacity—Or may I, with your permission, mention to your brother"——

"Not for the world, Mr Waverley!"——

"What am I to understand?" said Edward. "Is there any fatal bar—has any prepossession"——

"None, sir," answered Flora. "I owe it to myself to say, that I never yet saw the person, on whom I thought with reference to the present subject."

"The shortness of our acquaintance, perhaps—If Miss Mac-Ivor will deign to give me time"——

"I have not even that excuse. Captain Waverley's character is so open—is, in short, of that nature, that it cannot be misconstrued, either in its strength or its weakness."

"And for that weakness you despise me?" said Edward.

"Forgive me, Mr Waverley—and remember it is but within this half hour that there existed between us a barrier of a nature to me insurmountable, since I never could think of an officer in the service of the Elector of Hanover in any other light than as a casual acquaintance. Permit me then to arrange my ideas upon so unexpected a topic, and in less than an hour I will be ready to give you such reasons for the resolution I shall express, as may be satisfactory at least, if not pleasing to you." So saying, Flora withdrew, leaving Waverley to meditate upon the manner in which she had received his addresses.

Ere he could make up his mind whether to believe his suit had been acceptable or no, Fergus re-entered the apartment. "What, *à la mort*, Waverley?" he cried. "Come down with me to the court, and you shall see a sight worth all the tirades of your romances. An hundred firelocks, my friend, and as many broadswords, just arrived from good friends; and two or three hundred stout fellows almost fighting which shall first possess them.—But let me look at you closer—Why, a true Highlander would say you had been blighted by an evil eye. —Or can it be this silly girl that has thus blanked your spirit?—Never mind her, dear Edward; the wisest of her sex are fools in what regards the business of life."

"Indeed, my good friend," answered Waverley, "all that I can charge against your sister is, that she is too sensible, too reasonable."

"If that be all, I ensure you for a louis-d'or against the mood lasting four-and-twenty hours. No woman was ever steadily sensible for that period; and I will engage, if that will please you, Flora shall be as unreasonable to-morrow as any of her sex. You must learn, my dear Edward, to consider women *en mousquetaire*." So saying, he seized Waverley's arm, and dragged him off to review his military preparations.

## CHAPTER XXVII.

### *Upon the same Subject.*

FERGUS MAC-IVOR had too much tact and delicacy to renew the subject which he had interrupted. His head was, or appeared to be, so full of guns, broadswords, bonnets, canteens, and tartan hose, that Waverley could not for some time draw his attention to any other topic.

"Are you to take the field so soon, Fergus," he asked, "that you are making all these martial preparations?"

"When we have settled that you go with me, you shall know all; but otherwise, the knowledge might rather be prejudicial to you."

"But are you serious in your purpose, with such inferior forces, to rise against an established government? It is mere frenzy."

"*Laissez faire à Don Antoine*—I shall take good care of myself. We shall at least use the compliment of Conan, who never got a stroke but he gave one. I would not, however," continued the Chieftain, "have you think me mad enough to stir till a favourable opportunity: I will not slip my dog before the game's afoot. But, once more, will you join with us, and you shall know all?"

"How can I?" said Waverley; "I, who have so lately held that commission which is now posting back to those that gave it? My accepting it implied a promise of fidelity, and an acknowledgment of the legality of the government."

"A rash promise," answered Fergus, "is not a steel handcuff; it may be shaken off, especially when it was given under deception, and has been repaid by insult. But if you cannot immediately make up your mind to a glorious revenge, go to England, and ere you cross the Tweed, you will hear tidings that will make the world ring; and if Sir Everard be the gallant old cavalier I have heard him described by some of our *honest* gentlemen of the year one thousand seven hundred and fifteen, he will find you a better horse-troop and a better cause than you have lost."

"But your sister, Fergus?"

"Out, hyperbolical fiend!" replied the Chief, laughing; "how vexest thou this man!—Speak'st thou of nothing but of ladies?"

"Nay, be serious, my dear friend," said Waverley; "I feel that the happiness of my future life must depend upon the answer which Miss Mac-Ivor shall make to what I ventured to tell her this morning."

"And is this your very sober earnest," said Fergus, more gravely, "or are we in the land of romance and fiction?"

"My earnest, undoubtedly. How could you suppose me jesting on such a subject?"

"Then, in very sober earnest," answered his friend, "I am very glad to hear it; and so highly do I think of Flora, that you are the only man in England for whom I would say so much.—But before you shake my hand so warmly, there is more to be considered.—Your own family —will they approve your connecting yourself with the sister of a high-born Highland beggar?"

"My uncle's situation," said Waverley, "his general opinions, and his uniform indulgence, entitle me to say, that birth and personal qualities are all he would look to in such a connection. And where can I find both united in such excellence as in your sister?"

"O nowhere!—*cela va sans dire*," replied Fergus with a smile. "But your father will expect a father's prerogative in being consulted."

"Surely; but his late breach with the ruling powers removes all apprehension of objection on his part, especially as I am convinced that my uncle will be warm in my cause."

"Religion perhaps," said Fergus, "may make obstacles, though we are not bigotted Catholics."

"My grandmother was of the Church of Rome, and her religion was never objected to by my family.—Do not think of *my* friends, dear Fergus; let me rather have your influence where it may be more necessary to remove obstacles—I mean with your lovely sister."

"My lovely sister," replied Fergus, "like her loving brother, is very apt to have a pretty decisive will of her own, by which, in this case, you must be ruled; but you shall not want my interest, nor my counsel. And, in the first place, I will give you one hint—Loyalty is her ruling passion; and since she could spell an English book, she has been in love with the memory of the gallant Captain Wogan, who renounced the service of the usurper Cromwell to join the standard of Charles II., marched a handful of cavalry from London to the Highlands to join Middleton, then in arms for the king, and at length died gloriously in the royal cause. Ask her to show you some verses she made on his history and fate; they have been much admired, I assure you. The next point is—I think I saw Flora go up towards the waterfall a short time since—follow, man, follow! don't allow the garrison time to strengthen its purposes of resistance—*Alerta à la muraille!* Seek Flora out, and learn her decision as soon as you can, and Cupid go with you, while I go to look over belts and cartouch-boxes."

Waverley ascended the glen with an anxious and throbbing heart. Love, with all its romantic train of hopes, fears, and wishes, was mingled with other feelings of a nature less easily defined. He could not but remember how much this morning had changed his fate, and into what a complication of perplexity it was likely to plunge him. Sunrise had seen him possessed of an esteemed rank in the honourable profession of arms, his father to all appearance rapidly rising in the favour of his sovereign;—all this had passed away like a dream— he himself was dishonoured, his father disgraced, and he had become involuntarily the confident at least, if not the accomplice, of plans, dark, deep, and dangerous, which must infer either the subversion of the government he had so lately served, or the destruction of all who had participated in them. Should Flora even listen to his suit favourably, what prospect was there of its being brought to a happy termination, amid the tumult of an impending insurrection? Or how could he make the selfish request that she should leave Fergus, to whom she was so much attached, and, retiring with him to England, wait, as a distant spectator, the success of her brother's undertaking, or the ruin of all his hopes and fortunes?— Or, on the other hand, to engage himself, with no other aid than his single arm, in the dangerous and precipitate counsels of the Chieftain,—to be whirled along by him, the partaker of all his desperate and impetuous motions, renouncing almost the power of judging, or deciding upon the rectitude or prudence of his actions,—this was no pleasing prospect for the secret pride of Waverley to stoop to. And yet what other conclusion remained, saving the rejection of his addresses by Flora, an alternative not to be thought of in the present high-wrought state of his feelings, with anything short of mental agony. Pondering the doubtful and dangerous prospect before him, he at length arrived near the cascade, where, as Fergus had augured, he found Flora seated.

She was quite alone, and as soon as she observed his approach, she rose, and came to meet him. Edward attempted to say something within the verge of ordinary compliment and conversation, but found himself unequal to the task. Flora seemed at first equally embarrassed, but recovered herself more speedily, and (an unfavourable augury for Waverley's suit) was the first to enter upon the subject of their last interview. "It is too important, in every point of view, Mr Waverley, to permit me to leave you in doubt on my sentiments."

"Do not speak them speedily," said Waverley, much agitated, "unless they are such as I fear, from your manner, I must not dare to anticipate. Let time—let my future conduct—let your brother's influence "——

"Forgive me, Mr Waverley," said Flora, her complexion a little heightened, but her voice firm and composed. "I should incur my own heavy censure, did I delay expressing my sincere conviction that I can never regard you otherwise than as a valued friend. I should do you the highest injustice did I conceal my sentiments for a moment—I see I distress you, and I grieve for it, but better now than later; and O, better a thousand times, Mr Waverley, that you should feel a present momentary disappointment, than the long and heart-sickening griefs which attend a rash and ill-assorted marriage!"

"Good God!" exclaimed Waverley, "why should you anticipate such consequences from a union, where birth is equal, where fortune is favourable, where, if I may venture to say so, the tastes are similar, where you allege no preference for another, where you even express a favourable opinion of him whom you reject?"

"Mr Waverley, I *have* that favourable opinion," answered Flora; "and so strongly, that though I would rather have been silent on the grounds of my resolution, you shall command them, if you exact such a mark of my esteem and confidence."

She sat down upon a fragment of rock, and Waverley, placing himself near her, anxiously pressed for the explanation she offered.

"I dare hardly," she said, "tell you the situation of my feelings, they are so different from those usually ascribed to young women at my period of life; and I dare hardly touch upon what I conjecture to be the nature of yours, lest I should give offence where I would willingly administer consolation. For myself, from my infancy till this day, I have had but one wish—the restoration of my royal benefactors to their rightful throne. It is impossible to express to you the devotion of my feelings to this single subject; and I will frankly confess, that it has so occupied my mind as to exclude every thought respecting what is called my own settlement in life. Let me but live to see the day of that happy restoration, and a Highland cottage, a French convent, or an English palace, will be alike indifferent to me."

"But, dearest Flora, how is your enthusiastic zeal for the exiled family inconsistent with my happiness?"

"Because you seek, or ought to seek, in the object of your attachment, a heart whose principal delight should be in augmenting your domestic felicity, and returning your affection, even to the height of romance. To a man of less keen sensibility, and less enthusiastic tenderness of disposition, Flora Mac-Ivor might give content, if not happiness; for, were the irrevocable words spoken, never would she be deficient in the duties which she vowed."

"And why,—why, Miss Mac-Ivor, should you think yourself a more valuable treasure to one who is less capable of loving, of admiring you, than to me?"

"Simply because the tone of our affections would be more in unison, and because his more blunted sensibility would not require the return of enthusiasm which I have not to bestow. But you, Mr Waverley, would for ever refer to the idea of domestic happiness which your imagination is capable of painting, and whatever fell short of that ideal representation would be construed into coolness and indifference, while you might consider the enthusiasm with which I regarded the success of the royal family, as defrauding your affection of its due return."

"In other words, Miss Mac-Ivor, you cannot love me?" said her suitor dejectedly.

"I could esteem you, Mr Waverley, as much, perhaps more, than any man I have ever seen; but I cannot love you as you ought to be loved. O! do not, for your own sake, desire so hazardous an experiment! The woman whom you marry, ought to have affections and opinions moulded upon yours. Her studies ought to be your studies;—her wishes, her feelings, her hopes, her fears, should all mingle with yours. She should enhance your pleasures, share your sorrows, and cheer your melancholy."

"And why will not you, Miss Mac-Ivor, who can so well describe a happy union, why will not you be yourself the person you describe?"

"Is it possible you do not yet comprehend me?" answered Flora. "Have I not told you, that every keener sensation of my mind is bent exclusively towards an event, upon which, indeed, I have no power but those of my earnest prayers?"

"And might not the granting the suit I solicit," said

Waverley, too earnest on his purpose to consider what he was about to say, "even advance the interest to which you have devoted yourself? My family is wealthy and powerful, inclined in principles to the Stewart race, and should a favourable opportunity "——

"A favourable opportunity!" said Flora, somewhat scornfully,—"Inclined in principles!—Can such lukewarm adherence be honourable to yourselves, or gratifying to your lawful sovereign?—Think, from my present feelings, what I should suffer when I held the place of member in a family, where the rights which I hold most sacred are subjected to cold discussion, and only deemed worthy of support when they shall appear on the point of triumphing without it!"

"Your doubts," quickly replied Waverley, "are unjust as far as concerns myself. The cause that I shall assert, I dare support through every danger, as undauntedly as the boldest who draws sword in its behalf."

"Of that," answered Flora, "I cannot doubt for a moment. But consult your own good sense and reason rather than a prepossession hastily adopted, probably only because you have met a young woman possessed of the usual accomplishments, in a sequestered and romantic situation. Let your part in this great and perilous drama rest upon conviction, and not on a hurried, and probably a temporary feeling."

Waverley attempted to reply, but his words failed him. Every sentiment that Flora had uttered vindicated the strength of his attachment; for even her loyalty, although wildly enthusiastic, was generous and noble, and disdained to avail itself of any indirect means of supporting the cause to which she was devoted.

After walking a little way in silence down the path, Flora thus resumed the conversation.—"One word more, Mr Waverley, ere we bid farewell to this topic for ever; and forgive my boldness if that word have the air of advice. My brother Fergus is anxious that you should join him in his present enterprise. But do not consent to this; you could not, by your single exertions, further his success, and you would inevitably share his fall, if it be God's pleasure that fall he must. Your character would also suffer irretrievably. Let me beg you will return to your own country; and, having publicly freed yourself from every tie to the usurping government, I trust you will see cause, and find opportunity, to serve your injured sovereign with effect, and stand forth, as your loyal ancestors, at the head of your natural followers and adherents, a worthy representative of the house of Waverley."

"And should I be so happy as thus to distinguish myself, might I not hope"——

"Forgive my interruption," said Flora. "The present time only is ours, and I can but explain to you with candour the feelings which I now entertain; how they might be altered by a train of events too favourable perhaps to be hoped for, it were in vain even to conjecture: Only be assured, Mr Waverley, that, after my brother's honour and happiness, there is none which I shall more sincerely pray for than for yours."

With these words she parted from him, for they were now arrived where two paths separated. Waverley reached the castle amidst a medley of conflicting passions. He avoided any private interview with Fergus, as he did not find himself able either to encounter his raillery, or reply to his solicitations. The wild revelry of the feast, for Mac-Ivor kept open table for his clan, served in some degree to stun reflection. When their festivity was ended, he began to consider how he should again meet Miss Mac-Ivor after the painful and interesting explanation of the morning. But Flora did not appear. Fergus, whose eyes flashed when he was told by Cathleen that her mistress designed to keep her apartment that evening, went himself in quest of her; but apparently his remonstrances were in vain, for he returned with a heightened complexion, and manifest symptoms of displeasure. The rest of the evening passed on without any allusion, on the part either of Fergus or Waverley, to the subject which engrossed the reflections of the latter, and perhaps of both.

When retired to his own apartment, Edward endeavoured to sum up the business of the day. That the repulse he had received from Flora, would be persisted in for the present, there was no doubt. But could he hope for ultimate success in case circumstances permitted the renewal of his suit? Would the enthusiastic loyalty, which at this animating moment left no room for a softer passion, survive, at least in its engrossing force, the success or the failure of the present political machinations? And if so, could he hope that the interest which she had acknowledged him to possess in her favour, might be improved into a warmer attachment? He taxed his memory to recall every word she had used, with the appropriate looks and gestures which had enforced them, and ended by finding himself in the same state of uncertainty. It was very late before sleep brought relief to the tumult of his mind, after the most painful and agitating day which he had ever passed.


## CHAPTER XXVIII.

### *A Letter from Tully-Veolan.*

In the morning, when Waverley's troubled reflections had for some time given way to repose, there came music to his dreams, but not the voice of Selma. He imagined himself transported back to Tully-Veolan, and that he heard Davie Gellatley singing in the court those matins which used generally to be the first sounds that disturbed his repose while a guest of the Baron of Bradwardine. The notes which suggested this vision continued, and waxed louder, until Edward awoke in earnest. The illusion, however, did not seem entirely dispelled. The apartment was in the fortress of Ian nan Chaistel, but it was still the voice of Davie Gellatley that made the following lines resound under the window :—

> My heart's in the Highlands, my heart is not here,
> My heart's in the Highlands a-chasing the deer;
> A-chasing the wild deer, and following the roe,
> My heart's in the Highlands wherever I go. [1]

Curious to know what could have determined Mr Gellatley on an excursion of such unwonted extent, Edward began to dress himself in all haste, during which operation the minstrelsy of Davie changed its tune more than once :—

> There's nought in the Highlands but syboes and leeks,
> And lang-leggit callants gaun wanting the breeks;
> Wanting the breeks, and without hose and shoon,
> But we'll a' win the breeks when King Jamie comes hame. [2]

By the time Waverley was dressed and had issued forth, David had associated himself with two or three of the numerous Highland loungers who always graced the gates of the castle with their presence, and was capering and dancing full merrily in the doubles and full career of a Scotch foursome reel, to the music of his own whistling.

---

[1] These lines form the burden of an old song to which Burns wrote additional verses. (S.)

[2] These lines are also ancient, and I believe to the tune of

> We'll never hae peace till Jamie comes hame;

to which Burns likewise wrote some verses. (S.)

In this double capacity of dancer and musician, he continued, until an idle piper, who observed his zeal, obeyed the unanimous call of *Seid suas*, (*i.e.* blow up,) and relieved him from the latter part of his trouble. Young and old then mingled in the dance as they could find partners. The appearance of Waverley did not interrupt David's exercise, though he contrived, by grinning, nodding, and throwing one or two inclinations of the body into the graces with which he performed the Highland fling, to convey to our hero symptoms of recognition. Then, while busily employed in setting, whooping all the while, and snapping his fingers over his head, he of a sudden prolonged his side-step until it brought him to the place where Edward was standing, and, still keeping time to the music like Harlequin in a pantomime, he thrust a letter into our hero's hand, and continued his saltation without pause or intermission. Edward, who perceived that the address was in Rose's hand-writing, retired to peruse it, leaving the faithful bearer to continue his exercise until the piper or he should be tired out.

The contents of the letter greatly surprised him. It had originally commenced with, *Dear Sir;* but these words had been carefully erased, and the monosyllable, *Sir*, substituted in their place. The rest of the contents shall be given in Rose's own language.

"I fear I am using an improper freedom by intruding upon you, yet I cannot trust to any one else to let you know some things which have happened here, with which it seems necessary you should be acquainted. Forgive me, if I am wrong in what I am doing; for, alas! Mr Waverley, I have no better advice than that of my own feelings:—my dear father is gone from this place, and when he can return to my assistance and protection, God alone knows. You have probably heard, that in consequence of some troublesome news from the Highlands, warrants were sent out for apprehending several gentlemen in these parts, and, among others, my dear father. In spite of all my tears and entreaties that he would surrender himself to the government, he joined with Mr Falconer and some other gentlemen, and they have all gone northwards, with a body of about forty horsemen. So I am not so anxious concerning his immediate safety, as about what may follow afterwards, for these troubles are only beginning. But all this is nothing to you, Mr Waverley, only I thought you would be glad to learn that my father has escaped, in case you happen to have heard that he was in danger.

"The day after my father went off, there came a party of soldiers to Tully-Veolan, and behaved very rudely to Bailie Macwheeble; but the officer was very civil to me, only said his duty obliged him to search for arms and papers. My father had provided against this by taking away all the arms except the old useless things which hung in the hall, and he had put all his papers out of the way. But oh! Mr Waverley, how shall I tell you, that they made strict inquiry after you, and asked when you had been at Tully-Veolan, and where you now were. The officer is gone back with his party, but a non-commissioned officer and four men remain as a sort of garrison in the house. They have hitherto behaved very well, as we are forced to keep them in good humour. But these soldiers have hinted as if on your falling into their hands you would be in great danger; I cannot prevail on myself to write what wicked falsehoods they said, for I am sure they are falsehoods; but you will best judge what you ought to do. The party that returned carried off your servant prisoner, with your two horses, and everything that you left at Tully-Veolan. I hope God will protect you, and that you will get safe home to England, where you used to tell me there was no military violence nor fighting among clans permitted, but every thing was done according to an equal law that protected all who were harmless and innocent. I hope you will exert your indulgence as to my boldness in writing to you, where it seems to me, though perhaps erroneously, that your safety and honour are concerned. I am sure—at least I think, my father would approve of my writing; for Mr Rubric is fled to his cousin's at the Duchran, to be out of danger from the soldiers and the Whigs, and Bailie Macwheeble does not like to meddle (he says) in other men's concerns, though I hope what may serve my father's friend at such a time as this, cannot be termed improper interference. Farewell, Captain Waverley! I shall probably never see you more; for it would be very improper to wish you to call at Tully-Veolan just now, even if these men were gone; but I will always remember with gratitude your kindness in assisting so poor a scholar as myself, and your attentions to my dear, dear father.

"I remain your obliged servant,
"Rose Comyne Bradwardine.

"P.S.—I hope you will send me a line by David Gellatley, just to say you have received this, and that you will take care of yourself; and forgive me if I entreat you, for your own sake, to join none of these unhappy cabals, but escape, as fast as possible, to your own fortunate country.—My compliments to my dear Flora, and to Glennaquoich. Is she not as handsome and accomplished as I described her?"

Thus concluded the letter of Rose Bradwardine, the contents of which both surprised and affected Waverley. That the Baron should fall under the suspicions of government, in consequence of the present stir among the partizans of the house of Stewart, seemed only the natural consequence of his political predilections; but how *he* himself should have been involved in such suspicions, conscious that until yesterday he had been free from harbouring a thought against the prosperity of the reigning family, seemed inexplicable. Both at Tully-Veolan and Glennaquoich, his hosts had respected his engagements with the existing government, and though enough passed by accidental innuendo that might induce him to reckon the Baron and the Chief among those disaffected gentlemen who were still numerous in Scotland, yet until his own connection with the army had been broken off by the resumption of his commission, he had no reason to suppose that they nourished any immediate or hostile attempts against the present establishment. Still he was aware that unless he meant at once to embrace the proposal of Fergus Mac-Ivor, it would deeply concern him to leave the suspicious neighbourhood without delay, and repair where his conduct might undergo a satisfactory examination. Upon this he the rather determined, as Flora's advice favoured his doing so, and because he felt inexpressible repugnance at the idea of being accessory to the plague of civil war. Whatever were the original rights of the Stewarts, calm reflection told him, that, omitting the question how far James the Second could forfeit those of his posterity, he had, according to the united voice of the whole nation, justly forfeited his own. Since that period, four monarchs had reigned in peace and glory over Britain, sustaining and exalting the character of the nation abroad, and its liberties at home. Reason asked, was it worth while to disturb a government so long settled and established, and to plunge a kingdom into all the miseries of civil war, for the purpose of replacing upon the throne the descendants of a monarch by whom it had been wilfully forfeited? If, on the other hand, his own final conviction of the goodness of their cause, or the commands of his father or uncle, should recommend to him allegiance to the Stewarts, still it was necessary to clear his own character by showing that he had not, as seemed to be falsely insinuated, taken any step to this purpose, during his holding the commission of the reigning monarch.

The affectionate simplicity of Rose, and her anxiety for his safety,—his sense too of her unprotected state, and of the terror and actual dangers to which she might be exposed, made an impression upon his mind, and he instantly wrote to thank her in the kindest terms for her solicitude on his account, to express his earnest good wishes for her welfare and that of her father, and to assure her of his own safety. The feelings which this task excited were speedily lost in the necessity which he now saw of bidding farewell to Flora Mac-Ivor, perhaps for ever. The pang attending this reflection was inexpressible; for her high-minded elevation of character, her self-devotion to the cause which she had embraced, united to her scrupulous rectitude as to the means of serving it, had vindicated to his judgment the choice adopted by his passions. But time pressed, calumny was busy with his fame, and every hour's delay increased the power to injure it. His departure must be instant.

With this determination he sought out Fergus, and communicated to him the contents of Rose's letter, with his own resolution instantly to go to Edinburgh, and put into the hands of some one or other of those persons of influence to whom he had letters from his father, his exculpation from any charge which might be preferred against him.

"You run your head into the lion's mouth," answered Mac-Ivor. "You do not know the severity of a government harassed by just apprehensions, and a consciousness of their own illegality and insecurity. I shall have to deliver you from some dungeon in Stirling or Edinburgh Castle."

"My innocence, my rank, my father's intimacy with Lord M——, General G——, &c., will be a sufficient protection," said Waverley.

"You will find the contrary," replied the Chieftain; "these gentlemen will have enough to do about their own matters. Once more, will you take the plaid, and stay a little while with us among the mists and the crows, in the bravest cause ever sword was drawn in ?"[1]

"For many reasons, my dear Fergus, you must hold me excused."

"Well then," said Mac-Ivor, "I shall certainly find you exerting your poetical talents in elegies upon a prison, or your antiquarian researches in detecting the Oggam[2] character, or some Punic hieroglyphic upon the key-stones of a vault, curiously arched.   Or what say you to *un petit pendement bien joli?* against which awkward ceremony I don't warrant you, should you meet a body of the armed west-country Whigs."

"And why should they use me so ?" said Waverley.

"For a hundred good reasons," answered Fergus: "First, you are an Englishman ; secondly, a gentleman ; thirdly, a prelatist abjured ; and, fourthly, they have not had an opportunity to exercise their talents on such a subject this long while.   But don't be cast down, beloved : all will be done in the fear of the Lord."

"Well, I must run my hazard."

"You are determined, then ?"

"I am."

"Wilful will do't," said Fergus ;—"but you cannot go on foot, and I shall want no horse, as I must march on foot at the head of the children of Ivor ; you shall have brown Dermid."

"If you will sell him, I shall certainly be much obliged."

"If your proud English heart cannot be obliged by a gift or loan, I will not refuse money at the entrance of a campaign : his price is twenty guineas. [Remember, reader, it was Sixty Years since.]   And when do you propose to depart ?"

"The sooner the better," answered Waverley.

"You are right, since go you must, or rather, since go you will : I will take Flora's pony, and ride with you as far as Bally-Brough.—Callum Beg, see that our horses are ready, with a pony for yourself, to attend and carry Mr Waverley's baggage as far as —— (naming a small town,) where he can have a horse and guide to Edinburgh. Put on a Lowland dress, Callum, and see you keep your

---

[1] A Highland rhyme on Glencairn's Expedition, in 1650, has these lines—

"We'll bide a while among ta crows,
We'll wiske ta sword and bend ta bows."                    (S.)

[2] The Oggam is a species of the old Irish character.   The idea of the correspondence betwixt the Celtic and Punic, founded on a scene in Plautus, was not started till General Vallancey set up his theory, long after the date of Fergus Mac-Ivor.   (S.)

tongue close, if you would not have me cut it out: Mr
Waverley rides Dermid." Then turning to Edward, "You
will take leave of my sister?"

"Surely—that is, if Miss Mac-Ivor will honour me so
far."

"Cathleen, let my sister know Mr Waverley wishes to
bid her farewell before he leaves us.—But Rose Bradwardine, her situation must be thought of—I wish she were
here—And why should she not?—There are but four
red-coats at Tully-Veolan, and their muskets would be
very useful to us."

To these broken remarks Edward made no answer; his
ear indeed received them, but his soul was intent upon
the expected entrance of Flora. The door opened—It
was but Cathleen, with her lady's excuse, and wishes for
Captain Waverley's health and happiness.


## CHAPTER XXIX.

*Waverley's Reception in the Lowlands after his
Highland Tour.*

IT was noon when the two friends stood at the top of
the pass of Bally-Brough. "I must go no farther," said
Fergus Mac-Ivor, who during the journey had in vain
endeavoured to raise his friend's spirits. "If my cross-
grained sister has any share in your dejection, trust me
she thinks highly of you, though her present anxiety
about the public cause prevents her listening to any
other subject. Confide your interest to me; I will not
betray it, providing you do not again assume that vile
cockade."

"No fear of that, considering the manner in which it
has been recalled. Adieu, Fergus; do not permit your
sister to forget me."

"And adieu, Waverley; you may soon hear of her with
a prouder title. Get home, write letters, and make
friends as many and as fast as you can; there will
speedily be unexpected guests on the coast of Suffolk, or
my news from France has deceived me."[1]

---

[1] The sanguine Jacobites, during the eventful years 1745-6, kept up the spirits
of their party by the rumour of descents from France on behalf of the Chevalier
St George. (S.)

Thus parted the friends; Fergus returning back to his castle, while Edward, followed by Callum Beg, the latter transformed from point to point into a Low-country groom, proceeded to the little town of ——.

Edward paced on under the painful and yet not altogether embittered feelings, which separation and uncertainty produce in the mind of a youthful lover. I am not sure if the ladies understand the full value of the influence of absence, nor do I think it wise to teach it them, lest, like the Clelias and Mandanes of yore, they should resume the humour of sending their lovers into banishment. Distance, in truth, produces in idea the same effect as in real perspective. Objects are softened, and rounded, and rendered doubly graceful; the harsher and more ordinary points of character are mellowed down, and those by which it is remembered are the more striking outlines that mark sublimity, grace, or beauty. There are mists too in the mental, as well as the natural horizon, to conceal what is less pleasing in distant objects, and there are happy lights, to stream in full glory upon those points which can profit by brilliant illumination.

Waverley forgot Flora Mac-Ivor's prejudices in her magnanimity, and almost pardoned her indifference towards his affection, when he recollected the grand and decisive object which seemed to fill her whole soul. She, whose sense of duty so wholly engrossed her in the cause of a benefactor, what would be her feelings in favour of the happy individual who should be so fortunate as to awaken them? Then came the doubtful question, whether he might not be that happy man,—a question which fancy endeavoured to answer in the affirmative, by conjuring up all she had said in his praise, with the addition of a comment much more flattering than the text warranted. All that was commonplace, all that belonged to the everyday world, was melted away and obliterated in those dreams of imagination, which only remembered with advantage the points of grace and dignity that distinguished Flora from the generality of her sex, not the particulars which she held in common with them. Edward was, in short, in the fair way of creating a goddess out of a high-spirited, accomplished, and beautiful young woman; and the time was wasted in castle-building, until, at the descent of a steep hill, he saw beneath him the market-town of ——.

The Highland politeness of Callum Beg—there are few

nations, by the way, who can boast of so much natural
politeness as the Highlanders[1]—the Highland civility of
his attendant had not permitted him to disturb the
reveries of our hero.  But observing him rouse himself at
the sight of the village, Callum pressed closer to his side,
and hoped "when they cam to the public, his honour wad
not say nothing about Vich Ian Vohr, for ta people were
bitter Whigs, deil burst tem."

Waverley assured the prudent page that he would be
cautious ; and as he now distinguished, not indeed the
ringing of bells, but the tinkling of something like a
hammer against the side of an old mossy, green, inverted
porridge-pot, that hung in an open booth, of the size and
shape of a parrot's cage, erected to grace the east end of a
building resembling an old barn, he asked Callum Beg if
it were Sunday.

"Could na say just preceesely—Sunday seldom cam
aboun the pass of Bally-Brough."

On entering the town, however, and advancing towards
the most apparent public-house which presented itself,
the numbers of old women, in tartan screens and red
cloaks, who streamed from the barn-resembling building,
debating, as they went, the comparative merits of the
blessed youth Jabesh Rentowel, and that chosen vessel
Maister Goukthrapple, induced Callum to assure his temporary master, "that it was either ta muckle Sunday hersell, or ta little government Sunday that they ca'd ta fast."

On alighting at the sign of the Seven-branched Golden
Candlestick, which, for the further delectation of the
guests, was graced with a short Hebrew motto, they were
received by mine host, a tall thin puritanical figure, who
seemed to debate with himself whether he ought to give
shelter to those who travelled on such a day.  Reflecting,
however, in all probability, that he possessed the power
of mulcting them for this irregularity, a penalty which
they might escape by passing into Gregor Duncanson's,
at the sign of the Highlander and the Hawick Gill, Mr
Ebenezer Cruickshanks condescended to admit them into
his dwelling.

To this sanctified person Waverley addressed his request, that he would procure him a guide, with a saddle-
horse, to carry his portmanteau to Edinburgh.

---

[1] The Highlander, in former times, had always a high idea of his own gentility,
and was anxious to impress the same upon those with whom he conversed.  His
language abounded in the phrases of courtesy and compliment; and the habit of
carrying arms, and mixing with those who did so, made it particularly desirable
they should use cautious politeness in their intercourse with each other.  (S.)

"And whar may ye be coming from?" demanded mine host of the Candlestick.

"I have told you where I wish to go; I do not conceive any further information necessary either for the guide or his saddle-horse."

"Hem! Ahem!" returned he of the Candlestick, somewhat disconcerted at this rebuff. "It's the general fast, sir, and I cannot enter into ony carnal transactions on sic a day, when the people should be humbled, and the backsliders should return, as worthy Mr Goukthrapple said; and moreover when, as the precious Mr Jabesh Rentowel did weel observe, the land was mourning for covenants burnt, broken, and buried."

"My good friend," said Waverley, "if you cannot let me have a horse and guide, my servant shall seek them elsewhere."

"Aweel! Your servant?—and what for gangs he not forward wi' you himsell?"

Waverley had but very little of a captain of horse's spirit within him—I mean of that sort of spirit which I have been obliged to when I happened, in a mail-coach, or diligence, to meet some military man who has kindly taken upon him the disciplining of the waiters, and the taxing of reckonings. Some of this useful talent our hero had, however, acquired during his military service, and on this gross provocation it began seriously to arise, "Look ye, sir; I came here for my own accommodation, and not to answer impertinent questions. Either say you can, or cannot, get me what I want; I shall pursue my course in either case."

Mr Ebenezer Cruickshanks left the room with some indistinct muttering; but whether negative or acquiescent, Edward could not well distinguish. The hostess, a civil, quiet, laborious drudge, came to take his orders for dinner, but declined to make answer on the subject of the horse and guide; for the Salique law, it seems, extended to the stables of the Golden Candlestick.

From a window which overlooked the dark and narrow court in which Callum Beg rubbed down the horses after their journey, Waverley heard the following dialogue betwixt the subtle foot-page of Vich Ian Vohr and his landlord:

"Ye'll be frae the north, young man?" began the latter.

"And ye may say that," answered Callum.

"And ye'll hae ridden a lang way the day, it may weel be?"

"Sae lang, that I could weel tak a dram."

"Gudewife, bring the gill stoup. "

Here some compliments passed fitting the occasion, when my host of the Golden Candlestick, having, as he thought, opened his guest's heart by this hospitable propitiation, resumed his scrutiny.

"Ye'll no hae mickle better whisky than that aboon the Pass?"

"I am nae frae aboon the Pass?"

"Ye're a Highlandman by your tongue?"

"Na; I am but just Aberdeen-a-way."

"And did your master come frae Aberdeen wi' you?"

"Ay—that's when I left it mysell," answered the cool and impenetrable Callum Beg.

"And what kind of a gentleman is he?"

"I believe he is ane o' King George's state officers; at least he's aye for ganging on to the south, and he has a hantle o' siller, [1] and never grudges ony thing till a poor body, or in the way of a lawing." [2]

"He wants a guide and a horse frae hence to Edinburgh."

"Ay, and ye maun find it him forthwith."

"Ahem! It will be chargeable."

"He cares na for that a bodle." [3]

"Aweel, Duncan—did ye say your name was Duncan, or Donald?"

"Na, man—Jamie—Jamie Steenson—I telt ye before."

This last undaunted parry altogether foiled Mr Cruickshanks, who, though not quite satisfied either with the reserve of the master, or the extreme readiness of the man, was contented to lay a tax on the reckoning and horsehire, that might compound for his ungratified curiosity. The circumstance of its being the fast day was not forgotten in the charge, which, on the whole, did not, however, amount to much more than double what in fairness it should have been.

Callum Beg soon after announced in person the ratification of this treaty, adding, "Ta auld deevil was ganging to ride wi' ta Duinhé-wassel hersell."

"That will not be very pleasant, Callum, nor altogether safe, for our host seems a person of great curiosity; but a traveller must submit to these inconveniences. Meanwhile, my good lad, here is a trifle for you to drink Vich Ian Vohr's health."

The hawk's eye of Callum flashed delight upon a golden guinea, with which these last words were accompanied.

[1] A large supply of money.  [2] Tavern reckoning.  [3] A coin one-third of a penny.

He hastened, not without a curse on the intricacies of a Saxon breeches pocket, or *spleuchan*, as he called it, to deposit the treasure in his fob; and then, as if he conceived the benevolence called for some requital on his part, he gathered close up to Edward, with an expression of countenance peculiarly knowing, and spoke in an under tone, "If his honour thought ta auld deevil Whig carle was a bit dangerous, she could easily provide for him, and teil ane ta wiser."

"How, and in what manner?"

"Her ain sell," replied Callum, "could wait for him a wee bit frae the toun, and kittle his quarters wi' her *skene-occle*."

"Skene-occle! what's that?"

Callum unbuttoned his coat, raised his left arm, and, with an emphatic nod, pointed to the hilt of a small dirk, snugly deposited under it, in the lining of his jacket. Waverley thought he had misunderstood his meaning; he gazed in his face, and discovered in Callum's very handsome, though embrowned features, just the degree of roguish malice with which a lad of the same age in England would have brought forward a plan for robbing an orchard.

"Good God, Callum, would you take the man's life?"

"Indeed," answered the young desperado, "and I think he has had just a lang enough lease o't, when he's for betraying honest folk, that come to spend siller at his public."

Edward saw nothing was to be gained by argument, and therefore contented himself with enjoining Callum to lay aside all practices against the person of Mr Ebenezer Cruickshanks; in which injunction the page seemed to acquiesce with an air of great indifference.

"Ta Duinhé-wassel might please himsell; ta auld rudas loon[1] had never done Callum nae ill. But here's a bit line frae ta Tighearna, tat he bade me gie your honour ere I came back."

The letter from the Chief contained Flora's lines on the fate of Captain Wogan, whose enterprising character is so well drawn by Clarendon. He had originally engaged in the service of the Parliament, but had abjured that party upon the execution of Charles I.; and upon hearing that the royal standard was set up by the Earl of Glencairn and General Middleton in the Highlands of Scotland, took leave of Charles II., who was then at Paris, passed into England, assembled a body of cavaliers in the

[1] Bold rascal.

neighbourhood of London, and traversed the kingdom, which had been so long under domination of the usurper, by marches conducted with such skill, dexterity, and spirit, that he safely united his handful of horsemen with the body of Highlanders then in arms. After several months of desultory warfare, in which Wogan's skill and courage gained him the highest reputation, he had the misfortune to be wounded in a dangerous manner, and no surgical assistance being within reach, he terminated his short but glorious career.

There were obvious reasons why the politic Chieftain was desirous to place the example of this young hero under the eye of Waverley, with whose romantic disposition it coincided so peculiarly. But his letter turned chiefly upon some trifling commissions which Waverley had promised to execute for him in England, and it was only toward the conclusion that Edward found these words :— "I owe Flora a grudge for refusing us her company yesterday ; and as I am giving you the trouble of reading these lines, in order to keep in your memory your promise to procure me the fishing-tackle and cross-bow from London, I will enclose her verses on the Grave of Wogan. This I know will tease her ; for, to tell you the truth, I think her more in love with the memory of that dead hero, than she is likely to be with any living one, unless he shall tread a similar path. But English squires of our day keep their oak-trees to shelter their deer parks, or repair the losses of an evening at White's, and neither invoke them to wreath their brows, nor shelter their graves. Let me hope for one brilliant exception in a dear friend, to whom I would most gladly give a dearer title."

The verses were inscribed,

### TO AN OAK TREE.

*In the Church-Yard of ——, in the Highlands of Scotland, said to mark the Grave of Captain Wogan, killed in 1649.*

EMBLEM of England's ancient faith,
    Full proudly may thy branches wave,
Where loyalty lies low in death,
    And valour fills a timeless grave.

And thou, brave tenant of the tomb !
    Repine not if our clime deny,
Above thine honour'd sod to bloom.
    The flowerets of a milder sky.

These owe their birth to genial May,
    Beneath a fiercer sun they pine,
Before the winter storm decay—
    And can their worth be type of thine?

No! for, 'mid storms of Fate opposing,
  Still higher swell'd thy dauntless heart,
And, while Despair the scene was closing,
  Commenced thy brief but brilliant part.

'Twas then thou sought'st on Albyn's hill,
  (When England's sons the strife resign'd)
A rugged race resisting still,
  And unsubdued though unrefined.

Thy death's hour heard no kindred wail,
  No holy knell thy requiem rung;
Thy mourners were the plaided Gael,
  Thy dirge the clamorous pibroch sung.

Yet who, in Fortune's summer-shine
  To waste life's longest term away,
Would change that glorious dawn of thine,
  Though darken'd ere its noontide day?

Be thine the Tree whose dauntless boughs
  Brave summer's drought and winter's gloom!
Rome bound with oak her patriots' brows,
  As Albyn shadows Wogan's tomb.

Whatever might be the real merit of Flora Mac-Ivor's poetry, the enthusiasm which it intimated was well calculated to make a corresponding impression upon her lover. The lines were read—read again—then deposited in Waverley's bosom—then again drawn out, and read line by line, in a low and smothered voice, and with frequent pauses which prolonged the mental treat, as an epicure protracts, by sipping slowly, the enjoyment of a delicious beverage. The entrance of Mrs Cruickshanks, with the sublunary articles of dinner and wine, hardly interrupted this pantomime of affectionate enthusiasm.

At length the tall ungainly figure and ungracious visage of Ebenezer presented themselves. The upper part of his form, notwithstanding the season required no such defence, was shrouded in a large greatcoat, belted over his under habiliments, and crested with a huge cowl of the same stuff, which, when drawn over the head and hat, completely over-shadowed both, and being buttoned beneath the chin, was called a *trot-cozy*. His hand grasped a huge jockey-whip, garnished with brass mounting. His thin legs tenanted a pair of gambadoes, fastened at the sides with rusty clasps. Thus accoutred, he stalked into the midst of the apartment, and announced his errand in brief phrase:—" Yer horses are ready."

" You go with me yourself then, landlord ?"

" I do, as far as Perth ; where ye may be supplied with a guide to Embro', as your occasions shall require."

Thus saying, he placed under Waverley's eye the bill which he held in his hand ; and at the same time, self-invited, filled a glass of wine, and drank devoutly to a

blessing on their journey. Waverley stared at the man's
impudence, but, as their connection was to be short, and
promised to be convenient, he made no observation upon
it ; and, having paid his reckoning, expressed his intention to depart immediately.    He mounted Dermid
accordingly, and sallied forth from the Golden Candlestick, followed by the puritanical figure we have described,
after he had, at the expense of some time and difficulty,
and by the assistance of a "louping-on-stane," or structure
of masonry erected for the traveller's convenience in
front of the house, elevated his person to the back of a
long-backed, raw-boned, thin-gutted phantom of a broken-
down blood-horse, on which Waverley's portmanteau was
deposited.  Our hero, though not in a very gay humour,
could hardly help laughing at the appearance of his new
squire, and at imagining the astonishment which his
person and equipage would have excited at Waverley-
Honour.

Edward's tendency to mirth did not escape mine host
of the Candlestick, who, conscious of the cause, infused a
double portion of souring into the pharasaical leaven of
his countenance, and resolved internally that, in one way
or other, the young *Englisher* should pay dearly for the
contempt with which he seemed to regard him. Callum
also stood at the gate, and enjoyed, with undissembled
glee, the ridiculous figure of Mr Cruickshanks.  As
Waverley passed him, he pulled off his hat respectfully,
and, approaching his stirrup, bade him "Tak heed the
auld Whig deevil played him nae cantrip."[1]

Waverley once more thanked, and bade him farewell,
and then rode briskly onward, not sorry to be out of
hearing of the shouts of the children, as they beheld old
Ebenezer rise and sink in his stirrups, to avoid the con-
cussions occasioned by a hard trot upon a half-paved
street.  The village of —— was soon several miles behind
him.

## CHAPTER XXX.

*Shows that the Loss of a Horse's Shoe may be a serious
Inconvenience.*

THE manner and air of Waverley, but, above all, the
glittering contents of his purse, and the indifference with
which he seemed to regard them, somewhat overawed his

[1] Trick.

companion, and deterred him from making any attempts to enter upon conversation. His own reflections were moreover agitated by various surmises, and by plans of self-interest, with which these were intimately connected. The travellers journeyed, therefore, in silence, until it was interrupted by the annunciation, on the part of the guide, that his "naig had lost a fore-foot shoe, which, doubtless, his honour would consider it was his part to replace."

This was what lawyers call a *fishing question*, calculated to ascertain how far Waverley was disposed to submit to petty imposition. "My part to replace your horse's shoe, you rascal!" said Waverley, mistaking the purport of the intimation.

"Indubitably," answered Mr Cruickshanks; "though there was no preceese clause to that effect, it canna be expected that I am to pay for the casualties whilk may befall the puir naig while in your honour's service.— Nathless, if your honour"——

"O, you mean I am to pay the farrier; but where shall we find one?"

Rejoiced at discerning there would be no objection made on the part of his temporary master, Mr Cruickshanks assured him that Cairnvreckan, a village which they were about to enter, was happy in an excellent blacksmith; "but as he was a professor, he would drive a nail for no man on the Sabbath, or kirk-fast, unless it were in a case of absolute necessity, for which he always charged sixpence each shoe." The most important part of this communication, in the opinion of the speaker, made a very slight impression on the hearer, who only internally wondered what college this veterinary professor belonged to; not aware that the word was used to denote any person who pretended to uncommon sanctity of faith and manner.

As they entered the village of Cairnvreckan, they speedily distinguished the smith's house. Being also a *public*, it was two storeys high, and proudly reared its crest, covered with grey slate, above the thatched hovels by which it was surrounded. The adjoining smithy betokened none of the Sabbatical silence and repose which Ebenezer had augured from the sanctity of his friend. On the contrary, hammer clashed and anvil rang, the bellows groaned, and the whole apparatus of Vulcan appeared to be in full activity. Nor was the labour of a rural and pacific nature. The master smith, benempt, as his sign intimated, John Mucklewrath, with two assistants, toiled busily in arranging, repairing, and furbishing old muskets, pistols, and swords, which lay scattered around his work-shop in military confusion. The open shed, containing the forge, was crowded with persons who came and went as if receiving and communicating important news; and a single glance at the aspect of the people who traversed the street in haste, or stood assembled in groups, with eyes elevated, and hands uplifted, announced that some extraordinary intelligence was agitating the public mind of the municipality of Cairnvreckan. "There is some news," said mine host of the Candlestick, pushing his lantern-jawed visage and bare-boned nag rudely forward into the crowd—"there is some news; and if it please my Creator, I will forthwith obtain speirings[1] thereof."

Waverley, with better regulated curiosity than his attendant's, dismounted, and gave his horse to a boy who stood idling near. It arose, perhaps from the shyness of his character in early youth, that he felt dislike at applying to a stranger even for casual information, without previously glancing at his physiognomy and appearance. While he looked about in order to select the person with whom he would most willingly hold communication, the buzz around saved him in some degree the trouble of interrogatories. The names of Lochiel, Clanronald, Glengarry, and other distinguished Highland Chiefs, among whom Vich Ian Vohr was repeatedly mentioned, were as familiar in men's mouths as household words; and from the alarm generally expressed, he easily conceived that their descent into the Lowlands, at the head of their armed tribes, had either already taken place, or was instantly apprehended.

Ere Waverley could ask particulars, a strong, large-boned, hard-featured woman, about forty, dressed as if her clothes had been flung on with a pitchfork, her cheeks flushed with a scarlet red where they were not smutted with soot and lampblack, jostled through the crowd, and, brandishing high a child of two years old, which she danced in her arms, without regard to its screams of terror, sang forth, with all her might,—

> "Charlie is my darling, my darling, my darling,
> Charlie is my darling,
> The young Chevalier!"

"D'ye hear what's come ower ye now," continued the

---
[1] Tidings.

virago, "ye whingeing[1] Whig carles[2]? D'ye hear wha's coming to cow your cracks?[3]

> 'Little wot ye wha's coming,
> Little wot ye wha's coming,
> A' the wild Macraws are coming.' "

The Vulcan of Cairnvreckan, who acknowledged his Venus in this exulting Bacchante, regarded her with a grim and ire-foreboding countenance, while some of the senators of the village hastened to interpose. "Whisht, gudewife; is this a time, or is this a day, to be singing your ranting fule sangs in?—a time when the wine of wrath is poured out without mixture in the cup of indignation, and a day when the land should give testimony against popery, and prelacy, and quakerism, and independency, and supremacy, and erastianism, and antinomianism, and a' the errors of the church?"

"And that's a' your Whiggery," re-echoed the Jacobite heroine; "that's a' your Whiggery, and your presbytery, ye cut-lugged, graning carles![4] What! d'ye think the lads wi' the kilts will care for yer synods and yer presbyteries, and yer buttock-mail, and yer stool o' repentance? Vengeance on the black face o't! mony an honester woman's been set upon it than streeks[5] doon beside ony Whig in the country. I mysell"——

Here John Mucklewrath, who dreaded her entering upon a detail of personal experience, interposed his matrimonial authority. "Gae hame, and be d——, (that I should say sae,) and put on the sowens[6] for supper."

"And you, ye doil'd[7] dotard," replied his gentle help-mate, her wrath, which had hitherto wandered abroad over the whole assembly, being at once and violently impelled into its natural channel, "*ye* stand there hammering dog-heads for fules that will never snap them at a Highlandman, instead of earning bread for your family, and shoeing this winsome young gentleman's horse that's just come frae the north! I'se warrant him nane of your whingeing King George folk, but a gallant Gordon, at the least o' him."

The eyes of the assembly were now turned upon Waverley, who took the opportunity to beg the smith to shoe his guide's horse with all speed, as he wished to proceed on his journey;—for he had heard enough to make him sensible that there would be danger in delaying long in this place. The smith's eyes rested on him with

---

[1] Whining.  [2] Boors.  [3] Cut short your boasting talk.
[4] Groaning boors.  [5] Lies.  [6] Flummery made of oat-meal.  [7] Stupid.

a look of displeasure and suspicion, not lessened by the
eagerness with which his wife enforced Waverley's mandate.  "D'ye hear what the weel-favoured young gentleman says, you drunken ne'er-do-good?"

"And what may your name be, sir?" quoth Mucklewrath.

"It is of no consequence to you, my friend, provided I
pay your labour."

"But it may be of consequence to the state, sir," replied
an old farmer, smelling strongly of whisky and peat-
smoke; "and I doubt we maun delay your journey till
you have seen the Laird."

"You certainly," said Waverley, haughtily, "will find it
both difficult and dangerous to detain me, unless you can
produce some proper authority."

There was a pause and a whisper among the crowd—
"Secretary Murray;" "Lord Lewis Gordon;" "Maybe
the Chevalier himsell!"  Such were the surmises that
passed hurriedly among them, and there was obviously
an increased disposition to resist Waverley's departure.
He attempted to argue mildly with them, but his
voluntary ally, Mrs Mucklewrath, broke in upon and
drowned his expostulations, taking his part with an
abusive violence, which was all set down to Edward's
account by those on whom it was bestowed.  "Ye'll stop
ony gentleman that's the Prince's freend?" for she too,
though with other feelings, had adopted the general
opinion respecting Waverley.  "I daur ye to touch him,"
spreading abroad her long and muscular fingers, garnished
with claws which a vulture might have envied.  "I'll set
my ten commandments in the face o' the first loon[1] that
lays a finger on him."

"Gae hame, gudewife," quoth the farmer aforesaid; "it
wad better set you to be nursing the gudeman's bairns
than to be deaving[2] us here."

"*His* bairns?" retorted the Amazon, regarding her
husband with a grin of ineffable contempt—"*His* bairns!

> "O gin ye were dead, gudeman,
>   And a green turf on your head, gudeman!
> Then I wad ware[3] my widowhood
>   Upon a ranting Highlandman."

This canticle, which excited a suppressed titter among
the younger part of the audience, totally overcame the
patience of the taunted man of the anvil.  "Diel be in
me but I'll put this het gad[4] down her throat!" cried he,

[1] Rascal.     [2] Deafening.     [3] Spend.     [4] Hot rod.

in an ecstasy of wrath, snatching a bar from the forge; and he might have executed his threat, had he not been withheld by a part of the mob, while the rest endeavoured to force the termagant out of his presence.

Waverley meditated a retreat in the confusion, but his horse was nowhere to be seen. At length he observed, at some distance, his faithful attendant, Ebenezer, who, as soon as he had perceived the turn matters were likely to take, had withdrawn both horses from the press, and, mounted on the one, and holding the other, answered the loud and repeated calls of Waverley for his horse. "Na, na! if ye are nae friend to kirk and the king, and are detained as siccan [1] a person, ye maun [2] answer to honest men of the country for breach of contract; and I maun keep the naig and the walise for damage and expense, in respect my horse and mysell will lose to-morrow's day's-wark, besides the afternoon preaching."

Edward, out of patience, hemmed in and hustled by the rabble on every side, and every moment expecting personal violence, resolved to try measures of intimidation, and at length drew a pocket-pistol, threatening, on the one hand, to shoot whomsoever dared to stop him, and, on the other, menacing Ebenezer with a similar doom, if he stirred a foot with the horses. The sapient Partridge says, that one man with a pistol, is equal to a hundred unarmed, because, though he can shoot but one of the multitude, yet no one knows but that he himself may be that luckless individual. The *levy en masse* of Cairn-vreckan would therefore probably have given way, nor would Ebenezer, whose natural paleness had waxed three shades more cadaverous, have ventured to dispute a mandate so enforced, had not the Vulcan of the village, eager to discharge upon some more worthy object the fury which his helpmate had provoked, and not ill satisfied to find such an object in Waverley, rushed at him with the red-hot bar of iron, with such determination, as made the discharge of his pistol an act of self-defence. The unfortunate man fell; and while Edward, thrilled with a natural horror at the incident, neither had presence of mind to unsheathe his sword, nor to draw his remaining pistol, the populace threw themselves upon him, disarmed him, and were about to use him with great violence, when the appearance of a venerable clergyman, the pastor of the parish, put a curb on their fury.

This worthy man (none of the Goukthrapples or Ren-

---

[1] Such kind of.    [2] Must.

towels) maintained his character with the common people, although he preached the practical fruits of Christian faith, as well as its abstract tenets, and was respected by the higher orders, notwithstanding he declined soothing their speculative errors by converting the pulpit of the gospel into a school of heathen morality. Perhaps it is owing to this mixture of faith and practice in his doctrine, that, although his memory has formed a sort of era in the annals of Cairnvreckan, so that the parishioners, to denote what befell Sixty Years since, still say it happened "in good Mr Morton's time," I have never been able to discover which he belonged to, the evangelical, or the moderate party in the kirk. Nor do I hold the circumstance of much moment, since, in my own remembrance, the one was headed by an Erskine, the other by a Robertson.[1]

Mr Morton had been alarmed by the discharge of the pistol, and the increasing hubbub around the smithy. His first attention, after he had directed the bystanders to detain Waverley, but to abstain from injuring him, was turned to the body of Mucklewrath, over which his wife, in a revulsion of feeling, was weeping, howling, and tearing her elf-locks, in a state little short of distraction. On raising up the smith, the first discovery was, that he was alive; and the next, that he was likely to live as long as if he had never heard the report of a pistol in his life. He had made a narrow escape, however; the bullet had grazed his head, and stunned him for a moment or two, which trance terror and confusion of spirit had prolonged somewhat longer. He now arose to demand vengeance on the person of Waverley, and with difficulty acquiesced in the proposal of Mr Morton, that he should be carried before the Laird, as a justice of peace, and placed at his disposal. The rest of the assistants unanimously agreed to the measure recommended; even Mrs Mucklewrath, who had begun to recover from her hysterics, whimpered forth, "She wadna say naething against what the minister proposed; he was e'en ower gude for his trade, and she hoped to see him wi' a dainty decent bishop's gown on his back; a comelier sight than your Geneva cloaks and bands, I wis."

---

[1] The Rev. John Erskine, D.D., an eminent Scottish divine, and a most excellent man, headed the Evangelical party in the Church of Scotland at the time when the celebrated Dr Robertson, the historian, was the leader of the Moderate party. These two distinguished persons were colleagues in the Old Grey Friar's Church, Edinburgh; and, however much they differed in church politics, preserved the most perfect harmony as private friends, and as clergymen serving the same cure. (S.)

All controversy being thus laid aside, Waverley, escorted by the whole inhabitants of the village who were not bed-ridden, was conducted to the house of Cairnvreckan, which was about half a mile distant.

## CHAPTER XXXI.

### *An Examination.*

MAJOR MELVILLE of Cairnvreckan, an elderly gentleman, who had spent his youth in the military service, received Mr Morton with great kindness, and our hero with civility, which the equivocal circumstances wherein Edward was placed rendered constrained and distant.

The nature of the smith's hurt was inquired into, and as the actual injury was likely to prove trifling, and the circumstances in which it was received rendered the infliction, on Edward's part, a natural act of self-defence, the Major conceived he might dismiss that matter, on Waverley's depositing in his hands a small sum for the benefit of the wounded person.

"I could wish, sir," continued the major, "that my duty terminated here ; but it is necessary that we should have some further inquiry into the cause of your journey through the country at this unfortunate and distracted time."

Mr Ebenezer Cruickshanks now stood forth, and communicated to the magistrate all he knew or suspected, from the reserve of Waverley, and the evasions of Callum Beg. The horse upon which Edward rode, he said, he knew to belong to Vich Ian Vohr, though he dared not tax Edward's former attendant with the fact, lest he should have his house and stables burnt over his head some night by that godless gang, the Mac-Ivors. He concluded by exaggerating his own services to kirk and state, as having been the means, under God, (as he modestly qualified the assertion,) of attaching this suspicious and formidable delinquent. He intimated hopes of future reward, and of instant reimbursement for loss of time, and even of character, by travelling on the state business on the fast-day.

To this Major Melville answered, with great composure, that so far from claiming any merit in this affair, Mr Cruickshanks ought to deprecate the imposition of a very heavy fine for neglecting to lodge, in terms of the recent proclamation, an account with the nearest magistrate of any stranger who came to his inn; that, as Mr Cruickshanks boasted so much of religion and loyalty, he should not impute this conduct to disaffection, but only suppose that his zeal for kirk and state had been lulled asleep by the opportunity of charging a stranger with double horse-hire; that, however, feeling himself incompetent to decide singly upon the conduct of a person of such importance, he should reserve it for consideration of the next quarter-sessions. Now our history for the present saith no more of him of the Candlestick, who wended dolorous and malcontent back to his own dwelling.

Major Melville then commanded the villagers to return to their homes, excepting two, who officiated as constables, and whom he directed to wait below. The apartment was thus cleared of every person but Mr Morton, whom the Major invited to remain; a sort of factor, who acted as clerk; and Waverley himself. There ensued a painful and embarrassed pause, till Major Melville, looking upon Waverley with much compassion, and often consulting a paper or memorandum which he held in his hand, requested to know his name.—"Edward Waverley."

"I thought so; late of the —— dragoons, and nephew of Sir Everard Waverley of Waverley-Honour?"

"The same."

"Young gentleman, I am extremely sorry that this painful duty has fallen to my lot."

"Duty, Major Melville, renders apologies superfluous."

"True, sir; permit me, therefore, to ask you how your time has been disposed of since you obtained leave of absence from your regiment, several weeks ago, until the present moment?"

"My reply," said Waverley, "to so general a question must be guided by the nature of the charge which renders it necessary. I request to know what that charge is, and upon what authority I am forcibly detained to reply to it?"

"The charge, Mr Waverley, I grieve to say, is of a very high nature, and affects your character both as a soldier and a subject. In the former capacity, you are charged with spreading mutiny and rebellion among the men you commanded, and setting them the example of desertion, by prolonging your own absence from the regiment, contrary to the express orders of your commanding officer. The civil crime of which you stand accused is that of high treason, and levying war against the king, the highest delinquency of which a subject can be guilty.'

"And by what authority am I detained to reply to such heinous calumnies?"

"By one which you must not dispute, nor I disobey."

He handed to Waverley a warrant from the Supreme Criminal Court of Scotland, in full form, for apprehending and securing the person of Edward Waverley, Esq., suspected of treasonable practices, and other high crimes and misdemeanours.

The astonishment which Waverley expressed at this communication was imputed by Major Melville to conscious guilt, while Mr Morton was rather disposed to construe it into the surprise of innocence unjustly suspected. There was something true in both conjectures; for although Edward's mind acquitted him of the crime with which he was charged, yet a hasty review of his own conduct convinced him he might have great difficulty in establishing his innocence to the satisfaction of others.

"It is a very painful part of this painful business," said Major Melville, after a pause, "that, under so grave a charge, I must necessarily request to see such papers as you have on your person."

"You shall, sir, without reserve," said Edward, throwing his pocket-book and memorandums upon the table; "there is but one with which I could wish you would dispense."

"I am afraid, Mr Waverley, I can indulge you with no reservation."

"You shall see it then, sir; and as it can be of no service, I beg it may be returned."

He took from his bosom the lines he had that morning received, and presented them with the envelope. The Major perused them in silence, and directed his clerk to make a copy of them. He then wrapped the copy in the envelope, and placing it on the table before him, returned the original to Waverley, with an air of melancholy gravity.

After indulging the prisoner, for such our hero must now be considered, with what he thought a reasonable time for reflection, Major Melville resumed his examination, premising, that as Mr Waverley seemed to object to general questions, his interrogatories should be as specific as his information permitted. He then proceeded in his investigation, dictating, as he went on, the import of the questions and answers to the amanuensis, by whom it was written down.

"Did Mr Waverley know one Humphry Houghton, a non-commissioned officer in Gardiner's dragoons?"

"Certainly; he was sergeant of my troop, and son of a tenant of my uncle."

"Exactly—and had a considerable share of your confidence, and an influence among his comrades?"

"I had never occasion to repose confidence in a person of his description," answered Waverley. "I favoured Sergeant Houghton as a clever, active young fellow, and I believe his fellow-soldiers respected him accordingly."

"But you used through this man," answered Major Melville, "to communicate with such of your troop as were recruited upon Waverley-Honour?"

"Certainly; the poor fellows, finding themselves in a regiment chiefly composed of Scotch or Irish, looked up to me in any of their little distresses, and naturally made their countrymen, and sergeant, their spokesman on such occasions."

"Sergeant Houghton's influence," continued the Major, "extended, then, particularly over those soldiers who followed you to the regiment from your uncle's estate?"

"Surely;—but what is that to the present purpose?"

"To that I am just coming, and I beseech your candid reply. Have you, since leaving the regiment, held any correspondence, direct or indirect, with this Sergeant Houghton?"

"I!—I hold correspondence with a man of his rank and situation!—How, or for what purpose?"

"That you are to explain;—but did you not, for example, send to him for some books?"

"You remind me of a trifling commission," said Waverley, "which I gave Sergeant Houghton, because my servant could not read. I do recollect I bade him, by letter, select some books, of which I sent him a list, and send them to me at Tully-Veolan."

"And of what description were those books?"

"They related almost entirely to elegant literature; they were designed for a lady's perusal."

"Were there not, Mr Waverley, treasonable tracts and pamphlets among them?"

"There were some political treatises, into which I hardly looked. They had been sent to me by the officiousness of a kind friend, whose heart is more to be esteemed than his prudence or political sagacity: they seemed to be dull compositions."

"That friend," continued the persevering inquirer,

"was a Mr Pembroke, a nonjuring clergyman, the author of two treasonable works, of which the manuscripts were found among your baggage?"

"But of which, I give you my honour as a gentleman," replied Waverley, "I never read six pages."

"I am not your judge, Mr Waverley; your examination will be transmitted elsewhere. And now to proceed—Do you know a person that passes by the name of Wily Will, or Will Ruthven?"

"I never heard of such a name till this moment."

"Did you never through such a person, or any other person, communicate with Sergeant Humphry Houghton, instigating him to desert, with as many of his comrades as he could seduce to join him, and unite with the Highlanders and other rebels now in arms under the command of the young Pretender?"

"I assure you I am not only entirely guiltless of the plot you have laid to my charge, but I detest it from the very bottom of my soul, nor would I be guilty of such treachery to gain a throne, either for myself or any other man alive."

"Yet when I consider this envelope in the handwriting of one of those misguided gentlemen who are now in arms against their country, and the verses which it enclosed, I cannot but find some analogy between the enterprise I have mentioned and the exploit of Wogan, which the writer seems to expect you should imitate."

Waverley was struck with the coincidence, but denied that the wishes or expectations of the letter-writer were to be regarded as proofs of a charge otherwise chimerical.

"But, if I am rightly informed, your time was spent, during your absence from the regiment, between the house of this Highland Chieftain, and that of Mr Bradwardine, of Bradwardine, also in arms for this unfortunate cause?"

"I do not mean to disguise it; but I do deny, most resolutely, being privy to any of their designs against the government."

"You do not, however, I presume, intend to deny, that you attended your host Glennaquoich to a rendezvous, where, under a pretence of a general hunting match, most of the accomplices of his treason were assembled to concert measures for taking arms?"

"I acknowledge having been at such a meeting," said Waverley; "but I neither heard nor saw anything which could give it the character you affix to it."

"From thence you proceeded," continued the magistrate, "with Glennaquoich and a part of his clan, to join the army of the young Pretender, and returned, after having paid your homage to him, to discipline and arm the remainder, and unite them to his bands on their way southward?"

"I never went with Glennaquoich on such an errand. I never so much as heard that the person whom you mention was in the country."

He then detailed the history of his misfortune at the hunting match, and added, that on his return he found himself suddenly deprived of his commission, and did not deny that he then, for the first time, observed symptoms which indicated a disposition in the Highlanders to take arms; but added, that having no inclination to join their cause, and no longer any reason for remaining in Scotland, he was now on his return to his native country, to which he had been summoned by those who had a right to direct his motions, as Major Melville would perceive from the letters on the table.

Major Melville accordingly perused the letters of Richard Waverley, of Sir Everard, and of Aunt Rachel; but the inferences he drew from them were different from what Waverley expected. They held the language of discontent with government, threw out no obscure hints of revenge, and that of poor Aunt Rachel, which plainly asserted the justice of the Stewart cause, was held to contain the open avowal of what the others only ventured to insinuate.

"Permit me another question, Mr Waverley," said Major Melville,—"Did you not receive repeated letters from your commanding-officer, warning you and commanding you to return to your post, and acquainting you with the use made of your name to spread discontent among your soldiers?"

"I never did, Major Melville. One letter, indeed, I received from him, containing a civil intimation of his wish that I would employ my leave of absence otherwise than in constant residence at Bradwardine, as to which, I own, I thought he was not called on to interfere; and, finally, I received, on the same day on which I observed myself superseded in the Gazette, a second letter from Colonel Gardiner, commanding me to join the regiment, an order which, owing to my absence, already mentioned and accounted for, I received too late to be obeyed. If there were any intermediate letters, and certainly from the Colonel's high character I think it probable that there were, they have never reached me."

"I have omitted, Mr Waverley," continued Major Melville, "to inquire after a matter of less consequence, but which has nevertheless been publicly talked of to your disadvantage. It is said, that a treasonable toast having been proposed in your hearing and presence, you, holding his majesty's commission, suffered the task of resenting it to devolve upon another gentleman of the company. This, sir, cannot be charged against you in a court of justice; but if, as I am informed, the officers of your regiment requested an explanation of such a rumour, as a gentleman and soldier, I cannot but be surprised that you did not afford it to them."

This was too much. Beset and pressed on every hand by accusations, in which gross falsehoods were blended with such circumstances of truth as could not fail to procure them credit,—alone, unfriended, and in a strange land, Waverley almost gave up his life and honour for lost, and, leaning his head upon his hand, resolutely refused to answer any farther questions, since the fair and candid statement he had already made had only served to furnish arms against him.

Without expressing either surprise or displeasure at the change in Waverley's manner, Major Melville proceeded composedly to put several other queries to him. "What does it avail me to answer you?" said Edward, sullenly. "You appear convinced of my guilt, and wrest every reply I have made to support your own preconceived opinion. Enjoy your supposed triumph, then, and torment me no further. If I am capable of the cowardice and treachery your charge burdens me with, I am not worthy to be believed in any reply I can make to you. If I am not deserving of your suspicion—and God and my own conscience bear evidence with me that it is so—then I do not see why I should, by my candour, lend my accusers arms against my innocence. There is no reason I should answer a word more, and I am determined to abide by this resolution." And again he resumed his posture of sullen and determined silence.

"Allow me," said the magistrate, "to remind you of one reason that may suggest the propriety of a candid and open confession. The inexperience of youth, Mr Waverley, lays it open to the plans of the more designing and artful; and one of your friends at least—I mean Mac-Ivor of Glennaquoich—ranks high in the latter class, as, from your apparent ingenuousness, youth, and unacquaintance with the manners of the Highlands, I should be disposed to place you among the former. In such a case, a false step, or error like yours, which I shall be happy to consider as involuntary, may be atoned for, and I would willingly act as intercessor. But as you must necessarily be acquainted with the strength of the individuals in this country who have assumed arms, with their means, and with their plans, I must expect you will merit this mediation on my part by a frank and candid avowal of all that has come to your knowledge upon these heads. In which case, I think I can venture to promise that a very short personal restraint will be the only ill consequence that can arise from your accession to these unhappy intrigues."

Waverley listened with great composure until the end of this exhortation, when, springing from his seat, with an energy he had not yet displayed, he replied, "Major Melville, since that is your name, I have hitherto answered your questions with candour, or declined them with temper, because their import concerned myself alone; but as you presume to esteem me mean enough to commence informer against others, who received me, whatever may be their public misconduct, as a guest and friend,—I declare to you that I consider your questions as an insult infinitely more offensive than your calumnious suspicions; and that, since my hard fortune permits me no other mode of resenting them than by verbal defiance, you should sooner have my heart out of my bosom, than a single syllable of information on subjects which I could only become acquainted with in the full confidence of unsuspecting hospitality."

Mr Morton and the Major looked at each other; and the former, who, in the course of the examination, had been repeatedly troubled with a sorry rheum, had recourse to his snuff-box and his handkerchief.

"Mr Waverley," said the Major, "my present situation prohibits me alike from giving or receiving offence, and I will not protract a discussion which approaches to either. I am afraid I must sign a warrant for detaining you in custody, but this house shall for the present be your prison. I fear I cannot persuade you to accept a share of our supper,—(Edward shook his head)—but I will order refreshments in your apartment."

Our hero bowed and withdrew, under guard of the

officers of justice, to a small but handsome room, where, declining all offers of food or wine, he flung himself on the bed, and, stupified by the harassing events and mental fatigue of this miserable day, he sunk into a deep and heavy slumber. This was more than he himself could have expected; but it is mentioned of the North-American Indians, when at the stake of torture, that on the least intermission of agony, they will sleep until the fire is applied to awaken them.

## CHAPTER XXXII.

### A Conference, and the Consequence.

MAJOR MELVILLE had detained Mr Morton during his examination of Waverley, both because he thought he might derive assistance from his practical good sense and approved loyalty, and also because it was agreeable to have a witness of unimpeached candour and veracity to proceedings which touched the honour and safety of a young Englishman of high rank and family, and the expectant heir of a large fortune. Every step he knew would be rigorously canvassed, and it was his business to place the justice and integrity of his own conduct beyond the limits of question.

When Waverley retired, the laird and clergyman of Cairnvreckan sat down in silence to their evening meal. While the servants were in attendance, neither chose to say anything on the circumstances which occupied their minds, and neither felt it easy to speak upon any other. The youth and apparent frankness of Waverley stood in strong contrast to the shades of suspicion which darkened around him, and he had a sort of naiveté and openness of demeanour, that seemed to belong to one unhackneyed in the ways of intrigue, and which pleaded highly in his favour.

Each mused over the particulars of the examination, and each viewed it through the medium of his own feelings. Both were men of ready and acute talent, and both were equally competent to combine various parts of evidence, and to deduce from them the necessary conclusions. But the wide difference of their habits and education often occasioned a great discrepancy in their respective deductions from admitted premises.

Major Melville had been versed in camps and cities; he
was vigilant by profession, and cautious from experience,
had met with much evil in the world, and therefore,
though himself an upright magistrate and an honourable
man, his opinions of others were always strict, and sometimes unjustly severe. Mr Morton, on the contrary, had
passed from the literary pursuits of a college, where he
was beloved by his companions, and respected by his
teachers, to the ease and simplicity of his present charge,
where his opportunities of witnessing evil were few, and
never dwelt upon, but in order to encourage repentance
and amendment; and where the love and respect of his
parishioners repaid his affectionate zeal in their behalf,
by endeavouring to disguise from him what they knew
would give him the most acute pain, namely, their own
occasional transgressions of the duties which it was the
business of his life to recommend. Thus it was a common
saying in the neighbourhood, (though both were popular
characters,) that the laird knew only the ill in the parish,
and the minister only the good.

A love of letters, though kept in subordination to his
clerical studies and duties, also distinguished the Pastor
of Cairnvreckan, and had tinged his mind in earlier days
with a slight feeling of romance, which no after incidents
of real life had entirely dissipated. The early loss of an
amiable young woman, whom he had married for love,
and who was quickly followed to the grave by an only
child, had also served, even after the lapse of many years,
to soften a disposition naturally mild and contemplative.
His feelings on the present occasion were therefore likely
to differ from those of the severe disciplinarian, strict
magistrate, and distrustful man of the world.

When the servants had withdrawn, the silence of both
parties continued, until Major Melville, filling his glass,
and pushing the bottle to Mr Morton, commenced.

"A distressing affair this, Mr Morton. I fear this
youngster has brought himself within the compass of a
halter."

"God forbid!" answered the clergyman.

"Marry, and amen," said the temporal magistrate;
"but I think even your merciful logic will hardly deny
the conclusion."

"Surely, Major," answered the clergyman, "I should
hope it might be averted, for aught we have heard to-
night."

"Indeed!" replied Melville. "But, my good parson,

you are one of those who would communicate to every criminal the benefit of clergy."

"Unquestionably I would : Mercy and long-suffering are the grounds of the doctrine I am called to teach."

"True, religiously speaking ; but mercy to a criminal may be gross injustice to the community. I don't speak of this young fellow in particular, who I heartily wish may be able to clear himself, for I like both his modesty and his spirit. But I fear he has rushed upon his fate."

"And why? Hundreds of misguided gentlemen are now in arms against the government, many, doubtless, upon principles which education and early prejudice have gilded with the names of patriotism and heroism ;—Justice, when she selects her victims from such a multitude, (for surely all will not be destroyed,) must regard the moral motive. He whom ambition, or hope of personal advantage, has led to disturb the peace of a well-ordered government, let him fall a victim to the laws ; but surely youth, misled by the wild visions of chivalry and imaginary loyalty, may plead for pardon."

"If visionary chivalry and imaginary loyalty come within the predicament of high treason," replied the magistrate, "I know no court in Christendom, my dear Mr Morton, where they can sue out their Habeas Corpus."

"But I cannot see that this youth's guilt is at all established to my satisfaction," said the clergyman.

"Because your good-nature blinds your good sense," replied Major Melville. "Observe now : This young man, descended of a family of hereditary Jacobites, his uncle the leader of the Tory interest in the county of ——, his father a disobliged and discontented courtier, his tutor a non-juror, and the author of two treasonable volumes—this youth, I say, enters into Gardiner's dragoons, bringing with him a body of young fellows from his uncle's estate, who have not stickled at avowing, in their way, the high-church principles they learned at Waverley-Honour, in their disputes with their comrades. To these young men Waverley is unusually attentive ; they are supplied with money beyond a soldier's wants, and inconsistent with his discipline ; and are under the management of a favourite sergeant, through whom they hold an unusually close communication with their captain, and affect to consider themselves as independent of the other officers, and superior to their comrades."

"All this, my dear Major, is the natural consequence of

their attachment to their young landlord, and of their finding themselves in a regiment levied chiefly in the north of Ireland and the west of Scotland, and of course among comrades disposed to quarrel with them, both as Englishmen, and as members of the Church of England."

"Well said, parson!" replied the magistrate.—"I would some of your synod heard you—But let me go on. This young man obtains leave of absence, goes to Tully-Veolan —the principles of the Baron of Bradwardine are pretty well known, not to mention that this lad's uncle brought him off in the year fifteen; he engages there in a brawl, in which he is said to have disgraced the commission he bore; Colonel Gardiner writes to him, first mildly, then more sharply—I think you will not doubt his having done so, since he says so; the mess invite him to explain the quarrel, in which he is said to have been involved; he neither replies to his commander nor his comrades. In the meanwhile, his soldiers become mutinous and disorderly, and at length, when the rumour of this unhappy rebellion becomes general, his favourite Sergeant Houghton, and another fellow, are detected in correspondence with a French emissary, accredited, as he says, by Captain Waverley, who urges him, according to the men's confession, to desert with the troop and join their captain, who was with Prince Charles. In the meanwhile this trusty captain is, by his own admission, residing at Glennaquoich with the most active, subtle, and desperate Jacobite in Scotland; he goes with him at least as far as their famous hunting rendezvous, and I fear a little farther. Meanwhile two other summonses are sent him; one warning him of the disturbances in his troop, another peremptorily ordering him to repair to the regiment, which, indeed, common sense might have dictated, when he observed rebellion thickening all round him. He returns an absolute refusal, and throws up his commission."

"He had been already deprived of it," said Mr Morton.

"But he regrets," replied Melville, "that the measure had anticipated his resignation. His baggage is seized at his quarters, and at Tully-Veolan, and is found to contain a stock of pestilent Jacobitical pamphlets, enough to poison a whole country, besides the unprinted lucubrations of his worthy friend and tutor Mr Pembroke."

"He says he never read them," answered the minister.

"In an ordinary case I should believe him," replied the magistrate, "for they are as stupid and pedantic in composition as mischievous in their tenets. But can you suppose anything but value for the principles they maintain, would induce a young man of his age to lug such trash about with him? Then, when news arrive of the approach of the rebels, he sets out in a sort of disguise, refusing to tell his name; and, if yon old fanatic tell truth, attended by a very suspicious character, and mounted on a horse known to have belonged to Glennaquoich, and bearing on his person letters from his family expressing high rancour against the house of Brunswick, and a copy of verses in praise of one Wogan, who abjured the service of the Parliament to join the Highland insurgents, when in arms to restore the house of Stewart, with a body of English cavalry—the very counterpart of his own plot—and summed up with a 'Go thou and do likewise,' from that loyal subject, and most safe and peaceable character, Fergus Mac-Ivor of Glennaquoich, Vich Ian Vohr, and so forth. And, lastly," continued Major Melville, warming in the detail of his arguments, "where do we find this second edition of Cavalier Wogan? Why, truly, in the very track most proper for execution of his design, and pistolling the first of the king's subjects who ventures to question his intentions."

Mr Morton prudently abstained from argument, which he perceived would only harden the magistrate in his opinion, and merely asked how he intended to dispose of the prisoner?

"It is a question of some difficulty, considering the state of the country," said Major Melville.

"Could you not detain him (being such a gentleman-like young man) here in your own house, out of harm's way, till this storm blow over?"

"My good friend," said Major Melville, "neither your house nor mine will be long out of harm's way, even were it legal to confine him here. I have just learned that the commander-in-chief, who marched into the Highlands to seek out and disperse the insurgents, has declined giving them battle at Corryerick, and marched on northward with all the disposable force of government to Inverness, John-o'-Groat's house, or the devil, for what I know, leaving the road to the Low Country open and undefended to the Highland army."

"Good God!" said the clergyman. "Is the man a coward, a traitor, or an idiot?"

"None of the three, I believe," answered Melville. "Sir John has the commonplace courage of a common soldier, is honest enough, does what he is commanded, and under-

stands what is told him, but is as fit to act for himself in
circumstances of importance, as I, my dear parson, to
occupy your pulpit."

This important public intelligence naturally diverted
the discourse from Waverley for some time; at length,
however, the subject was resumed.

"I believe," said Major Melville, "that I must give
this young man in charge to some of the detached parties
of armed volunteers, who were lately sent out to overawe
the disaffected districts. They are now recalled towards
Stirling, and a small body comes this way to-morrow or
next day, commanded by the westland man—what's his
name?—You saw him, and said he was the very model of
one of Cromwell's military saints."

"Gilfillan, the Cameronian," answered Mr Morton. "I
wish the young gentleman may be safe with him.
Strange things are done in the heat and hurry of minds
in so agitating a crisis, and I fear Gilfillan is of a sect
which has suffered persecution without learning mercy."

"He has only to lodge Mr Waverley in Stirling Castle,"
said the Major: "I will give strict injunctions to treat
him well. I really cannot devise any better mode for
securing him, and I fancy you would hardly advise me to
encounter the responsibility of setting him at liberty."

"But you will have no objection to my seeing him to-
morrow in private?" said the minister.

"None, certainly; your loyalty and character are my
warrant. But with what view do you make the request?"

"Simply," replied Mr Morton, "to make the experiment whether he may not be brought to communicate to
me some circumstances which may hereafter be useful to
alleviate, if not to exculpate his conduct."

The friends now parted and retired to rest, each filled
with the most anxious reflections on the state of the
country.


# CHAPTER XXXIII.

## A Confident.

WAVERLEY awoke in the morning, from troubled dreams
and unrefreshing slumbers, to a full consciousness of the
horrors of his situation. How it might terminate he
knew not. He might be delivered up to military law,
which, in the midst of civil war, was not likely to be

scrupulous in the choice of its victims, or the quality of
the evidence. Nor did he feel much more comfortable at
the thoughts of a trial before a Scottish court of justice,
where he knew the laws and forms differed in many
respects from those of England, and had been taught to
believe, however erroneously, that the liberty and rights
of the subject were less carefully protected. A sentiment
of bitterness rose in his mind against the government,
which he considered as the cause of his embarrassment
and peril, and he cursed internally his scrupulous
rejection of Mac-Ivor's invitation to accompany him to
the field.

"Why did not I," he said to himself, "like other men
of honour, take the earliest opportunity to welcome to
Britain the descendant of her ancient kings, and lineal
heir of her throne? Why did not I

> ' Unthread the rude eye of rebellion,
> And welcome home again discarded faith,
> Seek out Prince Charles, and fall before his feet?'

All that has been recorded of excellence and worth in the
house of Waverley has been founded upon their loyal
faith to the house of Stewart. From the interpretation
which this Scotch magistrate has put upon the letters of
my uncle and father, it is plain that I ought to have
understood them as marshalling me to the course of my
ancestors; and it has been my gross dulness, joined to the
obscurity of expression which they adopted for the sake
of security, that has confounded my judgment. Had I
yielded to the first generous impulse of indignation, when I
learned that my honour was practised upon, how different
had been my present situation! I had then been free and
in arms, fighting, like my forefathers, for love, for loyalty,
and for fame. And now I am here, netted and in the
toils, at the disposal of a suspicious, stern, and cold-
hearted man, perhaps to be turned over to the solitude of
a dungeon, or the infamy of a public execution. O,
Fergus! how true has your prophecy proved; and how
speedy, how very speedy, has been its accomplishment!"

While Edward was ruminating on these painful subjects of contemplation, and very naturally, though not
quite so justly, bestowing upon the reigning dynasty that
blame which was due to chance, or, in part at least, to his
own unreflecting conduct, Mr Morton availed himself of
Major Melville's permission to pay him an early visit.

Waverley's first impulse was to intimate a desire that
he might not be disturbed with questions or conversation;

but he suppressed it upon observing the benevolent and reverend appearance of the clergyman who had rescued him from the immediate violence of the villagers.

"I believe, sir," said the unfortunate young man, "that in any other circumstances I should have had as much gratitude to express to you as the safety of my life may be worth; but such is the present tumult of my mind, and such is my anticipation of what I am yet likely to endure, that I can hardly offer you thanks for your interposition."

Mr Morton replied, "that, far from making any claim upon his good opinion, his only wish and the sole purpose of his visit was to find out the means of deserving it. My excellent friend, Major Melville," he continued, "has feelings and duties as a soldier and public functionary, by which I am not fettered; nor can I always coincide in opinions which he forms, perhaps with too little allowance for the imperfections of human nature." He paused, and then proceeded: "I do not intrude myself on your confidence, Mr Waverley, for the purpose of learning any circumstances, the knowledge of which can be prejudicial either to yourself or to others; but I own my earnest wish is, that you would intrust me with any particulars which could lead to your exculpation. I can solemnly assure you they will be deposited with a faithful, and, to the extent of his limited powers, a zealous agent."

"You are, sir, I presume, a Presbyterian clergyman?"— Mr Morton bowed—"Were I to be guided by the prepossessions of education, I might distrust your friendly professions in my case; but I have observed that similar prejudices are nourished in this country against your professional brethren of the Episcopal persuasion, and I am willing to believe them equally unfounded in both cases."

"Evil to him that thinks otherwise," said Mr Morton; "or who holds church government and ceremonies as the exclusive gage of Christian faith or moral virtue."

"But," continued Waverley, "I cannot perceive why I should trouble you with a detail of particulars, out of which, after revolving them as carefully as possible in my recollection, I find myself unable to explain much of what is charged against me. I know, indeed, that I am innocent, but I hardly see how I can hope to prove myself so."

"It is for that very reason, Mr Waverley," said the clergyman, "that I venture to solicit your confidence. My knowledge of individuals in this country is pretty general, and can upon occasion be extended. Your situation will, I fear, preclude your taking those active steps for recovering intelligence, or tracing imposture, which I would willingly undertake in your behalf; and if you are not benefited by my exertions, at least they cannot be prejudicial to you."

Waverley, after a few minutes' reflection, was convinced that his reposing confidence in Mr Morton, so far as he himself was concerned, could hurt neither Mr Bradwardine nor Fergus Mac-Ivor, both of whom had openly assumed arms against the government, and that it might possibly, if the professions of his new friend corresponded in sincerity with the earnestness of his expression, be of some service to himself. He therefore ran briefly over most of the events with which the reader is already acquainted, suppressing his attachment to Flora, and indeed neither mentioning her nor Rose Bradwardine in the course of his narrative.

Mr Morton seemed particularly struck with the account of Waverley's visit to Donald Bean Lean. "I am glad," he said, "you did not mention this circumstance to the Major. It is capable of great misconstruction on the part of those who do not consider the power of curiosity and the influence of romance as motives of youthful conduct. When I was a young man like you, Mr Waverley, any such hair-brained expedition (I beg your pardon for the expression) would have had inexpressible charms for me. But there are men in the world who will not believe that danger and fatigue are often incurred without any very adequate cause, and therefore who are sometimes led to assign motives of action entirely foreign to the truth. This man Bean Lean is renowned through the country as a sort of Robin Hood, and the stories which are told of his address and enterprise are the common tales of the winter fire-side. He certainly possesses talents beyond the rude sphere in which he moves; and, being neither destitute of ambition nor encumbered with scruples, he will probably attempt, by every means, to distinguish himself during the period of these unhappy commotions." Mr Morton then made a careful memorandum of the various particulars of Waverley's interview with Donald Bean, and the other circumstances which he had communicated.

The interest which this good man seemed to take in his misfortunes, above all, the full confidence he appeared to repose in his innocence, had the natural effect of softening Edward's heart, whom the coldness of Major Melville had taught to believe that the world was leagued to oppress him. He shook Mr Morton warmly by the hand, and, assuring him that his kindness and sympathy had relieved his mind of a heavy load, told him, that whatever might be his own fate, he belonged to a family who had both gratitude and the power of displaying it. The earnestness of his thanks called drops to the eyes of the worthy clergyman, who was doubly interested in the cause for which he had volunteered his services, by observing the genuine and undissembled feelings of his young friend.

Edward now enquired if Mr Morton knew what was likely to be his destination.

"Stirling Castle," replied his friend; "and so far I am well pleased for your sake, for the governor is a man of honour and humanity. But I am more doubtful of your treatment upon the road; Major Melville is involuntarily obliged to intrust the custody of your person to another."

"I am glad of it," answered Waverley. "I detest that cold-blooded calculating Scotch magistrate. I hope he and I shall never meet more: he had neither sympathy with my innocence nor with my wretchedness; and the petrifying accuracy with which he attended to every form of civility, while he tortured me by his questions, his suspicions, and his inferences, was as tormenting as the racks of the Inquisition. Do not vindicate him, my dear sir, for that I cannot bear with patience; tell me rather who is to have the charge of so important a state prisoner as I am."

"I believe a person called Gilfillan, one of the sect who are termed Cameronians."

"I never heard of them before."

"They claim," said the clergyman, "to represent the more strict and severe Presbyterians, who, in Charles Second's and James Second's days, refused to profit by the Toleration, or Indulgence, as it was called, which was extended to others of that religion. They held conventicles in the open fields, and being treated with great violence and cruelty by the Scottish government, more than once took arms during those reigns. They take their name from their leader, Richard Cameron."

"I recollect," said Waverley;—"but did not the triumph of Presbytery at the Revolution extinguish that sect?"

"By no means," replied Morton; "that great event fell yet far short of what they proposed, which was nothing less than the complete establishment of the

Presbyterian Church, upon the grounds of the old Solemn
League and Covenant. Indeed, I believe they scarce
knew what they wanted; but being a numerous body of
men, and not unacquainted with the use of arms, they
kept themselves together as a separate party in the state,
and at the time of the Union had nearly formed a most
unnatural league with their old enemies, the Jacobites,
to oppose that important national measure. Since that
time their numbers have gradually diminished; but a
good many are still to be found in the western counties,
and several, with a better temper than in 1707, have now
taken arms for government. This person, whom they
call Gifted Gilfillan, has been long a leader among them,
and now heads a small party, which will pass here to-day,
or to-morrow, on their march towards Stirling, under
whose escort Major Melville proposes you shall travel. I
would willingly speak to Gilfillan in your behalf; but,
having deeply imbibed all the prejudices of his sect, and
being of the same fierce disposition, he would pay little
regard to the remonstrances of an Erastian divine, as he
would politely term me.—And now, farewell, my young
friend; for the present, I must not weary out the Major's
indulgence, that I may obtain his permission to visit you
again in the course of the day."

## CHAPTER XXXIV.

### *Things mend a little.*

ABOUT noon, Mr Morton returned, and brought an
invitation from Major Melville that Mr Waverley would
honour him with his company to dinner, notwithstanding
the unpleasant affair which detained him at Cairnvreckan,
from which he should heartily rejoice to see Mr Waverley
completely extricated. The truth was, that Mr Morton's
favourable report and opinion had somewhat staggered
the preconceptions of the old soldier concerning Edward's
supposed accession to the mutiny in the regiment; and in
the unfortunate state of the country, the mere suspicion
of disaffection, or an inclination to join the insurgent
Jacobites, might infer criminality indeed, but certainly
not dishonour. Besides, a person whom the Major trusted
had reported to him, (though, as it proved, inaccurately,)
a contradiction of the agitating news of the preceding

evening. According to this second edition of the intelligence, the Highlanders had withdrawn from the Lowland frontier with the purpose of following the army in their march to Inverness. The Major was at a loss, indeed, to reconcile his information with the well-known abilities of some of the gentlemen in the Highland army, yet it was the course which was likely to be most agreeable to others. He remembered the same policy had detained them in the north in the year 1715, and he anticipated a similar termination to the insurrection, as upon that occasion.

This news put him in such good-humour, that he readily acquiesced in Mr Morton's proposal to pay some hospitable attention to his unfortunate guest, and voluntarily added, he hoped the whole affair would prove a youthful *escapade*, which might be easily atoned by a short confinement. The kind mediator had some trouble to prevail on his young friend to accept the invitation. He dared not urge to him the real motive, which was a good-natured wish to secure a favourable report of Waverley's case from Major Melville to Governor Blakeney. He remarked, from the flashes of our hero's spirit, that touching upon this topic would be sure to defeat his purpose. He therefore pleaded, that the invitation argued the Major's disbelief of any part of the accusation which was inconsistent with Waverley's conduct as a soldier and man of honour, and that to decline his courtesy might be interpreted into a consciousness that it was unmerited. In short, he so far satisfied Edward that the manly and proper course was to meet the Major on easy terms, that, suppressing his strong dislike again to encounter his cold and punctilious civility, Waverley agreed to be guided by his new friend.

The meeting, at first, was stiff and formal enough. But Edward having accepted the invitation, and his mind being really soothed and relieved by the kindness of Morton, held himself bound to behave with ease, though he could not affect cordiality. The Major was somewhat of a *bon vivant*, and his wine was excellent. He told his old campaign stories, and displayed much knowledge of men and manners. Mr Morton had an internal fund of placid and quiet gaiety, which seldom failed to enliven any small party in which he found himself pleasantly seated. Waverley, whose life was a dream, gave ready way to the predominating impulse, and became the most lively of the party. He had at all times remarkable natural powers of conversation, though easily silenced by discouragement. On the present occasion, he piqued himself upon leaving on the minds of his companions a favourable impression of one who, under such disastrous circumstances, could sustain his misfortunes with ease and gaiety. His spirits, though not unyielding, were abundantly elastic, and soon seconded his efforts. The trio were engaged in very lively discourse, apparently delighted with each other, and the kind host was pressing a third bottle of Burgundy, when the sound of a drum was heard at some distance. The Major, who, in the glee of an old soldier, had forgot the duties of a magistrate, cursed, with a muttered military oath, the circumstances which recalled him to his official functions. He rose and went towards the window, which commanded a very near view of the high-road, and he was followed by his guests.

The drum advanced, beating no measured martial tune, but a kind of rub-a-dub-dub, like that with which the fire-drum startles the slumbering artizans of a Scotch burgh. It is the object of this history to do justice to all men : I must therefore record, in justice to the drummer, that he protested he could beat any known march or point of war known in the British army, and had accordingly commenced with " Dumbarton's Drums," when he was silenced by Gifted Gilfillan, the commander of the party, who refused to permit his followers to move to this profane and even, as he said, persecutive tune, and commanded the drummer to beat the 119th Psalm. As this was beyond the capacity of the drubber of sheepskin, he was fain to have recourse to the inoffensive row-dow-dow, as a harmless substitute for the sacred music which his instrument or skill was unable to achieve. This may be held a trifling anecdote, but the drummer in question was no less than town-drummer of Anderton. I remember his successor in office a member of that enlightened body, the British Convention : Be his memory, therefore, treated with due respect.

## CHAPTER XXXV.

### A Volunteer Sixty Years since.

On hearing the unwelcome sound of the drum, Major Melville hastily opened a sashed door, and stepped out

upon a sort of terrace which divided his house from the
high-road from which the martial music proceeded.
Waverley and his new friend followed him, though probably he would have dispensed with their attendance.
They soon recognised in solemn march, first, the performer upon the drum; secondly, a large flag of four
compartments, on which were inscribed the words Covenant, Kirk, King, Kingdoms. The person who was
honoured with this charge was followed by the commander of the party, a thin, dark, rigid-looking man,
about sixty years old. The spiritual pride, which, in
mine Host of the Candlestick, mantled in a sort of super-
cilious hypocrisy, was, in this man's face, elevated and
yet darkened by genuine and undoubting fanaticism. It
was impossible to behold him without imagination placing him in some strange crisis, where religious zeal was
the ruling principle. A martyr at the stake, a soldier in
the field, a lonely and banished wanderer consoled by
the intensity and supposed purity of his faith under
every earthly privation; perhaps a persecuting inquis-
itor, as terrific in power as unyielding in adversity; any
of these seemed congenial characters to this personage.
With these high traits of energy, there was something in
the affected precision and solemnity of his deportment
and discourse, that bordered upon the ludicrous; so
that, according to the mood of the spectator's mind, and
the light under which Mr Gilfillan presented himself, one
might have feared, admired, or laughed at him. His
dress was that of a west-country peasant, of better
materials indeed than that of the lower rank, but in no
respect affecting either the mode of the age, or of the
Scottish gentry at any period. His arms were a broadsword and pistols, which, from the antiquity of their
appearance, might have seen the rout of Pentland, or
Bothwell Brigg.

As he came up a few steps to meet Major Melville, and
touched solemnly, but slightly, his huge and overbrimmed
blue bonnet, in answer to the Major who had courteously
raised a small triangular gold-laced hat, Waverley was
irresistibly impressed with the idea that he beheld a
leader of the Roundheads of yore, in conference with one
of Marlborough's captains.

The group of about thirty armed men who followed
this gifted commander, was of a motley description.
They were in ordinary Lowland dresses, of different
colours, which, contrasted with the arms they bore, gave

them an irregular and mobbish appearance; so much is the eye accustomed to connect uniformity of dress with the military character. In front were a few who apparently partook of their leader's enthusiasm; men obviously to be feared in a combat where their natural courage was exalted by religious zeal. Others puffed and strutted, filled with the importance of carrying arms, and all the novelty of their situation, while the rest, apparently fatigued with their march, dragged their limbs listlessly along, or straggled from their companions to procure such refreshments as the neighbouring cottages and alehouses afforded.—Six grenadiers of Ligonier's, thought the Major to himself, as his mind reverted to his own military experience, would have sent all these fellows to the right about.

Greeting, however, Mr Gilfillan civilly, he requested to know if he had received the letter he had sent to him upon his march, and could undertake the charge of the state prisoner whom he there mentioned, as far as Stirling Castle.. "Yea," was the concise reply of the Cameronian leader, in a voice which seemed to issue from the very *penetralia* of his person.

"But your escort, Mr Gilfillan, is not so strong as I expected," said Major Melville.

"Some of the people," replied Gilfillan, "hungered and were athirst by the way, and tarried until their poor souls were refreshed with the word."

"I am sorry, sir," replied the Major, "you did not trust to your refreshing your men at Cairnvreckan; whatever my house contains is at the command of persons employed in the service."

"It was not of creature-comforts I spake," answered the Covenanter, regarding Major Melville with something like a smile of contempt; "howbeit, I thank you; but the people remained waiting upon the precious Mr Jabesh Rentowel, for the out-pouring of the afternoon exhortation."

"And have you, sir," said the Major, "when the rebels are about to spread themselves through this country, actually left a great part of your command at a field-preaching?"

Gilfillan again smiled scornfully as he made this indirect answer,—"Even thus are the children of this world wiser in their generation than the children of light?"

"However, sir," said the Major, "as you are to take charge of this gentleman to Stirling, and deliver him,

with these papers, into the hands of Governor Blakeney,
I beseech you to observe some rules of military discipline
upon your march. For example, I would advise you to
keep your men more closely together, and that each, in
his march, should cover his file-leader, instead of straggling like geese upon a common ; and, for fear of surprise,
I further recommend to you to form a small advance-
party of your best men, with a single vidette in front of
the whole march, so that when you approach a village or
a wood "—(Here the Major interrupted himself)—" But as
I don't observe you listen to me, Mr Gilfillan, I suppose I
need not give myself the trouble to say more upon the
subject. You are a better judge, unquestionably, than I
am, of the measures to be pursued ; but one thing I would
have you well aware of, that you are to treat this gentleman, your prisoner, with no rigour nor incivility, and
are to subject him to no other restraint than is necessary
for his security."

"I have looked into my commission," said Mr Gilfillan,
"subscribed by a worthy and professing nobleman, William, Earl of Glencairn ; nor do I find it therein set down
that I am to receive any charges or commands anent my
doings from Major William Melville of Cairnvreckan."

Major Melville reddened even to the well-powdered ears
which appeared beneath his neat military side-curls, the
more so as he observed Mr Morton smile at the same
moment. "Mr Gilfillan," he answered, with some asperity,
" I beg ten thousand pardons for interfering with a person
of your importance. I thought, however, that as you
have been bred a grazier, if I mistake not, there might be
occasion to remind you of the difference between Highlanders and Highland cattle ; and if you should happen
to meet with any gentleman who has seen service, and is
disposed to speak upon the subject, I should still imagine
that listening to him would do you no sort of harm. But
I have done, and have only once more to recommend this
gentleman to your civility, as well as to your custody.—
Mr Waverley, I am truly sorry we should part in this
way ; but I trust, when you are again in this country, I
may have an opportunity to render Cairnvreckan more
agreeable than circumstances have permitted on this
occasion."

So saying, he shook our hero by the hand. Morton
also took an affectionate farewell, and Waverley, having
mounted his horse, with a musketeer leading it by the
bridle, and a file upon each side to prevent his escape, set

forward upon the march with Gilfillan and his party.
Through the little village they were accompanied with
the shouts of the children, who cried out, "Eh! see to the
Southland gentleman, that's gaun to be hanged for shooting lang John Mucklewrath, the smith!"

## CHAPTER XXXVI.

### An Incident.

THE dinner hour of Scotland Sixty Years since was
two o'clock. It was therefore about four o'clock of a
delightful autumn afternoon that Mr Gilfillan commenced
his march, in hopes, although Stirling was eighteen miles
distant, he might be able, by becoming a borrower of the
night for an hour or two, to reach it that evening. He
therefore put forth his strength, and marched stoutly
along at the head of his followers, eyeing our hero from
time to time, as if he longed to enter into controversy
with him. At length, unable to resist the temptation, he
slackened his pace till he was alongside of his prisoner's
horse, and after marching a few steps in silence abreast
of him, he suddenly asked,—"Can ye say wha the carle[1]
was wi' the black coat and the mousted[2] head, that was
wi' the Laird of Cairnvreckan?"

"A Presbyterian clergyman," answered Waverley.

"Presbyterian!" answered Gilfillan contemptuously;
"a wretched Erastian, or rather an obscured Prelatist,—
a favourer of the black Indulgence; ane of thae dumb
dogs that canna bark: they tell ower a clash o' terror and
a clatter o' comfort in their sermons, without ony sense,
or savour, or life—Ye've been fed in siccan a fauld,[3] be-
like?"

"No; I am of the Church of England," said Waverley.

"And they're just neighbour-like," replied the Covenanter; "and nae wonder they gree sae weel. Wha wad
hae thought the goodly structure of the Kirk of Scotland,
built up by our fathers in 1642, wad hae been defaced by
carnal ends and the corruptions of the time;—ay, wha
wad hae thought the carved work of the sanctuary would
hae been sae soon cut down!"

To this lamentation, which one or two of the assistants
chorussed with a deep groan, our hero thought it un-

---

[1] Man.   [2] Bald.   [3] Such a fold.

necessary to make any reply. Whereupon Mr Gilfillan, resolving that he should be a hearer at least, if not a disputant, proceeded in his Jeremiade.

"And now is it wonderful, when, for lack of exercise anent the call to the service of the altar and the duty of the day, ministers fall into sinful compliances with patronage, and indemnities, and oaths, and bonds, and other corruptions,—is it wonderful, I say, that you, sir, and other sic-like unhappy persons, should labour to build up your auld Babel of iniquity, as in the bluidy persecuting saint-killing times? I trow, gin ye werena blinded wi' the graces and favours, and services and enjoyments, and employments and inheritances, of this wicked world, I could prove to you, by the Scripture, in what a filthy rag ye put your trust; and that your surplices, and your copes and vestments, are but cast-off garments of the muckle harlot, that sitteth upon seven hills, and drinketh of the cup of abomination. But, I trow, ye are deaf as adders upon that side of the head; ay, ye are deceived with her enchantments, and ye traffic with her merchandise, and ye are drunk with the cup of her fornication!"

How much longer this military theologist might have continued his invective, in which he spared nobody but the scattered remnant of *hill-folk*, as he called them, is absolutely uncertain. His matter was copious, his voice powerful, and his memory strong; so that there was little chance of his ending his exhortation till the party had reached Stirling, had not his attention been attracted by a pedlar who had joined the march from a cross-road, and who sighed or groaned with great regularity at all fitting pauses of his homily.

"And what may ye be, friend?" said the Gifted Gilfillan.

"A puir pedlar, that's bound for Stirling, and craves the protection of your honour's party in these kittle[1] times. Ah! your honour has a notable faculty in searching and explaining the secret,—ay, the secret and obscure and incomprehensible causes of the backslidings of the land; ay, your honour touches the root o' the matter."

"Friend," said Gilfillan, with a more complacent voice than he had hitherto used, "honour not me. I do not go out to park-dikes, and to steadings, and to market-towns, to have herds and cottars, and burghers pull off their bonnets to me as they do to Major Melville o' Cairnvreckan, and ca' me laird, or captain, or honour;—no; my

                              [1] Difficult.

sma' means, whilk are not aboon twenty thousand merk,[1] have had the blessing of increase, but the pride of my heart has not increased with them; nor do I delight to be called captain, though I have the subscribed commission of that gospel-searching nobleman, the Earl of Glencairn, in whilk I am so designated. While I live, I am and will be called Habakkuk Gilfillan, who will stand up for the standards of doctrine agreed on by the ance-famous Kirk of Scotland, before she trafficked with the accursed Achan, while he has a plack[2] in his purse, or a drap o' bluid in his body."

"Ah," said the pedlar, "I have seen your land about Mauchlin—a fertile spot! your lines have fallen in pleasant places!—And siccan a breed o' cattle is not in ony laird's land in Scotland."

"Ye say right,—ye say right, friend," retorted Gilfillan eagerly, for he was not inaccessible to flattery upon this subject,—"Ye say right; they are the real Lancashire, and there's no the like o' them even at the Mains of Kilmaurs;" and he then entered into a discussion of their excellences, to which our readers will probably be as indifferent as our hero. After this excursion, the leader returned to his theological discussions, while the pedlar, less profound upon those mystic points, contented himself with groaning, and expressing his edification at suitable intervals.

"What a blessing it would be to the puir blinded popish nations among whom I hae sojourned, to have siccan a light to their paths! I hae been as far as Muscovia in my sma' trading way, as a travelling merchant; and I hae been through France, and the Low Countries, and a' Poland, and maist feck[3] o' Germany, and O! it would grieve your honour's soul to see the murmuring, and the singing, and massing, that's in the kirk, and the piping that's in the quire, and the heathen-ish dancing and dicing upon the Sabbath!"

This set Gilfillan off upon the Book of Sports and the Covenant, and the Engagers, and the Protesters, and the Whiggamore's Raid, and the Assembly of Divines at Westminster, and the Longer and Shorter Catechism, and the Excommunication at Torwood, and the slaughter of Archbishop Sharp. This last topic, again, led him into the lawfulness of defensive arms, on which subject he uttered much more sense than could have been expected from

---

[1] Scottish coin of the value of thirteen pence and one-third of a penny.
[2] Scottish coin, one-third of a penny.  [3] Most part.

some other parts of his harangue, and attracted even
Waverley's attention, who had hitherto been lost in his
own sad reflections.   Mr Gilfillan then considered the
lawfulness of a private man's standing forth as the avenger
of public oppression, and as he was labouring with great
earnestness, the cause of Mas James Mitchell, who fired
at the Archbishop of St Andrews some years before
the prelate's assassination on Magus Muir, an incident
occurred which interrupted his harangue.

The rays of the sun were lingering on the very verge of
the horizon, as the party ascended a hollow and somewhat
steep path, which led to the summit of a rising ground.
The country was unenclosed, being part of a very extensive
heath or common ; but it was far from level, exhibiting
in many places hollows filled with furze and broom ; in
others, little dingles of stunted brushwood.   A thicket of
the latter description crowned the hill up which the party
ascended.   The foremost of the band, being the stoutest
and most active, had pushed on, and, having surmounted
the ascent, were out of ken for the present.   Gilfillan, with
the pedlar, and the small party who were Waverley's more
immediate guard, were near the top of the ascent, and the
remainder straggled after them at a considerable interval.

Such was the situation of matters, when the pedlar,
missing, as he said, a little doggie which belonged to him,
began to halt and whistle for the animal.   This signal,
repeated more than once, gave offence to the rigour of his
companion, the rather because it appeared to indicate in-
attention to the treasures of theological and controversial
knowledge which was pouring out for his edification.   He
therefore signified gruffly, that he could not waste his
time in waiting for an useless cur.

"But if your honour wad consider the case of Tobit"——

"Tobit!" exclaimed Gilfillan, with great heat ; "Tobit
and his dog baith are altogether heathenish and apocryphal,
and none but a prelatist or a papist would draw them
into question.   I doubt I hae been mista'en in you, friend."

"Very likely," answered the pedlar, with great composure ; "but ne'ertheless, I shall take leave to whistle
again upon puir Bawty."

This last signal was answered in an unexpected manner ;
for six or eight stout Highlanders, who lurked among the
copse and brushwood, sprung into the hollow way, and
began to lay about them with their claymores.   Gilfillan,
unappalled at this undesirable apparition, cried out manfully, "The sword of the Lord and of Gideon !" and,

drawing his broadsword, would probably have done as much credit to the good old cause as any of its doughty champions at Drumclog, when, behold! the pedlar, snatching a musket from the person who was next him, bestowed the butt of it with such emphasis on the head of his late instructor in the Cameronian creed, that he was forthwith levelled to the ground. In the confusion which ensued the horse which bore our hero was shot by one of Gilfillan's party, as he discharged his firelock at random. Waverley fell with, and indeed under, the animal, and sustained some severe contusions. But he was almost instantly extricated from the fallen steed by two High-landers, who, each seizing him by the arm, hurried him away from the scuffle and from the high-road. They ran with great speed, half supporting and half dragging our hero, who could, however, distinguish a few dropping shots fired about the spot which he had left. This, as he afterwards learned, proceeded from Gilfillan's party, who had now assembled, the stragglers in front and rear having joined the others. At their approach the High-landers drew off, but not before they had rifled Gilfillan and two of his people, who remained on the spot grievous-ly wounded. A few shots were exchanged betwixt them and the Westlanders; but the latter, now without a commander, and apprehensive of a second ambush, did not make any serious effort to recover their prisoner, judging it more wise to proceed on their journey to Stirling, carrying with them their wounded captain and comrades.

## CHAPTER XXXVII.

### *Waverley is still in Distress.*

THE velocity, and indeed violence, with which Waver-ley was hurried along, nearly deprived him of sensation; for the injury he had received from his fall prevented him from aiding himself so effectually as he might other-wise have done. When this was observed by his conduc-tors, they called to their aid two or three others of the party, and swathing our hero's body in one of their plaids, divided his weight by that means among them, and trans-ported him at the same rapid rate as before, without any exertion of his own. They spoke little, and that in Gaelic; and did not slacken their pace till they had run nearly

two miles, when they abated their extreme rapidity, but
continued still to walk very fast, relieving each other
occasionally.

Our hero now endeavoured to address them, but was
only answered with " *Cha n'eil Beurl' agam,*" *i.e.* " I have
no English," being, as Waverley well knew, the constant
reply of a Highlander, when he either does not understand, or does not choose to reply to, an Englishman or
Lowlander. He then mentioned the name of Vich Ian
Vohr, concluding that he was indebted to his friendship
for his rescue from the clutches of Gifted Gilfillan ; but
neither did this produce any mark of recognition from
his escort.

The twilight had given place to moonshine when the
party halted upon the brink of a precipitous glen, which,
as partly enlightened by the moonbeams, seemed full of
trees and tangled brushwood. Two of the Highlanders
dived into it by a small foot-path, as if to explore its
recesses, and one of them returning in a few minutes, said
something to his companions, who instantly raised their
burden, and bore him, with great attention and care,
down the narrow and abrupt descent. Notwithstanding
their precautions, however, Waverley's person came more
than once into contact, rudely enough, with the projecting
stumps and branches which overhung the pathway.

At the bottom of the descent, and, as it seemed, by the
side of a brook, (for Waverley heard the rushing of a considerable body of water, although its stream was invisible
in the darkness,) the party again stopped before a small
and rudely-constructed hovel. The door was open, and
the inside of the premises appeared as uncomfortable and
rude as its situation and exterior foreboded. There was
no appearance of a floor of any kind ; the roof seemed
rent in several places ; the walls were composed of loose
stones and turf, and the thatch of branches of trees. The
fire was in the centre, and filled the whole wigwam with
smoke, which escaped as much through the door as by
means of a circular aperture in the roof. An old Highland sibyl, the only inhabitant of this forlorn mansion,
appeared busy in the preparation of some food. By the
light which the fire afforded, Waverley could discover
that his attendants were not of the clan of Ivor, for
Fergus was particularly strict in requiring from his
followers that they should wear the tartan striped in the
mode peculiar to their race ; a mark of distinction anciently general through the Highlands, and still main-

tained by those Chiefs who were proud of their lineage, or jealous of their separate and exclusive authority.

Edward had lived at Glennaquoich long enough to be aware of a distinction which he had repeatedly heard noticed, and now satisfied that he had no interest with his attendants, he glanced a disconsolate eye around the interior of the cabin. The only furniture, excepting a washing-tub, and a wooden press, called in Scotland an *ambry*, sorely decayed, was a large wooden bed, planked, as is usual, all around, and opening by a sliding panel. In this recess the Highlanders deposited Waverley, after he had by signs declined any refreshment. His slumbers were broken and unrefreshing ; strange visions passed before his eyes, and it required constant and reiterated efforts of mind to dispel them. Shivering, violent head-ache, and shooting pains in his limbs, succeeded these symptoms; and in the morning it was evident to his Highland attendants or guard, for he knew not in which light to consider them, that Waverley was quite unfit to travel.

After a long consultation among themselves, six of the party left the hut with their arms, leaving behind an old and a young man. The former addressed Waverley, and bathed the contusions, which swelling and livid colour now made conspicuous. His own portmanteau, which the Highlanders had not failed to bring off, supplied him with linen, and, to his great surprise, was, with all its un-diminished contents, freely resigned to his use. The bed-ding of his couch seemed clean and comfortable, and his aged attendant closed the door of the bed, for it had no curtain, after a few words of Gaelic, from which Waver-ley gathered that he exhorted him to repose. So behold our hero for a second time the patient of a Highland Esculapius, but in a situation much more uncomfortable than when he was the guest of the worthy Tomanrait.

The symptomatic fever which accompanied the injuries he had sustained, did not abate till the third day, when it gave way to the care of his attendants and the strength of his constitution, and he could now raise himself in his bed, though not without pain. He observed, however, that there was a great disinclination, on the part of the old woman who acted as his nurse, as well as on that of the elderly Highlander, to permit the door of the bed to be left open, so that he might amuse himself with observing their motions ; and at length, after Waverley had repeatedly drawn open, and they had as frequently shut, the hatchway of his cage, the old gentleman put an end to the contest, by securing it on the outside with a nail so effectually, that the door could not be drawn till this exterior impediment was removed.

While musing upon the cause of this contradictory spirit in persons whose conduct intimated no purpose of plunder, and who, in all other points, appeared to consult his welfare and his wishes, it occurred to our hero, that, during the worst crisis of his illness, a female figure, younger than his old Highland nurse, had appeared to flit around his couch. Of this, indeed, he had but a very indistinct recollection, but his suspicions were confirmed when, attentively listening, he often heard, in the course of the day, the voice of another female conversing in whispers with his attendant. Who could it be? And why should she apparently desire concealment? Fancy immediately roused herself and turned to Flora Mac-Ivor. But after a short conflict between his eager desire to believe she was in his neighbourhood, guarding, like an angel of mercy, the couch of his sickness, Waverley was compelled to conclude that his conjecture was altogether improbable; since, to suppose she had left her comparatively safe situation at Glennaquoich to descend into the Low Country, now the seat of civil war, and to inhabit such a lurking-place as this, was a thing hardly to be imagined. Yet his heart bounded as he sometimes could distinctly hear the trip of a light female step glide to or from the door of the hut, or the suppressed sounds of a female voice, of softness and delicacy, hold dialogue with the hoarse inward croak of old Janet, for so he understood his antiquated attendant was denominated.

Having nothing else to amuse his solitude, he employed himself in contriving some plan to gratify his curiosity, in despite of the sedulous caution of Janet and the old Highland janizary, for he had never seen the young fellow since the first morning. At length, upon accurate examination, the infirm state of his wooden prison-house appeared to supply the means of gratifying his curiosity, for out of a spot which was somewhat decayed he was able to extract a nail. Through this minute aperture he could perceive a female form, wrapped in a plaid, in the act of conversing with Janet. But, since the days of our grandmother Eve, the gratification of inordinate curiosity has generally borne its penalty in disappointment. The form was not that of Flora, nor was the face visible; and, to crown his vexation, while he laboured with the nail to enlarge the hole, that he might obtain a more complete view, a slight noise betrayed his purpose, and the object of his curiosity instantly disappeared; nor, so far as he could observe, did she again revisit the cottage.

All precautions to blockade his view were from that time abandoned, and he was not only permitted, but assisted, to rise, and quit what had been, in a literal sense, his couch of confinement. But he was not allowed to leave the hut; for the young Highlander had now rejoined his senior, and one or other was constantly on the watch. Whenever Waverley approached the cottage door, the sentinel upon duty civilly, but resolutely, placed himself against it and opposed his exit, accompanying his action with signs which seemed to imply there was danger in the attempt, and an enemy in the neighbourhood. Old Janet appeared anxious and upon the watch; and Waverley, who had not yet recovered strength enough to attempt to take his departure in spite of the opposition of his hosts, was under the necessity of remaining patient. His fare was, in every point of view, better than he could have conceived; for poultry, and even wine, were no strangers to his table. The Highlanders never presumed to eat with him, and, unless in the circumstance of watching him, treated him with great respect. His sole amusement was gazing from the window, or rather the shapeless aperture which was meant to answer the purpose of a window, upon a large and rough brook, which raged and foamed through a rocky channel, closely canopied with trees and bushes, about ten feet beneath the site of his house of captivity.

Upon the sixth day of his confinement, Waverley found himself so well, that he began to meditate his escape from this dull and miserable prison-house, thinking any risk which he might incur in the attempt preferable to the stupifying and intolerable uniformity of Janet's retirement. The question indeed occurred, whither he was to direct his course when again at his own disposal. Two schemes seemed practicable, yet both attended with danger and difficulty. One was to go back to Glenna-quoich, and join Fergus Mac-Ivor, by whom he was sure to be kindly received; and in the present state of his mind, the rigour with which he had been treated fully absolved him, in his own eyes, from his allegiance to the existing government. The other project was to endeavour to attain a Scottish seaport, and thence to take shipping for England. His mind wavered between these plans,

and probably, if he had effected his escape in the manner
he proposed, he would have been finally determined by
the comparative facility by which either might have been
executed. But his fortune had settled that he was not to
be left to his option.

Upon the evening of the seventh day the door of the
hut suddenly opened, and two Highlanders entered, whom
Waverley recognised as having been a part of his original
escort to this cottage. They conversed for a short time
with the old man and his companion, and then made
Waverley understand, by very significant signs, that he
was to prepare to accompany them. This was a joyful
communication. What had already passed during his
confinement made it evident that no personal injury was
designed to him ; and his romantic spirit, having recovered
during his repose much of that elasticity which anxiety,
resentment, disappointment, and the mixture of unpleasant
feelings excited by his late adventures had for a time
subjugated, was now wearied with inaction. His passion
for the wonderful, although it is the nature of such
dispositions to be excited by that degree of danger which
merely gives dignity to the feeling of the individual
exposed to it, had sunk under the extraordinary and
apparently insurmountable evils by which he appeared
environed at Cairnvreckan. In fact, this compound of
intense curiosity and exalted imagination forms a peculiar
species of courage, which somewhat resembles the light
usually carried by a miner,—sufficiently competent, indeed,
to afford him guidance and comfort during the ordinary
perils of his labour, but certain to be extinguished should
he encounter the more formidable hazard of earth-damps
or pestiferous vapours. It was now, however, once more
rekindled, and with a throbbing mixture of hope, awe,
and anxiety, Waverley watched the group before him, as
those who were just arrived snatched a hasty meal, and
the others assumed their arms, and made brief preparations for their departure.

As he sat in the smoky hut, at some distance from the
fire, around which the others were crowded, he felt a
gentle pressure upon his arm. He looked round—It was
Alice, the daughter of Donald Bean Lean. She showed
him a packet of papers in such a manner that the motion
was remarked by no one else, put her finger for a second
to her lips, and passed on, as if to assist old Janet in
packing Waverley's clothes in his portmanteau. It was
obviously her wish that he should not seem to recognise

her ; yet she repeatedly looked back at him, as an opportunity occurred of doing so unobserved, and when she saw that he remarked what she did, she folded the packet with great address and speed in one of his shirts, which she deposited in the portmanteau.

Here then was fresh food for conjecture. Was Alice his unknown warden, and was this maiden of the cavern the tutelar genius that watched his bed during his sickness? Was he in the hands of her father? and if so, what was his purpose? Spoil, his usual object, seemed in this case neglected ; for not only Waverley's property was restored, but his purse, which might have tempted this professional plunderer, had been all along suffered to remain in his possession. All this perhaps the packet might explain ; but it was plain from Alice's manner that she desired he should consult it in secret. Nor did she again seek his eye after she had satisfied herself that her manœuvre was observed and understood. On the contrary, she shortly afterwards left the hut, and it was only as she tript out from the door, that, favoured by the obscurity, she gave Waverley a parting smile and nod of significance, ere she vanished in the dark glen.

The young Highlander was repeatedly despatched by his comrades as if to collect intelligence. At length, when he had returned for the third or fourth time, the whole party arose, and made signs to our hero to accompany them. Before his departure, however, he shook hands with old Janet, who had been so sedulous in his behalf, and added substantial marks of his gratitude for her attendance.

"God bless you ! God prosper you, Captain Waverley !" said Janet, in good Lowland Scotch, though he had never hitherto heard her utter a syllable, save in Gaelic. But the impatience of his attendants prohibited his asking any explanation.


## CHAPTER XXXVIII.

### A Nocturnal Adventure.

THERE was a moment's pause when the whole party had got out of the hut ; and the Highlander who assumed the command, and who, in Waverley's awakened recollection, seemed to be the same tall figure who had acted as

Donald Bean Lean's lieutenant, by whispers and signs
imposed the strictest silence. He delivered to Edward a
sword and steel pistol, and, pointing up the track, laid
his hand on the hilt of his own claymore, as if to make
him sensible they might have occasion to use force to
make good their passage. He then placed himself at the
head of the party, who moved up the pathway in single
or Indian file, Waverley being placed nearest to their
leader. He moved with great precaution, as if to avoid
giving any alarm, and halted as soon as he came to the
verge of the ascent. Waverley was soon sensible of the
reason, for he heard at no great distance an English
sentinel call out "All's well." The heavy sound sunk on
the night-wind down the woody glen, and was answered
by the echoes of its banks. A second, third, and fourth
time the signal was repeated fainter and fainter, as if at
a greater and greater distance. It was obvious that a
party of soldiers were near, and upon their guard, though
not sufficiently so to detect men skilful in every art of
predatory warfare, like those with whom he now watched
their ineffectual precautions.

When these sounds had died upon the silence of the
night, the Highlanders began their march swiftly, yet
with the most cautious silence. Waverley had little time,
or indeed disposition, for observation, and could only
discern that they passed at some distance from a large
building, in the windows of which a light or two yet
seemed to twinkle. A little farther on, the leading Highlander snuffed the wind like a setting spaniel, and then
made a signal to his party again to halt. He stooped
down upon all fours, wrapped up in his plaid, so as to be
scarce distinguishable from the heathy ground on which
he moved, and advanced in this posture to reconnoitre.
In a short time he returned, and dismissed his attendants
excepting one; and, intimating to Waverley that he must
imitate his cautious mode of proceeding, all three crept
forward on hands and knees.

After proceeding a greater way in this inconvenient
manner than was at all comfortable to his knees and
shins, Waverley perceived the smell of smoke, which
probably had been much sooner distinguished by the
more acute nasal organs of his guide. It proceeded from
the corner of a low and ruinous sheep-fold, the walls of
which were made of loose stones, as is usual in Scotland.
Close by this low wall the Highlander guided Waverley,
and, in order probably to make him sensible of his

danger, or perhaps to obtain the full credit of his own dexterity, he intimated to him, by sign and example, that he might raise his head so as to peep into the sheep-fold. Waverley did so, and beheld an out-post of four or five soldiers lying by their watch-fire. They were all asleep, except the sentinel, who paced backwards and forwards with his firelock on his shoulder, which glanced red in the light of the fire as he crossed and re-crossed before it in his short walk, casting his eye frequently to that part of the heavens from which the moon, hitherto obscured by mist, seemed now about to make her appearance.

In the course of a minute or two, by one of those sudden changes of atmosphere incident to a mountainous country, a breeze arose, and swept before it the clouds which had covered the horizon, and the night planet poured her full effulgence upon a wide and blighted heath, skirted indeed with copsewood, and stunted trees in the quarter from which they had come, but open and bare to the observation of the sentinel in that to which their course tended. The wall of the sheep-fold indeed concealed them as they lay, but any advance beyond its shelter seemed impossible without certain discovery.

The Highlander eyed the blue vault, but far from blessing the useful light with Homer's or rather Pope's benighted peasant, he muttered a Gaelic curse upon the unseasonable splendour of *Mac-Farlane's buat* (*i.e.* lantern[1]). He looked anxiously around for a few minutes, and then apparently took his resolution. Leaving his attendant with Waverley, after motioning to Edward to remain quiet, and giving his comrade directions in a brief whisper, he retreated, favoured by the irregularity of the ground, in the same direction and in the same manner as they had advanced. Edward, turning his head after him, could perceive him crawling on all fours with the dexterity of an Indian, availing himself of every bush and inequality to escape observation, and never passing over the more exposed parts of his track until the sentinel's back was turned from him. At length he reached the thickets and underwood which partly covered the moor in that direction, and probably extended to the verge of the glen where Waverley had been so long an inhabitant. The Highlander disappeared, but it was only for a few minutes, for he suddenly issued forth from a different part of the thicket, and advancing boldly upon the open heath, as if to invite discovery, he levelled his piece, and

[1] Note 15. Mac-Farlane's Lantern.

fired at the sentinel. A wound in the arm proved a
disagreeable interruption to the poor fellow's meteorologi-
cal observations, as well as to the tune of Nancy Dawson,
which he was whistling. He returned the fire in-
effectually, and his comrades, starting up at the alarm,
advanced alertly towards the spot from which the first
shot had issued. The Highlander, after giving them a
full view of his person, dived among the thickets, for his
*ruse de guerre* had now perfectly succeeded.

While the soldiers pursued the cause of their disturbance
in one direction, Waverley, adopting the hint of his
remaining attendant, made the best of his speed in that
which his guide originally intended to pursue, and which
now (the attention of the soldiers being drawn to a
different quarter) was unobserved and unguarded. When
they had run about a quarter of a mile, the brow of a
rising ground, which they had surmounted, concealed
them from further risk of observation. They still heard,
however, at a distance, the shouts of the soldiers as they
hallooed to each other upon the heath, and they could
also hear the distant roll of a drum beating to arms in
the same direction. But these hostile sounds were now
far in their rear, and died away upon the breeze as they
rapidly proceeded.

When they had walked about half an hour, still along
open and waste ground of the same description, they
came to the stump of an ancient oak, which, from its
relics, appeared to have been at one time a tree of very
large size. In an adjacent hollow they found several
Highlanders, with a horse or two. They had not joined
them above a few minutes, which Waverley's attendant
employed, in all probability, in communicating the cause
of their delay, (for the words "Duncan Duroch" were
often repeated,) when Duncan himself appeared, out of
breath indeed, and with all the symptoms of having run
for his life, but laughing, and in high spirits at the
success of the stratagem by which he had baffled his
pursuers. This indeed Waverley could easily conceive
might be a matter of no great difficulty to the active
mountaineer, who was perfectly acquainted with the
ground, and traced his course with a firmness and confidence to which his pursuers must have been strangers.
The alarm which he excited seemed still to continue, for
a dropping shot or two were heard at a great distance,
which seemed to serve as an addition to the mirth of
Duncan and his comrades.

The mountaineer now resumed the arms with which he had intrusted our hero, giving him to understand that the dangers of the journey were happily surmounted. Waverley was then mounted upon one of the horses, a change which the fatigue of the night and his recent illness rendered exceedingly acceptable. His portmanteau was placed on another pony, Duncan mounted a third, and they set forward at a round pace, accompanied by their escort. No other incident marked the course of that night's journey, and at the dawn of morning they attained the banks of a rapid river. The country around was at once fertile and romantic. Steep banks of wood were broken by corn fields, which this year presented an abundant harvest, already in a great measure cut down.

On the opposite bank of the river, and partly surrounded by a winding of its stream, stood a large and massive castle, the half-ruined turrets of which were already glittering in the first rays of the sun.[1] It was in form an oblong square, of size sufficient to contain a large court in the centre. The towers at each angle of the square rose higher than the walls of the building, and were in their turn surmounted by turrets, differing in height, and irregular in shape. Upon one of these a sentinel watched, whose bonnet and plaid, streaming in the wind, declared him to be a Highlander, as a broad white ensign, which floated from another tower, announced that the garrison was held by the insurgent adherents of the House of Stewart.

Passing hastily through a small and mean town, where their appearance excited neither surprise nor curiosity in the few peasants whom the labours of the harvest began to summon from their repose, the party crossed an ancient and narrow bridge of several arches, and turning to the left, up an avenue of huge old sycamores, Waverley found himself in front of the gloomy yet picturesque structure which he had admired at a distance. A huge iron-grated door, which formed the exterior defence of the gateway, was already thrown back to receive them ; and a second, heavily constructed of oak, and studded thickly with iron nails, being next opened, admitted them into the interior court-yard. A gentleman, dressed in the Highland garb, and having a white cockade in his bonnet, assisted Waverley to dismount from his horse, and with much courtesy bid him welcome to the castle.

The governor, for so we must term him, having con-

1 Note 16. Castle of Doune.

ducted Waverley to a half-ruinous apartment, where,
however, there was a small camp-bed, and having offered
him any refreshment which he desired, was then about
to leave him.

"Will you not add to your civilities," said Waverley,
after having made the usual acknowledgment, "by
having the kindness to inform me where I am, and
whether or not I am to consider myself as a prisoner?"

"I am not at liberty to be so explicit upon this subject
as I could wish. Briefly, however, you are in the Castle
of Doune, in the district of Menteith, and in no danger
whatever."

"And how am I assured of that?"

"By the honour of Donald Stewart, governor of the
garrison and lieutenant-colonel in the service of his Royal
Highness Prince Charles Edward." So saying, he hastily
left the apartment, as if to avoid further discussion.

Exhausted by the fatigues of the night, our hero now
threw himself upon the bed, and was in a few minutes
fast asleep.


## CHAPTER XXXIX.

### *The Journey is continued.*

BEFORE Waverley awakened from his repose, the day
was far advanced, and he began to feel that he had passed
many hours without food. This was soon supplied in form
of a copious breakfast, but Colonel Stewart, as if wishing
to avoid the queries of his guest, did not again present
himself. His compliments were, however, delivered by a
servant, with an offer to provide anything in his power
that could be useful to Captain Waverley on his journey,
which he intimated would be continued that evening.
To Waverley's further inquiries, the servant opposed the
impenetrable barrier of real or affected ignorance and
stupidity. He removed the table and provisions, and
Waverley was again consigned to his own meditations.

As he contemplated the strangeness of his fortune,
which seemed to delight in placing him at the disposal of
others, without the power of directing his own motions,
Edward's eye suddenly rested upon his portmanteau,
which had been deposited in his apartment during his
sleep. The mysterious appearance of Alice, in the cottage

of the glen, immediately rushed upon his mind, and he was about to secure and examine the packet which she had deposited among his clothes, when the servant of Colonel Stewart again made his appearance, and took up the portmanteau upon his shoulders.

"May I not take out a change of linen, my friend ?"

"Your honour sall get ane o' the Colonel's ain ruffled sarks, but this maun gang in the baggage-cart."

And so saying, he very coolly carried off the portmanteau, without waiting further remonstrance, leaving our hero in a state where disappointment and indignation struggled for the mastery. In a few minutes he heard a cart rumble out of the rugged court-yard, and made no doubt that he was now dispossessed, for a space at least, if not for ever, of the only documents which seemed to promise some light upon the dubious events which had of late influenced his destiny. With such melancholy thoughts he had to beguile about four or five hours of solitude.

When this space was elapsed, the trampling of horse was heard in the court-yard, and Colonel Stewart soon after made his appearance to request his guest to take some further refreshment before his departure. The offer was accepted, for a late breakfast had by no means left our hero incapable of doing honour to dinner, which was now presented. The conversation of his host was that of a plain country gentleman, mixed with some soldier-like sentiments and expressions. He cautiously avoided any reference to the military operations or civil politics of the time ; and to Waverley's direct inquiries concerning some of these points, replied, that he was not at liberty to speak upon such topics.

When dinner was finished, the governor arose, and, wishing Edward a good journey, said, that having been informed by Waverley's servant that his baggage had been sent forward, he had taken the freedom to supply him with such changes of linen as he might find necessary, till he was again possessed of his own. With this compliment he disappeared. A servant acquainted Waverley an instant afterwards, that his horse was ready.

Upon this hint he descended into the court-yard, and found a trooper holding a saddled horse, on which he mounted, and sallied from the portal of Doune Castle, attended by about a score of armed men on horseback. These had less the appearance of regular soldiers than of individuals who had suddenly assumed arms from some pressing motive of unexpected emergency. Their uniform, which was blue and red, an affected imitation of that of French chasseurs, was in many respects incomplete, and sate awkwardly upon those who wore it. Waverley's eye, accustomed to look at a well-disciplined regiment, could easily discover that the motions and habits of his escort were not those of trained soldiers, and that, although expert enough in the management of their horses, their skill was that of huntsmen or grooms, rather than of troopers. The horses were not trained to the regular pace so necessary to execute simultaneous and combined movements and formations; nor did they seem *bitted* (as it is technically expressed) for the use of the sword. The men, however, were stout, hardy-looking fellows, and might be individually formidable as irregular cavalry. The commander of this small party was mounted upon an excellent hunter, and although dressed in uniform, his change of apparel did not prevent Waverley from recognising his old acquaintance, Mr Falconer of Balmawhapple.

Now, although the terms upon which Edward had parted with this gentleman were none of the most friendly, he would have sacrificed every recollection of their foolish quarrel, for the pleasure of enjoying once more the social intercourse of question and answer, from which he had been so long secluded. But apparently the remembrance of his defeat by the Baron of Bradwardine, of which Edward had been the unwilling cause, still rankled in the mind of the low-bred, and yet proud laird. He carefully avoided giving the least sign of recognition, riding doggedly at the head of his men, who, though scarce equal in numbers to a sergeant's party, were denominated Captain Falconer's troop, being preceded by a trumpet, which sounded from time to time, and a standard, borne by Cornet Falconer, the laird's younger brother. The lieutenant, an elderly man, had much the air of a low sportsman and boon companion; an expression of dry humour predominated in his countenance over features of a vulgar cast, which indicated habitual intemperance. His cocked hat was set knowingly upon one side of his head, and while he whistled the "Bob of Dumblain," under the influence of half a mutchkin of brandy, he seemed to trot merrily forward, with a happy indifference to the state of the country, the conduct of the party, the end of the journey, and all other sublunary matters whatever.

From this wight, who now and then dropped alongside of his horse, Waverley hoped to acquire some information, or at least to beguile the way with talk.

"A fine evening, sir," was Edward's salutation.

"Ow, ay, sir! a bra'[1] night," replied the lieutenant, in broad Scotch of the most vulgar description.

"And a fine harvest, apparently," continued Waverley, following up his first attack.

"Ay, the aits[2] will be got bravely in: but the farmers, deil burst them, and the corn-mongers, will make the auld price gude against them as has horses till keep."

"You perhaps act as quarter-master, sir?"

"Ay, quarter-master, riding-master, and lieutenant," answered this officer of all work. "And, to be sure, wha's fitter to look after the breaking and the keeping of the poor beasts than mysell, that bought and sold every ane o' them?"

"And pray, sir, if it be not too great a freedom, may I beg to know where we are going just now?"

"A fule's errand, I fear," answered this communicative personage.

"In that case," said Waverley, determined not to spare civility, "I should have thought a person of your appearance would not have been found on the road."

"Vera true, vera true, sir," replied the officer, "but every why has its wherefore. Ye maun ken,[3] the laird there bought a' thir beasts frae me to munt his troop, and agreed to pay for them according to the necessities and prices of the time. But then he hadna the ready penny, and I hae been advised his bond will not be worth a boddle[4] against the estate, and then I had a' my dealers to settle wi' at Martinmas; and so as he very kindly offered me this commission, and as the auld *Fifteen*[5] wad never help me to my siller for sending out naigs against the government, why, conscience! sir, I thought my best chance for payment was e'en to *gae out*[6] mysell; and ye may judge, sir, as I hae dealt a' my life in halters, I

---

[1] Splendid.      [2] Oats.      [3] Know.      [4] Small copper coin.

[5] The Judges of the Supreme Court of Session in Scotland are proverbially termed, among the country people, the Fifteen.

[6] To *go out*, or *to have been out*, in Scotland, was a conventional phrase similar to that of the Irish respecting a man having been *up*, both having reference to an individual who had been engaged in insurrection. It was accounted ill-breeding in Scotland, about forty years since, to use the phrase *rebellion* or *rebel*, which might be interpreted by some of the parties present as a personal insult. It was also esteemed more polite even for staunch Whigs to denominate Charles Edward the Chevalier, than to speak of him as the Pretender; and this kind of accommodating courtesy was usually observed in society where individuals of each party mixed on friendly terms. (S.)

think na mickle[1] o' putting my craig[2] in peril of a St Johnstone's tippet."

"You are not, then, by profession a soldier?" said Waverley.

"Na, na; thank God," answered this doughty partisan, "I wasna bred at sae short a tether; I was brought up to hack and manger. I was bred a horse-couper, sir; and if I might live to see you at Whitson-tryst, or at Stagshawbank, or the winter fair at Hawick, and ye wanted a spanker that would lead the field, I'se be caution I would serve ye easy; for Jamie Jinker was ne'er the lad to impose upon a gentleman. Ye're a gentleman, sir, and should ken a horse's points; ye see that through-ganging thing that Balmawhapple's on; I selled her till him. She was bred out of Lick-the-Ladle, that wan the king's plate at Caverton-Edge, by Duke Hamilton's White-Foot," &c. &c. &c.

But as Jinker was entered full sail, upon the pedigree of Balmawhapple's mare, having already got as far as great-grandsire and great-grand-dam, and while Waverley was watching for an opportunity to obtain from him intelligence of more interest, the noble captain checked his horse until they came up, and then, without directly appearing to notice Edward, said sternly to the genealogist, "I thought, lieutenant, my orders were preceese, that no one should speak to the prisoner?"

The metamorphosed horse-dealer was silenced of course, and slunk to the rear, where he consoled himself by entering into a vehement dispute upon the price of hay with a farmer, who had reluctantly followed his laird to the field, rather than give up his farm, whereof the lease had just expired. Waverley was therefore once more consigned to silence, foreseeing that further attempts at conversation with any of the party would only give Balmawhapple a wished-for opportunity to display the insolence of authority, and the sulky spite of a temper naturally dogged, and rendered more so by habits of low indulgence and the incense of servile adulation.

In about two hours' time, the party were near the Castle of Stirling, over whose battlements the union flag was brightened as it waved in the evening sun. To shorten his journey, or perhaps to display his importance and insult the English garrison, Balmawhapple, inclining to the right, took his route through the royal park, which

---

[1] Much.        [2] Throat.

reaches to and surrounds the rock upon which the fortress is situated.

With a mind more at ease, Waverley could not have failed to admire the mixture of romance and beauty which renders interesting the scene through which he was now passing—the field which had been the scene of the tournaments of old—the rock from which the ladies beheld the contest, while each made vows for the success of some favourite knight—the towers of the Gothic church, where these vows might be paid—and, surmounting all, the fortress itself, at once a castle and palace, where valour received the prize from royalty, and knights and dames closed the evening amid the revelry of the dance, the song, and the feast. All these were objects fitted to arouse and interest a romantic imagination.

But Waverley had other objects of meditation, and an incident soon occurred of a nature to disturb meditation of any kind. Balmawhapple, in the pride of his heart, as he wheeled his little body of cavalry round the base of the castle, commanded his trumpet to sound a flourish, and his standard to be displayed. This insult produced apparently some sensation ; for when the cavalcade was at such distance from the southern battery as to admit of a gun being depressed so as to bear upon them, a flash of fire issued from one of the embrazures upon the rock ; and ere the report with which it was attended could be heard, the rushing sound of a cannon-ball passed over Balmawhapple's head, and the bullet, burying itself in the ground at a few yards' distance, covered him with the earth which it drove up. There was no need to bid the party trudge. In fact, every man acting upon the impulse of the moment, soon brought Mr Jinker's steeds to show their nettle, and the cavaliers, retreating with more speed than regularity, never took to a trot, as the lieutenant afterwards observed, until an intervening eminence had secured them from any repetition of so undesirable a compliment on the part of Stirling Castle. I must do Balmawhapple, however, the justice to say, that he not only kept the rear of his troop, and laboured to maintain some order among them, but, in the height of his gallantry, answered the fire of the castle by discharging one of his horse-pistols at the battlements ; although, the distance being nearly half a mile, I could never learn that this measure of retaliation was attended with any particular effect.

The travellers now passed the memorable field of Ban-

nockburn, and reached the Torwood, a place glorious or
terrible to the recollections of the Scottish peasant, as the
feats of Wallace, or the cruelties of Wude Willie Grime,
predominate in his recollection.    At Falkirk, a town
formerly famous in Scottish history, and soon to be again
distinguished as the scene of military events of importance, Balmawhapple proposed to halt and repose for the
evening.    This was performed with very little regard to
military discipline, his worthy quarter-master being
chiefly solicitous to discover where the best brandy might
be come at.    Sentinels were deemed unnecessary, and the
only vigils performed were those of such of the party as
could procure liquor.    A few resolute men might easily
have cut off the detachment ; but of the inhabitants some
were favourable, many indifferent, and the rest overawed.
So nothing memorable occurred in the course of the
evening, except that Waverley's rest was sorely interrupted by the revellers hallooing forth their Jacobite
songs, without remorse or mitigation of voice.

Early in the morning they were again mounted, and on
the road to Edinburgh, though the pallid visages of some
of the troop betrayed that they had spent a night of
sleepless debauchery.    They halted at Linlithgow, distinguished by its ancient palace, which, Sixty Years since,
was entire and habitable, and whose venerable ruins, *not
quite Sixty Years since,* very narrowly escaped the unworthy fate of being converted into a barrack for French
prisoners.    May repose and blessings attend the ashes of
the patriotic statesman, who, amongst his last services to
Scotland, interposed to prevent this profanation !

As they approached the metropolis of Scotland, through
a champaign and cultivated country, the sounds of war
began to be heard.    The distant, yet distinct report of
heavy cannon, fired at intervals, apprized Waverley that
the work of destruction was going forward.    Even Balmawhapple seemed moved to take some precautions, by
sending an advanced party in front of his troop, keeping the
main body in tolerable order, and moving steadily forward.

Marching in this manner they speedily reached an
eminence, from which they could view Edinburgh stretching along the ridgy hill which slopes eastward from the
Castle.    The latter, being in a state of siege, or rather of
blockade, by the northern insurgents, who had already
occupied the town for two or three days, fired at intervals
upon such parties of Highlanders as exposed themselves,
either on the main street, or elsewhere in the vicinity of

the fortress. The morning being calm and fair, the effect of this dropping fire was to invest the Castle in wreaths of smoke, the edges of which dissipated slowly in the air, while the central veil was darkened ever and anon by fresh clouds poured forth from the battlements; the whole giving, by the partial concealment, an appearance of grandeur and gloom, rendered more terrific when Waverley reflected on the cause by which it was produced, and that each explosion might ring some brave man's knell.

Ere they approached the city, the partial cannonade had wholly ceased. Balmawhapple, however, having in his recollection the unfriendly greeting which his troop had received from the battery at Stirling, had apparently no wish to tempt the forbearance of the artillery of the Castle. He therefore left the direct road, and sweeping considerably to the southward, so as to keep out of the range of the cannon, approached the ancient palace of Holyrood, without having entered the walls of the city. He then drew up his men in front of that venerable pile, and delivered Waverley to the custody of a guard of Highlanders, whose officer conducted him into the interior of the building.

A long, low, and ill-proportioned gallery, hung with pictures, affirmed to be the portraits of kings, who, if they ever flourished at all, lived several hundred years before the invention of painting in oil colours, served as a sort of guard chamber, or vestibule, to the apartments which the adventurous Charles Edward now occupied in the palace of his ancestors. Officers, both in the Highland and Lowland garb, passed and repassed in haste, or loitered in the hall, as if waiting for orders. Secretaries were engaged in making out passes, musters, and returns. All seemed busy, and earnestly intent upon something of importance; but Waverley was suffered to remain seated in the recess of a window, unnoticed by any one, in anxious reflection upon the crisis of his fate, which seemed now rapidly approaching.

## CHAPTER XL.

### An Old and a New Acquaintance.

WHILE he was deep sunk in his reverie, the rustle of tartans was heard behind him, a friendly arm clasped his shoulders, and a friendly voice exclaimed,

"Said the Highland prophet sooth? Or must second-sight go for nothing?"

Waverley turned, and was warmly embraced by Fergus Mac-Ivor. "A thousand welcomes to Holyrood, once more possessed by her legitimate sovereign! Did I not say we should prosper, and that you would fall into the hands of the Philistines if you parted from us?"

"Dear Fergus!" said Waverley, eagerly returning his greeting, "it is long since I have heard a friend's voice. Where is Flora?"

"Safe, and a triumphant spectator of our success."

"In this place?" said Waverley.

"Ay, in this city at least," answered his friend, "and you shall see her; but first you must meet a friend whom you little think of, who has been frequent in his inquiries after you."

Thus saying, he dragged Waverley by the arm out of the guard chamber, and, ere he knew where he was conducted, Edward found himself in a presence room, fitted up with some attempt at royal state.

A young man, wearing his own fair hair, distinguished by the dignity of his mien and the noble expression of his well-formed and regular features, advanced out of a circle of military gentlemen and Highland chiefs, by whom he was surrounded. In his easy and graceful manners Waverley afterwards thought he could have discovered his high birth and rank, although the star on his breast, and the embroidered garter at his knee, had not appeared as its indications.

"Let me present to your Royal Highness," said Fergus, bowing profoundly——

"The descendant of one of the most ancient and loyal families in England," said the young Chevalier, interrupting him. "I beg your pardon for interrupting you, my dear Mac-Ivor; but no master of ceremonies is necessary to present a Waverley to a Stewart."

Thus saying, he extended his hand to Edward with the utmost courtesy, who could not, had he desired it, have avoided rendering him the homage which seemed due to his rank, and was certainly the right of his birth. "I am sorry to understand, Mr Waverley, that, owing to circumstances which have been as yet but ill explained, you have suffered some restraint among my followers in Perthshire, and on your march here; but we are in such a situation that we hardly know our friends, and I am even at this moment uncertain whether I can have the pleasure of considering Mr Waverley as among mine."

He then paused for an instant; but before Edward could adjust a suitable reply, or even arrange his ideas as to its purport, the Prince took out a paper, and then proceeded :—" I should indeed have no doubts upon this subject, if I could trust to this proclamation, set forth by the friends of the Elector of Hanover, in which they rank Mr Waverley among the nobility and gentry who are menaced with the pains of high-treason for loyalty to their legitimate sovereign. But I desire to gain no adherents save from affection and conviction; and if Mr Waverley inclines to prosecute his journey to the south, or to join the forces of the Elector, he shall have my passport and free permission to do so; and I can only regret, that my present power will not extend to protect him against the probable consequences of such a measure.—But," continued Charles Edward, after another short pause, "if Mr Waverley should, like his ancestor, Sir Nigel, determine to embrace a cause which has little to recommend it but its justice, and follow a prince who throws himself upon the affections of his people to recover the throne of his ancestors, or perish in the attempt, I can only say, that among these nobles and gentlemen he will find worthy associates in a gallant enterprise, and will follow a master who may be unfortunate, but, I trust, will never be ungrateful."

The politic Chieftain of the race of Ivor knew his advantage in introducing Waverley to this personal interview with the royal Adventurer. Unaccustomed to the address and manners of a polished court, in which Charles was eminently skilful, his words and his kindness penetrated the heart of our hero, and easily outweighed all prudential motives. To be thus personally solicited for assistance by a Prince, whose form and manners, as well as the spirit which he displayed in this singular enterprise, answered his ideas of a hero of romance; to be courted by him in the ancient halls of his paternal palace, recovered by the sword which he was already bending towards other conquests, gave Edward, in his own eyes, the dignity and importance which he had ceased to consider as his attributes. Rejected, slandered, and threatened upon the one side, he was irresistibly attracted to the cause which the prejudices of education, and the political principles of his family, had already recommended as the most just. These thoughts rushed through his mind like a torrent, sweeping before them every consideration of an opposite tendency,—the time, besides, admitted of no deliberation,—and Waverley, kneeling to Charles Edward, devoted his heart and sword to the vindication of his rights !

The Prince (for, although unfortunate in the faults and follies of his forefathers, we shall here, and elsewhere, give him the title due to his birth) raised Waverley from the ground, and embraced him with an expression of thanks too warm not to be genuine. He also thanked Fergus Mac-Ivor repeatedly for having brought him such an adherent, and presented Waverley to the various noblemen, chieftains, and officers who were about his person, as a young gentleman of the highest hopes and prospects, in whose bold and enthusiastic avowal of his cause they might see an evidence of the sentiments of the English families of rank at this important crisis.[1] Indeed, this was a point much doubted among the adherents of the house of Stewart ; and as a well-founded disbelief in the co-operation of the English Jacobites kept many Scottish men of rank from his standard, and diminished the courage of those who had joined it, nothing could be more seasonable for the Chevalier than the open declaration in his favour of the representative of the house of Waverley-Honour, so long known as cavaliers and royalists. This Fergus had foreseen from the beginning. He really loved Waverley, because their feelings and projects never thwarted each other ; he hoped to see him united with Flora, and he rejoiced that they were effectually engaged in the same cause. But as we before hinted, he also exulted as a politician in beholding secured to his party a partisan of such consequence ; and he was far from being insensible to the personal importance which he himself gained with the Prince, from having so materially assisted in making the acquisition.

Charles Edward, on his part, seemed eager to show his

[1] The Jacobite sentiments were general among the western counties, and in Wales. But although the great families of the Wynnes, the Wyndhams, and others, had come under an actual obligation to join Prince Charles if he should land, they had done so under the express stipulation, that he should be assisted by an auxiliary army of French, without which they foresaw the enterprise would be desperate. Wishing well to his cause, therefore, and watching an opportunity to join him, they did not, nevertheless, think themselves bound in honour to do so, as he was only supported by a body of wild mountaineers, speaking an uncouth dialect, and wearing a singular dress. The race up to Derby struck them with more dread than admiration. But it was difficult to say what the effect might have been, had either the battle of Preston or Falkirk been fought and won during the advance into England. (S.)

attendants the value which he attached to his new
adherent, by entering immediately, as in confidence, upon
the circumstances of his situation. "You have been
secluded so much from intelligence, Mr Waverley, from
causes of which I am but indistinctly informed, that I
presume you are even yet unacquainted with the important particulars of my present situation. You have,
however, heard of my landing in the remote district of
Moidart, with only seven attendants, and of the numerous
chiefs and clans whose loyal enthusiam at once placed a
solitary adventurer at the head of a gallant army. You
must also, I think, have learned, that the commander-in-
chief of the Hanoverian Elector, Sir John Cope, marched
into the Highlands at the head of a numerous and well-
appointed military force, with the intention of giving us
battle, but that his courage failed him when we were
within three hours' march of each other, so that he fairly
gave us the slip, and marched northward to Aberdeen,
leaving the Low Country open and undefended. Not to
lose so favourable an opportunity, I marched on to this
metropolis, driving before me two regiments of horse,
Gardiner's and Hamilton's, who had threatened to cut to
pieces every Highlander that should venture to pass Stirling; and while discussions were carrying forward among
the magistracy and citizens of Edinburgh, whether they
should defend themselves or surrender, my good friend
Lochiel (laying his hand on the shoulder of that gallant
and accomplished chieftain) saved them the trouble of
farther deliberation, by entering the gates with five
hundred Camerons. Thus far, therefore, we have done
well; but, in the meanwhile, this doughty general's nerves
being braced by the keen air of Aberdeen, he has taken
shipping for Dunbar, and I have just received certain
information that he landed there yesterday. His purpose
must unquestionably be, to march towards us to recover
possession of the capital. Now there are two opinions in
my council of war: one, that being inferior probably in
numbers, and certainly in discipline and military appointments, not to mention our total want of artillery, and the
weakness of our cavalry, it will be safest to fall back
towards the mountains, and there protract the war until
fresh succours arrive from France, and the whole body of
the Highland clans shall have taken arms in our favour.
The opposite opinion maintains, that a retrograde movement, in our circumstances, is certain to throw utter
discredit on our arms and undertaking; and, far from

gaining us new partisans, will be the means of disheartening those who have joined our standard. The officers who use these last arguments, among whom is your friend Fergus Mac-Ivor, maintain, that if the Highlanders are strangers to the usual military discipline of Europe, the soldiers whom they are to encounter are no less strangers to their peculiar and formidable mode of attack ; that the attachment and courage of the chiefs and gentlemen are not to be doubted ; and that as they will be in the midst of the enemy, their clansmen will as surely follow them ; in fine, that having drawn the sword we should throw away the scabbard, and trust our cause to battle and to the God of Battles. Will Mr Waverley favour us with his opinion in these arduous circumstances ?"

Waverley coloured high betwixt pleasure and modesty at the distinction implied in this question, and answered, with equal spirit and readiness, that he could not venture to offer an opinion as derived from military skill, but that the counsel would be far the most acceptable to him which should first afford him an opportunity to evince his zeal in his Royal Highness's service.

"Spoken like a Waverley !" answered Charles Edward ; " and that you may hold a rank in some degree corresponding to your name, allow me, instead of the captain's commission which you have lost, to offer you the brevet rank of major in my service, with the advantage of acting as one of my aides-de-camp until you can be attached to a regiment, of which I hope several will be speedily embodied."

"Your Royal Highness will forgive me," answered Waverley, (for his recollection turned to Balmawhapple and his scanty troop,) "if I decline accepting any rank until the time and place where I may have interest enough to raise a sufficient body of men to make my command useful to your Royal Highness's service. In the meanwhile, I hope for your permission to serve as a volunteer under my friend Fergus Mac-Ivor."

"At least," said the Prince, who was obviously pleased with this proposal, "allow me the pleasure of arming you after the Highland fashion." With these words, he unbuckled the broadsword which he wore, the belt of which was plated with silver, and the steel basket-hilt richly and curiously inlaid. "The blade," said the Prince, "is a genuine Andrea Ferrara ; it has been a sort of heir-loom in our family ; but I am convinced I put it into better hands than my own, and will add to it pistols of the same workmanship.—Colonel Mac-Ivor, you must have much to say to your friend; I will detain you no longer from your private conversation; but remember, we expect you both to attend us in the evening. It may be perhaps the last night we may enjoy in these halls, and as we go to the field with a clear conscience, we will spend the eve of battle merrily."

Thus licensed, the Chief and Waverley left the presence-chamber.

## CHAPTER XLI.

### The Mystery begins to be cleared up.

"How do you like him?" was Fergus's first question, as they descended the large stone staircase.

"A prince to live and die under," was Waverley's enthusiastic answer.

"I knew you would think so when you saw him, and I intended you should have met earlier, but was prevented by your sprain. And yet he has his foibles, or rather he has difficult cards to play, and his Irish Officers,[1] who are much about him, are but sorry advisers,—they cannot discriminate among the numerous pretensions that are set up. Would you think it—I have been obliged for the present to suppress an earl's patent, granted for services rendered ten years ago, for fear of exciting the jealousy, forsooth, of C—— and M——. But you were very right, Edward, to refuse the situation of aide-de-camp. There are two vacant, indeed, but Clanronald and Lochiel, and almost all of us, have requested one for young Aberchallader, and the Lowlanders and the Irish party are equally desirous to have the other for the Master of F——. Now, if either of these candidates were to be superseded in your favour, you would make enemies. And then I am surprised that the Prince should have

[1] Divisions early showed themselves in the Chevalier's little army, not only amongst the independent chieftains, who were far too proud to brook subjection to each other, but betwixt the Scotch, and Charles's governor O'Sullivan, an Irishman by birth, who, with some of his countrymen bred in the Irish-Brigade in the service of the King of France, had an influence with the Adventurer, much resented by the Highlanders, who were sensible that their own clans made the chief or rather the only strength of his enterprise. There was a feud, also, between Lord George Murray, and John Murray of Broughton, the Prince's secretary, whose disunion greatly embarrassed the affairs of the Adventurer. In general, a thousand different pretensions divided their little army, and finally contributed in no small degree to its overthrow. (S.)

offered you a majority, when he knows very well that
nothing short of lieutenant-colonel will satisfy others
who cannot bring one hundred and fifty men to the field.
'But patience, cousin, and shuffle the cards!' It is all
very well for the present, and we must have you properly
equipped for the evening in your new costume; for, to
say truth, your outward man is scarce fit for a court."

"Why," said Waverley, looking at his soiled dress, "my
shooting jacket has seen service since we parted; but
that, probably, you, my friend, know as well or better
than I."

"You do my second-sight too much honour," said
Fergus. "We were so busy, first with the scheme of
giving battle to Cope, and afterwards with our operations
in the Lowlands, that I could only give general directions
to such of our people as were left in Perthshire to respect
and protect you, should you come in their way. But let
me hear the full story of your adventures, for they have
reached us in a very partial and mutilated manner."

Waverley then detailed at length the circumstances
with which the reader is already acquainted, to which
Fergus listened with great attention. By this time they
had reached the door of his quarters, which he had taken
up in a small paved court, retiring from the street called
the Canongate, at the house of a buxom widow of forty,
who seemed to smile very graciously upon the handsome
young Chief, she being a person with whom good looks
and good-humour were sure to secure an interest, whatever might be the party's political opinions. Here Callum
Beg received them with a smile of recognition. "Callum,"
said the Chief, "call Shemus an Snachad," (James of the
Needle.) This was the hereditary tailor of Vich Ian Vohr.
"Shemus, Mr Waverley is to wear the *cath dath*, (battle
colour, or tartan;) his trews must be ready in four hours.
You know the measure of a well-made man; two double
nails to the small of the leg"——

"Eleven from haunch to heel, seven round the waist—
I give your honour leave to hang Shemus, if there's a pair
of sheers in the Highlands that has a baulder sneck[1] than
her's ain at the *cumadh an truais*," (shape of the trews.)

"Get a plaid of Mac-Ivor tartan, and sash," continued
the Chieftain, "and a blue bonnet of the Prince's pattern,
at Mr Mouat's in the Crames. My short green coat, with
silver lace and silver buttons, will fit him exactly, and I
have never worn it. Tell Ensign Maccombich to pick out

[1] Certain click with the scissors

a handsome target from among mine. The Prince has given Mr Waverley broadsword and pistols, I will furnish him with a dirk and purse; add but a pair of low-heeled shoes, and then, my dear Edward, (turning to him,) you will be a complete son of Ivor."

These necessary directions given, the Chieftain resumed the subject of Waverley's adventures. "It is plain," he said, "that you have been in the custody of Donald Bean Lean. You must know that when I marched away my clan to join the Prince, I laid my injunctions on that worthy member of society to perform a certain piece of service, which done, he was to join me with all the force he could muster. But instead of doing so, the gentleman, finding the coast clear, thought it better to make war on his own account, and has scoured the country, plundering, I believe, both friend and foe, under pretence of levying black mail, sometimes as if by my authority, and sometimes (and be cursed to his consummate impudence) in his own great name! Upon my honour, if I live to see the cairn of Benmore again, I shall be tempted to hang that fellow! I recognise his hand particularly in the mode of your rescue from that canting rascal Gilfillan, and I have little doubt that Donald himself played the part of the pedlar on that occasion; but how he should not have plundered you, or put you to ransom, or availed himself in some way or other of your captivity for his own advantage, passes my judgment."

"When and how did you hear the intelligence of my confinement?" asked Waverley.

"The Prince himself told me," said Fergus, "and inquired very minutely into your history. He then mentioned your being at that moment in the power of one of our northern parties—you know I could not ask him to explain particulars—and requested my opinion about disposing of you. I recommended that you should be brought here as a prisoner, because I did not wish to prejudice you farther with the English government, in case you pursued your purpose of going southward. I knew nothing, you must recollect, of the charge brought against you of aiding and abetting high treason, which, I presume, had some share in changing your original plan. That sullen, good-for-nothing brute, Balmawhapple, was sent to escort you from Doune, with what he calls his troop of horse. As to his behaviour, in addition to his natural antipathy to everything that resembles a gentleman, I presume his adventure with Bradwardine rankles

in his recollection, the rather that I daresay his mode of
telling that story contributed to the evil reports which
reached your quondam regiment."

"Very likely," said Waverley; "but now surely, my
dear Fergus, you may find time to tell me something of
Flora."

"Why," replied Fergus, "I can only tell you that she
is well, and residing for the present with a relation in
this city. I thought it better she should come here, as
since our success a good many ladies of rank attend our
military court; and I assure you, that there is a sort of
consequence annexed to the near relative of such a
person as Flora Mac-Ivor, and where there is such a
justling of claims and requests, a man must use every
fair means to enhance his importance."

There was something in this last sentence which grated
on Waverley's feelings. He could not bear that Flora
should be considered as conducing to her brother's preferment, by the admiration which she must unquestionably
attract; and although it was in strict correspondence
with many points of Fergus's character, it shocked him as
selfish, and unworthy of his sister's high mind and his
own independent pride. Fergus, to whom such manœuvres were familiar, as to one brought up at the French
court, did not observe the unfavourable impression which
he had unwarily made upon his friend's mind, and concluded by saying, "that they could hardly see Flora
before the evening, when she would be at the concert and
ball, with which the Prince's party were to be entertained. She and I had a quarrel about her not appearing
to take leave of you. I am unwilling to renew it, by
soliciting her to receive you this morning; and perhaps
my doing so might not only be ineffectual, but prevent
your meeting this evening."

While thus conversing, Waverley heard in the court,
before the windows of the parlour, a well-known voice.
"I aver to you, my worthy friend," said the speaker,
"that it is a total dereliction of military discipline; and
were you not as it were a *tyro*, your purpose would
deserve strong reprobation. For a prisoner of war is on
no account to be coerced with fetters, or debinded *in
ergastulo*, as would have been the case had you put this
gentleman into the pit of the peel-house at Balmawhapple. I grant, indeed, that such a prisoner may for
security be coerced *in carcere*, that is, in a public prison."

The growling voice of Balmawhapple was heard as

taking leave in displeasure, but the word, "land-louper," alone was distinctly audible. He had disappeared before Waverley reached the house, in order to greet the worthy Baron of Bradwardine. The uniform in which he was now attired, a blue coat, namely, with gold lace, a scarlet waistcoat and breeches, and immense jack-boots, seemed to have added fresh stiffness and rigidity to his tall, perpendicular figure; and the consciousness of military command and authority had increased, in the same proportion, the self-importance of his demeanour, and dogmatism of his conversation.

He received Waverley with his usual kindness, and expressed immediate anxiety to hear an explanation of the circumstances attending the loss of his commission in Gardiner's dragoons; "not," he said, "that he had the least apprehension of his young friend having done aught which could merit such ungenerous treatment as he had received from government, but because it was right and seemly that the Baron of Bradwardine should be, in point of trust and in point of power, fully able to refute all calumnies against the heir of Waverley-Honour, whom he had so much right to regard as his own son."

Fergus Mac-Ivor, who had now joined them, went hastily over the circumstances of Waverley's story, and concluded with the flattering reception he had met from the young Chevalier. The Baron listened in silence; and at the conclusion shook Waverley heartily by the hand, and congratulated him upon entering the service of his lawful Prince. "For," continued he, "although it has been justly held in all nations a matter of scandal and dishonour to infringe the *sacramentum militare*, and that whether it was taken by each soldier singly, whilk the Romans denominated *per conjurationem*, or by one soldier in name of the rest, yet no one ever doubted that the allegiance so sworn was discharged by the *dimissio*, or discharging of a soldier, whose case would be as hard as that of colliers, salters, and other *adscripti glebæ*, or slaves of the soil, were it to be accounted otherwise. This is something like the brocard expressed by the learned Sanchez in his work *De Jure-jurando*, which you have questionless consulted upon this occasion. As for those who have calumniated you by leasing-making, I protest to Heaven I think they have justly incurred the penalty of the *Memnonia lex*, also called *Lex Rhemnia*, which is prelected upon by Tullius in his oration *In Verrem*. I should have deemed, however, Mr Waverley, that before destining yourself to any special service in the army of the Prince, ye might have inquired what rank the old Bradwardine held there, and whether he would not have been peculiarly happy to have had your services in the regiment of horse which he is now about to levy."

Edward eluded this reproach by pleading the necessity of giving an immediate answer to the Prince's proposal, and his uncertainty at the moment whether his friend the Baron was with the army, or engaged upon service elsewhere.

This punctilio being settled, Waverley made inquiry after Miss Bradwardine, and was informed she had come to Edinburgh with Flora Mac-Ivor, under guard of a party of the Chieftain's men. This step was indeed necessary, Tully-Veolan having become a very unpleasant, and even dangerous place of residence for an unprotected young lady, on account of its vicinity to the Highlands, and also to one or two large villages, which, from aversion as much to the Caterans as zeal for presbytery, had declared themselves on the side of government, and formed irregular bodies of partisans, who had frequent skirmishes with the mountaineers, and sometimes attacked the houses of the Jacobite gentry in the braes, or frontier betwixt the mountain and plain.

"I would propose to you," continued the Baron, "to walk as far as my quarters in the Luckenbooths, and to admire in your passage the High Street, whilk is, beyond a shadow of dubitation, finer than any street, whether in London or Paris. But Rose, poor thing, is sorely discomposed with the firing of the Castle, though I have proved to her from Blondel and Coehorn, that it is impossible a bullet can reach these buildings ; and, besides, I have it in charge from his Royal Highness to go to the camp, or leaguer of our army, to see that the men do *conclamare vasa*, that is, truss up their bag and baggage for tomorrow's march."

"That will be easily done by most of us," said Mac-Ivor, laughing.

"Craving your pardon, Colonel Mac-Ivor, not quite so easily as ye seem to opine. I grant most of your folk left the Highlands, expedited as it were, and free from the incumbrance of baggage; but it is unspeakable the quantity of useless sprechery [1] which they have collected on their march. I saw one fellow of yours (craving your pardon once more) with a pier-glass upon his back."

[1] Plunder.

"Ay," said Fergus, still in good-humour, "he would have told you, if you had questioned him, *a ganging*[1] *foot is aye getting.*—But come, my dear Baron, you know as well as I, that a hundred Uhlans, or a single troop of Schmirschitz's Pandours, would make more havoc in a country than the knight of the mirror and all the rest of our clans put together."

"And that is very true likewise," replied the Baron; "they are, as the heathen author says, *ferociores in aspectu, mitiores in actu,* of a horrid and grim visage, but more benign in demeanour than their physiognomy or aspect might infer. — But I stand here talking to you two youngsters, when I should be in the King's Park."

"But you will dine with Waverley and me on your return? I assure you, Baron, though I can live like a Highlander when needs must, I remember my Paris education, and understand perfectly *faire la meilleure chère.*"

"And wha the deil doubts it," quoth the Baron, laughing, "when ye bring only the cookery, and the gude toun must furnish the materials?—Weel, I have some business in the toun too: But I'll join you at three, if the vivers[2] can tarry so long."

So saying, he took leave of his friends, and went to look after the charge which had been assigned him.

## CHAPTER XLII.

### *A Soldier's Dinner.*

JAMES OF THE NEEDLE was a man of his word, when whisky was no party to the contract; and upon this occasion Callum Beg, who still thought himself in Waverley's debt, since he had declined accepting compensation at the expense of mine Host of the Candlestick's person, took the opportunity of discharging the obligation, by mounting guard over the hereditary tailor of Sliochd nan Ivor; and, as he expressed himself, "targed him tightly"[3] till the finishing of the job. To rid himself of this restraint, Shemus's needle flew through the tartan like lightning; and as the artist kept chanting some dreadful skirmish of Fin Macoul, he accomplished at least three stitches to the death of every hero. The

[1] Going.    [2] Victuals.    [3] Kept him in order.

dress was, therefore, soon ready, for the short coat fitted
the wearer, and the rest of the apparel required little
adjustment.

Our hero having now fairly assumed the "garb of old
Gaul," well calculated as it was to give an appearance of
strength to a figure, which, though tall and well-made,
was rather elegant than robust, I hope my fair readers
will excuse him if he looked at himself in the mirror
more than once, and could not help acknowledging that
the reflection seemed that of a very handsome young
fellow. In fact, there was no disguising it. His light-
brown hair,—for he wore no periwig, notwithstanding
the universal fashion of the time,—became the bonnet
which surmounted it. His person promised firmness
and agility, to which the ample folds of the tartan
added an air of dignity. His blue eye seemed of that
kind,

> "Which melted in love, and which kindled in war;"

and an air of bashfulness, which was in reality the
effect of want of habitual intercourse with the world,
gave interest to his features, without injuring their grace
or intelligence.

"He's a pratty man—a very pratty man," said Evan
Dhu (now Ensign Maccombich) to Fergus's buxom landlady.

"He's vera weel," said the Widow Flockhart, "but no
naething sae weel-far'd [1] as your colonel, ensign."

"I wasna comparing them," quoth Evan, "nor was I
speaking about his being weel-favoured; but only that
Mr Waverley looks clean-made and *deliver*, [2] and like a
proper lad o' his quarters, that will not cry barley in a
brulzie. [3] And, indeed, he's gleg [4] aneuch at the broadsword and target. I hae played wi' him mysell at Glennaquoich, and sae has Vich Ian Vohr, often of a Sunday
afternoon."

"Lord forgie ye, Ensign Maccombich," said the alarmed
Presbyterian; "I'm sure the colonel wad never do the
like o' that!"

"Hout! hout! Mrs Flockhart," replied the ensign,
"we're young blude, ye ken; and young saints, auld
deils."

"But will ye fight wi' Sir John Cope the morn, Ensign
Maccombich?" demanded Mrs Flockhart of her guest.

"Troth I'se ensure him, an he'll bide us, Mrs Flockhart,"
replied the Gael.

[1] Well favoured.   [2] Agile.   [3] Brawl.   [4] Expert.

"And will ye face thae tearing chields, the dragoons, Ensign Maccombich?" again inquired the landlady.

"Claw for claw, as Conan said to Satan, Mrs Flockhart, and the deevil tak the shortest nails."

"And will the colonel venture on the bagganets himsell?"

"Ye may swear it, Mrs Flockhart; the very first man will he be, by Saint Phedar."

"Merciful goodness! and if he's killed amang the redcoats!" exclaimed the soft-hearted widow.

"Troth, if it should sae befall, Mrs Flockhart, I ken ane that will no be living to weep for him. But we maun a' live the day, and have our dinner; and there's Vich Ian Vohr has packed his *dorlach*,[1] and Mr Waverley's wearied wi' majoring yonder afore the muckle pier-glass; and that grey auld stoor carle,[2] the Baron o' Bradwardine, that shot young Ronald of Ballenkeirock, he's coming down the close wi' that droghling coghling bailie body they ca' Macwhupple, just like the Laird o' Kittlegab's French cook, wi' his turnspit doggie trindling ahint him, and I am as hungry as a gled,[3] my bonny dow; sae bid Kate set on the broo,[4] and do you put on your pinners,[5] for ye ken Vich Ian Vohr winna sit down till ye be at the head o' the table;—and dinna forget the pint bottle o' brandy, my woman."

This hint produced dinner. Mrs Flockhart, smiling in her weeds like the sun through a mist, took the head of the table, thinking within herself, perhaps, that she cared not how long the rebellion lasted, that brought her into company so much above her usual associates. She was supported by Waverley and the Baron, with the advantage of the Chieftain *vis-à-vis*. The men of peace and of war, that is, Bailie Macwheeble and Ensign Maccombich, after many profound congés to their superiors and each other, took their places on each side of the Chieftain. Their fare was excellent, time, place, and circumstances considered, and Fergus's spirits were extravagantly high. Regardless of danger, and sanguine from temper, youth, and ambition, he saw in imagination all his prospects crowned with success, and was totally indifferent to the probable alternative of a soldier's grave. The Baron apologized slightly for bringing Macwheeble. They had been providing, he said, for the expenses of the campaign. "And, by my faith," said the old man, "as I think this will be my last, so I just end where I began—

<hr>

[1] Dagger.　[2] Austere man.　[3] Hawk.　[4] Broth.　[5] Flowing head-dress.

I hae evermore found the sinews of war, as a learned
author calls the *caisse militaire*, mair difficult to come by
than either its flesh, blood, or bones."

"What! have you raised our only efficient body of
cavalry, and got ye none of the louis-d'or out of the
Doutelle, to help you?"[1]

"No, Glennaquoich; cleverer fellows have been before
me."

"That's a scandal," said the young Highlander; "but
you will share what is left of my subsidy: It will save
you an anxious thought to-night, and will be all one
to-morrow, for we shall all be provided for, one way or
other, before the sun sets." Waverley, blushing deeply,
but with great earnestness, pressed the same request.

"I thank ye baith, my good lads," said the Baron, "but
I will not infringe upon your peculium. Bailie Macwheeble
has provided the sum which is necessary."

Here the Bailie shifted and fidgeted about in his seat,
and appeared extremely uneasy. At length, after several
preliminary hems, and much tautological expression of
his devotion to his honour's service, by night or day,
living or dead, he began to insinuate, "that the Banks had
removed a' their ready cash into the Castle; that, nae
doubt, Sandie Goldie, the silversmith, would do mickle
for his honour; but there was little time to get the
wadset[2] made out; and, doubtless, if his honour Glennaquoich, or Mr Wauverley, could accommodate"——

"Let me hear of no such nonsense, sir," said the Baron,
in a tone which rendered Macwheeble mute, "but proceed
as we accorded before dinner, if it be your wish to remain
in my service."

To this peremptory order the Bailie, though he felt as if
condemned to suffer a transfusion of blood from his own
veins into those of the Baron, did not presume to make
any reply. After fidgeting a little while longer, however,
he addressed himself to Glennaquoich, and told him, if
his honour had mair ready siller than was sufficient
for his occasions in the field, he could put it out at use for
his honour in safe hands, and at great profit, at this time.

At this proposal Fergus laughed heartily, and answered,
when he had recovered his breath,—"Many thanks,
Bailie; but you must know, it is a general custom among
us soldiers to make our landlady our banker.—Here, Mrs
Flockhart," said he, taking four or five broad pieces out

---

[1] The Doutelle was an armed vessel, which brought a small supply of money and
arms from France for the use of the insurgents.  (S.)          [2] Bond.

of a well-filled purse, and tossing the purse itself, with its remaining contents, into her apron, "these will serve my occasions; do you take the rest: be my banker if I live, and my executor if I die; but take care to give something to the Highland cailliachs[1] that shall cry the coronach loudest for the last Vich Ian Vohr."

"It is the *testamentum militare*," quoth the Baron, "whilk, amang the Romans, was privilegiate to be nuncupative." But the soft heart of Mrs Flockhart was melted within her at the Chieftain's speech; she set up a lamentable blubbering, and positively refused to touch the bequest, which Fergus was therefore obliged to resume.

"Well, then," said the Chief, "if I fall, it will go to the grenadier that knocks my brains out, and I shall take care he works hard for it."

Bailie Macwheeble was again tempted to put in his oar; for where cash was concerned, he did not willingly remain silent. "Perhaps he had better carry the gowd to Miss Mac-Ivor, in case of mortality, or accidents of war. It might tak the form of a *mortis causa* donation in the young leddie's favour, and wad cost but the scrape of a pen to mak it out."

"The young lady," said Fergus, "should such an event happen, will have other matters to think of than these wretched louis-d'or."

"True—undeniable—there's nae doubt o' that; but your honour kens that a full sorrow"——

"Is endurable by most folk more easily than a hungry one?—True, Bailie, very true; and I believe there may even be some who would be consoled by such a reflection for the loss of the whole existing generation. But there is a sorrow which knows neither hunger nor thirst; and poor Flora"——He paused, and the whole company sympathized in his emotion.

The Baron's thoughts naturally reverted to the unprotected state of his daughter, and the big tear came to the veteran's eye. "If I fall, Macwheeble, you have all my papers and know all my affairs; be just to Rose."

The Bailie was a man of earthly mould, after all; a good deal of dirt and dross about him, undoubtedly, but some kindly and just feelings he had, especially where the Baron or his young mistress were concerned. He set up a lamentable howl. "If that doleful day should come, while Duncan Macwheeble had a boddle, it should be Miss

[1] Old women, on whom devolved the duty of lamenting for the dead, which the Irish call *Keenning*. (S.)

Rose's. He wald scroll for a plack[1] the sheet, or she
kenn'd what it was to want ; if indeed a' the bonnie
baronie o' Bradwardine and Tully-Veolan, with the
fortalice and manor-place thereof, (he kept sobbing and
whining at every pause,) tofts, crofts, mosses, muirs—
outfield, infield—buildings—orchards—dovecots—with the
right of net and coble in the water and loch of Veolan—
teinds, parsonage and vicarage—annexis, connexis—rights
of pasturage—fuel, feal, and divot—parts, pendicles, and
pertinents whatsoever—(here he had recourse to the end
of his long cravat to wipe his eyes, which overflowed, in
spite of him, at the ideas which this technical jargon
conjured up)—all as more fully described in the proper
evidents and titles thereof—and lying within the parish
of Bradwardine, and the shire of Perth—if, as aforesaid,
they must a' pass from my master's child to Inch-Grabbit,
wha's a Whig and a Hanoverian, and be managed by his
doer, Jamie Howie, wha's no fit to be a birlieman, [2] let be
a bailie."——

The beginning of this lamentation really had something
affecting, but the conclusion rendered laughter irresistible.
"Never mind, Bailie," said Ensign Maccombich, "for the
gude auld times of rugging and riving (pulling and
tearing) are come back again, an' Sneckus Mac-Snackus,
(meaning probably, annexis, connexis,) and a' the rest of
your friends, maun gie place to the langest claymore."

"And that claymore shall be ours, Bailie," said the
Chieftain, who saw that Macwheeble looked very blank at
this intimation.

> " 'We'll give them the metal our mountain affords,
>                 Lillibulero, bullen a la,
> And in place of broad-pieces, we'll pay with broadswords,
>                 Lero, lero, &c.
> With duns and with debts we will soon clear our score,
>                 Lillibulero, &c.
> For the man that s thus paid will crave payment no more,
>                 Lero, lero,' &c. [3]

But come, Bailie, be not cast down ; drink your wine
with a joyous heart ; the Baron shall return safe and
victorious to Tully-Veolan, and unite Killancureit's laird-
ship with his own, since the cowardly half-bred swine
will not turn out for the Prince like a gentleman."

"To be sure, they lie maist ewest," [4] said the Bailie,
wiping his eyes, "and should naturally fa' under the same
factory."

---

[1] Penny.          [2] Petty burgh officer.
[3] These lines, or something like them, occur in an old Magazine of the period.  (S.)
[4] Contiguous.

"And I," proceeded the Chieftain, "shall take care of myself, too; for you must know, I have to complete a good work here, by bringing Mrs Flockhart into the bosom of the Catholic church, or at least half way, and that is to your Episcopal meeting-house. O Baron! if you heard her fine counter-tenor admonishing Kate and Matty in the morning, you, who understand music, would tremble at the idea of hearing her shriek in the psalmody of Haddo's Hole."

"Lord forgie you, colonel, how ye rin on! But I hope your honours will tak tea before ye gang to the palace, and I maun gang and mask it for you."

So saying, Mrs Flockhart left the gentlemen to their own conversation, which, as might be supposed, turned chiefly upon the approaching events of the campaign.

## CHAPTER XLIII.

### The Ball.

ENSIGN MACCOMBICH having gone to the Highland camp upon duty, and Bailie Macwheeble having retired to digest his dinner, and Evan Dhu's intimation of martial law, in some blind change-house, Waverley, with the Baron and the Chieftain, proceeded to Holyrood-House. The two last were in full tide of spirits, and the Baron rallied in his way our hero upon the handsome figure which his new dress displayed to advantage. "If you have any design upon the heart of a bonny Scotch lassie, I would premonish you, when you address her, to remember and quote the words of Virgilius:—

> 'Nunc insanus amor duri me Martis in armis,
> Tela inter media atque adversos detinet hostes:'

Whilk verses Robertson of Struan, Chief of the Clan Donnochy, (unless the claims of Lude ought to be preferred *primo loco*,) has thus elegantly rendered:

> 'For cruel love has gartan'd low my leg,
> And clad my hurdies in a philabeg.'

Although, indeed, ye wear the trews, a garment whilk I approve maist of the twa, as mair ancient and seemly."

"Or rather," said Fergus, "hear my song:

> 'She wadna hae a Lowland laird,
>   Nor be an English lady;
> But she's away with Duncan Græme,
>   And he's row'd her in his plaidy.'"

By this time they reached the palace of Holyrood, and were announced respectively as they entered the apartments.

It is but too well known how many gentlemen of rank, education, and fortune, took a concern in the ill-fated and desperate undertaking of 1745. The ladies, also, of Scotland very generally espoused the cause of the gallant and handsome young Prince, who threw himself upon the mercy of his countrymen, rather like a hero of romance than a calculating politician. It is not, therefore, to be wondered that Edward, who had spent the greater part of his life in the solemn seclusion of Waverley-Honour, should have been dazzled at the liveliness and elegance of the scene now exhibited in the long-deserted halls of the Scottish palace. The accompaniments, indeed, fell short of splendour, being such as the confusion and hurry of the time admitted; still, however, the general effect was striking, and, the rank of the company considered, might well be called brilliant.

It was not long before the lover's eye discovered the object of his attachment. Flora Mac-Ivor was in the act of returning to her seat, near the top of the room, with Rose Bradwardine by her side. Among much elegance and beauty, they had attracted a great degree of the public attention, being certainly two of the handsomest women present. The Prince took much notice of both, particularly of Flora, with whom he danced; a preference which she probably owed to her foreign education, and command of the French and Italian languages.

When the bustle attending the conclusion of the dance permitted, Edward, almost intuitively, followed Fergus to the place where Miss Mac-Ivor was seated. The sensation of hope, with which he had nursed his affection in absence of the beloved object, seemed to vanish in her presence, and, like one striving to recover the particulars of a forgotten dream, he would have given the world at that moment to have recollected the grounds on which he had founded expectations which now seemed so delusive. He accompanied Fergus with downcast eyes, tingling ears, and the feelings of the criminal, who, while the melancholy cart moves slowly through the crowds that have assembled to behold his execution, receives no clear sensation either from the noise which fills his ears, or the tumult on which he casts his wandering look.

Flora seemed a little—a very little—affected and discomposed at his approach. "I bring you an adopted son of Ivor," said Fergus.

"And I receive him as a second brother," replied Flora. There was a slight emphasis on the word, which would have escaped every ear but one that was feverish with apprehension. It was, however, distinctly marked, and, combined with her whole tone and manner, plainly intimated, "I will never think of Mr Waverley as a more intimate connection." Edward stopped, bowed, and looked at Fergus, who bit his lip; a movement of anger, which proved that he also had put a sinister interpretation on the reception which his sister had given his friend. "This, then, is an end of my day-dream!" Such was Waverley's first thought, and it was so exquisitely painful as to banish from his cheek every drop of blood.

"Good God!" said Rose Bradwardine, "he is not yet recovered!"

These words, which she uttered with great emotion, were overheard by the Chevalier himself, who stepped hastily forward, and, taking Waverley by the hand, inquired kindly after his health, and added, that he wished to speak with him. By a strong and sudden effort, which the circumstances rendered indispensable, Waverley recovered himself so far as to follow the Chevalier in silence to a recess in the apartment.

Here the Prince detained him some time, asking various questions about the great Tory and Catholic families of England, their connections, their influence, and the state of their affections towards the house of Stewart. To these queries Edward could not at any time have given more than general answers, and it may be supposed that, in the present state of his feelings, his responses were indistinct even to confusion. The Chevalier smiled once or twice at the incongruity of his replies, but continued the same style of conversation, although he found himself obliged to occupy the principal share of it, until he perceived that Waverley had recovered his presence of mind. It is probable that this long audience was partly meant to further the idea which the Prince desired should be entertained among his followers, that Waverley was a character of political influence. But it appeared, from his concluding expressions, that he had a different and good-natured motive, personal to our hero, for prolonging the conference. "I cannot resist the temptation," he said, "of boasting of my own discretion as a lady's confident. You see, Mr Waverley, that I know all, and I assure you I am deeply interested in the affair. But, my good young friend, you must put a more severe restraint upon your feelings. There are many here whose eyes can see as clearly as mine, but the prudence of whose tongues may not be equally trusted."

So saying, he turned easily away, and joined a circle of officers at a few paces' distance, leaving Waverley to meditate upon his parting expression, which, though not intelligible to him in its whole purport, was sufficiently so in the caution which the last word recommended. Making, therefore, an effort to show himself worthy of the interest which his new master had expressed, by instant obedience to his recommendation, he walked up to the spot where Flora and Miss Bradwardine were still seated, and having made his compliments to the latter, he succeeded, even beyond his own expectation, in entering into conversation upon general topics.

If, my dear reader, thou hast ever happened to take post-horses at ——, or at ——, (one at least of which blanks, or more probably both, you will be able to fill up from an inn near your own residence,) you must have observed, and doubtless with sympathetic pain, the reluctant agony with which the poor jades at first apply their galled necks to the collars of the harness. But when the irresistible arguments of the post-boy have prevailed upon them to proceed a mile or two, they will become callous to the first sensation; and being *warm in the harness*, as the said post-boy may term it, proceed as if their withers were altogether unwrung. This simile so much corresponds with the state of Waverley's feelings in the course of this memorable evening, that I prefer it (especially as being, I trust, wholly original) to any more splendid illustration, with which Byshe's Art of Poetry might supply me.

Exertion, like virtue, is its own reward; and our hero had, moreover, other stimulating motives for persevering in a display of affected composure and indifference to Flora's obvious unkindness. Pride, which supplies its caustic as an useful, though severe, remedy for the wounds of affection, came rapidly to his aid. Distinguished by the favour of a Prince; destined, he had room to hope, to play a conspicuous part in the revolution which awaited a mighty kingdom; excelling, probably, in mental acquirements, and equalling at least in personal accomplishments, most of the noble and distinguished persons with whom he was now ranked; young, wealthy, and high-born,—could he, or ought he, to droop beneath the frown of a capricious beauty?

> "O nymph, unrelenting and cold as thou art,
> My bosom is proud as thine own."

With the feeling expressed in these beautiful lines, (which, however, were not then written,)[1] Waverley determined upon convincing Flora that he was not to be depressed by a rejection, in which his vanity whispered that perhaps she did her own prospects as much injustice as his. And, to aid this change of feeling, there lurked the secret and unacknowledged hope, that she might learn to prize his affection more highly, when she did not conceive it to be altogether within her own choice to attract or repulse it. There was a mystic tone of encouragement, also, in the Chevalier's words, though he feared they only referred to the wishes of Fergus in favour of an union between him and his sister. But the whole circumstances of time, place, and incident, combined at once to awaken his imagination, and to call upon him for a manly and decisive tone of conduct, leaving to fate to dispose of the issue. Should he appear to be the only one sad and disheartened on the eve of battle, how greedily would the tale be commented upon by the slander which had been already but too busy with his fame? Never, never, he internally resolved, shall my unprovoked enemies possess such an advantage over my reputation.

Under the influence of these mixed sensations, and cheered at times by a smile of intelligence and approbation from the Prince as he passed the group, Waverley exerted his powers of fancy, animation, and eloquence, and attracted the general admiration of the company. The conversation gradually assumed the tone best qualified for the display of his talents and acquisitions. The gaiety of the evening was exalted in character, rather than checked, by the approaching dangers of the morrow. All nerves were strung for the future, and prepared to enjoy the present. This mood of mind is highly favourable for the exercise of the powers of imagination, for poetry, and for that eloquence which is allied to poetry. Waverley, as we have elsewhere observed, possessed at times a wonderful flow of rhetoric; and, on the present occasion, he touched more than once the higher notes of feeling, and then again ran off in a wild voluntary of fanciful mirth. He was supported and excited by kindred

---

[1] They occur in Miss Seward's fine verses, beginning—

"To thy rocks, stormy Lannow, adieu.                    (S.)

spirits, who felt the same impulse of mood and time ; and even those of more cold and calculating habits were hurried along by the torrent. Many ladies declined the dance, which still went forward, and, under various pretences, joined the party to which the "handsome young Englishman" seemed to have attached himself. He was presented to several of the first rank, and his manners, which for the present were altogether free from the bashful restraint by which, in a moment of less excitement, they were usually clouded, gave universal delight.

Flora Mac-Ivor appeared to be the only female present who regarded him with a degree of coldness and reserve ; yet even she could not suppress a sort of wonder at talents, which, in the course of their acquaintance, she had never seen displayed with equal brilliancy and impressive effect. I do not know whether she might not feel a momentary regret at having taken so decisive a resolution upon the addresses of a lover, who seemed fitted so well to fill a high place in the highest stations of society. Certainly she had hitherto accounted among the incurable deficiencies of Edward's disposition, the *mauvaise honte*, which, as she had been educated in the first foreign circles, and was little acquainted with the shyness of English manners, was, in her opinion, too nearly related to timidity and imbecility of disposition. But if a passing wish occurred that Waverley could have rendered himself uniformly thus amiable and attractive, its influence was momentary ; for circumstances had arisen since they met, which rendered, in her eyes, the resolution she had formed respecting him, final and irrevocable.

With opposite feelings, Rose Bradwardine bent her whole soul to listen. She felt a secret triumph at the public tribute paid to one, whose merit she had learned to prize too early and too fondly. Without a thought of jealousy, without a feeling of fear, pain, or doubt, and undisturbed by a single selfish consideration, she resigned herself to the pleasure of observing the general murmur of applause. When Waverley spoke, her ear was exclusively filled with his voice ; when others answered, her eye took its turn of observation, and seemed to watch his reply. Perhaps the delight which she experienced in the course of that evening, though transient, and followed by much sorrow, was in its nature the most pure and disinterested which the human mind is capable of enjoying.

"Baron," said the Chevalier, "I would not trust my

mistress in the company of your young friend. He is really, though perhaps somewhat romantic, one of the most fascinating young men whom I have ever seen."

"And by my honour, sir," replied the Baron, "the lad can sometimes be as dowff as a sexagenary like myself. If your Royal Highness had seen him dreaming and dozing about the banks of Tully-Veolan like an hypochondriac person, or, as Burton's *Anatomia* hath it, a phrenesiac or lethargic patient, you would wonder where he hath sae suddenly acquired all this fine sprack festivity and jocularity."

"Truly," said Fergus Mac-Ivor, "I think it can only be the inspiration of the tartans ; for, though Waverley be always a young fellow of sense and honour, I have hitherto often found him a very absent and inattentive companion."

"We are the more obliged to him," said the Prince, "for having reserved for this evening qualities which even such intimate friends had not discovered.—But come, gentlemen, the night advances, and the business of tomorrow must be early thought upon. Each take charge of his fair partner, and honour a small refreshment with your company."

He led the way to another suite of apartments, and assumed the seat and canopy at the head of a long range of tables, with an air of dignity mingled with courtesy, which well became his high birth and lofty pretensions. An hour had hardly flown away when the musicians played the signal for parting, so well known in Scotland.[1]

"Good night, then," said the Chevalier, rising ; "Good night, and joy be with you !—Good night, fair ladies, who have so highly honoured a proscribed and banished Prince. —Good night, my brave friends ; may the happiness we have this evening experienced be an omen of our return to these our paternal halls, speedily and in triumph, and of many and many future meetings of mirth and pleasure in the palace of Holyrood !"

When the Baron of Bradwardine afterwards mentioned this adieu of the Chevalier, he never failed to repeat, in a melancholy tone,

> " Audiit, et voti Phœbus succedere partem
> Mente dedit ; partem volucres dispersit in auras ; "

[1] Which is, or was wont to be, the old air of " Good night and joy be wi' you a' ! " (S.)

"which," as he added, "is weel rendered into English metre by my friend Bangour :

> "'Ae half the prayer wi' Phœbus grace did find,
> The t'other half he whistled down the wind.'"

# CHAPTER XLIV.

## The March.

THE conflicting passions and exhausted feelings of Waverley had resigned him to late but sound repose. He was dreaming of Glennaquoich, and had transferred to the halls of Ian nan Chaistel the festal train which so lately graced those of Holyrood. The pibroch too was distinctly heard ; and this at least was no delusion, for the "proud step of the chief piper" of the "chlain Mac-Ivor" was perambulating the court before the door of his Chieftain's quarters, and, as Mrs Flockhart, apparently no friend to his minstrelsy, was pleased to observe, "garring[1] the very stane-and-lime wa's dingle wi' his screeching." Of course it soon became too powerful for Waverley's dream, with which it had at first rather harmonized.

The sound of Callum's brogues in his apartment (for Mac-Ivor had again assigned Waverley to his care) was the next note of parting. "Winna yere honour bang up ? Vich Ian Vohr and ta Prince are awa to the lang green glen ahint the clachan, tat they ca' the King's Park,[2] and mony ane's on his ain shanks the day that will be carried on ither folk's ere night."

Waverley sprung up, and, with Callum's assistance and instructions, adjusted his tartans in proper costume. Callum told him also, " tat his leather *dorlach* wi' the lock on her was come frae Doune, and she was awa again in the wain wi' Vich Ian Vohr's walise."

By this periphrasis Waverley readily apprehended his portmanteau was intended. He thought upon the mysterious packet of the maid of the cavern, which seemed always to escape him when within his very grasp. But this was no time for indulgence of curiosity ; and having declined Mrs Flockhart's compliment of a *morning,* *i.e.* a matutinal dram, being probably the only man in the

---

[1] Causing.
[2] The main body of the Highland army encamped, or rather bivouacked, in that part of the King's Park which lies towards the village of Duddingston. (S.)

Chevalier's army by whom such a courtesy would have been rejected, he made his adieus, and departed with Callum.

"Callum," said he, as they proceeded down a dirty close to gain the southern skirts of the Canongate, "what shall I do for a horse?"

"Ta deil ane ye maun think o'," said Callum. "Vich Ian Vohr's marching on foot at the head o' his kin, (not to say ta Prince, wha does the like,) wi' his target on his shoulder; and ye maun e'en be neighbour-like."

"And so I will, Callum—give me my target;—so, there we are fixed. How does it look?"

"Like the bra' Highlander tat's painted on the board afore the mickle change-house they ca' Luckie Middle-mass's," answered Callum; meaning, I must observe, a high compliment, for, in his opinion, Luckie Middlemass's sign was an exquisite specimen of art. Waverley, however, not feeling the full force of this polite simile, asked him no farther questions.

Upon extricating themselves from the mean and dirty suburbs of the metropolis, and emerging into the open air, Waverley felt a renewal both of health and spirits, and turned his recollection with firmness upon the events of the preceding evening, and with hope and resolution toward those of the approaching day.

When he had surmounted a small craggy eminence, call St Leonard's Hill, the King's Park, or the hollow between the mountain of Arthur's seat, and the rising grounds on which the southern part of Edinburgh is now built, lay beneath him, and displayed a singular and animating prospect. It was occupied by the army of the Highlanders, now in the act of preparing for their march. Waverley had already seen something of the kind at the hunting-match which he attended with Fergus Mac-Ivor; but this was on a scale of much greater magnitude, and incomparably deeper interest. The rocks, which formed the back-ground of the scene, and the very sky itself, rang with the clang of the bagpipers, summoning forth, each with his appropriate pibroch, his chieftain and clan. The mountaineers, rousing themselves from their couch under the canopy of heaven, with the hum and bustle of a confused and irregular multitude, like bees alarmed and arming in their hives, seemed to possess all the pliability of movement fitted to execute military manœuvres. Their motions appeared spontaneous and confused, but the result was order and regularity; so that

a general must have praised the conclusion, though a
martinet might have ridiculed the method by which it
was attained.

The sort of complicated medley created by the hasty
arrangements of the various clans under their respective
banners, for the purpose of getting into the order of
march, was in itself a gay and lively spectacle. They
had no tents to strike, having generally, and by choice,
slept upon the open field, although the autumn was now
waning, and the nights began to be frosty. For a little
space, while they were getting into order, there was
exhibited a changing, fluctuating, and confused appearance of waving tartans and floating plumes, and of
banners displaying the proud gathering word of Clanronald, *Ganion Coheriga*—(Gainsay who dares); *Loch-
Sloy*, the watchword of the Mac-Farlanes; *Forth, fortune,
and fill the fetters*, the motto of the Marquis of Tullibardine; *Bydand*, that of Lord Lewis Gordon; and the
appropriate signal words and emblems of many other
chieftains and clans.

At length the mixed and wavering multitude arranged
themselves into a narrow and dusky column of great
length, stretching through the whole extent of the valley.
In the front of the column the standard of the Chevalier
was displayed, bearing a red cross upon a white ground,
with the motto *Tandem Triumphans*. The few cavalry,
being chiefly Lowland gentry, with their domestic servants and retainers, formed the advanced guard of the
army; and their standards, of which they had rather
too many in respect of their numbers, were seen waving
upon the extreme verge of the horizon. Many horsemen
of this body, among whom Waverley accidentally remarked Balmawhapple, and his lieutenant, Jinker, (which
last, however, had been reduced, with several others, by
the advice of the Baron of Bradwardine, to the situation
of what he called reformed officers, or reformadoes,) added
to the liveliness, though by no means to the regularity, of
the scene, by galloping their horses as fast forward as the
press would permit, to join their proper station in the
van. The fascinations of the Circes of the High Street,
and the potations of strength with which they had been
drenched over night, had probably detained these heroes
within the walls of Edinburgh somewhat later than was
consistent with their morning duty. Of such loiterers,
the prudent took the longer and circuitous, but more open
route, to attain their place in the march, by keeping at

some distance from the infantry, and making their way through the enclosures to the right, at the expense of leaping over or pulling down the dry-stone fences. The irregular appearance and vanishing of these small parties of horsemen, as well as the confusion occasioned by those who endeavoured, though generally without effect, to press to the front through the crowd of Highlanders, maugre their curses, oaths, and opposition, added to the picturesque wildness, what it took from the military regularity, of the scene.

While Waverley gazed upon this remarkable spectacle, rendered yet more impressive by the occasional discharge of cannon-shot from the Castle at the Highland guards as they were withdrawn from its vicinity to join their main body, Callum, with his usual freedom of interference, reminded him that Vich Ian Vohr's folk were nearly at the head of the column of march which was still distant, and that "they would gang very fast after the cannon fired." Thus admonished, Waverley walked briskly forward, yet often casting a glance upon the darksome clouds of warriors who were collected before and beneath him. A nearer view, indeed, rather diminished the effect impressed on the mind by the more distant appearance of the army The leading men of each clan were well armed with broadsword, target, and fusee, to which all added the dirk, and most the steel pistol. But these consisted of gentlemen, that is, relations of the chief, however distant, and who had an immediate title to his countenance and protection. Finer and hardier men could not have been selected out of any army in Christendom; while the free and independent habits which each possessed, and which each was yet so well taught to subject to the command of his chief, and the peculiar mode of discipline adopted in Highland warfare, rendered them equally formidable by their individual courage and high spirit, and from their rational conviction of the necessity of acting in unison, and of giving their national mode of attack the fullest opportunity of success.

But, in a lower rank to these, there were found individuals of an inferior description, the common peasantry of the Highland country, who, although they did not allow themselves to be so called, and claimed often, with apparent truth, to be of more ancient descent than the masters whom they served, bore, neverthelesss, the livery of extreme penury, being indifferently accoutred, and worse armed, half naked, stinted in growth, and miserable in aspect. Each important clan had some of those Helots attached to them;—thus, the Mac-Couls, though tracing their descent from Comhal, the father of Finn or Fingal, were a sort of Gibeonites, or hereditary servants to the Stewarts of Appine ; the Macbeths descended from the unhappy monarch of that name, were subjects to the Morays, and clan Donnochy, or Robertsons of Athole ; and many other examples might be given, were it not for the risk of hurting any pride of clanship which may yet be left, and thereby drawing a Highland tempest into the shop of my publisher. Now these same Helots, though forced into the field by the arbitrary authority of the chieftains under whom they hewed wood, and drew water, were, in general, very sparingly fed, ill-dressed, and worse armed. The latter circumstance was indeed owing chiefly to the general disarming act, which had been carried into effect ostensibly through the whole Highlands, although most of the chieftains contrived to elude its influence, by retaining the weapons of their own immediate clansmen, and delivering up those of less value, which they collected from these inferior satellites. It followed, as a matter of course, that, as we have already hinted, many of these poor fellows were brought to the field in a very wretched condition.

From this it happened, that, in bodies, the van of which were admirably well armed in their own fashion, the rear resembled actual banditti. Here was a pole-axe, there a sword without a scabbard ; here a gun without a lock, there a scythe set straight upon a pole ; and some had only their dirks, and bludgeons or stakes pulled out of hedges. The grim, uncombed, and wild appearance of these men, most of whom gazed with all the admiration of ignorance upon the most ordinary production of domestic art, created surprise in the Lowlands, but it also created terror. So little was the condition of the Highlands known at that late period, that the character and appearance of their population, while thus sallying forth as military adventurers, conveyed to the south-country Lowlanders as much surprise as if an invasion of African Negroes, or Esquimaux Indians, had issued forth from the northern mountains of their own native country. It cannot therefore be wondered if Waverley, who had hitherto judged of the Highlanders generally, from the samples which the policy of Fergus had from time to time exhibited, should have felt damped and astonished at the daring attempt of a body not then exceeding four thousand men, and of whom not above half the number, at the utmost, were armed, to change the fate, and alter the dynasty, of the British kingdoms.

As he moved along the column, which still remained stationary, an iron gun, the only piece of artillery possessed by the army which meditated so important a revolution, was fired as the signal of march. The Chevalier had expressed a wish to leave this useless piece of ordnance behind him; but, to his surprise, the Highland chiefs interposed to solicit that it might accompany their march, pleading the prejudices of their followers, who, little accustomed to artillery, attached a degree of absurd importance to this field-piece, and expected it would contribute essentially to a victory which they could only owe to their own muskets and broadswords. Two or three French artillerymen were therefore appointed to the management of this military engine, which was drawn along by a string of Highland ponies, and was, after all, only used for the purpose of firing signals.[1]

No sooner was its voice heard upon the present occasion, than the whole line was in motion. A wild cry of joy from the advancing battalions rent the air, and was then lost in the shrill clangour of the bagpipes, as the sound of these, in their turn, was partially drowned by the heavy tread of so many men put at once into motion. The banners glittered and shook as they moved forward, and the horse hastened to occupy their station as the advanced guard, and to push on reconnoitring parties to ascertain and report the motions of the enemy. They vanished from Waverley's eye as they wheeled round the base of Arthur's Seat, under the remarkable ridge of basaltic rocks which fronts the little lake of Duddingston.

The infantry followed in the same direction, regulating their pace by another body which occupied a road more to the southward. It cost Edward some exertion of activity to attain the place which Fergus's followers occupied in the line of march.

## CHAPTER XLV.

*An Incident gives rise to unavailing Reflections.*

WHEN Waverley reached that part of the column which was filled by the clan of Mac-Ivor, they halted, formed,

[1] Note 17.    Field-piece in the Highland army.

and received him with a triumphant flourish upon the bagpipes, and a loud shout of the men, most of whom knew him personally, and were delighted to see him in the dress of their country and of their sept. "You shout," said a Highlander of a neighbouring clan to Evan Dhu, "as if the Chieftain were just come to your head."

"*Mar e Bran is e a brathair*, If it be not Bran, it is Bran's brother," was the proverbial reply of Maccombich.[1]

"O, then, it is the handsome Sassenach Duinhé-wassel, that is to be married to Lady Flora?"

"That may be, or it may not be; and it is neither your matter nor mine, Gregor."

Fergus advanced to embrace the volunteer, and afford him a warm and hearty welcome; but he thought it necessary to apologize for the diminished numbers of his battalion, (which did not exceed three hundred men,) by observing, he had sent a good many out upon parties.

The real fact, however, was, that the defection of Donald Bean Lean had deprived him of at least thirty hardy fellows, whose services he had fully reckoned upon, and that many of his occasional adherents had been recalled by their several chiefs to the standards to which they most properly owed their allegiance. The rival chief of the great northern branch also of his own clan, had mustered his people, although he had not yet declared either for the government or for the Chevalier, and by his intrigues had in some degree diminished the force with which Fergus took the field. To make amends for these disappointments, it was universally admitted that the followers of Vich Ian Vohr, in point of appearance, equipment, arms, and dexterity in using them, equalled the most choice troops which followed the standard of Charles Edward. Old Ballenkeiroch acted as his major; and, with the other officers who had known Waverley when at Glennaquoich, gave our hero a cordial reception, as the sharer of their future dangers and expected honours.

The route pursued by the Highland army, after leaving the village of Duddingstone, was, for some time, the common post-road betwixt Edinburgh and Haddington, until they crossed the Esk, at Musselburgh, when, instead of keeping the low grounds towards the sea, they turned more inland, and occupied the brow of the eminence called Carberry Hill, a place already distinguished in

---

[1] Bran, the well-known dog of Fingal, is often the theme of Highland proverb as well as song. (S.)

Scottish history, as the spot where the lovely Mary surrendered herself to her insurgent subjects. This direction was chosen because the Chevalier had received notice that the army of the government, arriving by sea from Aberdeen, had landed at Dunbar, and quartered the night before to the west of Haddington, with the intention of falling down towards the sea-side, and approaching Edinburgh by the lower coast-road. By keeping the height, which overhung that road in many places, it was hoped the Highlanders might find an opportunity of attacking them to advantage. The army therefore halted upon the ridge of Carberry Hill, both to refresh the soldiers, and as a central situation, from which their march could be directed to any point that the motions of the enemy might render most advisable. While they remained in this position, a messenger arrived in haste to desire Mac-Ivor to come to the Prince, adding, that their advanced post had had a skirmish with some of the enemy's cavalry, and that the Baron of Bradwardine had sent in a few prisoners.

Waverley walked forward out of the line to satisfy his curiosity, and soon observed five or six of the troopers, who, covered with dust, had galloped in to announce that the enemy were in full march westward along the coast. Passing still a little farther on, he was struck with a groan which issued from a hovel. He approached the spot, and heard a voice, in the provincial English of his native county, which endeavoured, though frequently interrupted by pain, to repeat the Lord's Prayer. The voice of distress always found a ready answer in our hero's bosom. He entered the hovel, which seemed to be intended for what is called, in the pastoral counties of Scotland, a *smearing-house ;* and in its obscurity Edward could only at first discern a sort of red bundle ; for those who had stripped the wounded man of his arms, and part of his clothes, had left him the dragoon-cloak in which he was enveloped.

"For the love of God," said the wounded man, as he heard Waverley's step, "Give me a single drop of water !"

"You shall have it," answered Waverley, at the same time raising him in his arms, bearing him to the door of the hut, and giving him some drink from his flask.

"I should know that voice," said the man ; but, looking on Waverley's dress with a bewildered look,—"no, this is not the young squire !"

This was the common phrase by which Edward was

distinguished on the estate of Waverley-Honour, and the sound now thrilled to his heart with the thousand recollections which the well-known accents of his native country had already contributed to awaken. "Houghton!" he said, gazing on the ghastly features which death was fast disfiguring, "can this be you?"

"I never thought to hear an English voice again," said the wounded man; "they left me to live or die here as I could, when they found I would say nothing about the strength of the regiment. But, O squire! how could you stay from us so long, and let us be tempted by that fiend of the pit, Ruffin?—we should have followed you through flood and fire, to be sure."

"Ruffin! I assure you, Houghton, you have been vilely imposed upon."

"I often thought so," said Houghton, "though they showed us your very seal; and so Timms was shot, and I was reduced to the ranks."

"Do not exhaust your strength in speaking," said Edward; "I will get you a surgeon presently."

He saw Mac-Ivor approaching, who was now returning from head-quarters, where he had attended a council of war, and hastened to meet him. "Brave news!" shouted the Chief; "we shall be at it in less than two hours. The Prince has put himself at the head of the advance, and, as he drew his sword, called out, 'My friends, I have thrown away the scabbard.' Come, Waverley, we move instantly."

"A moment,—a moment; this poor prisoner is dying;—where shall I find a surgeon?"

"Why, where should you? We have none, you know, but two or three French fellows, who, I believe, are little better than *garçons apothicaires.*"

"But the man will bleed to death."

"Poor fellow!" said Fergus, in a momentary fit of compassion; then instantly added, "But it will be a thousand men's fate before night; so come along."

"I cannot; I tell you he is a son of a tenant of my uncle's."

"O, if he's a follower of yours, he must be looked to; I'll send Callum to you; but *diaoul!—ceade millia molligheart*," continued the impatient Chieftain,—"what made an old soldier, like Bradwardine, send dying men here to cumber us?"

Callum came with his usual elertness; and, indeed, Waverley rather gained than lost in the opinion of the

Highlanders, by his anxiety about the wounded man. They would not have understood the general philanthropy, which rendered it almost impossible for Waverley to have passed any person in such distress; but, as apprehending that the sufferer was one of his *following*,[1] they unanimously allowed that Waverley's conduct was that of a kind and considerate chieftain, who merited the attachment of his people. In about a quarter of an hour poor Humphrey breathed his last, praying his young master, when he returned to Waverley-Honour, to be kind to old Job Houghton and his dame, and conjuring him not to fight with these wild petticoat-men against old England.

When his last breath was drawn, Waverley, who had beheld with sincere sorrow, and no slight tinge of remorse, the final agonies of mortality, now witnessed for the first time, commanded Callum to remove the body into the hut. This the young Highlander performed, not without examining the pockets of the defunct, which, however, he remarked, had been pretty well spung'd. He took the cloak, however, and proceeding with the provident caution of a spaniel hiding a bone, concealed it among some furze, and carefully marked the spot, observing, that if he chanced to return that way, it would be an excellent rokelay for his auld mother Elspat.

It was by a considerable exertion that they regained their place in the marching column, which was now moving rapidly forward to occupy the high grounds above the village of Tranent, between which and the sea lay the purposed march of the opposite army.

This melancholy interview with his late sergeant forced many unavailing and painful reflections upon Waverley's mind. It was clear, from the confession of the man, that Colonel Gardiner's proceedings had been strictly warranted, and even rendered indispensable, by the steps taken in Edward's name to induce the soldiers of his troop to mutiny. The circumstance of the seal, he now, for the first time, recollected, and that he had lost it in the cavern of the robber, Bean Lean. That the artful villain had secured it, and used it as the means of carrying on an intrigue in the regiment for his own purposes, was sufficiently evident; and Edward had now little doubt that in the packet placed in his portmanteau by his daughter, he should find farther light upon his proceedings. In the meanwhile, the repeated expostulation of Houghton,—

[1] *Scottice* for followers. (S.)

"Ah, squire, why did you leave us?" rung like a knell in
his ears.

"Yes," he said, "I have indeed acted towards you with
thoughtless cruelty. I brought you from your paternal
fields, and the protection of a generous and kind landlord,
and when I had subjected you to all the rigour of military
discipline, I shunned to bear my own share of the burden,
and wandered from the duties I had undertaken, leaving
alike those whom it was my business to protect, and my
own reputation, to suffer under the artifices of villany.
O, indolence and indecision of mind! if not in yourselves
vices, to how much exquisite misery and mischief do you
frequently prepare the way!"


# CHAPTER XLVI.

### The Eve of Battle.

ALTHOUGH the Highlanders marched on very fast, the
sun was declining when they arrived upon the brow of
those high grounds which command an open and extensive
plain stretching northward to the sea, on which are situated, but at a considerable distance from each other, the
small villages of Seaton and Cockenzie, and the larger
one of Preston. One of the low coast-roads to Edinburgh
passed through this plain, issuing upon it from the
enclosures of Seaton-house, and at the town or village of
Preston again entering the defiles of an enclosed country.
By this way the English general had chosen to approach
the metropolis, both as most commodious for his cavalry,
and being probably of opinion that, by doing so, he would
meet in front with the Highlanders advancing from
Edinburgh in the opposite direction. In this he was
mistaken; for the sound judgment of the Chevalier, or of
those to whose advice he listened, left the direct passage
free, but occupied the strong ground by which it was
overlooked and commanded.

When the Highlanders reached the heights above the
plain described, they were immediately formed in array
of battle along the brow of the hill. Almost at the same
instant the van of the English appeared issuing from
among the trees and enclosures of Seaton, with the
purpose of occupying the level plain between the high
ground and the sea; the space which divided the armies

being only about half a mile in breadth. Waverley could plainly see the squadrons of dragoons issue, one after another, from the defilés, with their videttes in front, and form upon the plain, with their front opposed to that of the Prince's army. They were followed by a train of field-pieces, which, when they reached the flank of the dragoons, were also brought into line, and pointed against the heights. The march was continued by three or four regiments of infantry marching in open column, their fixed bayonets showing like successive hedges of steel, and their arms glancing like lightning, as, at a signal given, they also at once wheeled up, and were placed in direct opposition to the Highlanders. A second train of artillery, with another regiment of horse, closed the long march, and formed on the left flank of the infantry, the whole line facing southward.

While the English army went through these evolutions, the Highlanders showed equal promptitude and zeal for battle. As fast as the clans came upon the ridge which fronted their enemy, they were formed into line, so that both armies got into complete order of battle at the same moment. When this was accomplished, the Highlanders set up a tremendous yell, which was re-echoed by the heights behind them. The regulars, who were in high spirits, returned a loud shout of defiance, and fired one or two of their cannon upon an advanced post of the Highlanders. The latter displayed great earnestness to proceed instantly to the attack, Evan Dhu urging to Fergus, by way of argument, that "the *sidier roy* was tottering like an egg upon a staff, and that they had a' the vantage of the onset, for even a haggis (God bless her!) could charge down hill."

But the ground through which the mountaineers must have descended, although not of great extent, was impracticable in its character, being not only marshy, but intersected with walls of dry stone, and traversed in its whole length by a very broad and deep ditch, circumstances which must have given the musketry of the regulars dreadful advantages, before the mountaineers could have used their swords, on which they were taught to rely. The authority of the commanders was therefore interposed to curb the impetuosity of the Highlanders, and only a few marksmen were sent down the descent to skirmish with the enemy's advanced posts, and to reconnoitre the ground.

Here then was a military spectacle of no ordinary

interest, or usual occurrence. The two armies, so different in aspect and discipline, yet each admirably
trained in its own peculiar mode of war, upon whose
conflict the temporary fate at least of Scotland appeared
to depend, now faced each other like two gladiators in
the arena, each meditating upon the mode of attacking
their enemy. The leading officers, and the general's staff
of each army, could be distinguished in front of their
lines, busied with spy-glasses to watch each other's
motions, and occupied in despatching the orders and
receiving the intelligence conveyed by the aides-de-camp
and orderly men, who gave life to the scene by galloping
along in different directions, as if the fate of the day
depended upon the speed of their horses. The space
between the armies was at times occupied by the partial
and irregular contest of individual sharp-shooters, and a
hat or bonnet was occasionally seen to fall, as a wounded
man was borne off by his comrades. These, however,
were but trifling skirmishes, for it suited the views of
neither party to advance in that direction. From the
neighbouring hamlets, the peasantry cautiously showed
themselves, as if watching the issue of the expected
engagement ; and at no great distance in the bay were
two square-rigged vessels, bearing the English flag,
whose tops and yards were crowded with less timid
spectators.

When this awful pause had lasted for a short time,
Fergus, with another chieftain, received orders to detach
their clans towards the village of Preston, in order to
threaten the right flank of Cope's army, and compel him
to a change of position. To enable him to execute these
orders, the Chief of Glennaquoich occupied the church-
yard of Tranent, a commanding situation, and a convenient place, as Evan Dhu remarked, "for any gentleman
who might have the misfortune to be killed, and chanced
to be curious about Christian burial." To check or
dislodge this party, the English general detached two
guns, escorted by a strong party of cavalry. They
approached so near, that Waverley could plainly recognise the standard of the troop he had formerly commanded, and hear the trumpets and kettle-drums sound
the signal of advance, which he had so often obeyed.
He could hear, too, the well-known word given in the
English dialect, by the equally well-distinguished voice
of the commanding officer, for whom he had once felt
so much respect. It was at that instant, that, looking

around him, he saw the wild dress and appearance of his Highland associates, heard their whispers in an uncouth and unknown language, looked upon his own dress, so unlike that which he had worn from his infancy, and wished to awake from what seemed at the moment a dream, strange, horrible, and unnatural. "Good God!" he muttered, "am I then a traitor to my country, a renegade to my standard, and a foe, as that poor dying wretch expressed himself, to my native England!"

Ere he could digest or smother the recollection, the tall military form of his late commander came full in view, for the purpose of reconnoitring. "I can hit him now," said Callum, cautiously raising his fusee over the wall under which he lay couched, at scarce sixty yards' distance.

Edward felt as if he was about to see a parricide committed in his presence; for the venerable grey hair and striking countenance of the veteran recalled the almost paternal respect with which his officers universally regarded him. But ere he could say "Hold!" an aged Highlander, who lay beside Callum Beg, stopped his arm. "Spare your shot," said the seer, "his hour is not yet come. But let him beware of to-morrow—I see his winding-sheet high upon his breast."

Callum, flint to other considerations, was penetrable to superstition. He turned pale at the words of the *Taishatr*, and recovered his piece. Colonel Gardiner, unconscious of the danger he had escaped, turned his horse round, and rode slowly back to the front of his regiment.

By this time the regular army had assumed a new line, with one flank inclined towards the sea, and the other resting upon the village of Preston; and, as similar difficulties occurred in attacking their new position, Fergus and the rest of the detachment were recalled to their former post. This alteration created the necessity of a corresponding change in General Cope's army, which was again brought into a line parallel with that of the Highlanders. In these manœuvres on both sides the day-light was nearly consumed, and both armies prepared to rest upon their arms for the night in the lines which they respectively occupied.

"There will be nothing done to-night," said Fergus to his friend Waverley; "ere we wrap ourselves in our plaids, let us go see what the Baron is doing in the rear of the line."

When they approached his post, they found the good
old careful officer, after having sent out his night patrols,
and posted his sentinels, engaged in reading the Evening
Service of the Episcopal Church to the remainder of his
troop. His voice was loud and sonorous, and though his
spectacles upon his nose, and the appearance of Saunders
Sanderson, in military array, performing the functions of
clerk, had something ludicrous, yet the circumstances of
danger in which they stood, the military costume of the
audience, and the appearance of their horses, saddled and
picquetted behind them, gave an impressive and solemn
effect to the office of devotion.

"I have confessed to-day, ere you were awake,"
whispered Fergus to Waverley; "yet I am not so strict
a Catholic as to refuse to join in this good man's
prayers."

Edward assented, and they remained till the Baron had
concluded the service.

As he shut the book, "Now, lads," said he, "have at
them in the morning, with heavy hands and light consciences." He then kindly greeted Mac-Ivor and Waverley, who requested to know his opinion of their situation.
"Why, you know Tacitus saith, '*In rebus bellicis maxime
dominatur Fortuna*,' which is equiponderate with our
vernacular adage, 'Luck can maist in the mellee.' But
credit me, gentlemen, yon man is not a deacon o' his
craft. He damps the spirits of the poor lads he commands, by keeping them on the defensive, whilk of itself
implies inferiority or fear. Now will they lie on their
arms yonder, as anxious and as ill at ease as a toad under
a harrow, while our men will be quite fresh and blithe for
action in the morning. Well, good night.—One thing
troubles me, but if to-morrow goes well off, I will consult
you about it, Glennaquoich."——

"I could almost apply to Mr Bradwardine the character which Henry gives of Fluellen," said Waverley, as his
friend and he walked towards their *bivouac:*

> " Though it appears a little out of fashion,
>     There is much care and valour in this 'Scotchman.' "

"He has seen much service," answered Fergus, "and
one is sometimes astonished to find how much nonsense
and reason are mingled in his composition. I wonder
what can be troubling his mind—probably something
about Rose.—Hark! the English are setting their watch."
The roll of the drum and shrill accompaniment of the

fifes swelled up the hill—died away—resumed its thunder
—and was at length hushed. The trumpets and kettle-
drums of the cavalry were next heard to perform the
beautiful and wild point of war appropriated as a signal
for that piece of nocturnal duty, and then finally sunk
upon the wind with a shrill and mournful cadence.

The friends, who had now reached their post, stood
and looked round them ere they lay down to rest. The
western sky twinkled with stars, but a frost-mist, rising
from the ocean, covered the eastern horizon, and rolled in
white wreaths along the plain where the adverse army
lay couched upon their arms. Their advanced posts were
pushed as far as the side of the great ditch at the bottom
of the descent, and had kindled large fires at different
intervals, gleaming with obscure and hazy lustre through
the heavy fog which encircled them with a doubtful
halo.

The Highlanders, "thick as leaves in Valumbrosa," lay
stretched upon the ridge of the hill, buried (excepting
their sentinels) in the most profound repose. "How
many of these brave fellows will sleep more soundly
before to-morrow night, Fergus!" said Waverley, with an
involuntary sigh.

"You must not think of that," answered Fergus, whose
ideas were entirely military. "You must only think of
your sword, and by whom it was given. All other reflections are now TOO LATE."

With the opiate contained in this undeniable remark,
Edward endeavoured to lull the tumult of his conflicting
feelings. The Chieftain and he, combining their plaids,
made a comfortable and warm couch. Callum, sitting
down at their head, (for it was his duty to watch upon
the immediate person of the Chief,) began a long mournful song in Gaelic, to a low and uniform tune, which, like
the sound of the wind at a distance, soon lulled them to
sleep.

## CHAPTER XLVII.

### The Conflict.

WHEN Fergus Mac-Ivor and his friend had slept for a
few hours, they were awakened, and summoned to attend
the Prince. The distant village-clock was heard to toll

three as they hastened to the place where he lay. He was already surrounded by his principal officers and the chiefs of clans. A bundle of pease-straw, which had been lately his couch, now served for his seat. Just as Fergus reached the circle, the consultation had broken up. "Courage, my brave friends!" said the Chevalier, "and each one put himself instantly at the head of his command; a faithful friend [1] has offered to guide us by a practicable, though narrow and circuitous route, which, sweeping to our right, traverses the broken ground and morass, and enables us to gain the firm and open plain, upon which the enemy are lying. This difficulty surmounted, Heaven and your good swords must do the rest."

The proposal spread unanimous joy, and each leader hastened to get his men into order with as little noise as possible. The army, moving by its right from off the ground on which they had rested, soon entered the path through the morass, conducting their march with astonishing silence and great rapidity. The mist had not risen to the higher grounds, so that for some time they had the advantage of star-light. But this was lost as the stars faded before approaching day, and the head of the marching column, continuing its descent, plunged as it were into the heavy ocean of fog, which rolled its white waves over the whole plain, and over the sea by which it was bounded. Some difficulties were now to be encountered, inseparable from darkness, a narrow, broken, and marshy path, and the necessity of preserving union in the march. These, however, were less inconvenient to Highlanders, from their habits of life, than they would have been to any other troops, and they continued a steady and swift movement.

As the clan of Ivor approached the firm ground, following the track of those who preceded them, the challenge of a patrol was heard through the mist, though they could not see the dragoon by whom it was made—"Who goes there?"

"Hush," cried Fergus, "hush! Let none answer, as he values his life—Press forward;" and they continued their march with silence and rapidity.

The patrol fired his carbine upon the body, and the report was instantly followed by the clang of his horse's feet as he galloped off. "*Hylax in limine latrat*," said the Baron of Bradwardine, who heard the shot; "that loon[2] will give the alarm."

[1] Note 18. Anderson of Whitburgh.    [2] Rascal.

The clan of Fergus had now gained the firm plain, which had lately borne a large crop of corn. But the harvest was gathered in, and the expanse was unbroken by tree, bush, or interruption of any kind. The rest of the army were following fast, when they heard the drums of the enemy beat the general. Surprise, however, had made no part of their plan, so they were not disconcerted by this intimation that the foe was upon his guard and prepared to receive them. It only hastened their dispositions for the combat, which were very simple.

The Highland army, which now occupied the eastern end of the wide plain, or stubble field, so often referred to, was drawn up in two lines, extending from the morass towards the sea. The first was destined to charge the enemy, the second to act as a reserve. The few horse, whom the Prince headed in person, remained between the two lines. The Adventurer had intimated a resolution to charge in person at the head of his first line; but his purpose was deprecated by all around him, and he was with difficulty induced to abandon it.

Both lines were now moving forward, the first prepared for instant combat. The clans, of which it was composed, formed each a sort of separate phalanx, narrow in front, and in depth ten, twelve, or fifteen files, according to the strength of the following. The best-armed and best-born, for the words were synonymous, were placed in front of each of these irregular subdivisions. The others in the rear shouldered forward the front, and by their pressure added both physical impulse, and additional ardour and confidence, to those who were first to encounter the danger.

"Down with your plaid, Waverley," cried Fergus, throwing off his own; "we'll win silks for our tartans before the sun is above the sea."

The clansmen on every side stript their plaids, prepared their arms, and there was an awful pause of about three minutes, during which the men, pulling off their bonnets, raised their faces to heaven, and uttered a short prayer; then pulled their bonnets over their brows, and began to move forward at first slowly. Waverley felt his heart at that moment throb as it would have burst from his bosom. It was not fear, it was not ardour,—it was a compound of both, a new and deep y energetic impulse, that with its first emotion chilled and astounded, then fevered and maddened his mind. The sounds around him combined to exalt his enthusiasm; the pipes played, and the clans rushed forward, each in its own dark column. As they advanced they mended their pace, and the muttering sounds of the men to each other began to swell into a wild cry.

At this moment, the sun, which was now risen above the horizon, dispelled the mist. The vapours rose like a curtain, and showed the two armies in the act of closing. The line of the regulars was formed directly fronting the attack of the Highlanders; it glittered with the appointments of a complete army, and was flanked by cavalry and artillery. But the sight impressed no terror on the assailants.

"Forward, sons of Ivor," cried their Chief, "or the Camerons will draw the first blood!"—They rushed on with a tremendous yell.

The rest is well known. The horse, who were commanded to charge the advancing Highlanders in the flank, received an irregular fire from their fusees as they ran on, and, seized with a disgraceful panic, wavered, halted, disbanded, and galloped from the field. The artillerymen, deserted by the cavalry, fled after discharging their pieces, and the Highlanders, who dropped their guns when fired, and drew their broadswords, rushed with headlong fury against the infantry.

It was at this moment of confusion and terror, that Waverley remarked an English officer, apparently of high rank, standing alone and unsupported by a field-piece, which, after the flight of the men by whom it was wrought, he had himself levelled and discharged against the clan of Mac-Ivor, the nearest group of Highlanders within his aim. Struck with his tall, martial figure, and eager to save him from inevitable destruction, Waverley outstripped for an instant even the speediest of the warriors, and, reaching the spot first, called to him to surrender. The officer replied by a thrust with his sword, which Waverley received in his target, and in turning it aside the Englishman's weapon broke. At the same time the battle-axe of Dugald Mahony was in the act of descending upon the officer's head. Waverley intercepted and prevented the blow, and the officer, perceiving further resistance unavailing, and struck with Edward's generous anxiety for his safety, resigned the fragment of his sword, and was committed by Waverley to Dugald, with strict charge to use him well, and not to pillage his person, promising him, at the same time, full indemnification for the spoil.

On Edward's right the battle for a few minutes raged

fierce and thick. The English infantry, trained in the
wars in Flanders, stood their ground with great courage.
But their extended files were pierced and broken in many
places by the close masses of the clans; and in the personal struggle which ensued, the nature of the Highlanders' weapons, and their extraordinary fierceness and
activity, gave them a decided superiority over those who
had been accustomed to trust much to their array and
discipline, and felt that the one was broken and the other
useless. Waverley, as he cast his eyes towards this scene
of smoke and slaughter, observed Colonel Gardiner,
deserted by his own soldiers in spite of all his attempts to
rally them, yet spurring his horse through the field to
take the command of a small body of infantry, who, with
their backs arranged against the wall of his own park,
(for his house was close by the field of battle,) continued
a desperate and unavailing resistance. Waverley could
perceive that he had already received many wounds, his
clothes and saddle being marked with blood. To save
this good and brave man, became the instant object of his
most anxious exertions. But he could only witness his
fall. Ere Edward could make his way among the Highlanders, who, furious and eager for spoil, now thronged
upon each other, he saw his former commander brought
from his horse by the blow of a scythe, and beheld him
receive, while on the ground, more wounds than would
have let out twenty lives. When Waverley came up, however, perception had not entirely fled. The dying warrior
seemed to recognise Edward, for he fixed his eye upon him
with an upbraiding, yet sorrowful look, and appeared to
struggle for utterance. But he felt that death was dealing
closely with him, and resigning his purpose, and folding
his hands as if in devotion, he gave up his soul to his
Creator. The look with which he regarded Waverley in
his dying moments, did not strike him so deeply at that
crisis of hurry and confusion, as when it recurred to his
imagination at the distance of some time.[1]

Loud shouts of triumph now echoed over the whole field.
The battle was fought and won, and the whole baggage,
artillery, and military stores of the regular army remained
in possession of the victors. Never was a victory more
complete. Scarce any escaped from the battle, excepting
the cavalry, who had left it at the very onset, and even
these were broken into different parties and scattered all
over the country. So far as our tale is concerned, we have

[1] Note 19. Death of Colonel Gardiner.

only to relate the fate of Balmawhapple, who, mounted
on a horse as headstrong and stiff-necked as his rider,
pursued the flight of the dragoons above four miles from
the field of battle, when some dozen of the fugitives took
heart of grace, turned round, and, cleaving his skull with
their broadswords, satisfied the world that the unfortunate
gentleman had actually brains, the end of his life thus
giving proof of a fact greatly doubted during its progress.
His death was lamented by few. Most of those who knew
him agreed in the pithy observation of Ensign Maccombich, that there "was mair *tint* (lost) at Sheriff-Muir."
His friend, Lieutenant Jinker, bent his eloquence only to
exculpate his favourite mare from any share in contribut-
ing to the catastrophe. "He had tauld the laird a
thousand times," he said, "that it was a burning shame
to put a martingale upon the puir thing, when he would
needs ride her wi' a curb of half a yard lang ; and that he
could na but bring himsell (not to say her) to some mischief, by flinging her down, or otherwise ; whereas, if he
had had a wee bit rinnin ring on the snaffle, she wad ha'
rein'd as cannily as a cadger's pownie."

Such was the elegy of the Laird of Balmawhapple.[1]


## CHAPTER XLVIII.

### *An unexpected Embarrassment.*

WHEN the battle was over, and all things coming into
order, the Baron of Bradwardine, returning from the duty
of the day, and having disposed those under his command
in their proper stations, sought the Chieftain of Glennaquoich and his friend Edward Waverley. He found
the former busied in determining disputes among his
clansmen about points of precedence and deeds of valour,
besides sundry high and doubtful questions concerning
plunder. The most important of the last respected the
property of a gold watch, which had once belonged to
some unfortunate English officer. The party against
whom judgment was awarded, consoled himself by
observing, "She (*i.e.* the watch, which he took for a
living animal) died the very night Vich Ian Vohr gave
her to Murdoch ;" the machine having, in fact, stopped
for want of winding up.

[1] Note 20.   Laird of Balmawhapple.

It was just when this important question was decided, that the Baron of Bradwardine, with a careful and yet important expression of countenance, joined the two young men. He descended from his reeking charger, the care of which he recommended to one of his grooms. "I seldom ban, sir," said he to the man; "but if you play any of your hound's-foot tricks, and leave puir Berwick before he's sorted, to rin after spuilzie,[1] deil be wi' me if I do not give your craig a thraw."[2] He then stroked with great complacency the animal which had borne him through the fatigues of the day, and having taken a tender leave of him,—"Weel, my good young friends, a glorious and decisive victory," said he; "but these loons[3] of troopers fled ower soon. I should have liked to have shown you the true points of the *prœlium equestre*, or equestrian combat, whilk their cowardice has postponed, and which I hold to be the pride and terror of warfare. Weel, I have fought once more in this old quarrel, though I admit I could not be so far *ben*[4] as you lads, being that it was my point of duty to keep together our handful of horse. And no cavalier ought in anywise to begrudge honour that befalls his companions, even though they are ordered upon thrice his danger, whilk, another time, by the blessing of God, may be his own case.—But, Glennaquoich, and you, Mr Waverley, I pray ye to give me your best advice on a matter of mickle weight, and which deeply affects the honour of the house of Bradwardine.—I crave your pardon, Ensign Maccombich, and yours, Inveraughlin, and yours, Edderalshendrach, and yours, sir."

The last person he addressed was Ballenkeiroch, who, remembering the death of his son, loured on him with a look of savage defiance. The Baron, quick as lightning at taking umbrage, had already bent his brow, when Glennaquoich dragged his major from the spot, and remonstrated with him, in the authoritative tone of a chieftain, on the madness of reviving a quarrel in such a moment.

"The ground is cumbered with carcasses," said the old mountaineer, turning sullenly away; "*one more* would hardly have been kenn'd upon it; and if it wasna for yoursell, Vich Ian Vohr, that one should be Bradwardine's or mine."

The chief soothed while he hurried him away; and then returned to the Baron. "It is Ballenkeiroch," he said, in an under and confidential voice, "father of the

---

[1] Spoil.  [2] Throat a twist.  [3] Rascals.  [4] Deeply engaged.

young man who fell eight years since in the unlucky affair
at the Mains."

"Ah!" said the Baron, instantly relaxing the doubtful
sternness of his features, "I can take mickle frae a man
to whom I have unhappily rendered sic a displeasure as
that. Ye were right to apprise me, Glennaquoich; he
may look as black as midnight at Martinmas ere Cosmo
Comyne Bradwardine shall say he does him wrang. Ah!
I have nae male lineage, and I should bear with one I
have made childless, though you are aware the blood-wit[1]
was made up to your ain satisfaction by assythment,[2]
and that I have since expedited letters of slains.[3]—Weel,
as I have said, I have no male issue, and yet it is needful
that I maintain the honour of my house; and it is on that
score I prayed ye for your peculiar and private attention."

The two young men awaited to hear him, in anxious
curiosity.

"I doubt na, lads," he proceeded, "but your education
has been sae seen to, that ye understand the true nature
of the feudal tenures?"

Fergus, afraid of an endless dissertation, answered,
"Intimately, Baron," and touched Waverley, as a signal
to express no ignorance.

"And ye are aware, I doubt not, that the holding of
the Barony of Bradwardine is of a nature alike honourable and peculiar, being blanch, (which Craig opines
ought to be Latinated *blancum*, or rather *francum*, a free
holding,) *pro servitio detrahendi, seu exuendi, caligas regis
post battalliam*." Here Fergus turned his falcon eye
upon Edward, with an almost imperceptible rise of his
eyebrow, to which his shoulders corresponded in the
same degree of elevation. "Now, twa points of dubitation occur to me upon this topic. First, whether this
service, or feudal homage, be at any event due to the person of the Prince, the words being, *per expressum, caligas*
REGIS, the boots of the king himself; and I pray your
opinion anent that particular before we proceed farther."

"Why, he is Prince Regent," answered Mac-Ivor, with
laudable composure of countenance; "and in the court
of France all the honours are rendered to the person of
the Regent which are due to that of the King. Besides,
were I to pull off either of their boots, I would render
that service to the young Chevalier ten times more
willingly than to his father."

---

[1] Fine paid for effusion of blood.   [2] Compensation.   [3] Letters, in case of
slaughter, soliciting for the pardon of the offender.

"Ay, but I talk not of personal predilections. However, your authority is of great weight as to the usages of the court of France : And doubtless the Prince, as *alter ego*, may have a right to claim the *homagium* of the great tenants of the crown, since all faithful subjects are commanded, in the commission of regency, to respect him as the King's own person. Far, therefore, be it from me to diminish the lustre of his authority, by withholding this act of homage, so peculiarly calculated to give it splendour ; for I question if the Emperor of Germany hath his boots taken off by a free baron of the empire. But here lieth the second difficulty—The Prince wears no boots, but simply brogues and trews."

This last dilemma had almost disturbed Fergus's gravity.

"Why," said he, "you know, Baron, the proverb tells us, 'It's ill taking the breeks off a Highlandman,'—and the boots are here in the same predicament."

"The word *caligæ*, however," continued the Baron, "though I admit that, by family tradition, and even in our ancient evidents, it is explained *lie* BOOTS, means, in its primitive sense, rather sandals ; and Caius Cæsar, the nephew and successor of Caius Tiberius, received the agnomen of Caligula, *a caligulis, sive caligis levioribus, quibus adolescentior usus fuerat in exercitu Germanici patris sui.* And the *caligæ* were also proper to the monastic bodies ; for we read in an ancient Glossarium, upon the rule of St Benedict, in the Abbey of St Amand, that *caligæ* were tied with latchets."

"That will apply to the brogues," said Fergus.

"It will so, my dear Glennaquoich, and the words are express ; *Caligæ dictæ sunt quia ligantur ; nam socci non ligantur, sed tantum intromittuntur ;* that is, *caligæ* are denominated from the ligatures, wherewith they are bound ; whereas *socci*, which may be analogous to our mules, whilk the English denominate slippers, are only slipped upon the feet. The words of the charter are also alternative, *exuere, seu detrahere ;* that is, to *undo*, as in the case of sandals or brogues ; and to *pull off*, as we say vernacularly, concerning boots. Yet I would we had more light ; but I fear there is little chance of finding hereabout any erudite author, *de re vestiaria.*"

"I should doubt it very much," said the Chieftain, looking around on the straggling Highlanders, who were returning loaded with spoils of the slain, "though the *res vestiaria* itself seems to be in some request at present."

This remark coming within the Baron's idea of jocularity, he honoured it with a smile, but immediately resumed what to him appeared very serious business.

"Bailie Macwheeble indeed holds an opinion, that this honorary service is due, from its very nature, *si petatur tantum;* only if his Royal Highness shall require of the great tenant of the crown to perform that personal duty; and indeed he pointed out the case in Dirleton's Doubts and Queries, Grippit *versus* Spicer, anent the eviction of an estate *ob non solutum canonem*, that is, for non-payment of a feu-duty of three pepper-corns a year, whilk were taxt to be worth seven-eighths of a penny Scots, in whilk the defender was assoilzied. But I deem it safest, wi' your good favour, to place myself in the way of rendering the Prince this service, and to proffer performance thereof; and I shall cause the Bailie to attend with a schedule of a protest, whilk he has here prepared, (taking out a paper,) intimating, that if it shall be his Royal Highness's pleasure to accept of other assistance at pulling off his *caligæ*, (whether the same shall be rendered boots or brogues,) save that of the said Baron of Bradwardine, who is in presence ready and willing to perform the same, it shall in nowise impinge upon or prejudice the right of the said Cosmo Comyne Bradwardine to perform the said service in future; nor shall it give any esquire, valet of the chamber, squire, or page, whose assistance it may please his Royal Highness to employ, any right, title, or ground, for evicting from the said Cosmo Comyne Bradwardine the estate and barony of Bradwardine, and others held as aforesaid, by the due and faithful performance thereof."

Fergus highly applauded this arrangement; and the Baron took a friendly leave of them, with a smile of contented importance upon his visage.

"Long live our dear friend, the Baron," exclaimed the Chief, as soon as he was out of hearing, "for the most absurd original that exists north of the Tweed! I wish to heaven I had recommended him to attend the circle this evening with a boot-ketch under his arm. I think he might have adopted the suggestion, if it had been made with suitable gravity."

"And how can you take pleasure in making a man of his worth so ridiculous?"

"Begging pardon, my dear Waverley, you are as ridiculous as he. Why, do you not see that the man's whole mind is wrapped up in this ceremony? He has heard and thought of it since infancy, as the most august privilege and ceremony in the world ; and I doubt not but the expected pleasure of performing it was a principal motive with him for taking up arms. Depend upon it, had I endeavoured to divert him from exposing himself, he would have treated me as an ignorant, conceited coxcomb, or perhaps might have taken a fancy to cut my throat ; a pleasure which he once proposed to himself upon some point of etiquette, not half so important, in his eyes, as this matter of boots or brogues, or whatever the *caligæ* shall finally be pronounced by the learned. But I must go to head-quarters, to prepare the Prince for this extraordinary scene. My information will be well taken, for it will give him a hearty laugh at present, and put him on his guard against laughing, when it might be very *mal-à-propos*. So, *au revoir*, my dear Waverley."

## CHAPTER XLIX.

### *The English Prisoner.*

THE first occupation of Waverley, after he departed from the Chieftain, was to go in quest of the officer whose life he had saved. He was guarded, along with his companions in misfortune, who were very numerous, in a gentleman's house near the field of battle.

On entering the room, where they stood crowded together, Waverley easily recognised the object of his visit, not only by the peculiar dignity of his appearance, but by the appendage of Dugald Mahony, with his battle-axe, who had stuck to him from the moment of his captivity, as if he had been skewered to his side. This close attendance was, perhaps, for the purpose of securing his promised reward from Edward, but it also operated to save the English gentleman from being plundered in the scene of general confusion ; for Dugald sagaciously argued, that the amount of the salvage which he might be allowed, would be regulated by the state of the prisoner, when he should deliver him over to Waverley. He hastened to assure Waverley, therefore, with more words than he usually employed, that he had "keepit ta *sidier roy* haill, and that he wasna a plack the waur since the fery moment when his honour forbad her to gie him a bit clamhewit wi' her Lochaber-axe."

Waverley assured Dugald of a liberal recompence, and, approaching the English officer, expressed his anxiety to do anything which might contribute to his convenience under his present unpleasant circumstances.

"I am not so inexperienced a soldier, sir," answered the Englishman, "as to complain of the fortune of war. I am only grieved to see those scenes acted in our own island, which I have often witnessed elsewhere with comparative indifference."

"Another such day as this," said Waverley, "and I trust the cause of your regrets will be removed, and all will again return to peace and order."

The officer smiled and shook his head. "I must not forget my situation so far as to attempt a formal confutation of that opinion; but, notwithstanding your success, and the valour which achieved it, you have undertaken a task to which your strength appears wholly inadequate.

At this moment Fergus pushed into the press.

"Come, Edward, come along; the Prince has gone to Pinkie-house for the night; and we must follow, or lose the whole ceremony of the *caligæ*. Your friend, the Baron, has been guilty of a great piece of cruelty; he has insisted upon dragging Bailie Macwheeble out to the field of battle. Now, you must know, the Bailie's greatest horror is an armed Highlander, or a loaded gun; and there he stands, listening to the Baron's instructions concerning the protest; ducking his head like a sea-gull at the report of every gun and pistol that our idle boys are firing upon the fields; and undergoing, by way of penance, at every symptom of flinching, a severe rebuke from his patron, who would not admit the discharge of a whole battery of cannon, within point-blank distance, as an apology for neglecting a discourse, in which the honour of his family is interested."

"But how has Mr Bradwardine got him to venture so far?" said Edward.

"Why, he had come as far as Musselburgh, I fancy, in hopes of making some of our wills; and the peremptory commands of the Baron dragged him forward to Preston after the battle was over. He complains of one or two of our ragamuffins having put him in peril of his life, by presenting their pieces at him; but as they limited his ransom to an English penny, I don't think we need trouble the provost-martial upon that subject.—So, come along, Waverley."

"Waverley!" said the English officer, with great emotion; "the nephew of Sir Everard Waverley, of —— shire?"

"The same, sir," replied our hero, somewhat surprised at the tone in which he was addressed.

"I am at once happy and grieved," said the prisoner, "to have met with you."

"I am ignorant, sir," answered Waverley, "how I have deserved so much interest."

"Did your uncle never mention a friend called Talbot?"

"I have heard him talk with great regard of such a person," replied Edward; "a colonel, I believe, in the army, and the husband of Lady Emily Blandeville; but I thought Colonel Talbot had been abroad."

"I am just returned," answered the officer; "and being in Scotland, thought it my duty to act where my services promised to be useful. Yes, Mr Waverley, I am that Colonel Talbot, the husband of the lady you have named; and I am proud to acknowledge, that I owe alike my professional rank and my domestic happiness to your generous and noble-minded relative. Good God! that I should find his nephew in such a dress, and engaged in such a cause!"

"Sir," said Fergus, haughtily, "the dress and cause are those of men of birth and honour."

"My situation forbids me to dispute your assertion," said Colonel Talbot; "otherwise it were no difficult matter to show, that neither courage nor pride of lineage can gild a bad cause. But, with Mr Waverley's permission, and yours, sir, if yours also must be asked, I would willingly speak a few words with him on affairs connected with his own family."

"Mr Waverley, sir, regulates his own motions.—You will follow me, I supppose, to Pinkie," said Fergus, turning to Edward, "when you have finished your discourse with this new acquaintance?" So saying, the Chief of Glennaquoich adjusted his plaid with rather more than his usual air of haughty assumption, and left the apartment.

The interest of Waverley readily procured for Colonel Talbot the freedom of adjourning to a large garden, belonging to his place of confinement. They walked a few paces in silence, Colonel Talbot apparently studying how to open what he had to say; at length he addressed Edward.

"Mr Waverley, you have this day saved my life; and yet I would to God that I had lost it, ere I had found you wearing the uniform and cockade of these men."

"I forgive your reproach, Colonel Talbot; it is well meant, and your education and prejudices render it natural. But there is nothing extraordinary in finding a man, whose honour has been publicly and unjustly assailed, in the situation which promised most fair to afford him satisfaction on his calumniators."

"I should rather say, in the situation most likely to confirm the reports which they have circulated," said Colonel Talbot, "by following the very line of conduct ascribed to you. Are you aware, Mr Waverley, of the infinite distress, and even danger, which your present conduct has occasioned to your nearest relatives?"

"Danger!"

"Yes, sir, danger. When I left England, your uncle and father had been obliged to find bail to answer a charge of treason, to which they were only admitted by the exertion of the most powerful interest. I came down to Scotland, with the sole purpose of rescuing you from the gulf into which you have precipitated yourself; nor can I estimate the consequences to your family, of your having openly joined the rebellion, since the very suspicion of your intention was so perilous to them. Most deeply do I regret, that I did not meet you before this last and fatal error."

"I am really ignorant," said Waverley, in a tone of reserve, "why Colonel Talbot should have taken so much trouble on my account."

"Mr Waverley," answered Talbot, "I am dull at apprehending irony; and therefore I shall answer your words according to their plain meaning. I am indebted to your uncle for benefits greater than those which a son owes to a father. I acknowledge to him the duty of a son; and as I know there is no manner in which I can requite his kindness so well as by serving you, I will serve you, if possible, whether you will permit me or no. The personal obligation which you have this ·day laid me under, (although, in common estimation, as great as one human being can bestow on another,) adds nothing to my zeal on your behalf; nor can that zeal be abated by any coolness with which you may please to receive it."

"Your intentions may be kind, sir," said Waverley, drily; "but your language is harsh, or at least peremptory."

"On my return to England," continued Colonel Talbot,

"after long absence, I found your uncle, Sir Everard Waverley, in the custody of a king's messenger, in consequence of the suspicion brought upon him by your conduct. He is my oldest friend—how often shall I repeat it—my best benefactor! he sacrificed his own views of happiness to mine—he never uttered a word, he never harboured a thought, that benevolence itself might not have thought or spoken. I found this man in confinement, rendered harsher to him by his habits of life, his natural dignity of feeling, and—forgive me, Mr Waverley, —by the cause through which this calamity had come upon him. I cannot disguise from you my feelings upon this occasion; they were most painfully unfavourable to you. Having, by my family interest, which you probably know is not inconsiderable, succeeded in obtaining Sir Everard's release, I set out for Scotland. I saw Colonel Gardiner, a man whose fate alone is sufficient to render this insurrection for ever execrable. In the course of conversation with him, I found, that, from late circumstances, from a re-examination of the persons engaged in the mutiny, and from his original good opinion of your character, he was much softened towards you; and I doubted not, that if I could be so fortunate as to discover you, all might yet be well. But this unnatural rebellion has ruined all. I have, for the first time, in a long and active military life, seen Britons disgrace themselves by a panic flight, and that before a foe without either arms or discipline: And now I find the heir of my dearest friend—the son, I may say, of his affections—sharing a triumph, for which he ought the first to have blushed. Why should I lament Gardiner! his lot was happy, compared to mine!"

There was so much dignity in Colonel Talbot's manner, such a mixture of military pride and manly sorrow, and the news of Sir Everard's imprisonment was told in so deep a tone of feeling, that Edward stood mortified, abashed, and distressed, in presence of the prisoner, who owed to him his life not many hours before. He was not sorry when Fergus interrupted their conference a second time.

"His Royal Highness commands Mr Waverley's attendance." Colonel Talbot threw upon Edward a reproachful glance, which did not escape the quick eye of the Highland Chief. "His *immediate* attendance," he repeated, with considerable emphasis. Waverley turned again towards the Colonel.

"We shall meet again," he said; "in the meanwhile, every possible accommodation"——

"I desire none," said the Colonel; "let me fare like the meanest of those brave men, who, on this day of calamity, have preferred wounds and captivity to flight; I would almost exchange places with one of those who have fallen, to know that my words have made a suitable impression on your mind."

"Let Colonel Talbot be carefully secured," said Fergus to the Highland officer, who commanded the guard over the prisoners; "it is the Prince's particular command; he is a prisoner of the utmost importance."

"But let him want no accommodation suitable to his rank," said Waverley.

"Consistent always with secure custody," reiterated Fergus. The officer signified his acquiescence in both commands, and Edward followed Fergus to the garden-gate, where Callum Beg, with three saddle-horses, awaited them. Turning his head, he saw Colonel Talbot re-conducted to his place of confinement by a file of Highlanders; he lingered on the threshold of the door, and made a signal with his hand towards Waverley, as if enforcing the language he had held towards him.

"Horses," said Fergus, as he mounted, "are now as plenty as blackberries; every man may have them for the catching. Come, let Callum adjust your stirrups, and let us to Pinkie-house [1] as fast as these *ci-devant* dragoon-horses choose to carry us."

# CHAPTER L.

## *Rather unimportant.*

"I WAS turned back," said Fergus to Edward, as they galloped from Preston to Pinkie-House, "by a message from the Prince. But, I suppose, you know the value of this most noble Colonel Talbot as a prisoner. He is held one of the best officers among the red-coats; a special friend and favourite of the Elector himself, and of that dreadful hero, the Duke of Cumberland, who has been summoned from his triumphs at Fontenoy, to come over and devour us poor Highlanders alive. Has he been telling you how

---

[1] Charles Edward took up his quarters after the battle at Pinkie-house, adjoining to Musselburgh.  (S.)

the bells of St James's ring? Not 'turn again, Whittington,' like those of Bow, in the days of yore?"

"Fergus!" said Waverley, with a reproachful look.

"Nay, I cannot tell what to make of you," answered the Chief of Mac-Ivor, "you are blown about with every wind of doctrine. Here have we gained a victory, unparalleled in history—and your behaviour is praised by every living mortal to the skies—and the Prince is eager to thank you in person—and all our beauties of the White Rose are pulling caps for you,—and you, the *preux chevalier* of the day, are stooping on your horse's neck like a butterwoman riding to market, and looking as black as a funeral!"

"I am sorry for poor Colonel Gardiner's death: he was once very kind to me."

"Why, then, be sorry for five minutes, and then be glad again; his chance to-day may be ours to-morrow; and what does it signify? The next best thing to victory is honourable death; but it is a *pis-aller*, and one would rather a foe had it than one's self."

"But Colonel Talbot has informed me that my father and uncle are both imprisoned by government on my account."

"We'll put in bail, my boy; old Andrew Ferrara[1] shall lodge his security; and I should like to see him put to justify it in Westminster-Hall!"

"Nay, they are already at liberty, upon bail of a more civic disposition."

"Then why is thy noble spirit cast down, Edward? Dost think that the Elector's ministers are such doves as to set their enemies at liberty at this critical moment, if they could or durst confine and punish them? Assure thyself that either they have no charge against your relations on which they can continue their imprisonment, or else they are afraid of our friends, the jolly cavaliers of old England. At any rate, you need not be apprehensive upon their account; and we will find some means of conveying to them assurances of your safety."

Edward was silenced, but not satisfied, with these reasons. He had now been more than once shocked at the small degree of sympathy which Fergus exhibited for the feelings even of those whom he loved, if they did not correspond with his own mood at the time, and more especially if they thwarted him while earnest in a favourite pursuit. Fergus sometimes indeed observed, that he

[1] Note, 21. Andrea de Ferrara.

had offended Waverley, but, always intent upon some
favourite plan or project of his own, he was never sufficiently aware of the extent or duration of his displeasure,
so that the reiteration of these petty offences somewhat
cooled the volunteer's extreme attachment to his officer.

The Chevalier received Waverley with his usual favour,
and paid him many compliments on his distinguished
bravery. He then took him apart, made many inquiries
concerning Colonel Talbot, and when he had received all
the information which Edward was able to give concerning him and his connections, he proceeded,—"I cannot
but think, Mr Waverley, that since this gentleman is so
particularly connected with our worthy and excellent
friend, Sir Everard Waverley, and since his lady is of the
house of Blandeville, whose devotion to the true and
loyal principles of the Church of England is so generally
known, the Colonel's own private sentiments cannot be
unfavourable to us, whatever mask he may have assumed
to accommodate himself to the times."

"If I am to judge from the language he this day held
to me, I am under the necessity of differing widely from
your Royal Highness."

"Well, it is worth making a trial at least. I therefore
intrust you with the charge of Colonel Talbot, with
power to act concerning him as you think most advisable;
and I hope you will find means of ascertaining what are
his real dispositions towards our Royal Father's restoration."

"I am convinced," said Waverley, bowing, "that if
Colonel Talbot chooses to grant his parole, it may be
securely depended upon; but if he refuses it, I trust your
Royal Highness will devolve on some other person than
the nephew of his friend, the task of laying him under
the necessary restraint."

"I will trust him with no person but you," said the
Prince, smiling, but peremptorily repeating his mandate;
"it is of importance to my service that there should
appear to be a good intelligence between you, even if you
are unable to gain his confidence in earnest. You will
therefore receive him into your quarters, and in case he
declines giving his parole, you must apply for a proper
guard. I beg you will go about this directly. We return
to Edinburgh to-morrow."

Being thus remanded to the vicinity of Preston,
Waverley lost the Baron of Bradwardine's solemn act of
homage. So little, however, was he at this time in love

with vanity, that he had quite forgotten the ceremony in which Fergus had laboured to engage his curiosity. But next day, a formal Gazette was circulated, containing a detailed account of the battle of Gladsmuir, as the Highlanders chose to denominate their victory. It concluded with an account of the Court afterwards held by the Chevalier at Pinkie-house, which contained this among other high-flown descriptive paragraphs:

"Since that fatal treaty which annihilates Scotland as an independent nation, it has not been our happiness to see her princes receive, and her nobles discharge, those acts of feudal homage, which, founded upon the splendid actions of Scottish valour, recall the memory of her early history, with the manly and chivalrous simplicity of the ties which united to the Crown the homage of the warriors by whom it was repeatedly upheld and defended. But on the evening of the 20th, our memories were refreshed with one of those ceremonies which belong to the ancient days of Scotland's glory. After the circle was formed, Cosmo Comyne Bradwardine, of that ilk, colonel in the service, &c. &c. &c. came before the Prince, attended by Mr D. Macwheeble, the Bailie of his ancient barony of Bradwardine, (who, we understand, has been lately named a commissary), and, under form of instrument, claimed permission to perform, to the person of his Royal Highness, as representing his father, the service used and wont, for which, under a charter of Robert Bruce, (of which the original was produced and inspected by the Masters of his Royal Highness's Chancery for the time being) the claimant held the barony of Bradwardine, and lands of Tully-Veolan. His claim being admitted and registered, his Royal Highness having placed his foot upon a cushion, the Baron of Bradwardine, kneeling upon his right knee, proceeded to undo the latchet of the brogue, or low-heeled Highland shoe, which our gallant young hero wears in compliment to his brave followers. When this was performed, his Royal Highness declared the ceremony completed; and embracing the gallant veteran, protested that nothing but compliance with an ordinance of Robert Bruce, could have induced him to receive even the symbolical performance of a menial office from hands which had fought so bravely to put the crown upon the head of his father. The Baron of Bradwardine then took instruments in the hands of Mr Commissary Macwheeble, bearing, that all points and circumstances of the act of homage had been

*rite et solenniter acta et peracta ;* and a corresponding
entry was made in the protocol of the Lord High
Chamberlain, and in the record of Chancery. We understand that it is in contemplation of his Royal Highness,
when his Majesty's pleasure can be known, to raise
Colonel Bradwardine to the peerage, by the title of
Viscount Bradwardine, of Bradwardine and Tully-Veolan,
and that, in the meanwhile, his Royal Highness, in his
father's name and authority, has been pleased to grant
him an honourable augmentation to his paternal coat of
arms, being a budget or boot-jack, disposed saltier-wise
with a naked broadsword, to be borne in the dexter
cantle of the shield ; and, as an additional motto, on a
scroll beneath, the words, 'Draw and draw off.'"

Were it not for the recollection of Fergus's raillery,
thought Waverley to himself, when he had perused this
long and grave document, how very tolerably would all
this sound, and how little should I have thought of
connecting it with any ludicrous idea ! Well, after all,
everything has its fair, as well as its seamy side ; and
truly I do not see why the Baron's boot-jack may not
stand as fair in heraldry as the water-buckets, waggons,
cart-wheels, plough-socks, shuttles, candlesticks, and other
ordinaries, conveying ideas of anything save chivalry,
which appear in the arms of some of our most ancient
gentry.—This, however, is an episode in respect to the
principal story.

When Waverley returned to Preston, and rejoined
Colonel Talbot, he found him recovered from the strong
and obvious emotions with which a concurrence of unpleasing events had affected him. He had regained his
natural manner, which was that of an English gentleman
and soldier, manly, open, and generous, but not unsuscep-
tible of prejudice against those of a different country, or
who opposed him in political tenets. When Waverley
acquainted Colonel Talbot with the Chevalier's purpose
to commit him to his charge, "I did not think to have
owed so much obligation to that young gentleman," he
said, "as is implied in this destination. I can at least
cheerfully join in the prayer of the honest Presbyterian
clergyman, that, as he has come among us seeking an
earthly crown, his labours may be speedily rewarded with
a heavenly one.[1] I shall willingly give my parole not to

[1] The clergyman's name was Mac-Vicar. Protected by the cannon of the Castle,
he preached every Sunday in the West Kirk, while the Highlanders were in possession of Edinburgh; and it was in presence of some of the Jacobites that he
prayed for Prince Charles Edward in the terms quoted in the text. (S.)

attempt an escape without your knowledge, since, in fact, it was to meet you that I came to Scotland; and I am glad it has happened even under this predicament. But I suppose we shall be but a short time together. Your Chevalier, (that is a name we may both give to him,) with his plaids and blue caps, will, I presume, be continuing his crusade southward?"

"Not as I hear; I believe the army makes some stay in Edinburgh, to collect reinforcements."

"And to besiege the Castle?" said Talbot, smiling sarcastically. "Well, unless my old commander, General Preston, turn false metal, or the Castle sink into the North Loch, events which I deem equally probable, I think we shall have some time to make up our acquaintance. I have a guess that this gallant Chevalier has a design that I should be your proselyte; and, as I wish you to be mine, there cannot be a more fair proposal, than to afford us fair conference together. But, as I spoke to-day under the influence of feelings I rarely give way to, I hope you will excuse my entering again upon controversy till we are somewhat better acquainted."

## CHAPTER LI.

### Intrigues of Love and Politics.

It is not necessary to record in these pages the triumphant entrance of the Chevalier into Edinburgh after the decisive affair of Preston. One circumstance, however, may be noticed, because it illustrates the high spirit of Flora Mac-Ivor. The Highlanders, by whom the Prince was surrounded, in the license and extravagance of this joyful moment, fired their pieces repeatedly, and one of these having been accidentally loaded with ball, the bullet grazed the young lady's temple as she waved her handkerchief from a balcony.[1] Fergus, who beheld the accident, was at her side in an instant; and, on seeing that the wound was trifling, he drew his broadsword, with the purpose of rushing down upon the man by whose

[1] The incident here said to have happened to Flora Mac-Ivor, actually befell Miss Nairne, a lady with whom the author had the pleasure of being acquainted. As the Highland army rushed into Edinburgh, Miss Nairne, like other ladies who approved of their cause, stood waving her handkerchief from a balcony, when a ball from a Highlander's musket, which was discharged by accident, grazed her forehead. "Thank God," said she, the instant she recovered, "that the accident happened to me, whose principles are known. Had it befallen a Whig, they would have said it was done on purpose." (S.)

carelessness she had incurred so much danger, when, holding him by the plaid, "Do not harm the poor fellow," she cried; "for Heaven's sake, do not harm him! but thank God with me that the accident happened to Flora Mac-Ivor; for had it befallen a Whig, they would have pretended that the shot was fired on purpose."

Waverley escaped the alarm which this accident would have occasioned to him, as he was unavoidably delayed by the necessity of accompanying Colonel Talbot to Edinburgh.

They performed the journey together on horse-back, and for some time, as if to sound each other's feelings and sentiments, they conversed upon general and ordinary topics.

When Waverley again entered upon the subject which he had most at heart, the situation, namely, of his father and his uncle, Colonel Talbot seemed now rather desirous to alleviate than to aggravate his anxiety. This appeared particularly to be the case when he heard Waverley's history, which he did not scruple to confide to him.

"And so," said the Colonel, "there has been no malice prepense, as lawyers, I think, term it, in this rash step of yours; and you have been trepanned into the service of this Italian knight-errant by a few civil speeches from him and one or two of his Highland recruiting sergeants? It is sadly foolish, to be sure, but not nearly so bad as I was led to expect. However, you cannot desert, even from the Pretender, at the present moment,—that seems impossible. But I have little doubt that, in the dissensions incident to this heterogeneous mass of wild and desperate men, some opportunity may arise, by availing yourself of which, you may extricate yourself honourably from your rash engagement before the bubble burst. If this can be managed, I would have you go to a place of safety in Flanders, which I shall point out. And I think I can secure your pardon from government after a few months' residence abroad."

"I cannot permit you, Colonel Talbot," answered Waverley, "to speak of any plan which turns on my deserting an enterprise in which I may have engaged hastily, but certainly voluntarily, and with the purpose of abiding the issue."

"Well," said Colonel Talbot, smiling, "leave me my thoughts and hopes at least at liberty, if not my speech. But have you never examined your mysterious packet?"

"It is in my baggage," replied Edward; "we shall find it in Edinburgh."

In Edinburgh they soon arrived. Waverley's quarters had been assigned to him, by the Prince's express orders, in a handsome lodging, where there was accommodation for Colonel Talbot. His first business was to examine his portmanteau, and, after a very short search, out tumbled the expected packet. Waverley opened it eagerly. Under a blank cover, simply addressed to E. Waverley, Esq., he found a number of open letters. The uppermost were two from Colonel Gardiner, addressed to himself. The earliest in date was a kind and gentle remonstrance for neglect of the writer's advice, respecting the disposal of his time during his leave of absence, the renewal of which, he reminded Captain Waverley, would speedily expire. "Indeed," the letter proceeded, "had it been otherwise, the news from abroad, and my instructions from the War-office, must have compelled me to recall it, as there is great danger, since the disaster in Flanders, both of foreign invasion and insurrection among the disaffected at home. I therefore entreat you will repair, as soon as possible, to the head-quarters of the regiment; and I am concerned to add, that this is still the more necessary, as there is some discontent in your troop, and I postpone enquiry into particulars until I can have the advantage of your assistance."

The second letter, dated eight days later, was in such a style as might have been expected from the Colonel's receiving no answer to the first. It reminded Waverley of his duty, as a man of honour, an officer, and a Briton; took notice of the increasing dissatisfaction of his men, and that some of them had been heard to hint, that their Captain encouraged and approved of their mutinous behaviour; and, finally, the writer expressed the utmost regret and surprise that he had not obeyed his commands by repairing to head-quarters, reminded him that his leave of absence had been recalled, and conjured him, in a style in which paternal remonstrance was mingled with military authority, to redeem his error by immediately joining his regiment. "That I may be certain," concluded the letter, "that this actually reaches you, I despatch it by Corporal Tims, of your troop, with orders to deliver it into your own hand."

Upon reading these letters, Waverley, with great bitterness of feeling, was compelled to make the *amende honorable* to the memory of the brave and excellent writer; for surely, as Colonel Gardiner must have had every reason to conclude they had come safely to hand, less could not follow, on their being neglected, than that third and final summons, which Waverley actually received at Glennaquoich, though too late to obey it. And his being superseded, in consequence of his apparent neglect of this last command, was so far from being a harsh or severe proceeding, that it was plainly inevitable. The next letter he unfolded was from the Major of the regiment, acquainting him that a report, to the disadvantage of his reputation, was public in the country, stating, that one Mr Falconer of Ballihopple, or some such name, had proposed, in his presence, a treasonable toast, which he permitted to pass in silence, although it was so gross an affront to the royal family, that a gentleman in company, not remarkable for his zeal for government, had nevertheless taken the matter up, and that, supposing the account true, Captain Waverley had thus suffered another, comparatively unconcerned, to resent an affront directed against him personally as an officer, and to go out with the person by whom it was offered. The Major concluded, that no one of Captain Waverley's brother officers could believe this scandalous story, but that it was necessarily their joint opinion that his own honour, equally with that of the regiment, depended upon its being instantly contradicted by his authority, &c. &c. &c.

"What do you think of all this?" said Colonel Talbot, to whom Waverley handed the letters after he had perused them.

"Think! it renders thought impossible. It is enough to drive me mad."

"Be calm, my young friend; let us see what are these dirty scrawls that follow."

The first was addressed, "For Master W. Ruffin These." —"Dear sur, sum of our yong gulpins will not bite, thof I tuold them you shoed me the squoire's own seel. But Tims will deliver you the lettrs as desired, and tell ould Addem he gave them to squoir's hond, as to be sure yours is the same, and shall be ready for signal, and hoy for Hoy Church and Sachefrel, as fadur sings at harvest-whome.

"Yours, deer Sur,

"H. H.

"Poscriff. Do'e tell squoire we longs to heer from him, and has dootings about his not writing himself, and Lifetenant Bottler is smoky."

"This Ruffin, I suppose, then, is your Donald of the Cavern, who has intercepted your letters, and carried on a correspondence with the poor devil Houghton, as if under your authority?"

"It seems too true. But who can Addem be?"

"Possibly Adam, for poor Gardiner, a sort of pun on his name."

The other letters were to the same purpose, and they soon received yet more complete light upon Donald Bean's machinations.

John Hodges, one of Waverley's servants, who had remained with the regiment, and had been taken at Preston, now made his appearance. He had sought out his master, with the purpose of again entering his service. From this fellow they learned, that some time after Waverley had gone from the head-quarters of the regiment, a pedlar, called Ruthven, Ruffin, or Rivane, known among the soldiers by the name of Wily Will, had made frequent visits to the town of Dundee. He appeared to possess plenty of money, sold his commodities very cheap, seemed always willing to treat his friends at the ale-house, and easily ingratiated himself with many of Waverley's troop, particularly Sergeant Houghton, and one Tims, also a non-commissioned officer. To these he unfolded, in Waverley's name, a plan for leaving the regiment and joining him in the Highlands, where report said the clans had already taken arms in great numbers. The men, who had been educated as Jacobites, so far as they had any opinion at all, and who knew their landlord, Sir Everard, had always been supposed to hold such tenets, easily fell into the snare. That Waverley was at a distance in the Highlands, was received as a sufficient excuse for transmitting his letters through the medium of the pedlar; and the sight of his well-known seal seemed to authenticate the negotiations in his name, where writing might have been dangerous. The cabal, however, began to take air, from the premature mutinous language of those concerned. Wily Will justified his appellative; for, after suspicion arose, he was seen no more. When the *Gazette* appeared, in which Waverley was superseded, great part of his troop broke out into actual mutiny, but were surrounded and disarmed by the rest of the regiment. In consequence of the sentence of a court-martial, Houghton and Tims were condemned to be shot, but afterwards permitted to cast lots for life. Houghton, the survivor, showed much penitence, being convinced, from the rebukes and explanations of Colonel Gardiner, that he had really engaged in a very heinous crime. It is remarkable, that as soon as the poor fellow was satisfied of this, he became also convinced that the instigator had acted without authority from Edward, saying, "If it was dishonourable and against Old England, the squire could know nought about it; he never did, or thought to do, anything dishonourable, no more didn't Sir Everard, nor none of them afore him, and in that belief he would live and die that Ruffen had done it all of his own head."

The strength of conviction with which he expressed himself upon this subject, as well as his assurances that the letters intended for Waverley had been delivered to Ruthven, made that revolution in Colonel Gardiner's opinion which he expressed to Talbot.

The reader has long since understood that Donald Bean Lean played the part of tempter on this occasion. His motives were shortly these. Of an active and intriguing spirit, he had been long employed as a subaltern agent and spy by those in the confidence of the Chevalier, to an extent beyond what was suspected even by Fergus Mac-Ivor, whom, though obliged to him for protection, he regarded with fear and dislike. To success in this political department, he naturally looked for raising himself by some bold stroke above his present hazardous and precarious trade of rapine. He was particularly employed in learning the strength of the regiments in Scotland, the character of the officers, &c., and had long had his eye upon Waverley's troop, as open to temptation. Donald even believed that Waverley himself was at bottom in the Stewart interest, which seemed confirmed by his long visit to the Jacobite Baron of Bradwardine. When, therefore, he came to his cave with one of Glennaquoich's attendants, the robber, who could never appreciate his real motive, which was mere curiosity, was so sanguine as to hope that his own talents were to be employed in some intrigue of consequence, under the auspices of this wealthy young Englishman. Nor was he undeceived by Waverley's neglecting all hints and openings afforded for explanation. His conduct passed for prudent reserve, and somewhat piqued Donald Bean, who, supposing himself left out of a secret where confidence promised to be advantageous, determined to have his share in the drama, whether a regular part were assigned him or not. For this purpose, during Waverley's sleep, he possessed himself of his seal, as a token to be used to any of the troopers whom he might discover to be possessed of the captain's confidence. His first journey to Dundee, the town where the regiment was quartered, undeceived him in his original supposition, but opened to him a new field of action. He knew there would be no service so well rewarded by the friends of the Chevalier, as seducing a part of the regular army to his standard. For this purpose he opened the machinations with which the reader is already acquainted, and which form a clue to all the intricacies and obscurities of the narrative previous to Waverley's leaving Glennaquoich.

By Colonel Talbot's advice, Waverley declined detaining in his service the lad whose evidence had thrown additional light on these intrigues. He represented to him it would be doing the man an injury to engage him in a desperate undertaking, and that, whatever should happen, his evidence would go some length, at least, in explaining the circumstances under which Waverley himself had embarked in it. Waverley therefore wrote a short state of what had happened, to his uncle and his father, cautioning them, however, in the present circumstances, not to attempt to answer his letter. Talbot then gave the young man a letter to the commander of one of the English vessels of war cruising in the frith, requesting him to put the bearer ashore at Berwick, with a pass to proceed to ——shire. He was then furnished with money to make an expeditious journey, and directed to get on board the ship by means of bribing a fishing-boat, which, as they afterwards learned, he easily effected.

Tired of the attendance of Callum Beg, who, he thought, had some disposition to act as a spy on his motions, Waverley hired as a servant a simple Edinburgh swain, who had mounted the white cockade in a fit of spleen and jealousy, because Jenny Jop had danced a whole night with Corporal Bullock of the Fusileers.

## CHAPTER LII.

### Intrigues of Society and Love.

COLONEL TALBOT became more kindly in his demeanour towards Waverley after the confidence he had reposed in him, and as they were necessarily much together, the character of the Colonel rose in Waverley's estimation.

There seemed at first something harsh in his strong
expressions of dislike and censure, although no one was
in the general case more open to conviction. The habit
of authority had also given his manners some peremptory
hardness, notwithstanding the polish which they had
received from his intimate acquaintance with the higher
circles. As a specimen of the military character, he
differed from all whom Waverley had as yet seen. The
soldiership of the Baron of Bradwardine was marked by
pedantry; that of Major Melville by a sort of martinet
attention to the minutiæ and technicalities of discipline,
rather suitable to one who was to manœuvre a battalion,
than to him who was to command an army; the military
spirit of Fergus was so much warped and blended with
his plans and political views, that it was less that of a
soldier than of a petty sovereign. But Colonel Talbot
was in every point the English soldier. His whole soul
was devoted to the service of his king and country, without feeling any pride in knowing the theory of his art
with the Baron, or its practical minutiæ with the Major,
or in applying his science to his own particular plans of
ambition, like the Chieftain of Glennaquoich. Added to
this, he was a man of extended knowledge and cultivated
taste, although strongly tinged, as we have already
observed, with those prejudices which are peculiarly
English.

The character of Colonel Talbot dawned upon Edward
by degrees; for the delay of the Highlanders in the
fruitless siege of Edinburgh Castle occupied several
weeks, during which Waverley had little to do, excepting
to seek such amusement as society afforded. He would
willingly have persuaded his new friend to become
acquainted with some of his former intimates. But the
Colonel, after one or two visits, shook his head, and
declined farther experiment. Indeed he went farther,
and characterised the Baron as the most intolerable
formal pedant he had ever had the misfortune to meet
with, and the Chief of Glennaquoich as a Frenchified
Scotchman, possessing all the cunning and plausibility
of the nation where he was educated, with the proud,
vindictive, and turbulent humour of that of his birth.
"If the devil," he said, "had sought out an agent
expressly for the purpose of embroiling this miserable
country, I do not think he could find a better than such
a fellow as this, whose temper seems equally active,
supple, and mischievous, and who is followed, and

implicitly obeyed, by a gang of such cut-throats as those whom you are pleased to admire so much."

The ladies of the party did not escape his censure. He allowed that Flora Mac-Ivor was a fine woman, and Rose Bradwardine a pretty girl. But he alleged that the former destroyed the effect of her beauty by an affectation of the grand airs which she had probably seen practised in the mock court of St Germains. As for Rose Bradwardine, he said it was impossible for any mortal to admire such a little uninformed thing, whose small portion of education was as ill adapted to her sex or youth, as if she had appeared with one of her father's old campaign-coats upon her person for her sole garment. Now much of this was mere spleen and prejudice in the excellent Colonel, with whom the white cockade on the breast, the white rose in the hair, and the Mac at the beginning of a name, would have made a devil out of an angel; and indeed he himself jocularly allowed, that he could not have endured Venus herself, if she had been announced in a drawing-room by the name of Miss Mac-Jupiter.

Waverley, it may easily be believed, looked upon these young ladies with very different eyes. During the period of the siege, he paid them almost daily visits, although he observed with regret that his suit made as little progress in the affections of the former, as the arms of the Chevalier in subduing the fortress. She maintained with rigour the rule she had laid down of treating him with indifference, without either affecting to avoid him, or to shun intercourse with him. Every word, every look, was strictly regulated to accord with her system, and neither the dejection of Waverley, nor the anger which Fergus scarcely suppressed, could extend Flora's attention to Edward beyond that which the most ordinary politeness demanded. On the other hand, Rose Bradwardine gradually rose in Waverley's opinion. He had several opportunities of remarking, that, as her extreme timidity wore off, her manners assumed a higher character; that the agitating circumstances of the stormy time seemed to call forth a certain dignity of feeling and expression, which he had not formerly observed; and that she omitted no opportunity within her reach to extend her knowledge and refine her taste.

Flora Mac-Ivor called Rose her pupil, and was attentive to assist her in her studies, and to fashion both her taste and understanding. It might have been remarked by a

very close observer, that in the presence of Waverley she
was much more desirous to exhibit her friend's excellences
than her own.  But I must request of the reader to
suppose, that this kind and disinterested purpose was
concealed by the most cautious delicacy, studiously shunning the most distant approach to affectation.  So that it
was as unlike the usual exhibition of one pretty woman
affecting to *proner* another, as the friendship of David
and Jonathan might be to the intimacy of two Bond-
street loungers.  The fact is, that though the effect was
felt, the cause could hardly be observed.  Each of the
ladies, like two excellent actresses, was perfect in her
parts, and performed them to the delight of the audience ;
and such being the case, it was almost impossible to
discover that the elder constantly ceded to her friend that
which was most suitable to her talents.

But to Waverley, Rose Bradwardine possessed an at-
traction which few men can resist, from the marked
interest which she took in everything that affected him.
She was too young and too inexperienced to estimate the
full force of the constant attention which she paid to him.
Her father was too abstractedly immersed in learned and
military discussions to observe her partiality, and Flora
Mac-Ivor did not alarm her by remonstrance, because she
saw in this line of conduct the most probable chance
of her friend securing at length a return of affection.

The truth is, that in her first conversation after their
meeting, Rose had discovered the state of her mind to
that acute and intelligent friend, although she was not
herself aware of it.  From that time, Flora was not only
determined upon the final rejection of Waverley's addresses, but became anxious that they should, if possible,
be transferred to her friend.  Nor was she less interested
in this plan, though her brother had from time to time
talked, as between jest and earnest, of paying his suit to
Miss Bradwardine.  She knew that Fergus had the true
continental latitude of opinion respecting the institution
of marriage, and would not have given his hand to an
angel, unless for the purpose of strengthening his alliances,
and increasing his influence and wealth.  The Baron's
whim of transferring his estate to the distant heir male,
instead of his own daughter, was therefore likely to be an
insurmountable obstacle to his entertaining any serious
thoughts of Rose Bradwardine.  Indeed, Fergus's brain
was a perpetual workshop of scheme and intrigue, of
every possible kind and description ; while, like many a

mechanic of more ingenuity than steadiness, he would often unexpectedly, and without any apparent motive, abandon one plan, and go earnestly to work upon another, which was either fresh from the forge of his imagination, or had at some former period been flung aside half finished. It was therefore often difficult to guess what line of conduct he might finally adopt upon any given occasion.

Although Flora was sincerely attached to her brother, whose high energies might indeed have commanded her admiration even without the ties which bound them together, she was by no means blind to his faults, which she considered as dangerous to the hopes of any woman, who should found her ideas of a happy marriage in the peaceful enjoyment of domestic society, and the exchange of mutual and engrossing affection. The real disposition of Waverley, on the other hand, notwithstanding his dreams of tented fields and military honour, seemed exclusively domestic. He asked and received no share in the busy scenes which were constantly going on around him, and was rather annoyed than interested by the discussion of contending claims, rights, and interests, which often passed in his presence. All this pointed him out as the person formed to make happy a spirit like that of Rose, which corresponded with his own.

She remarked this point in Waverley's character one day while she sat with Miss Bradwardine. " His genius and elegant taste," answered Rose, " cannot be interested in such trifling discussions. What is it to him, for example, whether the Chief of the Macindallaghers, who has brought out only fifty men, should be a colonel or a captain? and how could Mr Waverley be supposed to interest himself in the violent altercation between your brother and young Corrinaschian, whether the post of honour is due to the eldest cadet of a clan or the youngest?"

"My dear Rose, if he were the hero you suppose him, he would interest himself in these matters, not indeed as important in themselves, but for the purpose of mediating between the ardent spirits who actually do make them the subject of discord. You saw when Corrinaschian raised his voice in great passion, and laid his hand upon his sword, Waverley lifted his head as if he had just awaked from a dream, and asked, with great composure, what the matter was."

"Well, and did not the laughter they fell into at his

absence of mind, serve better to break off the dispute, than anything he could have said to them?"

"True, my dear," answered Flora; "but not quite so creditably for Waverley as if he had brought them to their senses by force of reason."

"Would you have him peace-maker general between all the gunpowder Highlanders in the army? I beg your pardon, Flora, your brother, you know, is out of the question; he has more sense than half of them. But can you think the fierce, hot, furious spirits, of whose brawls we see much and hear more, and who terrify me out of my life every day in the world, are at all to be compared to Waverley?"

"I do not compare him with those uneducated men, my dear Rose. I only lament, that, with his talents and genius, he does not assume that place in society for which they eminently fit him, and that he does not lend their full impulse to the noble cause in which he has enlisted. Are there not Lochiel, and P——, and M——, and G——, all men of the highest education, as well as the first talents,—why will he not stoop like them to be alive and useful?—I often believe his zeal is frozen by that proud cold-blooded Englishman, whom he now lives with so much."

"Colonel Talbot?—he is a very disagreeable person, to be sure. He looks as if he thought no Scottish woman worth the trouble of handing her a cup of tea. But Waverley is so gentle, so well informed"——

"Yes," said Flora, smiling, "he can admire the moon, and quote a stanza from Tasso."

"Besides, you know how he fought," added Miss Bradwardine.

"For mere fighting," answered Flora, "I believe all men (that is, who deserve the name) are pretty much alike; there is generally more courage required to run away. They have besides, when confronted with each other, a certain instinct for strife, as we see in other male animals, such as dogs, bulls, and so forth. But high and perilous enterprise is not Waverley's forte. He would never have been his celebrated ancestor Sir Nigel, but only Sir Nigel's eulogist and poet. I will tell you where he will be at home, my dear, and in his place,—in the quiet circle of domestic happiness, lettered indolence, and elegant enjoyments, of Waverley-Honour. And he will refit the old library in the most exquisite Gothic taste, and garnish its shelves with the rarest and most valuable volumes ;—and he will draw plans and landscapes, and write verses, and rear temples, and dig grottoes ;—and he will stand in a clear summer night in the colonnade before the hall, and gaze on the deer as they stray in the moonlight, or lie shadowed by the boughs of the huge old fantastic oaks ;—and he will repeat verses to his beautiful wife, who will hang upon his arm ;—and he will be a happy man."

And she will be a happy woman, thought poor Rose. But she only sighed, and dropped the conversation.

## CHAPTER LIII.

### Fergus, a Suitor.

WAVERLEY had, indeed, as he looked closer into the state of the Chevalier's Court, less reason to be satisfied with it. It contained, as they say an acorn includes all the ramifications of the future oak, as many seeds of *tracasserie* and intrigue, as might have done honour to the Court of a large empire. Every person of consequence had some separate object, which he pursued with a fury that Waverley considered as altogether disproportioned to its importance. Almost all had their reasons for discontent, although the most legitimate was that of the worthy old Baron, who was only distressed on account of the common cause.

"We shall hardly," said he one morning to Waverley, when they had been viewing the castle,—"we shall hardly gain the obsidional crown, which you wot well was made of the roots or grain which takes root within the place besieged, or it may be of the herb woodbind, *paretaria*, or pellitory ; we shall not, I say, gain it by this same blockade or leaguer of Edinburgh Castle." For this opinion, he gave most learned and satisfactory reasons, that the reader may not care to hear repeated.

Having escaped from the old gentleman, Waverley went to Fergus's lodgings by appointment, to await his return from Holyrood-House. "I am to have a particular audience to-morrow," said Fergus to Waverley, overnight, "and you must meet me to wish me joy of the success which I securely anticipate."

The morrow came, and in the Chief's apartment he found Ensign Maccombich waiting to make report of his

turn of duty in a sort of ditch which they had dug across
the Castle-hill, and called a trench. In a short time the
Chief's voice was heard on the stair in a tone of impatient
fury :—"Callum,—why, Callum Beg,—Diaoul !" He entered the room with all the marks of a man agitated by
a towering passion ; and there were few upon whose
features rage produced a more violent effect. The veins
of his forehead swelled when he was in such agitation ;
his nostril became dilated ; his cheek and eye inflamed ;
and his look that of a demoniac. These appearances of
half-suppressed rage were the more frightful, because they
were obviously caused by a strong effort to temper
with discretion an almost ungovernable paroxysm of
passion, and resulted from an internal conflict of the
most dreadful kind, which agitated his whole frame of
mortality.

As he entered the apartment, he unbuckled his broadsword, and throwing it down with such violence, that the
weapon rolled to the other end of the room, "I know not
what," he exclaimed, "withholds me from taking a solemn
oath that I will never more draw it in his cause :—Load
my pistols, Callum, and bring them hither instantly ;—
instantly !" Callum, whom nothing ever startled, dis-
mayed, or disconcerted, obeyed very coolly. Evan Dhu,
upon whose brow the suspicion that his Chief had been
insulted, called up a corresponding storm, swelled in
sullen silence, awaiting to learn where or upon whom
vengeance was to descend.

"So, Waverley, you are there," said the Chief, after a
moment's recollection ;—"Yes, I remember I asked you to
share my triumph, and you have come to witness my—
disappointment we shall call it." Evan now presented
the written report he had in his hand, which Fergus threw
from him with great passion. "I wish to God," he said,
"the old den would tumble down upon the heads of the
fools who attack, and the knaves who defend it ! I see,
Waverley, you think I am mad—leave us, Evan, but be
within call."

"The Colonel's in an unco kippage,"[1] said Mrs Flockhart
to Evan as he descended ; "I wish he may be weel,—the
very veins on his brent brow are swelled like whip-cord ;
wad he no tak something ?"

"He usually lets blood for these fits," answered the
Highland Ancient with great composure.

When this officer left the room, the Chieftain gradually

_____
[1] Rage.

reassumed some degree of composure. "I know, Waverley," he said, "that Colonel Talbot has persuaded you to curse ten times a day your engagement with us;—nay, never deny it, for I am at this moment tempted to curse my own. Would you believe it, I made this very morning two suits to the Prince, and he has rejected them both; what do you think of it?"

"What can I think," answered Waverley, "till I know what your requests were?"

"Why, what signifies what they were, man? I tell you it was I that made them; I, to whom he owes more than to any three who have joined the standard; for I negotiated the whole business, and brought in all the Perthshire men when not one would have stirred. I am not likely, I think, to ask anything very unreasonable, and if I did, they might have stretched a point.—Well, but you shall know all, now that I can draw my breath again with some freedom.—You remember my earl's patent; it is dated some years back, for services then rendered; and certainly my merit has not been diminished, to say the least, by my subsequent behaviour. Now, sir, I value this bauble of a coronet as little as you can, or any philosopher on earth; for I hold that the chief of such a clan as the Sliochd nan Ivor is superior in rank to any earl in Scotland. But I had a particular reason for assuming this cursed title at this time. You must know that I learned accidentally that the Prince has been pressing that old foolish Baron of Bradwardine to disinherit his male heir, or nineteenth or twentieth cousin, who has taken a command in the Elector of Hanover's militia, and to settle his estate upon your pretty little friend Rose; and this, as being the command of his king and overlord, who may alter the destination of a fief at pleasure, the old gentleman seems well reconciled to."

"And what becomes of the homage?"

"Curse the homage!—I believe Rose is to pull off the queen's slipper on her coronation-day, or some such trash. Well, sir, as Rose Bradwardine would always have made a suitable match for me, but for this idiotical predilection of her father for the heir-male, it occurred to me there now remained no obstacle, unless that the Baron might expect his daughter's husband to take the name of Bradwardine, (which you know would be impossible in my case,) and that this might be evaded by my assuming the title to which I had so good a right, and which, of course, would supersede that difficulty. If she was to be also Vis-

countess Bradwardine, in her own right, after her father's
demise, so much the better; I could have no objection."

"But, Fergus," said Waverley, "I had no idea that you
had any affection for Miss Bradwardine, and you are
always sneering at her father."

"I have as much affection for Miss Bradwardine, my
good friend, as I think it necessary to have for the future
mistress of my family, and the mother of my children.
She is a very pretty, intelligent girl, and is certainly of
one of the very first Lowland families; and, with a little
of Flora's instructions and forming, will make a very good
figure. As to her father, he is an original, it is true, and
an absurd one enough; but he has given such severe
lessons to Sir Hew Halbert, that dear defunct the Laird
of Balmawhapple, and others, that nobody dare laugh at
him, so his absurdity goes for nothing. I tell you there
could have been no earthly objection—none. I had
settled the thing entirely in my own mind."

"But had you asked the Baron's consent," said Waverley,
"or Rose's?"

"To what purpose? To have spoke to the Baron before
I had assumed my title would have only provoked a premature and irritating discussion on the subject of the
change of name, when, as Earl of Glennaquoich, I had
only to propose to him to carry his d—d bear and boot-
jack *party per pale*, or in a scutcheon of pretence, or in a
separate shield perhaps—anyway that would not blemish
my own coat-of-arms. And as to Rose, I don't see what
objection she could have made, if her father was satisfied."

"Perhaps the same that your sister makes to me, you
being satisfied."

Fergus gave a broad stare at the comparison which this
supposition implied, but cautiously suppressed the answer
which rose to his tongue. "O, we should easily have
arranged all that.—So, sir, I craved a private interview,
and this morning was assigned; and I asked you to meet
me here, thinking, like a fool, that I should want your
countenance as bride's-man. Well—I state my pretensions—they are not denied—the promises so repeatedly
made, and the patent granted—they are acknowledged.
But I propose, as a natural consequence, to assume the
rank which the patent bestowed—I have the old story of
the jealousy of C———— and M———— trumpt up
against me—I resist this pretext, and offer to procure
their written acquiescence, in virtue of the date of my
patent as prior to their silly claims—I assure you I would

have had such a consent from them, if it had been at the point of the sword—And then out comes the real truth; and he dares to tell me, to my face, that my patent must be suppressed for the present, for fear of disgusting that rascally coward and *faineant*—(naming the rival chief of his own clan) who has no better title to be a chieftain than I to be Emperor of China; and who is pleased to shelter his dastardly reluctance to come out, agreeable to his promise twenty times pledged, under a pretended jealousy of the Prince's partiality to me. And, to leave this miserable driveller without a pretence for his cowardice, the Prince asks it as a personal favour of me, forsooth, not to press my just and reasonable request at this moment. After this, put your faith in princes!"

"And did your audience end here?"

"End? O no! I was determined to leave him no pretence for his ingratitude, and I therefore stated, with all the composure I could muster,—for I promise you I trembled with passion,—the particular reasons I had for wishing that his Royal Highness would impose upon me any other mode of exhibiting my duty and devotion, as my views in life made, what at any other time would have been a mere trifle, at this crisis a severe sacrifice; and then I explained to him my full plan."

"And what did the Prince answer?"

"Answer? why—it is well it is written, Curse not the king, no, not in thy thought!—why, he answered, that truly he was glad I had made him my confident, to prevent more grievous disappointment, for he could assure me, upon the word of a prince, that Miss Bradwardine's affections were engaged, and he was under a particular promise to favour them. 'So, my dear Fergus,' said he, with his most gracious cast of smile, 'as the marriage is utterly out of question, there need be no hurry, you know, about the earldom.' And so he glided off, and left me *planté la*."

"And what did you do?"

"I'll tell you what I *could* have done at that moment—sold myself to the devil or the Elector, whichever offered the dearest revenge. However I am now cool. I know he intends to marry her to some of his rascally Frenchmen, or his Irish officers, but I will watch them close; and let the man that would supplant me look well to himself.—*Bisogna coprirsi, Signor.*"

After some further conversation, unnecessary to be detailed, Waverley took leave of the Chieftain, whose fury had now subsided into a deep and strong desire of vengeance, and returned home, scarce able to analyze the mixture of feelings which the narrative had awakened in his own bosom.

## CHAPTER LIV.

*" To one Thing constant never."*

"I AM the very child of caprice," said Waverley to himself, as he bolted the door of his apartment, and paced it with hasty steps—" What is it to me that Fergus Mac-Ivor should wish to marry Rose Bradwardine?—I love her not—I might have been loved by her perhaps—but I rejected her simple, natural, and affecting attachment, instead of cherishing it into tenderness, and dedicated myself to one who will never love mortal man, unless old Warwick, the King-maker, should arise from the dead. The Baron too—I would not have cared about his estate, and so the name would have been no stumbling-block. The devil might have taken the barren moors, and drawn off the royal *caligæ*, for anything I would have minded. But, framed as she is for domestic affection and tenderness, for giving and receiving all those kind and quiet attentions which sweeten life to those who pass it together, she is sought by Fergus Mac-Ivor. He will not use her ill, to be sure—of that he is incapable—but he will neglect her after the first month; he will be too intent on subduing some rival chieftain, or circumventing some favourite at court, on gaining some heathy hill and lake, or adding to his bands some new troop of caterans, to inquire what she does, or how she amuses herself.

> ' And then will canker sorrow eat her bud,
> And chase the native beauty from her cheek;
> And she will look as hollow as a ghost,
> And dim and meagre as an ague fit,
> And so she'll die.'

And such a catastrophe of the most gentle creature on earth might have been prevented, if Mr Edward Waverley had had his eyes!—Upon my word, I cannot understand how I thought Flora so much, that is, so *very* much, handsomer than Rose. She is taller indeed, and her manner more formed; but many people think Miss Bradwardine's more natural; and she is certainly much younger. I should think Flora is two years older than I am—I will look at them particularly this evening."

And with this resolution Waverley went to drink tea (as the fashion was Sixty Years since) at the house of a lady of quality, attached to the cause of the Chevalier, where he found, as he expected, both the ladies. All rose as he entered, but Flora immediately resumed her place, and the conversation in which she was engaged. Rose, on the contrary, almost imperceptibly made a little way in the crowded circle for his advancing the corner of a chair.—" Her manner, upon the whole, is most engaging," said Waverley to himself.

A dispute occurred whether the Gaelic or Italian language was most liquid, and best adapted for poetry : the opinion for the Gaelic, which probably might not have found supporters elsewhere, was here fiercely defended by seven Highland ladies, who talked at the top of their lungs, and screamed the company deaf, with examples of Celtic *euphonia*. Flora, observing the Lowland ladies sneer at the comparison, produced some reasons to show that it was not altogether so absurd ; but Rose, when asked for her opinion, gave it with animation in praise of Italian, which she had studied with Waverley's assistance, "She has a more correct ear than Flora, though a less accomplished musician," said Waverley to himself. " I suppose Miss Mac-Ivor will next compare Mac-Murrough nan Fonn to Ariosto ! "

Lastly, it so befell that the company differed whether Fergus should be asked to perform on the flute, at which he was an adept, or Waverley invited to read a play of Shakspeare ; and the lady of the house good-humouredly undertook to collect the votes of the company for poetry or music, under the condition, that the gentlemen whose talents were not laid under contribution that evening, should contribute them to enliven he next. It chanced that Rose had the casting vote. Now Flora, who seemed to impose it as a rule upon herself never to countenance any proposal which might seem to encourage Waverley, had voted for music, providing the Baron would take his violin to accompany Fergus. " I wish you joy of your taste, Miss Mac-Ivor," thought Edward, as they sought for his book. " I thought it better when we were at Glennaquoich ; but certainly the Baron is no great performer, and Shakspeare is worth listening to."

Romeo and Juliet was selected, and Edward read with taste, feeling, and spirit, several scenes from that play. All the company applauded with their hands, and many with their tears. Flora, to whom the drama was well known, was among the former; Rose, to whom it was altogether new, belonged to the latter class of admirers. "She has more feeling too," said Waverley, internally.

The conversation turning upon the incidents of the play, and upon the characters, Fergus declared that the only one worth naming, as a man of fashion and spirit, was Mercutio. "I could not," he said, "quite follow all his old-fashioned wit, but he must have been a very pretty fellow, according to the ideas of his time."

"And it was a shame," said Ensign Maccombich, who usually followed his Colonel everywhere, "for that Tibbert, or Taggart, or whatever was his name, to stick him under the other gentleman's arm while he was redding[1] the fray."

The ladies, of course, declared loudly in favour of Romeo, but this opinion did not go undisputed. The mistress of the house, and several other ladies, severely reprobated the levity with which the hero transfers his affections from Rosalind to Juliet. Flora remained silent until her opinion was repeatedly requested, and then answered, she thought the circumstance objected to, not only reconcilable to nature, but such as in the highest degree evinced the art of the poet. "Romeo is described," said she, "as a young man, peculiarly susceptible of the softer passions; his love is at first fixed upon a woman who could afford it no return; this he repeatedly tells you,—

'From love's weak, childish bow she lives unharmed;'

and again,—

'She hath forsworn to love.'

Now, as it was impossible that Romeo's love, supposing him a reasonable being, could continue to subsist without hope, the poet has, with great art, seized the moment when he was reduced actually to despair, to throw in his way an object more accomplished than her by whom he had been rejected, and who is disposed to repay his attachment. I can scarce conceive a situation more calculated to enhance the ardour of Romeo's affection for Juliet, than his being at once raised by her from the state of drooping melancholy in which he appears first upon the scene, to the ecstatic state in which he exclaims—

'—— come what sorrow can,
It cannot countervail the exchange of joy
That one short moment gives me in her sight.'"

"Good now, Miss Mac-Ivor," said a young lady of

[1] Settling.

quality, "do you mean to cheat us out of our prerogative? will you persuade us love cannot subsist
without hope, or that the lover must become fickle if the
lady is cruel? O fie! I did not expect such an unsenti-
mental conclusion."

"A lover, my dear Lady Betty," said Flora, "may, I
conceive, persevere in his suit under very discouraging
circumstances. Affection can (now and then) withstand
very severe storms of rigour, but not a long polar frost of
downright indifference. Don't, even with *your* attractions, try the experiment upon any lover whose faith you
value. Love will subsist on wonderfully little hope, but
not altogether without it."

"It will be just like Duncan Mac-Girdie's mare," said
Evan, "if your ladyships please; he wanted to use her
by degrees to live without meat, and just as he had put
her on a straw a-day, the poor thing died!"

Evan's illustration set the company a-laughing, and
the discourse took a different turn. Shortly afterwards
the party broke up, and Edward returned home, musing
on what Flora had said. "I will love my Rosalind no
more," said he; "she has given me a broad enough hint
for that; and I will speak to her brother, and resign my
suit. But for a Juliet—would it be handsome to interfere with Fergus's pretensions?—though it is impossible
they can ever succeed: and should they miscarry, what
then?—why then *alors comme alors*." And with this
resolution, of being guided by circumstances, did our
hero commit himself to repose.

## CHAPTER LV.

### *A brave Man in Sorrow.*

IF my fair readers should be of opinion that my hero's
levity in love is altogether unpardonable, I must remind
them, that all his griefs and difficulties did not arise from
that sentimental source. Even the lyric poet, who
complains so feelingly of the pains of love, could not
forget, that, at the same time, he was "in debt and in
drink," which, doubtless, were great aggravations of his
distress. There were, indeed, whole days in which Waverley thought neither of Flora nor Rose Bradwardine,
but which were spent in melancholy conjectures on the

probable state of matters at Waverley-Honour, and the
dubious issue of the civil contest in which he was
pledged. Colonel Talbot often engaged him in discussions upon the justice of the cause he had espoused.
"Not," he said, "that it is possible for you to quit it at
this present moment, for, come what will, you must stand
by your rash engagement. But I wish you to be aware
that the right is not with you; that you are fighting
against the real interests of your country; and that you
ought, as an Englishman and a patriot, to take the first
opportunity to leave this unhappy expedition before the
snow-ball melts."

In such political disputes, Waverley usually opposed
the common arguments of his party, with which it is
unnecessary to trouble the reader. But he had little to
say when the Colonel urged him to compare the strength
by which they had undertaken to overthrow the government, with that which was now assembling very rapidly
for its support. To this statement Waverley had but one
answer: "If the cause I have undertaken be perilous,
there would be the greater disgrace in abandoning it."
And in his turn he generally silenced Colonel Talbot, and
succeeded in changing the subject.

One night, when, after a long dispute of this nature,
the friends had separated, and our hero had retired to
bed, he was awakened about midnight by a suppressed
groan. He started up and listened; it came from the
apartment of Colonel Talbot, which was divided from his
own by a wainscotted partition, with a door of communication. Waverley approached this door, and distinctly heard one or two deep-drawn sighs. What could
be the matter? The Colonel had parted from him,
apparently, in his usual state of spirits. He must have
been taken suddenly ill. Under this impression, he
opened the door of communication very gently, and perceived the Colonel, in his night-gown, seated by a table,
on which lay a letter and picture. He raised his head
hastily, as Edward stood uncertain whether to advance or
retire, and Waverley perceived that his cheeks were
stained with tears.

As if ashamed at being found giving away to such
emotion, Colonel Talbot rose with apparent displeasure,
and said, with some sternness, "I think, Mr Waverley,
my own apartment, and the hour, might have secured
even a prisoner against "——

"Do not say intrusion, Colonel Talbot; I heard you

breathe hard, and feared you were ill ; that alone could
have induced me to break in upon you."

"I am well," said the Colonel, " perfectly well."

"But you are distressed," said Edward : "is there anything can be done ?"

"Nothing, Mr Waverley ; I was only thinking of home,
and some unpleasant occurrences there."

"Good God, my uncle !" exclaimed Waverley.

"No, it is a grief entirely my own. I am ashamed you
should have seen it disarm me so much ; but it must
have its course at times, that it may be at others more
decently supported. I would have kept it secret from
you ; for I think it will grieve you, and yet you can
administer no consolation. But you have surprised me,
—I see you are surprised yourself,—and I hate mystery.
Read that letter."

The letter was from Colonel Talbot's sister, and in these
words :

"'I received yours, my dearest brother, by Hodges. Sir
E. W. and Mr R. are still at large, but are not permitted
to leave London. I wish to heaven I could give you as
good an account of matters in the square. But the news
of the unhappy affair at Preston came upon us, with the
dreadful addition that you were among the fallen. You
know Lady Emily's state of health, when your friendship
for Sir E. induced you to leave her. She was much
harassed with the sad accounts from Scotland of the rebellion having broken out ; but kept up her spirits, as, she
said, it became your wife, and for the sake of the future
heir, so long hoped for in vain. Alas, my dear brother,
these hopes are now ended ! Notwithstanding all my
watchful care, this unhappy rumour reached her without
preparation. She was taken ill immediately ; and the
poor infant scarce survived its birth. Would to God this
were all ! But although the contradiction of the horrible
report by your own letter has greatly revived her spirits,
yet Dr —— apprehends, I grieve to say, serious, and even
dangerous, consequences to her health, especially from
the uncertainty in which she must necessarily remain for
some time, aggravated by the ideas she has formed of the
ferocity of those with whom you are a prisoner.

"Do therefore, my dear brother, as soon as this reaches
you, endeavour to gain your release, by parole, by ransom, or any way that is practicable. I do not exaggerate
Lady Emily's state of health ; but I must not—dare not

—suppress the truth. Ever, my dear Philip, your most affectionate sister, "LUCY TALBOT."

Edward stood motionless when he had perused this letter; for the conclusion was inevitable, that, by the Colonel's journey in quest of him, he had incurred this heavy calamity. It was severe enough, even in its irremediable part; for Colonel Talbot and Lady Emily, long without a family, had fondly exulted in the hopes which were now blasted. But this disappointment was nothing to the extent of the threatened evil; and Edward, with horror, regarded himself as the original cause of both.

Ere he could collect himself sufficiently to speak, Colonel Talbot had recovered his usual composure of manner, though his troubled eye denoted his mental agony.

"She is a woman, my young friend, who may justify even a soldier's tears." He reached him the miniature, exhibiting features which fully justified the eulogium; "and yet, God knows, what you see of her there is the least of the charms she possesses—possessed I should perhaps say—but God's will be done."

"You must fly—you must fly instantly to her relief. It is not—it shall not be too late."

"Fly? how is it possible? I am a prisoner—upon parole."

"I am your keeper—I restore your parole—I am to answer for you."

"You cannot do so consistently with your duty; nor can I accept a discharge from you, with due regard to my own honour—you would be made responsible."

"I will answer it with my head, if necessary," said Waverley impetuously. "I have been the unhappy cause of the loss of your child, make me not the murderer of your wife."

"No, my dear Edward," said Talbot, taking him kindly by the hand, "you are in no respect to blame; and if I concealed this domestic distress for two days, it was lest your sensibility should view it in that light. You could not think of me, hardly knew of my existence, when I left England in quest of you. It is a responsibility, Heaven knows, sufficiently heavy for mortality, that we must answer for the foreseen and direct result of our actions,—for their indirect and consequential operation, the great and good Being, who alone can foresee the dependence of human events on each other, hath not pronounced his frail creatures liable."

"But that you should have left Lady Emily," said Waverley with much emotion, "in the situation of all others the most interesting to a husband, to seek a"——

"I only did my duty," answered Colonel Talbot, calmly, "and I do not, ought not, to regret it. If the path of gratitude and honour were always smooth and easy, there would be little merit in following it ; but it moves often in contradiction to our interest and passions, and sometimes to our better affections. These are the trials of life, and this, though not the least bitter," (the tears came unbidden to his eyes,) "is not the first which it has been my fate to encounter—But we will talk of this to-morrow," he said, wringing Waverley's hands. "Good night ; strive to forget it for a few hours. It will dawn, I think, by six, and it is now past two. Good night."

Edward retired, without trusting his voice with a reply.

## CHAPTER LVI.

### *Exertion.*

WHEN Colonel Talbot entered the breakfast-parlour next morning, he learned from Waverley's servant that our hero had been abroad at an early hour, and was not yet returned. The morning was well advanced before he again appeared. He arrived out of breath, but with an air of joy that astonished Colonel Talbot.

"There," said he, throwing a paper on the table, "there is my morning's work. Alick, pack up the Colonel's clothes. Make haste, make haste."

The Colonel examined the paper with astonishment. It was a pass from the Chevalier to Colonel Talbot, to repair to Leith, or any other port in possession of his Royal Highness's troops, and there to embark for England or elsewhere, at his free pleasure ; he only giving his parole of honour not to bear arms against the house of Stewart for the space of a twelvemonth.

"In the name of God," said the Colonel, his eyes sparkling with eagerness, "how did you obtain this ?"

"I was at the Chevalier's levee as soon as he usually rises. He was gone to the camp at Duddingston. I pursued him thither ; asked and obtained an audience—but I will tell you not a word more, unless I see you begin to pack."

"Before I know whether I can avail myself of this passport, or how it was obtained ?"

"O, you can take out the things again, you know.— Now I see you busy, I will go on. When I first mentioned your name, his eyes sparkled almost as bright as yours did two minutes since. 'Had you,' he earnestly asked, 'shown any sentiments favourable to his cause?' 'Not in the least, nor was there any hope you would do so.' His countenance fell. I requested your freedom. 'Impossible,' he said;—'your importance, as a friend and confident of such and such personages, made my request altogether extravagant.' I told him my own story and yours; and asked him to judge what my feelings must be by his own. He has a heart, and a kind one, Colonel Talbot, you may say what you please. He took a sheet of paper, and wrote the pass with his own hand. 'I will not trust myself with my council,' he said; 'they will argue me out of what is right. I will not endure that a friend, valued as I value you, should be loaded with the painful reflections which must afflict you in case of further misfortune in Colonel Talbot's family; nor will I keep a brave enemy a prisoner under such circumstances. Besides,' said he, 'I think I can justify myself to my prudent advisers, by pleading the good effect such lenity will produce on the minds of the great English families with whom Colonel Talbot is connected.'"

"There the politician peeped out," said the Colonel.

"Well, at least he concluded like a king's son :—'Take the passport; I have added a condition for form's sake; but if the Colonel objects to it, let him depart without giving any parole whatever. I come here to war with men, but not to distress or endanger women.'"

"Well, I never thought to have been so much indebted to the Pretend——"

"To the Prince," said Waverley, smiling.

"To the Chevalier," said the Colonel; "it is a good travelling name, and which we may both freely use. Did he say anything more?"

"Only asked if there was anything else he could oblige me in; and when I replied in the negative, he shook me by the hand, and wished all his followers were as considerate, since some friends of mine not only asked all he had to bestow, but many things which were entirely out of his power, or that of the greatest sovereign upon earth. Indeed, he said, no prince seemed, in the eyes of his followers, so like the Deity as himself, if you were to judge from the extravagant requests which they daily preferred to him."

"Poor young gentleman,' said the Colonel, "I suppose he begins to feel the difficulties of his situation. Well, dear Waverley, this is more than kind, and shall not be forgotten while Philip Talbot can remember anything. My life—pshaw—let Emily thank you for that—this is a favour worth fifty lives. I cannot hestitate on giving my parole in the circumstances : there it is—(he wrote it out in form)—And now, how am I to get off?"

"All that is settled : your baggage is packed, my horses wait, and a boat has been engaged, by the Prince's permission, to put you on board the *Fox* frigate. I sent a messenger down to Leith on purpose."

"That will do excellently well. Captain Beaver is my particular friend : he will put me ashore at Berwick or Shields, from whence I can ride post to London ;—and you must intrust me with the packet of papers which you recovered by means of your Miss Bean Lean. I may have an opportunity of using them to your advantage.—But I see your Highland friend, Glen——what do you call his barbarous name? and his orderly with him—I must not call him his orderley cut-throat any more, I suppose. See how he walks as if the world were his own, with the bonnet on one side of his head, and his plaid puffed out across his breast ! I should like now to meet that youth where my hands were not tied : I would tame his pride, or he should tame mine."

"For shame, Colonel Talbot ! you swell at sight of tartan, as the bull is said to do at scarlet. You and Mac-Ivor have some points not much unlike, so far as national prejudice is concerned."

"The latter part of this discourse took place in the street. They passed the Chief, the Colonel and he sternly and punctiliously greeting each other, like two duellists before they take their ground. It was evident the dislike was mutual. "I never see that surly fellow that dogs his heels," said the Colonel, after he had mounted his horse, "but he reminds me of lines I have somewhere heard—upon the stage, I think :

> ——'Close behind him
> Stalks sullen Bertram, like a sorcerer's fiend,
> Pressing to be employed.'"

"I assure you, Colonel," said Waverley, "that you judge too harshly of the Highlanders."

"Not a whit, not a whit ; I cannot spare them a jot ; I

cannot bate them an ace. Let them stay in their own
barren mountains, and puff and swell, and hang their
bonnets on the horns of the moon, if they have a mind ;
but what business have they to come where people wear
breeches, and speak an intelligible language ?—I mean
intelligible in comparison to their gibberish, for even the
Lowlanders talk a kind of English little better than the
Negroes in Jamaica. I could pity the Pr——, I mean the
Chevalier himself, for having so many desperadoes about
him. And they learn their trade so early. There is a
kind of subaltern imp, for example, a sort of sucking
devil, whom your friend Glena—Glenamuck there, has
sometimes in his train. To look at him, he is about
fifteen years ; but he is a century old in mischief and
villainy. He was playing at quoits the other day in the
court ; a gentleman, a decent-looking person enough,
came past, and as a quoit hit his shin, he lifted his cane :
But my young bravo whips out his pistol, like Beau
Clincher in the Trip to the Jubilee, and had not a scream
of *Gardez l'eau*, from an upper window, set all parties a
scampering for fear of the inevitable consequences, the
poor gentleman would have lost his life by the hands of
that little cockatrice."

"A fine character you'll give of Scotland upon your
return, Colonel Talbot."

"O, Justice Shallow," said the Colonel, "will save me
the trouble—'Barren, barren, beggars all, beggars all.
Marry, good air,'—and that only when you are fairly out
of Edinburgh, and not yet come to Leith, as is our case
at present."

In a short time they arrived at the seaport :—

> "The boat rock'd at the pier of Leith,
>   Full loud the wind blew down the ferry ;
> The ship rode at the Berwick Law "——

"Farewell, Colonel ; may you find all as you would wish
it ! Perhaps we may meet sooner than you expect : they
talk of an immediate route to England."

"Tell me nothing of that," said Talbot ; "I wish to
carry no news of your motions."

"Simply, then, adieu. Say, with a thousand kind
greetings, all that is dutiful and affectionate to Sir
Everard and Aunt Rachel—Think of me as kindly as you
can—speak of me as indulgently as your conscience will
permit, and once more adieu."

"And adieu, my dear Waverley ; many, many thanks for
your kindness. Unplaid yourself on the first opportunity.

I shall ever think on you with gratitude, and the worst of my censure shall be, *Que diable alloit il faire dans cette galere?*"

And thus they parted, Colonel Talbot going on board of the boat, and Waverley returning to Edinburgh.

## CHAPTER LVII.

### The March.

IT is not our purpose to intrude upon the province of history. We shall therefore only remind our readers, that about the beginning of November the Young Chevalier, at the head of about six thousand men at the utmost, resolved to peril his cause on an attempt to penetrate into the centre of England, although aware of the mighty preparations which were made for his reception. They set forward on this crusade in weather which would have rendered any other troops incapable of marching, but which in reality gave these active mountaineers advantages over a less hardy enemy. In defiance of a superior army lying upon the Borders, under Field-Marshal Wade, they besieged and took Carlisle, and soon afterwards prosecuted their daring march to the southward.

As Colonel Mac-Ivor's regiment marched in the van of the clans, he and Waverley, who now equalled any Highlander in the endurance of fatigue, and was become somewhat acquainted with their language, were perpetually at its head. They marked the progress of the army, however, with very different eyes. Fergus, all air and fire, and confident against the world in arms, measured nothing but that every step was a yard nearer London. He neither asked, expected, nor desired any aid, except that of the clans, to place the Stewarts once more on the throne; and when by chance a few adherents joined the standard, he always considered them in the light of new claimants upon the favours of the future monarch, who, he concluded, must therefore subtract for their gratification so much of the bounty which ought to be shared among his Highland followers.

Edward's views were very different. He could not but observe, that in those towns in which they proclaimed James the Third, "no man cried, God bless him." The mob stared and listened, heartless, stupified, and dull, but gave few signs even of that boisterous spirit, which induces them to shout upon all occasions, for the mere exercise of their most sweet voices. The Jacobites had been taught to believe that the north-western counties abounded with wealthy squires and hardy yeomen, devoted to the cause of the White Rose. But of the wealthier Tories they saw little. Some fled from their houses, some feigned themselves sick, some surrendered themselves to the government as suspected persons. Of such as remained, the ignorant gazed with astonishment, mixed with horror and aversion, at the wild appearance, unknown language, and singular garb, of the Scottish clans. And to the more prudent, their scanty numbers, apparent deficiency in discipline, and poverty of equipment, seemed certain tokens of the calamitous termination of their rash undertaking. Thus the few who joined them were such as bigotry of political principle blinded to consequences, or whose broken fortunes induced to hazard all on a risk so desperate.

The Baron of Bradwardine being asked what he thought of these recruits, took a long pinch of snuff, and answered drily, "that he could not but have an excellent opinion of them, since they resembled precisely the followers who attached themselves to the good King David at the cave of Adullam ; *videlicet*, every one that was in distress, and every one that was in debt, and every one that was discontented, which the vulgate renders bitter of soul ; and doubtless," he said, "they will prove mighty men of their hands, and there is much need that they should, for I have seen many a sour look cast upon us."

But none of these considerations moved Fergus. He admired the luxuriant beauty of the country, and the situation of many of the seats which they passed. "Is Waverley-Honour like that house, Edward ?"

"It is one-half larger."

"Is your uncle's park as fine a one as that ?"

"It is three times as extensive, and rather resembles a forest than a mere park."

"Flora will be a happy woman."

"I hope Miss Mac-Ivor will have much reason for happiness, unconnected with Waverley-Honour."

"I hope so too ; but, to be mistress of such a place, will be a pretty addition to the sum total."

"An addition, the want of which, I trust, will be amply supplied by some other means."

"How," said Fergus, stopping short, and turning upon Waverley—"How am I to understand that, Mr Waverley?—Had I the pleasure to hear you aright?"

"Perfectly right, Fergus."

"And I am to understand that you no longer desire my alliance, and my sister's hand?"

"Your sister has refused mine," said Waverley, "both directly, and by all the usual means by which ladies repress undesired attentions."

"I have no idea," answered the Chieftain, "of a lady dismissing or a gentleman withdrawing his suit, after it has been approved of by her legal guardian, without giving him an opportunity of talking the matter over with the lady. You did not, I suppose, expect my sister to drop into your mouth like a ripe plum, the first moment you chose to open it?"

"As to the lady's title to dismiss her lover, Colonel," replied Edward, "it is a point which you must argue with her, as I am ignorant of the customs of the Highlands in that particular. But as to my title to acquiesce in a rejection from her without an appeal to your interest, I will tell you plainly, without meaning to undervalue Miss Mac-Ivor's admitted beauty and accomplishments, that I would not take the hand of an angel, with an empire for her dowry, if her consent were extorted by the importunity of friends and guardians, and did not flow from her own free inclination."

"An angel, with the dowry of an empire," repeated Fergus, in a tone of bitter irony, "is not very likely to be pressed upon a ——shire squire. But, sir," changing his tone, "if Flora Mac-Ivor have not the dowry of an empire, she is *my* sister; and that is sufficient at least to secure her against being treated with anything approaching to levity."

"She is Flora Mac-Ivor, sir," said Waverley, with firmness, "which to me, were I capable of treating *any* woman with levity, would be a more effectual protection."

The brow of the Chieftain was now fully clouded, but Edward felt too indignant at the unreasonable tone which he had adopted, to avert the storm by the least concession. They both stood still while this short dialogue passed, and Fergus seemed half disposed to say something more violent, but, by a strong effort, suppressed his passion, and, turning his face forward, walked sullenly on. As they had always hitherto walked together,

and almost constantly side by side, Waverley pursued
his course silently in the same direction, determined to
let the Chief take his own time in recovering the
good-humour which he had so unreasonably discarded,
and firm in his resolution not to bate him an inch of
dignity.

After they had marched on in this sullen manner about
a mile, Fergus resumed the discourse in a different tone.
"I believe I was warm, my dear Edward, but you provoke
me with your want of knowledge of the world. You have
taken pet at some of Flora's prudery, or high-flying
notions of loyalty, and now, like a child, you quarrel
with the plaything you have been crying for, and beat
me, your faithful keeper, because my arm cannot reach
to Edinburgh to hand it to you. I am sure, if I was
passionate, the mortification of losing the alliance of such
a friend, after your arrangement had been the talk of
both Highlands and Lowlands, and that without so much
as knowing why or wherefore, might well provoke calmer
blood than mine. I shall write to Edinburgh, and put all
to rights; that is, if you desire I should do so; as indeed
I cannot suppose that your good opinion of Flora, it
being such as you have often expressed to me, can be at
once laid aside."

"Colonel Mac-Ivor," said Edward, who had no mind to
be hurried farther or faster than he chose, in a matter
which he had already considered as broken off, "I am
fully sensible of the value of your good offices; and
certainly, by your zeal on my behalf in such an affair,
you do me no small honour. But as Miss Mac-Ivor has
made her election freely and voluntarily, and as all my
attentions in Edinburgh were received with more than
coldness, I cannot, in justice either to her or myself,
consent that she should again be harassed upon this topic.
I would have mentioned this to you some time since, but
you saw the footing upon which we stood together, and
must have understood it. Had I thought otherwise, I
would have earlier spoken; but I had a natural reluctance to enter upon a subject so painful to us both."

"O, very well, Mr Waverley," said Fergus, haughtily,
"the thing is at an end. I have no occasion to press my
sister upon any man."

"Nor have I any occasion to court repeated rejection
from the same young lady," answered Edward, in the
same tone.

"I shall make due inquiry, however," said the Chieftain,

without noticing the interruption, "and learn what my sister thinks of all this : we will then see whether it is to end here."

"Respecting such inquiries, you will of course be guided by your own judgment," said Waverley. "It is, I am aware, impossible Miss Mac-Ivor can change her mind ; and were such an unsupposable case to happen, it is certain I will not change mine. I only mention this to prevent any possibility of future misconstruction."

Gladly at this moment would Mac-Ivor have put their quarrel to a personal arbitrement ; his eye flashed fire, and he measured Edward as if to choose where he might best plant a mortal wound. But although we do not now quarrel according to the modes and figures of Caranza or Vincent Saviola, no one knew better than Fergus that there must be some decent pretext for a mortal duel. For instance, you may challenge a man for treading on your corn in a crowd, or for pushing you up to the wall, or for taking your seat in the theatre ; but the modern code of honour will not permit you to found a quarrel upon your right of compelling a man to continue addresses to a female relative, which the fair lady has already refused. So that Fergus was compelled to stomach this supposed affront, until the whirligig of time, whose motion he promised himself he would watch most sedulously, should bring about an opportunity of revenge.

Waverley's servant always led a saddle-horse for him in the rear of the battalion to which he was attached, though his master seldom rode. But now, incensed at the domineering and unreasonable conduct of his late friend, he fell behind the column, and mounted his horse, resolving to seek the Baron of Bradwardine, and request permission to volunteer in his troop, instead of the Mac-Ivor regiment.

A happy time of it I should have had, thought he, after he was mounted, to have been so closely allied to this superb specimen of pride and self-opinion and passion. A colonel! why, he should have been a generalissimo. A petty chief of three or four hundred men ! his pride might suffice for the Cham of Tartary—the Grand Seignior—the Great Mogul ! I am well free of him. Were Flora an angel, she would bring with her a second Lucifer of ambition and wrath for a brother-in-law.—

The Baron, whose learning (like Sancho's jests while in the Sierra Morena) seemed to grow mouldy for want of exercise, joyfully embraced the opportunity of Waverley's

offering his service in his regiment, to bring it into some
exertion. The good-natured old gentleman, however,
laboured to effect a reconciliation between the two
quondam friends. Fergus turned a cold ear to his remonstrances, though he gave them a respectful hearing;
and as for Waverley, he saw no reason why he should be
the first in courting a renewal of the intimacy which the
Chieftain had so unreasonably disturbed. The Baron
then mentioned the matter to the Prince, who, anxious to
prevent quarrels in his little army, declared, he would
himself remonstrate with Colonel Mac-Ivor on the un-
reasonableness of his conduct. But, in the hurry of their
march, it was a day or two before he had an opportunity
to exert his influence in the manner proposed.

In the meanwhile, Waverley turned the instructions
he had received while in Gardiner's dragoons to some
account, and assisted the Baron in his command as a
sort of adjutant. "*Parmi les aveugles un borgne est roi,*"
says the French proverb; and the cavalry, which consisted chiefly of Lowland gentlemen, their tenants and
servants, formed a high opinion of Waverley's skill, and a
great attachment to his person. This was indeed partly
owing to the satisfaction which they felt at the distinguished English volunteer's leaving the Highlanders to
rank among them; for there was a latent grudge between
the horse and foot, not only owing to the difference of the
services, but because most of the gentlemen, living near
the Highlands, had at one time or other had quarrels
with the tribes in their vicinity, and all of them looked
with a jealous eye on the Highlanders' avowed pretensions
to superior valour, and utility in the Prince's service.

# CHAPTER LVIII.

### The Confusion of King Agramant's Camp.

It was Waverley's custom sometimes to ride a little
apart from the main body, to look at any object of
curiosity which occurred on the march. They were now
in Lancashire, when, attracted by a castellated old hall,
he left the squadron for half an hour, to take a survey
and slight sketch of it. As he returned down the avenue,
he was met by Ensign Maccombich. This man had contracted a sort of regard for Edward since the day of his

first seeing him at Tully-Veolan, and introducing him to the Highlands. He seemed to loiter, as if on purpose to meet with our hero. Yet, as he passed him, he only approached his stirrup, and pronounced the single word, "Beware!" and then walked swiftly on, shunning all further communication.

Edward, somewhat surprised at this hint, followed with his eyes the course of Evan, who speedily disappeared among the trees. His servant Alick Polwarth, who was in attendance, also looked after the Highlander, and then riding up close to his master, said,

"The ne'er be in me, sir, if I think you're safe amang thae Highland rintherouts."

"What do you mean, Alick?" said Waverley.

"The Mac-Ivors, sir, hae gotten it into their heads, that ye hae affronted their young leddy, Miss Flora; and I hae heard mae than ane say, they wadna tak muckle to mak a black-cock o' ye; and ye ken weel eneugh there's mony o' them wadna mind a bawbee[1] the weising[2] a ball through the Prince himsell, an the Chief gae them the wink—or whether he did or no, if they thought it a thing that would please him when it was dune."

Waverley, though confident that Fergus Mac-Ivor was incapable of such treachery, was by no means equally sure of the forbearance of his followers. He knew, that where the honour of the Chief or his family was supposed to be touched, the happiest man would be he that could first avenge the stigma; and he had often heard them quote a proverb, "That the best revenge was the most speedy and most safe." Coupling this with the hint of Evan, he judged it most prudent to set spurs to his horse and ride briskly back to the squadron. Ere he reached the end of the long avenue, however, a ball whistled past him, and the report of a pistol was heard.

"It was that deevil's buckie,[3] Callum Beg," said Alick; "I saw him whisk away through amang the reises."[4]

Edward, justly incensed at this act of treachery, galloped out of the avenue, and observed the battalion of Mac-Ivor at some distance moving along the common, in which it terminated. He also saw an individual running very fast to join the party; this he concluded was the intended assassin, who, by leaping an enclosure, might easily make a much shorter path to the main body than he could find on horseback. Unable to contain himself, he commanded Alick to go to the Baron of Bradwardine,

[1] Halfpenny.     [2] Sending.     [3] Quarrelsome person.     [4] Brushwood.

who was at the head of his regiment about half a mile in
front, and acquaint him with what had happened. He
himself immediately rode up to Fergus's regiment. The
Chief himself was in the act of joining them. He was on
horseback, having returned from waiting on the Prince.
On perceiving Edward approaching, he put his horse in
motion towards him.

"Colonel Mac-Ivor," said Waverley, without any farther
salutation, "I have to inform you that one of your people
has this instant fired at me from a lurking-place."

"As that," answered Mac-Ivor, "excepting the circumstance of a lurking-place, is a pleasure which I presently
propose to myself, I should be glad to know which of my
clansmen dared to anticipate me."

"I shall certainly be at your command whenever you
please;—the gentleman who took your office upon himself
is your page there, Callum Beg."

"Stand forth from the ranks, Callum! Did you fire at
Mr Waverley?"

"No," answered the unblushing Callum.

"You did," said Alick Polwarth, who was already
returned, having met a trooper by whom he despatched
an account of what was going forward to the Baron of
Bradwardine, while he himself returned to his master at
full gallop, neither sparing the rowels of his spurs, nor the
sides of his horse. "You did; I saw you as plainly as I
ever saw the auld kirk at Coudingham."

"You lie," replied Callum, with his usual impenetrable
obstinacy. The combat between the knights would certainly, as in the days of chivalry, have been preceded by
an encounter between the squires, (for Alick was a stout-
hearted Merseman, and feared the bow of Cupid far more
than a Highlander's dirk or claymore,) but Fergus, with
his usual tone of decision, demanded Callum's pistol.
The cock was down, the pan and muzzle were black with
the smoke; it had been that instant fired.

"Take that," said Fergus, striking the boy upon the
head with the heavy pistol-butt with his whole force,—
"take that for acting without orders, and lying to
disguise it." Callum received the blow without appearing
to flinch from it, and fell without sign of life. "Stand
still, upon your lives!" said Fergus to the rest of the
clan; "I blow out the brains of the first man who inter-
feres between Mr Waverley and me." They stood motionless; Evan Dhu alone showed symptoms of vexation and
anxiety. Callum lay on the ground bleeding copiously,

but no one ventured to give him any assistance. It seemed as if he had gotten his death-blow.

"And now for you, Mr Waverley; please to turn your horse twenty yards with me upon the common." Waverley complied; and Fergus, confronting him when they were a little way from the line of march, said, with great affected coolness, "I could not but wonder, sir, at the fickleness of taste which you were pleased to express the other day. But it was not an angel, as you justly observed, who had charms for you, unless she brought an empire for her fortune. I have now an excellent commentary upon that obscure text."

"I am at a loss even to guess at your meaning, Colonel Mac-Ivor, unless it seems plain that you intend to fasten a quarrel upon me."

"Your affected ignorance shall not serve you, sir. The Prince,—the Prince himself, has acquainted me with your manœuvres. I little thought that your engagements with Miss Bradwardine were the reason of your breaking off your intended match with my sister. I suppose the information that the Baron had altered the destination of his estate, was quite a sufficient reason for slighting your friend's sister, and carrying off your friend's mistress."

"Did the Prince tell you I was engaged to Miss Bradwardine?" said Waverley. "Impossible."

"He did, sir," answered Mac-Ivor; "so, either draw and defend yourself, or resign your pretensions to the lady."

"This is absolute madness," exclaimed Waverley, "or some strange mistake!"

"O! no evasion! draw your sword!" said the infuriated Chieftain,—his own already unsheathed.

"Must I fight in a madman's quarrel?"

"Then give up now, and for ever, all pretensions to Miss Bradwardine's hand."

"What title have you," cried Waverley, utterly losing command of himself,—"what title have you, or any man living, to dictate such terms to me?" And he also drew his sword.

At this moment, the Baron of Bradwardine, followed by several of his troop, came up on the spur, some from curiosity, others to take part in the quarrel, which they indistinctly understood had broken out between the Mac-Ivors and their corps. The clan, seeing them approach, put themselves in motion to support their Chieftain, and

a scene of confusion commenced, which seemed likely to
terminate in bloodshed. A hundred tongues were in
motion at once. The Baron lectured, the Chieftain
stormed, the Highlanders screamed in Gaelic, the horsemen cursed and swore in Lowland Scotch. At length
matters came to such a pass, that the Baron threatened
to charge the Mac-Ivors unless they resumed their ranks,
and many of them, in return, presented their fire-arms at
him and the other troopers. The confusion was privately
fostered by old Ballenkeiroch, who made no doubt that
his own day of vengeance was arrived, when, behold! a
cry arose of "Room! make way! *place à Monseigneur!
place à Monseigneur!*" This announced the approach
of the Prince, who came up with a party of Fitz-
James's foreign dragoons that acted as his body guard.
His arrival produced some degree of order. The Highlanders re-assumed their ranks, the cavalry fell in and
formed squadron, and the Baron and Chieftain were
silent.

The Prince called them and Waverley before him.
Having heard the original cause of the quarrel through
the villainy of Callum Beg, he ordered him into custody
of the provost-marshal for immediate execution, in the
event of his surviving the chastisement inflicted by his
Chieftain. Fergus, however, in a tone betwixt claiming
a right and asking a favour, requested he might be left to
his disposal, and promised his punishment should be ex-
emplary. To deny this might have seemed to encroach on
the patriarchal authority of the Chieftains, of which they
were very jealous, and they were not persons to be
disobliged. Callum was therefore left to the justice of
his own tribe.

The Prince next demanded to know the new cause of
quarrel between Colonel Mac-Ivor and Waverley. There
was a pause. Both gentlemen found the presence of the
Baron of Bradwardine (for by this time all three had
approached the Chevalier by his command) an insurmountable barrier against entering upon a subject where
the name of his daughter must unavoidably be mentioned.
They turned their eyes on the ground, with looks in which
shame and embarrassment were mingled with displeasure.
The Prince, who had been educated amongst the discontented and mutinous spirits of the court of St Germains,
where feuds of every kind were the daily subject of
solicitude to the dethroned sovereign, had served his
apprenticeship, as old Frederick of Prussia would have

said, to the trade of royalty. To promote or restore concord among his followers was indispensable. Accordingly he took his measures.

"Monsieur de Beaujeu!"

"Monseigneur!" said a very handsome French cavalry officer, who was in attendance.

"Ayez la bonté d'alligner ces montagnards là, ainsi que la cavalerie, s'il vous plait, et de les remettre à la marche. Vous parlez si bien l'Anglois, cela ne vous donneroit pas beaucoup de peine."

"Ah! pas de tout, Monseigneur," replied Mons. le Compte de Beaujeu, his head bending down to the neck of his little prancing highly managed charger. Accordingly he *piaffed* away, in high spirits and confidence, to the head of Fergus's regiment, although understanding not a word of Gaelic, and very little English.

"Messieurs les sauvages Ecossois—dat is—gentilmans savages, have the goodness d'arranger vous."

The clan, comprehending the order more from the gesture than the words, and seeing the Prince himself present, hastened to dress their ranks.

"Ah! ver well! dat is fort bien!" said the Count de Beaujeu. "Gentilmans sauvages—mais, très bien—Eh bien!—Qu' est ce que vous appellez visage, Monsieur?" (to a lounging trooper who stood by him) "Ah, oui! *face* —Je vous remercie, Monsieur.—Gentilshommes, have de goodness to make de face to de right par file, dat is, by files.—Marsh!—Mais, très bien—encore, Messieurs; il faut vous mettre à la marche . . . . Marchez donc, au nom de Dieu, parceque j'ai oublié le mot Anglois—mais vous étes des braves gens, et me comprenez très bien."

The Count next hastened to put the cavalry in motion. "Gentilmans cavalry, you must fall in—Ah! par ma foi, I did not say fall off! I am a fear de little gross fat gentilman is moche hurt. Ah, mon Dieu! c'est le Commissaire qui nous a apporté les prémières nouvelles de cet maudit fracas. Je suis trop faché, Monsieur!"

But poor Macwheeble, who, with a sword stuck across him, and a white cockade as large as a pancake, now figured in the character of a commissary, being overturned in the bustle occasioned by the troopers hastening to get themselves in order in the Prince's presence, before he could rally his galloway, slunk to the rear amid the unrestrained laughter of the spectators.

"Eh bien, Messieurs, wheel to de right—Ah! dat is it! —Eh, Monsieur de Bradwardine, ayez la bonté de vous

mettre à la tête de votre régiment, car, par Dieu, je n'en
puis plus ! "

The Baron of Bradwardine was obliged to go to the
assistance of Monsieur de Beaujeu, after he had fairly
expended his few English military phrases.  One purpose
of the Chevalier was thus answered.  The other he proposed was, that in the eagerness to hear and comprehend
commands issued through such an indistinct medium in
his own presence, the thoughts of the soldiers in both
corps might get a current different from the angry
channel in which they were flowing at the time.

Charles Edward was no sooner left with the Chieftain
and Waverley, the rest of his attendants being at some
distance, than he said, " If I owed less to your disinterested
friendship, I could be most seriously angry with both of
you for this very extraordinary and causeless broil, at a
moment when my father's service so decidedly demands
the most perfect unanimity.  But the worst of my
situation is, that my very best friends hold they have
liberty to ruin themselves, as well as the cause they are
engaged in, upon the slightest caprice."

Both the young men protested their resolution to
submit every difference to his arbitration.  "Indeed,"
said Edward, "I hardly know of what I am accused.  I
sought Colonel Mac-Ivor merely to mention to him that I
had narrowly escaped assassination at the hand of his
immediate dependent, a dastardly revenge, which I knew
him to be incapable of authorising.  As to the cause for
which he is disposed to fasten a quarrel upon me, I am
ignorant of it, unless it be that he accuses me, most
unjustly, of having engaged the affections of a young lady
in prejudice of his pretensions."

"If there is an error," said the Chieftain, "it arises
from a conversation which I held this morning with his
Royal Highness himself."

"With me ?" said the Chevalier ; "how can Colonel
Mac-Ivor have so far misunderstood me ?"

He then led Fergus aside, and, after five minutes'
earnest conversation, spurred his horse towards Edward.
"Is it possible—nay, ride up, Colonel, for I desire no
secrets—Is it possible, Mr Waverley, that I am mistaken
in supposing that you are an accepted lover of Miss
Bradwardine ? a fact of which I was by circumstances,
though not by communication from you, so absolutely
convinced, that I alleged it to Vich Ian Vohr this morning as a reason why, without offence to him, you might

not continue to be ambitious of an alliance, which to an unengaged person, even though once repulsed, holds out too many charms to be lightly laid aside."

"Your Royal Highness," said Waverley, "must have founded on circumstances altogether unknown to me, when you did me the distinguished honour of supposing me an accepted lover of Miss Bradwardine. I feel the distinction implied in the supposition, but I have no title to it. For the rest, my confidence in my own merit is too justly slight to admit of my hoping for success in any quarter after positive rejection."

The Chevalier was silent for a moment, looking steadily at them both, and then said, "Upon my word, Mr Waverley, you are a less happy man than I conceived I had very good reason to believe you. But now, gentlemen, allow me to be umpire in this matter, not as Prince Regent, but as Charles Stewart, a brother adventurer with you in the same gallant cause. Lay my pretensions to be obeyed by you entirely out of view, and consider your own honour, and how far it is well, or becoming, to give our enemies the advantage, and our friends the scandal, of showing that, few as we are, we are not united. And forgive me if I add, that the names of the ladies who have been mentioned, crave more respect from us all than to be made themes of discord."

He took Fergus a little apart, and spoke to him very earnestly for two or three minutes, and then returning to Waverley, said, "I believe I have satisfied Colonel Mac-Ivor, that his resentment was founded upon a misconception, to which, indeed, I myself gave rise ; and I trust Mr Waverley is too generous to harbour any recollection of what is past, when I assure him that such is the case.— You must state this matter properly to your clan, Vich Ian Vohr, to prevent a recurrence of their precipitate violence." Fergus bowed. "And now, gentlemen, let me have the pleasure to see you shake hands."

They advanced coldly, and with measured steps, each apparently reluctant to appear most forward in concession. They did, however, shake hands, and parted, taking a respectful leave of the Chevalier.

Charles Edward [1] then rode to the head of the Mac-Ivors, threw himself from his horse, begged a drink out of old Ballenkeiroch's cantine, and marched about half a mile along with them, inquiring into the history and connections of Sliochd nan Ivor, adroitly using the

[1] Note 22. Prince Charles Edward.

few words of Gaelic he possessed, and affecting a great
desire to learn it more thoroughly. . He then mounted his
horse once more, and galloped to the Baron's cavalry,
which was in front, halted them, and examined their
accoutrements and state of discipline ; took notice of the
principal gentlemen, and even of the cadets ; inquired
after their ladies, and commended their horses ; rode
about an hour with the Baron of Bradwardine, and
endured three long stories about Field-Marshal the Duke
of Berwick.

"Ah, Beaujeu, mon cher ami," said he as he returned to
his usual place in the line of march, "que mon métier de
prince errant est ennuyant, par fois. Mais, courage !
c'est le grand jeu, après tout."


# CHAPTER LIX

### A Skirmish.

THE reader need hardly be reminded, that, after a
council of war held at Derby on the 5th of December, the
Highlanders relinquished their desperate attempt to
penetrate farther into England, and, greatly to the
dissatisfaction of their young and daring leader, positively determined to return northward. They commenced
their retreat accordingly, and, by the extreme celerity of
their movements, outstripped the motions of the Duke of
Cumberland, who now pursued them with a very large
body of cavalry.

This retreat was a virtual resignation of their towering
hopes. None had been so sanguine as Fergus Mac-Ivor ;
none, consequently, was so cruelly mortified at the
change of measures. He argued, or rather remonstrated,
with the utmost vehemence at the council of war ; and,
when his opinion was rejected, shed tears of grief and
indignation. From that moment his whole manner was
so much altered, that he could scarcely have been recognised for the same soaring and ardent spirit, for whom
the whole earth seemed too narrow but a week before.
The retreat had continued for several days, when Edward,
to his surprise, early on the 12th of December, received a
visit from the Chieftain in his quarters, in a hamlet about
half way between Shap and Penrith.

Having had no intercourse with the Chieftain since

their rupture, Edward waited with some anxiety an explanation of this unexpected visit; nor could he help being surprised, and somewhat shocked, with the change in his appearance. His eye had lost much of its fire; his cheek was hollow, his voice was languid, even his gait seemed less firm and elastic than it was wont; and his dress, to which he used to be particularly attentive, was now carelessly flung about him. He invited Edward to walk out with him by the little river in the vicinity; and smiled in a melancholy manner when he observed him take down and buckle on his sword.

As soon as they were in a wild sequestered path by the side of the stream, the Chief broke out,—"Our fine adventure is now totally ruined, Waverley, and I wish to know what you intend to do:—nay, never stare at me, man. I tell you I received a packet from my sister yesterday, and, had I got the information it contains sooner, it would have prevented a quarrel, which I am always vexed when I think of. In a letter written after our dispute, I acquainted her with the cause of it; and she now replies to me, that she never had, nor could have, any purpose of giving you encouragement; so that it seems I have acted like a madman.—Poor Flora! she writes in high spirits; what a change will the news of this unhappy retreat make in her state of mind!"

Waverley, who was really much affected by the deep tone of melancholy with which Fergus spoke, affectionately entreated him to banish from his remembrance any unkindness which had arisen between them, and they once more shook hands, but now with sincere cordiality. Fergus again inquired of Waverley what he intended to do. "Had you not better leave this luckless army, and get down before us into Scotland, and embark for the Continent from some of the eastern ports that are still in our possession? When you are out of the kingdom, your friends will easily negotiate your pardon; and, to tell you the truth, I wish you would carry Rose Bradwardine with you as your wife, and take Flora also under your joint protection."—Edward looked surprised—"She loves you, and I believe you love her, though, perhaps, you have not found it out, for you are not celebrated for knowing your own mind very pointedly." He said this with a sort of smile.

"How," answered Edward, "can you advise me to desert the expedition in which we are all embarked?"

"Embarked?" said Fergus; "the vessel is going to

pieces, and it is full time for all who can, to get into the long-boat and leave her."

"Why, what will other gentlemen do?" answered Waverley, "and why did the Highland Chiefs consent to this retreat, if it is so ruinous?"

"O," replied Mac-Ivor, "they think that, as on former occasions, the heading, hanging, and forfeiting, will chiefly fall to the lot of the Lowland gentry; that they will be left secure in their poverty and their fastnesses, there, according to their proverb, 'to listen to the wind upon the hill till the waters abate.' But they will be disappointed; they have been too often troublesome to be so repeatedly passed over, and this time John Bull has been too heartily frightened to recover his good-humour for some time. The Hanoverian ministers always deserved to be hanged for rascals; but now, if they get the power in their hands,—as, sooner or later, they must, since there is neither rising in England nor assistance from France,—they will deserve the gallows as fools, if they leave a single clan in the Highlands in a situation to be again troublesome to government. Ay, they will make root-and-branch-work, I warrant them."

"And while you recommend flight to me," said Edward, —"a counsel which I would rather die than embrace,— what are your own views?"

"O," answered Fergus, with a melancholy air, "my fate is settled. Dead or captive I must be before to-morrow."

"What do you mean by that, my friend?" said Edward. "The enemy is still a day's march in our rear, and if he comes up, we are still strong enough to keep him in check. Remember Gladsmuir."

"What I tell you is true notwithstanding, so far as I am individually concerned."

"Upon what authority can you found so melancholy a prediction?" asked Waverley.

"On one which never failed a person of my house. I have seen," he said, lowering his voice, "I have seen the Bodach Glas."

"Bodach Glas?"

"Yes: Have you been so long at Glennaquoich, and never heard of the Grey Spectre? though indeed there is a certain reluctance among us to mention him."

"No, never."

"Ah? it would have been a tale for poor Flora to have told you. Or, if that hill were Benmore, and that long

blue lake, which you see just winding towards yon mountainous country, were Loch Tay, or my own Loch an Ri,
the tale would be better suited with scenery. However,
let us sit down on this knoll; even Saddleback and
Ulswater will suit what I have to say better than the
English hedgerows, enclosures, and farm-houses. You
must know, then, that when my ancestor, Ian nan Chaistel, wasted Northumberland, there was associated with
him in the expedition a sort of Southland Chief, or captain
of a band of Lowlanders, called Halbert Hall. In their
return through the Cheviots, they quarrelled about the
division of the great booty they had acquired, and came
from words to blows. The Lowlanders were cut off to a
man, and their chief fell the last, covered with wounds by
the sword of my ancestor. Since that time, his spirit has
crossed the Vich Ian Vohr of the day when any great
disaster was impending, but especially before approaching
death. My father saw him twice: once before he was
made prisoner at Sheriff-Muir; another time on the
morning of the day on which he died."

"How can you, my dear Fergus, tell such nonsense with
a grave face?"

"I do not ask you to believe it; but I tell you the truth,
ascertained by three hundred years' experience at least,
and last night by my own eyes."

"The particulars, for heaven's sake!" said Waverley,
with eagerness.

"I will, on condition you will not attempt a jest on the
subject.—Since this unhappy retreat commenced, I have
scarce ever been able to sleep for thinking of my clan, and
of this poor Prince, whom they are leading back like a
dog in a string, whether he will or no, and of the downfall
of my family. Last night I felt so feverish that I left my
quarters, and walked out, in hopes the keen frosty air
would brace my nerves—I cannot tell how much I dislike
going on, for I know you will hardly believe me. However—I crossed a small footbridge, and kept walking
backwards and forwards, when I observed with surprise,
by the clear moonlight, a tall figure in a grey plaid, such
as shepherds wear in the south of Scotland, which, move
at what pace I would, kept regularly about four yards
before me."

"You saw a Cumberland peasant in his ordinary dress,
probably."

"No: I thought so at first, and was astonished at the
man's audacity in daring to dog me. I called to him, but

received no answer. I felt an anxious throbbing at my heart, and to ascertain what I dreaded, I stood still, and turned myself on the same spot successively to the four points of the compass—By Heaven, Edward, turn where I would, the figure was instantly before my eyes, at precisely the same distance! I was then convinced it was the Bodach Glas. My hair bristled, and my knees shook. I manned myself, however, and determined to return to my quarters. My ghastly visitant glided before me (for I cannot say he walked,) until he reached the foot-bridge: there he stopped, and turned full round. I must either wade the river, or pass him as close as I am to you. A desperate courage, founded on the belief that my death was near, made me resolve to make my way in despite of him. I made the sign of the cross, drew my sword, and uttered, 'In the name of God, Evil Spirit, give place!' 'Vich Ian Vohr,' it said, in a voice that made my very blood curdle, 'beware of to-morrow!' It seemed at that moment not half a yard from my sword's point; but the words were no sooner spoken than it was gone, and nothing appeared further to obstruct my passage. I got home, and threw myself on my bed, where I spent a few hours heavily enough; and this morning, as no enemy was reported to be near us, I took my horse, and rode forward to make up matters with you. I would not willingly fall until I am in charity with a wronged friend."

Edward had little doubt that this phantom was the operation of an exhausted frame and depressed spirits, working on the belief common to all Highlanders in such superstitions. He did not the less pity Fergus, for whom, in his present distress, he felt all his former regard revive. With the view of diverting his mind from these gloomy images, he offered, with the Baron's permission, which he knew he could readily obtain, to remain in his quarters till Fergus's corps should come up, and then to march with them as usual. The Chief seemed much pleased, yet hesitated to accept the offer.

"We are, you know, in the rear,—the post of danger in a retreat."

"And therefore the post of honour."

"Well," replied the Chieftain, "let Alick have your horse in readiness, in case we should be overmatched, and I shall be delighted to have your company once more."

The rear-guard were late in making their appearance, having been delayed by various accidents, and by the badness of the roads. At length they entered the hamlet.

When Waverley joined the clan Mac-Ivor, arm-in-arm with their Chieftain, all the resentment they had entertained against him seemed blown off at once. Evan Dhu received him with a grin of congratulation; and even Callum, who was running about as active as ever, pale indeed, and with a great patch on his head, appeared delighted to see him.

"That gallows-bird's skull," said Fergus, "must be harder than marble: the lock of the pistol was actually broken."

"How could you strike so young a lad so hard?" said Waverley, with some interest.

"Why, if I did not strike hard sometimes, the rascals would forget themselves."

They were now in full march, every caution being taken to prevent surprise. Fergus's people, and a fine clan regiment from Badenoch, commanded by Cluny Mac-Pherson, had the rear. They had passed a large open moor, and were entering into the enclosures which surround a small village called Clifton. The winter sun had set, and Edward began to rally Fergus upon the false predictions of the Grey Spirit. "The ides of March are not past," said Mac-Ivor, with a smile; when, suddenly, casting his eyes back on the moor, a large body of cavalry was indistinctly seen to hover upon its brown and dark surface. To line the enclosures facing the open ground, and the road by which the enemy must move from it upon the village, was the work of a short time. While these manœuvres were accomplishing, night sunk down, dark and gloomy, though the moon was at full. Sometimes, however, she gleamed forth a dubious light upon the scene of action.

The Highlanders did not long remain undisturbed in the defensive position they had adopted. Favoured by the night, one large body of dismounted dragoons attempted to force the enclosures, while another, equally strong, strove to penetrate by the high-road. Both were received by such a heavy fire as disconcerted their ranks, and effectually checked their progress. Unsatisfied with the advantage thus gained, Fergus, to whose ardent spirit the approach of danger seemed to restore all its elasticity, drawing his sword, and calling out "Claymore!" encouraged his men, by voice and example, to break through the hedge which divided them, and rush down upon the enemy. Mingling with the dismounted dragoons, they forced them, at the sword-point, to fly to the open moor,

where a considerable number were cut to pieces. But
the moon, which suddenly shone out, showed to the
English the small number of assailants, disordered by
their own success. Two squadrons of horse moving to the
support of their companions, the Highlanders endeavoured
to recover the enclosures. But several of them, amongst
others their brave Chieftain, were cut off and surrounded
before they could effect their purpose. Waverley, looking
eagerly for Fergus, from whom, as well as from the retreating body of his followers, he had been separated in
the darkness and tumult, saw him, with Evan Dhu and
Callum, defending themselves desperately against a dozen
of horsemen, who were hewing at them with their long
broadswords. The moon was again at that moment
totally overclouded, and Edward, in the obscurity, could
neither bring aid to his friends, nor discover which way
lay his own road to rejoin the rear-guard. After once or
twice narrowly escaping being slain or made prisoner by
parties of the cavalry whom he encountered in the darkness, he at length reached an enclosure, and clambering
over it, concluded himself in safety, and on the way to the
Highland forces, whose pipes he heard at some distance.
For Fergus hardly a hope remained, unless that he might
be made prisoner. Revolving his fate with sorrow and
anxiety, the superstition of the Bodach Glas recurred to
Edward's recollection, and he said to himself, with internal surprise, "What, can the devil speak truth?"[1]

## CHAPTER LX.

### Chapter of Accidents.

EDWARD was in a most unpleasant and dangerous
situation. He soon lost the sound of the bagpipes; and,
what was yet more unpleasant, when, after searching long

[1] The following account of the skirmish at Clifton is extracted from the manuscript Memoirs of Evan Macpherson of Cluny, Chief of the clan Macpherson, who
had the merit of supporting the principal brunt of that spirited affair. The
Memoirs appear to have been composed about 1755, only ten years after the action
had taken place. They were written in France, where that gallant Chief resided
in exile, which accounts for some Gallicisms which occur in the narrative.

"In the Prince's return from Derby back towards Scotland, my Lord George
Murray, Lieutenant-General, cheerfully charg'd himself with the command of the
rear; a post, which, altho' honourable, was attended with great danger, many
difficulties, and no small fatigue: for the Prince being apprehensive that his retreat to Scotland might be cut off by Marischall Wade, who lay to the northward

in vain, and scrambling through many enclosures, he at length approached the high-road, he learned, from the unwelcome noise of kettle-drums and trumpets, that the English cavalry now occupied it, and consequently were between him and the Highlanders. Precluded, therefore, from advancing in a straight direction, he resolved to avoid the English military, and endeavour to join his friends by making a circuit to the left, for which a beaten path, deviating from the main road in that direction, seemed to afford facilities. The path was muddy, and the night dark and cold ; but even these inconveniences were hardly felt amidst the apprehensions which falling into the hands of the King's forces reasonably excited in his bosom.

After walking about three miles, he at length reached a hamlet. Conscious that the common people were in general unfavourable to the cause he had espoused, yet

of him with an armie much supperior to what H. R. H. had, while the Duke of Comberland with his whole cavalrie followed hard in the rear, was obliged to hasten his marches. It was not, therefore, possible for the artilirie to march so fast as the Prince's army, in the depth of winter, extremely bad weather, and the worst roads in England; so Lord George Murray was obliged often to continue his marches long after it was dark almost every night, while at the same time he had frequent allarms and disturbances from the Duke of Comberland's advanc'd parties. Towards the evening of the twentie-eight December 1745, the Prince entered the town of Penrith, in the Province of Comberland. But as Lord George Murray could not bring up the artilirie so fast as he wou'd have wish'd, he was oblig'd to pass the night six miles short of that town, together with the regiment of MacDonel of Glengarrie, which that day happened to have the arrear guard. The Prince, in order to refresh his armie, and to give My Lord George and the artilirie time to come up, resolved to sejour the 29th at Penrith; so ordered his little army to appear in the morning under arms, in order to be reviewed, and to know in what manner the numbers stood from his haveing entered England. It did not at that time amount to 5000 foot in all, with about 400 cavalrie, compos'd of the noblesse who serv'd as volunteers, part of whom form'd a first troop of guards for the Prince, under the command of My Lord Elchoe, now Comte de Weems, who being proscribed, is presently in France. Another part formed a second troup of guards under the command of My Lord Balmirino, who was beheaded at the Tower of London. A third part serv'd under My Lord le Comte de Kilmarnock, who was likewise beheaded at the Tower. A fourth part serv'd under my Lord Pitsligow, who is also proscribed, which cavalrie, tho' very few in numbers, being all Noblesse, were very brave, and of infinite advantage to the foot, not only in the day of battle, but in serving as advanced guards on the several marches, and in patroling dureing the night on the different roads which led towards the towns where the army happened to quarter.

"While this small army was out in a body on the 29th December, upon a riseing ground to the northward of Penrith, passing review, Mons. de Cluny, with his tribe, was ordered to the Bridge of Clifton, about a mile to southward of Penrith, after having pass'd in review before Mons. Pattullo, who was charged with the inspection of the troops, and was likeways Quarter Master General of the army, and is now in France. They remained under arms at the Bridge, waiting the arrival of My Lord George Murray with the artilirie, whom Mons. de Cluny had orders to cover in passing the bridge. They arrived about sunsett closly pursued by the Duke of Comberland with the whole body of his cavalrie, reckoned upwards of 3000 strong, about a thousand of whom, as near as might be computed, dismounted, in order to cut off the passage of the artilirie towards the bridge, while the Duke and the others remained on horseback in order to attack the rear. My

desirous, if possible, to procure a horse and guide to
Penrith, where he hoped to find the rear, if not the main
body, of the Chevalier's army, he approached the alehouse
of the place. There was a great noise within : he paused
to listen. A round English oath or two, and the burden
of a campaign song, convinced him the hamlet also was
occupied by the Duke of Cumberland's soldiers. Endeavouring to retire from it as softly as possible, and
blessing the obscurity which hitherto he had murmured
against, Waverley groped his way the best he could along
a small paling, which seemed the boundary of some
cottage garden. As he reached the gate of this little
enclosure, his outstretched hand was grasped by that of a
female, whose voice at the same time uttered, "Edward
is't thou, man ?"

Here is some unlucky mistake, thought Edward,
struggling, but gently, to disengage himself.

Lord George Murray advanced, and although he found Mons. de Cluny and his
tribe in good spirits under arms, yet the circumstance appear'd extremely delicate.
The numbers were vastly unequall, and the attack seem'd very dangerous; so My
Lord George declin'd giving orders to such time as he ask'd Mons. de Cluny's
oppinion. 'I will attack them with all my heart,' says Mons. de Cluny, 'if you
order me.' 'I do order it then,' answered My Lord George, and immediately
went on himself along with Mons. de Cluny, and fought sword in hand on foot, at
the head of the single tribe of Macphersons. They in a moment made their way
through a strong hedge of thorns, under the cover whereof the cavalrie had taken
their station, in the strugle of passing which hedge My Lord George Murray, being
dressed *en montagnard*, as all the army were, lost his bonet and wig; so continued
to fight bear-headed during the action. They at first made a brisk discharge
of their fire arms on the enemy, then attacked them with their sabres, and made
a great slaughter a considerable time, which obliged Comberland and his cavalrie
to fly with precipitation and in great confusion; in so much, that if the Prince had
been provided in a sufficient number of cavalrie to have taken advantage of the
disorder, it is beyond question that the Duke of Comberland and the bulk of his
cavalrie had been taken prisoners. By this time it was so dark that it was not
possible to view or number the slain who filled all the ditches which happened to
be on the ground where they stood. But it was computed that, besides those who
went off wounded, upwards of a hundred at least were left on the spot, among
whom was Colonel Honywood, who commanded the dismounted cavalrie, whose
sabre of considerable value Mons. de Cluny brought off and still preserves; and
his tribe lykeways brought off many arms;—the Colonel was afterwards taken up,
and, his wounds being dress'd, with great difficultie recovered. Mons. de Cluny
lost only in the action twelve men, of whom some haveing been only wounded,
fell afterwards into the hands of the enemy, and were sent as slaves to America,
whence several of them returned, and one of them is now in France, a sergeant in
the Regiment of Royal Scots. How soon the accounts of the enemy's approach
had reached the Prince, H. R. H. had immediately ordered Mi-Lord le Comte de
Nairne, Brigadier, who, being proscribed, is now in France, with the three batal-
ions of the Duke of Athol, the batalion of the Duke of Perth, and some other
troups under his command, in order to support Cluny, and to bring off the artilirie.
But the action was intirely over, before the Comte de Nairne, with his command,
cou'd reach nigh to the place. They therefore return'd ali to Penrith, and the
artilirie marched up in good order. Nor did the Duke of Comberland ever afterwards dare to come within a day's march of the Prince and his army dureing the
course of all that retreat, which was conducted with great prudence and safety
when in some manner surrounded by enemies."

"Naen o' thy foun, now, man, or the red cwoats will hear thee; they hae been houlerying and poulerying every ane that past alehouse door this noight to make them drive their waggons and sick loike. Come into feyther's, or they'll do ho a mischief."

A good hint, thought Waverley, following the girl through the little garden into a brick-paved kitchen, where she set herself to kindle a match at an expiring fire, and with the match to light a candle. She had no sooner looked on Edward, than she dropped the light, with a shrill scream of "O feyther, feyther!"

The father, thus invoked, speedily appeared—a sturdy old farmer, in a pair of leather breeches, and boots pulled on without stockings, having just started from his bed; the rest of his dress was only a Westmoreland statesman's robe-de-chambre,—that is, his shirt. His figure was displayed to advantage, by a candle which he bore in his left hand; in his right he brandished a poker.

"What hast ho here, wench?"

"O!" cried the poor girl, almost going off in hysterics, "I thought it was Ned Williams, and it is one of the plaid-men."

"And what was thee ganging to do wi' Ned Williams at this time o' noight?" To this, which was, perhaps, one of the numerous class of questions more easily asked than answered, the rosy-cheeked damsel made no reply, but continued sobbing and wringing her hands.

"And thee, lad, dost ho know that the dragoons be a town? dost ho know that, mon? ad, they'll sliver thee loike a turnip, mon."

"I know my life is in great danger," said Waverley, "but if you can assist me, I will reward you handsomely. I am no Scotchman, but an unfortunate English gentleman."

"Be ho Scot or no," said the honest farmer, "I wish thou hadst kept the other side of the hallan. But since thou art here, Jacob Jopson will betray no man's bluid; and the plaids were gay canny, and did not do so much mischief when they were here yesterday." Accordingly, he set seriously about sheltering and refreshing our hero for the night. The fire was speedily rekindled, but with precaution against its light being seen from without. The jolly yeoman cut a rasher of bacon, which Cicely soon broiled, and her father added a swingeing tankard of his best ale. It was settled, that Edward should remain there till the troops marched in the morning, then hire or buy a horse from the farmer, and, with the best

directions that could be obtained, endeavour to overtake
his friends. A clean, though coarse bed, received him
after the fatigues of this unhappy day.

With the morning arrived the news that the Highlanders had evacuated Penrith, and marched off towards
Carlisle ; that the Duke of Cumberland was in possession
of Penrith, and that detachments of his army covered the
roads in every direction. To attempt to get through un-
discovered would be an act of the most frantic temerity.
Ned Williams (the right Edward) was now called to
council by Cicely and her father. Ned, who perhaps did
not care that his handsome namesake should remain too
long in the same house with his sweetheart, for fear of
fresh mistakes, proposed that Waverley, exchanging his
uniform and plaid for the dress of the country, should go
with him to his father's farm near Ulswater, and remain
in that undisturbed retirement until the military movements in the country should have ceased to render his
departure hazardous. A price was also agreed upon, at
which the stranger might board with Farmer Williams, if
he thought proper, till he could depart with safety. It
was of moderate amount ; the distress of his situation,
among this honest and simple-hearted race, being considered as no reason for increasing their demand.

The necessary articles of dress were accordingly procured, and, by following by-paths, known to the young
farmer, they hoped to escape any unpleasant rencontre.
A recompense for their hospitality was refused peremptorily by old Jopson and his cherry-cheeked daughter ; a
kiss paid the one, and a hearty shake of the hand the
other. Both seemed anxious for their guest's safety, and
took leave of him with kind wishes.

In the course of their route, Edward, with his guide,
traversed those fields which the night before had been the
scene of action. A brief gleam of December's sun shone
sadly on the broad heath, which, towards the spot where
the great north-west road entered the enclosures of Lord
Lonsdale's property, exhibited dead bodies of men and
horses, and the usual companions of war, a number of
carrion-crows, hawks, and ravens.

"And this, then, was thy last field," said Waverley to
himself, his eye filling at the recollection of the many
splendid points of Fergus's character, and of their former
intimacy, all his passions and imperfections forgotten—
"here fell the last Vich Ian Vohr, on a nameless heath ;
and in an obscure night-skirmish was quenched that

ardent spirit, who thought it little to cut a way for his
master to the British throne! Ambition, policy, bravery,
all far beyond their sphere, here learned the fate of
mortals. The sole support, too, of a sister, whose spirit,
as proud and unbending, was even more exalted than
thine own; here ended all thy hopes for Flora, and the
long and valued line which it was thy boast to raise yet
more highly by thy adventurous valour!"

As these ideas pressed on Waverley's mind, he resolved
to go upon the open heath, and search if, among the
slain, he could discover the body of his friend, with the
pious intention of procuring for him the last rites of
sepulture. The timorous young man who accompanied
him remonstrated upon the danger of the attempt, but
Edward was determined. The followers of the camp had
already stripped the dead of all they could carry away;
but the country-people, unused to scenes of blood, had
not yet approached the field of action, though some stood
fearfully gazing at a distance. About sixty or seventy
dragoons lay slain within the first enclosure, upon the
high-road, and on the open moor. Of the Highlanders,
not above a dozen had fallen, chiefly those who, venturing
too far on the moor, could not regain the strong ground.
He could not find the body of Fergus among the slain.
On a little knoll, separated from the others, lay the carcasses of three English dragoons, two horses, and the
page Callum Beg, whose hard skull a trooper's broadsword had, at length, effectually cloven. It was possible
his clan had carried off the body of Fergus; but it was
also possible he had escaped, especially as Evan Dhu,
who would never leave his Chief, was not found among
the dead; or he might be prisoner, and the less formidable denunciation inferred from the appearance of the
Bodach Glas might have proved the true one. The
approach of a party, sent for the purpose of compelling
the country-people to bury the dead, and who had
already assembled several peasants for that purpose, now
obliged Edward to rejoin his guide, who awaited him in
great anxiety and fear under shade of the plantations.

After leaving this field of death, the rest of their
journey was happily accomplished. At the house of
Farmer Williams, Edward passed for a young kinsman,
educated for the church, who was come to reside their till
the civil tumults permitted him to pass through the
country. This silenced suspicion among the kind and
simple yeomanry of Cumberland, and accounted suffi-

ciently for the grave manners and retired habits of the
new guest. The precaution became more necessary than
Waverley had anticipated, as a variety of incidents
prolonged his stay at Fasthwaite, as the farm was called.

A tremendous fall of snow rendered his departure
impossible for more than ten days. When the roads
began to become a little practicable, they successively
received news of the retreat of the Chevalier into Scotland; then, that he had abandoned the frontiers, retiring
upon Glasgow; and that the Duke of Cumberland had
formed the siege of Carlisle. His army, therefore, cut
off all possibility of Waverley's escaping into Scotland in
that direction. On the eastern border, Marshal Wade,
with a large force, was advancing upon Edinburgh, and
all along the frontier, parties of militia, volunteers, and
partisans, were in arms to suppress insurrection, and
apprehend such stragglers from the Highland army as
had been left in England. The surrender of Carlisle, and
the severity with which the rebel garrison were threatened,
soon formed an additional reason against venturing upon
a solitary and hopeless journey through a hostile country
and a large army, to carry the assistance of a single
sword to a cause which seemed altogether desperate.

In this lonely and secluded situation, without the
advantage of company or conversation with men of cultivated minds, the arguments of Colonel Talbot often
recurred to the mind of our hero. A still more anxious
recollection haunted his slumbers—it was the dying look
and gesture of Colonel Gardiner. Most devoutly did he
hope, as the rarely occurring post brought news of
skirmishes with various success, that it might never
again be his lot to draw his sword in civil conflict. Then
his mind turned to the supposed death of Fergus, to the
desolate situation of Flora, and, with yet more tender
recollection, to that of Rose Bradwardine, who was
destitute of the devoted enthusiasm of loyalty, which,
to her friend, hallowed and exalted misfortune. These
reveries he was permitted to enjoy, undisturbed by
queries or interruption; and it was in many a winter
walk by the shores of Ulswater, that he acquired a more
complete mastery of a spirit tamed by adversity, than his
former experience had given him; and that he felt
himself entitled to say firmly, though perhaps with a
sigh, that the romance of his life was ended, and that its
real history had now commenced. He was soon called
upon to justify his pretensions by reason and philosophy.

## CHAPTER LXI.

### A Journey to London.

THE family at Fasthwaite were soon attached to Edward.
He had, indeed, that gentleness and urbanity which almost
universally attracts corresponding kindness ; and to their
simple ideas his learning gave him consequence, and his
sorrows interest. The last he ascribed, evasively, to the
loss of a brother in the skirmish near Clifton ; and in that
primitive state of society, where the ties of affection were
highly deemed of, his continued depression excited sympathy, but not surprise.

In the end of January, his more lively powers were
called out by the happy union of Edward Williams, the
son of his host, with Cicely Jopson. Our hero would not
cloud with sorrow the festivity attending the wedding
of two persons to whom he was so highly obliged. He
therefore exerted himself, danced, sung, played at the
various games of the day, and was the blithest of the
company. The next morning, however, he had more
serious matters to think of.

The clergyman who had married the young couple was
so much pleased with the supposed student of divinity,
that he came next day from Penrith on purpose to pay
him a visit. This might have been a puzzling chapter had
he entered into any examination of our hero's supposed
theological studies ; but fortunately he loved better to
hear and communicate the news of the day. He brought
with him two or three old newspapers, in one of which
Edward found a piece of intelligence that soon rendered
him deaf to every word which the Reverend Mr Twigtythe
was saying upon the news from the north, and the prospect
of the Duke's speedily overtaking and crushing the rebels.
This was an article in these, or nearly these words :

"Died at his house, in Hill Street, Berkeley-Square,
upon the 10th inst. Richard Waverley, Esq., second son of
Sir Giles Waverley of Waverley-Honour, &c. &c. He died
of a lingering disorder, augmented by the unpleasant
predicament of suspicion in which he stood, having been
obliged to find bail to a high amount, to meet an impending
accusation of high-treason. An accusation of the same
grave crime hangs over his elder brother, Sir Everard
Waverley, the representative of that ancient family ; and
we understand the day of his trial will be fixed early in

the next month, unless Edward Waverley, son of the deceased Richard, and heir to the Baronet, shall surrender himself to justice. In that case, we are assured it is his Majesty's gracious purpose to drop further proceedings upon the charge against Sir Everard. This unfortunate young gentleman is ascertained to have been in arms in the Pretender's service, and to have marched along with the Highland troops into England. But he has not been heard of since the skirmish at Clifton, on the 18th December last."

Such was this distracting paragraph.—"Good God!" exclaimed Waverley, "am I then a parricide?—Impossible! My father, who never showed the affection of a father while he lived, cannot have been so much affected by my supposed death as to hasten his own; no, I will not believe it,—it were distraction to entertain for a moment such a horrible idea. But it were, if possible, worse than parricide to suffer any danger to hang over my noble and generous uncle, who has ever been more to me than a father, if such evil can be averted by any sacrifice on my part!"

While these reflections passed like the stings of scorpions through Waverley's sensorium, the worthy divine was startled in a long disquisition on the battle of Falkirk by the ghastliness which they communicated to his looks, and asked him if he was ill? Fortunately the bride, all smirk and blush, had just entered the room. Mrs Williams was none of the brightest of women, but she was good-natured, and readily concluding that Edward had been shocked by disagreeable news in the papers, interfered so judiciously, that, without exciting suspicion, she drew off Mr Twig-tythe's attention, and engaged it until he soon after took his leave. Waverley then explained to his friends, that he was under the necessity of going to London with as little delay as possible.

One cause of delay, however, did occur, to which Waverley had been very little accustomed. His purse, though well stocked when he first went to Tully-Veolan, had not been reinforced since that period; and although his life since had not been of a nature to exhaust it hastily, for he had lived chiefly with his friends or with the army, yet he found, that, after settling with his kind landlord, he should be too poor to encounter the expense of travelling post. The best course, therefore, seemed to be, to get into the great north road about Borough-bridge, and there take a place in the Northern Diligence, a huge old-fashioned tub, drawn by three horses, which completed the journey from Edinburgh to London (God willing, as the advertisement expressed it) in three weeks. Our hero, therefore, took an affectionate farewell of his Cumberland friends, whose kindness he promised never to forget, and tacitly hoped one day to acknowledge, by substantial proofs of gratitude. After some petty difficulties and vexatious delays, and after putting his dress into a shape better befitting his rank, though perfectly plain and simple, he accomplished crossing the country, and found himself in the desired vehicle *vis-à-vis* to Mrs Nosebag, the lady of Lieutenant Nosebag, adjutant and riding-master of the —— dragoons, a jolly woman of about fifty, wearing a blue habit, faced with scarlet, and grasping a silver-mounted horse-whip.

This lady was one of those active members of society who take upon them *faire le frais de conversation*. She had just returned from the north, and informed Edward how nearly her regiment had cut the petticoat people into ribands at Falkirk, "only somehow there was one of those nasty, awkward marshes, that they are never without in Scotland, I think, and so our poor dear little regiment suffered something, as my Nosebag says, in that unsatisfactory affair. You, sir, have served in the dragoons?" Waverley was taken so much at unawares, that he acquiesced.

"O, I knew it at once; I saw you were military from your air, and I was sure you could be none of the foot-wobblers, as my Nosebag calls them. What regiment, pray?" Here was a delightful question. Waverley, however, justly concluded that this good lady had the whole army-list by heart; and, to avoid detection by adhering to truth, answered, "Gardiner's dragoons, ma'am; but I have retired some time."

"O aye, those as won the race at the battle of Preston, as my Nosebag says. Pray, sir, were you there?"

"I was so unfortunate, madam," he replied, "as to witness that engagement."

"And that was a misfortune that few of Gardiner's stood to witness, I believe, sir ha! ha! ha! I beg your pardon; but a soldier's wife loves a joke."

Devil confound you, thought Waverley; what infernal luck has penned me up with this inquisitive hag!

Fortunately the good lady did not stick long to one subject. "We are coming to Ferrybridge, now," she said, "where there was a party of *ours* left to support the

beadles, and constables, and justices, and these sort of
creatures that are examining papers and stopping rebels,
and all that." They were hardly in the inn before she
dragged Waverley to the window, exclaiming, "Yonder
comes Corporal Bridoon, of our poor dear troop; he's
coming with the constable man; Bridoon's one of my
lambs, as Nosebag calls 'em. Come, Mr —— a—a,—pray,
what's your name, sir?"

"Butler, ma'am," said Waverley, resolved rather to
make free with the name of a former fellow-officer, than
run the risk of detection by inventing one not to be found
in the regiment.

"O, you got a troop lately, when that shabby fellow,
Waverley, went over to the rebels? Lord, I wish our old
cross Captain Crump would go over to the rebels, that
Nosebag might get the troop!—Lord, what can Bridoon
be standing swinging on the bridge for? I'll be hanged
if he a'nt hazy, as Nosebag says.—Come, sir, as you and I
belong to the service, we'll go put the rascal in mind of
his duty."

Waverley, with feelings more easily conceived than
described, saw himself obliged to follow this doughty
female commander. The gallant trooper was as like a
lamb as a drunk corporal of dragoons, about six feet high,
with very broad shoulders, and very thin legs, not to
mention a great scar across his nose, could well be. Mrs
Nosebag addressed him with something which, if not an
oath, sounded very like one, and commanded him to
attend to his duty. "You be d—d for a ——," commenced
the gallant cavalier; but, looking up in order to suit the
action to the words, and also to enforce the epithet which
he meditated, with an adjective applicable to the party,
he recognised the speaker, made his military salam, and
altered his tone.—"Lord love your handsome face, Madam
Nosebag, is it you? Why, if a poor fellow does happen
to fire a slug of a morning, I am sure you were never the
lady to bring him to harm."

. "Well, you rascallion, go, mind your duty; this gentleman and I belong to the service; but be sure you look
after that shy cock in the slouched hat that sits in the
corner of the coach. I believe he's one of the rebels in
disguise."

"D—n her gooseberry wig," said the corporal, when
she was out of hearing, "that gimlet-eyed jade—mother
adjutant, as we call her—is a greater plague to the
regiment than prevot-marshal, sergeant-major, and old

Hubble-de-Shuff, the colonel, into the bargain,—Come.
Master Constable, let's see if this shy cock, as she calls
him, (who, by the way, was a Quaker from Leeds, with
whom Mrs Nosebag had had some tart argument on the
legality of bearing arms,) will stand godfather to a sup of
brandy, for your Yorkshire ale is cold on my stomach."

The vivacity of this good lady, as it helped Edward out
of this scrape, was like to have drawn him into one or
two others. In every town where they stopped, she
wished to examine the corps de garde if there was one,
and once very narrowly missed introducing Waverley to
a recruiting-sergeant of his own regiment. Then she
Captain'd and Butler'd him till he was almost mad with
vexation and anxiety; and never was he more rejoiced
in his life at the termination of a journey, than when
the arrival of the coach in London freed him from the
attentions of Madam Nosebag.


## CHAPTER LXII.

### *What's to be done next?*

It was twilight when they arrived in town; and having
shaken off his companions, and walked through a good
many streets, to avoid the possibility of being traced by
them, Edward took a hackney-coach and drove to Colonel
Talbot's house, in one of the principal squares at the
west end of the town. That gentleman, by the death of
relations, had succeeded since his marriage to a large
fortune, possessed considerable political interest, and
lived in what is called great style.

When Waverley knocked at his door, he found it at
first difficult to procure admittance, but at length was
shown into an apartment where the Colonel was at table.
Lady Emily, whose very beautiful features were still
pallid from indisposition, sate opposite to him. The
instant he heard Waverley's voice, he started up and
embraced him. "Frank Stanley, my dear boy, how d'ye
do?—Emily, my love, this is young Stanley."

The blood started to the lady's cheek as she gave Waverley a reception, in which courtesy was mingled with
kindness, while her trembling hand and faltering voice
showed how much she was startled and discomposed.
Dinner was hastily replaced, and while Waverley was

engaged in refreshing himself, the Colonel proceeded—
"I wonder you have come here, Frank; the Doctors tell
me the air of London is very bad for your complaints.
You should not have risked it. But I am delighted to see
you, and so is Emily, though I fear we must not reckon
upon your staying long."

"Some particular business brought me up," muttered
Waverley.

"I supposed so, but I sha'nt allow you to stay long,—
Spontoon," (to an elderly military-looking servant out of
livery,) "take away these things, and answer the bell
yourself, if I ring. Don't let any of the other fellows
disturb us—My nephew and I have business to talk
of."

When the servants had retired, "In the name of God,
Waverley, what has brought you here? It may be as
much as your life is worth."

"Dear Mr Waverley," said Lady Emily, "to whom I
owe so much more than acknowledgments can ever pay,
how could you be so rash?"

"My father—my uncle—this paragraph,"—he handed
the paper to Colonel Talbot.

"I wish to Heaven these scoundrels were condemned to
be squeezed to death in their own presses," said Talbot.
"I am told there are not less than a dozen of their papers
now published in town, and no wonder that they are
obliged to invent lies to find sale for their journals. It is
true, however, my dear Edward, that you have lost your
father; but as to this flourish of his unpleasant situation
having grated upon his spirits, and hurt his health—the
truth is—for though it is harsh to say so now, yet it will
relieve your mind from the idea of weighty responsibility
—the truth then is, that Mr Richard Waverley, through
this whole business, showed great want of sensibility,
both to your situation and that of your uncle; and the
last time I saw him, he told me, with great glee, that as I
was so good as take charge of your interests, he had
thought it best to patch up a separate negotiation for
himself, and make his peace with government through
some channels which former connections left still open to
him."

"And my uncle, my dear uncle?"

"Is in no danger whatever. It is true (looking at the
date of the paper) there was a foolish report some time
ago to the purport here quoted, but it is entirely false.
Sir Everard is gone down to Waverley-Honour, freed from

all uneasiness, unless upon your own account. But you are in peril yourself—your name is in every proclamation —warrants are out to apprehend you. How and when did you come here?"

Edward told his story at length, suppressing his quarrel with Fergus; for, being himself partial to Highlanders, he did not wish to give any advantage to the Colonel's national prejudice against them.

"Are you sure it was your friend Glen's foot-boy you saw dead in Clifton Moor?"

"Quite positive."

"Then that little limb of the devil has cheated the gallows, for cut-throat was written in his face; though" (turning to Lady Emily) "it was a very handsome face too.—But for you, Edward, I wish you would go down again to Cumberland, or rather I wish you had never stirred from thence, for there is an embargo in all the seaports, and a strict search for the adherents of the Pretender; and the tongue of that confounded woman will wag in her head like the clack of a mill, till somehow or other she will detect Captain Butler to be a feigned personage."

"Do you know anything," asked Waverley, "of my fellow-traveller?"

"Her husband was my sergeant-major for six years; she was a buxom widow, with a little money—he married her—was steady, and got on by being a good drill. I must send Spontoon to see what she is about; he will find her out among the old regimental connections. To-morrow you must be indisposed, and keep your room from fatigue. Lady Emily is to be your nurse, and Spontoon and I your attendants. You bear the name of a near relation of mine, whom none of my present people ever saw, except Spontoon, so there will be no immediate danger. So pray feel your head ache and your eyes grow heavy as soon as possible, that you may be put upon the sick list; and, Emily, do you order an apartment for Frank Stanley, with all the attentions which an invalid may require."

In the morning the Colonel visited his guest. "Now," said he, "I have some good news for you. Your reputation as a gentleman and officer is effectually cleared of neglect of duty, and accession to the mutiny in Gardiner's regiment. I have had a correspondence on this subject with a very zealous friend of yours, your Scottish parson, Morton; his first letter was addressed to Sir Everard; but I relieved the good Baronet of the trouble of answer-

ing it.   You must know that your free-booting acquaintance, Donald of the Cave, has at length fallen into the
hands of the Philistines.   He was driving off the cattle of a
certain proprietor, called Killan—something or other——"

"Killancureit ?"

"The same—now the gentleman being, it seems, a great
farmer, and having a special value for his breed of cattle,
being, moreover, rather of a timid disposition, had got a
party of soldiers to protect his property.   So Donald run
his head unawares into the lion's mouth, and was defeated
and made prisoner.   Being ordered for execution, his
conscience was assailed on the one hand by a Catholic
priest, on the other by your friend Morton.   He repulsed the Catholic chiefly on account of the doctrine of
extreme unction, which this economical gentleman considered as an excessive waste of oil.   So his conversion
from a state of impenitence fell to Mr Morton's share,
who, I dare say, acquitted himself excellently, though, I
suppose, Donald made but a queer kind of Christian after
all.   He confessed, however, before a magistrate, one
Major Melville, who seems to have been a correct, friendly
sort of person, his full intrigue with Houghton, explaining
particularly how it was carried on, and fully acquitting
you of the least accession to it.   He also mentioned his
rescuing you from the hands of the volunteer officer, and
sending you, by orders of the Pret—Chevalier, I mean—as
a prisoner to Doune, from whence he understood you
were carried prisoner to Edinburgh.   These are particulars which cannot but tell in your favour.   He hinted
that he had been employed to deliver and protect you,
and rewarded for doing so ; but he would not confess by
whom, alleging, that though he would not have minded
breaking any ordinary oath to satisfy the curiosity of Mr
Morton, to whose pious admonitions he owed so much, yet,
in the present case, he had been sworn to silence upon
the edge of his dirk,[1] which, it seems, constituted, in his
opinion, an inviolable obligation."

"And what is become of him ?"

"Oh, he was hanged at Stirling after the rebels raised
the siege, with his lieutenant, and four plaids besides ;
he having the advantage of a gallows more lofty than his
friends."

"Well, I have little cause either to regret or rejoice at
his death ; and yet he has done me both good and harm
to a very considerable extent."

[1] Note 23.   Oath upon the Dirk.

"His confession, at least, will serve you materially, since it wipes from your character all those suspicions which gave the accusation against you a complexion of a nature different from that with which so many unfortunate gentlemen, now, or lately, in arms against the government, may be justly charged. Their treason—I must give it its name, though you participate in its guilt—is an action arising from mistaken virtue, and therefore cannot be classed as a disgrace, though it be doubtless highly criminal. Where the guilty are so numerous, clemency must be extended to far the greater number; and I have little doubt of procuring a remission for you, providing we can keep you out of the claws of justice, till she has selected and gorged upon her victims; for in this, as in other cases, it will be according to the vulgar proverb, 'First come, first served.' Besides, government are desirous at present to intimidate the English Jacobites, among whom they can find few examples for punishment. This is a vindictive and timid feeling which will soon wear off, for, of all nations, the English are least blood-thirsty by nature. But it exists at present, and you must, therefore, be kept out of the way in the meantime."

Now entered Spontoon with an anxious countenance. By his regimental acquaintances, he had traced out Madam Nosebag, and found her full of ire, fuss, and fidget, at discovery of an impostor, who had travelled from the north with her under the assumed name of Captain Butler of Gardiner's dragoons. She was going to lodge an information on the subject, to have him sought for as an emissary of the Pretender; but Spontoon, (an old soldier,) while he pretended to approve, contrived to make her delay her intention. No time, however, was to be lost: the accuracy of this good dame's description might probably lead to the discovery that Waverley was the pretended Captain Butler; an identification fraught with danger to Edward, perhaps to his uncle, and even to Colonel Talbot. Which way to direct his course was now, therefore, the question.

"To Scotland," said Waverley.

"To Scotland?" said the Colonel; "with what purpose? not to engage again with the rebels, I hope?"

"No—I considered my campaign ended, when, after all my efforts, I could not rejoin them; and now, by all accounts, they are gone to make a winter campaign in the Highlands, where such adherents as I am would rather be burdensome than useful. Indeed, it seems

likely that they only prolong the war to place the
Chevalier's person out of danger, and then to make some
terms for themselves. To burden them with my presence
would merely add another party, whom they would not
give up, and could not defend. I understand they left
almost all their English adherents in garrison at Carlisle,
for that very reason:—and on a more general view,
Colonel, to confess the truth, though it may lower me in
your opinion, I am heartily tired of the trade of war, and
am, as Fletcher's Humorous Lieutenant says, 'even as
weary of this fighting'"———

"Fighting! pooh, what have you seen but a skirmish
or two?—Ah! if you saw war on the grand scale—sixty
or a hundred thousand men in the field on each side!"

"I am not at all curious, Colonel—Enough, says our
homely proverb, is as good as a feast. The plumed troops
and the big war used to enchant me in poetry; but the
night marches, vigils, couches under the wintry sky, and
such accompaniments of the glorious trade, are not at all
to my taste in practice:—then for dry blows, I had *my* fill
of fighting at Clifton, where I escaped by a hair's-breadth
half-a-dozen times; and you, I should think"——— He
stopped.

"Had enough of it at Preston? you mean to say,"
answered the Colonel, laughing; "but 'tis my vocation, Hal."

"It is not mine though," said Waverley; "and having
honourably got rid of the sword, which I drew only as a
volunteer, I am quite satisfied with my military experience,
and shall be in no hurry to take it up again."

"I am very glad you are of that mind,—but then what
would you do in the north?"

"In the first place, there are some seaports on the
eastern coast of Scotland still in the hands of the
Chevalier's friends; should I gain any of them, I can
easily embark for the Continent."

"Good—your second reason?"

"Why, to speak the very truth, there is a person in
Scotland upon whom I now find my happiness depends
more than I was always aware, and about whose situation
I am very anxious."

"Then Emily was right, and there is a love affair in the
case after all?—And which of these two pretty Scotch-
women, whom you insisted upon my admiring, is the
distinguished fair? not Miss Glen—— I hope."

"No."

"Ah, pass for the other; simplicity may be improved,

but pride and conceit never. Well, I don't discourage
you; I think it will please Sir Everard, from what he said
when I jested with him about it; only I hope that
intolerable papa, with his brogue, and his snuff, and his
Latin, and his insufferable long stories about the Duke of
Berwick, will find it necessary hereafter to be an inhabitant of foreign parts. But as to the daughter, though
I think you might find as fitting a match in England, yet
if your heart be really set upon this Scotch rose-bud, why
the Baronet has a great opinion of her father and of his
family, and he wishes much to see you married and settled,
both for your own sake and for that of the three ermines
passant, which may otherwise pass away altogether. But
I will bring you his mind fully upon the subject, since
you are debarred correspondence for the present, for I
think you will not be long in Scotland before me."

"Indeed! and what can induce you to think of returning to Scotland? No relenting longings towards the land
of mountains and floods, I am afraid."

"None, on my word; but Emily's health is now, thank
God, re-established, and, to tell you the truth, I have
little hopes of concluding the business which I have at
present most at heart, until I can have a personal interview with his Royal Highness the Commander-in-Chief;
for, as Fluellen says, 'the duke doth love me well, and I
thank heaven I have deserved some love at his hands.'
I am now going out for an hour or two to arrange matters
for your departure; your liberty extends to the next room,
Lady Emily's parlour, where you will find her when you
are disposed for music, reading, or conversation. We
have taken measures to exclude all servants but Spontoon,
who is as true as steel."

In about two hours Colonel Talbot returned, and found
his young friend conversing with his lady; she pleased
with his manners and information, and he delighted at
being restored, though but for a moment, to the society
of his own rank, from which he had been for some time
excluded.

"And now," said the Colonel, "hear my arrangements,
for there is little time to lose. This youngster, Edward
Waverley, alias Williams, alias Captain Butler, must
continue to pass by his fourth *alias* of Francis Stanley,
my nephew: he shall set out to-morrow for the North,
and the chariot shall take him the first two stages. Spontoon shall then attend him; and they shall ride post as
far as Huntingdon; and the presence of Spontoon, well

known on the road as my servant, will check all disposition to enquiry. At Huntingdon you will meet the
real Frank Stanley. He is studying at Cambridge; but,
a little while ago, doubtful if Emily's health would
permit me to go down to the North myself, I procured
him a passport from the secretary of state's office to go in
my stead. As he went chiefly to look after you, his
journey is now unnecessary. He knows your story; you
will dine together at Huntingdon; and perhaps your wise
heads may hit upon some plan for removing or diminishing
the danger of your farther progress northward. And now,
(taking out a morocco case,) let me put you in funds for
the campaign."

"I am ashamed, my dear Colonel,"——

"Nay," said Colonel Talbot; "you should command my
purse in any event; but this money is your own. Your
father, considering the chance of your being attainted,
left me his trustee for your advantage. So that you are
worth above £15,000, besides Brerewood Lodge—a very
independent person, I promise you. There are bills here
for £200; any larger sum you may have, or credit abroad,
as soon as your motions require it."

The first use which occurred to Waverley of his newly-
acquired wealth, was to write to honest Farmer Jopson,
requesting his acceptance of a silver tankard on the part
of his friend Williams, who had not forgotten the night
of the eighteenth December last. He begged him at the
same time carefully to preserve for him his Highland
garb and accoutrements, particularly the arms, curious in
themselves, and to which the friendship of the donors
gave additional value. Lady Emily undertook to find
some suitable token of remembrance, likely to flatter the
vanity and please the taste of Mrs Williams; and the
Colonel, who was a kind of farmer, promised to send the
Ulswater patriarch an excellent team of horses for cart
and plough.

One happy day Waverley spent in London; and,
travelling in the manner projected, he met with Frank
Stanley at Huntingdon. The two young men were
acquainted in a minute.

"I can read my uncle's riddle," said Stanley; "the
cautious old soldier did not care to hint to me that I
might hand over to you this passport, which I have no
occasion for; but if it should afterwards come out as the
rattle-pated trick of a young Cantab, *cela ne tire à rien*.
You are therefore to be Francis Stanley, with this pass-

port." This proposal appeared in effect to alleviate a great part of the difficulties which Edward must otherwise have encountered at every turn; and accordingly he scrupled not to avail himself of it, the more especially as he had discarded all political purposes from his present journey, and could not be accused of furthering machinations against the government while travelling under protection of the secretary's passport.

The day passed merrily away. The young student was inquisitive about Waverley's campaigns, and the manners of the Highlands, and Edward was obliged to satisfy his curiosity by whistling a pibroch, dancing a strathspey, and singing a Highland song. The next morning Stanley rode a stage northward with his new friend, and parted from him with great reluctance, upon the remonstrances of Spontoon, who, accustomed to submit to discipline, was rigid in enforcing it.

# CHAPTER LXIII.

## *Desolation.*

WAVERLEY riding post, as was the usual fashion of the period, without any adventure save one or two queries, which the talisman of his passport sufficiently answered, reached the borders of Scotland. Here he heard the tidings of the decisive battle of Culloden. It was no more than he had long expected, though the success at Falkirk had thrown a faint and setting gleam over the arms of the Chevalier. Yet it came upon him like a shock, by which he was for a time altogether unmanned. The generous, the courteous, the noble-minded Adventurer, was then a fugitive, with a price upon his head; his adherents, so brave, so enthusiastic, so faithful, were dead, imprisoned, or exiled. Where, now, was the exalted and high-souled Fergus, if, indeed, he had survived the night at Clifton? Where the pure-hearted and primitive Baron of Bradwardine, whose foibles seemed foils to set off the disinterestedness of his disposition, the genuine goodness of his heart, and his unshaken courage? Those who clung for support to these fallen columns, Rose and Flora, where were they to be sought, and in what distress must not the loss of their natural protectors have involved them? Of Flora, he thought with the regard of a brother for a sister;

of Rose, with a sensation yet more deep and tender. It might be still his fate to supply the want of those guardians they had lost. Agitated by these thoughts he precipitated his journey.

When he arrived in Edinburgh, where his inquiries must necessarily commence, he felt the full difficulty of his situation. Many inhabitants of that city had seen and known him as Edward Waverley; how, then, could he avail himself of a passport as Francis Stanley? He resolved, therefore, to avoid all company, and to move northward as soon as possible. He was, however, obliged to wait a day or two in expectation of a letter from Colonel Talbot, and he was also to leave his own address, under his feigned character, at a place agreed upon. With this latter purpose he sallied out in the dusk through the well-known streets, carefully shunning observation, but in vain: one of the first persons whom he met at once recognised him. It was Mrs Flockhart, Fergus Mac-Ivor's good-humoured landlady.

"Gude guide us, Mr Waverley, is this you? na, ye needna be feared for me. I wad betray nae gentleman in your circumstances—eh, lack a-day! lack a-day! here's a change o' markets; how merry Colonel Mac-Ivor and you used to be in our house!" And the good-natured widow shed a few natural tears. As there was no resisting her claim of acquaintance, Waverley acknowledged it with a good grace, as well as the danger of his own situation. "As it's near the darkening, sir, wad ye just step in by to our house, and tak a dish o' tea? and I am sure if ye like to sleep in the little room, I wad tak care ye are no disturbed, and naebody wad ken ye; for Kate and Matty, the limmers,[1] gaed aff wi' twa o' Hawley's dragoons, and I hae twa new queans instead o' them."

Waverley accepted her invitation, and engaged her lodging for a night or two, satisfied he should be safer in the house of this simple creature than anywhere else. When he entered the parlour, his heart swelled to see Fergus's bonnet, with the white cockade, hanging beside the little mirror.

"Ay," said Mrs Flockhart, sighing, as she observed the direction of his eyes, "the puir Colonel bought a new ane just the day before they marched, and I winna let them tak that ane doun, but just to brush it ilka day mysell; and whiles I look at it till I just think I hear him cry to Callum to bring him his bonnet, as he used to

[1] Loose mannered women.

do when he was ganging out.—It's unco silly[1]—the neighbours ca' me a Jacobite—but they may say their say—I am sure it's no for that—but he was as kind-hearted a gentleman as ever lived, and as weel-fa'rd too. Oh, d'ye ken, sir, when he is to suffer?"

"Suffer! Good heaven!—Why, where is he?"

"Eh, Lord's sake! d'ye no ken? The poor Hieland body, Dugald Mahony, cam here a while syne, wi' ane o' his arms cuttit off, and a sair clour[2] in the head—ye'll mind Dugald, he carried aye an axe on his shouther—and he cam here just begging, as I may say, for something to eat. Aweel, he tauld us the Chief, as they ca'd him, (but I aye ca' him the Colonel,) and Ensign Maccombich, that ye mind weel, were ta'en somewhere beside the English border, when it was sae dark that his folk never missed him till it was ower late, and they were like to gang clean daft.[3] And he said that little Callum Beg, (he was a bauld mischievous callant that,) and your honour, were killed that same night in the tuilzie,[4] and mony mae braw[5] men. But he grat[6] when he spak o' the Colonel, ye never saw the like. And now the word gangs the Colonel is to be tried, and to suffer wi' them that were ta'en at Carlisle."

"And his sister?"

"Ay, that they ca'd the Lady Flora—weel, she's away up to Carlisle to him, and lives wi' some grand Papist lady thereabouts to be near him."

"And," said Edward, "the other young lady?"

"Whilk other? I ken only of ae sister the Colonel had."

"I mean Miss Bradwardine," said Edward.

"Ou, ay; the laird's daughter," said his landlady. "She was a very bonny lassie, poor thing, but far shyer than Lady Flora."

"Where is she, for God's sake?"

"Ou, wha kens where ony o' them is now? puir things, they're sair ta'en doun for their white cockades and their white roses; but she gaed north to her father's in Perthshire, when the government troops cam back to Edinbro'. There was some pretty men amang them, and ane Major Whacker was quartered on me, a very ceevil gentleman,—but O, Mr Waverley, he was naething sae weel fa'rd as the puir Colonel."

"Do you know what is become of Miss Bradwardine's father?"

"The auld laird? na, naebody kens that; but they say
he fought very hard in that bluidy battle at Inverness;
and Deacon Clank, the white-iron smith, says, that the
government folk are sair agane him for having been *out*
twice; and troth he might hae ta'en warning, but there's
nae fule like an auld fule—the puir Colonel was only out
ance."

Such conversation contained almost all the good-natured
widow knew of the fate of her late lodgers and acquaintances; but it was enough to determine Edward, at all
hazards, to proceed instantly to Tully-Veolan, where he
concluded he should see, or at least hear something of
Rose.  He therefore left a letter for Colonel Talbot at the
place agreed upon, signed by his assumed name, and
giving for his address the post-town next to the Baron's
residence.

From Edinburgh to Perth he took post-horses, resolving
to make the rest of his journey on foot; a mode of
travelling to which he was partial, and which had the
advantage of permitting a deviation from the road when
he saw parties of military at a distance.  His campaign
had considerably strengthened his constitution, and improved his habits of enduring fatigue.  His baggage he
sent before him as opportunity occurred.

As he advanced northward, the traces of war became
visible.  Broken carriages, dead horses, unroofed cottages,
trees felled for palisades, and bridges destroyed, or only
partially repaired,—all indicated the movements of hostile
armies.  In those places where the gentry were attached
to the Stewart cause, their houses seemed dismantled or
deserted, the usual course of what may be called orna-
mental labour was totally interrupted, and the inhabitants
were seen gliding about, with fear, sorrow, and dejection
on their faces.

It was evening when he approached the village of
Tully-Veolan, with feelings and sentiments—how different
from those which attended his first entrance!  Then, life
was so new to him, that a dull or disagreeable day was
one of the greatest misfortunes which his imagination
anticipated, and it seemed to him that his time ought only
to be consecrated to elegant or amusing study, and relieved by social or youthful frolic.  Now, how changed!
how saddened, yet how elevated was his character, within
the course of a very few months !  Danger and misfortune
are rapid, though severe teachers.  "A sadder and a
wiser man," he felt, in internal confidence and mental

dignity, a compensation for the gay dreams which, in his case, experience had so rapidly dissolved.

As he approached the village, he saw, with surprise and anxiety, that a party of soldiers were quartered near it, and, what was worse, that they seemed stationary there. This he conjectured from a few tents which he beheld glimmering upon what was called the Common Moor. To avoid the risk of being stopped and questioned in a place where he was so likely to be recognised, he made a large circuit, altogether avoiding the hamlet, and approaching the upper gate of the avenue by a by-path well known to him. A single glance announced that great changes had taken place. One half of the gate, entirely destroyed, and split up for firewood, lay in piles, ready to be taken away; the other swung uselessly about upon its loosened hinges. The battlements above the gate were broken and thrown down, and the carved Bears, which were said to have done sentinel's duty upon the top for centuries, now, hurled from their posts, lay among the rubbish. The avenue was cruelly wasted. Several large trees were felled and left lying across the path; and the cattle of the villagers, and the more rude hoofs of dragoon horses, had poached into black mud the verdant turf, which Waverley had so much admired.

Upon entering the courtyard, Edward saw the fears realized which these circumstances had excited. The place had been sacked by the King's troops, who, in wanton mischief, had even attempted to burn it; and though the thickness of the walls had resisted the fire, unless to a partial extent, the stables and out-houses were totally consumed. The towers and pinnacles of the main building were scorched and blackened; the pavement of the court broken and shattered; the doors torn down entirely, or hanging by a single hinge; the windows dashed in and demolished, and the court strewed with articles of furniture broken into fragments. The accessaries of ancient distinction, to which the Baron, in the pride of his heart, had attached so much importance and veneration, were treated with peculiar contumely. The fountain was demolished, and the spring, which had supplied it, now flooded the courtyard. The stone basin seemed to be destined for a drinking-trough for cattle, from the manner in which it was arranged upon the ground. The whole tribe of Bears, large and small, had experienced as little favour as those at the head of the avenue, and one or two of the family pictures, which

seemed to have served as targets for the soldiers, lay on
the ground in tatters. With an aching heart, as may
well be imagined, Edward viewed this wreck of a mansion
so respected. But his anxiety to learn the fate of the
proprietors, and his fears as to what that fate might be,
increased with every step. When he entered upon the
terrace, new scenes of desolation were visible. The balustrade was broken down, the walls destroyed, the borders
overgrown with weeds, and the fruit-trees cut down or
grubbed up. In one copartment of this old-fashioned
garden were two immense horse-chestnut trees, of whose
size the Baron was particularly vain: too lazy, perhaps, to
cut them down, the spoilers, with malevolent ingenuity,
had mined them, and placed a quantity of gunpowder in
the cavity. One had been shivered to pieces by the explosion, and the fragments lay scattered around, encum-
bering the ground it had so long shadowed. The other
mine had been more partial in its effect. About one-
fourth of the trunk of the tree was torn from the mass,
which, mutilated and defaced on the one side, still spread
on the other its ample and undiminished boughs.[1]

Amid these general marks of ravage, there were some
which more particularly addressed the feelings of Waverley. Viewing the front of the building, thus wasted and
defaced, his eyes naturally sought the little balcony
which more properly belonged to Rose's apartment—her
*troisième*, or rather *cinquième étage*. It was easily discovered, for beneath it lay the stage-flowers and shrubs,
with which it was her pride to decorate it, and which had
been hurled from the bartizan : several of her books were
mingled with broken flower-pots and other remnants.
Among these, Waverley distinguished one of his own, a
small copy of Ariosto, and gathered it as a treasure,
though wasted by the wind and rain.

While plunged in the sad reflections which the scene
excited, he was looking around for some one who might
explain the fate of the inhabitants, he heard a voice from
the interior of the building singing, in well-remembered
accents, an old Scottish song :

> "They came upon us in the night,
> And brake my bower and slew my knight:
> My servants a' for life did flee,
> And left us in extremity.

---

[1] A pair of chestnut trees, destroyed, the one entirely, and the other in part, by
such a mischievous and wanton act of revenge, grew at Invergarry Castle, the
fastness of MacDonald of Glengarry. (S.)

They slew my knight, to me sae dear;
They slew my knight and drave his gear; [1]
The moon may set, the sun may rise,
But a deadly sleep has closed his eyes."

Alas, thought Edward, is it thou? Poor helpless being, art thou alone left, to gibber and moan, and fill with thy wild and unconnected scraps of minstrelsy the halls that protected thee!—He then called, first low, and then louder, "Davie—Davie Gellatley!"

The poor simpleton showed himself from among the ruins of a sort of green-house, that once terminated what was called the Terrace-Walk, but at first sight of a stranger retreated, as if in terror. Waverley, remembering his habits, began to whistle a tune to which he was partial, which Davie had expressed great pleasure in listening to, and had picked up from him by the ear. Our hero's minstrelsy no more equalled that of Blondel, than poor Davie resembled Cœur de Lion ; but the melody had the same effect, of producing recognition. Davie again stole from his lurking-place, but timidly, while Waverley, afraid of frightening him, stood making the most encouraging signals he could devise.—"It's his ghaist," muttered Davie ; yet, coming nearer, he seemed to acknowledge his living acquaintance. The poor fool himself appeared the ghost of what he had been. The peculiar dress in which he had been attired in better days, showed only miserable rags of its whimsical finery, the lack of which was oddly supplied by the remnants of tapestried hangings, window-curtains, and shreds of pictures, with which he had bedizened his tatters. His face, too, had lost its vacant and careless air, and the poor creature looked hollow-eyed, meagre, half-starved, and nervous to a pitiable degree. After long hesitation, he at length approached Waverley with some confidence, stared him sadly in the face, and said, "A' dead and gane—a' dead and gane."

"Who are dead?" said Waverley, forgetting the incapacity of Davie to hold any connected discourse.

"Baron—and Bailie—and Saunders Saunderson—and Lady Rose, that sang sae sweet—A' dead and gane—dead and gane ;

But follow, follow me,
While glowworms light the lea,
I'll show ye where the dead should be—

[1] The first three couplets are from an old ballad, called the Border Widow's Lament. (S.)

Each in his shroud,
  While winds pipe loud,
    And the red moon peeps dim through the cloud.
Follow, follow me;
  Brave should he be
  That treads by night the dead man's lea."

With these words, chanted in a wild and earnest tone, he made a sign to Waverley to follow him, and walked rapidly towards the bottom of the garden, tracing the bank of the stream, which, it may be remembered, was its eastern boundary. Edward, over whom an involuntary shuddering stole at the import of his words, followed him in some hope of an explanation. As the house was evidently deserted, he could not expect to find among the ruins any more rational informer.

Davie, walking very fast, soon reached the extremity of the garden, and scrambled over the ruins of the wall that once had divided it from the wooded glen in which the old Tower of Tully-Veolan was situated. He then jumped down into the bed of the stream, and, followed by Waverley, proceeded at a great pace, climbing over some fragments of rock, and turning with difficulty round others. They passed beneath the ruins of the castle; Waverley followed, keeping up with his guide with difficulty, for the twilight began to fall. Following the descent of the stream a little lower, he totally lost him, but a twinkling light, which he now discovered among the tangled copse-wood and bushes, seemed a surer guide. He soon pursued a very uncouth path; and by its guidance at length reached the door of a wretched hut. A fierce barking of dogs was at first heard, but it stilled at his approach. A voice sounded from within, and he held it most prudent to listen before he advanced.

"Wha hast thou brought here, thou unsonsy villain, thou?" said an old woman, apparently in great indignation. He heard Davie Gellatley, in answer, whistle a part of the tune by which he had recalled himself to the simpleton's memory, and had now no hesitation to knock at the door. There was a dead silence instantly within, except the deep growling of the dogs; and he next heard the mistress of the hut approach the door, not probably for the sake of undoing a latch, but of fastening a bolt. To prevent this, Waverley lifted the latch himself.

In front was an old wretched-looking woman, exclaiming, "Wha comes into folk's houses in this gate, at this time o' the night?" On one side, two grim and half-starved deer greyhounds laid aside their ferocity at his appearance and seemed to recognise him. On the other side, half concealed by the open door, yet apparently seeking that concealment reluctantly, with a cocked pistol in his right hand, and his left in the act of drawing another from his belt, stood a tall bony gaunt figure in the remnants of a faded uniform, and a beard of three weeks' growth.

It was the Baron of Bradwardine.—It is unnecessary to add, that he threw aside his weapon, and greeted Waverley with a hearty embrace.

# CHAPTER LXIV.

## Comparing of Notes.

THE Baron's story was short, when divested of the adages and commonplaces, Latin, English, and Scotch, with which his erudition garnished it. He insisted much upon his grief at the loss of Edward and of Glennaquoich, fought the fields of Falkirk and Culloden, and related how, after all was lost in the last battle, he had returned home, under the idea of more easily finding shelter among his own tenants, and on his own estate, than elsewhere. A party of soldiers had been sent to lay waste his property, for clemency was not the order of the day. Their proceedings, however, were checked by an order from the civil court. The estate, it was found, might not be forfeited to the crown, to the prejudice of Malcolm Bradwardine of Inch-Grabbit, the heir-male, whose claim could not be prejudiced by the Baron's attainder, as deriving no right through him, and who, therefore, like other heirs of entail in the same situation, entered upon possession. But, unlike many in similar circumstances, the new laird speedily showed that he intended utterly to exclude his predecessor from all benefit or advantage in the estate, and that it was his purpose to avail himself of the old Baron's evil fortune to the full extent. This was the more ungenerous, as it was generally known, that, from a romantic idea of not prejudicing this young man's right as heir-male, the Baron had refrained from settling his estate on his daughter.

This selfish injustice was resented by the country people, who were partial to their old master, and irritated against his successor. In the Baron's own words, "The matter did not coincide with the feelings of the commons of Bradwardine, Mr Waverley; and the tenants were slack and repugnant in payment of their mails and duties; and when my kinsman came to the village wi' the new factor, Mr James Howie, to lift the rents, some wanchancy person—I suspect John Heatherblutter, the auld game-keeper, that was out wi' me in the year fifteen —fired a shot at him in the gloaming, whereby he was so affrighted, that I may say with Tullius in Catilinam, *Abiit, evasit, erupit, effugit.* He fled, sir, as one may say, incontinent to Stirling. And now he hath advertised the estate for sale, being himself the last substitute in the entail.—And if I were to lament about sic matters, this would grieve me mair than its passing from my immediate possession, whilk, by the course of nature, must have happened in a few years. Whereas now it passes from the lineage that should have possessed it in *sæcula sæculorum.* But God's will be done, *humana perpessi sumus.* Sir John of Bradwardine—Black Sir John, as he is called —who was the common ancestor of our house and the Inch-Grabbits, little thought such a person would have sprung from his loins. Meantime, he has accused me to some of the *primates,* the rulers for the time, as if I were a cut-throat, and an abettor of bravoes and assassinates, and coupe-jarrets.[1] And they have sent soldiers here to abide on the estate, and hunt me like a partridge upon the mountains, as Scripture says of good King David, or like our valiant Sir William Wallace,—not that I bring myself into comparison with either.—I thought, when I heard you at the door, they had driven the auld deer to his den at last; and so I e'en proposed to die at bay, like a buck of the first head.—But now, Janet, canna ye gie us something for supper?"

"Ou ay, sir, I'll brander the moor-fowl that John Heatherblutter brought in this morning; and ye see puir Davie's roasting the black hen's eggs.—I daur say, Mr Wauverley, ye never kend that a' the eggs that were sae weel roasted at supper in the Ha'-house were aye turned by our Davie?—there's no the like o' him ony gate for powtering[2] wi' his fingers amang the het peat-ashes, and roasting eggs." Davie all this while lay with his nose almost in the fire, nuzzling among the ashes, kicking his heels, mumbling to himself, turning the eggs as they lay in the hot embers, as if to confute the proverb, that "there

[1] Those who hamstring others.    [2] Trifling.

goes reason to roasting of eggs," and justify the eulogium
which poor Janet poured out upon

"Him whom she loved, her idiot boy."

"Davie's no sae silly as folk tak him for, Mr Wauverley;
he wadna hae brought you here unless he had kend ye
was a friend to his Honour—indeed the very dogs kend ye,
Mr Wauverley, for ye was aye kind to beast and body.—
I can tell you a story o' Davie, wi' his Honour's leave:
His Honour, ye see, being under hiding in thae sair times
—the mair's the pity—he lies a' day, and whiles a' night,
in the cove in the dern hag;[1] but though it's a bieldy[2]
eneugh bit, and the auld gudeman o' Corse-Cleugh has
panged[3] it wi' a kemple[4] o' strae amaist, yet when the
country's quiet, and the night very cauld, his Honour
whiles creeps doun here to get a warm at the ingle, and a
sleep amang the blankets, and gangs awa in the morning.
And so, ae morning, siccan a fright as I got! Twa unlucky
red-coats were up for black-fishing, or some siccan ploy—
for the neb o' them's never out o' mischief—and they
just got a glisk o' his Honour as he gaed into the wood,
and banged aff a gun at him. I out like a jer-falcon, and
cried,—'Wad they shoot an honest woman's poor innocent
bairn?' And I fleyt[5] at them, and threepit[6] it was my
son; and they damned and swuir at me that it was the
auld rebel, as the villains ca'd his Honour; and Davie was
in the wood, and heard the tuilzie, and he, just out o' his
ain head, got up the auld grey mantle that his Honour had
flung off him to gang the faster, and he cam out o' the
very same bit o' the wood, majoring and looking about
sae like his Honour, that they were clean beguiled, and
thought they had letten aff their gun at crack-brained
Sawney, as they ca' him; and they gae me saxpence, and
twa saumon fish, to sae naething about it.—Na, na, Davie's
no just like other folk, puir fallow; but he's no sae silly
as folk tak him for.—But, to be sure, how can we do
eneugh for his Honour, when we and ours have lived on
his ground this twa hundred years; and when he keepit
my puir Jamie at school and college, and even at the Ha'-
house, till he gaed to a better place; and when he saved
me frae being ta'en to Perth as a witch—Lord forgi'e them
that would touch sic a puir silly auld body!—and has
maintained puir Davie at heck and manger maist feck[7] o'
his life?"

---

[1] Hidden peat-moss.     [2] Protected.     [3] Crammed.     [4] Chopped heap.
[5] Scolded.     [6] Asserted.     [7] Part.

Waverley at length found an opportunity to interrupt
Janet's narrative, by an enquiry after Miss Bradwardine.

"She's weel and safe, thank God! at the Duchran,"
answered the Baron; "the laird's distantly related to us,
and more nearly to my chaplain, Mr Rubrick; and, though
he be of Whig principles, yet he's not forgetful of auld
friendship at this time. The Bailie's doing what he can
to save something out of the wreck for puir Rose; but I
doubt, I doubt, I shall never see her again, for I maun lay
my banes in some far country."

"Hout na, your Honour," said old Janet, "ye were just
as ill aff in the feifteen, and got the bonnie baronie back,
an' a'.—And now the eggs is ready, and the muir-cock's
brandered, and there's ilk ane a trencher and some saut,
and the heel o' the white loaf that cam frae the Bailie's;
and there's plenty o' brandy in the greybeard that Luckie
Maclearie sent doun, and winna ye be suppered like
princes?"

"I wish one Prince, at least of our acquaintance, may be
no worse of," said the Baron to Waverley, who joined him
in cordial hopes for the safety of the unfortunate Chevalier.

They then began to talk of their future prospects. The
Baron's plan was very simple. It was, to escape to
France, where, by the interest of his old friends, he hoped
to get some military employment, of which he still conceived himself capable. He invited Waverley to go with
him, a proposal in which he acquiesced, providing the
interest of Colonel Talbot should fail in procuring his
pardon. Tacitly he hoped the Baron would sanction his
addresses to Rose, and give him a right to assist him in
his exile; but he forbore to speak on this subject until
his own fate should be decided. They then talked of
Glennaquoich, for whom the Baron expressed great
anxiety, although, he observed, he was "the very Achilles
of Horatius Flaccus,—

> Impiger, iracundus, inexorabilis, acer.

Which," he continued, "has been thus rendered (vernacularly) by Struan Robertson:

> A fiery etter-cap, a fractious chiel,
> As het as ginger, and as stieve [1] as steel."

Flora had a large and unqualified share of the good old
man's sympathy.

It was now wearing late. Old Janet got into some kind
of kennel behind the hallan [2]; Davie had been long asleep

----

[1] Firm.          [2] Partition.

and snoring between Ban and Buscar. These dogs had followed him to the hut after the mansion-house was deserted, and there constantly resided ; and their ferocity, with the old woman's reputation of being a witch, contributed a good deal to keep visitors from the glen. With this view, Bailie Macwheeble provided Janet underhand with meal for their maintenance, and also with little articles of luxury for his patron's use, in supplying which much precaution was necessarily used. After some compliments, the Baron occupied his usual couch, and Waverley reclined in an easy chair of tattered velvet, which had once garnished the state bedroom of Tully-Veolan, (for the furniture of this mansion was now scattered through all the cottages in the vicinity,) and went to sleep as comfortably as if he had been in a bed of down.

## CHAPTER LXV.

### *More Explanation.*

WITH the first dawn of day, old Janet was scuttling about the house to wake the Baron, who usually slept sound and heavily.

"I must go back," he said to Waverley, "to my cove ; will you walk down the glen wi' me ?"

They went out together, and followed a narrow and entangled footpath, which the occasional passage of anglers, or wood-cutters, had traced by the side of the stream. On their way, the Baron explained to Waverley, that he would be under no danger in remaining a day or two at Tully-Veolan, and even in being seen walking about, if he used the precaution of pretending that he was looking at the estate as agent or surveyor for an English gentleman, who designed to be purchaser. With this view, he recommended to him to visit the Bailie, who still lived at the factor's house, called Little Veolan, about a mile from the village, though he was to remove at next term. Stanley's passport would be an answer to the officer who commanded the military ; and as to any of the country people who might recognise Waverley, the Baron assured him he was in no danger of being betrayed by them.

"I believe," said the old man, "half the people of the

barony know that their poor auld laird is somewhere
hereabout ; for I see they do not suffer a single bairn to
come here a bird-nesting ; a practice, whilk, when I was
in full possession of my power as baron, I was unable
totally to inhibit. Nay, I often find bits of things in my
way, that the poor bodies, God help them! leave there,
because they think they may be useful to me. I hope
they will get a wiser master, and as kind a one as I
was."

A natural sigh closed the sentence ; but the quiet
equanimity with which the Baron endured his misfortunes, had something in it venerable and even sublime.
There was no fruitless repining, no turbid melancholy ;
he bore his lot, and the hardships which it involved, with
a good-humoured, though serious composure, and used
no violent language against the prevailing party.

"I did what I thought my duty," said the good old man,
"and questionless they are doing what they think theirs.
It grieves me sometimes to look upon these blackened walls
of the house of my ancestors ; but doubtless officers cannot always keep the soldier's hand from depredation and
spuilzie; and Gustavus Adolphus himself, as ye may read
in Colonel Munro his Expedition with the worthy Scotch
regiment called Mackay's regiment, did often permit it.
—Indeed I have myself seen as sad sights as Tully-Veolan
now is, when I served with the Mareschal Duke of Berwick. To be sure we may say with Virgilius Maro,
*Fuimus Troes*—and there's the end of an auld sang. But
houses and families and men have a' stood lang eneugh
when they have stood till they fall with honour; and now
I hae gotten a house that is not unlike a *domus ultima*"—
they were now standing below a steep rock. "We poor
Jacobites," continued the Baron, looking up, "are now
like the conies in Holy Scripture, (which the great
traveller Pococke calleth Jerboa,) a feeble people, that
make our abode in the rocks. So, fare ye well, my good
lad, till we meet at Janet's in the even ; for I must get
into my Patmos, which is no easy matter for my auld stiff
limbs."

With that he began to ascend the rock, striding, with
the help of his hands, from one precarious footstep to
another, till he got about half way up, where two or
three bushes concealed the mouth of a hole, resembling
an oven, into which the Baron insinuated, first his head
and shoulders, and then, by slow gradation, the rest of
his long body ; his legs and feet finally disappearing,

coiled up like a huge snake entering his retreat, or a long pedigree introduced with care and difficulty into the narrow pigeon-hole of an old cabinet. Waverley had the curiosity to clamber up and look in upon him in his den, as the lurking-place might well be termed. Upon the whole, he looked not unlike that ingenious puzzle, called *a reel in a bottle*, the marvel of children, (and of some grown people too, myself for one,) who can neither comprehend the mystery how it has got in, or how it is to be taken out. The cave was very narrow, too low in the roof to admit of his standing, or almost of his sitting up, though he made some awkward attempts at the latter posture. His sole amusement was the perusal of his old friend Titus Livius, varied by occasionally scratching Latin proverbs and texts of Scripture with his knife on the roof and walls of his fortalice, which were of sandstone. As the cave was dry, and filled with clean straw and withered fern, "it made," as he said, coiling himself up with an air of snugness and comfort which contrasted strangely with his situation, "unless when the wind was due north, a very passable *gite*[1] for an old soldier." Neither, as he observed, was he without sentries for the purpose of reconnoitring. Davie and his mother were constantly on the watch, to discover and avert danger ; and it was singular what instances of address seemed dictated by the instinctive attachment of the poor simpleton, when his patron's safety was concerned.

With Janet, Edward now sought an interview. He had recognised her at first sight as the old woman who had nursed him during his sickness after his delivery from Gifted Gilfillan. The hut also, though a little repaired, and somewhat better furnished, was certainly the place of his confinement ; and he now recollected on the common moor of Tully-Veolan the trunk of a large decayed tree, called the *trysting-tree*, which he had no doubt was the same at which the Highlanders rendezvoused on that memorable night. All this he had combined in his imagination the night before ; but reasons, which may probably occur to the reader, prevented him from catechising Janet in the presence of the Baron.

He now commenced the task in good earnest ; and the first question was, Who was the young lady that visited the hut during his illness? Janet paused for a little ; and then observed, that to keep the secret now, would neither do good nor ill to anybody.

[1] Refuge.

"It was just a leddy, that hasna her equal in the world —Miss Rose Bradwardine!"

"Then Miss Rose was probably also the author of my deliverance," inferred Waverley, delighted at the confirmation of an idea which local circumstances had already induced him to entertain.

"I wot weel, Mr Wauverley, and that was she e'en; but sair, sair angry and affronted wad she hae been, puir thing, if she had thought ye had been ever to ken a word about the matter; for she gar'd me speak aye Gaelic when ye was in hearing, to mak ye trow we were in the Hielands. I can speak it weil eneugh, for my mother was a Hieland woman."

A few more questions now brought out the whole mystery respecting Waverley's deliverance from the bondage in which he left Cairnvreckan. Never did music sound sweeter to an amateur, than the drowsy tautology, with which old Janet detailed every circumstance, thrilled upon the ears of Waverley. But my reader is not a lover, and I must spare his patience, by attempting to condense within reasonable compass, the narrative which old Janet spread through a harangue of nearly two hours.

When Waverley communicated to Fergus the letter he had received from Rose Bradwardine, by Davie Gellatley, giving an account of Tully-Veolan being occupied by a small party of soldiers, that circumstance had struck upon the busy and active mind of the Chieftain. Eager to distress and narrow the posts of the enemy, desirous to prevent their establishing a garrison so near him, and willing also to oblige the Baron,—for he often had the idea of marriage with Rose floating through his brain,— he resolved to send some of his people to drive out the red-coats, and to bring Rose to Glennaquoich. But just as he had ordered Evan with a small party on this duty, the news of Cope's having marched into the Highlands to meet and disperse the forces of the Chevalier, ere they came to a head, obliged him to join the standard with his whole forces.

He sent to order Donald Bean to attend him; but that cautious freebooter, who well understood the value of a separate command, instead of joining, sent various apologies which the pressure of the times compelled Fergus to admit as current, though not without the internal resolution of being revenged on him for his procrastination, time and place convenient. However, as he could not amend the matter, he issued orders to Donald to descend into the Low Country, drive the soldiers from Tully-Veolan, and, paying all respect to the mansion of the Baron, to take his abode somewhere near it, for protection of his daughter and family, and to harass and drive away any of the armed volunteers, or small parties of military, which he might find moving about the vicinity.

As this charge formed a sort of roving commission, which Donald proposed to interpret in the way most advantageous to himself, as he was relieved from the immediate terrors of Fergus, and as he had, from former secret services, some interest in the councils of the Chevalier, he resolved to make hay while the sun shone. He achieved, without difficulty, the task of driving the soldiers from Tully-Veolan; but although he did not venture to encroach upon the interior of the family, or to disturb Miss Rose, being unwilling to make himself a powerful enemy in the Chevalier's army,

"For well he knew the Baron's wrath was deadly;"

yet he set about to raise contributions and exactions upon the tenantry, and otherwise to turn the war to his own advantage. Meanwhile he mounted the white cockade, and waited upon Rose with a pretext of great devotion for the service in which her father was engaged, and many apologies for the freedom he must necessarily use for the support of his people. It was at this moment that Rose learned, by open-mouthed fame, with all sorts of exaggeration, that Waverley had killed the smith at Cairnvreckan, in an attempt to arrest him; had been cast into a dungeon by Major Melville of Cairnvreckan, and was to be executed by martial law within three days. In the agony which these tidings excited, she proposed to Donald Bean the rescue of the prisoner. It was the very sort of service which he was desirous to undertake, judging it might constitute a merit of such a nature as would make amends for any peccadilloes which he might be guilty of in the country. He had the art, however, pleading all the while duty and discipline, to hold off, until poor Rose, in the extremity of her distress, offered to bribe him to the enterprise with some valuable jewels which had been her mother's.

Donald Bean, who had served in France, knew, and perhaps over-estimated, the value of these trinkets. But he also perceived Rose's apprehensions of its being discovered that she had parted with her jewels for Waver-

ley's liberation. Resolved this scruple should not part
him and the treasure, he voluntarily offered to take an
oath that he would never mention Miss Rose's share in
the transaction ; and foreseeing convenience in keeping
the oath, and no probable advantage in breaking it, he
took the engagement—in order, as he told his lieutenant,
to deal handsomely by the young lady—in the only mode
and form which, by a mental paction with himself, he
considered as binding—he swore secrecy upon his drawn
dirk. He was the more especially moved to this act of
good faith by some attentions that Miss Bradwardine
showed to his daughter Alice, which, while they gained
the heart of the mountain damsel, highly gratified the
pride of her father. Alice, who could now speak a little
English, was very communicative in return for Rose's
kindness, readily confided to her the whole papers respecting the intrigue with Gardiner's regiment, of which
she was the depositary, and as readily undertook, at her
instance, to restore them to Waverley without her father's
knowledge. "For they may oblige the bonnie young
lady and the handsome young gentleman," said Alice,
"and what use has my father for a whin bits o' scarted
paper?"[1]

The reader is aware that she took an opportunity of
executing this purpose on the eve of Waverley's leaving
the glen.

How Donald executed his enterprise, the reader is
aware. But the expulsion of the military from Tully-
Veolan had given alarm, and, while he was lying in wait
for Gilfillan, a strong party, such as Donald did not care
to face, was sent to drive back the insurgents in their
turn, to encamp there, and to protect the country. The
officer, a gentleman and a disciplinarian, neither intruded
himself on Miss Bradwardine, whose unprotected situation
he respected, nor permitted his soldiers to commit any
breach of discipline. He formed a little camp, upon an
eminence, near the house of Tully-Veolan, and placed
proper guards at the passes in the vicinity. This unwelcome news reached Donald Bean Lean as he was
returning to Tully-Veolan. Determined, however, to
obtain the guerdon of his labour, he resolved, since
approach to Tully-Veolan was impossible, to deposit his
prisoner in Janet's cottage, a place, the very existence of
which could hardly have been suspected even by those
who had long lived in the vicinity, unless they had been

[1] Few pieces of scratched paper.

guided thither, and which was utterly unknown to
Waverley himself. This effected, he claimed and received
his reward. Waverley's illness was an event which
deranged all their calculations. Donald was obliged to
leave the neighbourhood with his people, and to seek more
free course for his adventures elsewhere. At Rose's
earnest entreaty, he left an old man, a herbalist, who was
supposed to understand a little of medicine, to attend
Waverley during his illness.

In the meanwhile, new and fearful doubts started in
Rose's mind. They were suggested by old Janet, who
insisted, that a reward having been offered for the apprehension of Waverley, and his own personal effects being
so valuable, there was no saying to what breach of faith
Donald might be tempted. In an agony of grief and
terror, Rose took the daring resolution of explaining to
the Prince himself the danger in which Mr Waverley
stood, judging that, both as a politician, and a man of
honour and humanity, Charles Edward would interest
himself to prevent his falling into the hands of the
opposite party. This letter she at first thought of sending
anonymously, but naturally feared it would not, in that
case, be credited. She therefore subscribed her name,
though with reluctance and terror, and consigned it in
charge to a young man, who, at leaving his farm to join
the Chevalier's army, made it his petition to her to have
some sort of credentials to the Adventurer, from whom
he hoped to obtain a commission.

The letter reached Charles Edward on his descent to
the Lowlands, and, aware of the political importance of
having it supposed that he was in correspondence with
the English Jacobites, he caused the most positive orders
to be transmitted to Donald Bean Lean, to transmit
Waverley, safe and uninjured, in person or effects, to the
governor of Doune Castle. The freebooter durst not
disobey, for the army of the Prince was now so near him
that punishment might have followed ; besides, he was a
politician as well as a robber, and was unwilling to cancel
the interest created through former secret services, by
being refractory on this occasion. He therefore made a
virtue of necessity, and transmitted orders to his lieutenant to convey Edward to Doune, which was safely
accomplished in the mode mentioned in a former chapter.
The governor of Doune was directed to send him to
Edinburgh as a prisoner, because the Prince was apprehensive that Waverley, if set at liberty, might have

resumed his purpose of returning to England, without
affording him an opportunity of a personal interview. In
this, indeed, he acted by the advice of the Chieftain of
Glennaquoich, with whom it may be remembered the
Chevalier communicated upon the mode of disposing of
Edward, though without telling him how he came to learn
the place of his confinement.

This, indeed, Charles Edward considered as a lady's
secret; for although Rose's letter was couched in the
most cautious and general terms, and professed to be
written merely from motives of humanity, and zeal for
the Prince's service, yet she expressed so anxious a wish
that she should not be known to have interfered, that the
Chevalier was induced to suspect the deep interest which
she took in Waverley's safety. This conjecture, which
was well founded, led, however, to false inferences. For
the emotion which Edward displayed on approaching
Flora and Rose at the ball of Holyrood, was placed by
the Chevalier to the account of the latter; and he concluded that the Baron's views about the settlement of
his property, or some such obstacle, thwarted their
mutual inclinations. Common fame, it is true, frequently
gave Waverley to Miss Mac-Ivor; but the Prince knew
that common fame is very prodigal in such gifts; and,
watching attentively the behaviour of the ladies towards
Waverley, he had no doubt that the young Englishman
had no interest with Flora, and was beloved by Rose
Bradwardine. Desirous to bind Waverley to his service,
and wishing also to do a kind and friendly action,
the Prince next assailed the Baron on the subject of
settling his estate upon his daughter. Mr Bradwardine
acquiesced; but the consequence was, that Fergus was
immediately induced to prefer his double suit for a wife
and an earldom, which the Prince rejected in the manner
we have seen. The Chevalier, constantly engaged in his
own multiplied affairs, had not hitherto sought any explanation with Waverley, though often meaning to do so.
But after Fergus's declaration, he saw the necessity of
appearing neutral between the rivals, devoutly hoping
that the matter, which now seemed fraught with the
seeds of strife, might be permitted to lie over till the
termination of the expedition. When on the march to
Derby, Fergus, being questioned concerning his quarrel
with Waverley, alleged as the cause, that Edward was
desirous of retracting the suit he had made to his sister,
the Chevalier plainly told him, that he had himself ob-

served Miss Mac-Ivor's behaviour to Waverley, and that he was convinced Fergus was under the influence of a mistake in judging of Waverley's conduct, who, he had every reason to believe, was engaged to Miss Bradwardine. The quarrel which ensued between Edward and the chieftain is, I hope, still in the remembrance of the reader. These circumstances will serve to explain such points of our narrative as, according to the custom of story-tellers, we deemed it fit to leave unexplained, for the purpose of exciting the reader's curiosity.

When Janet had once finished the leading facts of this narrative, Waverley was easily enabled to apply the clue which they afforded, to other mazes of the labyrinth in which he had been engaged. To Rose Bradwardine, then, he owed the life which he now thought he could willingly have laid down to serve her. A little reflection convinced him, however, that to live for her sake was more convenient and agreeable, and that, being possessed of independence, she might share it with him either in foreign countries or in his own. The pleasure of being allied to a man of the Baron's high worth, and who was so much valued by his uncle Sir Everard, was also an agreeable consideration, had anything been wanting to recommend the match. His absurdities, which had appeared grotesquely ludicrous during his prosperity, seemed, in the sunset of his fortune, to be harmonized and assimilated with the noble features of his character, so as to add peculiarity without exciting ridicule. His mind occupied with such projects of future happiness, Edward sought Little Veolan, the habitation of Mr Duncan Macwheeble.

## CHAPTER LXVI.

Now is Cupid a child of conscience—he makes restitution.
*Shakspeare.*

MR DUNCAN MACWHEEBLE, no longer Commissary or Bailie, though still enjoying the empty name of the latter dignity, had escaped proscription by an early secession from the insurgent party, and by his insignificance.

Edward found him in his office, immersed among papers and accounts. Before him was a large bicker of oatmeal-porridge, and at the side thereof, a horn-spoon and a bottle of two-penny. Eagerly running his eye over a voluminous law-paper, he from time to time shovelled an immense spoonful of these nutritive viands into his capacious mouth. A potbellied Dutch bottle of brandy which stood by, intimated either that this honest limb of the law had taken his *morning* already, or that he meant to season his porridge with such digestive; or perhaps both circumstances might reasonably be inferred. His night-cap and morning-gown had whilome been of tartan, but, equally cautious and frugal, the honest Bailie had got them dyed black, lest their original ill-omened colour might remind his visitors of his unlucky excursion to Derby. To sum up the picture, his face was daubed with snuff up to the eyes, and his fingers with ink up to the knuckles. He looked dubiously at Waverley as he approached the little green rail which fenced his desk and stool from the approach of the vulgar. Nothing could give the Bailie more annoyance than the idea of his acquaintance being claimed by any of the unfortunate gentlemen, who were now so much more likely to need assistance than to afford profit. But this was the rich young Englishman—who knew what might be his situation?—he was the Baron's friend too—what was to be done?

While these reflections gave an air of absurd perplexity to the poor man's visage, Waverley, reflecting on the communication he was about to make to him, of a nature so ridiculously contrasted with the appearance of the individual, could not help bursting out a-laughing, as he checked the propensity to exclaim with Syphax,—

> "Cato's a proper person to intrust
> A love-tale with."

As Mr Macwheeble had no idea of any person laughing heartily, who was either encircled by peril or oppressed by poverty, the hilarity of Edward's countenance greatly relieved the embarrassment of his own, and, giving him a tolerably hearty welcome to Little Veolan, he asked what he would choose for breakfast. His visitor had, in the first place, something for his private ear, and begged leave to bolt the door. Duncan by no means liked this precaution, which savoured of danger to be apprehended; but he could not now draw back.

Convinced he might trust this man, as he could make it his interest to be faithful, Edward communicated his present situation and future schemes to Macwheeble. The wily agent listened with apprehension when he

found Waverley was still in a state of proscription—was
somewhat comforted by learning that he had a passport
—rubbed his hands with glee when he mentioned the
amount of his present fortune—opened huge eyes when
he heard the brilliancy of his future expectations—but
when he expressed his intention to share them with Miss
Rose Bradwardine, ecstacy had almost deprived the
honest man of his senses. The Bailie started from his
three-footed stool like the Pythoness from her tripod;
flung his best wig out of the window, because the block
on which it was placed stood in the way of his career;
chucked his cap to the ceiling, caught it as it fell;
whistled Tullochgorum; danced a Highland fling with
inimitable grace and agility, and then threw himself
exhausted into a chair, exclaiming, "Lady Wauverley?—
ten thousand a-year, the least penny!—Lord preserve
my poor understanding!"—

"Amen with all my heart," said Waverley; "but now,
Mr Macwheeble, let us proceed to business." This word
had somewhat a sedative effect, but the Bailie's head, as
he expressed himself, was still "in the bees." He mended
his pen, however, marked half a dozen sheets of paper
with an ample marginal fold, whipped down Dallas of St
Martin's Styles from a shelf, where that venerable work
roosted with Stair's Institutions, Dirleton's Doubts, Bal-
four's Practiques, and a parcel of old account-books—
opened the volume at the article Contract of Marriage,
and prepared to make what he called a "sma' minute, to
prevent parties frae resiling."

With some difficulty, Waverley made him comprehend
that he was going a little too fast. He explained to him
that he should want his assistance, in the first place, to
make his residence safe for the time, by writing to the
officer at Tully-Veolan, that Mr Stanley, an English
gentleman nearly related to Colonel Talbot, was upon a
visit of business at Mr Macwheeble's, and, knowing the
state of the country, had sent his passport for Captain
Foster's inspection. This produced a polite answer from
the officer, with an invitation to Mr Stanley to dine with
him, which was declined, (as may easily be supposed,)
under pretence of business.

Waverley's next request was, that Mr Macwheeble
would despatch a man and horse to ——, the post-town at
which Colonel Talbot was to address him, with directions
to wait there until the post should bring a letter for Mr
Stanley, and then to forward it to Little Veolan with all

speed. In a moment, the Bailie was in search of his
apprentice, (or servitor, as he was called Sixty Years
since,) Jock Scriever, and in not much greater space of
time, Jock was on the back of the white pony.

"Tak care ye guide him weel, sir, for he's aye been
short in the wind since—a hem—Lord be gude to me !
(in a low voice,) I was gaun to come out wi'—since I rode
whip and spur to fetch the Chevalier to redd Mr Wauverley and Vich Ian Vohr; and an uncanny coup [1] I gat for
my pains.—Lord forgie your honour ! I might hae broken
my neck—but troth it was in a venture, mae ways nor
ane; but this maks amends for a'. Lady Wauverley !—
ten thousand a-year !—Lord be gude unto me ! "

"But you forget, Mr Macwheeble, we want the Baron's
consent—the lady's—"

"Never fear, I'se be caution for them—I'se gie you my
personal warrandice—ten thousand a-year ! it dings
Balmawhapple out and out—a year's rent's worth a' Balmawhapple, fee and life-rent ! Lord make us thankful ! "

To turn the current of his feelings, Edward inquired if
he had heard anything lately of the Chieftain of Glennaquoich?

"Not one word," answered Macwheeble, "but that he
was still in Carlisle Castle, and was soon to be panelled
for his life. I dinna wish the young gentleman ill," he
said, "but I hope that they that hae got him will keep
him, and no let him back to this Hieland border to plague
us wi' black mail, and a' manner o' violent, wrongous, and
masterfu' oppression and spoliation, both by himself and
others of his causing, sending, and hounding out ; and he
couldna tak care o' the siller when he had gotten it neither,
but flang it a' into yon idle quean's lap at Edinburgh—
but light come light gane. For my part, I never wish to
see a kilt in the country again, nor a red coat, nor a gun,
for that matter, unless it were to shoot a paitrick :—they're
a' tarr'd wi' ae stick. And when they have done ye wrang,
even when ye hae gotten decreet of spuilzie,[2] oppression,
and violent profits against them, what better are ye ?—
they hae na a plack [3] to pay ye ; ye need never extract it."

With such discourse, and the intervening topics of
business, the time passed until dinner, Macwheeble meanwhile promising to devise some mode of introducing
Edward at the Duchran, where Rose at present resided,
without risk of danger or suspicion ; which seemed no
very easy task, since the laird was a very zealous friend

[1] Unchancy upset.    [2] Spoil.    [3] Small copper coin.

to government. The poultry-yard had been laid under requisition, and cockyleeky and Scotch collops soon reeked in the Bailie's little parlour. The landlord's cork-screw was just introduced into the muzzle of a pint-bottle of claret, (cribbed possibly from the cellars of Tully-Veolan,) when the sight of the grey pony, passing the window at full trot, induced the Bailie, but with due precaution, to place it aside for the moment. Enter Jock Scriever with a packet for Mr Stanley; it is Colonel Talbot's seal; and Edward's fingers tremble as he undoes it. Two official papers, folded, signed, and sealed in all formality, drop out. They were hastily picked up by the Bailie, who had a natural respect for everything resembling a deed, and, glancing slily on their titles, his eyes, or rather spectacles, are greeted with " Protection by his Royal Highness to the person of Cosmo Comyne Bradwardine, Esq., of that ilk, commonly called Baron of Bradwardine, forfeited for his accession to the late rebellion." The other proves to be a protection of the same tenor in favour of Edward Waverley, Esq. Colonel Talbot's letter was in these words :—

"MY DEAR EDWARD,

"I am just arrived here, and yet I have finished my business; it has cost me some trouble though, as you shall hear. I waited upon his Royal Highness immediately on my arrival, and found him in no very good humour for my purpose. Three or four Scotch gentlemen were just leaving his levee. After he had expressed himself to me very courteously; 'Would you think it,' he said, 'Talbot, here have been half a dozen of the most respectable gentlemen, and best friends to government north of the Forth, Major Melville of Cairnvreckan, Rubrick of Duchran, and others, who have fairly wrung from me, by their downright importunity, a present protection, and the promise of a future pardon, for that stubborn old rebel whom they call Baron of Bradwardine. They allege that his high personal character, and the clemency which he showed to such of our people as fell into the rebels' hands, should weigh in his favour; especially as the loss of his estate is likely to be a severe enough punishment. Rubrick has undertaken to keep him at his own house till things are settled in the country; but it's a little hard to be forced in a manner to pardon such a mortal enemy to the House of Brunswick.' This was no favourable moment for opening my business; however, I said I was rejoiced to learn that his Royal Highness was in the course of granting such requests, as it emboldened me to present one of the like nature in my own name. He was very angry, but I persisted ; I mentioned the uniform support of our three votes in the house, touched modestly on services abroad, though valuable only in his Royal Highness's having been pleased kindly to accept them, and founded pretty strongly on his own expressions of friendship and good-will. He was embarrassed, but obstinate. I hinted the policy of detaching, on all future occasions, the heir of such a fortune as your uncle's from the machinations of the disaffected. But I made no impression. I mentioned the obligations which I lay under to Sir Everard, and to you personally, and claimed, as the sole reward of my services, that he would be pleased to afford me the means of evincing my gratitude. I perceived that he still meditated a refusal, and, taking my commission from my pocket, I said, (as a last resource,) that as his Royal Highness did not, under these pressing circumstances, think me worthy of a favour which he had not scrupled to grant to other gentlemen, whose services I could hardly judge more important than my own, I must beg leave to deposit, with all humility, my commission in his Royal Highness's hands, and to retire from the service. He was not prepared for this ; he told me to take up my commission ; said some handsome things of my services, and granted my request. You are therefore once more a free man, and I have promised for you that you will be a good boy in future, and remember what you owe to the lenity of government. Thus you see *my* prince can be as generous as *yours.* I do not pretend, indeed, that he confers a favour with all the foreign graces and compliments of your Chevalier errant ; but he has a plain English manner, and the evident reluctance with which he grants your request, indicates the sacrifice which he makes of his own inclination to your wishes. My friend, the adjutant-general, has procured me a duplicate of the Baron's protection, (the original being in Major Melville's possession,) which I send to you, as I know that if you can find him you will have pleasure in being the first to communicate the joyful intelligence. He will of course repair to the Duchran without loss of time, there to ride quarantine for a few weeks. As for you, I give you leave to escort him thither, and to stay a week there, as I understand a certain fair lady is in that quarter. And I have the pleasure to tell you, that whatever progress you can make in her good graces will be highly agreeable to Sir

Everard and Mrs Rachel, who will never believe your views and prospects settled, and the three ermines passant in actual safety, until you present them with a Mrs Edward Waverley. Now, certain love-affairs of my own —a good many years since—interrupted some measures which were then proposed in favour of the three ermines passant; so I am bound in honour to make them amends. Therefore make good use of your time, for, when your week is expired, it will be necessary that you go to London to plead your pardon in the law courts.

"Ever, dear Waverley, yours most truly,

"PHILIP TALBOT."

## CHAPTER LXVII.

Happy's the wooing
That's not long a-doing.

WHEN the first rapturous sensation occasioned by these excellent tidings had somewhat subsided, Edward proposed instantly to go down to the glen to acquaint the Baron with their import. But the cautious Bailie justly observed, that if the Baron were to appear instantly in public, the tenantry and villagers might become riotous in expressing their joy, and give offence to "the powers that be," a sort of persons for whom the Bailie always had unlimited respect. He therefore proposed that Mr Waverley should go to Janet Gellatley's, and bring the Baron up under cloud of night to Little Veolan, where he might once more enjoy the luxury of a good bed. In the meanwhile, he said, he himself would go to Captain Foster, and show him the Baron's protection, and obtain his countenance for harbouring him that night, and he would have horses ready on the morrow to set him on his way to the Duchran along with Mr Stanley, "whilk denomination, I apprehend, your honour will for the present retain," said the Bailie.

"Certainly, Mr Macwheeble; but will you not go down to the glen yourself in the evening to meet your patron?"

"That I wad wi' a' my heart; and mickle obliged to your honour for putting me in mind o' my bounden duty. But it will be past sunset afore I get back frae the Captain's, and at these unsonsy[1] hours the glen has a bad

[1] Unseasonable.

name—there's something no that canny about auld Janet
Gellatley. The Laird he'll no believe thae things, but he
was aye ower rash and venturesome—and feared neither
man nor deevil—and sae's seen o't. But right sure am I
Sir George Mackenyie says, that no divine can doubt
there are witches, since the Bible says thou shalt not
suffer them to live ; and that no lawyer in Scotland can
doubt it, since it is punishable with death by our law.
So there's baith law and gospel for it. An his honour
winna believe the Leviticus, he might aye believe the
Statute-Book—but he may take his ain way o't ; it's a'
ane to Duncan Macwheeble. However, I shall send to ask
up auld Janet this e'en ; it's best no to lightly them that
have that character—and we'll want Davie to turn the
spit, for I'll gar Eppie put down a fat goose to the fire for
your honours to your supper."

When it was near sunset, Waverley hastened to the
hut ; and he could not but allow that superstition had
chosen no improper locality, or unfit object, for the
foundation of her fantastic terrors. It resembled exactly
the description of Spenser :

> "There, in a gloomy hollow glen, she found
>     A little cottage built of sticks and reeds,
> In homely wise, and wall'd with sods around,
>     In which a witch did dwell in loathly weeds,
>     And wilful want, all careless of her needs;
>     So choosing solitary to abide
> Far from all neighbours, that her devilish deeds,
>     And hellish arts, from people she might hide,
> And hurt far off, unknown, whomsoever she espied."

He entered the cottage with these verses in his memory.
Poor old Janet, bent double with age, and bleared with
peat-smoke, was tottering about the hut with a birch
broom, muttering to herself as she endeavoured to make
her hearth and floor a little clean for the reception of her
expected guests. Waverley's step made her start, look
up, and fall a-trembling, so much had her nerves been on
the rack for her patron's safety. With difficulty Waverley
made her comprehend that the Baron was now safe from
personal danger ; and when her mind had admitted that
joyful news, it was equally hard to make her believe that
he was not to enter again upon possession of his estate.
"It behoved to be," she said, " he wad get it back again ;
naebody wad be sae gripple[1] as to tak his gear after
they had gi'en him a pardon : and for that Inch-Grabbit,
I could whiles wish mysell a witch for his sake, if I werena
feared the Enemy wad tak me at my word." Waverley

_____
[1] Rapacious.

then gave her some money, and promised that her fidelity should be rewarded. "How can I be rewarded, sir, sae weel, as just to see my auld maister and Miss Rose come back and bruik their ain ?" [1]

Waverley now took leave of Janet, and soon stood beneath the Baron's Patmos. At a low whistle, he observed the veteran peeping out to reconnoitre, like an old badger with his head out of his hole. "Ye hae come rather early, my good lad," said he, descending; "I question if the redcoats hae beat the tattoo yet, and we're not safe till then."

"Good news cannot be told too soon," said Waverley ; and with infinite joy communicated to him the happy tidings. The old man stood for a moment in silent devotion, then exclaimed, "Praise be to God !—I shall see my bairn again."

"And never, I hope, to part with her more," said Waverley.

"I trust in God, not, unless it be to win the means of supporting her ; for my things are but in a bruckle [2] state ;—but what signifies warld's gear ?"

"And if," said Waverley modestly, "there were a situation in life which would put Miss Bradwardine beyond the uncertainty of fortune, and in the rank to which she was born, would you object to it, my dear Baron, because it would make one of your friends the happiest man in the world ?" The Baron turned, and looked at him with great earnestness. "Yes," continued Edward, "I shall not consider my sentence of banishment as repealed, unless you will give me permission to accompany you to the Duchran, and "——

The Baron seemed collecting all his dignity to make a suitable reply to what, at another time, he would have treated as the propounding a treaty of alliance between the houses of Bradwardine and Waverley. But his efforts were in vain ; the father was too mighty for the Baron ; the pride of birth and rank were swept away ;—in the joyful surprise, a slight convulsion passed rapidly over his features as he gave way to the feelings of nature, threw his arms around Waverley's neck, and sobbed out,—"My son, my son ! if I had been to search the world, I would have made my choice here." Edward returned the embrace with great sympathy of feeling, and for a little while they both kept silence. At length it was broken by Edward. "But Miss Bradwardine ?"

[1] Enjoy their own.    [2] Uncertain.

"She had never a will but her old father's; besides, you are a likely youth, of honest principles, and high birth; no, she never had any other will than mine, and in my proudest days I could not have wished a mair eligible espousal for her than the nephew of my excellent old friend, Sir Everard.—But I hope, young man, ye deal na rashly in this matter? I hope ye hae secured the approbation of your ain friends and allies, particularly of your uncle, who is *in loco parentis?* Ah! we maun tak heed o' that." Edward assured him that Sir Everard would think himself highly honoured in the flattering reception his proposal had met with, and that it had his entire approbation; in evidence of which, he put Colonel Talbot's letter into the Baron's hand. The Baron read it with great attention. "Sir Everard," he said, "always despised wealth in comparison of honour and birth; and indeed he hath no occasion to court the *Diva Pecunia.* Yet I now wish, since this Malcom turns out such a parricide, for I can call him no better, as to think of alienating the family inheritance—I now wish (his eyes fixed on a part of the roof which was visible above the trees) that I could have left Rose the auld hurley-house,[1] and the riggs[2] belanging to it.—And yet," said he, resuming more cheerfully, "it's may be as weel as it is; for, as Baron of Bradwardine, I might have thought it my duty to insist upon certain compliances respecting name and bearings, whilk now, as a landless laird wi' a tocherless[3] daughter, no one can blame me for departing from."

Now, Heaven be praised! thought Edward, that Sir Everard does not hear these scruples! The three ermines passant and rampant bear would certainly have gone together by the ears.—He then, with all the ardour of a young lover, assured the Baron, that he sought for his happiness only in Rose's heart and hand, and thought himself as happy in her father's simple approbation, as if he had settled an earldom upon his daughter.

They now reached Little Veolan. The goose was smoking on the table, and the Bailie brandished his knife and fork. A joyous greeting took place between him and his patron. The kitchen, too, had its company. Auld Janet was established at the ingle-nook; Davie had turned the spit to his immortal honour; and even Ban and Buscar, in the liberality of Macwheeble's joy, had been stuffed to the throat with food, and now lay snoring on the floor.

---

[1] House out of repair.    [2] Cultivated lands.    [3] Dowerless.

The next day conducted the Baron and his young friend to the Duchran, where the former was expected, in consequence of the success of the nearly unanimous application of the Scottish friends of government in his favour. This had been so general and so powerful, that it was almost thought his estate might have been saved, had it not passed into the rapacious hands of his unworthy kinsman, whose right, arising out of the Baron's attainder, could not be affected by a pardon from the crown. The old gentleman, however, said, with his usual spirit, he was more gratified by the hold he possessed in the good opinion of his neighbours, than he would have been in being "rehabilitated and restored *in integrum*, had it been found practicable."

We shall not attempt to describe the meeting of the father and daughter,—loving each other so affectionately, and separated under such perilous circumstances. Still less shall we attempt to analyze the deep blush of Rose, at receiving the compliments of Waverley, or stop to inquire whether she had any curiosity respecting the particular cause of his journey to Scotland at that period. We shall not even trouble the reader with the hum-drum details of a courtship Sixty Years since. It is enough to say, that, under so strict a martinet as the Baron, all things were conducted in due form. He took upon himself, the morning after their arrival, the task of announcing the proposal of Waverley to Rose, which she heard with a proper degree of maiden timidity. Fame does, however, say, that Waverley had, the evening before, found five minutes to apprize her of what was coming, while the rest of the company were looking at three twisted serpents, which formed a *jet d'eau* in the garden.

My fair readers will judge for themselves ; but, for my part, I cannot conceive how so important an affair could be communicated in so short a space of time ; at least, it certainly took a full hour in the Baron's mode of conveying it.

Waverley was now considered as a received lover in all the forms. He was made, by dint of smirking and nodding on the part of the lady of the house, to sit next Miss Bradwardine at dinner, to be Miss Bradwardine's partner at cards. If he came into the room, she of the four Miss Rubricks who chanced to be next Rose, was sure to recollect that her thimble, or her scissors, were at the other end of the room, in order to leave the seat nearest to Miss Bradwardine vacant for his occupation. And sometimes,

if papa and mamma were not in the way to keep them on
their good behaviour, the misses would titter a little.
The old Laird of Duchran would also have his occasional
jest, and the old lady her remark. Even the Baron could
not refrain; but here Rose escaped every embarrassment
but that of conjecture, for his wit was usually couched in
a Latin quotation. The very footmen sometimes grinned
too broadly, the maid-servants giggled mayhap too loud,
and a provoking air of intelligence seemed to pervade
the whole family. Alice Bean, the pretty maid of the
cavern, who, after her father's *misfortune*, as she called it,
had attended Rose as fille-de-chambre, smiled and smirked
with the best of them. Rose and Edward, however,
endured all these little vexatious circumstances as other
folks have done before and since, and probably contrived
to obtain some indemnification, since they are not supposed, on the whole, to have been particularly unhappy
during Waverley's six days' stay at the Duchran.

It was finally arranged that Edward should go to
Waverley-Honour to make the necessary arrangements
for his marriage, thence to London to take the proper
measures for pleading his pardon, and return as soon as
possible to claim the hand of his plighted bride. He also
intended in his journey to visit Colonel Talbot; but,
above all, it was his most important object to learn the
fate of the unfortunate Chief of Glennaquoich; to visit
him at Carlisle, and to try whether anything could be
done for procuring, if not a pardon, a commutation at
least, or alleviation, of the punishment to which he was
almost certain of being condemned; and, in case of the
worst, to offer the miserable Flora an asylum with Rose,
or otherwise to assist her views in any mode which might
seem possible. The fate of Fergus seemed hard to be
averted. Edward had already striven to interest his
friend, Colonel Talbot, in his behalf; but had been given
distinctly to understand, by his reply, that his credit in
matters of that nature was totally exhausted.

The Colonel was still in Edinburgh, and proposed to
wait there for some months upon business confided to
him by the Duke of Cumberland. He was to be joined
by Lady Emily, to whom easy travelling and goat's whey
were recommended, and who was to journey northward,
under the escort of Francis Stanley. Edward, therefore,
met the Colonel at Edinburgh, who wished him joy in the
kindest manner on his approaching happiness, and cheerfully undertook many commissions which our hero was

necessarily obliged to delegate to his charge. But on the subject of Fergus he was inexorable. He satisfied Edward, indeed, that his interference would be unavailing; but, besides, Colonel Talbot owned that he could not conscientiously use any influence in favour of that unfortunate gentleman. "Justice," he said, "which demanded some penalty of those who had wrapped the whole nation in fear and in mourning, could not perhaps have selected a fitter victim. He came to the field with the fullest light upon the nature of his attempt. He had studied and understood the subject. His father's fate could not intimidate him; the lenity of the laws which had restored to him his father's property and rights could not melt him. That he was brave, generous, and possessed many good qualities, only rendered him the more dangerous; that he was enlightened and accomplished, made his crime the less excusable; that he was an enthusiast in a wrong cause, only made him the more fit to be its martyr. Above all, he had been the means of bringing many hundreds of men into the field, who, without him, would never have broken the peace of the country.

"I repeat it," said the Colonel, "though Heaven knows with a heart distressed for him as an individual, that this young gentleman has studied and fully understood the desperate game which he has played. He threw for life or death, a coronet or a coffin; and he cannot now be permitted, with justice to the country, to draw stakes because the dice have gone against him."

Such was the reasoning of those times, held even by brave and humane men towards a vanquished enemy. Let us devoutly hope, that, in this respect at least, we shall never see the scenes, or hold the sentiments, that were general in Britain Sixty Years since.

## CHAPTER LXVIII.

To-morrow? O that's sudden!—Spare him, spare him!
*Shakspeare.*

EDWARD, attended by his former servant Alick Polwarth, who had re-entered his service at Edinburgh, reached Carlisle while the commission of Oyer and Terminer on his unfortunate associates was yet sitting. He had pushed forward in haste, not, alas! with the most distant hope of saving Fergus, but to see him for the last time. I ought to have mentioned, that he had furnished funds for the defence of the prisoners in the most liberal manner, as soon as he heard that the day of trial was fixed. A solicitor, and the first counsel, accordingly attended; but it was upon the same footing on which the first physicians are usually summoned to the bedside of some dying man of rank; the doctors to take the advantage of some incalculable chance of an exertion of nature—the lawyers to avail themselves of the barely possible occurrence of some legal flaw. Edward pressed into the court, which was extremely crowded; but by his arriving from the north, and his extreme eagerness and agitation, it was supposed he was a relation of the prisoners, and people made way for him. It was the third sitting of the court, and there were two men at the bar. The verdict of GUILTY was already pronounced. Edward just glanced at the bar during the momentous pause which ensued. There was no mistaking the stately form and noble features of Fergus Mac-Ivor, although his dress was squalid, and his countenance tinged with the sickly yellow hue of long and close imprisonment. By his side was Evan Maccombich. Edward felt sick and dizzy as he gazed on them; but he was recalled to himself as the Clerk of Arraigns pronounced the solemn words: "Fergus Mac-Ivor of Glennaquoich, otherwise called Vich Ian Vohr, and Evan Mac-Ivor, in the Dhu of Tarrascleugh, otherwise called Evan Dhu, otherwise called Evan Maccombich, or Evan Dhu Maccombich—you, and each of you, stand attainted of high treason. What have you to say for yourselves why the Court should not pronounce judgment against you, that you die according to law?"

Fergus, as the presiding Judge was putting on the fatal cap of judgment, placed his own bonnet upon his head, regarded him with a steadfast and stern look, and replied in a firm voice, "I cannot let this numerous audience suppose that to such an appeal I have no answer to make. But what I have to say, you would not bear to hear, for my defence would be your condemnation. Proceed, then, in the name of God, to do what is permitted to you. Yesterday, and the day before, you have condemned loyal and honourable blood to be poured forth like water. Spare not mine. Were that of all my ancestors in my veins, I would have peril'd it in this quarrel." He resumed his seat, and refused again to rise.

Evan Maccombich looked at him with great earnestness, and, rising up, seemed anxious to speak; but the confusion of the court, and the perplexity arising from thinking in a language different from that in which he was wont to express himself, kept him silent. There was a murmur of compassion among the spectators, from the idea that the poor fellow intended to plead the influence of his superior as an excuse for his crime. The Judge commanded silence, and encouraged Evan to proceed.

"I was only ganging to say, my lord," said Evan, in what he meant to be an insinuating manner, "that if your excellent honour, and the honourable Court, would let Vich Ian Vohr go free just this once, and let him gae back to France, and no to trouble King George's government again, that ony six o' the very best of his clan will be willing to be justified in his stead; and if you'll just let me gae down to Glennaquoich, I'll fetch them up to ye mysell, to head or hang, and you may begin wi' me the very first man."

Notwithstanding the solemnity of the occasion, a sort of laugh was heard in the court at the extraordinary nature of the proposal. The Judge checked this indecency, and Evan, looking sternly around, when the mumur abated, "If the Saxon gentlemen are laughing," he said, "because a poor man, such as me, thinks my life, or the life of six of my degree, is worth that of Vich Ian Vohr, it's like enough they may be very right; but if they laugh because they think I would not keep my word, and come back to redeem him, I can tell them they ken neither the heart of a Hielandman, nor the honour of a gentleman."

There was no farther inclination to laugh among the audience, and a dead silence ensued.

The Judge then pronounced upon both prisoners the sentence of the law of high treason, with all its horrible accompaniments. The execution was appointed for the ensuing day. "For you, Fergus Mac-Ivor," continued the Judge, "I can hold out no hope of mercy. You must prepare against to-morrow for your last sufferings here, and your great audit hereafter."

"I desire nothing else, my lord," answered Fergus, in the same manly and firm tone.

The hard eyes of Evan, which had been perpetually bent on his Chief, were moistened with a tear. "For you, poor ignorant man," continued the Judge, "who, following the ideas in which you have been educated,

have this day given us a striking example how the loyalty
due to the king and state alone, is, from your unhappy
ideas of clanship, transferred to some ambitious individual, who ends by making you the tool of his crimes
—for you, I say, I feel so much compassion, that if you
can make up your mind to petition for grace, I will
endeavour to procure it for you.  Otherwise——"

"Grace me no grace," said Evan; "since you are to
shed Vich Ian Vohr's blood, the only favour I would
accept from you, is—to bid them loose my hands and gie
me my claymore, and bide you just a minute sitting
where you are!"

"Remove the prisoners," said the Judge; "his blood be
upon his own head."

Almost stupified with his feelings, Edward found that
the rush of the crowd had conveyed him out into the street,
ere he knew what he was doing.  His immediate wish
was to see and speak with Fergus once more.  He applied
at the Castle where his unfortunate friend was confined,
but was refused admittance.  "The High Sheriff," a non-
commissioned officer said, "had requested of the governor
that none should be admitted to see the prisoner excepting his confessor and his sister."

"And where was Miss Mac-Ivor?"  They gave him the
direction.  It was the house of a respectable Catholic
family near Carlisle.

Repulsed from the gate of the Castle, and not venturing to make application to the High Sheriff or Judges in
his own unpopular name, he had recourse to the solicitor
who came down in Fergus's behalf.  This gentleman told
him, that it was thought the public mind was in danger
of being debauched by the account of the last moments of
these persons, as given by the friends of the Pretender;
that there had been a resolution, therefore, to exclude all
such persons as had not the plea of near kindred for
attending [upon them.  Yet, he promised (to oblige the
heir of Waverley-Honour) to get him an order for admittance to the prisoner the next morning, before his irons
were knocked off for execution.

Is it of Fergus Mac-Ivor they speak thus, thought
Waverley, or do I dream?  Of Fergus the bold, the
chivalrous, the free-minded?  The lofty chieftain of a
tribe devoted to him?  Is it he, that I have seen lead the
chase and head the attack,—the brave, the active, the
young, the noble, the love of ladies, and the theme of
song,—is it he who is ironed like a malefactor; who is to

be dragged on a hurdle to the common gallows; to die a lingering and cruel death, and to be mangled by the hand of the most outcast of wretches? Evil indeed was the spectre, that boded such a fate as this to the brave Chief of Glennaquoich!

With a faltering voice he requested the solicitor to find means to warn Fergus of his intended visit, should he obtain permission to make it. He then turned away from him, and, returning to the inn, wrote a scarcely intelligible note to Flora Mac-Ivor, intimating his purpose to wait upon her that evening. The messenger brought back a letter in Flora's beautiful Italian hand, which seemed scarce to tremble even under this load of misery. "Miss Flora Mac-Ivor," the letter bore, "could not refuse to see the dearest friend of her dear brother, even in her present circumstances of unparalleled distress."

When Edward reached Miss Mac-Ivor's present place of abode, he was instantly admitted. In a large and gloomy tapestried apartment, Flora was seated by a latticed window, sewing what seemed to be a garment of white flannel. At a little distance sat an elderly woman, apparently a foreigner, and of a religious order. She was reading in a book of Catholic devotion, but when Waverley entered, laid it on the table and left the room. Flora rose to receive him, and stretched out her hand, but neither ventured to attempt speech. Her fine complexion was totally gone; her person considerably emaciated; and her face and hands as white as the purest statuary marble, forming a strong contrast with her sable dress and jet-black hair. Yet, amid these marks of distress, there was nothing negligent or ill-arranged about her attire; even her hair, though totally without ornament, was disposed with her usual attention to neatness. The first words she uttered were, "Have you seen him?"

"Alas, no," answered Waverley, "I have been refused admittance."

"It accords with the rest," she said; "but we must submit. Shall you obtain leave, do you suppose?"

"For—for—to-morrow," said Waverley; but muttering the last word so faintly that it was almost unintelligible.

"Ay, then or never," said Flora, "until"—she added, looking upward, "the time when, I trust, we shall all meet. But I hope you will see him while earth yet bears him. He always loved you at his heart, though—but it is vain to talk of the past."

"Vain indeed!" echoed Waverley.

"Or even of the future, my good friend," said Flora, "so far as earthly events are concerned ; for how often have I pictured to myself the strong possibility of this horrid issue, and tasked myself to consider how I could support my part ; and yet how far has all my antici- pation fallen short of the unimaginable bitterness of this hour !"

"Dear Flora, if your strength of mind"——

"Ay, there it is," she answered, somewhat wildly ; "there is, Mr Waverley, there is a busy devil at my heart, that whispers—but it were madness to listen to it—that the strength of mind on which Flora prided herself has murdered her brother !"

"Good God ! how can you give utterance to a thought so shocking ?"

"Ay, is it not so ? but yet it haunts me like a phantom ; I know it is unsubstantial and vain ; but it *will* be present ; will intrude its horrors on my mind ; will whisper that my brother, as volatile as ardent, would have divided his energies amid a hundred objects. It was I who taught him to concentrate them, and to gage all on this dreadful and desperate cast. Oh that I could recollect that I had but once said to him, 'He that striketh with the sword, shall die by the sword ;' that I had but once said, Remain at home ; reserve yourself, your vassals, your life, for enterprises within the reach of man. But O, Mr Waverley, I spurred his fiery temper, and half of his ruin at least lies with his sister !"

The horrid idea which she had intimated, Edward endeavoured to combat by every incoherent argument that occurred to him. He recalled to her the principles on which both thought it their duty to act, and in which they had been educated.

"Do not think I have forgotten them," she said, looking up, with eager quickness ; "I do not regret his attempt, because it was wrong ! O no ! on that point I am armed ; but because it was impossible it could end otherwise than thus."

"Yet it did not always seem so desperate and hazardous as it was ; and it would have been chosen by the bold spirit of Fergus, whether you had approved it or no ; your counsels only served to give unity and consistence to his conduct ; to dignify, but not to precipitate, his resolution." Flora had soon ceased to listen to Edward, and was again intent upon her needle-work.

"Do you remember," she said, looking up with a ghastly

smile, "you once found me making Fergus's bride-favours and now I am sewing his bridal-garment. Our friends here," she continued, with suppressed emotion, "are to give hallowed earth in their chapel to the bloody relics of the last Vich Ian Vohr. But they will not all rest together; no—his head!—I shall not have the last miserable consolation of kissing the cold lips of my dear, dear Fergus!"

The unfortunate Flora here, after one or two hysterical sobs, fainted in her chair. The lady, who had been attending in the anteroom, now entered hastily, and begged Edward to leave the room, but not the house.

When he was recalled, after the space of nearly half an hour, he found that, by a strong effort, Miss Mac-Ivor had greatly composed herself. It was then he ventured to urge Miss Bradwardine's claim, to be considered as an adopted sister, and empowered to assist her plans for the future.

"I have had a letter from my dear Rose," she replied, "to the same purpose. Sorrow is selfish and engrossing, or I would have written to express, that, even in my own despair, I felt a gleam of pleasure at learning her happy prospects, and at hearing that the good old Baron has escaped the general wreck. Give this to my dearest Rose; it is her poor Flora's only ornament of value, and was the gift of a princess." She put into his hands a case, containing the chain of diamonds with which she used to decorate her hair. "To me it is in future useless. The kindness of my friends has secured me a retreat in the convent of the Scottish Benedictine nuns in Paris. To-morrow—if indeed I can survive to-morrow—I set forward on my journey with this venerable sister. And now, Mr Waverley, adieu! May you be as happy with Rose as your amiable dispositions deserve; and think sometimes on the friends you have lost. Do not attempt to see me again; it would be mistaken kindness."

She gave him her hand, on which Edward shed a torrent of tears, and, with a faltering step, withdrew from the apartment, and returned to the town of Carlisle. At the inn, he found a letter from his law friend, intimating, that he would be admitted to Fergus next morning, as soon as the Castle gates were opened, and permitted to remain with him till the arrival of the Sheriff gave signal for the fatal procession.

## CHAPTER LXIX.

—— A darker departure is near,
The death drum is muffled, and sable the bier.
                                        *Campbell.*

AFTER a sleepless night, the first dawn of morning
found Waverley on the esplanade in front of the old
Gothic gate of Carlisle Castle. But he paced it long in
every direction, before the hour when, according to the
rules of the garrison, the gates were opened, and the
drawbridge lowered. He produced his order to the
sergeant of the guard, and was admitted.

The place of Fergus's confinement was a gloomy and
vaulted apartment in the central part of the Castle; a
huge old tower, supposed to be of great antiquity, and
surrounded by outworks seemingly of Henry VIII.'s time,
or somewhat later. The grating of the large old-fashioned
bars and bolts, withdrawn for the purpose of admitting
Edward, was answered by the clash of chains, as the unfortunate Chieftain, strongly and heavily fettered, shuffled
along the stone floor of his prison, to fling himself into his
friend's arms.

"My dear Edward," he said, in a firm and even cheerful
voice, "this is truly kind. I heard of your approaching
happiness with the highest pleasure. And how does
Rose? and how is our old whimsical friend the Baron?
Well, I trust, since I see you at freedom—And how will
you settle precedence between the three ermines passant
and the bear and boot-jack?"

"How, O how, my dear Fergus, can you talk of such
things at such a moment?"

"Why, we have entered Carlisle with happier auspices,
to be sure—on the 16th of November last, for example,
when we marched in, side by side, and hoisted the white
flag on these ancient towers. But I am no boy, to sit
down and weep, because the luck has gone against me.
I knew the stake which I risked; we played the game
boldly, and the forfeit shall be paid manfully. And now,
since my time is short, let me come to the questions that
interest me most—the Prince? has he escaped the blood-
hounds?"

"He has, and is in safety."

"Praised be God for that! Tell me the particulars of
his escape."

Waverley communicated that remarkable history, so far as it had then transpired, to which Fergus listened with deep interest. He then asked after several other friends; and made many minute inquiries concerning the fate of his own clansmen. They had suffered less than other tribes who had been engaged in the affair; for, having in a great measure dispersed and returned home after the captivity of their Chieftain, according to the universal custom of the Highlanders, they were not in arms when the insurrection was finally suppressed, and consequently were treated with less rigour. This Fergus heard with great satisfaction.

"You are rich," he said, "Waverley, and you are generous. When you hear of these poor Mac-Ivors being distressed about their miserable possessions by some harsh overseer or agent of government, remember you have worn their tartan, and are an adopted son of their race. The Baron, who knows our manners, and lives near our country, will apprize you of the time and means to be their protector. Will you promise this to the last Vich Ian Vohr?"

Edward, as may well be believed, pledged his word; which he afterwards so amply redeemed, that his memory still lives in these glens by the name of the Friend of the Sons of Ivor.

"Would to God," continued the Chieftain, "I could bequeath to you my rights to the love and obedience of this primitive and brave race:—or at least, as I have striven to do, persuade poor Evan to accept of his life upon their terms; and be to you, what he has been to me, the kindest,—the bravest,—the most devoted——"

The tears which his own fate could not draw forth, fell fast for that of his foster-brother.

"But," said he, drying them, "that cannot be. You cannot be to them Vich Ian Vohr; and these three magic words," said he, half smiling, "are the only *Open Sesame* to their feelings and sympathies, and poor Evan must attend his foster-brother in death, as he has done through his whole life."

"And I am sure," said Maccombich, raising himself from the floor, on which, for fear of interrupting their conversation, he had lain so still, that, in the obscurity of the apartment, Edward was not aware of his presence,— "I am sure Evan never desired or deserved a better end than just to die with his Chieftain."

"And now," said Fergus, "while we are upon the subject of clanship—what think you now of the prediction of
the Bodach Glas?"—Then, before Edward could answer,
"I saw him again last night—he stood in the slip of
moonshine, which fell from that high and narrow window,
towards my bed. Why should I fear him, I thought—to-
morrow, long ere this time, I shall be as immaterial as he.
'False Spirit,' I said, 'art thou come to close thy walks
on earth, and to enjoy thy triumph in the fall of the last
descendant of thine enemy!' The spectre seemed to
beckon and to smile, as he faded from my sight. What
do you think of it?—I asked the same question of the
priest, who is a good and sensible man; he admitted that
the church allowed that such apparitions were possible,
but urged me not to permit my mind to dwell upon it, as
imagination plays us such strange tricks. What do you
think of it?"

"Much as your confessor," said Waverley, willing to
avoid dispute upon such a point at such a moment. A
tap at the door now announced that good man, and
Edward retired while he administered to both prisoners
the last rites of religion, in the mode which the Church of
Rome prescribes.

In about an hour he was re-admitted; soon after, a file
of soldiers entered with a blacksmith, who struck the
fetters from the legs of the prisoners.

"You see the compliment they pay to our Highland strength and courage—we have lain chained here
like wild beasts, till our legs are cramped into palsy,
and when they free us, they send six soldiers with
loaded muskets to prevent our taking the castle by
storm!"

Edward afterwards learned that these severe precautions had been taken in consequence of a desperate
attempt of the prisoners to escape, in which they had
very nearly succeeded.

Shortly afterwards the drums of the garrison beat to
arms. "This is the last turn-out," said Fergus, "that
I shall hear and obey. And now, my dear, dear
Edward, ere we part let us speak of Flora—a subject
which awakes the tenderest feeling that yet thrills
within me."

"We part not _here!_" said Waverley.

"O yes, we do; you must come no farther. Not that
I fear what is to follow for myself," he said proudly:
"Nature has her tortures as well as art; and how happy

should we think the man who escapes from the throes of a mortal and painful disorder, in the space of a short half hour? And this matter, spin it out as they will, cannot last longer. But what a dying man can suffer firmly, may kill a living friend to look upon.—This same law of high treason," he continued, with astonishing firmness and composure, "is one of the blessings, Edward, with which your free country has accommodated poor old Scotland—her own jurisprudence, as I have heard, was much milder. But I suppose one day or other—when there are no longer any wild Highlanders to benefit by its tender mercies—they will blot it from their records, as levelling them with a nation of cannibals. The mummery, too, of exposing the senseless head—they have not the wit to grace mine with a paper coronet; there would be some satire in that, Edward. I hope they will set it on the Scotch gate though, that I may look, even after death, to the blue hills of my own country, which I love so dearly. The Baron would have added,

'Moritur, et moriens dulces reminiscitur Argos.'"

A bustle, and the sound of wheels and horses' feet, was now heard in the courtyard of the Castle. "As I have told you why you must not follow me, and these sounds admonish me that my time flies fast, tell me how you found poor Flora?"

Waverley, with a voice interrupted by suffocating sensations, gave some account of the state of her mind.

"Poor Flora!" answered the Chief, "she could have borne her own sentence of death, but not mine. You Waverley, will soon know the happiness of mutual affection in the married state—long, long may Rose and you enjoy it!—but you can never know the purity of feeling which combines two orphans, like Flora and me, left alone as it were in the world, and being all in all to each other from our very infancy. But her strong sense of duty, and predominant feeling of loyalty, will give new nerve to her mind after the immediate and acute sensation of this parting has passed away. She will then think of Fergus as of the heroes of our race, upon whose deeds she loved to dwell."

"Shall she not see you then?" asked Waverley. "She seemed to expect it."

"A necessary deceit will spare her the last dreadful parting. I could not part with her without tears, and I cannot bear that these men should think they have

power to extort them. She was made to believe she
would see me at a later hour, and this letter, which
my confessor will deliver, will apprize her that all is
over."

An officer now appeared, and intimated that the High
Sheriff and his attendants waited before the gate of the
Castle, to claim the bodies of Fergus Mac-Ivor and Evan
Maccombich. "I come," said Fergus. Accordingly, supporting Edward by the arm, and followed by Evan Dhu
and the priest, he moved down the stairs of the tower,
the soldiers bringing up the rear. The court was
occupied by a squadron of dragoons and a battalion of
infantry, drawn up in hollow square. Within their ranks
was the sledge, or hurdle, on which the prisoners were to
be drawn to the place of execution, about a mile distant
from Carlisle. It was painted black, and drawn by a
white horse. At one end of the vehicle sat the Execu-
tioner, a horrid-looking fellow, as beseemed his trade,
with the broad axe in his hand; at the other end, next
the horse, was an empty seat for two persons. Through
the deep and dark Gothic archway, that opened on the
drawbridge, were seen on horseback the High Sheriff and
his attendants, whom the etiquette betwixt the civil and
military powers did not permit to come farther. "This
is well GOT UP for a closing scene," said Fergus, smiling
disdainfully as he gazed around upon the apparatus of
terror. Evan Dhu exclaimed with some eagerness, after
looking at the dragoons, "These are the very chields that
galloped off at Gladsmuir, before we could kill a dozen
o' them. They look bold enough now, however." The
priest entreated him to be silent.

The sledge now approached, and Fergus, turning round,
embraced Waverley, kissed him on each side of the face,
and stepped nimbly into his place. Evan sat down by
his side. The priest was to follow in a carriage belonging
to his patron, the Catholic gentleman at whose house
Flora resided. As Fergus waved his hand to Edward, the
ranks closed around the sledge, and the whole procession
began to move forward. There was a momentary stop
at the gateway, while the governor of the Castle and
the High Sheriff went through a short ceremony, the
military officer there delivering over the persons of the
criminals to the civil power. "God save King George!"
said the High Sheriff. When the formality concluded,
Fergus stood erect in the sledge, and, with a firm
and steady voice, replied, "God save King *James!*".

These were the last words which Waverley heard him speak.

The procession resumed its march, and the sledge vanished from beneath the portal, under which it had stopped for an instant. The dead-march was then heard, and its melancholy sounds were mingled with those of a muffled peal, tolled from the neighbouring cathedral. The sound of the military music died away as the procession moved on ; the sullen clang of the bells was soon heard to sound alone.

The last of the soldiers had now disappeared from under the vaulted archway through which they had been filing for several minutes ; the courtyard was now totally empty, but Waverley still stood there as if stupified, his eyes fixed upon the dark pass where he had so lately seen the last glimpse of his friend. At length, a female servant of the governor's, struck with compassion at the stupified misery which his countenance expressed, asked him if he would not walk into her master's house and sit down ? She was obliged to repeat her question twice ere he comprehended her, but at length it recalled him to himself. Declining the courtesy by a hasty gesture, he pulled his hat over his eyes, and leaving the Castle, walked as swiftly as he could through the empty streets, till he regained his inn, then rushed into an apartment, and bolted the door.

In about an hour and a half, which seemed an age of unutterable suspense, the sound of the drums and fifes, performing a lively air, and the confused murmur of the crowd which now filled the streets, so lately deserted, apprised him that all was finished, and that the military and populace were returning from the dreadful scene. I will not attempt to describe his sensations.

In the evening the priest made him a visit, and informed him that he did so by directions of his deceased friend, to assure him that Fergus Mac-Ivor had died as he lived, and remembered his friendship to the last. He added, he had also seen Flora, whose state of mind seemed more composed since all was over. With her, and sister Theresa, the priest proposed next day to leave Carlisle, for the nearest seaport from which they could embark for France. Waverley forced on this good man a ring of some value, and a sum of money to be employed (as he thought might gratify Flora) in the services of the Catholic church, for the memory of his friend. "*Fungarque inani munere,*" he repeated, as the ecclesiastic retired. "Yet why not class

these acts of remembrance with other honours, with
which affection, in all sects, pursues the memory of the
dead ?"

The next morning ere daylight he took leave of the
town of Carlisle, promising to himself never again to
enter its walls. He dared hardly look back towards the
Gothic battlements of the fortified gate under which he
passed, for the place is surrounded with an old wall.
"They're no there," said Alick Polwarth, who guessed the
cause of the dubious look which Waverley cast backward,
and who, with the vulgar appetite for the horrible, was
master of each detail of the butchery,—"The heads are
ower the Scotch yate, as they ca' it. It's a great pity of
Evan Dhu, who was a very weel-meaning, good-natured
man, to be a Hielandman ; and indeed so was the Laird o'
Glennaquoich too, for that matter, when he wasna in ane
o' his tirrivies." [1]


## CHAPTER LXX.

### *Dulce Domum.*


THE impression of horror with which Waverley left
Carlisle softened by degrees into melancholy, a gradation
which was accelerated by the painful, yet soothing, task
of writing to Rose ; and, while he could not suppress his
own feelings of the calamity, he endeavoured to place it
in a light which might grieve her, without shocking her
imagination. The picture which he drew for her benefit
he gradually familiarized to his own mind, and his next
letters were more cheerful, and referred to the prospects
of peace and happiness which lay before them. Yet,
though his first horrible sensations had sunk into melancholy, Edward had reached his native country before he
could, as usual on former occasions, look round for
enjoyment upon the face of nature.

He then, for the first time since leaving Edinburgh,
began to experience that pleasure which almost all feel
who return to a verdant, populous, and highly cultivated
country, from scenes of waste desolation, or of solitary
and melancholy grandeur. But how were those feelings
enhanced when he entered on the domain so long

[1] Fits of passion.

possessed by his forefathers; recognised the old oaks of Waverley-Chace; thought with what delight he should introduce Rose to all his favourite haunts; beheld at length the towers of the venerable hall arise above the woods which embowered it, and finally threw himself into the arms of the venerable relations to whom he owed so much duty and affection!

The happiness of their meeting was not tarnished by a single word of reproach. On the contrary, whatever pain Sir Everard and Mrs Rachel had felt during Waverley's perilous engagement with the young Chevalier, it assorted too well with the principles in which they had been brought up, to incur reprobation, or even censure. Colonel Talbot also had smoothed the way, with great address, for Edward's favourable reception, by dwelling upon his gallant behaviour in the military character, particularly his bravery and generosity at Preston; until, warmed at the idea of their nephew's engaging in single combat, making prisoner, and saving from slaughter, so distinguished an officer as the Colonel himself, the imagination of the Baronet and his sister ranked the exploits of Edward with those of Wilibert, Hildebrand, and Nigel, the vaunted heroes of their line.

The appearance of Waverley, embrowned by exercise, and dignified by the habits of military discipline, had acquired an athletic and hardy character, which not only verified the Colonel's narration, but surprised and delighted all the inhabitants of Waverley-Honour. They crowded to see, to hear him, and to sing his praises. Mr Pembroke, who secretly extolled his spirit and courage in embracing the genuine cause of the Church of England, censured his pupil gently, nevertheless, for being so careless of his manuscripts, which indeed, he said, had occasioned him some personal inconvenience, as, upon the Baronet's being arrested by a King's messenger, he had deemed it prudent to retire to a concealment called "The Priest's Hole," from the use it had been put to in former days; where, he assured our hero, the butler had thought it safe to venture with food only once in the day, so that he had been repeatedly compelled to dine upon victuals either absolutely cold, or, what was worse, only half warm, not to mention that sometimes his bed had not been arranged for two days together. Waverley's mind involuntarily turned to the Patmos of the Baron of Bradwardine, who was well pleased with Janet's fare, and a few bunches of straw stowed in a cleft in the front of a sand-cliff; but he made no remarks upon a contrast which could only mortify his worthy tutor.

All was now in a bustle to prepare for the nuptials of Edward, an event to which the good old Baronet and Mrs Rachel looked forward as if to the renewal of their own youth. The match, as Colonel Talbot had intimated, had seemed to them in the highest degree eligible, having every recommendation but wealth, of which they themselves had more than enough. Mr Clippurse was, therefore, summoned to Waverley-Honour, under better auspices than at the commencement of our story. But Mr Clippurse came not alone; for, being now stricken in years, he had associated with him a nephew, a younger vulture, (as our English Juvenal, who tells the tale of Swallow the attorney, might have called him,) and they now carried on business as Messrs Clippurse and Hookem. These worthy gentlemen had directions to make the necessary settlements on the most splendid scale of liberality, as if Edward were to wed a peeress in her own right, with her paternal estate tacked to the fringe of her ermine.

But before entering upon a subject of proverbial delay, I must remind my reader of the progress of a stone rolled down hill by an idle truant boy (a pastime at which I was myself expert in my more juvenile years:) it moves at first slowly, avoiding by inflection every obstacle of the least importance; but when it has attained its full impulse, and draws near the conclusion of its career, it smokes and thunders down, taking a rood at every spring, clearing hedge and ditch like a Yorkshire huntsman, and becoming most furiously rapid in its course when it is nearest to being consigned to rest for ever. Even such is the course of a narrative, like that which you are perusing. The earlier events are studiously dwelt upon, that you, kind reader, may be introduced to the character rather by narrative, than by the duller medium of direct description; but when the story draws near its close, we hurry over the circumstances, however important, which your imagination must have forestalled, and leave you to suppose those things, which it would be abusing your patience to relate at length.

We are, therefore, so far from attempting to trace the dull progress of Messrs Clippurse and Hookem, or that of their worthy official brethren, who had the charge of suing out the pardons of Edward Waverley and his intended father-in-law, that we can but touch upon matters more attractive. The mutual epistles, for example, which were exchanged between Sir Everard and the Baron upon this occasion, though matchless specimens of eloquence in their way, must be consigned to merciless oblivion. Nor can I tell you at length, how worthy Aunt Rachel, not without a delicate and affectionate allusion to the circumstances which had transferred Rose's maternal diamonds to the hands of Donald Bean Lean, stocked her casket with a set of jewels that a duchess might have envied. Moreover, the reader will have the goodness to imagine that Job Houghton and his dame were suitably provided for, although they could never be persuaded that their son fell otherwise than fighting by the young squire's side ; so that Alick, who, as a lover of truth, had made many needless attempts to expound the real circumstances to them, was finally ordered to say not a word more upon the subject. He indemnified himself, however, by the liberal allowance of desperate battles, grisly executions, and raw-head and bloody-bone stories, with which he astonished the servants'-hall.

But although these important matters may be briefly told in narrative, like a newspaper report of a Chancery suit, yet, with all the urgency which Waverley could use, the real time which the law proceedings occupied, joined to the delay occasioned by the mode of travelling at that period, rendered it considerably more than two months ere Waverley, having left England, alighted once more at the mansion of the Laird of Duchran to claim the hand of his plighted bride.

The day of his marriage was fixed for the sixth after his arrival. The Baron of Bradwardine, with whom bridals, christenings, and funerals, were festivals of high and solemn import, felt a little hurt, that, including the family of the Duchran, and all the immediate vicinity who had title to be present on such an occasion, there could not be above thirty persons collected. "When he was married," he observed, "three hundred horse of gentlemen born, besides servants, and some score or two of Highland lairds, who never got on horseback, were present on the occasion."

But his pride found some consolation in reflecting, that he and his son-in-law having been so lately in arms against government, it might give matter of reasonable fear and offence to the ruling powers, if they were to collect together the kith, kin, and allies of their houses, arrayed in effeir of war, as was the ancient custom of

Scotland on these occasions—"And, without dubitation,"
he concluded with a sigh, "many of those who would
have rejoiced most freely upon these joyful espousals,
are either gone to a better place, or are now exiles from
their native land."

The marriage took place on the appointed day. The
Reverend Mr Rubrick, kinsman to the proprietor of the
hospitable mansion where it was solemnized, and chaplain
to the Baron of Bradwardine, had the satisfaction to unite
their hands ; and Frank Stanley acted as bridesman,
having joined Edward with that view soon after his
arrival. Lady Emily and Colonel Talbot had proposed
being present ; but Lady Emily's health, when the day
approached, was found inadequate to the journey. In
amends, it was arranged that Edward Waverley and his
lady, who, with the Baron, proposed an immediate journey to Waverley-Honour, should, in their way, spend a
few days at an estate which Colonel Talbot had been
tempted to purchase in Scotland as a very great bargain,
and at which he proposed to reside for some time.

## CHAPTER LXXI.

"This is no mine ain house, I ken by the bigging o't."
                                                    *Old Scng.*

THE nuptial party travelled in great style. There was
a coach and six after the newest pattern, which Sir
Everard had presented to his nephew, that dazzled with
its splendour the eyes of one half of Scotland ; there was
the family coach of Mr Rubrick ;—both these were
crowded with ladies, and there were gentlemen on horseback, with their servants to the number of a round score.
Nevertheless, without having the fear of famine before his
eyes, Bailie Macwheeble met them in the road, to entreat
that they would pass by his house at Little Veolan. The
Baron stared, and said his son and he would certainly
ride by Little Veolan, and pay their compliments to the
Bailie, but could not think of bringing with them the
"haill *comitatus nuptialis*, or matrimonial procession."
He added, "that, as he understood that the barony had
been sold by its unworthy possessor, he was glad to see
his old friend Duncan had regained his situation under

the new *Dominus*, or proprietor." The Bailie ducked, bowed, and fidgeted, and then again insisted upon his invitation; until the Baron, though rather piqued at the pertinacity of his instances, could not nevertheless refuse to consent, without making evident sensations which he was anxious to conceal.

He fell into a deep study as they approached the top of the avenue, and was only startled from it by observing that the battlements were replaced, the ruins cleared away and (most wonderful of all) that the two great stone Bears, those mutilated Dagons of his idolatry, had resumed their posts over the gateway. "Now this new proprietor," said he to Edward, "has shown mair *gusto*, as the Italians call it, in the short time he has had this domain, than that hound Malcolm, though I bred him here mysell, has acquired *vita adhuc durante.*—And now I talk of hounds, is not yon Ban and Buscar, who come scouping up the avenue with Davie Gellatley?"

"I vote we should go to meet them, sir," said Waverley, "for I believe the present master of the house is Colonel Talbot, who will expect to see us. We hesitated to mention to you at first that he had purchased your ancient patrimonial property, and even yet if you do not incline to visit him, we can pass on to the Bailie's."

The Baron had occasion for all his magnanimity. However, he drew a long breath, took a long snuff, and observed, since they had brought him so far, he could not pass the Colonel's gate, and he would be happy to see the new master of his old tenants. He alighted accordingly, as did the other gentlemen and ladies;—he gave his arm to his daughter, and as they descended the avenue, pointed out to her how speedily the "*Diva Pecunia* of the Southron —their tutelary deity, he might call her—had removed the marks of spoliation."

In truth, not only had the felled trees been removed, but, their stumps being grubbed up, and the earth round them levelled and sown with grass, every mark of devastation, unless to an eye intimately acquainted with the spot, was already totally obliterated. There was a similar reformation in the outward man of Davie Gellatley, who met them, every now and then stopping to admire the new suit which graced his person, in the same colours as formerly, but bedizened fine enough to have served Touchstone himself. He danced up with his usual ungainly frolics, first to the Baron, and then to Rose, passing his hands over his clothes, crying, "*Bra', bra' Davie,*" and

scarce able to sing a bar to an end of his thousand-and-one
songs, for the breathless extravagance of his joy. The
dogs also acknowledged their old master with a thousand
gambols. "Upon my conscience, Rose," ejaculated the
Baron, "the gratitude o' thae dumb brutes, and of that puir
innocent, brings the tears into my auld een, while that
schellum[1] Malcolm—but I'm obliged to Colonel Talbot for
putting my hounds into such good condition, and likewise
for puir Davie. But, Rose, my dear, we must not permit
them to be a life-rent burden upon the estate."

As he spoke, Lady Emily, leaning upon the arm of her
husband, met the party at the lower gate, with a thousand
welcomes. After the ceremony of introduction had been
gone through, much abridged by the ease and excellent
breeding of Lady Emily, she apologized for having used a
little art to wile them back to a place which might awaken
some painful reflections—"But as it was to change
masters, we were very desirous that the Baron "——

"Mr Bradwardine, madam, if you please," said the old
gentleman.

"Mr Bradwardine, then, and Mr Waverley, should see
what we have done towards restoring the mansion of your
fathers to its former state."

The Baron answered with a low bow. Indeed, when he
entered the court, excepting that the heavy stables, which
had been burnt down, were replaced by buildings of a
lighter and more picturesque appearance, all seemed as
much as possible restored to the state in which he had
left it when he assumed arms some months before. The
pigeon-house was replenished; the fountain played with
its usual activity, and not only the Bear who predominated
over its basin, but all the other Bears whatsoever, were
replaced on their several stations, and renewed or repaired
with so much care, that they bore no tokens of the violence
which had so lately descended upon them. While these
minutiæ had been so heedfully attended to, it is scarce
necessary to add, that the house itself had been thoroughly
repaired, as well as the gardens, with the strictest attention to maintain the original character of both, and to
remove, as far as possible, all appearance of the ravage
they had sustained. The Baron gazed in silent wonder;
at length he addressed Colonel Talbot.

"While I acknowledge my obligation to you, sir, for
the restoration of the badge of our family, I cannot but
marvel that you have nowhere established your own crest,

[1] Rascal.

whilk is, I believe, a mastiff, anciently called a talbot; as
the poet has it,

A talbot strong—a sturdy tyke.

At least such a dog is the crest of the martial and renowned Earls of Shrewsbury, to whom your family are
probably blood relations."

"I believe," said the Colonel, smiling, "our dogs are
whelps of the same litter—for my part, if crests were to
dispute precedence, I should be apt to let them, as the
proverb says, 'fight dog, fight bear.'"

As he made this speech, at which the Baron took
another long pinch of snuff, they had entered the house,
that is, the Baron, Rose, and Lady Emily, with young
Stanley, and the Bailie, for Edward and the rest of the
party remained on the terrace, to examine a new green-
house stocked with the finest plants.   The Baron resumed
his favourite topic : "However it may please you to
derogate from the honour of your burgonet, Colonel
Talbot, which is doubtless your humour, as I have seen in
other gentlemen of birth and honour in your country, I
must again repeat it as a most ancient and distinguished
bearing, as well as that of my young friend Francis
Stanley, which is the eagle and child."

"The bird and bantling they call it in Derbyshire, sir,"
said Stanley.

"Ye're a daft callant,[1] sir," said the Baron, who had a
great liking to this young man, perhaps because he sometimes teazed him—"Ye're a daft callant, and I must
correct you some of these days," shaking his great brown
fist at him.   "But what I meant to say, Colonel Talbot,
is, that yours is an ancient *prosapia*, or descent, and since
you have lawfully and justly acquired the estate for you
and yours, which I have lost for me and mine, I wish it
may remain in your name as many centuries as it has
done in that of the late proprietor's."

"That," answered the Colonel, "is very handsome, Mr
Bradwardine, indeed."

"And yet, sir, I cannot but marvel that you, Colonel,
whom I noted to have so much of the *amor patriæ*, when
we met in Edinburgh, as even to vilipend other countries,
should have chosen to establish your Lares, or household
gods, *procul a patriæ finibus*, and in a manner to expatriate
yourself."

"Why, really, Baron, I do not see why, to keep the

[1] Frolicsome lad.

secret of these foolish boys, Waverley and Stanley, and of
my wife, who is no wiser, one old soldier should continue
to impose upon another. You must know then that I have
so much of that same prejudice in favour of my native
country, that the sum of money which I advanced to the
seller of this extensive barony has only purchased for me
a box in ——shire, called Brerewood Lodge, with about
two hundred and fifty acres of land, the chief merit
of which is, that it is within a very few miles of Waverley-
Honour."

"And who, then, in the name of Heaven, has bought
this property ? "

"That," said the Colonel, "it is this gentleman's profession to explain."

The Bailie, whom this reference regarded, and who had
all this while shifted from one foot to another with great
impatience, "like a hen," as he afterwards said, "upon a
het girdle ; "[1] and chuckling, he might have added, like
the said hen in all the glory of laying an egg,—now
pushed forward. "That I can, that I can, your Honour ; "
drawing from his pocket a budget of papers, and untying
the red tape with a hand trembling with eagerness.
"Here is the disposition and assignation, by Malcolm
Bradwardine of Inch-Grabbit, regularly signed and tested
in terms of the statute, whereby, for a certain sum of
sterling money presently contented and paid to him, he
has disponed, alienated, and conveyed, the whole estate
and barony of Bradwardine, Tully-Veolan, and others,
with the fortalice and manor-place"——

"For God's sake, to the point, sir ; I have all that by
heart," said the Colonel.

"To Cosmo Comyne Bradwardine, Esq.," pursued the
Bailie, "his heirs and assignees, simply and irredeemably
—to be held either *a me vel de me*"——

"Pray read short, sir."

"On the conscience of an honest man, Colonel, I read
as short as is consistent with style.—Under the burden
and reservation always"——

"Mr Macwheeble, this would outlast a Russian winter
—give me leave. In short, Mr Bradwardine, your family
estate is your own once more in full property, and at
your absolute disposal, but only burdened with the sum
advanced to re-purchase it, which I understand is utterly
disproportioned to its value."

"An auld sang—an auld sang, if it please your honours,"

[1] Circular iron plate for toasting cakes.

cried the Bailie, rubbing his hands; "look at the rental book."

"Which sum being advanced by Mr Edward Waverley, chiefly from the price of his father's property which I bought from him, is secured to his lady your daughter, and her family by this marriage."

"It is a catholic security," shouted the Bailie, "to Rose Comyne Bradwardine *alias* Wauverley, in liferent, and the children of the said marriage, in fee: and I made up a wee bit minute of an antenuptial contract, *intuitu matrimonij*, so it cannot be subject to reduction hereafter, as a donation *inter virum et uxorem*."

It is difficult to say whether the worthy Baron was most delighted with the restitution of his family property, or with the delicacy and generosity that left him unfettered to pursue his purpose in disposing of it after his death, and which avoided, as much as possible, even the appearance of laying him under pecuniary obligation. When his first pause of joy and astonishment was over, his thoughts turned to the unworthy heir-male, who, he pronounced, had sold his birth-right, like Esau, for a mess o' pottage.

"But wha cookit the parritch for him?" exclaimed the Bailie; "I wad like to ken that;—wha, but your honour's to command, Duncan Macwheeble? His honour, young Mr Wauverley, put it a' into my hand frae the beginning —frae the first calling o' the summons, as I may say. I circumvented them—I played at bogle about the bush wi' them—I cajolled them; and if I havena gien Inch-Grabbit and Jamie Howie a bonnie begunk,[1] they ken themselves. Him a writer! I didna gae slapdash to them wi' our young bra' bridegroom, to gar them haud up the market: na, na; I scared them wi' our wild tenantry, and the Mac-Ivors, that are but ill settled yet, till they durstna on ony errand whatsoever gang ower the door-stane after gloaming, for fear John Heatherblutter, or some siccan dare-the-deil, should tak a baff[2] at them: then, on the other hand, I beflumm'd them wi' Colonel Talbot—wad they offer to keep up the price again' the Duke's friend? did they na ken wha was master? had they na seen eneugh, by the sad example of mony a puir misguided unhappy body"—

"Who went to Derby, for example, Mr Macwheeble?" said the Colonel to him, aside.

"O whisht, Colonel, for the love o' God? let that

[1] Cheat.   [2] Stroke.

flee stick i' the wa'. There were mony good folk at
Derby; and it's ill speaking of halters,"—with a sly
cast of his eye toward the Baron, who was in a deep
reverie.

Starting out of it at once, he took Macwheeble by the
button, and led him into one of the deep window recesses,
whence only fragments of their conversation reached the
rest of the party. It certainly related to stamp-paper
and parchment; for no other subject, even from the
mouth of his patron, and he, once more, an efficient one,
could have arrested so deeply the Bailie's reverent and
absorbed attention.

"I understand your honour perfectly; it can be dune
as easy as taking out a decreet in absence."

"To her and him, after my demise, and to their heirs-
male,—but preferring the second son, if God shall bless
them with two, who is to carry the name and arms of
Bradwardine of that Ilk, without any other name or
armorial bearings whatsoever."

"Tut, your honour!" whispered the Bailie, "I'll mak a
slight jotting the morn; it will cost but a charter of
resignation *in favorem* ; and I'll hae it ready for the next
term in Exchequer."

Their private conversation ended, the Baron was now
summoned to do the honours of Tully-Veolan to new
guests. These were, Major Melville of Cairnvreckan,
and the Reverend Mr Morton, followed by two or three
others of the Baron's acquaintances, who had been made
privy to his having again acquired the estate of his
fathers. The shouts of the villagers were also heard
beneath in the courtyard; for Saunders Saunderson, who
had kept the secret for several days with laudable
prudence, had unloosed his tongue upon beholding the
arrival of the carriages.

But, while Edward received Major Melville with politeness, and the clergyman with the most affectionate and
greatful kindness, his father-in-law looked a little awkward, as uncertain how he should answer the necessary
claims of hospitality to his guests, and forward the
festivity of his tenants. Lady Emily relieved him, by
intimating, that, though she must be an indifferent
representative of Mrs Edward Waverley in many respects, she hoped the Baron would approve of the
entertainment she had ordered, in expectation of so
many guests; and that they would find such other
accommodations provided, as might in some degree

support the ancient hospitality of Tully-Veolan. It is impossible to describe the pleasure which this assurance gave the Baron, who, with an air of gallantry half appertaining to the stiff Scottish laird, and half to the officer in the French service, offered his arm to the fair speaker, and led the way in something between a stride and a minuet step, into the large dining parlour, followed by all the rest of the good company.

By dint of Saunderson's directions and exertions, all here, as well as in the other apartments, had been disposed as much as possible according to the old arrangement ; and where new movables had been necessary, they had been selected in the same character with the old furniture. There was one addition to this fine old apartment, however, which drew tears into the Baron's eyes. It was a large and spirited painting, representing Fergus Mac-Ivor and Waverley in their Highland dress, the scene a wild, rocky, and mountainous pass, down which the clan were descending in the background. It was taken from a spirited sketch, drawn while they were in Edinburgh by a young man of high genius, and had been painted on a full-length scale by an eminent London artist. Raeburn himself, (whose Highland Chiefs do all but walk out of the canvass) could not have done more justice to the subject ; and the ardent, fiery, and impetuous character of the unfortunate Chief of Glennaquoich was finely contrasted with the contemplative, fanciful, and enthusiastic expression of his happier friend. Beside this painting hung the arms which Waverley had borne in the unfortunate civil war. The whole piece was beheld with admiration, and deeper feelings.

Men must, however, eat, in spite both of sentiment and vertu ; and the Baron, while he assumed the lower end of the table, insisted that Lady Emily should do the honours of the head, that they might, he said, set a meet example to the *young fôlk*. After a pause of deliberation, employed in adjusting in his own brain the precedence between the Presbyterian kirk and Episcopal church of Scotland, he requested Mr Morton, as the stranger, would crave a blessing, observing that Mr Rubrick, who was at *home*, would return thanks for the distinguished mercies it had been his lot to experience. The dinner was excellent. Saunderson attended in full costume, with all the former domestics, who had been collected, excepting one or two, that had not been heard of since the affair of Culloden. The cellars were stocked with wine which was pronounced to be superb, and it had been contrived that the Bear of the Fountain, in the courtyard, should (for that night only) play excellent brandy punch for the benefit of the lower orders.

When the dinner was over, the Baron, about to propose a toast, cast a somewhat sorrowful look upon the sideboard, which, however, exhibited much of his plate, that had either been secreted, or purchased by neighbouring gentlemen from the soldiery, and by them gladly restored to the original owner.

"In the late times," he said, "those must be thankful who have saved life and land; yet when I am about to pronounce this toast, I cannot but regret an old heirloom, Lady Emily—a *poculum potatorium*, Colonel Talbot"——

Here the Baron's elbow was gently touched by his Major Domo, and, turning round, he beheld in the hands of Alexander ab Alexandro, the celebrated cup of Saint Duthac, the Blessed Bear of Bradwardine! I question if the recovery of his estate afforded him more rapture. "By my honour," he said, "one might almost believe in brownies and fairies, Lady Emily, when your ladyship is in presence!"

"I am truly happy," said Colonel Talbot, "that by the recovery of this piece of family antiquity, it has fallen within my power to give you some token of my deep interest in all that concerns my young friend Edward. But that you may not suspect Lady Emily for a sorceress, or me for a conjurer, which is no joke in Scotland, I must tell you that Frank Stanley, your friend, who has been seized with a tartan fever ever since he heard Edward's tales of old Scottish manners, happened to describe to us at second hand this remarkable cup. My servant, Spontoon, who, like a true old soldier, observes everything and says little, gave me afterwards to understand that he thought he had seen the piece of plate Mr Stanley mentioned, in the possession of a certain Mrs Nosebag, who, having been originally the helpmate of a pawnbroker, had found opportunity, during the late unpleasant scenes in Scotland, to trade a little in her old line, and so became the depositary of the more valuable part of the spoil of half the army. You may believe the cup was speedily recovered; and it will give me very great pleasure if you allow me to suppose, that its value is not diminished by having been restored through my means."

A tear mingled with the wine which the Baron filled, as

he proposed a cup of gratitude to Colonel Talbot, and "The Prosperity of the united Houses of Waverley-Honour and Bradwardine !"——

It only remains for me to say, that as no wish was ever uttered with more affectionate sincerity, there are few which, allowing for the necessary mutability of human events, have been, upon the whole, more happily fulfilled.

## CHAPTER LXXII.

### *A Postscript, which should have been a Preface.*

OUR journey is now finished, gentle reader ; and if your patience has accompanied me through these sheets, the contract is, on your part, strictly fulfilled. Yet, like the driver who has received his full hire, I still linger near you, and make, with becoming diffidence, a trifling additional claim upon your bounty and good nature. You are as free, however, to shut the volume of the one petitioner, as to close your door in the face of the other.

This should have been a prefatory chapter, but for two reasons : First, that most novel readers, as my own conscience reminds me, are apt to be guilty of the sin of omission respecting that same matter of prefaces ; Secondly, that it is a general custom with that class of students, to begin with the last chapter of a work ; so that, after all, these remarks, being introduced last in order, have still the best chance to be read in their proper place.

There is no European nation, which, within the course of half a century, or little more, has undergone so complete a change as this kingdom of Scotland. The effects of the insurrection of 1745,—the destruction of the patriarchal power of the Highland chiefs,—the abolition of the heritable jurisdictions of the Lowland nobility and barons,—the total eradication of the Jacobite party, which, averse to intermingle with the English, or adopt their customs, long continued to pride themselves upon maintaining ancient Scottish manners and customs,—commenced this innovation. The gradual influx of wealth, and extension of commerce, have since united to render the present people of Scotland a class of beings as different from their grandfathers, as the existing English are from those of Queen Elizabeth's time. The political

and economical effects of these changes have been traced
by Lord Selkirk with great precision and accuracy. But
the change, though steadily and rapidly progressive, has,
nevertheless, been gradual; and like those who drift down
the stream of a deep and smooth river, we are not aware
of the progress we have made until we fix our eye on the
now distant point from which we have been drifted.
Such of the present generation as can recollect the last
twenty or twenty-five years of the eighteenth century,
will be fully sensible of the truth of this statement;
especially if their acquaintance and connections lay among
those, who, in my younger time, were facetiously called
"folks of the old leven," who still cherished a lingering,
though hopeless attachment, to the house of Stewart.
This race has now almost entirely vanished from the land,
and with it, doubtless, much absurd political prejudice;
but also, many living examples of singular and disinterested attachment to the principles of loyalty which
they received from their fathers, and of old Scottish faith,
hospitality, worth, and honour.

It was my accidental lot, though not born a Highlander,
(which may be an apology for much bad Gaelic) to reside,
during my childhood and youth, among persons of the
above description; and now, for the purpose of preserving
some idea of the ancient manners of which I have
witnessed the almost total extinction, I have embodied
in imaginary scenes, and ascribed to fictitious characters,
a part of the incidents which I then received from those
who were actors in them. Indeed, the most romantic
parts of this narrative are precisely those which have a
foundation in fact. The exchange of mutual protection
between a Highland gentleman and an officer of rank in
the king's service, together with the spirited manner in
which the latter asserted his right to return the favour
he had received, is literally true. The accident by a
musket-shot, and the heroic reply imputed to Flora, relate
to a lady of rank not long deceased. And scarce a
gentleman who was "in hiding," after the battle of
Culloden, but could tell a tale of strange concealments,
and of wild and hair's-breadth 'scapes, as extraordinary as
any which I have ascribed to my heroes. Of this, the
escape of Charles Edward himself, as the most prominent,
is the most striking example. The accounts of the battle
of Preston and skirmish at Clifton, are taken from the
narrative of intelligent eye-witnesses, and corrected from
the History of the Rebellion by the late venerable author

of Douglas. The Lowland Scottish gentlemen, and the subordinate characters, are not given as individual portraits, but are drawn from the general habits of the period, of which I have witnessed some remnants in my younger days, and partly gathered from tradition.

It has been my object to describe these persons, not by a caricatured and exaggerated use of the national dialect, but by their habits, manners, and feelings ; so as in some distant degree to emulate the admirable Irish portraits drawn by Miss Edgeworth, so different from the "Teagues" and "dear joys," who so long, with the most perfect family resemblance to each other, occupied the drama and the novel.

I feel no confidence, however, in the manner in which I have executed my purpose. Indeed, so little was I satisfied with my production, that I laid it aside in an unfinished state, and only found it again by mere accident among other waste papers in an old cabinet, the drawers of which I was rummaging, in order to accommodate a friend with some fishing tackle, after it had been mislaid for several years. Two works upon similar subjects, by female authors, whose genius is highly creditable to their country, have appeared in the interval ; I mean Mrs Hamilton's Glenburnie, and the late account of Highland Superstitions. But the first is confined to the rural habits of Scotland, of which it has given a picture with striking and impressive fidelity ; and the traditional records of the respectable and ingenious Mrs Grant of Laggan, are of a nature distinct from the fictitious narrative which I have here attempted.

I would willingly persuade myself, that the preceding work will not be found altogether uninteresting. To elder persons it will recall scenes and characters familiar to their youth ; and to the rising generation the tale may present some idea of the manners of their forefathers.

Yet I heartily wish that the task of tracing the evanescent manners of his own country had employed the pen of the only man in Scotland who could have done it justice,—of him so eminently distinguished in elegant literature, and whose sketches of Colonel Caustic and Umphraville are perfectly blended with the finer traits of national character. I should in that case have had more pleasure as a reader, than I shall ever feel in the pride of a successful author, should these sheets confer upon me that envied distinction. And as I have inverted

the usual arrangement, placing these remarks at the end
of the work to which they refer, I will venture on a
second violation of form, by closing the whole with a
Dedication ;

THESE VOLUMES

BEING RESPECTFULLY INSCRIBED

TO

*OUR SCOTTISH ADDISON,*

# HENRY MACKENZIE.

BY

AN UNKNOWN ADMIRER

OF

HIS GENIUS.

# NOTES TO WAVERLEY.

### Note 1.—TITUS LIVIUS.

The attachment to this classic was, it is said, actually displayed, in the manner mentioned in the text, by an unfortunate Jacobite in that unhappy period. He escaped from the jail in which he was confined for a hasty trial and certain condemnation, and was retaken as he hovered around the place in which he had been imprisoned, for which he could give no better reason than the hope of recovering his favourite *Titus Livius*. I am sorry to add, that the simplicity of such a character was found to form no apology for his guilt as a rebel, and that he was condemned and executed.

### Note 2.—NICHOLAS AMHURST.

Nicholas Amhurst, a noted political writer, who conducted for many years a paper called the Craftsman, under the assumed name of Caleb D'Anvers. He was devoted to the Tory interest, and seconded, with much ability, the attacks of Pulteney on Sir Robert Walpole. He died in 1742, neglected by his great patrons, and in the most miserable circumstances.

"Amhurst survived the downfall of Walpole's power, and had reason to expect a reward for his labours. If we excuse Bolingbroke, who had only saved the shipwreck of his fortunes, we shall be at a loss to justify Pulteney, who could with ease have given this man a considerable income. The utmost of his generosity to Amhurst, that I ever heard of, was a hogshead of claret! He died, it is supposed, of a broken heart; and was buried at the charge of his honest printer, Richard Francklin." —(*Lord Chesterfield's Characters Reviewed*, p. 42.)

### Note 3.—COLONEL GARDINER.

I have now given in the text, the full name of this gallant and excellent man, and proceed to copy the account of his remarkable conversion, as related by Dr Doddridge.

"This memorable event," says the pious writer, "happened towards the middle of July 1719. The major had spent the evening (and, if I mistake not, it was the Sabbath) in some gay company, and had an unhappy assignation with a married woman, whom he was to attend exactly at twelve. The company broke up about eleven; and not judging it convenient to antici-

pate the time appointed, he went into his chamber to kill the
tedious hour, perhaps with some amusing book, or some other
way. But it very accidentally happened, that he took up a
religious book, which his good mother or aunt had, without his
knowledge, slipped into his portmanteau. It was called, if I
remember the title exactly, The Christian Soldier, or Heaven
taken by Storm, and it was written by Mr Thomas Watson.
Guessing by the title of it that he would find some phrases of his
own profession spiritualized in a manner which he thought might
afford him some diversion, he resolved to dip into it; but he
took no serious notice of anything it had in it; and yet while
this book was in his hand, an impression was made upon his
mind (perhaps God only knows how) which drew after it a train
of the most important and happy consequences. He thought he
saw an unusual blaze of light fall upon the book which he was
reading, which he at first imagined might happen by some
accident in the candle; but lifting up his eyes, he apprehended
to his extreme amazement, that there was before him, as it were
suspended in the air, a visible representation of the Lord Jesus
Christ upon the cross, surrounded on all sides with a glory; and
was impressed, as if a voice, or something equivalent to a voice,
had come to him, to this effect (for he was not confident as to the
words), 'Oh, sinner! did I suffer this for thee, and are these thy
returns!' Struck with so amazing a phenomenon as this, there
remained hardly any life in him, so that he sunk down in the
arm-chair in which he sat, and continued, he knew not how long,
insensible."

"With regard to this vision," says the ingenious Dr Hibbert,
"the appearance of our Saviour on the cross, and the awful
words repeated, can be considered in no other light than as so
many recollected images of the mind, which, probably, had their
origin in the language of some urgent appeal to repentance, that
the colonel might have casually read, or heard delivered. From
what cause, however, such ideas were rendered as vivid as actual
impressions, we have no information to be depended upon. This
vision was certainly attended with one of the most important of
consequences, connected with the Christian dispensation—the
conversion of a sinner. And hence no single narrative has,
perhaps, done more to confirm the superstitious opinion that
apparitions of this awful kind cannot arise without a divine
fiat." Dr Hibbert adds, in a note—"A short time before the
vision, Colonel Gardiner had received a severe fall from his horse.
Did the brain receive some slight degree of injury from the
accident, so as to predispose him to this spiritual illusion?"—
(Hibbert's Philosophy of Apparitions, Edinburgh, 1824, p. 190.)

## Note 4.—Scottish Inns.

The courtesy of an invitation to partake a traveller's meal, or
at least that of being invited to share whatever liquor the guest

called for, was expected by certain old landlords in Scotland even in the youth of the author. In requital, mine host was always furnished with the news of the country, and was probably a little of a humourist to boot. The devolution of the whole actual business and drudgery of the inn upon the poor gudewife, was very common among the Scottish Bonifaces. There was in ancient times, in the city of Edinburgh, a gentleman of good family, who condescended, in order to gain a livelihood, to become the nominal keeper of a coffeehouse, one of the first places of the kind which had been opened in the Scottish metropolis. As usual, it was entirely managed by the careful and industrious Mrs B——; while her husband amused himself with field sports, without troubling his head about the matter. Once upon a time the premises having taken fire, the husband was met, walking up the High Street loaded with his guns and fishing-rods, and replied calmly to some one who enquired after his wife, "that the poor woman was trying to save a parcel of crockery, and some trumpery books;" the last being those which served her to conduct the business of the house.

There were many elderly gentlemen in the author's younger days, who still held it part of the amusement of a journey "to parley with mine host," who often resembled, in his quaint humour, mine Host of the Garter in the Merry Wives of Windsor; or Blague of the George in the Merry Devil of Edmonton. Sometimes the landlady took her share of entertaining the company. In either case the omitting to pay them due attention gave displeasure, and perhaps brought down a smart jest, as on the following occasion:—

A jolly dame who, not "Sixty Years since," kept the principal caravansary at Greenlaw, in Berwickshire, had the honour to receive under her roof a very worthy clergyman, with three sons of the same profession, each having a cure of souls: be it said in passing, none of the reverend party were reckoned powerful in the pulpit. After dinner was over, the worthy senior, in the pride of his heart, asked Mrs Buchan whether she ever had had such a party in her house before, "Here sit I," he said, "a placed minister of the Kirk of Scotland, and here sit my three sons, each a placed minister of the same kirk.— Confess, Luckie Buchan, you never had such a party in your house before." The question was not premised by any invitation to sit down and take a glass of wine or the like, so Mrs B. answered dryly, "Indeed sir, I cannot just say that ever I had such a party in my house before, except once in the forty-five, when I had a Highland piper here, with his three sons, all Highland pipers; *and deil a spring they could play amang them.*"

## Note 5.—STIRRUP-CUP.

I may here mention, that the fashion of compotation described in the text, was still occasionally practised in Scotland, in the author's youth. A company, after having taken leave of their host, often went to finish the evening at the clachan or village, in "womb of tavern." Their entertainer always accompanied them to take the stirrup-cup, which often occasioned a long and late revel.

The *Poculum Potatorium* of the valiant Baron his blessed Bear, has a prototype at the fine old Castle of Glammis, so rich in memorials of ancient times; it is a massive beaker of silver, double gilt, moulded into the shape of a lion, and holding about an English pint of wine. The form alludes to the family name of Strathmore, which is Lyon, and, when exhibited, the cup must necessarily be emptied to the Earl's health. The author ought perhaps to be ashamed of recording that he has had the honour of swallowing the contents of the Lion; and the recollection of the feat served to suggest the story of the Bear of Bradwardine. In the family of Scott of Thirlestane (not Thirlestane in the Forest, but the place of the same name in Roxburghshire) was long preserved a cup of the same kind, in the form of a jackboot. Each guest was obliged to empty this at his departure. If the guest's name was Scott, the necessity was doubly imperative.

When the landlord of an inn presented his guests with *deoch an doruis*, that is, the drink at the door, or the stirrup-cup, the draught was not charged in the reckoning. On this point a learned Bailie of the town of Forfar pronounced a very sound judgment.

A., an ale wife in Forfar, had brewed her "peck of malt," and set the liquor out of doors to cool; the cow of B., a neighbour of A., chanced to come by, and seeing the good beverage, was allured to taste it, and finally to drink it up. When A. came to take in her liquor, she found her tub empty, and from the cow's staggering and staring, so as to betray her intemperance, she easily divined the mode in which her "browst" had disappeared. To take vengeance on Crummie's ribs with a stick, was her first effort. The roaring of the cow brought B., her master, who remonstrated with his angry neighbour, and received in reply a demand for the value of the ale which Crummie had drunk up. B. refused payment and was conveyed before C., the Bailie, or sitting Magistrate. He heard the case patiently; and then demanded of the plaintiff A., whether the cow had sat down to her potation, or taken it standing. The plaintiff answered, she had not seen the deed committed, but she supposed the cow drank the ale while standing on her feet; adding, that had she been near, she would have made her use them to some purpose. The Bailie, on this admission, solemnly adjudged the cow's drink to be *deoch an doruis*—a stirrup-cup, for which no charge could be made, without violating the ancient hospitality of Scotland.

## Note 6.—Rob Roy.

An adventure, very similar to what is here stated, actually befell the late Mr Abercromby of Tullibody, grandfather of the

present Lord Abercromby, and father of the celebrated Sir
Ralph. When this gentleman, who lived to a very advanced
period of life, first settled in Stirlingshire, his cattle were
repeatedly driven off by the celebrated Rob Roy, or some of his
gang; and at length he was obliged, after obtaining a proper
safe-conduct, to make the cateran such a visit as that of Waverley to Bean Lean in the text. Rob received him with much
courtesy, and made many apologies for the accident, which must
have happened, he said, through some mistake. Mr Abercromby
was regaled with collops from two of his own cattle, which were
hung up by the heels in the cavern, and was dismissed in perfect
safety, after having agreed to pay in future a small sum of black-
mail, in consideration of which Rob Roy not only undertook to
forbear his herds in future, but to replace any that should be
stolen from him by other freebooters. Mr Abercromby said,
Rob Roy affected to consider him as a friend to the Jacobite
interest, and a sincere enemy to the Union. Neither of these
circumstances were true; but the laird thought it quite unnecessary to undeceive his Highland host at the risk of bringing on a
political dispute in such a situation. This anecdote I received
many years since (about 1792), from the mouth of the venerable
gentleman who was concerned in it.

## Note 7.—KIND GALLOWS OF CRIEFF.

This celebrated gibbet was, in the memory of the last generation, still standing at the western end of the town of Crieff, in
Perthshire. Why it was called the *kind* gallows, we are unable
to inform the reader with certainty; but it is alleged that the
Highlanders used to touch their bonnets as they passed a place,
which had been fatal to many of their countrymen, with the
ejaculation—"God bless her nain sell, and the Teil tamn you!"
It may therefore have been called kind, as being a sort of native
or kindred place of doom to those who suffered there, as in fulfil-
ment of a natural destiny.

## Note 8.—CATERANS.

The story of the bridegroom carried off by Caterans, on his
bridal-day, is taken from one which was told to the author by
the late Laird of Mac-Nab, many years since. To carry off
persons from the Lowlands, and to put them to ransom, was a
common practice with the wild Highlanders, as it is said to be
at the present day with the banditti in the South of Italy.
Upon the occasion alluded to, a party of Caterans carried off the
bridegroom, and secreted him in some cave near the mountain of
Schiehallion. The young man caught the small-pox before his
ransom could be agreed on; and whether it was the fine cool air
of the place, or the want of medical attendance, Mac-Nab did
not pretend to be positive; but so it was, that the prisoner
recovered, his ransom was paid, and he was restored to his

friends and bride, but always considered the Highland robbers as having saved his life, by their treatment of his malady.

### Note 9.—Highland Policy.

This sort of political game ascribed to Mac-Ivor was in reality played by several Highland chiefs, the celebrated Lord Lovat in particular, who used that kind of finesse to the uttermost. The Laird of Mac—— was also captain of an independent company, but valued the sweets of present pay too well to incur the risk of losing them in the Jacobite cause. His martial consort raised his clan, and headed it, in 1745. But the chief himself would have nothing to do with king-making, declaring himself for that monarch, and no other, who gave the Laird of Mac—— "half-a-guinea the day, and half-a-guinea the morn."

### Note 10.—Highland Discipline.

In explanation of the military exercise observed at the Castle of Glennaquoich, the author begs to remark, that the Highlanders were not only well practised in the use of the broadsword, fire-lock, and most of the manly sports and trials of strength common throughout Scotland, but also used a peculiar sort of drill, suited to their own dress and mode of warfare. There were, for instance, different modes of disposing the plaid, one when on a peaceful journey, another when danger was apprehended; one way of enveloping themselves in it when expecting undisturbed repose, and another which enabled them to start up with sword and pistol in hand on the slightest alarm.

Previous to 1720, or thereabouts, the belted plaid was universally worn, in which the portion which surrounded the middle of the wearer, and that which was flung around his shoulders, were all of the same piece of tartan. In a desperate onset, all was thrown away, and the clan charged bare beneath the doublet, save for an artificial arrangement of the shirt, which, like that of the Irish, was always ample, and for the sporran-mollach, or goat's skin purse.

The manner of handling the pistol and dirk was also part of the Highland manual exercise, which the author has seen gone through by men who had learned it in their youth.

### Note 11.—Dislike of the Scotch to Pork.

Pork, or swine's flesh, in any shape, was, till of late years, much abominated by the Scotch, nor is it yet a favourite food amongst them. King Jamie carried this prejudice to England, and is known to have abhorred pork almost as much as he did tobacco. Ben Jonson has recorded this peculiarity, where the gipsy in a masque, examining the king's hand, says,

> "—— you should by this line
> Love a horse, and a hound, but no part of a swine."
> *The Gipsies Metamorphosed.*

James's own proposed banquet for the Devil, was a loin of pork and a poll of ling, with a pipe of tobacco for digestion.

### Note 12.—A Scottish Dinner Table.

In the number of persons of all ranks who assembled at the same table, though by no means to discuss the same fare, the Highland chiefs only retained a custom which had been formerly universally observed throughout Scotland. "I myself," says the traveller, Fynes Morrison, in the end of Queen Elizabeth's reign, the scene being the Lowlands of Scotland, "was at a knight's house, who had many servants to attend him, that brought in his meat with their heads covered with blue caps, the table being more than half furnished with great platters of porridge, each having a little piece of sodden meat. And when the table was served, the servants did sit down with us; but the upper mess, instead of porridge, had a pullet, with some prunes in the broth."—(*Travels*, p. 155.)

Till within this last century, the farmers, even of a respectable condition, dined with their work-people. The difference betwixt those of high degree, was ascertained by the place of the party above or below the salt, or, sometimes, by a line drawn with chalk on the dining table. Lord Lovat, who knew well how to feed the vanity, and restrain the appetites, of his clansmen, allowed each sturdy Fraser, who had the slightest pretensions to be a Duinhé-wassal, the full honour of the sitting, but, at the same time, took care that his young kinsmen did not acquire at his table any taste for outlandish luxuries. His lordship was always ready with some honourable apology, why foreign wines and French brandy, delicacies which he conceived might sap the hardy habits of his cousins, should not circulate past an assigned point on the table.

### Note 13.—Conan the Jester.

In the Irish ballads, relating to Fion, (the Fingal of Mac-Pherson,) there occurs, as in the primitive poetry of most nations, a cycle of heroes, each of whom has some distinguishing attribute; upon these qualities, and the adventures of those possessing them, many proverbs are formed, which are still current in the Highlands. Among other characters, Conan is distinguished as in some respects a kind of Thersites, but brave and daring even to rashness. He had made a vow that he would never take a blow without returning it; and having, like other heroes of antiquity, descended to the infernal regions, he received a cuff from the Arch-fiend, who presided there, which he instantly returned, using the expression in the text. Sometimes the proverb is worded thus:—"Claw for claw, and the devil take the shortest nails, as Conan said to the devil."

## Note 14.—WATERFALL.

The description of the waterfall mentioned in this chapter is taken from that of Ledeard, at the farm so called on the northern side of Lochard, and near the head of the Lake, four or five miles from Aberfoyle. It is upon a small scale, but otherwise one of the most exquisite cascades it is possible to behold. The appearance of Flora with the harp, as described, has been justly censured as too theatrical and affected for the lady-like simplicity of her character. But something may be allowed to her French education, in which point and striking effect always make a considerable object.

## Note 15.—MAC-FARLANE'S LANTERN.

The Clan of Mac-Farlane, occupying the fastnesses of the western side of Loch Lomond, were great depredators on the Low Country, and as their excursions were made usually by night, the moon was proverbially called their lantern. Their celebrated pibroch of *Hoggil nam Bo*, which is the name of their gathering tune, intimates similar practices,—the sense being:—

> " We are bound to drive the bullocks,
>   All by hollows, hirsts and hillocks,
>     Through the sleet, and through the rain.
>   When the moon is beaming low
>   On frozen lake and hills of snow.
>   Bold and heartily we go;
>     And all for little gain."

## Note 16.—THE CASTLE OF DOUNE.

This noble ruin is dear to my recollection, from associations which have been long and painfully broken. It holds a commanding station on the banks of the river Teith, and has been one of the largest castles in Scotland. Murdoch, Duke of Albany, the founder of this stately pile, was beheaded on the Castlehill of Stirling, from which he might see the towers of Doune, the monument of his fallen greatness.

In 1745-6, as stated in the text, a garrison on the part of the Chevalier was put into the castle, then less ruinous than at present. It was commanded by Mr Stewart of Balloch, as governor for Prince Charles; he was a man of property near Callander. This castle became at that time the actual scene of a romantic escape made by John Home, the author of Douglas, and some other prisoners, who, having been taken at the battle of Falkirk, were confined there by the insurgents. The poet, who had in his own mind a large stock of that romantic and enthusiastic spirit of adventure, which he has described as animating the youthful hero of his drama, devised and undertook the perilous enterprise of escaping from his prison. He inspired his companions with his sentiments, and when every attempt at open force was deemed hopeless, they resolved to twist their bed-clothes into ropes, and thus to descend. Four persons, with Home himself, reached the ground in safety. But the rope broke with the fifth, who was a tall lusty man. The sixth was Thomas Barrow, a brave young Englishman, a particular friend of Home's. Determined to take the risk, even in such unfavourable circumstances, Barrow committed himself to the broken rope, slid down on it as far as it could assist him, and then let himself drop. His friends beneath succeeded in breaking his fall. Nevertheless, he dislocated his ankle, and had several of his ribs broken. His companions, however, were able to bear him off in safety.

The Highlanders next morning sought for their prisoners with great activity. An old gentleman told the author he remembered seeing the commander Stewart,

> "Bloody with spurring, fiery red with haste,"

riding furiously through the country in quest of the fugitives.

## Note 17.—Field-piece in the Highland Army.

This circumstance, which is historical, as well as the description that precedes it, will remind the reader of the war of La Vendée, in which the royalists, consisting chiefly of insurgent peasantry, attached a prodigious and even superstitious interest to the possession of a piece of brass ordnance, which they called Marie Jeane.

The Highlanders of an early period were afraid of cannon, with the noise and effect of which they were totally unacquainted. It was by means of three or four small pieces of artillery, that the Earls of Huntly and Errol, in James VI.'s time, gained a great victory at Glenlivat, over a numerous Highland army, commanded by the Earl of Argyle. At the battle of the Bridge of Dee, General Middleton obtained by his artillery a similar success, the Highlanders not being able to stand the discharge of *Musket's-Mother*, which was the name they bestowed on great-guns. In an old ballad on the battle of the Bridge of Dee, these verses occur:—

> "The Highlandmen are pretty men
> For handling sword and shield,
> But yet they are but simple men
> To stand a stricken field.
>
> The Highlandmen are pretty men
> For target and claymore,
> But yet they are but naked men
> To face the cannon's roar.
>
> For the cannon's roar on a summer night
> Like thunder in the air;
> Was never man in Highland garb
> Would face the cannon fair."

But the Highlanders of 1745 had got far beyond the simplicity of their forefathers, and showed throughout the whole war how little they dreaded artillery, although the common people still attached some consequence to the possession of the field-piece, which led to this disquisition.

### Note 18.—ANDERSON OF WHITBURGH.

The faithful friend who pointed out the pass by which the Highlanders moved from Tranent to Seaton, was Robert Anderson, junior, of Whitburgh, a gentleman of property in East Lothian. He had been interrogated by the Lord George Murray concerning the possibility of crossing the uncouth and marshy piece of ground which divided the armies, and which he described as impracticable. When dismissed, he recollected that there was a circuitous path leading eastward through the marsh into the plain, by which the Highlanders might turn the flank of Sir John Cope's position, without being exposed to the enemy's fire. Having mentioned his opinion to Mr Hepburn of Keith, who instantly saw its importance, he was encouraged by that gentleman to awake Lord George Murray, and communicate the idea to him. Lord George received the information with grateful thanks, and instantly awakened Prince Charles, who was sleeping in the field with a bunch of pease under his head. The Adventurer received with alacrity the news that there was a possibility of bringing an excellently provided army to a decisive battle with his own irregular forces. His joy on the occasion was not very consistent with the charge of cowardice brought against him by Chevalier Johnstone, a discontented follower, whose Memoirs possess at least as much of a romantic as a historical character. Even by the account of the Chevalier himself, the Prince was at the head of the second line of the Highland army during the battle, of which he says, "It was gained with such rapidity, that in the second line, where I was still by the side of the Prince, we saw no other enemy than those who were lying on the ground killed and wounded, *though we were not more than fifty paces behind our first line, running always as fast as we could to overtake them.*"

This passage in the Chevalier's Memoirs places the Prince within fifty paces of the heat of the battle, a position which would never have been the choice of one unwilling to take a share of its dangers. Indeed, unless the chiefs had complied with the young Adventurer's proposal to lead the van in person, it does not appear that he could have been deeper in the action.

### Note 19.—DEATH OF COLONEL GARDINER.

The death of this good Christian and gallant man is thus given by his affectionate biographer, Dr Doddridge, from the evidence of eye-witnesses :—

"He continued all night under arms, wrapped up in his cloak, and generally sheltered under a rick of barley, which happened to be in the field. About three in the morning he called his

domestic servants to him, of which there were four in waiting.
He dismissed three of them with most affectionate Christian
advice, and such solemn charges relating to the performance of
their duty, and the care of their souls, as seemed plainly to intimate that he apprehended it was at least very probable he was
taking his last farewell of them. There is great reason to
believe that he spent the little remainder of the time, which
could not be much above an hour, in those devout exercises of
soul which had been so long habitual to him, and to which so
many circumstances did then concur to call him. The army was
alarmed by break of day, by the noise of the rebels' approach,
and the attack was made before sunrise, yet when it was light
enough to discern what passed. As soon as the enemy came
within gun-shot they made a furious fire; and it is said that the
dragoons which constituted the left wing, immediately fled. The
Colonel at the beginning of the onset, which in the whole lasted
but a few minutes, received a wound by a bullet in his left
breast, which made him give a sudden spring in his saddle; upon
which his servant, who led the horse, would have persuaded him
to retreat, but he said it was only a wound in the flesh, and
fought on, though he presently after received a shot in his right
thigh. In the meantime, it was discerned that some of the
enemy fell by him, and particularly one man, who had made him
a treacherous visit but a few days before, with great profession
of zeal for the present establishment.

"Events of this kind pass in less time than the description of
them can be written, or than it can be read. The Colonel was
for a few moments supported by his men, and particularly by
that worthy person Lieutenant-Colonel Whitney, who was shot
through the arm here, and a few months after fell nobly at the
battle of Falkirk, and by Lieutenant West, a man of distinguished
bravery, as also by about fifteen dragoons, who stood by him to
the last. But after a faint fire, the regiment in general was
seized with a panic: and though their Colonel and some other
gallant officers did what they could to rally them once or twice,
they at last took a precipitate flight. And just in the moment
when Colonel Gardiner seemed to be making a pause to deliberate
what duty required him to do in such circumstances, an accident
happened, which must, I think, in the judgment of every worthy
and generous man, be allowed a sufficient apology for exposing
his life to so great hazard, when his regiment had left him.
He saw a party of the foot, who were then bravely fighting near
him, and whom he was ordered to support, had no officer to head
them; upon which he said eagerly, in the hearing of the person
from whom I had this account, 'These brave fellows will be cut
to pieces for want of a commander,' or words to that effect;
which while he was speaking, he rode up to them and cried out,
'Fire on, my lads, and fear nothing.' But just as the words
were out of his mouth, a Highlander advanced towards him with
a scythe fastened to a long pole, with which he gave him so

dreadful a wound on his right arm, that his sword dropped out of his hand ; and at the same time several others coming about him while he was thus dreadfully entangled with that cruel weapon, he was dragged off from his horse. The moment he fell, another Highlander, who, if the king's evidence at Carlisle may be credited (as I know not why they should not, though the unhappy creature died denying it), was one Mac-Naught, who was executed about a year after, gave him a stroke either with a broadsword or a Lochaber-axe (for my informant could not exactly distinguish) on the hinder part of his head, which was the mortal blow. All that his faithful attendant saw further at this time was, that as his hat was falling off, he took it in his left hand and waved it as a signal to him to retreat, and added, what were the last words he ever heard him speak, ' Take care of yourself ;' upon which the servant retired."—*Some remarkable Passages in the Life of Colonel James Gardiner, by P. Doddridge, D.D.* London, 1747, p. 187.

I may remark on this extract, that it confirms the account given in the text of the resistance offered by some of the English infantry. Surprised by a force of a peculiar and unusual description, their opposition could not be long or formidable, especially as they were deserted by the cavalry, and those who undertook to manage the artillery. But although the affair was soon decided, I have always understood that many of the infantry showed an inclination to do their duty.

### Note 20.—THE LAIRD OF BALMAWHAPPLE.

It is scarcely necessary to say that the character of this brutal young Laird is entirely imaginary. A gentleman, however, who resembled Balmawhapple in the article of courage only, fell at Preston in the manner described. A Perthshire gentleman of high honour and respectability, one of the handful of cavalry who followed the fortunes of Charles Edward, pursued the fugitive dragoons almost alone until near Saint Clement's Wells, where the efforts of some of the officers had prevailed on a few of them to make a momentary stand. Perceiving at this moment that they were pursued by only one man and a couple of servants, they turned upon him and cut him down with their swords. I remember, when a child, sitting on his grave, where the grass long grew rank and green, distinguishing it from the rest of the field. A female of the family then residing at Saint Clement's Wells used to tell me the tragedy of which she had been an eye-witness, and showed me in evidence one of the silver clasps of the unfortunate gentleman's waistcoat.

### Note 21.—ANDREA DE FERRARA.

The name of Andrea de Ferrara is inscribed on all the Scottish broadswords which are accounted of peculiar excellence.

Who this artist was, what were his fortunes, and when he flourished, have hitherto defied the research of antiquaries ; only it is in general believed that Andrea de Ferrara was a Spanish or Italian artificer, brought over by James the IV. or V. to instruct the Scots in the manufacture of sword blades. Most barbarous nations excel in the fabrication of arms ; and the Scots had attained great proficiency in forging swords, so early as the field of Pinkie ; at which period the historian Patten describes them as "all notably broad and thin, universally made to slice, and of such exceeding good temper, that as I never saw any so good, so I think it hard to devise better."—(*Account of Somerset's Expedition.*)

It may be observed, that the best and most genuine Andrea Ferraras have a crown marked on the blades.

## Note 22.—PRINCE CHARLES EDWARD.

The Author of Waverley has been charged with painting the young Adventurer in colours more amiable than his character deserved. But having known many individuals who were near his person, he. has been described according to the light in which those eye-witnesses saw his temper and qualifications. Something must be allowed, no doubt, to the natural exaggerations of those who remembered him as the bold and adventurous Prince, in whose cause they had braved death and ruin ; but is their evidence to give place entirely to that of a single malcontent?

I have already noticed the imputations thrown by the Chevalier Johnstone on the Prince's courage. But some part at least of that gentleman's tale is purely romantic. It would not, for instance, be supposed, that at the time he is favouring us with the highly wrought account of his amour with the adorable Peggie, the Chevalier Johnstone was a married man, whose grandchild is now alive, or that the whole circumstantial story concerning the outrageous vengeance taken by Gordon of Abbachie on a Presbyterian clergyman, is entirely apocryphal. At the same time it may be admitted, that the Prince, like others of his family, did not esteem the services done him by his adherents so highly as he ought. Educated in high ideas of his hereditary right, he has been supposed to have held every exertion and sacrifice made in his cause as too much the duty of the person making it to merit extravagant gratitude on his part. Dr King's evidence (which his leaving the Jacobite interest renders somewhat doubtful) goes to strengthen this opinion.

The ingenious editor of Johnstone's Memoirs has quoted a story said to be told by Helvetius, stating that Prince Charles Edward, far from voluntarily embarking on his daring expedition, was literally bound hand and foot, and to which he seems disposed to yield credit. Now, it being a fact as well known as any in his history, and, so far as I know, entirely undisputed, that the Prince's personal entreaties and urgency positively forced Boisdale and Lochiel into insurrection, when they were earnestly desirous that he would put off his attempt until he could obtain a sufficient force from France, it will be very difficult to reconcile his alleged reluctance to undertake the expedition, with his desperately insisting on carrying the rising into effect, against the advice and entreaty of his most powerful and most sage partizans. Surely a man who had been carried bound on board the vessel which brought him to so desperate an enterprise, would have taken the opportunity afforded by the reluctance of his partizans, to return to France in safety.

It is averred in Johnstone's Memoirs, that Charles Edward left the field of Culloden without doing the utmost to dispute the victory ; and, to give the evidence on both sides, there is in existence the more trustworthy testimony of Lord Elcho, who states, that he himself earnestly exhorted the Prince to charge at the head of the left wing, which was entire, and retrieve the day or die with honour. And on his counsel being declined, Lord Elcho took leave of him with a bitter execration, swearing he would never look on his face again, and kept his word.

On the other hand, it seems to have been the opinion of almost all the other officers, that the day was irretrievably lost, one wing of the Highlanders being entirely routed, the rest of the army out-numbered, out flanked, and in a condition totally hopeless. In this situation of things, the Irish officers who surrounded Charles's person interfered to force him off the field. A cornet who was close to the Prince, left a strong attestation, that he had seen Sir Thomas Sheridan seize the bridle of his horse, and turn him round. There is some discrepancy of evidence ; but the opinion of Lord Elcho, a man of fiery temper, and desperate at the ruin which he beheld impending, cannot fairly be taken, in prejudice of a character for courage which is intimated by the nature of the enterprise itself, by the Prince's eagerness to fight on all occasions, by his determination to advance from Derby to London, and by the presence of mind which he manifested during the romantic perils of his escape. The author is far from claiming for this unfortunate person the praise due to splendid talents ; but he continues to be of opinion, that at the period of his enterprise, he had a mind capable of facing danger and aspiring to fame.

That Charles Edward had the advantages of a graceful presence, courtesy, and an address and manner becoming his station, the author never heard disputed by any who approached his person, nor does he conceive that these qualities are overcharged in the present attempt to sketch his portrait. The following extracts corroborative of the general opinion respecting the Prince's amiable disposition, are taken from a manuscript account of his romantic expedition, by James Maxwell of Kirkconnell, of which I possess a copy, by the friendship of J. Menzies, Esq. of Pitfoddells. The author, though partial to the Prince, whom he faithfully followed, seems to have been a fair and candid man, and well acquainted with the intrigues among the Adventurer's council :—

"Everybody was mightily taken with the Prince's figure and personal behaviour. There was but one voice about them. Those whom interest or prejudice made a runaway to his cause, could not help acknowledging that they wished him well in all other respects, and could hardly blame him for his present undertaking. Sundry things had concurred to raise his character to the highest pitch, besides the greatness of the enterprise, and the conduct that had hitherto appeared in the execution of it. There were several instances of good-nature and humanity that had made a great impression on peoples' minds. I shall confine myself to two or three. Immediately after the battle, as the Prince was riding along the ground that Cope's army had occupied a few minutes before, one of the officers came up to congratulate him, and said, pointing to the killed, 'Sir, there are your enemies at your feet.' The Prince, far from exulting, expressed a great deal of compassion for his father's deluded subjects, whom he declared he was heartily sorry to see in that posture. Next day, while the Prince was at Pinkie-house, a citizen of Edinburgh came to make some representation to Secretary Murray about the tents that city was ordered to furnish against a certain day. Murray happened to be out of the way, which the Prince hearing of, called to have the gentleman brought to him, saying, he would rather despatch the business, whatever it was, himself, than have the gentleman wait, which he did, by granting everything that was asked. So much affability in a young prince, flushed with victory, drew encomiums even from his enemies. But what gave the people the highest idea of him, was the negative he gave to a thing that very nearly concerned his interest, and upon which the success of his enterprise perhaps depended. It was proposed to send one of the prisoners to London, to demand of that court a cartel for the exchange of prisoners taken, and to be taken, during this war, and to intimate that a refusal would be looked upon as a resolution on their part to give no quarter. It was visible a cartel would be of great advantage to the Prince's affairs; his friends would be more ready to declare for him if they had nothing to fear but the chance of war in the field; and if the court of London refused to settle a cartel, the Prince was authorised to treat his prisoners in the same manner the Elector of Hanover was determined to treat such of the Prince's friends as might fall into his hands : it was urged that a few examples would compel the court of London to comply. It was to be presumed that the officers of the English army would make a point of it. They had never engaged in the service, but upon such terms as are in use among all civilized nations, and it could be no stain upon their honour to lay down their commissions if these terms were not observed, and that owing to the obstinacy of their own Prince. Though this scheme was plausible, and representeed as very important, the Prince could never be brought into it ; it was below him, he said, to make empty threats, and he would never put such as those into execution ; he would never in cold blood take away lives which he had saved in heat of action, at the peril of his own. These were not the only proofs of good-nature the Prince gave about this time. Every day produced something new of this kind. These things softened the rigour of a military government, which was only imputed to the necessity of his affairs, and which he endeavoured to make as gentle and easy as possible."

It has been said, that the Prince sometimes exacted more state and ceremonial than seemed to suit his condition ; but, on the other hand, some strictness of etiquette was altogether indispensable where he must otherwise have been exposed to general intrusion. He could also endure, with a good grace, the retorts which his affectation of ceremony sometimes exposed him to. It is said, for example, that Grant of Glenmoriston having made a hasty march to join Charles, at the head of his clan, rushed into the Prince's presence at Holyrood, with unceremonious haste, without having attended to the duties of the toilet. The Prince received him kindly, but not without a hint that a previous interview with the barber might not have been wholly unnecessary. " It is not beardless boys," answered the displeased Chief, " who are to do your Royal Highness's turn." The Chevalier took the rebuke in good part.

On the whole, if Prince Charles had concluded his life soon after his miraculous escape, his character in history must have stood very high. As it was, his station is amongst those, a certain brilliant portion of whose life forms a remarkable contrast to all which precedes, and all which follows it.


## Note 23.—Oath upon the Dirk.

As the heathen deities contracted an indelible obligation if they swore by Styx, the Scottish Highlanders had usually some peculiar solemnity attached to an oath, which they intended should be binding on them. Very frequently it consisted in laying their hand, as they swore, on their own drawn dirk ; which dagger, becoming a party to the transaction, was invoked to punish any breach of faith. But by whatever ritual the oath was sanctioned, the party was extremely desirous to keep secret what the especial oath was, which he considered as irrevocable. This was a matter of great convenience, as he felt no scruple in breaking his asseveration, when made in any other form than that which he accounted as peculiarly solemn ; and therefore readily granted any engagement which bound him no longer than he inclined. Whereas, if the oath which he accounted inviolable was once publicly known, no party with whom he might have occasion to contract, would have rested satisfied with any other. Louis XI. of France practised the same sophistry, for he also had a peculiar species of oath, the only one which he

was ever known to respect, and which, therefore, he was very
unwilling to pledge.  The only engagement which that wily
tyrant accounted binding upon him, was an oath by the Holy
Cross of Saint Lo d'Angers, which contained a portion of the
True Cross.  If he prevaricated after taking this oath, Louis
believed he should die within the year.  The Constable Saint
Paul, being invited to a personal conference with Louis, refused
to meet the king unless he would agree to ensure him safe conduct under sanction of this oath.  But, says Comines, the king
replied, he would never again pledge that engagement to mortal
man, though he was willing to take any other oath which could
be devised.  The treaty broke off, therefore, after much
chaffering concerning the nature of the vow which Louis was to
take.  Such is the difference between the dictates of superstition
and those of conscience.